SPACETIME

BOOK ONE OF THE TIME-QUEST CHRONICLES

Patrick Sheridan

Lux Dictum
London

To my Mum – Survivor, rock of support,
and the first writer to encourage me to pick up a pen.

Chapter 1

IT ALL BEGAN one chill autumn evening. It could be said it began long before, or far in the future. But for me it was straightforward enough. It was the point of rude awakening from the mundane daydream of my life into the extraordinary roller coaster that was to engulf me.

Darkness was falling over London. Towering thunderclouds filled the sky. Majestic, sullen, they glowed dully in the dying sunlight. Angry raindrops and fitful gusts of wind rattled the windows of my flat. I shivered, sensing perhaps a portent of things to come, and shut out the vision of such elemental forces with a swiftly drawn curtain. Lighting a cigarette, I turned instead to the more comfortable certainties of Jazz F.M. and an early evening drink.

My mobile rang and I picked it up, groaning inwardly as Charles' enthusiastic tones assailed my ear. Charles was a nice enough guy in an oddball sort of way. But he expected everyone to tackle life with his own limitless brand of energy. He pursued an ever-changing series of obsessions which rarely stirred my interest, if at all.

'Hi Richard, all set?'

'I suppose so Charles.'

'Cheer up, you'll love it. I'll be over in a bit.'

I ended the call with a wry smile, wondering just how much I might enjoy the evening ahead. Charles worked in the accounts department of an architectural firm where I was a junior partner. He had recently inherited a cottage some way out of London, and had pestered me to come and see it for weeks. His excitement evoked considerable misgivings on my part regarding far-fetched renovation schemes, yet I had eventually agreed. But fate had worse in store than I had feared. Agreeing to spend Saturday with Charles was only the foot in the door: I found myself manoeuvred into an eventful Friday evening as well.

'It's amazing Richard, you know, all sixties stuff, live, terrific atmosphere!'

Retro rock bashes were Charles' latest thing. Unsurprisingly, he had achieved little success in discovering kindred spirits to share this latest revelation. But he was so keen I hadn't the heart to refuse, and had capitulated wearily. It had also occurred to me that perhaps it was time I did something different, and without Melissa for a change.

I had never really had much luck with women. They might show initial interest, but as soon as I opened my mouth everything went wrong. I never knew what to say, and only the most inane remarks seemed to surface at such moments. Melissa and I had been an item for almost two years, but the relationship had never been particularly intense. It had come about almost by default: she didn't seem to mind my random conversation, and we kept ending up at the same parties with no one else to talk to. I finished my drink and hesitated before pouring another. I had been feeling uneasy about Melissa for some time. At least, I felt uneasy about something, but was unsure if I could lay it all at Melissa's door.

There seemed to be a kind of emptiness seeping into my life. Nothing was quite the same anymore. I sighed gloomily, wondering what had happened to all those high, bright dreams. Not that my life had ever been particularly happy. Family life had been rather bleak. I had no siblings, and my parents had fought for as long as I could remember. Mostly I recalled feeling somehow responsible for their frustrated ambitions. My father left when I was thirteen, and my mother was ill for a long time before her death. That had been a couple of years after I started work. But she had got me through university, found fulfilment in setting my feet on the first steps of the ladder. I had been determined to achieve better things; dreamt of stylish designs and an exciting lifestyle. Instead life seemed to be slipping through my fingers, usurped by a greying world of habit and financial necessity.

I glanced distastefully around the room. I had planned to do all kinds of things when I bought the flat, but it looked as boring and nondescript as ever. Even thinking about it seemed too much to contemplate. I stared irritably at the cigarette in my hand and stubbed it out in the ashtray. I had even started smoking again, and was drinking too much. I shook free of such thoughts with a self-mocking smile. They didn't help either. A couple of times lately I had glimpsed a downward spiral into darkly hypnotic depths.

Suddenly I felt better about going out that evening, perhaps Charles was right to keep charging at life like a bull at a proverbial red rag. I wondered what it would take to ignite that kind of passion in me, and smiled a little wistfully as Melissa drifted back to mind. I toyed with the idea of phoning her, but decided against it. She had been quite happy for me to spend the weekend with Charles. She seemed to have been more tied up with her job lately, taking work home, and we were spending less time together.

Charles' arrival was announced by a cheerful tooting outside.

'His horn even sounds like him,' I grumbled to myself. I waved through the window and scooped up my jacket. Yet my heart felt a little lighter. I was surprised by a trickle of anticipation at the evening ahead. It did feel good to be doing something new after all.

The rain had stopped, and I tugged the jacket around me against the damp autumn air. Charles sat jauntily in his car, the wheels ploughed deep into a sodden pile of auburn leaves in the gutter. It was a few days before Guy Fawkes, and somewhere nearby a firework went off with a desultory wail. I marvelled at how peculiarly English the whole thing was; arbitrary, anonymous bangs and screeches echoing around the country for days in celebration of someone not quite managing to blow up parliament.

Charles was determined I would enjoy the evening ahead. He had insisted he drove so I could 'have a good drink'. It seemed slightly illogical that someone practically a teetotaller believed I had to get legless to have a good time. But I supposed I may have given him that impression at the last office party. I eased myself gingerly into the finely tuned environment of gleaming gadgets and booming bass and we were off, zooming stylishly along wet shiny roads illuminated by dull orange streetlights and the electric rainbows of glaring headlights.

'Do you good to get out on your own,' said Charles, nodding sagely to himself, 'lots of great people there, you know, nice girls and everything.'

'Charles,' I sighed, 'I am not the type to run around with other women.'

'Of course not,' he backtracked hastily, 'but it's not as if you're married or anything. Anyway, girls might like me more if there are two of us.'

I regarded him suspiciously. 'So this is just about meeting girls? I thought there were apps for that these days.'

'Yes – no,' he said agitatedly. 'I mean, of course there are, but they don't work for me. That's not really why we're going though. It's fun, really great. You'll see.'

'Have you tried dating apps?' I asked in surprise.

'Yes,' he said uncomfortably.

'And?' I pressed.

'Well, err, not many wanted a date,' he admitted.

'How many did you ask?' I enquired, fascinated.

'Thirty seven so far,' he said glumly.

'So how many dates did you get?'

'Three.'

'Oh dear,' I said, 'how did they work out?'

'They didn't,' he said. 'One didn't turn up. One went to the toilet and didn't come back, and the other was gender-fluid and exploring his – I mean her – preferences.'

I suppressed a grin but my heart went out to him. 'Oh well,' I said, 'maybe retro rock raves will work out better.'

He looked more cheerful. 'Yes I hope so. You can meet people too: you know, make new friends.'

'Hmm, friends,' I muttered. My social life was pretty unexciting too, and I fell into wondering what had happened to everyone. Married, a few of them, and others had moved away. Some had just drifted off. Or perhaps I was the one who had drifted off – me and Melissa.

'Probably bored them all to death,' I mused aloud.

'What? Bored?' exclaimed Charles, alarmed. His gaze darted back and forth from me to the road ahead like an anxious sparrow.

'Oh, sorry Charles,' I said with a rueful grin. 'Just thinking how boring I have become.'

'Ah,' he said, relieved, and beamed triumphantly. 'That's all going to change tonight, you'll see.'

It was uncanny how prophetic his words turned out to be.

We took a while to find somewhere to park, and Charles led me eagerly towards a disused sixties cinema. An authentically shabby venue, it seemed to me. The muffled clamour of live music hung heavily in the dank air. Volume reigned supreme over quality, but Charles was quite unabashed. He almost quivered with excitement as we shelled out the (surprisingly large) entry fee. We pushed through the doors, and the sound leaped to an ear-shattering crescendo.

The floor trembled, strobe lights flickered, and light projectors bathed everything in a melting kaleidoscope of psychedelic colour. A group on stage pounded out an iconic sixties song in a brilliant grotto of light. Everything else lurked dimly on the edge of the visual spectrum, camouflaged in swirling patterns of light and darkness. After a moment I made out a bar to our left. Two men stood there, mouths stretched wide: screaming in wild exhilaration at the deafening noise all around them.

'It's great isn't it!' bellowed Charles.

'It's madness,' I yelled.

'What?' bellowed back Charles.

I smiled apologetically and shook my head. Charles looked disconcerted for a moment, then brightened.

'I'll get the drinks!' he mouthed, making pantomime motions with his hand. He indicated some tables and chairs flashing intermittently in and out of view on one side. I headed towards them and half-felt my way into a seat. My heart was beginning to sink, and I peered unenthusiastically through the leaping shadows. The place was not crowded, but the combination of noise and lighting was disorientating. The beginnings of a nagging headache did not seem a good omen.

'I must be getting old,' I groaned, and tried to cultivate a frame of mind that would find it fun. I would certainly need a few drinks for that, I decided.

But in the space of a moment my old life ended. She appeared suddenly out of the flickering light and darkness. I jumped, a shock like a static charge passing through me. I grunted in surprise, unable to take my eyes off her. She was casually dressed, jeans, a T-shirt and a light jacket, and strikingly attractive even in that fluorescent mayhem. She had a great figure, but moved with a purposeful physical assurance quite out of place on the dance floor. The shifting light-show accentuated the fine contours of her face. Her eyes gleamed bright, luminous. Her hair flowed like black satin, alive with electric sparks of reflected colour. An odd, fatalistic calm seized me. My head said she wasn't coming to me but my heart told me she was. I tensed, yet there was something about her that disarmed me. Then she was standing over me, and leaned to call into my ear.

'Richard! Richard Walton! I must speak with you. Come with me.'

I was stunned, and hesitated before rising slowly to my feet. My mind was a whirl of confusion. I had no idea what was going on.

Charles appeared and gaped disbelievingly, a drink in either hand. My fleeting suspicion that he had set this up evaporated at the look on his face. A sense of the ridiculous bubbled up and I gave a self-conscious grin. Whatever was happening, it was worth it just to see Charles' astonishment.

I looked at her uncertainly, thoughts ricocheting about in my head. I wondered if I had heard her correctly – how she could possibly know my name. I half turned towards the entrance, but she grasped my arm impatiently and pulled me away. More mystified than ever, I allowed myself to be dragged back into the depths of the swirling light-show.

My mind raced, struggling to understand what she wanted. Strobe-lit dancers gyrated around us like shimmering statues, frozen in moments of time. A sense of unreality gripped me. I convinced myself that I must have misheard her, that she just wanted to dance. But she pushed on through the writhing figures. A dimly lit exit door swam into view and she strode towards it, thrusting open the release bar. She pulled me through and it swung back behind us with a crash.

'Hey!' I gasped, 'I'm going to have to pay to get back in.'

'You people are crazy,' she said with a half-smile on her face. 'Don't worry, I fixed the door. You can get back in.' She had a slight accent, one I could not place.

'Wait a minute,' I spluttered, belatedly trying to regain some control. 'What's this about? How do you know me? What do you want?'

'Over here,' she said.

The noise from the club was still very loud, and she pulled me several steps further. A high brick wall enclosed the narrow walkway, which followed the outside of the building to the road. She was little less than my own six feet, and surprisingly strong. There was a casual physical force about her which was quite intimidating. Then everything went quiet. The clamour from the dancehall ceased completely. It was surreal, we were isolated suddenly in a zone of silence. The only sound was a faint, indistinct clacking noise, as if we were surrounded by a random ensemble of whispering keyboards.

It was weird. But so was she. I regarded her uneasily. Something about her disturbed me deeply; fascinated and alarmed me in equal measure. She returned my gaze matter-of-factly.

'Well,' she said slowly, and shook her head wonderingly. 'You're better looking than I expected, but such a baby.'

10

Embarrassment flooded me. I was as discomforted by her familiarity as by her candid appraisal. Then I saw something else, a look I could not fathom…of amusement, even affection.

'I am not the girl for you,' she said with a mischievous smile, 'at least, not in that way. I am, shall we say, someone who means you well.'

In that moment something communicated itself beyond words. An overwhelming sense of déjà vu coursed through me, a confused remembering. It was like encountering an old friend unexpectedly in a foreign land. I felt another electrical charge, this time slow and sinuous. My skin tingled and the hair rose on my body. I shivered, a growing rush of exhilaration travelling the whole length of my being. She regarded me steadily, and I stared back doubtfully. Something unfathomable linked us. She saw my bewilderment and looked contrite, her lips twitching in the beginnings of a rueful smile. My traitorous mouth smiled tentatively in return. I could not deny the affinity I felt.

'Who…who are you?' I faltered.

'You must trust me,' she said gently, 'I know it's difficult.'

I nodded reluctantly, puzzled yet entranced. But my mood somersaulted abruptly. Something stirred in the back of my mind, and I felt an extraordinary flash of malevolence. I froze in shock.

Her eyes narrowed. 'Yes,' she said, 'there's that too.'

Now I was lost, totally confused, held together purely by the strength of her will. Too many bizarre things were happening and my mind could not track what was going on. I had the strangest feeling I was seeing my life from two separate viewpoints, and a wave of dizziness washed over me. I staggered and almost fell. She gripped my arms, staring intently into my eyes.

'This is hard for me too,' she said, 'but we must do this.'

Something inexplicable was happening, my sense of reality was changing. The déjà vu grew stronger again. There was a shift in the quality of my awareness, a heightened perception of everything around me. Incredulity struggled with fear, but deep down some fundamental certainty nagged, an unknown memory surfacing like a forgotten limb.

A measure of normality returned, and I tried to reject what was happening by becoming amazingly superficial. I remembered Charles standing there in astonishment holding our drinks.

'My God…..Charles!' I gasped, 'I've left him in there.'

PATRICK SHERIDAN

'You can catch up with him later,' she said impatiently, 'in fact you must.'

I frowned, amazed that she knew anything about Charles. Everything about her sudden appearance seemed full of riddles.

She spoke again. 'I know this must seem crazy to you. Just bear with me a little longer.'

'Crazy is the understatement of the century,' I grumbled, feeling for my cigarettes. A cigarette was just what I needed, I thought. But I could not have been more wrong. It had barely touched my lips when she snatched it away with a snort of disgust and tossed it over her shoulder.

I stared in astonishment. 'What did you do that for?' I demanded angrily, only to encounter a fierce glare in return. I continued more cautiously, 'you...err, don't like smoking?'

'Of course I don't like it!' she said irately, 'and neither do you!'

I sighed, rolling my eyes heavenward and wondering if this could all be a bad dream. I was suddenly weary, unable to imagine what was going to happen next.

Then I felt the cool touch of her fingers on my hand, and my mistrust faded again. I wondered what it was about her that affected me so much. She regarded me gravely, her eyes grey-green and brilliant with life and intelligence. Tiny gold flecks danced in their depths. I remembered what she had said, that she was not the girl for me. I could not understand it at all.

Again I felt the extraordinary rapport between us. For an instant I sensed resistance, a strange stab of resentment within me, but it was swept aside in a wave of empathy. Only the immediacy of the present mattered. The moment lingered, deepened, expanded. I was enthralled. An unseen energy palpitated between us. It vibrated in my body, in the concrete beneath my feet, in the bricks of the alley. Even the air we breathed seemed to resonate with power. I was gripped by the conviction that my life hung in the balance. I tottered precariously over a terrifying chasm of uncertainty, buffeted by forces I could not comprehend.

'There are things I must say to you,' she said.

'It had better be good to explain this,' I said shakily. 'I think I'm going out of my mind.'

For the first time she seemed irresolute, even evasive. She shook her head slowly, and I was surprised by an almost wistful curiosity in her gaze.

'I thought this would be so easy...' she faltered.

12

'Oh great!' I snapped, suddenly angry. All at once I couldn't bear the mystery any more. I regretted the flicker of distress that registered in her face, but I couldn't hold back now.

'Look,' I said quickly, 'I can't stand this. If you're crazy just say so. If this is some kind of game just tell me, OK? I've gone along with it because…well, I don't know why. I don't know who you are. I don't even know your name. I've hardly had a sane moment since I first saw you.'

'No,' she said a little sadly, 'I don't suppose you have. There's a lot I can't explain. It's not that I don't want to. I just don't know where to start, or even if I should. All right!' She flung up her hands in mock surrender as my anger began to explode again.

'My name is Alex.' She sighed, 'I shouldn't tell you that either. Please speak of it to no one… no one at all, no matter how close they are to you. If you do it could cause great harm to both of us. Now hear me out. It will sound unbelievable, but you will understand soon enough. You are about to acquire a valuable artefact, a highly advanced technological device shall we say. It will attract…it has already attracted…the attention of some very dangerous people…'

'Me!' I exclaimed doubtfully. Somehow I had not expected it to be about me. 'What do you mean? How am I supposed to acquire this… thing?'

'I said hear me out,' she said caustically, 'not jump in and interrupt at every possible moment!'

I backed off a little, still disbelieving.

'I am myself in possession of'…she paused briefly, closing her eyes for a moment…'such a device. You are aware of it. You are experiencing things you have never felt before, are you not?'

I swallowed uncomfortably. My safe, mundane world was eroding fast, but it was reluctant to go down without a fight and I tried to make light of it all.

'I know I shouldn't interrupt, but why is this thing so valuable if it just makes people crazy?'

She looked annoyed again. 'It affects our relationship with space and time. Much of what you are experiencing is discordance looping. It's because of me. I shouldn't be here, and before you ask, I can't really explain that either.'

'Oh well, thanks for clearing that up,' I said, exasperated. 'Have you got anything to say that actually makes sense?'

'These are serious matters,' she said sternly. 'It is foolish to be flippant about things you don't understand.'

I must have looked particularly vacant at that stage, because she began to speak as if I was a schoolboy.

'It is very important that you don't change your plans. You must go to Charles' house tomorrow.'

'You really know about Charles?' I said in amazement, 'I don't believe it. Have you been snooping on me?'

'Of course,' she said coolly, 'and so have a lot of other people. They have been watching you for weeks.'

The swirl of unreality lurched into full flood, and I felt cold fingers of fear within me. 'This is not just crazy,' I said heatedly, 'it is totally insane. People are watching me? Why would anyone want to watch me?'

She nodded. 'It's actually a good question. They know about the artefact of course, but it's hard to believe they plan to act openly. You are under intense surveillance, there are tracking devices on you.'

'You don't really expect me to buy this do you?' I said sceptically. 'Tell me this is some kind of joke.'

'I'm afraid it's the simple truth,' she said, 'I'm suppressing the bugs at the moment, but you should assume they will know where you are and what you are doing once I've gone. When you have the…artefact, you should be safe. It will negate anything like that.'

'You are right about one thing. It is unbelievable,' I said in frustration. 'None of this makes sense at all.'

'I don't understand it all myself,' she said calmly. 'I wasn't expecting them to be here. I came because of something they…or someone…did months ago, something much worse.'

Her manner changed as she spoke. Her eyes hardened, and she leaned forward to fix me with a glare that seemed to pierce my soul. I squirmed, feeling a pang of fear. More than fear…anger and implacable hatred. Some part of me, something deep inside, felt threatened.

'Why don't I like the sound of that?' I asked, feeling a stirring of dread.

'It's a Mindworm.' She spoke flatly, but with a small catch in her voice. 'A neural virus. They want to control you.'

A jolt flashed through me. I felt a blast of fury, and then pure, cold terror as something unwound itself inside my head. It disappeared into the back of my mind like a crab burrowing into the sand, and I froze in horror.

'Th…there was something there,' I yelped, too shocked to feel ashamed at the hysteria in my voice, 'something weird, it was horrible.'

'It didn't like the attention,' she said with some satisfaction. 'They like to work slowly and subtly. But there's little that's subtle about their purpose. Being exposed has upset its plans.'

I shuddered, waves of revulsion sweeping through me. 'Where does it come from? I've never heard of…something like that…it was awful.'

A shadow crossed her face. 'It's advanced technology,' she said, 'the effects are gradual, tailored to the psyche. This one I think is meant to distract you, degrade your effectiveness. Eventually perhaps to turn you into one of them, or drive you crazy in the process.'

'Why not just kill me?' I heard my voice squeak. 'This can't be real. It's a nightmare!'

'If so it's a nightmare you're already caught up in,' she said evenly. 'They can't act too openly, so it's a logical choice I suppose.'

'Why can't they act openly?' I asked distractedly, 'what do you mean?'

'Many different parties are mixed up in this. There would be repercussions if anyone interfered dramatically. Using the Mindworm is clever. It weakens you gradually. It is intended to bend events in their favour over time. Of course it's shocking, but forewarned is forearmed.'

Her cool composure steadied me a little.

'I can't believe it,' I said shakily, 'who would use 'advanced technology' in such a disgusting way?'

She laughed humourlessly. 'People use advanced technology in all sorts of disgusting ways. This is just something new. You know it's possible, you've experienced its existence. The point is, why? They are afraid. You are a threat to them. Think instead how to fight back.'

'Who are these people?' I demanded. 'Aren't there any good guys who can stop them?'

'We are the good guys,' she replied with a grimace. 'We have to deal with it.'

'All this stuff is way over my head,' I said tetchily. 'I don't understand what is happening, and I don't know what I can do about it. I'm nobody special.'

She looked amused. 'True, you don't look up to much at the moment. But that doesn't mean you are nobody special. I think you should have more faith in yourself.'

'I can't imagine why,' I said sulkily, 'I think you must have picked the wrong guy.'

'You are not the wrong guy,' she said, a twinkle reappearing in her eyes, 'and perhaps we will talk about who picked who another time. There is much more at stake here than just you, more than you can imagine.'

I felt the Mindworm shift a little.

'OK,' I thought, *'maybe this thing is like a bad tooth. I just have an anaesthetic and out it comes.'*

'If this thing is real, how do I get rid of it?'

Her encouraging air dropped a notch. 'They are not meant to be got rid of,' she admitted. 'You will have to try and find the answer from the people who created it.'

'How the hell can I do that?' I demanded furiously. 'Wait a minute, you must know. You know what this is all about. You can help me.'

'I can't,' she said, a note of anguish creeping into her voice. 'I've taken a big enough risk just coming here.'

'You said this 'artefact' will neutralise the bugs,' I remembered desperately, 'can't it neutralise this horrible thing as well?'

'It's different technology. It will not perceive the Mindworm as separate or alien. The neural virus is written into your DNA; downloaded as a customised genome which synthesizes your own proteins to construct itself in your brain.'

'You must help me,' I pleaded.

'I'm sorry,' she said, her gaze compassionate, 'only you can do it. It's a long term problem. It's been there a while but you've existed with it, haven't you? It will try to work its way into your life, exploit your weaknesses and drag you down. Stay positive. Try to remain separate from it. Recognise what it wants, and don't let it take control.'

'What about you?' I asked fearfully, 'where will you be?'

'I will be close for a day or two,' she answered, more subdued. 'I want to keep an eye on these people. I don't know what they are up to. But then I will be far from here.'

'You mean I won't see you again?' I asked quickly.

'No, I don't mean that,' she said, 'we will meet again.'

'Can't you tell me anything?' I begged.

'Their intervention has changed some things, but so will mine. The situation is not irretrievable. It may just work out in a slightly different way.' She paused. 'There is one thing. Don't try to fight it all by yourself. Get help.' She gripped my arms and stared deep into my eyes, 'especially from people who care about you.'

The intimacy in her gaze embarrassed me again. I wondered what Mellissa would think if she could see us, and realised I hadn't thought of her once since this extraordinary girl had appeared.

'Wait a minute!' I exclaimed, 'what about Melissa? How can I even begin to tell her...'

'Oh, I wouldn't worry about Mellissa,' said Alex, 'she's having an affair with Stinks.'

'What!' I stared in blank astonishment. For a moment her words seemed completely meaningless, and I wondered if she was just plain mad. Then a niggling suspicion flagged itself up.

'You...you're not talking about Dinks, by any chance?'

'Dinks, that's right. Forget about it, it's not important. You must go back to Charles. Don't say anything about this conversation, remember the bugs. Just make sure you go to his house tomorrow. Don't say anything about me before you get the artefact, and don't mention my name to anyone until you see me again.'

'Dinks!' I said aghast, 'you can't be serious! This is definitely a nightmare. I'm going to wake up in a minute!'

'I said it's not important!' she exclaimed crossly, 'now what are you doing?'

I was struggling to dig my mobile out of my pocket. 'I'm going to call her!' I said furiously, 'I'm going to find out if it's true, and if so I'm going to wring his neck.'

'It won't work,' she said, 'I've got a suppression field on. Have you listened to anything I've said?'

'Something's wrong with it,' I said dumbly, watching random patterns swim merrily about on the display.

'No, obviously not,' she concluded sharply, and tried again. 'After I leave the bugs will function correctly. At the moment they are just picking up all that noise in there. Be careful what you say, they'll be listening.'

'What?' I said blankly, looking up from my phone, and it was her turn to roll her eyes. But a second later everything changed. She concentrated briefly within herself and was abruptly radiating intense coiled energy, like a tiger about to spring.

'They are coming!' she hissed, and the strange zone of silence vanished. 'Remember everything I told you,' she said forcefully over the sudden commotion of music. 'Don't forget the bugs…and go back to Charles!'

She steered me firmly back towards the exit door as I stared in shock. I was astonished to see desperation, even the glint of tears in her eyes.

'Don't leave us, please!' she shouted, as the noise from the club grew loud. Then paradoxically she whipped open the exit door, thrust me through and slammed it behind me.

Chapter 2

I STOOD THERE stunned, surrounded by ear-splitting sound and flickering shadows once more. Her last impassioned plea had been as emotionally charged as it was absurd. It made no sense at all, yet I felt a deep, poignant wrench in my being. For long moments I floundered helplessly. My body jerked belatedly with an impulse to chase after her, but I felt unable to move. My mind was numb, failing to process what had happened. I tried to shake the stupor out of my head and resisted the urge to sink down to the floor.

Finally the thought of Charles roused some semblance of normality. I pushed my way unsteadily through the crowd of dancers, the noise and flashing lights an irrelevant distraction now. He was sitting at the same table looking rather glum, still nursing my drink. I clapped him on the shoulder, suddenly glad to see him. His face lit up, and we went through an elaborate pantomime of meaningless gestures before giving up on explanations. I tossed off my drink and set out to the bar for another, dragging him with me.

Attracting the attention of the barman, I ordered a half of beer for Charles and two double whiskies for myself. Charles' eyebrows shot up at the sight of my drinks, and stayed up as I downed them one after the other with unseemly haste. I shut my eyes, willing the burning liquid to soothe the trembling in my body, and suddenly I wanted more. I looked for the barman but checked myself, wondering if it was wise. I had never really liked drinking that much. Now I questioned if there might be something alien about the impulse.

I was shocked at my own paranoia. Yet the memory of the creature remained stark in my mind. It made me wonder if I was going mad. I could hardly believe the whole fantastic episode had taken place, never mind think coherently about it. I felt weirdly conflicted: half fascinated by the extraordinary girl who had gate-crashed my life and half appalled by the craziness of it all. I tried to cling to the belief there must be a

19

logical explanation, but could not imagine what it might be. It was all I could do to keep functioning at all. If nothing else I decided this was not the time to get obliterated. Instead I suddenly wanted to let off steam with a vengeance.

'Let's dance!' I yelled recklessly, miming my intention with wild abandon, and leapt out onto the dance floor. Charles followed, looking determined, and for the next two hours we gyrated wildly to the music. I had a couple more drinks, just enough to keep me anaesthetised. Charles almost got friendly with an eccentric looking blonde who danced reasonably close to him, while I pointedly ignored two different girls who seemed to pick up on the energy that drove me. I kept remembering Alex's face: her sudden appearance in that very place just a short time before.

'Well?' asked Charles excitedly, as we walked back to the car.

I had not decided until that moment what to say to him. Part of me feared I had imagined Alex's appearance, and another part that it was real. It was on the tip of my tongue to give him an amusing account of it all, but I held back at the last moment.

'Yes, it was great,' I prevaricated, 'I really enjoyed it.' I was surprised to realise it was true. I hadn't danced like that in a long time.

'Of course it was great!' exclaimed Charles impatiently, 'but that's not what I meant. What happened with the girl?'

Having avoided mentioning Alex once, it seemed somehow prudent to say nothing after all – at least until I had more time to think about it. I did not want to believe her warnings about eavesdroppers, but a more primal part of me was less certain. The alcohol cast a rosy glow over the evening's developments as well. It seemed kind of fun to play along with the drama her appearance had created.

'Which girl?' I asked, enjoying a little playful misdirection.

'The first one,' said Charles.

'Oh I don't know, danced for a bit. She seemed a little pushy.' I even grinned, wondering if Alex was listening as well.

'I didn't really think you would dance with anyone,' said Charles, 'what about Mellissa?'

All at once Alex's remark about Dinks came back to me. The fact that she knew anything about him was shocking, but her claim that he was involved with Mellissa was – well, unthinkable. I realised it was something I could check up on, and stopped dead in my tracks.

'What's wrong?' asked Charles.

'Nothing,' I said, setting off again, 'just something I'm wondering about her.'

'Really,' he said, 'after all this time?'

'What do you mean?' I demanded, suddenly suspicious.

'I don't mean anything,' he said hurriedly, 'I just thought you should know everything about her by now.'

'Hmm, I suppose I should,' I grunted noncommittally, and changed the subject. 'What time are we going tomorrow, not too early I hope?'

'Ah, tomorrow!' said Charles eagerly 'Yes, not too early. But not too late either, so we have plenty of time to see everything.'

I let his voice drone on as the car sped through the silent streets. The alcohol was starting to lose its edge and I began to feel a little morose. Other things Alex had said crowded back into my mind. I was starting to realise that I missed her sharply. She had burst into my life like a spectacular shooting star, and her dramatic departure had left an aching void inside me. I could not believe a stranger had turned my life upside down so quickly. She had talked about such crazy things. Yet the impact of her personality had been immense, and she had seemed so passionate about what she was saying. What really bugged me was that such a bizarre experience had felt somehow so profound.

I wished Charles goodnight, past caring that he was puzzled by my mood.

'Nine o'clock then,' he said, a hint of uncertainly in his voice.

'Sure,' I agreed with an absent wave, opening the front door and striding purposefully up the stairs. I had my phone out and Mellissa's number was ringing before I entered the flat. It rang for a long time.

'Hello – Richard.'

I frowned at the hesitation in her voice.

'Is Dinks there?' I was harsher than I meant to be, but the silence at the other end lasted much too long.

'What – what do you mean?'

There was no mistaking how flustered she was now, and I felt a burst of fury.

'How could you!' I shouted, 'Dinks, of all people!'

'Richard I – I was going to – '

My anger cooled suddenly, but a tumult of feelings swirled inside me: rejection, betrayal, and the slow recognition that Alex had been right. A fateful resignation seemed to distil itself from the turmoil: a sense that events in my life were moving beyond my control. I realised I had known the relationship was going nowhere, and suddenly a fling with Dinks did not surprise me.

'Forget it,' I said sadly. 'I wish you the best of luck. Goodbye Mellissa.'

'No! Wait – '

I cut the call. There was no way I could talk to her, not at that moment. Instead the inexplicable events at the club paraded through my mind again. It seemed Alex was not crazy: at least I thought with a crooked smile, not completely crazy. I felt oddly pleased until I remembered everything else, and a flutter of fear stirred in the pit of my stomach. I tried to contemplate the idea that strangers might be watching me: might have done something terrible to me, could be listening to me now. I shivered, searching for another explanation. But the thought that Alex was just a mad stalker prying into my life would not stick somehow.

I went back through everything I could remember about her dramatic appearance: the things she had said, the way she had looked, the way I had felt. It had seemed so real, yet it was so unbelievable. I could not imagine what this 'artefact' might be, and how it might be connected to me. I poured myself a nightcap and threw myself back on the bed, hands crossed behind my head. Thoughts whirled chaotically through my mind and I stared sightlessly at the ceiling. Alex, Melissa, Mindworms and mysterious artefacts. It seemed impossible to engage with any of it properly, and I drifted wearily into sleep.

The insistent jingle of my mobile dragged me out of dark, complicated dreams. I fumbled blindly and grunted into it, wincing at the daylight streaming through the window and Charles' metallic tones in my ear.

'Hi Richard, all set?'

'No, not again,' I muttered.

'Are you OK, Richard?' he asked anxiously. 'We're going to the cottage!'

'Yes, yes,' I grumbled, 'just had too much to drink.' I stretched and groaned. 'I'm not used to dancing like that either. Give me a chance to have a shower.'

'Great,' he said, happy again, 'say forty-five minutes?'

'Fine,' I agreed through gritted teeth.

My head throbbed, my mouth tasted awful and I realised in disgust that I was still fully dressed. But first things first: I glanced surreptitiously at my hand, and there written in smudged biro for precisely this moment was the word 'Alex'. Last night I had believed, at least partly, in the extraordinary girl who had hijacked my life. I had expected it would be different in the cold light of day, and so it was. Fear knotted my stomach, doubts clouded my mind and my heart ached in the strangest way. People were watching me, Melissa was gone and so was the girl who had exposed her. It was hard to accept it had all really happened. I felt the pressure of the everyday world: its stolid reality and workaday routine, and stared at the tiny letters half concealed in my palm. Yes, said my message to myself, some of it at least was true. It was not a message I wanted to hear though. At least a sizeable part of me did not. It took a real effort to accept it at all.

'*After all,*' I thought to myself, '*I only have to carry on with life as normal.*'

'*And then what?*' demanded a less certain part of me.

I reached for my cigarettes. They repulsed me now more than ever, and I suddenly wanted to be free of them. But they were a useful crutch, and I had an excuse. I was supposed to remain in character. I decided to wait and have one with a coffee, and heaved myself off the bed to head for the shower.

The journey into Hertfordshire was uneventful. Charles made a couple more attempts to broach the subject of Alex's appearance the night before, but I tried to sound bored and disinterested. I attempted to divert the conversation towards the cottage, but Charles did not want to talk about this either, at least not yet.

'Just wait until you see it!' he said brightly.

I fell to thinking about Alex again. '*Don't change your plans,*' she had said, '*go with Charles tomorrow.*' It felt weird having a complete stranger know my business, yet I felt reassured somehow that she knew where I was. It irritated me that I hoped to see her again, and I wondered at my own foolishness. I was still shell-shocked by everything that had happened and tried hopelessly to piece it all together, settling back restlessly into my seat.

I felt very different to the person who had set out for the club with Charles the evening before. Everything about Alex's appearance had been bizarre. Nothing she had said made any sense. Yet the impact of her words had been immense: had seemed so significant. My mind floundered helplessly as I tried to understand it all. She had told me I should have faith in myself. I remembered how she had looked when she said that – the urgent intensity of her personality. I wanted to believe her, but it all seemed as crazy as hell.

I supposed it was partly frustration. I felt helpless. Confused and out of my depth, with no real idea what was going on. But there was more to it than that. I was shaken by these baffling events, but it wasn't just uncertainty that unsettled me. There was excitement too. Something was happening in my life: a little too much no doubt; but something I wanted or needed. I felt alive again in a way I had forgotten was possible. A new self seemed to be awakening in me, or perhaps just a younger one. I found myself wondering what had happened to the old me: to my fascination with ancient civilizations and obscure scientific facts – my conviction that magical opportunities hovered on the horizon of life. Now a vital current of anticipation seemed to fizz in my veins: a sense that anything was possible. I realised that no matter what came of all this, a part of me could not regret it. *'Anyway,'* I thought wryly, *'all I have to do is forget that everything Alex said is impossible, and see what actually happens.'*

An hour or so after setting out from London we pulled into a short driveway off a pleasant country lane. We were a few miles from the busy A1 that led up towards the North of England. The cottage was traditional, sturdily built in local stone. Charles beamed at me, inviting appreciation of his good fortune, and I was duly impressed.

'Good old Aunt Jane!' he exclaimed happily, hopping out of the car. 'She always said she would leave it to me!' He stretched mightily, breathing in the rich country air with much satisfaction, and pointed eagerly up at an attic window. 'See that room! That's where I want the observatory!'

I couldn't help smiling. How Charles thought he was going to get planning permission for an observatory I couldn't imagine.

'Can we have a cup of tea first?' I suggested.

Sure enough, Charles had several building schemes in mind; and feeling rather irresponsible, I encouraged him to elaborate. It had occurred to me that an 'artefact' might be something we would discover in the house. It didn't quite make sense: it would presumably be 'acquired' by Charles rather than me. But it seemed as good an idea as any.

He was much gratified by the keen interest I took in everything, if a little puzzled at my efforts to investigate every nook and corner. The day would have passed pleasantly enough had I not constantly felt I should be looking over my shoulder. The weather was good for the time of year, and we opened the windows to air the place a little. It let in a rich chorus of birdsong and diffused farmyard aromas, and we enjoyed leisurely tea and biscuit breaks over the sturdy wooden kitchen table. The place seemed idyllic.

'Listen to them!' said Charles elatedly, 'the place is so full of birds it's not true. Isn't it amazing that so much noise can sound so peaceful!'

In the evening we drove out for a meal and a couple of drinks, stopping at a local pub. It was a nice enough place, but the clientele were not above a certain suspicion of strangers, and it reminded me of hidden watchers. I wondered who these mysterious people might be: clandestine agencies or criminals perhaps. I half expected Alex to pop out from somewhere and tell me. Perplexed anticipation became tinged with impatience. I wanted to have everything out in the open and get it over with. Eventually we took a bottle of wine back to the cottage to enjoy the novelty of a real fireplace. We scavenged some wood from an outhouse and settled by the hearth to watch it burn. Conversation became sporadic and companionable silences longer as we stared into the fire. My body relaxed, soaking up the warmth, and on impulse I reached out and switched off the single table lamp.

The transition in consciousness was so gradual I did not notice it at first. For a moment the flickering firelight reminded me of the flashing lights in the club, but such electronic wizardry seemed suddenly trivial and meaningless. I was spellbound by the incessant play of light and colour: the bright iridescent hues of the writhing tongues of flame as they delivered their cosy heat. The rich, acid tang of wood-smoke seeped deep into my nostrils, the spitting crackle of logs an elemental chorus evoking a more ancient alchemy. The incandescent heart of the fire seemed to resonate with the volcanic depths of the Earth: constantly changing, always the same; a mystic glow reflected in the gaze of countless human beings over thousands of years.

This was Alex's world I felt suddenly: an ancient, primeval planet which bore the tinsel of the twenty-first century with unhurried indifference. I sensed the presence of the Mindworm. It did not like such contemplation, and strangely it no longer scared me. It felt distant and feeble, pushed aside by the depth of the mood that engulfed me. I remained absolutely still, too lost in the experience to wonder at its nature. Some new depth of being was revealing itself, something timeless and immutable. Unseen energies palpitated all around me, and my vision expanded beyond the fleeting screen of stone cottage walls, far beyond my insubstantial form by the fire. I was awakening from a living dream, the sleep of ages falling away and unknown wonders sparking my imagination. How small, how foolish seemed the ant-like preoccupations of humanity: how tragic the obsessions of all those blinkered minds.

'They say you can see the future,' said Charles suddenly.

'What?' I grunted in surprise, startled from the intensity of my reverie. His words resonated uncannily with the trancelike state that had overtaken me.

'They say you can see the future in the flames,' explained Charles. 'Girls were supposed to, you know, see their future husbands when they looked into the fire.'

'Oh,' I muttered, struggling to focus, 'who knows? Maybe they did.'

Charles gave me an odd look. 'Are you all right?' he asked.

'*A good question,*' I thought, stunned by the strange state of perception I had drifted into. Back down on solid ground, it seemed extremely weird. I stared at Charles, trying to get my bearings. I had no idea what had happened, and there was no way I could explain it to him. I felt vacant, suspended in a kind of limbo. Then my mind spluttered back into action again. I remembered that strangers were supposed to be listening – now a prospect considerably less inconceivable than God-like visions of humanity. I suppressed a shudder, and tried to turn it into an elaborate yawn.

'Sure, I'm fine,' I said finally. 'Just tired I guess. Maybe it's time to crash.'

Sleep was slow in coming though. I lay in darkness, my head spinning with the startling events that were crashing in on my life. I wondered how the extraordinary vision of ant-like humanity might be related to Alex: who Alex was, and where she might be. I thought of Mellissa too, a lingering sense of loss mingling with the inexplicable void left by Alex's disappearance. Everything seemed to be falling apart, and I didn't think I could go on like this much longer.

I awoke surprisingly early next morning. My mind was full of the astounding experience of the night before, and I half-wondered if I had dreamt it. There was no sound from Charles' room. I gazed out at the peaceful countryside through my bedroom window. The rising sun shone brilliantly through a delicate mist drifting close to the ground, and the autumn landscape was suffused with a luminous, golden-pink glow. It was a magnificent sight, and I felt drawn to venture out and soothe my restless thoughts in its tranquil beauty.

The dawning day was quite magical. The sun's rays transformed glistening dew-drops into immaculate jewels scattered over the lush green grass. I walked slowly in dampened shoes, enjoying the rare foray into the natural world. The birdsong was absolutely enchanting. Childhood memories stirred as I took in deep, deliberate breaths of the earthy, pristine air. It seemed strange that I had lived so much of my life in the absence of such exhilarating vitality.

Alex's mysterious prophecy and the odd experience of the night before were far from my mind when it happened. A startling wave of disorientation washed over me: a bewildering sense of dislocation from my surroundings. The hair on my body lifted with a static charge and a burst of excitement blossomed. I recognised the familiar, tingling energy resonating all around me.

'Alex!' I thought elatedly.

There was a sensation of lightness, of expansion, as if my consciousness existed beyond the confines of my body. The air began to distort and shimmer: gossamer patterns of colour playing over a delicate energy field. A fleeting golden dust sparkled everywhere like a thousand tiny fireflies. There was a subdued reverberation: a hum of power. Then in the blink of an eye a man appeared, as completely and finally as if he had dropped from the sky.

Strangely enough it was disappointment rather than amazement that registered first. It wasn't Alex. Yet a similar sense of déjà vu unsettled me. I knew this man too – and he was also a stranger. He was small, almost petite, and not young, with neatly-cropped hair and a trimmed beard. He wore a loose flowing garment: a rich cream decorated with beautifully patterned coloured borders. An instant later I realised he was injured. His face was grey with pain, his breathing laboured, and there was a nasty scorched rent across his stomach and lower chest.

He stared wildly at me for a moment, and surprise and recognition registered.

'Richard!' he gasped, his words slightly accented, 'you were right, we were fools!'

Then his expression altered and he peered in consternation. 'But you are not...'

His voice dropped away, his eyes full of questions.

I gaped back at him, trying vainly to understand what was happening. But I recognised it had to be connected with Alex, and her warnings seemed suddenly crucial.

'Someone is watching us!' I blurted out. Alarm flitted across his face, and several things happened at once. He clutched hold of me: eyes closed in sudden concentration. Simultaneously I glimpsed rapid movement across the field. *Something* came straight towards us at an impossible speed. More than one, I realised in shock. Grotesque, insect-like beings blurred across the ground almost faster than the eye could follow.

Sudden bars of light, blindingly bright, stabbed viciously among them from somewhere behind me. They tracked the bizarre creatures as they darted aside, changing position so rapidly they seemed to blink in and out of existence. They froze into intermittent solidity to emit bright, venomous rods of their own, zipping back into a deadly dance with the rapid lightning that played among them. The air pulsated with power, but the strange creatures' weapons seemed less potent than the incoming fire. These shafts of light strobed a super-dense blue-white and repeated themselves at a frightening rate. They left negative afterimages in my vision. One of the creatures was struck, and then another: blasted, shattered, to the ground. They were men I saw, clad in strange armoured suits.

I had barely grasped this when another ripple of disorientation rocked me. Energy flowed everywhere, coursing through my body and crackling over the surface of my skin. Time seemed to slow, or perhaps it speeded up. The world began to fade. It became as insubstantial as a myth or a dream. Then in a heart-stopping moment of fear and wonder I passed beyond it.

I floated in a formless void, bombarded by myriad alarming perceptions. Unfathomable forces danced all around me: fascinating and beautiful. I was lost, adrift outside the walls of reality. Then trees, fields and bright blue sky came back into being, and I found myself sprawling with the injured man on solid earth. I felt paralysed with shock, my senses reeling. But amidst my bemusement I saw we were alone. The strange armoured men and the wicked spears of light had gone.

I sucked in a tremulous breath. 'Wh – what happened?' I gulped.

My voice died to a squeak as I realised the fields and trees were quite unfamiliar. Charles' house had vanished. We were in a completely different place, and I stared about myself in astonishment.

The man moaned piteously, shaking me from my stupor.

'You're hurt,' I croaked, attempting to disentangle myself from him. I looked around helplessly, trying not to panic, 'you need help.'

The man groaned again. 'No one can help me,' he gasped, tears of pain in his eyes, 'the damage is too great. I barely escaped.'

He turned to look at me, trembling with effort, and gazed at me uncertainly. Understanding seemed to grow slowly.

'Oh!' he whispered, and something like a sob escaped him.

'Can I do anything for you?' I asked shakily, 'get medical help?'

He ignored my words, staring at me for long, anguished moments.

'You must help me with this,' he muttered finally, pawing weakly at his throat. He closed his eyes grimly. Anxious seconds ticked by and I feared he was passing out. But the humming vibration started up again, different in pitch now. He stirred, feebly pulling his clothing aside to bare his neck and upper chest.

'Here,' he said, touching his chest below the neck.

I looked where he indicated, unsure what he wanted. For a moment I saw nothing. Then an insubstantial shape began to form, vibrating with an intensity that confused my vision. It grew suddenly solid: a hazy image snapping into focus. I stared, entranced. An extensive jewel-like necklace of stunning perfection had flashed into existence. Something about its nature made my head swim. It was wide and complex: sparkling crystals of scintillating colours worked into a gleaming composite web of mysterious structures and gold filament. But there was an elegance of form and function which transcended its exquisite artistry. It carried the indefinable stamp of technology and a potency that radiated from every molecule.

'Artefact' said my mind in fatalistic certainty, and I felt a reciprocal response like an echo inside me. I sensed the Mindworm's presence like a hitchhiking ghost. It had no doubts either. The centre of the broad front pendant sparkled with larger crystals, and one of them pulsed slowly with a bright, compelling radiance.

'It is prepared,' he rasped, his voice weaker by the moment. 'After I touch the key, lift the device off carefully.'

'What is it?' I asked nervously.

'You will know. There is no time. Do it now.'

He reached unsteadily for the pulsing crystal and pressed his thumb to it, transforming its slow blinking into a rapid oscillation. The sense that I was in over my head loomed large. Everything Alex had said was coming true, and in a more spectacular fashion than I could ever have imagined. There was a dreamlike inevitability about it all which held me transfixed, but his desperation compelled me as much as anything. I cautiously lifted the strange device over his head.

The light was beginning to fade from his eyes, but he spoke again with feeble urgency. His words were suddenly unclear, which confused me. I caught familiar sounds, but they seemed garbled somehow. I looked at the elaborate necklace. Its broad design would maximise contact with the body, and a substantial tail section would lay some way down the spine. I expected it to be warm with body heat, but it was cool to the touch.

The man spoke once more: the words barely intelligible but his intentions clear. He was urging me to put it on. I felt lost in the moment. I opened my shirt and lifted it cautiously over my head to place it into position. It felt alive, its energy purring softly against my skin. It seemed to reach out to me, a silent question, and await a response. The man spoke more words. I felt a tingling at the back of my neck. Something pushed into my mind and the unfamiliar sounds were recognisable again.

'Accept the Portal,' the man had said, 'use your right thumb.'

I hesitated then: I knew I hovered on the brink of something huge. But the hope and trust in his eyes dispelled my fears. I pressed the flickering crystal as he had done, and the device hummed contentedly. It resumed its slow blinking for a moment before the quality of its vibration subtly changed. It felt lighter, and as I glanced down it became fuzzily insubstantial again and vanished. Power flowed in my spine and my head, and my focus of awareness altered somehow. A new clarity of perception crystallised. Holographic images floated in the air about me: luminous green symbols resonating with dynamic purpose. Living energies invited engagement, but control hovered on the edge of comprehension. It was both thrilling and alarming: like taking delivery of a powerful vehicle I had no idea how to drive.

'What do I do with it?' I faltered.

'I have done all I can,' he gasped. His words were barely audible. 'Believe in yourself. You will find a way.'

'Are you sure there's nothing I can do for you?' I asked.

'You can do everything, you must. It is all before you.'

I frowned. More riddles, and I needed to know so much. 'Can't you tell me anything?'

He grimaced; a sad, quirky smile. 'It seems not,' he said, and died.

The shocking confrontation with mortality left me stunned. I knelt motionless for a long time, staring uselessly at the little man's corpse. It was almost as if I was willing him back to life. I felt very alone. His dogged courage awed me, and I felt a sense of loss beyond the death of a stranger. Only gradually did I begin to look around me. I had no idea where I was. All I knew was he had somehow moved us here, and it still looked like ordinary English countryside. The sun looked higher in the sky though. I had left my mobile at Charles' place and had no watch. I wondered how long we had spent among the extraordinary energy flows. It had seemed only seconds, but more time seemed to have passed than that.

Belatedly, I noticed the sense of oneness with the Portal had faded. The holographic images and its incredible sense of potency had gone. I looked down. There was nothing to see, yet I could still sense a subtle, vibrating presence there. I remembered how the device had opened out to me, and tried to call the experience back. For a moment I touched something, and a single luminous symbol glowed in the air. But my mind seemed to slip from the fleeting connection and the awareness vanished.

'Damn!' I thought, and wondered what to do next. I tried to stay calm and think clearly, but adrenalin, anxiety and confusion clouded my efforts.

'OK,' I told myself deliberately, 'Alex said I'd acquire an artefact, and I guess I've done that.'

My thoughts lurched on a few steps, and I swallowed nervously. One thing was clear. The dead man had counted on me to use the 'Portal': perhaps to face someone or something that had killed him. I looked again at the body in front of me, trying to take stock of its stark reality. I was sitting in a field with a corpse I could not explain. I could be in trouble with the police, I realised.

But worse, some deep and vicious game was being played out by people using technologies I had never heard of. A game I was somehow involved in. Why, or how I could not imagine. I thought of Alex: how she had tried to help me, how she had believed in me, and how the hapless corpse at my feet had believed in me too. A part of me wanted nothing to do with it all, yet I felt a sense of debt to both of them. However unlikely an adventurer I might be, I seemed in it up to my neck.

I considered what to do with the poor man's body. It seemed wrong to leave him lying there, and it also seemed prudent to hide him. I looked cautiously about and saw nothing but countryside. No sign of people. There was a gentle hollow in the land some seventy yards away where three fields met, sparsely populated with denuded trees and bushes. It was the most practical option, so I lifted him awkwardly into my arms and started towards the shallow refuge.

The earth was reasonably firm, the field fallow and thinly covered with grass and weeds. I felt a little squeamish at the macabre intimacy I shared with him. But such concerns faded as the weight of his body became increasingly burdensome. I stumbled along and almost lost my footing where the ground sloped into the tiny copse. Panting, I put the body down and half dragged, half carried it into the hollow.

'Sorry,' I said: ashamed at the lack of dignity I was affording him. I would like to have dug a grave but there was no means of doing so. I laid him at a point where a shallow bank leaned over the lowest part of the incline. It seemed better he lay in this peaceful spot than out in the open, and the longer it took for his body to be discovered the better. I stood regaining my breath for a while, wondering about the unfortunate little man – where he had come from and how he had known me. Finally I left him, resolving to return and bury him properly if I could.

I walked two or three hundred yards back across the field towards what might have been the sound of a distant car, and came across a lane. Looking behind me, I tried to fix the location of the improvised resting place in my mind. Then, choosing a direction at random, I set off walking. I was in a bit of a daze. The events of the past couple of days played out constantly in my mind. It was not long before I was kicking myself for accepting the strange device. I felt unsure why I had done it: how I could have got myself more involved in the whole frightening situation. But the jumble of fears and doubts gradually settled down as I considered everything Alex had said. I tried to accept it was a fate or destiny I could not escape from, and to think constructively about what to do next.

The only obvious course of action was to learn more about the Portal I wore. How, I had no idea. I felt concerned about Alex, especially now I knew the people she was up against were really dangerous. I wondered if she had taken part in the surreal firefight outside Charles' cottage, and worried about what might have happened to her. I felt bad about Charles too, abandoned without explanation, if not worse.

After about an hour I reached a village with a name I did not recognise, and one tiny shop which was annoyingly closed. I peered in the window, thinking a makeshift breakfast of biscuits and a soft drink would be better than nothing, and banged irritably on the door.

'You won't get her to open up, lad,' said a passing voice.

I looked up to see a middle aged lady beaming at me. She had a very short dog on a very long lead, which took advantage of the diversion to get tangled around my ankles.

'Why not?' I asked, unwilling to share her bonhomie.

'Doesn't open on Sundays luv,' she replied.

'It's Saturday, not Sunday,' I said grumpily, trying to step out of the lasso the dog had caught me in.

'Not last time I looked,' she quipped, peering sideways at me.

'Of course it's Saturday,' I insisted, then paused. 'What time is it?'

'Eleven fifteen,' she said, before adding with pointed irony: 'Sunday morning.'

'Sunday?' I said perplexedly, 'the fourth?'

'The twenty-sixth,' she replied severely.

'Don't be silly!' I exclaimed. The twenty-sixth had been weeks away.

'Are you on drugs?' she asked, looking alarmed.

'It's the fourth,' I said emphatically.

'No wonder you don't know what day it is!' she said disapprovingly: extricating her dog and edging away a little.

'Of course I know what day it is!' I retorted, dimly aware that a degree of uncertainty was forming in my mind. 'That is, err, I think I do.'

It was occurring to me I might have spent more time than I realised in that strange energy state.

'Are you all right, luv?' she asked, backing further away.

'Yes, sorry,' I temporised, 'are you sure it's the twenty-sixth? Of um, November I mean?'

'It certainly is,' she said crisply, giving the dog lead a hefty yank. 'Come on Foxy.'

I watched her stride away, feeling every bit the madman she thought me. She glanced apprehensively over her shoulder, and I returned a tentative wave which only sped her on her way. I felt totally confounded. Confused thoughts entangled themselves in my head. It seemed unbelievable that I had remained in that mysterious domain of light and power for several weeks.

It took a while for my overburdened brain to come up with another possibility: that I had travelled in time as well as space. Images flooded in – advanced technology, bizarre hi-tec warriors, strangers who already knew me. A creeping vibrational charge enveloped my being as realisation dawned: the same tingling, the hair rising on my skin, and the slow linger-ing thrill travelling the length of my body. But now it was tinged with real fear and I felt lightheaded, caught between wonder and disbelief at the first real inkling of what I had stumbled across.

The insect-like armoured men stuck in my mind, and I wondered if they were still looking for me. I thought over some of the things Alex had said: that the Portal would disable their surveillance bugs. That was reassuring, but I still felt I should get moving as soon as possible. I checked my wallet. There were credit & debit cards and cash, a bit over forty pounds. I had no real idea where to go or what to do. I just wanted to rest and think things over.

I headed for a phone booth further along the road. Unusually it was working, and I found the number of a local minicab company. An unenthusiastic female informed me that Sunday rates meant thirty pounds for a ride to the nearest town, and impotently outraged, I agreed. I was particularly annoyed because it meant using up most of my cash. I had seen enough movies to fear being traced through my cards.

The cab driver eventually arrived, and I pondered my next move during the ride back to civilisation, which in this case was the town of Banbury in Oxfordshire. I had mysteriously shifted over forty miles in space as well as weeks in time. In the end I decided to try and find out what had happened to Charles, although I knew it might be unsafe. Apart from my concern about him, I figured I might be able to borrow some money. The easiest way back to London was by train, but I did not have enough cash for a ticket. So I resolved to travel without one. It would have horrified me only a day (I should say weeks) before. But now it seemed a pretty minor issue. I had to get there somehow.

'British Rail tickets are absurdly overpriced anyway,' I thought to myself, nipping past the ticket booth as its occupant turned his back. I strode anxiously about the platform, feeling a little conspicuous among the scattering of passengers. I wondered if the bad guys could hack into the surveillance cameras, or if I was getting paranoid. I settled for turning my collar up, keeping my head down and feeling a little ridiculous.

I boarded the train with a resolute spring in my step. When a ticket inspector appeared half way through the journey I took refuge in the toilet. I waited until the handle was tried, sneaked a look after a couple of minutes and then darted across to the opposite stall, where I locked myself in again. The handle of my new refuge was tried in its turn a couple of times but I stayed put. No one investigated further before the train pulled into Marylebone Station, but I had to run past the ticket collector to get off the platform. I quickly disappeared among the busy crowd of people with no sign of pursuit.

Buying an underground ticket to Fulham Broadway made me honest again and I relaxed, but I still kept my head down. I deliberated how best to approach Charles' flat as the carriage rattled and banged its way through the dark, grimy tunnels. He lived on the first floor of a substantial Victorian block of flats. A service alley ran behind the building, where refuse was noisily collected on Tuesdays. I knew a back door opened from there into the main stairwell, and that it was often unlocked. I decided to give it a try, and it opened when I heaved on it.

But I was unsure of the next step. I feared someone might have bugged Charles too. I wondered what Alex or the previous owner of the Portal would have done. The reality of its existence hit me afresh: I had not fully realised it was mine until that moment. All at once the elusive vibration of its presence hummed within me. I felt a sudden focus of perception: a vital connection; and a tangible sense of the device formed in my mind's eye. Was Charles bugged? – I just had to look and see.

Subtle processes slipped into place, and a luminous latticework of shapes and symbols expanded from nowhere. A transparent hologram appeared all around me. It penetrated Charles' flat, the building and the street outside, clearly revealing their structure. Small points of light winked rapidly in several locations, and were instantly surrounded by glowing rotating spheres. I knew immediately that surveillance devices had been identified and suppressed. It felt quite safe to ring the bell, and two rotating globes inside the flat began to move towards the front door. Charles, I guessed, with bugs planted somewhere on him.

A wave of exhilaration swept through me: I had used the Portal! I reached through the connection I felt, scarcely aware of what I was doing. The device responded forcefully. A surge of energy uprooted the foundation of reality, and a familiar wave of disorientation began to flood my senses. The door opened and Charles appeared. He froze in shock: his eyes twin pools of incredulity. The world was dissolving into a mass of exotic energies. But suddenly Charles was screaming. My confidence wavered, and I crashed back down to earth, all sense of connection with the Portal gone.

Chapter 3

WE STARED AT each other, tiny golden whirls and sparks of light fading in the air between us. Charles was trembling. I was distressed at losing contact with the Portal. But I realised the situation had got wildly out of control.

'Sorry about that,' I said, attempting casual cheer, 'we have a lot to talk about,'

'Wh-what happened to you?' he squeaked.

I smiled at his slack-jawed incomprehension. 'What did you see just now?'

'Everything was disappearing,' he said dazedly. 'I thought you were a ghost. I thought I was dying. Are you a ghost?'

'I'm not a ghost. Do you want the long story or the short?'

'I don't know,' he said, his voice still shaky, 'where have you been?'

'OK,' I said, 'the long version. Let's go inside – and before I start, I didn't believe it either.'

I hadn't intended to jump in at the deep end with Charles. It happened by accident. Or perhaps not: I remember getting a little carried away with my supposed mastery of the Portal.

I left out Alex's name as requested, and the part about the Mindworm, and the strange experience by the fire. I left out quite a lot in fact, but related everything else more or less verbatim. I watched his nervous disbelief abate little by little as the tale unfolded. He looked doubtful and confused but increasingly fascinated. Towards the end his customary animation began to re-emerge, and a familiar gleam appeared in his eyes. I felt a wry sense of foreboding. All the signs of a born-again time traveller were in the ascendant.

'So what happened when I disappeared from your place?' I inquired eventually.

'Nothing happened,' he said disapprovingly, 'you disappeared.'

'You didn't see anything, or anyone?'

'No, I woke up and you weren't there, so I just waited around for ages. I tried ringing you, but your phone was in your room. Then I spent the rest of the day walking around the fields looking for you.'

'Sorry about that,' I said.

'So you haven't, err, been anywhere yet?' he asked with a new look of professional interest.

'No,' I replied, a little put out at how quickly he seemed to be adjusting to all this. 'Just here from three weeks ago. For me it was only last night that I stayed at your cottage.'

'That's amazing,' he said. 'Not much use but, you know, amazing.'

'What do you mean, not much use,' I said indignantly. 'We escaped from the bad guys!'

'I suppose so. It's certainly a big thing at work, and Melissa thinks you jumped in the river.'

'What?' I asked, confused.

'Jumped in the river up the road from the cottage: because you found out about Dinks. She's been ringing me all the time.'

I had my first good laugh for a long time. 'Jumped in the river, really?'

'She's very upset: keeps crying on the phone. She made me report you as a missing person.'

'OK, I suppose I ought to try and speak to her. What's happening at work?'

'They keep on about it all the time, as if it's my fault.'

'Not much I can do about that,' I said thoughtfully.

'Anyway, what I meant was – it's not much use compared to going somewhere interesting, you know, in the past or the future.' He paused. 'Does it go to the past?'

'I don't know.' I said. 'Wait a minute, yes I do. The girl and the old man must have come from the future. They already knew me, and she knew the Portal would appear.'

'It travels in space too,' pointed out Charles. 'You moved to a different place as well.'

'I guess,' I said cautiously, sensing a deep interest in sci-fi coming on. I was much more concerned about what I was going to do next.

'It's better than the matrix,' he decided excitedly. 'I want to check something out on the internet.'

'I wouldn't draw attention to any of this stuff if I were you,' I said. 'These guys might be monitoring our phones and computers too. We need to be careful. That laser fight was no joke.'

'Wow, and right outside Aunt Jane's cottage!' said Charles, his eyes shining.

'I'm serious Charles. People were dying.'

'OK,' he said, adopting a suitably clandestine air. 'What are we going to do then?'

'I'm not exactly sure. They have surveillance devices everywhere. They're in your flat and on you. The Portal showed them to me, and it suppressed them somehow.'

'What do you mean on me,' he asked, 'on my clothes, you mean?'

'I have no idea,' I said, 'I just see them.'

'Is it still suppressing them?' he asked, looking alarmed, and I felt a simultaneous stab of anxiety.

'I don't know,' I admitted, 'I hope so.'

I felt a faint tingling in my spine, and the strange sense of connection with the Portal surfaced briefly. The holographic image of the building glowed in my vision for a moment: the winking lights still enveloped by whirling spheres. I sighed in relief.

'Seems like it is,' I said thankfully. 'I don't really know how to use it yet, but it appears to be keeping tabs on things.'

'What did it do?' asked Charles, 'you looked like you were seeing something inside your head.'

'It kind of switches on in my mind and stuff happens. It showed me a hologram of the building and the bugs in it, with a sort of energy field suppressing them.'

'So you control it with your mind then?' he asked eagerly.

'I can't control it at all. Not yet anyway. But I think it's done through the mind, yes.'

'Wow!' sighed Charles enviously, 'you really have all the luck!'

'I'm not sure I quite see it that way,' I said irritably. 'It feels more like a bad dream!'

'Don't be silly,' he said, 'it's amazing!'

I gave him a lop-sided smile. 'Maybe, if so let's hope good things are going to come from it.'

'Of course they are,' he said cheerfully. 'Lots of incredible stuff is going to happen!'

I laughed. 'OK Charles, I give up. You're an incorrigible optimist. But you will have to be careful what you say and do when I'm not with you. The bad guys mustn't find out where I am, or even that you have seen me. I need time to learn how to use this thing, or for it to teach me. I think I need to stay missing, so these people think I've gone to some other time and place.'

'What about your flat?'

'I don't think I can go there. The Portal will suppress the bugs, but it's the first place they would look.'

'I don't mean that. What about, you know, your mortgage?'

'I don't think there's anything I can do,' I said reluctantly. 'If I make any payments, or try to sell it, I might as well make a public announcement that I'm here. I'll just have to let it go for now. Hopefully the bank won't jump on it too soon if I'm officially missing. Maybe I can do something about it later.'

'Hmm,' said Charles. 'I suppose you're right. It seems a shame though.'

'I feel like that about a lot of things right now,' I said with a grimace. 'I need to find somewhere else to stay for a while. I don't think it can be here either. Can you lend me some cash? I don't dare use my cards.'

'Yes, yes of course,' he replied uncertainly.

'I'll pay you back,' I said, a little surprised at his hesitation.

'It's not that,' he said, looking troubled. 'I was hoping we would, you know, be in this together.'

'Don't worry Charles, I'll keep in touch,' I assured him. 'We just need some time to figure this out. We don't want to attract attention before we really know what we're doing.' Something else occurred to me. 'Don't forget: Al – err, that girl knew about you, from the future.'

'Ah yes,' he exclaimed, his eyes brightening. 'OK. I've got a bit of cash, and I'll nip out and get some more from a cash machine.'

'Is it far?' I asked.

'No,' he said, 'about a hundred yards, why?'

'It might be too far for the Portal to control the bugs on you. I don't know how they work, what kind of information they transmit. I think it's best to assume these people can see and hear you at all times, just in case. Don't take too much money out either. It might look odd.'

'OK, got it,' said Charles, instantly transformed into a seasoned counter-surveillance operative.

'Do you mind if I make myself a sandwich or something?' I asked, 'I'm starving.'

'Of course not, help yourself,' he said.

I got stuck into a couple of cheese sandwiches and a mug of tea while he was gone. It was only then I realised I hadn't had a cigarette since leaving Charles's cottage. I had left them by my bed and not given them a thought since.

'*Extraordinary,*' I thought, and said so to Charles when he returned.

'So are you giving up then?' he asked, ever practical.

'I don't know,' I said, considering the matter. I felt a kind of reflex to light up, and wondered sourly if I could sense a vicarious echo from the Mindworm. 'Yes I think I probably am.'

Charles found a bag and threw in a few clothes and essential items. Only his loosest tracksuits had any chance of fitting me. But he also had a bulky jacket with a deep hood left over from a fishing craze the year before. It was a bit small but just about fitted, and he pressed it on me.

'Counter-surveillance,' he said knowingly, 'cameras.'

'You think?' I wondered. 'I thought that might be a bit far-fetched.'

He looked a little patronising. 'You don't think super-soldiers from the future can hack into surveillance systems?'

I smiled weakly. 'I suppose you're right.'

I shook his hand, and then on impulse gave him a hug. I left the building the same way I had entered. I needed somewhere to stay and had only about two hundred and fifty pounds, so I had to be extremely frugal. I took a tube ride towards a more suburban part of the city and wandered around looking at cards advertising cheap bedsits in newsagents' windows. I hoped my mysterious, hooded presence did not look too menacing or suspicious.

The first one I checked out was in the landlord's own house, which seemed a little personal. The second was perfect: a large run-down building crudely transformed into cell-like rooms, with seedy second hand furniture and worn out carpets. The landlord turned up in an equally cheap and worn out car, and asked for two weeks rent in advance. It was a large chunk of my current capital. I gave him a hundred pounds and persuaded him to wait until the weekend for the rest. Then I bought some meagre provisions and settled into my new surroundings, with very little idea of what to do next.

I sat on the creaky bed sipping a cup of coffee and tried to sense a connection with the Portal. But it had retreated into mysterious depths of its own, as if censuring my amateur theatrics outside Charles' flat. It remained stubbornly impervious to my efforts, and my mind skittered around the fact of its existence in a jumble of inconsequential nonsense. Such random thought processes were normal enough. But I found myself wondering if the Mindworm was involved, and my efforts to detect its presence turned the whole thing into something of a farce. So I abandoned the struggle. I decided to find a library in the morning and read up about mental discipline and meditation techniques. I had no idea if it would help, but it seemed as good an idea as any.

There was little else I could do but get some sleep. I headed off to check out the communal bathroom along the corridor, and surprised a pretty girl vacating it who jumped nervously at the sight of me. She scuttled back to her room and rapped quickly on the door. It was opened by an equally cautious young lady, who gave me a hard glance before closing it. It was odd, but I assumed it par for the course in the bleak bedsit world I had ventured into. I shrugged it off and lay distractedly on my uncomfortable bed. I tried not to think of all the weird, lonely people who had inhabited the room before me, and slept fitfully through the night.

I spent much of the following morning on the internet at the local library, increasingly bewildered by a plethora of esoteric breathing and visualisation techniques. Returning confused and uninspired to my dingy room, I sat cross-legged on the floor and sternly attempted to emulate some of the simpler exercises. But I succeeded only in feeling rather stupid. The self-evident solidity of the everyday world defied the existence of more nebulous levels of reality, despite my experience to the contrary. I gave up in disgust, and brooded instead on the endless riddles of the past few days. Mellissa came to mind and I thought about contacting her. I knew it was unwise. I even wondered if the Mindworm was prompting the idea. But anger, hurt and habit spurred a desire to see her.

A public place seemed safer, so I decided to watch out for her as she left work. I occupied myself with a couple more forays into half-digested New Age mental gymnastics. Then I had a coffee, and it was time to stake out her office. There was a sizeable book store with large plate glass windows opposite the block where she worked. I could loiter unobtrusively there with a clear view of the main entrance to her building. I had no real plan, just a desire to see her, but as the time drew near I grew increasingly uneasy. I wondered if there might be surveillance devices on her too, or if I was just being paranoid. I tried to sense some connection with the Portal but there was no response.

Then an unanticipated development threw me onto a different tack. Dinks sauntered along the street and stood nonchalantly on the pavement opposite, obviously waiting for her too. An intense desire to cross the road and strangle him possessed me. I had actually begun to turn towards the door when Melissa appeared, and the Portal purred into action. Two tell-tale winking lights glowed on her. Annoyingly there was even a bug on Dinks. I stared dumbly as the Portal's warning faded, a riot of feelings churning inside me.

The two of them set off together, chatting with a familiarity that pushed the two years I'd known Mellissa into ancient history. I felt empty, forcibly reminded that my old life was over. There was no way I could talk to her in the foreseeable future either. She would betray me one way or another, and anyone else I was connected with would inadvertently do the same. The reality of my predicament hit me afresh.

'I'm on my own,' I thought dismally, then grinned reluctantly to myself. *'OK, me and Charles.'*

I thought of Alex too, and my grin widened. I thrust the past behind me and set off back to my temporary home.

Next morning I idly considered further experimental introspection, before choosing instead to wander into the local park. It was a clear, chill autumn morning and brilliant rays of sunlight peeped intermittently through the trees. I sat on a bench and marvelled at the delicate spectrum of colours winking at me through the shifting leaves. It took me back to the magical morning in the field outside Charles' cottage, just before the time traveller had appeared. I thought I detected an indefinable hum in my body. It became stronger, or I became surer of it. I felt a trickle of anticipation, half expecting Alex or some other temporal voyager to appear. Instead the sensation continued to increase in depth and intensity until it seemed to transcend the physical limitations of my being.

I felt suddenly very light, as if merged within a subtle energetic field. Everything felt connected: a complex dance of patterns and frequencies. Memories of the strange primeval visions by the fire with

Charles returned, and I sensed a flash of unease. Yet this echo carried the taint of the Mindworm: it feared the experience more than I did.

The park basked in a dense, vibrant silence. Almost without volition I reached down to dig my fingers into a million blades of whispering grass. The world seemed a great mystery hovering on the brink of understanding. I had the oddest sensation I had been sleepwalking through life: dreaming on the cusp of long, slow ages of evolution without ever really questioning the fact of my existence. I was myself and yet not myself: rather, something much more than myself. Every facet of chaotic Nature appeared to vibrate within a unified field that was both self-aware and self-sustaining.

The perception receded slowly, but I remained transfixed. I tried to grasp its meaning as the dream-like tendrils of serenity drifted from me. I wondered if it had been triggered by the Portal. Yet the strange transcendence of self had been different from the dramatic, driven journey I had shared with the time traveller. It occurred to me that the extraordinary experience by the fire at Charles' place had happened before I ever laid eyes on the portal. I supposed that distorting time and space might affect the way I experienced reality: that effect might precede cause, or perhaps trigger other inexplicable things. My mood remained unsettled all day. I was no longer sure what was real, and fluctuated between excitement and cold prickles of doubt regarding my sanity. The uncertainty ate away at my confidence and resolution.

I returned to my room and tried to school my mind with hopeful mystic instructions – repeatedly having to snap out of protracted daydreams about Alex and Melissa. But memories of the unexpected happening in the park remained at the back of my mind, and it was somehow unsurprising when a second, far more powerful episode burst upon me that evening. I even relaxed in anticipation as I began to sense the background vibration, and was taken off guard by its sudden acceleration into mind-blowing intensity.

This time, instead of a gradual new awareness of the world around me, the world seemed to wake up and grab me by the throat. A vast sense of depth and time opened up, and my perspective was instantly and hugely transformed. My body seemed at first shrunken and tiny. I registered a brief spike of distress from the Mindworm before losing all sense of self completely. My vision soared, looking down once more on the ant-like obsessions of humanity, upon billions of blinkered minds.

Now I watched the march of history and the ascent of myriad dreams and aspirations. I saw the future: conflict, disaster and the rise of great and glorious things. A haze of uncertainty obscured the far reaches of time, and at its end towered an immense wall of light: invincible, unbearably bright and barring all knowledge of what lay beyond.

Something infinitely powerful emerged from that impenetrable barrier. A shining wonder beyond my wildest imaginings, even in this exalted state: a form so achingly beautiful that it enraptured consciousness itself. If this was advanced technology, I could not understand its nature or function. Its very image confounded comprehension. Something reached out and touched me. I glimpsed limitless pulsating energies gathered into a single, cohesive whole: myriad complexities focussed into an immaculate lens of perception. A laser-bright consciousness transfixed me, and I shrank back into a miniscule nucleus of being. I felt helpless and exposed: pinned within an immovable stasis like a bug under a microscope.

I felt a flicker of shock and vulnerability from the Mindworm too. We were trapped together, but now I did not fear the creature. Instead I felt revulsion and impatience to confront its shadowy form. I reached for it impulsively. For a moment it resisted: its brooding presence murky and blurred as it fought to elude my will. It writhed and slipped from my grasp like eddying shingle on a beach. Then I grasped it, and the contact was shockingly real. Time and space were subverted somehow. Light and energy fled, and I was immersed in a bizarre, negative world with all life sucked from it. I floated in an eternal purgatory without hope or purpose, and at its centre hovered the Mindworm: a strange, segmented creature, sleek, puissant and sophisticated.

'Why do you resist me? I can make you strong.'

The contact reverberated starkly in my being, its intrusion as unexpected as its meaning. Communication existed not in words but in direct assertions of will, a telepathic clash of resolve in a timeless void. I wavered, confused.

'You want me weak, not strong,' I insisted.

'You need knowledge and power; you have many trials to face.'

'I know what you are.'

A hive-like intellect glittered before me. 'You know only what others have told you. You are a pawn in a struggle you know nothing about. I can teach you many things: make you become what you need to be.'

45

'I don't want anything from you. I want to be myself.'
'You have little knowledge of what you are, or what you can become.'

I struggled to comprehend what was happening. The dead world in which I was suspended sapped my will, and I fought to free myself from its grip. I felt shocked and bewildered, trying to remember what Alex had told me about this creature.

'You want to destroy me.'

The Mindworm remained inscrutable: *'I can give you strength to face the unknown; to bear the unbearable.'*

'To become a creature like you?' I felt stronger as the idea crystallised. It was not truly alive. It could only orchestrate my feelings.

'These are your fears and inadequacies. I can help you with your burden: give you power and proficiency.'

Energy flowed from it, and images flashed through my consciousness. I glimpsed mastery, manipulation and control, and an encyclopaedia of knowledge – even schematics of the Portal and its functions. I felt a flicker of interest and it mushroomed into ghostly new perspectives and insights. I redoubled my efforts to resist even as I questioned my motives for doing so. I badly wanted knowledge, but I felt in deadly peril. Seductive doubts and persuasions circled in my head. Truth and illusion blurred as I tried to grasp what was real, and I sought for certainty from the core of my being. I hung for an endless time in a silent scream for deliverance.

A vision of Alex flared within me, a sudden smile bright with confidence. I felt a reciprocal spark, a pulse of life, and reached for it with the last of my strength. I glimpsed fine filaments disengage from delicate nerve endings: a separation of the creature from some essential part of myself. There was a sudden release, a rush of energy, and I burst from the fog of uncertainty in a surge of liberation.

I rode on a wave of joy, a primal song of life and contentment. I looked now upon a different vision: a luminous archetypal depiction of a long, slow evolution of matter over eons of time. The Earth pulsed with potent nurture. Lifeforms came and went: changed and transformed. They morphed into the roots of a majestic tree. Its topmost branches formed a nest in which lay a fabulous golden egg. Some lower branches atrophied, mutating into scuttling creatures which gathered around its base like parasitical insects. They ate relentlessly into the trunk of the tree, devouring the being that had spawned them. The egg vibrated with extraordinary power. It started to become transparent, but the image blurred as I tried to see into it. A snowstorm of static obscured my sight and rapidly consumed my whole existence. Oblivion beckoned; and I surrendered to sweet nothingness.

Long ages seemed to pass before consciousness returned. When I felt something resembling myself again I was sitting on the floor of my room, dazed and disorientated. I lurched to my feet, desperate to establish a hold on reality. I stumbled to a large, cracked mirror on the wall and gazed numbly into its depths. I looked wild and elated, lit up like a neon sign. My reflection was luminous with shimmering pixels of energy. High anxiety and excitement battled within me, and a dazzling vision burst through the shifting image. The portal blazed around my neck, gloriously beautiful, its crystals iridescent with colour. Luminous nodes of energy extended from it throughout my body. For a moment I shone like a living god; then the image faded and only a shell-shocked husk remained.

I was drained and exhausted, unable to conceive of a technology that could create such things. I sensed that the Mindworm's inroads into my psyche had been altered somehow, but how, or exactly what had happened I had no idea. I doubted I could take much more. I vacillated between a stunned incomprehension of everything to do with Alex and her world and a profound desire to run away. I crawled into bed and shut it from my mind, falling deeply asleep in moments.

It was dawn when I awoke, and I lay still for some time hoping the events of the evening before had been a dream. Only reluctantly did I allow that dreams seemed to have become relatively tame compared to reality, and swung myself wearily out of bed to face the impossible experience that life had become. I thought about the visions – or encounters – of the day before, and tried to make sense of them. It was hopeless. They were too strange, too fantastic, and I had no frame of reference. I tried to concentrate on how I felt instead. I definitely noticed a greater awareness of the Mindworm. It seemed to have lost some of its ability to hide from me. It was not communicating directly as it had during the 'event', but I sensed it could if it wanted to. In fact I had the distinct impression it was sulking.

'Hello,' I said internally. *'I know you're there.'*

There was no reply.

'What was all that about last night?' I asked more boldly. A thirst for information in the face of such unfathomable experiences outweighed any reservations about acknowledging its existence.

The silence continued. I had the impression of disorder and uncertainty on its part.

'Don't tell me you don't know what happened,' I mocked. *'I thought you were the source of all knowledge and power.'*

'It is an alien force. It seeks the end of humanity,' came a cryptic reply at length.

'Really?' I queried sceptically. Whatever happened had been frighteningly powerful, but it hadn't seemed exactly malevolent. *'It didn't seem to like Mindworms either,'* I suggested.

'I do not recognise that term,' it responded haughtily. *'I am a cybernetic augmentation device. The alien intervention has disrupted some of my functions. However, I may still assist you in certain ways.'*

'No thanks.' I ended the conversation. I suspected it would offer to teach me about the Portal, and did not want to give it any openings.

I bumped into one of the paranoid ladies down the hall again on my way to the bathroom. It reminded me I was not the only one with problems in life. I had seen little of them apart from such chance encounters. One disappeared during the day while the other remained in the room. Neither would make eye contact, nor return the most perfunctory greeting. The other tenants were private too, but would at least say hello.

I had some breakfast and contemplated the day ahead. I abandoned much of my interest in New Age techniques, now that I knew mysterious other-worldly events could manifest all by themselves. I thought constantly about the astonishing things that had happened, but remained little the wiser. The experience with the Mindworm seemed particularly bizarre. I continued to be aware of it, but felt more detached about its presence in some way, and more confident about dealing with it. It seemed subdued as well, which was fine with me.

No particular way forward occurred to me, so I retraced my movements of the day before and took a leisurely walk in the park. I sat on the bench for an hour but nothing happened, and I wandered despondently back to the bedsit. Yet about midday, just as I was considering a clandestine return to Charles' place, a brief hum of energy vibrated in my body. I felt a momentary link with the Portal, my vision began to shimmer, and a mixture of apprehension and excitement fluttered in my stomach. I tensed: perhaps tried too hard, and the experience ceased.

I suppressed a pang of annoyance and tried instead to feel encouraged that something had happened. An hour passed, and then another and I began to feel impatient again. I puzzled over the apparent disparity between the operation of the Portal and other, overpowering states of being that had overtaken me. There seemed to be two things going on. The little experience I had of the Portal seemed to relate to personal focus and control. But the overwhelming psychic tsunamis had been very different: spontaneous, on a vast scale, and seemingly imbued with quite a different agenda.

There was a third issue too, of course: the Mindworm. I felt equally baffled and ignorant about all of these things. The only thing I could really hang on to was Alex. If it hadn't been for her, I don't know what I would have done.

I became increasingly angry, longing for clarity and certainty. A need to know about Alex consumed me. I felt absolutely desperate to make the Portal work: to make some sort of progress. Perhaps it made a difference. I seemed to penetrate more deeply into myself, and energy was humming within me again. This time I felt steadier: intent, but more relaxed. A holographic display flickered briefly into life around me: the same luminous green. The series of symbols glowed and then faded in the air. There was a familiarity about them, but nothing I could grasp – a forgotten thought half-remembered. I was too determined to think of consequences. Power crackled around me, and I felt a wave of disorientation. The world warped, dissolved into fluid abstraction. And I sailed – alarmed but resolute – into a sea of light and power.

Yet I spent the briefest of moments in that strange, unearthly reality. I felt a kind of soft shunt, as if I had been propelled back into existence. The room swam into focus through sparkling golden dust. But I was still sitting on the floor, with everything apparently unchanged around me. Then I noticed something was different: the last vestiges of a setting sun lit the room. I felt goose bumps and a creeping thrill up my spine. It was hard to take in. I had used the Portal. Somehow, nothing had seemed completely real until that instant. I felt suddenly poised on the brink of limitless possibilities. It thrilled and terrified me, and my head swam with the burden of it.

Clambering unsteadily to my feet, I made my way over to peer out of the window. Everything looked normal enough, until I turned to see that a note had been pushed under the door. I picked it up to discover an irate communication from the landlord, berating me for failing to hand over the additional promised rent. It had been due on Saturday, which had been three days away. So I had jumped several days at least. I wanted to know how many and I was without a phone, so I set off impulsively for the shops.

Just walking along the pavement seemed surreal, as if I was experiencing a brand new existence. I marvelled at fascinating everyday details I had ignored for years. Either my recent experiences were still affecting me, or I was high on my first solo trip through time. There was a newsagent's at the end of the road, and the first paper I glanced at confirmed my achievement. I bought a copy anyway to savour the new reality it represented. It was Saturday evening, around eight thirty according to the newsagent's clock. I read the paper from cover to cover in a nearby café; turning the pages in a kind of wonder, and celebrated with a satisfyingly self-indulgent plate of fried food.

Chapter 4

SOMETHING WAS WRONG when I got back to the house. The front door was open, its lock hanging loosely from splintered wood. I glanced inside with growing alarm. My door was intact, but there were sounds of distress further along the corridor. I crept cautiously into the building. The door to the nervous girls' room had been forced as well, and I heard someone crying. It seemed I was not the object of the violence, and I hurried to investigate. The room was a mess. Furniture and possessions were scattered everywhere, and one of the girls was crouched sobbing on the floor with her face in her hands.

'What happened?' I gasped in dismay, 'are you all right?' I knelt down beside her.

She looked up and I stared in shock. She was bleeding from the nose, and there was a nasty gash on her forehead. There were dark, ugly swellings on her face too, and her cheeks glistened with tears.

'They have taken her,' she wept, an unfamiliar lilt to her words.

'Who did this?' I asked shakily. The idea of inflicting such violence on a woman horrified me. 'I'll call the police – and an ambulance.'

'No,' she said, her voice breaking. 'No police or ambulance. They can do nothing and neither can you.'

'The police will come anyway,' I said, 'the landlord will report the damage.'

'He will throw me out,' she muttered miserably. 'Just leave me alone.'

'No,' I insisted. 'Come and sit down – are you badly hurt?'

She was in shock. I picked up a chair and helped her into it despite her protests. Searching around, I grabbed a towel and soaked it in water at the tiny sink. I sponged carefully at the blood on her face, and she responded a little to my concern. She became calmer, though little less despairing. I coaxed some of her story from her, and the rest I filled in later.

Her name was Sophia: she was Greek, and working as a waitress in a restaurant in Soho. Her family had helped a relative across the border in Albania to get a Greek passport, hoping to improve her chances of finding work in the UK. But the contacts who contrived to arrange the passport had sold the details to someone in London. They had threatened to expose her cousin's dodgy documentation, and tried to force her into the clutches of a prostitution ring. She had escaped and gone to Sophia for help, and the mayhem was the work of enforcers who had tracked the girl down. They had abducted her, beating up Sophia in the process. She was inconsolable: unable to bear the thought of what her friend had been dragged into.

'We could do nothing, we could not escape them,' she said bitterly. 'We had no money. There was nowhere to go.'

My eye fell on a lottery ticket lying amidst the trashed belongings on the floor. It was a forlorn testimony to the odds they had struggled with, and several ideas crystallised at once.

'I may be able to help,' I said.

She looked unimpressed. 'What could you do?'

'Will you be all right for a while?' I asked: 'are you feeling better?'

'Yes, thank you,' she said listlessly. 'You have been kind, but you should not get involved in this. You cannot do anything'

'I will leave you for a while, but I'll be back,' I told her. 'Can I help you clear up first?'

'No, I can manage,' she replied dully.

'OK, I'll see you soon,' I said.

A mixture of excitement and trepidation churned inside me as I passed shell-shocked tenants peering out through their doors.

'Well, it didn't take long to get around to the old time-travelling lottery cliché,' I thought to myself, as I speed-walked down to the newsagent. *'But the girls need money as much as I do, and it's as good a way to try and use the Portal as any.'*

The week's lottery results had not long been announced, and the Indian proprietor produced a print-out with a flourish.

'Any luck boss?' he asked cheerfully.

'Maybe next time,' I said briefly, pocketing the numbers and setting off back to my room.

I still sensed a connection with the Portal, but had no real idea if it would respond to my wishes. I was determined to try though: eager to return to my point of departure three days earlier. For a long time nothing happened, while I doggedly continued to insist that it did. Finally something shifted – almost reluctantly it seemed – and the elusive hum of the Portal began to reverberate within me. Holographic symbols shimmered in the air, their meanings tantalisingly on the cusp of comprehension. I felt the connection gel: watched the data react to my will. There seemed an inherent inertia, a resistance to my desire to revisit the past. Then something slipped into place and engaged.

The boundaries of reality wavered, and ethereal energies engulfed me. I floated beyond the illusory walls of space-time once more, too exultant to feel fear. Almost instantly an image of my room reappeared. It was insubstantial and ghostlike, as if viewed through a veil, and I had the briefest glimpse of my former self sitting cross legged on the floor. But I was repelled by a shockingly powerful force, and tumbled back into the energy flow like a leaf in the wind.

I was suddenly sprawling on the ground in unfamiliar surroundings, with no idea what had happened. I scrambled to my feet in bemusement and struggled dazedly to get my bearings. Bouts of dizziness disorientated me, and it took a while to find out where and when I was. I had mysteriously rebounded from my original point of departure and appeared miles away from my bedsit, back in the afternoon of that same fateful Saturday. I made my way home with difficulty, but had still achieved what I set out to do. I had gone back in time – by a much narrower margin than I intended – but still with several hours to spare. I checked my pocket and I had the all-important results for the evening draw.

I was too fixated on my goal to wonder much about what had happened, and the sense of disorientation began to recede as I trundled along on the bus home. But I started to get strangely vivid flashbacks of my previous visit as I neared my destination. I did wonder if I was doing the right thing, and reaffirmed my motives to stay on track. I wanted to help the two girls, and I needed cash to further my mission. I was unsure if my resolute new mind-set was courageous or foolish, but pressed on regardless. A heady excitement bubbled inside me as I reached the newsagent, along with an odd double-take of myself arriving to buy a newspaper to confirm my first jump in time. I felt almost guilty as I chose the numbers and handed in the card, but elbowed the ethics of interdimensional morality aside.

A forceful pulse of déjà vu rocked me as he printed out the ticket, and a powerful distortion wave rippled in my vision. I felt a prickle of alarm. It was as if the fabric of reality had shrugged and readjusted itself. I wondered uneasily about it, conscious I was meddling with things I knew nothing about. The sense that my actions might have effects other than intended nagged at me, but I continued to thrust such misgivings away. I was committed now, and clasped the all-important ticket tightly in my pocket. I held it all the way back to the bedsit, and hid it carefully under the carpet.

Further doubts hit me when I caught the faint sound of Sophia's voice in her room as I visited the bathroom. I wondered how I could approach her, and if I could really prevent the brutal attack. It also occurred to me that if I did win the lottery, I would need a bank account to pay the prize cheque into. I could not use mine or Charles's, or even my own name, in case my unknown enemies were monitoring such things. The situation seemed less simple than it had first appeared. The dizziness reappeared and thoughts whirled in my head until it began to ache. I decided to take it one step at a time. If the ticket won I could be confident it was possible to change the future. I would still have time to warn Sophia before her friend's pursuers arrived.

My mind made up, I loitered restlessly through the remaining couple of hours; trying to ignore stark inner images of finding Sophia's shattered room, and disjointed fears about screwing up the space-time continuum. I felt too aggrieved at the people messing with my own life to worry too much about the greater hypothetical scheme of things. I had missed the landlord again, or rather missed his visit twice, and spent the final few minutes wondering what it would be like to be free of money worries. Finally the deadline passed for the draw, and I walked tentatively down to my favourite newsagent.

'Any luck boss?' he asked cheerfully again, producing the results' printout with the same flourish as before – or as he would be in a while if I hadn't changed things.

'I don't know, I'll check when I get home,' I said as casually as possible, pocketing the slip of paper: 'how many winners?'

'Two,' he said, beaming happily, 'nearly two million each.'

I had glimpsed the numbers and they looked right. It seemed weirdly unreal. It was a struggle to walk normally as I returned to the house. I made an effort to look unconcerned, and tried to divert the adrenalin into considering the practical difficulties of claiming the money. My stride kept speeding up, and barely repressed elation threatened to unseat my newly-fledged time travelling gravitas.

I stood comparing the results' print-out to the all-important ticket from under the carpet. I was almost ashamed at the wave of euphoria that washed over me. My gaze switched feverishly back and forth between the numbers, unable to cease confirming their extraordinary reality over and over again. The magical potency that radiated from the flimsy paper ticket was astounding.

My heart beat rapidly, but not just at the thought of new riches at my fingertips. The next step was to intervene in the fate of Sophia and her friend. A wisp of fear brushed through me: the hint of a thought that perhaps I could just stay out of it. Keep all the money and avoid the ugly situation altogether. It only crossed my mind for a fraction of a second, and it surprised me. But I knew in that instant I could not walk away, and a new, rippling sense of distortion rocked my sense of reality. The whole dramatic sequence of my interaction with Sophia flashed through my mind in shocking detail. Then the images were absorbed somehow within my present consciousness and vanished. I was going to do it.

I felt quite normal again as I tucked the ticket resolutely back under the carpet: a little nervous, but entirely determined. I marched out into the corridor to knock on their door. There was no answer. But I sensed a sudden stillness in the room within.

'Hello? It's Richard, from number five,' I called urgently: 'I need to talk to you. It's important.'

There was a further pause, and then a slight movement. A pulse of déjà vu passed through me and I wondered how Alex had felt as she approached me in the club. The door opened a crack to reveal the tiniest possible sliver of Sophia's profile. It was strange to glimpse her uninjured features.

'What do you want?' she asked guardedly.

'There are men coming here,' I said tersely, 'they are looking for your friend.'

Even through the tiny gap I saw her face turn white.

'Wh – what?' she gasped.

'The people she escaped from,' I hissed, 'they are coming here now.'

I heard a car pull up somewhere outside and realised belatedly that I did not know exactly when the attack had taken place, or how long the men had stayed in the house.

'Quickly!' I insisted, 'you had better hide in my room.'

'How do you know...' began Sophia shakily; but the other girl pushed past her with a low wail.

'Just come, now,' I urged, whipping their door shut as Sophia stumbled into the corridor after her friend. She continued to protest, but I shepherded them purposefully through my open door. I closed it hurriedly, and turned to face the fear and confusion in their eyes.

'How can you know this?' Sophia demanded furiously.

'Shh!' I whispered, 'keep quiet.'

There was a sudden crash outside as the front door smashed back against the wall, and harsh voices in the corridor. Both girls froze in horror. The language was foreign, but not to them. There was a second crash moments later as their bedsit door was forced. Faint curses and angry words signalled the discovery of their empty room.

I looked about me, and my heart began to race. There was nowhere the girls could hide if these guys came in. I had not really figured on putting myself in harm's way when this little adventure began. Now I was in line for quite a lot of harm if they checked other bedsits. They had not done so before, but they had found their prey that time around. The tone of the voices changed. One of them was on the phone. The conversation sounded progressively one-sided: silence apart from a series of grunts. Muffled bangs and thumps followed, and the crash of falling objects. The room was being trashed or searched. Finally heavy footsteps tramped past us, and out into the street.

We all stood rooted to the spot, suspended like statues for more than a minute. Then normal life gradually resumed: the sounds of other tenants venturing out to investigate the noise. Sophia's friend was trembling, and began to sob. Sophia comforted her, staring at me with frightened, suspicious eyes.

'Who are you? How did you know?' she demanded, her words hoarse with emotion.

'It's difficult to explain,' I said. 'Please speak softly. It's best no one knows you are in here.'

She toned down the volume, but not the urgency.

'Are you with them? I need to know. We have to find somewhere to go...' there was a catch in her voice, 'I have to leave my job. Oh God, I don't know what I'm going to do.'

'Well that brings me to the next thing: I need you to do something for me.'

She was abruptly cold: silent. There was a long pause before she spoke. 'What do you want from us?'

'Well, this is going to seem a bit weird. I need you to claim a lottery ticket.'

They both stared at me.

'A lottery ticket?' said Sophia disbelievingly.

'Yes, you see I have problems of my own. I have a winning lottery ticket, and I can't use my bank account. I need you to claim the ticket and split the money with me.'

They stared at me some more.

'For how much?' asked Sophia finally.

'I'm not exactly sure, quite a lot.'

'What do you call quite a lot?'

'Well, getting on for two million.'

The silence stretched into long seconds.

'This is a joke?'

'No, I have the ticket.'

I dug the magic item out from under the carpet, and took the printout from my pocket. I displayed them together, and they studied the scraps of paper suspiciously.

'This can't be real,' said Sophia at last.

'You have a phone?' I asked.

'Yes, no, I don't think...ah!' she was patting her pockets, and pulled out a mobile.

'Check it on the internet, or call someone,' I suggested.

She gave me one last sceptical look before her fingers moved swiftly over the keys. It did not take long for her to find what she was looking for. I suppressed a smile as she did exactly as I had, switching her eyes rapidly back and forth between the numbers.

'This is crazy,' she said in a stunned voice, 'what sort of man are you?'

'Someone a bit like you,' I ventured: 'in a difficult situation.'

For the first time there was some feeling in her eyes. 'If this is real, you would trust us to give you half?'

'Well I could try to find someone else...'

'Yes, yes, trust us!' hissed her friend excitedly.

'There is something very strange about all this,' said Sophia wonderingly. 'How did you know about those pigs coming for Kaltrina – and you just happen to have a lottery ticket you want us to cash?'

'It's difficult to explain,' I said awkwardly, 'sometimes I just know when things are going to happen. But I was happy to help. You can walk away if you want. Or phone the lottery people. It's up to you.'

'Phone lottery people!' urged Kaltrina.

'If you phone you need to know the ticket was brought here, at the Newsagents on the corner,' I said. 'You can say a friend got it if necessary. Tell them you have had a break-in and are changing your address. But remember, no publicity!'

Sophia scrutinised me uncertainly for a while. Then she took the ticket and dialled the number on the back. It was answered quickly, and she began to provide the information they asked for. Her voice was hesitant at first, but grew steadily in confidence and excitement. There were tears in her eyes as she ended the call.

'How can this be happening?' she asked, 'it's like a dream.'

In moments she had lit up like a lighthouse. I remembered the desolation I had witnessed in those same radiant features and I felt my own glow of satisfaction. It seemed astonishing that such fleeting changes in time could create such a change in fortune. I hoped there wouldn't be a price to pay for playing with fate. But it seemed our lives were being affected in randomly capricious ways as it was, and I refused to see any harm in an extra sprinkling of good luck.

'Just remember, money doesn't buy happiness,' I said with a smile.

We managed the whole business easily enough. The police came and questioned everyone in the building, and the incident was written off as a break-in. The landlord bad-temperedly got the doors fixed, and was unsurprised that the girls no longer wanted to stay there. They paid him their dues and left. Sophia found a temporary refuge for her and Kaltrina through a carefully vetted network of friends. They also obtained cash from somewhere in expectation of their good fortune. There were no further developments, other than the occasional appearance of dubious looking characters outside the house.

We met up a couple of times for meals on which they lavished some of their borrowed riches. They even had cash to spare for me. I got a pay-as-you-go phone to keep in touch, and was able to settle what I owed the landlord with some to spare. I was briefly tempted to try and jump forward in time to collect my share, but decided against it: worried I might end up badly out of time and place. So I occupied myself, ironically enough, in trying not to activate the portal instead. I also went house-hunting with my new partners in the lottery-winning business. They were not waiting until payday to look for somewhere to buy. They hauled me around as unofficial architectural adviser, but took no notice of anything I said when they fell in love with a substantial end-terrace house near Walthamstow. It stood solidly in a quiet, tree-lined avenue far from the scene of their recent misadventures. I understood the appeal. A little woodworm and rising damp could not compete with the secluded air of security it radiated.

The lottery company paid out the winnings in seven days. They got the cheque as promised: one million, seven hundred and eleven thousand, five hundred and twenty eight pounds and thirty six pence; and any doubts they might fail to honour our agreement were soon dissipated. I accompanied the girls to the bank to pick up my share a couple of days later: a certified cheque for half the amount, less thirty thousand pounds in cash nestled snugly in a large hold-all. The cheque was made out to 'Golden Enterprises Ltd', a suitably obscure company I hoped shortly to bring into existence.

'Are you sure is enough?' giggled Kaltrina, now a totally transformed person in a classy outfit.

'Sure,' I said nonchalantly, 'if I need more I'll just predict another draw.'

I had remained deliberately vague about my fortune-telling abilities, and they were too happy surfing their own wave of happiness to probe too deeply. I got a kiss from each of them, and a raised eyebrow from Sophia which might have suggested something more. I didn't need further complications in my life just then, but I would have loved Mellissa to see it. We promised to keep in touch and I waved goodbye from my taxi, basking in a contentment I had not felt in years.

I was looking forward to my next task. I had visited Charles one evening to tell him something was up, and asked him to take the day off. But I hadn't told him what to expect. I wanted to take my ill-gotten gains over to his place immediately, in daylight. Perhaps childishly, I also wanted to surprise him. I preferred to get my hands on the money first too. I was not one for counting my chickens before they hatched.

The taxi dropped me close to the back entrance of the building, and I was quickly inside with the bag. The Portal flickered briefly into life to pinpoint suppressed surveillance devices, and then Charles answered his doorbell.

'Richard,' he beamed, before eying the bag dubiously. 'Are you, err, going somewhere?'

'No,' I said. 'Well, yes I hope so. But this is something else. You'll be glad to hear I've finally done something useful with the Portal.'

'Really?' he asked eagerly.

'Yes,' I said, relishing the moment. I unzipped the bag and emptied a substantial heap of bundled twenty pound notes onto the floor. 'Funds for time travel HQ: cash plus a certified cheque for eight hundred and twenty five thousand, seven hundred and sixty four pounds and eighteen pence!'

Charles' face was a picture. He stared goggle-eyed at the dense wads of banknotes. His excitement surpassed all previous records, and he sat with rapt attention, eyes positively blazing as he drank in everything I had to tell him. Again I said nothing about astonishing cosmic occurrences and Mindworms though. It seemed too much to get my own head around, never mind him.

'It's amazing!' he kept saying as I finished. He got up repeatedly and did a little excited walk around the pile of money on the floor, waving his hands in the air. 'We can get everything we need, and, you know, explore!' He stopped suddenly. 'I could even give up work!' He seemed astonished at the idea, and turned enquiringly towards me.

'Yes, but not yet,' I said hastily, 'it may attract attention before we really know what we're doing.'

He nodded reluctantly. 'It's not fair though, you're having all the fun.'

'I wouldn't exactly call it fun Charles,' I said, 'more like living life at the sharp end. Anyway, you have an important job to do. You have to think about our finances. You can't actually do anything yet because of these bugs. But we are going to have to set up a company to run the money through. We'll have to get somewhere new as a base too.'

'Wow yes!' said Charles gleefully, 'we can start a whole network!'

I regarded him with some misgiving. 'I imagine we may have to do all kinds of things, but try not to get too carried away.'

'OK,' he agreed reluctantly, 'but how long do you think they'll keep watching?'

'I don't know,' I admitted. 'I've given it some thought, and I'm wondering if they were just trying to stop me getting the Portal in the first place, or catch me before I could use it. And don't forget that someone else attacked them when they appeared. They may no longer be watching at all. The bugs might be redundant. Hopefully we'll find out a bit more soon, but for now don't take any chances.'

'Right,' said Charles, slipping expertly into counter-espionage mode. 'Where are we going to keep the money?'

'I suggest here for now – hidden I mean – and don't take it out when I'm not around. I'll just take some cash for now. Keep some for yourself in a drawer or somewhere if you want some, just don't start splashing it about too much.'

We hid the cheque and most of the money inside a loose panel in the airing cupboard, right at the back behind the hot water tank. It was hard to get at, and we glued it shut. It was unlikely anyone would find it easily.

We talked a little more, and I returned to my bed sit with no clear idea what to do next. Back in my room I hid some of my cash under the carpet, had a cup of coffee and thought about trying again with the Portal. Having achieved one jump in time, the enormity of the task facing me hit home with a vengeance. The euphoria of my successful adventure with Sophia and Kaltrina had diminished, and everything appeared suddenly both much more real and much less achievable. I felt lost on the shores of a limitless ocean of time: an unimaginable milieu of possibilities. I had no idea where or when to look, or how to get there.

True, I had pulled off a minor miracle for the girls, and made myself some money. But I also sensed how lucky I had been, and how differently things could have turned out. Now I felt overshadowed by daunting otherworldly realities and unwanted responsibilities. I wondered what threat I could really be to my mysterious enemies; and what help I could give to someone as strong and capable as Alex.

It seemed crazy to leap blindly into alien times and places: that perhaps I should take things gradually instead. I reasoned that I had money, and could make more. Perhaps get myself a nice out-of-the-way place to live and prepare for the future. I began to warm to the idea, slipping into a pleasant daydream where I became an accomplished recluse: gradually mastering the Portal and all forms of expertise required to launch surgical commando raids through time. I only snapped out of it when I sensed a hint of smugness from the Mindworm, and realised the damned thing was probably orchestrating my mood. I grimaced irritably. I would most likely turn into a bigger couch potato than I already was in that scenario. Indignation at what these people had done fired me up again and I cast aside my doubts, determined to do the opposite of what the wretched creature wanted.

My enthusiasm re-kindled, I concentrated on everything I could remember about Alex: her warnings, her concern and her encouragement. My anger grew as the full horror of the Mindworm and everything it signified crystallised in my mind. I seemed to emerge from a kind of fog which bled some vital force from my existence. A sudden conviction that I had to find Alex flared in me: that I had to do something now. All at once a sense of her presence became bright and real. I seized the moment, and reached for the Portal with impulsive determination.

My mind was clear and focused on the device, and it seemed to trigger a reciprocal demand for engagement. It opened out to me, and I melded effortlessly with its subtle protocols. Luminous icons floated before me, and I sensed powerful responses fine-tuned to the slightest touch of will. But I felt no capacity of command and control. I hovered on the brink of infinite uncertainties. There was an instant – as the familiar sense of disorientation washed over me – when I might have backed away. I knew somehow this would be no small leap in space and time. But I clung to the image of Alex and embraced a sense of reckless abandonment. It felt almost preordained, and a great force seemed to impel me into the unknown.

Energy crackled everywhere and solid outlines wavered. The world began to undulate like a viscous ocean, and I dived beneath its surface in a sudden surge of resolve. Concrete reality faded and I raced wraith-like though insubstantial realms. I glimpsed a maze of pathways: golden tunnels of light laced with diaphanous rainbow hues. Awesome energies flowed about me. Yet I moved through a timeless present as though frozen in amber: suspended somehow in roaring silence. Just as coherent enquiry began to take conscious form, it was over. Solid ground reappeared through a haze of golden sparks, and I found myself staggering on long grass a world away from my London bedsit.

I had passed through overwhelmingly fabulous states of being, but there had been no real sense of direction: no greater perspective on it all. I stared around slowly, oddly serene despite my rapidly beating heart. It was dawn – or dusk: a faint red glow of sunlight smeared across a murky horizon. It was strange to be unsure of time – or of East or West. I had no sense of where I was. I felt far from home, yet strangely unfazed by it. A surreal sense of detachment buoyed my mood.

Dark, fast-drifting clouds intermittently masked a luminous full moon and a sprinkling of stars. It was warmer than London had been, and there was moisture in the air. Scattered clumps of trees were silhouetted starkly against the sky. An earthy tang of freshly turned soil and pungent manure hit me, and a looming quiet hung everywhere. There were no bright lights, no distant sounds and no busy civilization. Yet everything seemed expectant with life, saturated in a rich, still silence.

The moon waxed brighter through the clouds, its silvery luminescence eerily intense in the quiet landscape. I was standing on a grassy hillock above a wide, ploughed field. The furrows criss-crossed a gentle slope which ran downwards towards a distant huddle of buildings. It looked like a farm of sorts, and I thought I could make out dim lighting in a couple of windows.

There seemed only one course of action: to make my way down to the buildings and knock on someone's door. Forcing myself forward, I navigated the field's perimeter along a crude wooden fence running roughly where I wanted to go. I had supplemented my limited wardrobe and was wearing jeans and a shirt. I hoped they would not stand out too much if I was in another time. It became increasingly obvious it was evening. It was definitely darker when I found myself among the black silhouettes of barns and the sounds and smells of livestock. I picked my way past mysterious agricultural contraptions half hidden in the murk. Then, locating what appeared to be the rear of the main farmhouse, I began to circle around in search of a front entrance.

I couldn't resist peering in through one of the lighted windows. A very un-electric table lamp burned with a weird, potent radiance behind neat lace curtains. Its flame trembled minutely, casting a bright glow over a sparsely furnished room. Everything was crafted in wood, its contours sharply contrasted in light and shadow. Its construction was simple, but there was decorative detail too. I stared in silent fascination, knowing I was gazing into a world very different from my own.

'And just who might you be?' demanded a feminine voice sharply, and I jumped as a pale, indistinct shape moved from the shadows by the back door. The moon cleared the clouds at that moment, brightly illuminating a striking, dark haired woman in a long voluminous dress. There was a flood of déjà vu and a fleeting wild joy, for my first impression was she was Alex. My second was I was wrong. The third was that she seemed coolly determined to use the tiny pistol she was pointing at my head.

Chapter 5

'PLEASE STEP INTO the house,' she said, coldly polite, and indicated the door with her gun.

My mouth went dry. The pistol looked lethal despite its size, and facing a weapon that could blast a hole through me was unexpectedly unnerving.

'I – there's no need for the gun,' I faltered, struggling to keep calm. 'I don't mean any trouble.'

She tilted her head quizzically at the sound of my voice, but ushered me in with the pistol. A rich timber fragrance and a fatalistic sense of commitment settled on me as my foot crossed the threshold. I heard the door close and turned to face her, my breath catching sharply. She was not Alex, but there was an uncanny likeness. The same grey-green eyes regarded me dispassionately, and her luxurious black locks were tied loosely back in a bun. She was equally beautiful, but there were differences too. Her mouth was more generous, and her movements more graceful. Alex was like a diamond: brilliant, capable and strong. But the woman before me glowed like a softer gemstone, with a rich inner beauty. The formal elegance of her gown proclaimed her of an earlier time, and the vital reality of her existence seemed fantastic. I had an absurd urge to reach out and touch her. But I didn't doubt it would be a bad idea. There was certainly nothing yielding in her features. Only contempt and distaste showed in her gaze.

'Why are you creeping about out there in the dark?' she demanded fiercely. 'Are there not enough strange men in this house?'

Her voice was deep and musical, her accent difficult to judge. It was almost American: a hint of French perhaps. But she had no such problem with mine.

'You are English,' she stated, the first question evidently rhetorical. 'Why are you not in there with your friends?'

'I...don't know what you mean,' I said uncertainly, confused by her words and her likeness to Alex. 'I am, err, lost. I don't come from here.'

'And why are you staring at me like that,' she asked crossly, 'are you mad?'

'You...um, remind me of someone,' I gulped, struggling for dignity. 'Besides, I was not creeping about. I was looking for the front door.'

She laughed scornfully, 'better to say nothing than lie like a fool.'

I answered with a hopeless shrug and what I intended as a disarming smile. But it just seemed to confirm her opinions, and she turned her attention to my unfamiliar attire.

'What is this you are wearing, are these English clothes? I have never seen the like. If you are an English spy you will be caught immediately.'

I began to feel a little annoyed: no doubt unreasonably so.

'I am not a spy!' I retorted, 'and I wish you would stop pointing that thing at me. I am not a thief or a murderer either.'

'We will see what you are,' she said carelessly, and waved her pistol at me. 'This way: I think you should come and meet your friends.'

She indicated a doorway behind me, and I moved reluctantly through into a wide, wood-panelled hallway. It was high-ceilinged, and extended for a generous distance to a substantial front door at the far end. A sturdy pine staircase ran back up to the floor above us on my right. Three other doors opened off the passageway at ground level, all of them closed.

'This one,' she said brusquely, indicating the nearest door, 'kindly open it.'

I turned the brass doorknob with butterflies in my stomach. I had no idea what to expect. Part of me felt it could not really be happening, and I stepped into the unknown like an actor without a script. The room was spacious and occupied. A large, polished pine table occupied its centre, over which hung a simple candle-laden chandelier. Several men sat around it on tall-backed pine chairs; with documents, half-filled glasses and decanters of liquor scattered between them. The panelled walls were more elaborately worked than in the hallway, and sparsely adorned with prints and paintings. There were two other doors opposite, and a couple of windows at the far end. The men all looked up as we entered.

Several impressions hit me at once. There was a lot of hair: largely unkempt, with beards and moustaches much in evidence. The room stank of leather, sweat, horses and cigars. The two occupants on my side of the table wore dusty, hard-worn outfits, and I could see gun belts on their hips. Two others opposite were more neatly dressed, but their clothes were casual and unrefined.

Another man dominated the scene, the best dressed in the room. He sat directly across from the two ragged travellers, flanked by his two likely subordinates. He was big built, dark-haired and dark-complexioned, with a full beard and moustache. He stood up as soon as he saw me. A bright intelligence burned in his eyes – eyes that knew too much – and I was not surprised by the powerful wave of déjà vu that hit me. One thing did surprise me though: something I had not experienced before. It was bright and impenetrable, and reflected from him as though from a mirror. I did not need the flurry of holographic images to guess that he wore a Portal too.

'Who the hell are you?' he demanded furiously. But his features showed alarm and confusion.

'I found this one creeping about outside,' announced my captor contemptuously, but I detected a note of puzzlement at the man's reaction. I glanced at her and noticed the pistol had disappeared. I looked back resignedly at my mysterious counterpart: I would leave the next step to him.

'Gentlemen,' he said, recovering his self-possession, 'and lady,' he added with exaggerated politeness. 'I would be grateful if everyone other than my uninvited guest would leave the room.'

Instead the room received a great many more uninvited guests. One of the doors behind him burst inwards, and men crowded through with brutish-looking revolvers in their hands. Everyone else went for their guns, and all hell broke loose. The first shot seemed to reverberate endlessly: the shock of the pressure wave stunning in the confined space. Everything seemed to unfold in slow motion. Several guns went off almost simultaneously in a deafening, rolling thunderclap. A half seated man close to me was struck. I felt as much as heard the sickening slap of the bullet. The room was full of dense, sluggish clouds of smoke and I thought of the girl.

She seemed suddenly infinitely precious: perhaps because she looked so much like Alex. My fear skyrocketed when I saw she had half-pulled her tiny gun from her dress. I felt myself blur through an instant of time – a series of images of myself reaching for her – and seized her gun hand, hugging her tightly as I dived to the floor. The gunfire went on and on, an ear-splitting cacophony of sound that seemed to shatter my ears and my mind. I clung to her in terror, constantly expecting the hammer blow of a bullet in my back. After an endless time the noise slackened into the gut-wrenching moans of injured men. I raised my head, and the girl began to wriggle indignantly beneath me.

'Let me go you stupid man,' she shrieked, but I barely heard it, still deafened by the noise. I started to rise, glancing cautiously about me, and she fought her way free. She left her gun on the floor, and glared angrily at me as she got to her feet. I stood up and gazed in stunned disbelief at the carnage all around me. Men lay dead or badly wounded, spread-eagled over splintered chairs, broken glass and a rumpled floor rug, with growing pools of blood beneath them. Others clutched less serious wounds. The smoke began to thin, but the air remained heavy with the sour stench of gunpowder, the sickly scent of blood, and the whiff of opened bowels.

I was astonished at the way the gunfight had gone, given the surprise achieved by the attackers. The two rough-clad men were both on the floor, as was one of their better dressed companions, but the time traveller and his second sidekick had vanished. The other casualties were newcomers, six or seven of them. A further four men stood alert and tense, their revolvers at the ready and pointed mostly at me and the girl.

'Who are you?' she demanded angrily of the intruders, trembling visibly from shock, 'how dare you do this in my house?'

'I am sorry for this ma'am,' said an officer in a frayed grey frock coat, 'but it is a serious matter of spying against the Confederacy.' He looked apologetic, and tipped a non-existent hat. But he remained vigilant and did not lower his weapon.

'The Confederacy has no business here, this is Union land,' she snapped, 'and you are murdering people in my home.'

'It was your people started the murdering ma'am, resisting arrest,' he said more forcefully, 'and we have questions to ask. I would trouble you to wait out back while we clean up in here. Then we'll talk some more.'

My shell-shocked mind informed me that I had become a participant in the American Civil War, while the rest of me struggled to catch up. The dusty, tatty clothes these men wore were confederate uniforms. The guns were not stage props, and the dead and dying were a brutal fact of life. No flotillas of ambulances with blue flashing lights would come for them. The sense of unreality was overwhelming. Yet this was real, and twenty-first century London existed only in my memory. I felt numb and bemused by it all.

The officer nodded to one of his companions, who motioned me and the angry young woman out into the passage with his revolver. She stalked haughtily ahead of her supposed jailer, and I followed her quietly into the back room where we had first met. She seated herself disdainfully upon a bench by a rear window, and proceeded to studiously ignore my presence. I sat as close to her as I dared, and the trooper took a stool a little further away, holding his long handgun a little self-consciously across his knees. He looked several years younger than I was and a little shorter; with a sturdy build, bright blue eyes and fair curly hair. He barely looked old enough to own the heavy weapon he carried. Small ripples of déjà vu continued to flow through me. Even the boy soldier seemed oddly familiar. I felt horribly disorientated: cut adrift from everything I was used to in this strange new world.

Then the shock of the gunfight caught up with me. I shuddered, hardly able to believe I had lived through all that violence. My body hummed with adrenaline and I clasped my hands together to stop them shaking. I tried to remember what had happened: the men bursting in, the dream-like inevitability of the guns coming out and the barrels swinging round…I wondered if the strange timelessness of it all had been something to do with the Portal. It seemed a miracle we were both still alive. I turned to her. Tears glistened in her eyes. The violent invasion of her home had shaken her just as badly as me, if not more.

'I'm sorry this happened in your house,' I said awkwardly.

She glanced at me, her expression unreadable. But she dashed away her tears with an impatient gesture and looked away again without speaking. Her resemblance to Alex still shook me, and I felt driven to try again.

'I hope I didn't hurt you. I was trying to protect you.'

'You were trying to assist these murderers,' she said bitterly.

'Then why are they guarding me?' I asked.

'I don't know,' she retorted.

'Perhaps we should introduce ourselves,' I suggested a little more boldly.

'I cannot imagine why I would wish to know you sir,' she said sharply, and swivelled away to stare pointedly at the ceiling.

I resigned myself to silence, and fell back to considering everything that had happened. Many things were unclear. The sense of déjà vu I had felt as events unfolded had been overwhelmingly intense: more like I had experienced with Alex and the previous owner of the Portal than with Kaltrina and Sophia. The fact that my unwilling companion bore a striking resemblance to Alex seemed hardly a coincidence. Then there was the question of the gun she had been carrying; why she had referred to strange and unwelcome visitors in her home, and what the allegations of spying were all about. Most of all I wondered what another time traveller was doing at the centre of it all. I was still pondering these things when the Confederate officer entered the room with a slightly plump and rather timid looking lady of about thirty.

'Oh Mistress Jacqueline, thank goodness you are all right!' she exclaimed shakily.

'Yes Mary, I am quite well,' replied my fellow captive, who had regained some of her composure.

'So this is your Mistress,' said the officer. 'And can you tell me who this gentleman is?'

'No Captain,' said Mary, staring at me and my twenty-first century clothing nervously, 'I never seen him before.'

'It's Lieutenant, Ma'am, if that's all the same to you. However I thank you for your assistance. I hope my men will soon finish up in there, and you will be able put the rest to rights.'

Mary muttered her thanks and left the room wringing her hands. The Lieutenant turned to us.

'Miss Johnson is your name I believe. Can you tell me who this gentleman is?'

'I cannot,' said the girl with Alex's eyes. 'I have never seen him before tonight.'

The man looked grim. 'Then can you tell me who were the other gentlemen meeting together?'

'My stepfather and two of his men of business were the only people I knew in the room Lieutenant,' she said stiffly. 'The bushwhacker's were strangers, and had not long arrived.'

His eyes narrowed. 'What were you doing in the room Miss Johnson?'

'I found this man skulking outside the back and escorted him in to my stepfather,' she said, 'I was there less than a minute.'

'Yet you pulled a gun on my men?'

She appeared discomforted. 'It was foolish, I didn't think. They burst into my house.'

'I believe this gentleman saved your life,' he remarked.

She glared at me and said nothing.

He turned to me. 'Your name, sir?'

'Richard Walton.'

His eyebrows rose. 'You are English!'

'Yes.'

He stared at me for several seconds, and finally sighed.

'There is something mighty strange going on in this house,' he said flatly. 'I have confidential military documents and dead men on my hands, and no one knows anything or knows each other. I am charged with solving this treason, and my men and I have to get out of here. So you are both coming with me.'

'Now you are a kidnapper!' exclaimed my fiery companion. 'I will not go with you.'

The Lieutenant's eyes grew hard. 'I lost some good men today Ma'am,' he said shortly. 'I am in no mood for games. Don't force my hand.'

She was still for a moment. 'Very well,' she said reluctantly, 'but I will need some things, and to saddle my horse.'

'You have ten minutes,' he said curtly, and nodded to the guard: 'stay with her, Billy.'

He turned his attention to me as they left the room. 'What is your part in all this Mr Walton?'

'None of it is anything to do with me,' I said cautiously. 'I don't expect you to believe it, but I just arrived.'

'Just arrived from where?' he asked impatiently.

'That's a bit difficult to explain,' I admitted.

'The English are supposed to be on our side, is what I'm thinking.'

'My presence has nothing to do with politics,' I insisted. 'I was lost and came to the house for directions, that's all.'

He studied me silently for several seconds. 'Would you mind emptying your pockets sir?'

PATRICK SHERIDAN

'Not at all,' I said, cursing the fact that I had cash and my cheap new mobile phone on me. The money puzzled him: it was much too small and hi-tec for the times. The phone mystified him completely.

'This is English money?' he enquired, 'these appear to be of high value: twenty pounds apiece.'

'They are, err, Bills of Credit,' I temporised.

'What is this?' he asked, brandishing the phone. At least it wasn't switched on.

'Ah,' I said, my mind working feverishly. The only thing I could think of, bizarrely, was Charles and his fanciful observatory. 'That is for, err, calculating the positions of the stars. It is a hobby of mine.'

He looked doubtful. 'I've never seen something like this before. What is it made of?'

'It is a new kind of metal.'

'It is very small,' he observed.

'It only does simple calculations,' I said lamely.

'How does it work?' he asked suspiciously, examining it from different angles.

'It's broken.'

He stared, baffled, at the instrument for a little longer, then shook his head and slipped it into his pocket along with my money. He obviously had more immediate things on his mind.

'You are a mystery and no mistake,' he decided: 'no identification, strange clothes, foreign bills and an odd-looking instrument. You got a horse outside?'

'No,' I admitted awkwardly.

'Then how did you get here?'

'I am not exactly sure,' I said in an agony of embarrassment. 'I seem to have been robbed – stuck on the head maybe – and lost my memory of recent events. That's why I came to this house for help.'

His stare progressed from doubtful to extremely sceptical, and he gave a bitter laugh. 'Well I sure have some horses to spare.'

'I have um, not much experience with horses,' I confessed, and his scepticism edged towards incredulity.

'Then how were you travelling?' he demanded impatiently.

'As I said, I can't remember,' I repeated, feeling hopelessly compromised, 'perhaps in a, ah, stagecoach?'

72

He seemed to weigh the odds of my being a madman or an idiot, and finally shrugged.

'If you ain't used to horses you'll have to learn real quick,' he said.

He led me out to the front of the house, where half a dozen men worked purposefully around a dozen horses under the moonlight.

'You might have to tie him on boys,' he called out to them, 'or he might fall off!'

There were a few chuckles, and one of them assisted me in clambering onto one of the horses, radiating mute amusement at my clumsiness as he did so. I sat self-consciously on the animal feeling extremely ill at ease: my mount alarmed and indignant in its turn. 'Mistress Jacqueline' appeared after rather more than ten minutes, leading a horse with a side saddle and wearing some sort of divided skirt. Mary staggered next to her with two bulky bags, and after a heated discussion with the Lieutenant they were fastened over the saddle of another rider-less horse.

The dead and two seriously wounded men were left behind in the hopes of Union mercy, and two others rode with blood seeping from makeshift bandages. We set out at a brisk trot, travelling along a broad dirt track leading from the front of the house. I was thankful we were not going faster, but was horrified by the unseemly bouncing the innocuous pace appeared to generate. Infuriatingly it only happened to me. The Lieutenant dropped back, appraising my performance in mock astonishment.

'Well, that's one thing you didn't lie about,' he guffawed, 'you sure ain't ridden a horse before!'

I detected answering grins among the shadowy men around me. I even thought I caught a flicker of amusement from Jacqueline. But my equestrian ineptitude soon carried me beyond mere indignity. It passed into acute discomfort and before long into something like pure torture. We took a fork in the road and followed it for about twenty minutes, after which to my great relief we headed across country at a walking pace. It was still uncomfortable but far more bearable, and we travelled steadily through gently rolling hills and fairly open forested land. Time passed slowly in an unreal procession of aching tedium: a long waking dream of moonlight and shadow. It seemed to go on for ever before the lieutenant called a halt.

'We'll grab some food and sleep until first light,' he grunted.

A fire was kindled in a small hollow where it would be difficult to see closer than a hundred yards or so. Men went off to relieve themselves in the darkness and Jacqueline did likewise, picking her way out for some distance.

'Don't run off now, Miss Johnson,' called the Lieutenant, but her only answer was a defiant toss of her head. The moon was lower in the sky and shone less brightly, with clouds appearing in greater numbers. I hoped it would not mean rain, because there was no sign anyone was carrying tents or any other protection from the weather.

The pungent wood smoke stung my nostrils and made my eyes water. But the aroma of cooking was surprisingly good when pans and provisions were unpacked. The scene was intensely surreal. The flickering flames illuminating the soldiers' weathered faces and worn uniforms put me in mind of an old painting rather than real life. It wasn't merely the image. It was the vital, living presence of human existence in a bygone era that was so strange: everything different and everything the same. I suppose it disturbed innate assumptions about the permanence of my own twenty-first century existence. I thought of Charles: how thrilled he would be by the idea of something like this. In practice it was loaded with confusion and anxiety. I was living on my nerves, and it would have been even worse without Alex's trail before me.

Jacqueline returned, and I felt somehow gratified that she sat closer to me than the other soldiers. I wondered about her part in all this: who she was and how much she knew. Her resemblance to Alex seemed remarkable: she could have been her sister. Or, it occurred to me, one of her ancestors or descendants – and she had a stepfather who was a time traveller. Yet she had obviously not recognised my displacement in time the way he had. It seemed an unlikely web of intrigue or coincidence.

The young soldier Billy retrieved a metal bowl and spoon from a bag on my horse and put them into my hands, followed by a dollop of cooked food.

'What is it?' I asked, sniffing curiously.

'Salt beef and cornmeal, same as always,' he said cheerfully. He apparently considered himself personally responsible for me and Jacqueline and offered her the same, but she declined. I chewed the food tentatively. It was rough and appeared to contain a percentage of grit, but I was hungry. The men muttered between themselves, seemingly anxious to finish their food and get some sleep. I felt bad that Jacqueline wasn't eating and turned to her, trying to imitate Billy's cheerful air.

'Are you sure you won't have anything to eat? It tastes pretty good.'

'No thank you,' she said shortly.

I was silent for a moment and then tried again.

'Do you have a sister?' I ventured.

She looked at me in surprise. 'No, why would you ask?'

'You remind me of someone,' I admitted reticently.

'You said that before,' she remembered. 'It's an odd thing to say when you creep into someone's house.'

'I did not creep into your house,' I pointed out, 'I was creeping around it.'

She regarded me stonily for a moment.

'You are a very strange man,' she said finally.

'Do you get on with your stepfather?' I blurted out.

'And a very rude one,' she added, before turning her head away.

Billy came around with a coarse blanket for each of us, and bade us good night. Jacqueline buried herself in hers immediately, and turned on her side away from me, her head pillowed awkwardly on her arms. I covered myself and lay on my back, hands behind my head and watched the sky. It seemed weird how little the hundred and fifty years separating me from my own time meant to the twinkling stars above. I didn't think I would sleep, but was suddenly jerked awake from a bizarre dream in which Alex and Jacqueline were one person and speaking in two voices.

'Time to get up,' said Billy, 'rise and shine.'

I stared blearily around me. It was still quite dark, but there was a glimmer of light on the horizon and something was brewing on the fire. My body ached everywhere, and I stretched with a groan. I looked around at Jacqueline, who had turned during the night and was facing me. She opened one eye, and sat up crossly when she saw I was watching her.

'Coffee,' announced Billy, handing me a steaming metal mug. He did the same to Jacqueline and this time she took it, despite glowering darkly at him. She blew on it and sipped carefully and I did the same. It smelt and tasted nothing like coffee and there was no milk, but it was hot and sweet.

The Lieutenant sent two men riding back the way we had come as dawn broke. A short time later we were in the saddle again too, heading east. I tried to ease my tender muscles, shifting and flexing uncomfortably as the horse plodded steadily on, but I continued to feel like a punch bag. The rising sun bestowed the raw, untamed land with incredible beauty. There was a moment, as the fabulous red-gold eye of the sun peeped through distant mountains, when I seemed to touch the transcendent lucidity of some higher realm. But I let the awareness slip away. I had no idea what might activate the Portal, and I was reluctant to launch myself back into the unknown. Despite all the discomfort and uncertainty, I wanted to learn more about Jacqueline and her stepfather.

I tried to restart a conversation with her a couple of times as the morning wore on. I manoeuvred my horse alongside her with great difficulty, only to be dismissed with monosyllables and frosty looks. I had better luck with Billy, and achieved a few brief, disjointed and mutually confusing exchanges with him. I tried ineptly to extract the date, our geographical whereabouts and the current state of the war from him. But Billy's colloquialisms and my hazy knowledge of all things American allowed considerable scope for misunderstanding; and I remained little the wiser.

The two men re-joined us after several hours and we stopped for a late breakfast, or perhaps an early lunch. This time Jacqueline condescended to eat, and we drank our so-called coffee together in what I liked to think was our most equitable silence so far. We set off once more and sometime later passed a couple of dilapidated wooden huts. Further on the rough ground transformed itself into a track lined intermittently with structures in better repair: solidly built log cabins for the most part. The soldiers at the head of our little column pulled out their pistols and looked about cautiously. But we continued on without seeing a soul.

Then the track curved and widened, and all of a sudden there were a great many people. They stood mutely where the roadway circumnavigated a broad lake encroaching on the village. An assortment of mismatched buildings was concentrated there, and it seemed every occupant was present. At first the wailing seemed incongruous in the stillness. Then I made out a distraught woman inside the circle of onlookers. She clutched the limp body of a child: its clothes sodden with water. A few turned to look as we drew closer, but the prevailing mood made them indifferent to our presence. Their tragic silence spoke to us too, and we began to pass the scene in funereal solemnity.

I looked at the crumpled child, a boy of eight or nine. The woman's despair was palpable and somehow transformed the scene from someone else's problem into timeless human heartbreak. There was something odd about this perception, and I had a weird impression that something other than myself was watching through my eyes. A new sense of depth transcended my everyday nonchalant self. It was as if some timeless being was witnessing life unfold at the slow, ancient pace of the planet beneath my feet. It reminded me of my incomprehensible experience at Charles' cottage, but this seemed a more human perspective. The sombre crowd took on an archetypal pathos: a lost tribe of primordial children marooned in an era of darkness and ignorance. And something sparked in me – the germ of an idea – the hint of a suggestion.

I snapped out of the dream-like state with no time to question its veracity. In my time it would have probably been possible to resuscitate the boy. I considered my first aid training and wondered if I could do it.

'Yes,' I thought, 'maybe I could. But how will the crowd react if I try, and what if I fail?'

A paralysing moment of unreality gripped me. I knew I might hold the balance of life and death in this frozen tableau. But I doubted and feared to act.

'They will lynch you,' said the Mindworm dismissively – the first contact for days – 'and there is nothing to gain from it.'

I recoiled instinctively from its horrid urgings, but still hesitated. Then the unbearable anguish on the woman's face and an unaccountable desire to give Jacqueline a better opinion of me did the rest. I slid off my horse and was running before I dared to make a conscious decision, pushing my way through the crowd.

'How long was he under the water?' I demanded, breathless with fear and adrenalin.

'Hey you can't do nothing, he's dead,' rasped a sour faced man, snatching at my clothes.

The woman looked wildly at me, uncomprehending.

'Stop him, he's crazy,' called another.

'I said how long?' I shouted franticly, lightheaded at the chance I was taking.

Someone else moved to grab me.

'Bin five minutes,' she wailed, 'he's dead.'

I hoped it was less than five minutes. There was something else in her eyes now: a glimmer of hope that filled me with dread. I reached the still figure just as two men grasped me.

'Let me try!' I cried, and suddenly the woman was tearing at my assailants in fury.

'You leave him be!' she screamed at them.

I turned the boy to try and empty water from his lungs, and then laid him out and began to pump his heart. I stopped briefly for mouth-to-mouth resuscitation every so often and continued: counting the strokes out loud to myself to steady my nerves and to ward off the shocked silence of the crowd.

'You fool,' whispered the Mindworm, and I cringed inwardly as the seconds ticked by. But I continued on desperately. There was a singing in my ears and a grainy pattern forming in my vision. The consequences were unthinkable if I failed, and all I could think of was that I was failing…then the boy belched water, spluttering all over me. He gasped for breath, and stared at me in alarm.

'Ma!' he squealed, and wriggled away: grasping his mother, who burst into tears. I sank back on my haunches exhausted, eyes closed and the world spinning around me. Only slowly did I become aware that the crowd remained silent. I looked around. Many faces registered a similar vacillation between awe and fear, and several crossed themselves in alarm. Superstition was raising its head, I realised.

The Mindworm glowered dourly in my head. 'Now look what you have done.'

I thrust its loathsome presence aside and stood up, thinking frantically.

'It is something I learned from a doctor,' I announced, my heat thumping. 'If the, ah, spark of life is still there and you start him breathing again, he'll live. Another minute and it would have been too late.'

Some eyes lightened, and a more natural animation moved through my audience. The boy's mother was nodding and smiling, the tears trickling down her face. The tension hung for a moment longer and then passed. Suddenly everyone was smiling, and I suppressed a sigh of relief.

'Thank you, oh thank you sir,' cried the mother. I was shaken and thrilled, unable to believe I had really done it.

'He may still become ill from the water madam,' I felt obliged to say, putting on a formal if rather self-conscious tone. 'He may have some fever. But I hope he will be well.'

I glowed with self-satisfaction; but my contentment soared when I glanced back at my captors. Their hard-bitten faces were alight with wonder, and Jacqueline gazed in astonishment. My lowly status was unquestionably thrown into doubt.

The lieutenant beckoned me over.

'I don't know if you're a spy Mr Walton, but let me shake you by the hand,' he said with grudging admiration. 'I seen a lot of things, but if that don't beat the Dutch I don't know what does.'

Being complemented by a capable man leading a hard and dangerous life was embarrassing. All I had done was apply a little knowledge that others didn't have. Yet I had stuck my neck out when I don't have to. I had surprised myself.

'Thank you Lieutenant,' I said.

My new sense of pride sat awkwardly on me. The Mindworm appeared to be sulking: or had at least slid under its stone at the back of my mind. I wondered at the way it continued to communicate so directly with me. It seemed the mysterious high-energy confrontation had definitely changed something. It was preferable to the creature invisibly orchestrating my thoughts and feelings I supposed, and I hoped it was a good sign.

We set off again with some surprisingly good natured jibes between the Northern folk and the Southern soldiers, and rode with only a brief coffee stop until evening. The conundrums of my present predicament continued to revolve in my head, and en route I managed to manoeuvre my horse approximately alongside Jacqueline.

'Would you mind if I asked you again about your stepfather?' I enquired tentatively.

She narrowed her eyes slightly, but did not look away.

'You are still a strange man,' she said, 'but you did something wonderful.'

I found myself colouring a little. Somehow I was just as discomforted by her praise as by her hostility. She considered me curiously, her face tilted quizzically as she had when we first met.

'I do not get on well with my stepfather,' she said finally. 'My mother died not long after she married him, so my home is owned by a man who is a stranger to me.'

'He seems a forceful man,' I suggested.

'Yes, forceful and strange: just as you are kind and strange.'

'I'm not really that strange,' I said.

She burst into peals of laughter, and all of the men looked around at the rich outpouring of mirth. Finally she subsided into fits of giggles and dabbed at her eyes in amusement.

'Not that strange!' she repeated comically: 'creeping about in the dark in those outlandish clothes. Asking odd questions – don't know where you are, and don't know where you've been!'

'That does sound a bit strange,' I admitted.

She chuckled a little longer. 'Thank you,' she said finally.

'For what?' I asked.

'For making me laugh,' she said, 'I don't know how long it is since that happened.'

We stopped soon after dark, a more companionable mood binding our little group as we ate by the light of the campfire. The moon had yet to reach its zenith, and a vast swathe of stars spread their glittering beauty across the black velvet sky. There was no light pollution beyond the fire, and I could not take my eyes from the exquisite display above us. Several of the soldiers gazed up along with me.

'They say the stars are a long way off,' said Billy dreamily.

'How far do you reckon, Mr Walton?' asked the Lieutenant.

'Light years,' I said, trying to maintain my stargazing persona.

Jacqueline looked puzzled. I was unsure if it was because the Lieutenant had deferred to me, or because she didn't understand my answer.

'How do you mean?' asked Billy.

'It's how far light from the stars travels in a year,' I said, wondering if I should have kept my mouth shut.

'But you just see them straight away,' said Billy in a puzzled voice.

'No, you see them as they were when they gave out that light,' I said, digging myself deeper into the hole. 'Light is a kind of energy just like sound. It takes time to travel, it's just much faster. You can see, say, an explosion a long way off before you hear it can't you?'

'Yes,' said Billy slowly, thinking about it. 'But how can light be an energy?'

'You can feel the warmth of sunlight on your skin can't you?'

'I guess so,' he said, slower still, 'but the sun is hot and stars are cold.'

'The stars are other suns,' I said, 'they are just very far away.'

'The stars are all suns?' he gasped, 'but there are so many...' He gazed in awe at the countless pinpoints of light in the heavens above us, his mouth slack with astonishment. Everyone sat in silence, equally absorbed in the unthinkable.

Finally Billy spoke again. 'But moonlight's not warm.'

'Not so you can feel it,' I agreed, 'it doesn't reflect sunlight very well, and it absorbs most of the heat.'

'You mean moonlight comes from the sun?' he said in amazement.

'Yes,' I said, suppressing a smile.

'Oh,' said Billy, staring up at the moon as though seeing it for the first time. 'I guess that's right. How come I never thought about that before?'

'I suppose you just never talked about it with anyone before,' I suggested.

'It gives me goose bumps,' he admitted with a shiver.

'I read how fast sound travels: about one mile in five seconds,' said Jacqueline, joining in unexpectedly. 'But I don't remember reading that light takes time to get anywhere.'

'It does,' I said, wondering how to wind down the conversation, 'just too fast to measure on Earth.'

'Well then,' she asked curiously, 'how would you know?'

I was put on the spot, racking my brains to try and remember when the speed of light was discovered. I had a dim memory of reading about it once, but the details completely eluded me. It was annoying to have walked into a trap of my own making. To admit that I didn't know or couldn't remember would be ridiculous after the knowledgeable pose I had struck. At the very least I thought Jacqueline might start laughing at me again, and the Lieutenant's suspicions would be further aroused.

I felt the disquieting sense of an altered state of being and resisted at first, fearing the Portal was about to take me away to some other place and time. Then a sudden spark of that forgotten memory glimmered somewhere inside me. I felt a tingling excitement, wondering if the Portal was somehow retrieving the lost information. It grew from nowhere to crystallise vividly in my mind's eye: the detail even more complete than I remembered. The scientific observation had been made in the past few years. I was saved.

'By measuring apparent differences in the movements of the moons of Jupiter,' I replied: 'that is, as its orbit takes it nearer or further from the Earth.'

'I don't understand,' said Jacqueline.

'Do you really want to?' I asked.

'Of course!' she said indignantly.

'Well,' I said authoritatively, 'at certain times of the year Jupiter's orbit takes it nearer to the earth, and at other times further away. When the orbits of Jupiter's moons were observed; it was found that they appeared to be moving faster than their mathematically calculated orbits when Jupiter was nearest to Earth, and slower when it was further away.'

'How could that be?' she asked.

'That was exactly the question. The answer was that the shorter the distance light had to travel the more up-to-date the image was, and the longer it had to travel the older the image was. So from the closest distance the moons appear to be ahead of their calculated orbit, and from the furthest distance the opposite seems to be true.'

There was some muttering and scratching of heads among the soldiers, but Jacqueline brightened.

'Ah! I see,' she said, 'so you calculate the speed of light somehow from the differences in the positions of the moons.'

'Yes,' I said, impressed at her astuteness, 'all the distances are known.'

'And what is it calculated to be?'

'About a hundred and eighty six thousand miles a second,' I said, torn between a pride in knowledge and a reluctance to draw too much attention to myself. 'It takes more than eight minutes for the light of the sun to reach the Earth.'

There was a lengthy silence. 'You said the stars were 'light years' away,' said Jacqueline eventually, 'that would make the distances unimaginable.'

'Yes it would,' I admitted reluctantly. 'The distances are vast.'

'But how can you measure how far away they actually are?' she persisted.

This was something I did know. 'Simple trigonometry,' I said, feigning learned nonchalance: 'in the same way that the distance to the planets and our sun is known. In the case of the stars, the baseline is the diameter of the earth's orbit around the sun. It is just a matter of measuring the angle of a star in the sky in summer and again in winter. Then you can determine the distance, at least for the nearest stars. For those further away the change in angle is too slight.'

'And how far is it to the nearest star?' she asked, her eyes now alive with interest in the glowing firelight. Her sudden absorption in my amateur astronomy surprised me.

'A bit over four light years,' I said, 'about twenty five million, million miles.'

Billy was dumbfounded. 'Why would God make other suns so far away?' he cried incredulously.

'I don't know,' I said, ambushed by religion once more. 'Maybe our ideas about God are not big enough.'

A hush fell over the whole company as we lost ourselves in the infinity of stars above us. I gazed out at the tiny, myriad points of light, dimly realising my ignorance of the world around me even as they realised something of their own. The solid Earth of my childhood was gone. I thought of the awesome things I had witnessed: the extraordinary states of being that seemed to exist beyond the senses. The stars looked different to me now: as if pulsing with a secret life of their own. They had always invoked wonder in me. But now I felt I was looking upon a vast, luminous work-in-progress on an unthinkable scale: galaxies, suns and planets forming the outermost weaves of an unimaginable multidimensional reality. I tried to conceive of the complexities involved and met only towering silence.

'You are a very strange man,' reprised Jacqueline, not unkindly. She sounded a little sleepy now.

'Mr Walton,' said Billy in a lowered voice, 'I spoke to Jeb before he died. He said you flew in the air.'

'What?' I said, confused.

'When Miss Johnson pulled her gun: he said you flew in the air to stop her.'

'I – don't know what he meant,' I said awkwardly, remembering that weird timeless moment. 'Maybe he wasn't in his right mind.'

I felt Jacqueline's gaze on me, but she said nothing.

'I think she's right,' Billy said.

'What do you mean?' I asked.

'There sure is something strange about you.'

We were up drinking coffee again before dawn, and set off on another interminable ride. My body seemed to have more aches and pains than ever, and I wondered resignedly how long the journey would last. The Lieutenant had again sent a couple of men back in the direction we had come from, and this time they re-joined us earlier than expected. They thundered up with their horses lathered in sweat. There was a rapid, terse conversation just out of earshot, and we set off again at a brisk trot. I bounced about uncomfortably and asked Billy breathlessly what was up. He only nodded towards the Lieutenant. So I inexpertly manhandled my horse over to ask him what was happening. He looked a little irritable, but admitted that someone was coming after us.

'Most likely Miss Johnson's stepfather,' he said, 'there's a whole party of them a way back.'

'I don't know if I can stay on if you ride too fast,' I warned.

'We will have to move as fast as we can,' he said shortly. 'But we're meeting up with the army soon: ain't nothing they can do then.'

'I didn't know the Confederates were this far North, Lieutenant,' said Jacqueline, overhearing. 'Whereabouts are we going?'

'Little place called Gettysburg Ma'am,' he said, spurring his horse forward.

Chapter 6

I TRIED TO remember what I could about the battle of Gettysburg as we pushed rapidly on over increasingly hilly countryside. It had been a pivotal point in the Civil War, I knew that much, and a defeat for the Confederates but not decisively so. What I recalled most were descriptions of the huge numbers of dead and wounded from both armies left for the shocked local population to deal with afterwards: around the same as at the battle of Waterloo. There seemed an eerie sense of fatalism about the way events were carrying me towards such a cataclysmic episode in American history. It felt as if a violent storm was forming over the horizon, and sucking everything for miles around into a terrible vortex of destruction.

We travelled rapidly, and for me extremely painfully, stopping only for a brief meal about noon. Then we pushed on swiftly and started to pass the first outlying farms and scattered houses of Gettysburg in the early afternoon. Our escort began to relax and the pace slowed. But as we reached a fork in the road I glimpsed mounted soldiers approaching on our right, and instead of the anticipated Confederate uniforms they were clad in blue. There were shots and shouted challenges, and our whole party set off at a gallop, following the left fork further into town.

I clung frantically to my plunging mount, alternating between exhilaration and terror. But our impetuous dash was short lived. More blue uniforms appeared in front of us, a troop of cavalry twenty strong bringing carbines to bear on us. Several of the Lieutenant's men had drawn their pistols and looked for an escape, but there was nowhere to go. Our desperate cavalcade pulled up in a cloud of dust and snorting horses. There was silence as both sides took stock of the situation. Then the Lieutenant's men slowly raised their hands. A burly Union sergeant walked his horse forward with an affable grin on his face.

'Well boys, it looks like you rode up the wrong street,' he chuckled. His gaze switched to Jacqueline as she nudged her horse forward.

'Sergeant, these men abducted me from my home,' she announced loudly.

The man's demeanour changed: his face hardened and his men stirred grimly, shifting their grip on their weapons.

'This was not banditry sergeant,' she said hastily, 'I was taken on suspicion of a spying matter against the South.'

The sergeant relaxed a little but suspicion lingered, and he scratched his head in puzzlement.

'And are you a spy ma'am?' he asked, the more jovial side of his nature beginning to re-assert itself.

'Of course not,' she said in disgust. 'I demand to be taken to your commanding officer.'

'There I am in agreement with you ma'am,' he said, looking over to the Lieutenant. 'Sir, I would request that you and your men surrender your weapons and follow me.'

The Confederate soldiers began to stiffly comply, while the sergeant's attention was next diverted by me, presumably because of my unconventional clothing.

'Who might this gentleman be?' he enquired with exaggerated politeness.

'This gentleman was also abducted by these soldiers,' said Jacqueline with an equivocal glance in my direction.

'Is he a spy too?' the man asked, obviously enjoying himself again now.

'I have no idea,' she replied with an impatient toss of her head.

The sergeant shook his head theatrically, and signalled his men to take positions around our small party.

'You all come along with me,' he said, and we set off further into town.

The Lieutenant and his men looked dour, the Union soldiers grinned in delight, and Jacqueline glared imperiously at anyone who dared catch her eye.

I stared about me as we rode. This was the largest place I had seen so far, and it was strange to see brick buildings which would not have looked out of place in my own time. The people were different though: stamped by a dress code which seemed stern and severe. Their eyes were suspicious or awe-struck as they gathered in doorways to watch us pass by. This was a well-ordered world in which everyone knew their place, and did not presume to think beyond it. It seemed rigid and constrained, yet I sensed simplicity too: a freedom from the doubts and anxieties of twenty-first century autonomy. They had something real to be anxious about instead. War was at their door, but they little knew how entirely it was to engulf them.

We travelled unhurriedly for five or ten minutes, until we arrived at a fairly imposing municipal building of some kind. More union cavalry milled about outside it: some dismounted and cleaning equipment or watering their horses at wooden troughs. The sergeant slid off his horse and strode importantly into the building. He disappeared for some minutes before re-emerging with an officer, who inspected our party with considerable interest.

'Good afternoon ma'am,' he nodded to Jacqueline, and then saluted our late captor, 'Lieutenant.' He turned to me: 'and, ah, you sir. Would you three accompany me inside?'

He spoke to the sergeant. 'I want these other men inside too, locked up and searched. Check the gear on their horses as well. I want to know if they're carrying anything of interest.'

The sergeant assumed importance again, but looked slightly confused.

'What items of interest should I be looking for sir?' he asked.

'Use your imagination Sergeant,' replied the officer dryly. 'I imagine documents might be a good place to start.'

The sergeant nodded vigorously, duly firing up his imagination. He assigned some of his men to escort the confederate troopers into the building, and others to search their saddlebags. Jacqueline, the Lieutenant and I dismounted first, stepping into a spacious entrance hall. It had a high ceiling decorated with plaster reliefs. Several imposing doorways lined the ground floor, and a wide, ornate stairway ascended to an upper level.

The Union officer beckoned us to follow him across the hallway, and rapped smartly on one of the solid oak doors. There was an answering summons and he opened it, ushering us into a spacious office which showed signs of hurried occupation. Saddlebags and opened boxes were scattered about, and a heavy cavalry sabre and a couple of carbines slung haphazardly in a corner. I smelt the same pervasive aroma I had encountered in Jacqueline's house: leather, sweat, horses and cigars.

Another officer, obviously of higher rank, looked up from behind a desk over which a large map had been spread.

'Major, these are the prisoners,' announced the officer by the door. It triggered an outraged response from Jacqueline.

'I am not a prisoner,' she declared furiously. 'I am a law abiding citizen of the Union!'

'Very well ma'am,' said the Major, looking somewhat taken aback. 'However, first things first: I am Major Rufus Dawes of the 6th Wisconsin. May I know who I have the pleasure of addressing?'

'Miss Johnson sir,' said Jacqueline stiffly, slightly mollified.

'Well Miss Johnson, this seems to be a very irregular business, and it must be investigated.'

'Of course it must be investigated!' she affirmed tartly. 'But it is extremely hot, and I have been kidnapped and forced to ride across country for two days. I demand the return of my belongings, which are no doubt being rummaged through by your men, and I insist on finding a hotel room in which to wash and change.'

The man eyed her uncertainly for a moment or two, and then turned to his subordinate. 'Captain, detail one of the men to retrieve Miss Johnson's horse and belongings, and escort her to a suitable hotel. Let him remain there until she is, ah, refreshed, and then escort her back to this building.'

Jacqueline thanked him graciously, and walked out looking pleased with herself. The Major turned to the Lieutenant and me.

'What have you two gentlemen got to say about this matter?'

'Sir,' said the Lieutenant formally, 'I will not deny that this is an irregular business. My men and I followed two renegades suspected of working against the interests of the Southern States, and they led us to this lady's home. When we tried to apprehend them, there was a gunfight. I was carrying out my duty. That is all I have to say.'

The Major regarded him silently for a moment, and then raised an eyebrow at me.

'I was a visitor at the house, and knew nothing of what was going on there.'

I tried to emulate the Lieutenants objective tone. But it was the least important aspect of my delivery as far as the Major was concerned.

'You're English,' he said, his jaw clamping down tightly, and I sighed inwardly.

'Captain,' he said, as the man came back into the room. 'I want these two gentlemen searched thoroughly, and kept separate from the rest of their troop. I have a few things to attend to. I should be ready to see them in an hour or so. Can you send a runner to that Bureau of Military Information fellow – see if he can join us. I think you had better send a second man after Miss Johnson too. Make sure her baggage is searched after all, and make sure that she returns.'

The Lieutenant and I were taken back out through the entrance hall, and into a small windowless room. The Sergeant and another union soldier sifted through our clothes as we shed them, while a third stood guard by the door. My boxer shorts got a few stares, but body cavity searches did not appear to figure in contemporary espionage, and the process was relatively painless. The lieutenant was not as happy though. A number of documents were discovered in an inside pocket of his faded frock coat, along with my money and my phone.

We sat in the room with an impassive Union soldier for company, and neither of us spoke. We were in an awkward position, and it was unclear how things would turn out. I had a feeling I was the one with the most to fear. Everyone seemed to think I was on a covert mission for the British Government, which was supposed to be a friend to the South.

I contemplated the extraordinary reality of the room we sat in, its ancient clock ticking a hundred and fifty years in the past. There was still a part of me that could not accept it was real. I marvelled at the living vitality of the Confederate officer sitting next to me. Confined in an enclosed space, he smelt a little ripe. Unsurprising I supposed, in a life with little chance to bathe, but it emphasised the vigour of his presence. I savoured the untold stories ingrained in the scuffed wooden floor and the scratched plaster walls. It was just as mundane, engrossing and matter of fact as my own world, yet I knew that either could dissolve into dream-like oceans of light and power.

I wondered about reality: how material corporeality could disappear, and consciousness remain. I thought about that strange realm beyond space-time. I could not remember any physical existence in that state, any more than the material world itself, yet I had felt my essential being to be intact. I tried to imagine how it operated: what had actually been going on. The Portal seemed to open a door into another dimension where my sense of self could be extracted from material reality and resurrected in an entirely new space-time location. The strange thing was that they all seemed equally real. So I came full circle, and wondered if they were equally unreal as well. To say I was confused would be a considerable understatement.

I was snapped out of my reverie by the return of the Captain and the Sergeant, and we were marched back into the Major's office. It had been tidied up somewhat, and the sabre and carbines were gone. The fruits of the search – my money, mobile phone and a dozen folded documents, had been placed significantly on the desk. The Sergeant stood rigidly to one side, radiating intense satisfaction.

'Is this all,' asked the Major, 'nothing found anywhere else?'

'Nothing else sir,' affirmed the sergeant, 'the other men, the horses, even the lady's luggage – all checked.'

'What about the Bureau fellow, Captain?'

'No word yet sir.'

'Very well. Please shut the door.'

The Major picked up my money, and looked it over with a bemused air.

'What are these?' he enquired.

'Err, bills of credit,' I said.

'English?' he asked.

'Of course,' I said.

'I have never seen such workmanship. Why are they so small: for concealment?'

'No, it is a new, err…style.'

He directed a piercing stare at me, closely replicated by the Captain and the Sergeant, before shrugging and picking up my phone. He held it up at me, eyebrows raised inquiringly.

'It is an instrument for calculating the positions of the stars,' I said, sticking uncomfortably to my earlier story.

The Major looked sceptical, but the Lieutenant spoke up unexpectedly.

'I thought the same Major, but Mr Walton here does know a thing or two about that kind of stuff. He sure tied my head in knots, what with the moons of Jupiter, and the speed of light and all.'

The Major considered this for a moment, and then sighed and put the money and the banknotes into a drawer. He picked up the folded documents instead, and started to sift through them. Here he was much more at home, and quickly became intent on their contents.

'Where did these documents come from Lieutenant?' he asked.

'We found them in Miss Johnson's house,' replied the Lieutenant crisply, 'in a meeting with our two renegades and her stepfather.'

A pregnant silence fell in the room, penetrated only by the distant sound of hoof beats. They grew louder, and mixed with muffled cries as horses clattered to a halt somewhere outside. Shouted words echoed in the hallway, and then came a violent knocking on the Major's door. He looked up from the papers he was reading as the protestations of a union soldier outside were ignored. The door was forced open and Jacqueline's stepfather strode into the room, as big and formidable as I remembered him. The strange, mirror-like reflection of the Portal he wore excited tingling reactions all over me. Luminous images flickered in the air between us, and my own device grew more defined in my attention.

'I demand to see my daughter!' he bellowed, glaring around the room. A second man entered with him. The time-traveller was dressed in a militia uniform of impressive quality and ornamentation. Presumably of impressive rank too, because the Major suppressed his initial start of anger at the intrusion.

'May I know who you are sir?' he enquired, and his disruptive visitor drew himself up to his full height.

'I am Colonel Jeremiah Serrano of the 31st Regiment, Pennsylvania 2nd Reserve Volunteers,' he announced stridently, 'and my daughter was abducted by the Confederate scum you have here. These men have invaded my home sir, and I have pursued them with my Militia these past days. I claim rightful custody.'

The Major looked troubled. 'That may be so Colonel, but there are some serious questions about the documents this Southern officer claims to have found at your property.'

'Of course Major, but this is a political matter regarding sensitive military information, a sphere in which I am highly placed. I can assure you this matter is fully in hand, and has been politically sanctioned at the highest level. There is no need for you to take further responsibility upon yourself.'

'I'm not so sure Colonel,' said the Major slowly, 'you see, there are Confederate military documents here, which is all well and good. But among them are Union Army orders relating to my own Regiment, which I happen to know have not yet been –'

Events spiralled abruptly out of control, just as they had the last time I met this darkly mysterious man. A gunshot exploded with ear-splitting force, blasting the Major backwards. My heightened sense of the Portal's presence mushroomed, and reality became oddly distorted. Space-time seemed to gel into a strangely fluid mass, and everything around me slowed into a dreamlike dance.

There was a revolver in Jacqueline's stepfather's hand, wreathed in lazily swirling smoke. It shifted to unleash a long reverberating report into the sergeant, who stood gaping uncomprehendingly in a suspended moment of time. Then it swung towards the equally slow-moving Union Captain. But no such temporal inertia impeded my movements. I grabbed the weapon before it fired again, knocking it upwards, and was suddenly wrestling with a great bear of a man whose strength far outmatched my own.

I was aware of his grim-faced accomplice, moving in normal time but fast enough to exploit the unprepared Captain: his gun had already cleared his holster as the unfortunate officer started to go for his firearm. The Lieutenant was quicker off the mark, diving into the man in slow motion as he discharged a lingering detonation, and they fell struggling sluggishly together to the floor. The misplaced shot caught the Captain high on his left arm causing him to stagger in shock, but he continued to pull out his revolver. My own massive assailant finally wrenched his weapon free, throwing me against the desk. He whipped back towards the Captain, and their guns lined up together. They fired simultaneously, a long booming echo of sound, and both fell backwards. Jacqueline's stepfather slumped down against the door, and his gun clattered from his hand.

There was another prolonged gunshot, and the Lieutenants body was flung leadenly back from the man he grappled with. I knew he was as good as dead: the bullet erupted from between his shoulder blades. I burned with fury as his assailant began to climb lethargically to his feet, and dived unthinkingly for the fallen revolver. The Lieutenant's killer was hopelessly slow as he swung his gun towards me. I held the heavy weapon two handed and pulled the trigger without hesitation. But its recoil caught me unprepared. It jerked the barrel upwards and the bullet kicked out plaster above his head. He had still to line his gun up and I aimed lower, pulling the trigger twice more. I felt only savage satisfaction as his ruined body was blasted against the wall.

'That's more like it,' said the Mindworm smugly, *'but you shot the wrong guy. He could have helped you.'*

It seemed to revel in my rage, and I tried to shake it out of my head with a curse. I crawled over to where the Lieutenant lay. It had taken only seconds to turn the room into a charnel house. Everything was thick with the stench of gunpowder and death. Shouts were coming from the hallway outside, and someone was heaving at the door. But Jacqueline's stepfather lay jammed against it, and his bulk resisted all efforts to shift him. I reached the lieutenant, who now lay on his back. He was staring at the ceiling, bright red blood pooling on his chest and spreading beneath him.

'Looks like you weren't a spy after all,' he murmured drowsily, and I realised I was back in real-time.

'You did well Lieutenant, you gave me a chance,' I said, surprised at the emotion that choked me.

'Them stars,' he said dreamily, 'you think God's in them stars too?'

I thought of the awesome energies I had seen pulsing through the Cosmos.

'I think maybe God is in everything,' I said sadly. I could think of nothing else to say, and it seemed to ease him as his life drained away.

The pounding outside increased in volume, and I looked around to see Jacqueline's stepfather stirring, disturbed by the shuddering door. He opened his eyes with a groan. The side of his head was bleeding and he felt for the damage, inspecting the blood on his fingers.

'You stupid bastard,' he said dazedly, 'I was trying to help you.'

'I doubt it,' I snapped, still angered by the death all around me.

'Major Dawes!' Someone shouted through the door. 'What's going on in there? Are you all right?'

'Keep out, or he'll kill the Major!' called Jacqueline's stepfather, favouring me with a sardonic wink. His callus arrogance was extraordinary.

I became dimly aware that the hubbub outside the door was being eclipsed by shouting in the street, and I could hear gunshots in the distance.

'Colonel!' someone else called out, 'the graybacks are coming. We got to get out of here!'

'You go!' he shouted back, 'I'll meet you up at Culp's Hill.'

The shooting outside in the street intensified in volume.

'Time to leave,' said the hulking time traveller, heaving himself to his feet. I got up too, backing off and keeping the gun trained on him. I was afraid it might be empty, but he didn't know that. At least I hoped not.

'I just want the documents,' he said, stepping towards the desk.

'What about Jacqueline?' I asked sarcastically.

'There was only one civilian killed at Gettysburg,' he leered, 'and it wasn't her. It was the documents I came after, and you.'

He scooped up the pile of papers on the desk and thrust them into his elaborate frock coat, holding my gaze and daring me to stop him.

'You are a mystery,' he said, 'but you will have to wait for another day.'

He picked up a chair and faced me with it.

'Out of the way,' he said.

'What's that for?' I asked, fascinated by his supreme self-confidence.

'A plausible escape route,' he said, and launched the chair casually through the window.

'Au revoir.'

His words hung in the air like the grin of the Cheshire cat, consumed by the hum of an energetic field. The air around him shimmered: a gossamer pattern of iridescent colour, and he vanished in a fading haze of sparkling gold. I felt a sympathetic tug from my own Portal, like a dog straining at its leash. But I remained firmly planted in space-time.

I stood stunned for long moments. Dense layers of gun-smoke drifted lazily through the shattered window. There was no shouting now in the hallway, but the door handle turned cautiously and the door edged open. Jacqueline peered into the room, her eyes widening with horror. Her gaze took in the carnage and the weapon in my hand. She paled. Her mouth opened but no sound came, and I hurriedly dropped the gun.

'I didn't start it,' I muttered stupidly.

I looked beyond her into the hallway. The place seemed deserted, with bits and pieces of equipment scattered on the floor. The gunfire outside was constant now, and sounded very close.

I was numb, but felt a flicker of concern as I realised she had come through the chaos in the street.

'What are you doing here?' I said in sudden alarm, 'it sounds dangerous outside.'

'Not as dangerous as in here,' she said shakily. 'What have you done?'

'Your stepfather –' my voice dried up and I swallowed. 'He turned up with some men. It was just like what happened in your house.'

'I thought it might be him,' she said, her own voice catching. 'I saw his Militia galloping away with their tails between their legs. Where is he? Why, these are Northern officers – and is that the poor Lieutenant?'

'Your stepfather's gone,' I said dully. 'One of his men is here. They started shooting everyone: the Lieutenant fought them, and I shot the one who killed him.'

'I don't understand,' she said. 'They shot other Union officers? That makes no sense.'

'Your stepfather wanted the documents the Lieutenant found at your house. These other Union officers became suspicious. That's why he started shooting. How much do you really know about him?'

Her face darkened. 'There is much I don't know about him,' she said slowly, 'but there is much I don't know about you either.'

'Well, I guess we have more urgent things to worry about,' I said, 'we've got to get away from here. There's going to be a terrible battle.'

'There already is a terrible battle,' she said, 'but you're right: we need to move back with the Union soldiers.'

'It's kinda late for that,' said a voice behind her. Billy stood there, his eyes hard and cold. Several more of the Lieutenant's men were behind him. Their guards must have fled I realised. Billy pushed past us, and knelt at the Lieutenants body.

'He's gone,' he said briefly, and went to work collecting the weapons scattered about the floor. He passed the handguns out to his companions. 'Our boys will be here any minute,' he told them, and then looked slowly around the room.

'What happened here?' he demanded harshly.

'More or less the same as back at Jacq – at Miss Johnson's house,' I said unsteadily, 'except she wasn't here this time. Her stepfather turned up and everybody started shooting.'

'And here you are without a scratch again,' said Billy scathingly, 'and the lieutenant dead.'

'He helped me,' I said. 'If it wasn't for him I might be dead too.'

A little more humanity flickered in Billy's eyes, but he remained guarded.

'There's a lot of blue-bellies down,' he observed, watching for my reaction.

'They searched the Lieutenant and found he had picked up Union documents as well as Confederate at Miss Johnson's house. They got suspicious, and her stepfather and his man started shooting.'

'His own side?' asked Billy sharply.

'Yes.'

He shook his head, and gave a low whistle. 'Where's the papers now?'

'He took them.'

'Through the window?'

'Yes'. There was nothing else I could say.

The vicious crackle of gunfire was right outside the building now. The air filled with the tang of fresh gunpowder, and there were shouts between men in the street and some of Billy's companions at the entrance.

Billy turned to Jacqueline. 'You weren't here for the shooting?' he asked.

'I have just come back from the hotel,' she stated. 'I needed to bathe and change my clothes. I'm sorry about your Lieutenant.'

He looked pensive. 'I'm going to have to hand you over to someone else,' he said.

'This is outrageous,' she said angrily. 'This is a Northern town. You don't belong here, and I don't know anything about your ridiculous Southern secrets. Isn't there enough fighting out there to satisfy you?'

Billy looked a little rueful.

'Well, you sure ain't lost your fighting spirit ma'am. But I don't have a choice, or it'll be my hide they're after. There's going to be a lot of questions over this.'

Raucous voices sounded as more Confederate soldiers spilled into the entrance hall. Hyped up from the fighting, they were keen on finding valuables or eatables they could secrete about their persons. A minute or two later an officer arrived. He entered into a terse conversation with Billy and another of the Lieutenants men, interspersed with hard glances at me and Jacqueline. Agreement was reached, and Billy came across to us.

'You got to be interrogated,' he said, keeping a wary eye on Jacqueline. 'You can stay here for now, but you will probably be moved later.'

'Under the strongest protest,' she said. 'I will most certainly give this interrogator a piece of my mind.'

Billy lowered his voice. 'I think you had better be careful Miss Johnson. This is serious.'

He took us into the hall, and looked into the same small room I had occupied with the Lieutenant.

'I think it will have to be here for now,' he said, and Jacqueline marched into it with a characteristic toss of her head. I followed more soberly, still stunned by the shocking violence of the gunfight. We sat in silence for a minute, until Jacqueline turned to me.

'You are trembling,' she said.

'I've never shot anyone before,' I admitted.

'Most men seem happy enough about it,' she said bitterly.

'Not where I come from,' I said.

She eyed me curiously. 'Where exactly do you come from?'

'London.'

A flash of interest lit her eyes, 'Oh I would love to see London.'

She reminded me intensely of Alex at that moment. I had forgotten how beautiful she was. I was suddenly aware that she had bathed, and changed into an elegant green dress which made her look absolutely enchanting. There was a richness of style and presence about her very different from the busy twenty-first century women I was used to.

'You look perfect in that dress,' I stammered, my words sounding idiotic even as I said them.

She chuckled in amusement, blushing a little as she did so. 'You don't have much experience in paying compliments to ladies do you Mr Walton?'

'Not really,' I admitted.

She favoured me with one of her trademark looks, head tilted slightly, and eyes quizzical and considering.

'You look worried,' she said.

'I don't know what your stepfather is up to. Remember, Billy said this was serious.'

'Do you really not know?' she asked in puzzlement.

'No, he is as much a mystery to me as I am to him.'

'But you admit you are a mystery. Why did you come to my house, and in such a strange manner?'

'I can't explain. At least not at the moment: you will think I'm crazy.'

She laughed. 'I already think you're crazy, Mister Walton.'

'Can't you call me Richard?'

She regarded me speculatively. 'Very well, Richard, and you may call me Jacqueline, but that doesn't mean I have decided to trust you.'

'Can you trust me enough to tell me about your stepfather?'

'What do you want to know?'

'Can you say how he became involved in your life?'

She frowned. 'He appeared from nowhere, a bit like you. My father died when I was seventeen. Mister Jeremiah Serrano appeared a few years later: swept Mama off her feet it seemed.'

She sounded angry.

'Where is your mother now?' I asked tentatively.

'She died a year later, nearly eight months ago now,' she said. 'It was a fever; we never knew exactly what it was.'

'I'm sorry to hear that,' I said. 'What about your stepfather, how does he behave towards you?'

She looked at me. 'You know something about him don't you?'

I hesitated. 'Yes, but not why he is involved with your family.'

'Tell me what you know.'

'I'm sorry I really can't, not just now. But maybe he had something to gain by marrying your mother?'

She shrugged. 'Only the farm, and my uncle's legacy. But half of each goes to me.'

'Your uncle's legacy?'

'Oh, he just made guns. He bequeathed the company to Mama and me. Or at least, I will own my half when I am twenty five.'

'What happened to your mothers half?'

She pouted. 'He owns it now.'

'And if something happens to you?'

'I suppose my half would go to him too.' She stared at me. 'You don't think –'

'I don't know,' I said, 'is the company worth a lot of money?'

'It's not very big, although there is a lot more business with the war. My uncle was always more interested in inventing guns than selling them.'

'Hmm,' I mused.

'Is that all: hmm?' She seemed annoyed.

'Can I ask you something else?'

'I suppose so.'

'Do you normally carry a gun around with you?'

She looked down. 'It was a present from my uncle. I kept it locked away until a few months ago. I don't like my stepfather, but I never had a reason to be afraid of him. It's all the strange men coming to the house. They make me uneasy.'

'Do they come there a lot?'

'No, my stepfather is mostly away on business. But when he appears, usually other men come too.'

'He seems to be mixed up in all kinds of things,' I said. 'Maybe you should get some legal advice about safeguarding yourself and your inheritance.'

'I think I will,' she said and shivered. 'I feel as if someone has just walked over my grave.'

'Just a precaution that's all,' I said, trying to sound reassuring. 'It's probably nothing to worry about. Do you have anyone else in the family who can help you?'

'No,' she said, with her customary pride. 'I can look after myself.'

'If I can do anything to help I will,' I said.

'Why should you help me?' she asked sharply, a flash of suspicion returning, 'and what could you do anyway?'

'Well, in the first instance, because I know what it's like to have troubles come into your life,' I said defensively. 'As far as help is concerned: probably not much. I don't know where I'll be or what I'll be doing.'

It hit me again then. The vast gulf of time and space I was lost in. I really did have no idea what was going to happen to me. I thought of Alex. '*I will be far from here,*' she had said. My head swam. That could mean almost anything, and the enormity of the quest seemed to crush me.

'You look sad,' Jacqueline said. 'I am sorry. We are talking of my troubles but not of your own.'

'Don't worry about my problems: they are of a different kind...' I thought for a moment. 'At least, I think they are.'

She shook her head wryly. 'More riddles: I don't think I've ever met anyone quite like you Mr – Richard.'

'I hope that's a compliment,' I said with a smile, and she surprised me with a smile of her own.

'It's just an observation,' she said. 'I don't have much experience in paying compliments to gentlemen either, especially one as mysterious and artless as yourself.'

I grinned sheepishly. 'Can I ask you one last thing?'

'Very well,' she sighed.

'I'm surprised you came back, with all that fighting going on outside. Did the Union soldiers force you?'

She hesitated. 'We were on our way when we saw the fighting was getting nearer. The soldiers wanted to turn back, but I – insisted on coming. I don't know why. It felt important somehow. But I must admit, I did not think the Confederates would come this far into town.'

We shared our most sociable silence to date as the sounds of battle moved further away. It sounded as if the Union troops were being driven all the way back through the town. It all felt quite unreal, and I had to force myself to think about it rationally. The Southern soldiers I had met so far had acted decently enough. But there was no guarantee this would always be the case. I hoped Jacqueline and I would be in a better position with the incriminating papers gone. I also hoped the phone and the money in the draw would be overlooked. But I could not be sure.

I certainly did not feel I could rely on the Portal to get out of the situation. I thought enviously of the way Jacqueline's stepfather had disappeared at will, and wondered if I would ever achieve that sort of control. I contemplated the way my Portal had triggered the time dilation effect which had so enhanced my performance in the gunfight. It appeared to have been stimulated when my fellow time traveller did the same, or perhaps it had been an unconscious reaction to danger, I wasn't sure which. The same thing seemed to have happened back at Jacqueline's house too. I remained vaguely aware of the Mindworm brooding somewhere in the background. Yet I was no closer to understanding the creature than I was to achieving an effective connection with the Portal. I sensed a certain antipathy on the Mindworm's part towards Jacqueline, and on reflection this seemed to be missing where her stepfather was concerned. Perhaps it was a clue of sorts, but there were too many uncertainties to be sure of anything.

We were both dozing a little when the door opened, and Billy's face appeared.

'Good news Miss Johnson,' he said cheerfully, 'you can go back to your hotel and stay the night in comfort. A couple of the boys will keep watch, and bring you along when the Information Bureau people are ready for you. Mr Walton is coming with us now, and we'll all meet up again in a day or so.'

Jacqueline looked at me uncertainly, and then nodded.

'Very well,' she said, 'I will see you soon – Richard.'

She left on foot with an escort, and I went out with Billy to find our horses standing nearby. A couple of mounted men from the Lieutenant's original force were waiting for us. The street was crammed with triumphant Confederate soldiers, along with abandoned equipment and bloodied bodies from both armies. The dead lay in grotesque postures by the side of the road where they had fallen, or been dragged aside. Billy and I mounted and the four of us made our way slowly through the jubilant throng. There was almost a fairground atmosphere. The casual disregard for the dead seemed bizarre, but I supposed death had become pretty matter-of-fact for these men.

We rode back out of Gettysburg and began to circle around to the North West, where vast quantities of men and equipment were being managed on an industrial scale. It was a sea of organised mayhem. Large companies of soldiers were marching in, or sat resting under the trees with their packs and weapons. All around them teams of whickering horses hauled rattling wagons and canons with their ammunition trailers in a grim cacophony of creaking wheels. A heavy sense of fate seemed to hang over everything, and I studied the teeming mosaic of faces in fascination. It was extraordinary to see their mute absorption in the drama unfolding all around them.

It reminded me of the state of mind that had overtaken me at Charles' cottage, and again at my bedsit, of the human race marching blindly towards its collective doom like an army of ants. A subtle vibration reverberated in my being, and I sensed a powerful static charge all around me. I had little time to wonder at it. Energy pulsated intensely in my body and my sense of self swelled to encompass the whole epic tableaux in a new mantle of awareness. I felt almost suspended in the air, while the pace of life slowed to a profound and momentous present.

The vision spoke of timeless patience and detachment, but the grim martial carnival invoked a sad inner acuity. Men absurdly young and naïve held in thrall by forces beyond their knowledge and understanding. Half-grown children trapped in fatalistic resignation to the lottery of war: sheltering from brutal reality in the camaraderie of their companions. Manifold animations swam in the sea of personalities, but it was a primitive, tribal affair: a learned perception of the other. It seemed extraordinary that men would kill each other on such a scale.

The unforgiving revelation receded, and I contemplated its departure in bewilderment. It was as if some deeper, primal self was looking in at my life. Or, of course, that I was going mad. Or the Mindworm was playing tricks on me. Swirling uncertainties plagued me after such experience, but never when they were taking place. Their impact carried its own conviction: but appeared outlandish in the face of rational deliberation.

Looking back it is a wonder I coped at all. Yet I managed to proceed in the face of relentlessly frightening and mind-bending events. The human mind seems to shut out inconvenient or contradictory truths in the interests of self-preservation. I could not afford to indulge in self-doubt or paranoia. I was too busy dodging more concrete threats. At the time, I could only assume these strange experiences were something to do with the exotic dimensions opened up by the Portal. I knew it was dangerous, and I risked losing myself in mysterious and unknown realities. But once I had awoken into Alex's world, I was as consumed as a moth before a flame.

I gradually slipped back into the everyday world, and began to notice more mundane details of life around me. The variety of uniforms in the Confederate army surprised me, not only in style and design, but in quality and condition. Many men looked little better than tramps, with threadbare, mismatching jackets and pants. Their shoes and boots were in a terrible condition. Some were in bare feet. Yet other units appeared better equipped, and some officers, astonishingly, could have just come off stage in the most elaborate outfits the costume department had to offer.

We arrived at a large enclave of tents, dismounting to wait while a sentry reported our arrival. Billy and I were escorted to a large, broad tent with its sides tied back. It was obviously a command centre. A number of officers of various ranks sat around a wide, rough wooden table strewn with maps and notebooks. The most senior man present looked surprisingly young, but was apparent by the steel in his eyes and the deference of those around him. He looked up, and held me in an unyielding gaze for a moment.

'Good evening Mr Walton,' he said. 'Colonel Tyler Bennett, 14th North Carolina. I understand you have been involved in some unfortunate events concerning the security of the Southern States.'

'Yes I believe that is true,' I answered, 'but it was without knowledge or intent.'

'You are also English.'

I refrained from rolling my eyes, and tried to look harmless instead.

'I am informed,' he said, apparently unimpressed by my harmlessness, 'that Lieutenant Bowen discovered Confederate military documents at a meeting between Southern renegades and Northern agents.'

'So I understand,' I said.

'– a meeting at which you were also present.'

'I was the victim of circumstance,' I said, adding 'sir' for good measure. 'My presence was accidental, and in no way connected with these matters.'

'You will forgive me if I find that hard to accept.'

'I can understand that,' I admitted, swallowing uncomfortably.

'Do you know of the contents of these documents?'

'No, I have not looked at them.'

'I believe you claim that Miss Johnson's stepfather took these documents from Union soldiers in a gunfight today.'

'Yes, that is what happened.'

'Why would he do that if he was spying for the North?'

'It seems that military information from both sides was involved,' I said, feeling my position becoming increasingly complicated. 'When the Union officer – the Major discovered this, Miss Johnson's stepfather started shooting.'

The Colonel gave me a flat stare. 'What were you doing at this man's house?'

'I had, err, called there for help,' I said, cringing inwardly. 'I think I may have been robbed: knocked on the head. I cannot remember what happened.'

'You were without even a horse, I am told,' he said with more than a touch of impatience. 'Were you staying with Miss Johnson and her stepfather?'

'No, I had just arrived.'

'On foot?' he enquired ironically.

'Yes.' I said shortly.

He regarded me silently for several seconds. 'So you claim not to know them?'

'I don't know them,' I insisted. 'Well, I have got to know Miss Johnson a little, but I have barely met her stepfather. He seems a violent and unscrupulous man. My impression is that Miss Johnson does not trust him, or understand his interests or motives.'

'Hmm,' said the Colonel, ending the interview. 'I will request Captain Daniels to question you in detail about the events of the past few days, and I will make a decision when I receive his report.'

We were dismissed and marched off to a smaller tent, where Billy and his comrades were detailed to guard me. Soon afterwards a serious-minded Captain appeared, and began a meticulous re-examination of my recent adventures. It was a warm evening, and I envied Billy and his friends as they conversed in low voices out in the fresh air. The Captain scribbled copious notes, and I constantly told and retold different parts of the story to explain the actions of various people.

My mysterious appearance at Jacqueline's house, and my movements prior to this did not take long to emerge as the main sticking point. It was something I could give no account of. I just did not know enough about the times or the place to construct anything like a coherent story. I even appealed to the Portal for help in the hope it might trawl something from my memory. One or two vivid reconstructions of relevant historical events did start to form in my mind's eye. But that was unhelpful where the complex itinerary of a long land and sea journey was concerned; never mind a fictitious identity, a destination and a purpose.

'I can help with that,' said the Mindworm, *'just let me take over for a while, and I can give them everything they need to hear.'*

I didn't like the sound of that, but it was certainly tempting. I wavered for a moment before digging my heels in. I had no idea what 'let me take over for a while' actually meant, but I instinctively shied away from it, and my resentment at its intrusion into my life fuelled my rejection.

'Suit yourself,' it said condescendingly, *'but they will probably shoot you.'*

I stuck instead to the story that I had been hit on the head, and lost my memory. I hoped the Portal would get me out of the situation if it became too serious. My interrogator finally shut his note book and announced that he would return in the morning. It meant spending the night in the tent, and equipment was collected from the horses and dumped inside. Billy and his companions scrounged some food, and we sat and ate as the sun went down. My jailors were not inclined to talk much. They appeared uncomfortable about my interrogation, and I shared their mood. I was shattered by the day's events, and went to sleep surrounded by the ominous sounds of an army girding itself for war. I dreamed of violence, blood and death.

I was awoken early by the sound of horses and men on the march. Billy escorted me to the latrines, and we returned to find the inevitable breakfast of cornmeal and thin coffee waiting for us. But I was grateful for it. We sat in silence watching the bustling activity in the camp. I little enjoyed the leisure we had though. The prospect of further interrogation, and the relentless preparation for killing all around us weighed heavily on me. I thought disagreeably about Charles, and what he might make of this unique peephole into history. But even the thought of his enthusiastic tones faltered under the grim blanket of tension that hung over the camp.

The first canons opened up some distance away: a startling, intermittent barrage that built up into a rolling, thunderous bombardment. It was swiftly joined by the wicked crackling of massed musketry. We couldn't see anything. But the sound conjured the image of a wild, foreboding storm that had fallen from the sky and was rampaging up and down the shallow valley between the two armies. The sullen thunder of artillery and the rippling volleys of gunfire played back and forth as the morning crept on: rising and falling in intensity, distance and direction. Billy and his companions were visibly restless without sight or knowledge of the battlefield. Only a thin haze of gun smoke drifted back through the camp, and the occasional musket ball whizzed overhead. I sat thinking about Jacqueline: hoping we had been forgiven or forgotten amidst the titanic drama that was engulfing us.

My hopes were in vain. The punctilious Captain returned with a grim-faced colleague, who seemed familiar with the shadowy world of political intrigue and military subterfuge. Between them they picked their way through my statements all over again, while the Mindworm smirked palpably somewhere in my head. Finally they asked me point blank if the British Government had plans to abandon its support for the South. I maintained my innocence, but was hopelessly compromised. They were clearly dissatisfied, and their expressions were ominous as they departed.

The day dragged slowly on, punctuated by a mixture of rumour and news as messengers and wounded men passed by. The stumbling processions of wounded grew from a trickle to a stream: a shocking spectacle of pain, ruin and broken dreams, borne with shaky bravado. A casualty station was close by, and the screams were a horrific testimony to the harsh reality of war.

Billy appeared unfazed by the bloodshed though, and increasingly buoyed up by the news of the fighting.

'This could be it,' he said excitedly, 'we could thrash them Yankees for once and all, and get this war over with.'

Finally in the late afternoon the military intelligence officer returned, looking as severe and impenetrable as ever. He indicated that we should saddle up, and we all rode slowly out of the camp, passing a grotesque heap of discarded, bloody limbs behind the casualty station. We rode for a mile or so through light woodland alive with troops: some recovering from skirmishes and others waiting to go into action. Eventually we approached a small, whitewashed cottage, vacated or abandoned by its occupants. Two men in civilian outfits stood talking outside the open front door. It was screened by a thin grove of coniferous evergreens, and far from other habitation. The trees smelled vaguely of Cedar, a fragrance that reminds me of the house to this day.

'This is the Englishman,' announced the officer laconically, and the two men regarded me with stony eyes.

'Mr McCreedy is waiting for you,' said one, and inclined his head to indicate the open doorway. I dismounted in my customary ungainly fashion, and walked stiffly into the dim corridor, my eyes trying to adjust to the gloom. A door stood ajar, opening into a modest, low ceilinged room, and within it stood an odd-looking man, also in civilian clothes. He was an ill-favoured individual of medium height and a gawky, bony build. His face was pale and angular. One eye drooped and both were pitiless and cruel. He smiled coldly as I entered.

'Pleased to meet you Mr Walton,' he said evenly, and smashed his fist deep into my stomach. I sunk to my knees, unable even to gasp for breath. I had entered a whole new world of darkness and pain.

Chapter 7

'WHO IS JEREMIAH Serrano working for? Who do you represent in the English government? Why were you sent to this country?'

The questions went on endlessly, with so many vicious cuffs and jabs being delivered by different men that I could not have answered if I'd wanted to. When at last they stopped I was on my hands and knees spitting blood: my mind stunned, my body engulfed in pain, and my senses reeling. White lights sparked before my eyes, and my hearing was overlaid by a dull static roar.

'Well, now you know we mean business, perhaps you can give us some answers,' said Mr McCreedy venomously, peering down at me in great satisfaction.

'Are you crazy?' I gasped, shocked and terrified. 'I don't know anything about these things.'

'I think you do Mr Walton,' he sneered, 'and I think you are going to tell us.'

His two accomplices forced me up into a chair and bound me roughly to it; the repugnant Mr McCreedy firing the same relentless questions at me. Every attempt I made to protest my innocence just made his accusations louder and more insistent. Then they started hitting me again, and I could not move my body to ward off the blows. The helplessness and despair was as bad as the physical pain. I had no idea what they were talking about, and even less what I could say or do to stop them. There was no escape from the incessant violence.

At last there was a pause. They left me slumped in the chair, and took themselves off for a while, no doubt to discuss tactics. I struggled frantically to establish a link with the Portal. I just wanted to escape the pain, and I strained with all my might to do so. But my dazed mind could find no purchase, and the Portal did not seem inclined to help. I went nowhere, and when Mr McCreedy and his friends returned the nightmare continued.

The questions became more varied and wide ranging, but the end result was the same. I was beaten with calculated savagery until I began to lose all sense of who I was and what was happening. The questions, the blows, and the unbearable intervals of dread began to blur into one. Numbness crept through my body, and I felt consciousness slipping away. I knew I could not take much more. When it finally stopped I lolled limply in the chair, hardly caring what came next.

'Acting dumb is not going to help you Mr Walton,' said Mr McCreedy's baleful voice in my ear. 'We'll give you a night to think it over, and talk again in the morning.'

I was hauled roughly to my feet, and stumbled along between my captors into the back of the house, where I was half-thrown down some rickety steps into a cellar. Its earthen floor was surprisingly cool and comforting, and I surrendered thankfully to oblivion.

Morning signalled its presence through a couple of chinks of daylight, which penetrated the trapdoor at the top of the cellar steps. I regained consciousness slowly, staring bemusedly at dust motes circulating lazily in the dim beams of light. I tried to take stock of my situation. I felt weak and nauseous, and every part of my body burned dully. My head pounded and my nose was blocked and swollen. I could taste and smell nothing but blood, and my probing tongue discovered several loose teeth. I wasn't sure how I would react if Mr McCreedy and his men laid into me again. I was certainly frightened by the thought of a renewed beating. But a deeper horror lurked at the thought of him turning his attentions to Jacqueline. I did not believe she would be assaulted in any official capacity. But there was an unsavoury air about these people, and I imagined they would be capable of almost anything carried out in a clandestine manner. Presumably that was why I had been turned over to them.

I thought about the Portal. Despite the layers of pain, my awareness of the device seemed to have grown a little. I was badly shaken, but no longer shocked, and a cold anger underlay a new determination. But I hesitated to try and escape. I did not want to leave Jacqueline to face the situation alone.

It was strange how involved I had become in a reality which had held no existence for me only days before. I knew it could only be one of myriad scenarios playing out in space-time. I dimly grasped that these were superficial events, fleeting bubbles of reality on the cusp of profoundly mysterious dimensions of being. But it made my head hurt in a whole new way just to think of it. I supposed that tangible existence, however finite, was real enough for me.

I had got into this because of Alex as much as anything; and my concern for Jacqueline was no different. Her resemblance to Alex seemed an unlikely coincidence. I felt sure she was part of the puzzle, and I was reluctant to leave without knowing more. So I strove instead to steel myself for my imminent confrontation with the thugs upstairs.

'I can help you with the Portal, you know,' said the Mindworm conversationally. 'Or if you prefer, I can switch off the pain. All these high-minded ideas are making you suffer without reason. Jacqueline can look after herself, and no one will care if you are beaten to death. It is time you started thinking about yourself for a change.'

'Go away,' I replied irritably, 'or at least shut up.' But freedom from pain, and help with the Portal sounded very inviting in that cellar.

A great amount of musket fire started up somewhere: the noise muted, and direction and distance impossible to guess from my dingy prison. It was joined by the dull, booming bass of cannon, seemingly replied to from a distance, and the disembodied sound of violence settled into a sullen background clamour.

It was Billy who opened the trapdoor, and he came down to help me up the stairs. He looked ashamed, avoiding my eyes as he supported me out back to the crude toilet. I made my way stiffly and uncertainly beside him. We returned to eat some bread and cheese in the kitchen, and I had some water to wash it down with. I chewed carefully and painfully, favouring my loose teeth. Even my gums were sore and tender.

'I sure am sorry about this, Mr Walton,' he said at length, 'I don't like it at all. Can't you just tell them what they want to know? What's the point of getting yourself all beat up?'

'There's nothing to tell Billy,' I said wearily, slurring my words a little. 'I don't know what they're talking about. Don't feel bad, you treated me well enough.'

Shaking his head, Billy helped me back down the cellar steps, and I sat dozing fitfully in darkness for what seemed a very long time. After a while I began to feel a little better, and tried to force myself into a more optimistic frame of mind. But everything changed when I caught a familiar sound above the muffled, background tumult of war. It set me trembling with fear and adrenaline again: Jacqueline's voice raised in anger, punctuated by short pauses which I imagined filled with Mr

McCreedy's insidious, rasping tones. Finally heavy footsteps approached the trapdoor, and it was heaved open to reveal the two men who had delivered me there the night before.

'I hope you're not going to make us come down there and get you,' one said in surly tones.

I got to my feet, and made my way unsteadily up towards them. They seized me roughly, and frogmarched me back to the room where the beating had taken place. I was thrust through the door, and stood blinking in the unaccustomed light.

Jacqueline blanched as she saw me. Her face registered shock, fear and anger in quick succession. 'What have you done?' she gasped.

'Mr Walton has been rather unhelpful with our enquiries,' said Mr McCreedy unpleasantly. 'I thought it might help to jog your memory, Miss Johnson, if you see that we mean business.'

'This is disgraceful,' she said furiously. 'How dare you treat him like this? I demand that he receives medical treatment immediately.'

'You are in no place to demand anything,' sneered Mr McCreedy, 'and I would worry more about your own good health if I were you. Your family has been playing a dangerous game with the interests of the Southern States.'

'I have told you, I know nothing about my stepfather's affairs. I have known him little more than a year myself.'

'And what of Mr Walton?'

She hesitated. 'I have known Mr Walton only a few days. I do not know if he has any involvement with my stepfather. But in my estimation he is a decent man who has little interest in military or political affairs.'

The obnoxious man shifted his gaze backwards and forwards, as though seeking an invisible conduit between me and Jacqueline. Finally he closed his drooping eye almost completely, and fixed the other orb inscrutably on some distant realm.

'Very well,' he said at last, 'as you know, a great battle is being fought, and my men and I have much to occupy us. I will leave you both to consider your position. I trust we will find you more cooperative when we return.'

He turned and stalked out, followed by his men. A key turned in the lock, voices muttered in the hall, and a minute later several horses rode off outside. Jacqueline stepped quickly over and lightly touched my face, her eyes full of concern.

'What a loathsome toad that man is,' she said. 'He is a brute. Let me attend to this for you.'

She went to the door and hammered on it, waited a few moments and then hammered again. Eventually sounds emanated from the hall, and the door was opened. An awkward deputation stood there: Billy, with another of the Lieutenants men similarly discomforted behind him.

'Billy, this is disgraceful,' she said fiercely. 'I need warm salt water and a clean cloth for poor Mr Walton.'

'Miss Johnson,' he said hesitantly, 'I ain't sure we're supposed to...'

'Have you been ordered not to provide warm salt water and a clean cloth?'

'Well no ma'am, but...'

'Then please do it.'

Billy withdrew rapidly, relocking the door. I lowered myself awkwardly into my torture chair, and Jacqueline gently probed my face and head with her fingers, tracing lumps, swellings and dried blood.

'Do you have any serious injuries: anything fractured or broken?' she enquired anxiously.

'Probably mostly bruises,' I murmured through swollen lips. I felt rather self-conscious about the intimate attention I was getting. This close, her physical presence was kind of overwhelming. 'I think they could have done a lot more damage if they wanted to.'

'Could you not have told them what they wanted to know?' she asked.

'I don't know anything,' I groaned.

'Well, if that's true then I know how you feel. It is infuriating to be questioned about something you know nothing about. But you must own that there is some mystery about you, and you have given no real explanation of yourself.'

I suspected Mr McCreedy had left a listener in some advantageous spot to eavesdrop on our conversation. But there was little he could hear of an incriminating nature.

'I can't explain,' I muttered, 'I told you before: you'd think I was crazy. But I can tell you it had nothing to do with spying for the Confederacy, the Union, the English or anyone else.'

The key turned in the lock, and Billy reappeared, carrying a white enamel bowel equipped with warmish salt water and a rather ragged linen cloth.

'Here you are Miss Johnson,' he said, an uncertain look on his face. 'Now you two better decide to tell Mr McCreedy what he wants to know. He's a hard man and one used to getting his way. I'm sorry for this, but there's a war on.'

'How's the war going Billy?' I asked faintly, trying to show that I bore him no ill-will. 'It sounds like the end of the world out there.'

The vicious crackle and popping of distant musketry had risen to new levels of intensity, and the vibrations from the cannon fire were making my chair tremble.

'I reckon we're giving them Yankees something to think about,' he said proudly. 'General Lee is gonna whip them good.'

'Don't be too sure of that,' said Jacqueline snippily.

'Well, I'd better get going then, Ma'am; Mr Walton,' he said hurriedly. 'I guess you can holler if you need something. I sure hope everything goes all right with Mr McCreedy.'

He backed out of the room and locked the door. Jacqueline turned to me. She dipped the cloth into the bowel of water, and began to carefully dab at my face. I couldn't help flinching, and she bit her lip contritely, concentrating on her work. She reminded me of Alex again, and I was surprised by a rush of emotion that constricted my throat. I was unable to prevent a tear forming, and felt a dull flush of embarrassment as it trickled down my cheek.

Her eyes softened. 'Are you alone Richard? Do you have family or – anyone?'

'Not really,' I said.

She was silent for a moment.

'Can you really not tell me why you came to my house?'

'I was looking for someone.'

'At the back of the house?'

'I came across country.'

'Without a horse?'

'Yes.'

She sighed, 'you are right. I do think you are crazy.'

'But I haven't told you anything yet,' I protested weakly.

'Quite enough I think!' She sounded both amused and exasperated.

I looked into the bowel of water, which was distinctly red.

'Is my face a mess?'

'Cuts and bruises: it will look better when the swelling goes down. The dried blood and dirt makes it look worse than it is.'

She paused, obviously still trying to make up her mind about me.

'When you first saw me, you said I reminded you of someone?'

'Someone who looks quite like you, yes,' I admitted.

Her brow furrowed. 'Had you seen me out somewhere, is that why you came?'

I chuckled painfully. 'No, I didn't know you existed. I was just looking for, err – directions.'

She looked sceptical, but let it pass. 'Is this lady someone special to you?'

'Well, yes and no,' I croaked. 'It's difficult to explain. She may hold the key to clarifying some mysteries in my life.'

'What sort of mysteries?'

'A bit like yours. Strangers appearing, and doing things I don't understand.'

She looked pensive. 'Yes, I know how that feels.'

She continued to work carefully on my face, and I was moved by a depth of affinity with her. It was more than her looks that reminded me of Alex.

'It's not easy to know who to trust,' I sighed, 'especially when faced with so much that is unusual or unexpected.'

She eyed me curiously. 'You are certainly both unusual and unexpected Richard. Tell me, do you have a profession?'

'Architect,' I grunted, thankful to be on firm ground for a change.

'An Architect!' A flash of interest gleamed in her eyes. 'That is excellent! It is why I would love to see London – to see Europe. All those beautiful old buildings with their amazing histories: why, the Pantheon is nearly two thousand years old!'

'Yes,' I smiled stiffly, 'it is amazing.'

'Have you seen it?' she asked eagerly.

'Oww,' I gasped, 'you dabbed too hard.'

'Sorry,' she giggled, 'I forget myself when I think of these things.'

'Yes, I have seen it.'

'How wonderful,' she cried. 'So you have travelled.'

'I have travelled a little,' I admitted, 'but not as much as I would have liked.'

'What about your scientific pursuits, do you own a telescope?'

'A telescope?'

'Yes, for your astronomical studies.'

'Ouch!' I grunted again: this time seeking a diversion from the subject.

'I hardly touched you!' she protested.

'Sorry,' I said, rummaging about in my head for something to say about telescopes. An assortment of nineteenth century astronomical facts arose from somewhere inside me. It was odd, but seemed free of the Mindworm's insinuations. I sensed it resented this mysterious store of data in fact, and I assumed it was something to do with the Portal. But my faculties were shattered from the beating I had received, and I had to struggle to grasp enough to say something.

'They are rather expensive,' I achieved, 'but some local members have them.'

'Members?' she queried.

'The local Amateur Astronomical Society.'

'Oh I see,' she said. 'What sort of lens do you use?'

'Reflective telescopes are more common,' I muttered. 'They use mirrors instead of lenses... except the eyepiece. They give a clearer picture... and a larger area.'

'Really?' she exclaimed, ever curious. 'Why is that? How do they work?'

'It's complicated,' I groaned, 'at least, too complicated to explain at the moment.'

'Oh,' she said quickly, 'I am sorry to tax you at a time like this.'

She was silent for a while. But her enthusiasm fired up once more.

'How extraordinary it must be to see the moons of Jupiter,' she sighed – 'or Saturn's rings, or the craters on the Moon! And what of the stars: how do they look?'

'You can see many more stars on a clear night,' I said, inspired more by the discovery channel than anything else. 'They shine in different colours. The greater the magnification, the more stars you can see.'

She looked increasingly enraptured, and her excitement was infectious, even in my battered state.

'Maybe I will be able to show you one day,' I said.

She appeared to remember then that our acquaintance was slight, despite everything we had been through.

'Yes perhaps,' she said more reticently, 'I would like that.'

Fighting nearby seemed to have receded, but gunfire could still be heard far off. There were occasional cracks and thuds as spent bullets struck the outside of the building. There was danger everywhere, and Mr McCreedy could return at any time. I wondered if I should try to activate the Portal and take Jacqueline someplace else. But I worried about my inexperience with the device. Even if I managed to make it work we could end up anywhere – maybe somewhere even more dangerous – and I hesitated to take her away from everything she knew.

She continued to clean up my face. It was amazing how much better it made me feel. I was becoming increasingly relaxed, and a deep weariness began to settle on me.

'Now I'm feeling really sleepy,' I said, my eyes drooping.

'You need to rest,' she said and looked around the room, 'there is nothing to lie on except the floor, but there is a shawl over there which will do as a pillow.'

My body felt incredibly heavy. 'I'm sorry about this,' I said, a little ashamed at my weakness, 'but I think you're right…'

'Don't be silly,' she said lightly.

I barely made it to the floor before sleep overcame me. I dreamed intensely, but remembered little of it when I awoke, rather thick-headed, sometime later. I felt more normal in myself, although my body seemed one solid slab of aching discomfort. I sat up stiffly with a groan, to see her seated in my torture chair and gazing out of the window. The muffled background reverberation of gunfire appeared to have died down.

'I don't think it's a good idea to sit near the window,' I said. 'A stray bullet could strike at any time.'

'Ah, you are awake,' she said, turning to me. 'I believe they are striking the other side of the house. How are you feeling?'

'Better, thank you, although everything hurts,' I said. 'Do you know what time it is?'

'I suspect it is some time after noon,' she replied. 'I wonder if the battle is drawing to a close. The fighting seems to have diminished.'

'I hope that doesn't mean our unpleasant friends will be back,' I said.

But there was a commotion of horses outside even as I spoke. Muffled voices sounded inside the house. A murmured discussion took place, and then the conversation became more general. Instructions were issued. I heard Billy express some dissent, silenced by Mr McCreedy's obnoxious tones. Several people left on horses, and a couple of minutes later the door to our room was flung open. The man himself marched impatiently into the room, flanked by the same disagreeable duo as before.

'It seems you have not been forthcoming, even in private,' he said shortly. 'I am going to quit horsing around. I have no more time to waste.'

I wondered if I could attack them using the time-dilation effect, but I still felt physically weak and fuzzy from sleep. Before I could attempt anything I was seized, and the two men roped me roughly to the chair.

'What are you doing?' exclaimed Jacqueline angrily. 'What sort of people are you? Haven't you harmed Mr Walton enough?'

'Not to be trifled with is what we are Miss Johnson, and answerable to none,' snapped Mr McCreedy. 'We will have the answers we are looking for, and stop at nothing to get them. Do not think your sex will save you. No one will know what happens here, and Mr Walton will take any blame.'

Jacqueline stared at him in horror, her face drained of colour as he pulled an evil-looking knife from under his coat. He admired its edge with a professional air.

'Well,' he said, 'let us see what Mr Walton has to say first shall we?'

Too late I realised I could not get to her. Even if I succeeded in activating the Portal, I would not be able to take her with me.

A sudden, thunderous roar shattered the stillness outside: repeating and prolonging itself into a long drumroll of fury. Everyone in the room froze for a moment. The floor quivered, and the windows rattled violently. A series of artillery batteries were opening up. The battle was certainly not over. Probably the final push on the third day of fighting I realised: the start of the disastrous Confederate advance against the centre of the Union line. It was pretty much the only thing I could remember about the whole engagement. The massed cannon fire continued relentlessly, battery by battery, and Mr McCreedy smiled unpleasantly.

'The final attack has begun,' he said, speaking loud against the din. 'We will break the Union centre, and chase them all the way back to Washington. No one will know or care what happens to you here.'

There was a stunning crash, and the room vanished in an explosion of plaster dust. For some moments I had no idea what had happened. My ears had popped, and my mind was numb. When the cloud of dust thinned, Mr McCreedy and his henchmen had disappeared. I strained to see, and after a second made out their crumpled bodies. They had been smashed across the room. It took a little longer to make sense of it. A heavy projectile had burst clean through the house from the far side. An answering cannon ball from the Union artillery, I guessed. It had killed one of the men outright, and horribly injured another. Mr McCreedy had no obvious injuries, but was dead or unconscious: struck by debris perhaps. My face stung, peppered with plaster dust. I was shocked. Death had come suddenly. But it was deliverance too.

'Merciful heavens!' gasped Jacqueline, trying not to look at the obscenely disfigured bodies.

I belatedly woke up to the situation. 'Quick, untie me!' I yelled above the thunder of the artillery barrage, 'we have to get away from here.'

She stared in bemusement for an instant, and then began to fumble at the ropes binding me to the chair. Long seconds passed before they came free, and I got to my feet with an effort. Everything hurt, but I felt stronger, fuelled by adrenaline. I took her by the hand.

'We must make a run for it,' I urged. 'I don't think there's anyone else in the house.'

She nodded, wide-eyed. The door was unlocked and the corridor empty. We got to the entrance and peered out of the front door. Soldiers were in sight, but none were close by, or looking in our direction. We stepped outside. It felt dangerously exposed, and I forced myself to stay calm.

'This way,' I suggested: indicating a direction further away from the town and behind the Confederate lines. I hoped we might pass beyond the long avenue of confrontation between the two armies, and circle around to the Northern side. We moved at a stumbling run, Jacqueline hampered by her long dress, and me by my aching body. I flinched at the ear-splitting crack of cannon fire nearby. I could feel the pressure waves a hundred yards from the nearest Confederate battery: strangely more aware of the weight of atmosphere resisting the expanding gasses than the detonations themselves. I was nervous of return Union fire too, though it was not extensive. Only a couple of cannon balls whipped high through the trees above us. We came upon a group of Southern soldiers studying a map, and Jacqueline moved to avoid them.

'Don't give them reason for suspicion,' I said quickly, 'they probably know nothing about us.'

The soldiers merely looked concerned as I nodded to them.

'This is no place for civilians,' said one curtly, looking curiously at my clothes and the marks on my face, 'you must go to the rear.'

'My cousin has been injured,' said Jacqueline, improvising gamely. 'We are trying to get to my sister's house.'

'I would not advise you to stay in the area ma'am,' replied the soldier, 'the fighting is liable to get mighty hot.'

I turned to her as we hurried away. 'You are good at this,' I joked, 'are you sure you're not a spy?'

'I had to say something,' she said sharply. 'I did not want them to hear your accent.'

We spotted a sizeable contingent of Confederate infantry in the distance, and this time waited behind a large thicket of bushes to let them march by. Then we continued to make our way south, slowly climbing onto higher ground. We had gone a mile or two when the cannon fire died down, and soon afterwards the terrain brought us out into the open. We stood on the shallow, upper slope of an exposed escarpment, which dropped away steeply below. It formed a great viewing platform, overlooking miles of the long, shallow depression in the land between the two armies.

Some distance below and to our left, a great body of Confederate infantry emerged from the trees. They moved purposefully across the cornfields towards the Union lines opposite, tramping steadily through the thinning smoke of the artillery barrage. The line grew longer as we watched. More and more men came into view, their ranks stretching far back along the wide valley towards the town. The dense files of men advanced in ragged formations: separate regiments treading behind sword-wielding officers on horses. They moved with ominous determination, and sunlight glittered wickedly on thousands of bayonets up and down the line. From our vantage point they looked invincible, and I could only imagine how they appeared to the soldiers waiting across the valley.

'Oh no! How can they be withstood?' gasped Jacqueline, her voice almost a whisper.

Yet I knew they would be repulsed, driven back with appalling casualties. We were looking at Pickett's doomed charge at the centre of the Union lines: the high-water mark of the fortunes of the South, and harbinger of a downward spiral of decline and defeat. I shivered at the sight of so many men marching to their death. Once again I felt the touch of some deeper self: some mysterious, silent witness of the dramas of humanity, watching the ages turn with timeless knowledge and indifference. A still and profound detachment settled on me, and I sensed the Mindworm squirm. It feared this enigmatic state of being.

Words came back to me I had read years before. Everyone knew Oppenheimer's iconic quote from the Bhagavad Gita, on witnessing the detonation of the atomic bomb: *'Now I am become Death, the destroyer of worlds.'*

But I had looked it up, and other lines had stuck in my mind too for no apparent reason: *'I am time: world devouring, grown aged – all the warriors standing in the army of the enemies, they are already claimed by me.'* More words of Krishna on the battlefield of Kurukshetra: speaking of a greater destiny than the fortunes of men.

Such things had moved me in some profound and nameless manner, and then slipped away from any attempt to engage them. Was this what it was like to stand beyond time I wondered – to watch fate unfold like an inescapable dream? And if this was a dream how did I awake from it, and what did reality then become?

'They will not succeed,' I said distantly to Jacqueline, and simultaneously a storm of fire broke out along the Union lines. My trance-like state deepened, and I watched the battle unfold like a sad, antique movie. Southern soldiers went down in scores, their comrades forging stubbornly ahead through a pitiless hail of destruction. Clouds of dirty white smoke billowed across the battlefield, whipped and beaten about by lethal swathes of metal, and the immense band of men marched into the thickening haze as though erasing themselves from the story of their lives.

Raw courage and foolish bravado blurred in a dream-like parody of human folly. Men formed up as if on parade: marking time and dressing left and right to realign themselves with other regiments as bodies dropped in their ranks, and shuffled up to fill the gaps. They looked like children playing a game whose consequences they did not understand: believing themselves invulnerable and their cause inviolate. Abruptly the watcher began to withdraw, and I started to become myself again – still disengaged, but more personally aware. Sensation returned to my battered body, and I remembered our own predicament. I glanced back the way we had come, and saw distant figures riding in our direction through the trees. They looked very much as if they might be searching for us.

'Quickly, we must hurry!' I said to Jacqueline, shaking off the last of my stupor. I grasped her hand, and we hurried off.

I pushed away the alarming depth of experience that had engulfed me. It had been too alien; too penetrating; too profound, and I had more practical problems at hand. We passed more Southern troops on the slopes below us, but they were intent on the awful drama spread out before them. We continued for nearly a mile before I began to sense that we were approaching the furthest extent of the Confederate lines. The valley between the opposing sides had deepened, and the tiny figures on the low hills opposite remained Union men. But they marked the end of the high, hilly ground running south east of Gettysburg, and the Southern defences began to loop around to contain them.

'We will have to start moving down into the valley,' I said. 'We must try to circle around to the Union side.'

'There may be soldiers from both sides down there,' she said uneasily, 'it will be dangerous.'

'Sure it will,' I agreed, 'but we have most likely got Mr McCreedy's men chasing us, and I know who I would prefer to run into.'

We continued south; running, stumbling, and picking our way downwards across an uneven hillside strewn with rocks and stunted trees. The adrenaline was beginning to wear off, and I found it hard to keep up with Jacqueline. Twice we spotted more Southern troops, and moved higher up the slope to avoid them. The distant sounds of slaughter were dying away behind us as we arrived at last on lower ground. We crept among large, rugged boulders and sparse thickets of bush to get around to the Northern side. But as we splashed across a rocky stream, its water running an ominous pink from further up the valley, there was a shout behind us.

'Mr Walton, Miss Johnson, stop or we'll shoot!'

It was Billy's voice, and I turned to see him running towards us on foot with three other men, all waving their weapons. A fusillade of shots rang out from across the stream, and Billy and his comrades seemed to hit an invisible wall. They went down heavily, and a terrible, anguished gurgling sound started up from their position. I was surprised at the wrench I felt: yet another recent companion meeting a violent end.

Jacqueline and I had dropped fast enough too. Some of the rounds had passed very close. I called out as loudly as I could.

'Don't shoot! I am a civilian and there is a lady here.'

There was no answer for a moment, and then a voice called from some distance ahead. 'Come forward slowly, so we can see you.'

We had our chance, but I could not bear the awful noises coming from where Billy had fallen.

I gripped Jacqueline's arm. 'You go. I must see if I can do something for Billy first.'

She looked wildly at me. 'I don't think that's a good idea,' she hissed. 'I am sorry for him, but we must go while we can.'

'I can't just leave him,' I insisted, 'you will be safe now. I won't be long. Tell them I am following you.'

'Richard, no!' she cried. But I pushed her forward, and turned to crawl back towards Billy.

'I can see you ma'am, just come forward to us,' called a Union soldier.

I crawled frantically back towards the awful sounds of suffering: skinning my knees, and half-disbelieving the risk I was taking. It was further than it had seemed, and I was panting when I got there. I didn't know whether to feel relieved or foolish when I found the terrible sounds were not Billy's. He lay stunned and blinking about him: a tear in the front of his uniform, but no visible blood. Two others lay still, and another had been shot through the throat. His piteous gurgles died away into silence.

'Billy!' I said urgently, 'are you hit?'

He patted himself absently about the chest, and then fumbled inside his uniform, drawing out a wallet from an inner pocket. It was indented and torn, and he looked at it wonderingly.

'Grandpa's medals,' he murmured, chuckling weakly at the dull clunk of metal inside. 'He said they would bring me luck!'

They didn't bring me luck though. There was a pounding of feet and half dozen more Confederate soldiers threw themselves into the shallow hollow we lay in.

'Is this the Englishman?' asked one of them breathlessly, pointing his revolver at me.

A fresh burst of gunfire whistled overhead, and a couple of men with rifles shot back towards the stream Jacqueline had crossed. Those with handguns peered warily above the sparse foliage, looking for targets. There were shouts from the Union lines, and shots came from a new direction. Men were manoeuvring around our position, and the numbers of Union troops were increasing.

'We gotta get out of here!' shouted one of the Southern soldiers. 'Bring the Englishmen.'

He moved out from our refuge at a crouch, peering back towards the Northern lines, but a shot punched right through his head and he dropped like a stone. The firing escalated on both sides. The Confederate soldiers were shooting all around them, and gun-smoke began to obscure everything. Things were looking bad, and more of my captors were hit.

'You didn't ought to have come back for me,' said Billy dazedly. He had got shakily to his knees, and was trying to see through the smoke.

I sensed impending doom, and struggled desperately to activate the Portal. It was hard to focus with the chaos all around me. But my concentration problems were transcended in an instant. A group of Union soldiers burst out from somewhere close by, their carbines levelled with murderous intent. There was no time to think. Billy stared, his gun forgotten in his hand. But the Portal flared into life, and I jumped at him in the same moment.

It was less disorientating this time, and I felt a flash of elation as reality melded and flowed. I had acted purely on instinct, grabbing Billy almost reflexively. I had saved both of us, but he was less relieved: I could feel his silent scream as we fell through the void. Yet the greatest sensation was of loss – of leaving Jacqueline behind. We passed through an eternity of nothingness, if an ocean of power and beauty is nothingness, and a destination seemed to manifest of its own volition. Suddenly we were rolling on the ground together under a thick, warm deluge of drumming rain. The sky was dark with rainclouds and thunder was in the air.

Chapter 8

'AM I DEAD?' gasped Billy.

'No,' I said, squinting through the rain.

We were sprawled on a wide, hard-packed sandy roadway, crowded on either side by antiquated brick and timber buildings of conflicting quality and style. A wild clattering rang out above the clamour of the storm: a driverless wagon rattling and banging behind frantic, careering horses. There was a scream. Two children cowered directly in its path, and a woman stood frozen with horror on the far side of the rudimentary avenue.

Thrown from one desperate situation into another, life seemed to have become one continuous, crazy movie. I watched myself engage with the situation in surprise. Neither disembodied presence nor disapproving Mindworm persuaded me. Yet I hardly recognised my unhesitating rush to save them. I had no idea how the time dilation effect had triggered either. The flailing hoofs were only meters from the frozen children when I blurred across the street and scooped them up.

All three of us tumbled into a heap at the feet of the distressed woman. I lay shattered, and in no little pain. A desperate energy had fuelled me, but my ill-used body protested fiercely now it was over. I felt dizzy, my mind struggling with the kaleidoscope of events: Gettysburg gunfire bizarrely negated by the thunderous deluge that drenched me. And now children whisked from disaster under the wheels of a wagon. They struggled wailing from my grasp, and sought comfort from the equally hysterical female. Two men splashed through puddles after the careering wagon, and another converged on us through the downpour. Voluminous capes and three cornered hats suggested an earlier period in history to my inexpert eye.

I realised it would be ten times worse for Billy, and levered myself up with a groan. He was still crouched in the driving rain where I had left him, his face a mask of utter incomprehension. Water ran unheeded over his frozen stare, pouring in rivulets from his chin. I heaved myself to my feet, and lurched over to him. He still had the gun in his hand, and I laid my fingers over it.

'Put the gun away Billy,' I said as calmly as I could, 'there is no war here.'

He looked down at the weapon as if he had forgotten its existence, and replaced it into his holster as though in a dream. His trembling fingers failed to button down the cover.

'What happened? Where are we?' he asked in a strangled voice.

'Don't try to understand it,' I continued gently. 'We went through a kind of door into another place. It happened to me before. That's why I couldn't explain to your Lieutenant how I got to Jacqueline's – to Miss Johnson's house.'

'Are you sure I ain't dead?' he wondered.

'Yes I'm sure. But you would be if we hadn't come here. You remember those Union soldiers? They were going to shoot.'

'Then I must be dead,' he murmured numbly.

'No, you're alive. Feel the rain. We are just somewhere else.'

'You flew again,' he said.

I laughed a little wildly. 'Yes Billy, I suppose I did. Try not to think about it. Just take it one minute at a time, like in a battle. Can you do that?'

'I guess so,' he said doubtfully.

The rain was thinning, and the clouds growing lighter. I looked around to try and get my bearings. Many of the houses had crude shop fronts, and signs advertising a bewildering array of archaic services. *Tanner, Cooper, Vintner* and *Cordwainer* rang some bells, but the specifics were a mystery to me. Some buildings were quite substantial, three or four stories with steep tiled roofs. They were vaguely Tudor in style: the ground and first floors faced with patterned brickwork, and higher floors displaying exposed beams and plasterwork. But there were crown-glass sash windows as well as leaded casements, and an odd, indefinable quality about everything which took a few seconds to identify. The structures were all quite new.

Less identifiable and more crudely constructed buildings also looked relatively recent creations. The roadway was a compacted mass of shale and sand, uneven and rutted. Innumerable pieces of debris, large and small were ground into its surface, or had accumulated untidily on either side. The air was decidedly warm. There were few people in evidence, presumably due to the rain, but a burly man was speaking animatedly to the woman and children. She left, ushering her charges ahead of her, and he hurried across to us.

'Good day sir,' he said, lifting his Tricorn hat despite the rain, 'I am deeply indebted to you for the life of my niece and nephew. I beg you will tell me how I may be of service.'

'Well,' I said, thinking fast, 'my friend and I are in need of food and shelter. We would greatly appreciate any assistance you can offer.'

We certainly looked a sorry sight: soaking wet, our clothing torn and frayed, and my face battered and bruised. But he discounted our condition with beaming good will.

'Then it is settled. Please come in from this inclement weather, and we shall speak further.'

I helped Billy to his feet, and we followed our new benefactor towards a large Inn proclaiming itself 'The Three Crowns': this displayed on a signboard in bold red lettering, with bright golden images of its namesakes gleaming royally beneath the words. It was a big, three storied half-timbered building, with a frontage of sixty feet or so facing the sandy roadway. The Inn stretched back even further to the rear, and was separated from other structures by narrow lanes on both sides, and a smaller service alley behind it.

We entered by a side door, and found ourselves in a kind of anteroom between the ground floor public rooms and the kitchen, which was a single story add-on standing in a rear courtyard. The smell of cooking mingled with a curious locker-room odour that I couldn't pin down at first. The low, rough-plastered ceiling was set with a couple of heavy beams; the walls were plastered too, and the floor laid with bricks. A large brick fireplace occupied most of one wall, where two iron pots hung suspended over softly burning flames. Rough wooden tables formed a staging area for food bound for diners, and serving staff bustled back and forth.

The scene was imbued with a strong sense of déjà vu, as if I remembered it from a dream. I was unsure if it was triggered by the room or the two children by the fire. They looked like twins: a fair haired boy and girl of seven or eight. Their angelic features were screwed up in distress as they were scolded and dried off by the lady who had accompanied them outside. Our host spoke reassuringly to them for a moment, and then turned to us.

'I am William Bambridge, the proprietor of this establishment,' he said genially, 'may I know whom I have the honour of addressing?' A waft of body odour coincided with his proximity, and I realised the sour background smell was that of people unaccustomed to washing.

'My name is Richard Walton,' I relied, 'and this is, err, William Bonney.'

'It is a pleasure to meet you,' he said, pulling up two sturdy stools for us to sit on. 'Please dry yourselves by the fire while I procure your victuals, after which I will be pleased to discuss your situation.'

'Well we seem to have fallen on our feet,' I said to Billy, as the innkeeper disappeared into the kitchen. 'Last time I landed up in that gunfight at Jacqueline's house.'

'My name ain't William Bonney,' he said, leaning forward anxiously.

'Well I had to say something,' I grinned, 'you should be happy, he was a famous gunfighter.'

'Never heard of him,' he said disapprovingly.

He stared at his bizarre new surroundings with intense misgiving, obviously thinking things over.

'You mean you came from someplace else?' he said at last.

'Yes, and I felt as out of place in America as you do here.'

'Can we get back home?' he asked, his eyes pleading.

'Yes,' I said, 'well maybe not. I'm not exactly sure.'

'You don't know?' he gulped disbelievingly.

'It's a bit of a long story Billy. I'll try to explain later. For now, yes we should be able to get back, but I can't really say when.'

He was silent for a while.

'These people talk funny,' he said finally.

'Yes they are English, like me,' I suggested.

'No, not like you, they sound strange. I can't hardly understand them.'

I remembered how the Portal had translated the speech of its original owner, and wondered if it was adjusting the way I understood people now. The words seemed a little formal and old fashioned, but they were clear enough and easy to grasp. If the Portal was translating it appeared seamless, and I wondered how it worked.

I thought about the nature of reality, and of the mysterious dimensions of being beyond the fabric of space-time. For an instant I touched an astonishing energetic state which staggered me: an immaculate fountainhead of light generating multiple levels of reality. It was a blazing quantum fire which ignited even my own consciousness. Suddenly I was peering down into my own personal hologram of existence. I shared an essential cognisance with a living energy that existed everywhere. Everything was telepathic at every level.

'What's wrong?' asked Billy nervously.

I realised I was staring at him in astonishment. 'N-nothing,' I stammered, 'I just realised something...I think.'

But I hadn't realised anything really – merely glimpsed another layer of the mind-boggling conundrum that had usurped my existence. I tried to rationalise it. After all, even in my previous incarnation as an ordinary person I had known that my body was mostly empty space, that its molecules were forged in mighty suns, and this whole vast universe had expanded from a single, tiny point too small to see. Not that it had made any difference to the way I lived my life. But now I wondered if anything was real. I felt overwhelmed and lost – miserably reminded of the unfathomable gulf separating me from Alex, and now from Jacqueline too. I tried to shake off the ocean of impossibilities and think of Billy instead. Everything was far more difficult for him to understand than me.

'This is not just someplace else Billy,' I said slowly, 'it might be another time as well.'

'What do you mean?' he asked fearfully.

'We might not be in the same year that we left. William Bonney was a famous gunfighter around twenty years after the battle of Gettysburg. When I met you I had come from a hundred and fifty years in the future. Your time was ancient history to me.'

'This stuff is crazy,' he muttered, 'I get dizzy just thinking about it.'

'Would you rather be dead?'

'I guess not,' he sighed.

Mr Bambridge reappeared with a young lady in tow, who proved that body odour was not a uniquely male attribute in this environment. She placed two plates piled high with food on a table close by, and then returned with an unwieldy knife and two-tined fork for each of us, and two full tankards of drink. Everything was fashioned in a shiny grey metal. I wondered if it was silver at first, then realised it must be pewter.

'Please eat your fill,' said Mr Bambridge happily, indicating for us to move our stools over to the feast, 'I will speak with you afterwards.'

He left with the children and their chaperone, all of them speaking volubly together. I needed no further encouragement. It had been a long time since I had something substantial to eat, and I speared a large chunk of meat eagerly with my fork.   Billy appeared briefly at cross-purposes with himself. The enticing aromas of fresh bread, succulent meat and interesting pastries wrestled with his rejection of the impossible reality he found himself in.   His first tentative mouthful transformed him though. The battle was lost, or won, and he began eating faster than I was. I took a sip from the tankard. It was a strong, pungent beer, and I washed my food down with it gladly. I was a new man when I finished: thoroughly satiated, and even a little merry, while Billy's eyes glowed with ecstasy.

'I don't remember when I last had a feed like that,' he said, licking his lips in satisfaction.

'Nothing like good food to keep you down to earth,' I agreed, and it felt good to share the extraordinary transcendence of time and place with someone else. But it put me in mind of Jacqueline again, and I felt a pang of regret. I wondered what had become of her and if I would ever see her again.

'So what do we do now?' asked Billy, breaking into my thoughts.

'We try to survive. We figure out where we are, and what year it is, and take it from there.'

Mr Bambridge returned: still congenial, but shaking his head and whistling pensively to himself.

'Those twins are a worry to me and that's a fact,' he said. 'If not for you sir it would have been the end of them, and at no small risk to yourself. Barely a yard before the horses Mary said you were – come out of nowhere, and quick as a flash in all that rain. I can't thank you enough.'

'I am only happy I was in time,' I said, 'they look an engaging pair.'

'My brother's children, God rest his soul. He and his wife were taken by fever last year, and I care for them now. They are dear children, but always up to mischief. I don't have the time that I should for them. Ran out in the rain without a moment's thought, and the horses frightened by the thunder… it doesn't bear thinking about.' He paused, shaking his head again, and looked us over. 'I trust the food has been to your satisfaction?'

'Excellent thank you,' I said, 'it was most kind of you.'

'It is nothing,' he said. 'I would do more for you if I may. I see you are injured,' he nodded at the bruises on my face, 'and out in this weather without a cloak or a hat.'

'Our situation is not good,' I admitted, having thought about an explanation for our sorry state, 'our possessions have been taken from us.' It was true in a way, although really more the other way around.

'Ah, this town is a den of thieves,' he growled. 'I do not like to see good people down on their luck. I am a man of business here, and I have work for men such as yourselves – and lodgings here at the Inn if you are in need of them.'

'We would be grateful of both,' I smiled.

'You have not been long in Port Royal I take it?'

'Err, no,' I said. My mind went into overdrive as I braced myself for the next question. Port Royal, I remembered vaguely, had been a busy and notorious seaport in the West Indies. We would have arrived by ship, but once more I would be unable to give a credible account of the journey. To my great relief he did not press me further, and I assumed it was not unusual to find rootless strangers here.

'May I know your professions, sirs?' he asked.

'I am, ah, a bookkeeper, and my friend Billy is a stable hand.'

I had blurted out the first thing that came to mind. Bookkeeping was probably something I could manage, and I assumed Billy knew plenty about horses.

'Bookkeeping?' He stroked his chin thoughtfully. 'It may be that I will have such work for you in days to come. But in the meantime, what say you to honest labour in my warehouse on the docks?'

'We would be happy to accept sir,' I replied.

'It is settled then,' he said cheerfully. 'I will show you your lodgings. You may have a glass or two in the bar, and I will walk down to the warehouse with you in the morning.'

He led us out through another door into a sizeable back yard. The ground was lined with grimy brickwork, and the protruding kitchen took up much of the area on one side. The whole was enclosed by a high brick wall, with a gateway opening into the narrow alleyway at the rear.

Empty kegs and packing crates were stacked beside the kitchen, and several large barrels stood by a round brick well in the corner behind it. On the opposite side of the yard lurked an unmistakeable if eccentric construction: a crude wooden cubicle some eight feet wide by four deep, not very tall, with an ill-fitting door and a plain roof sloping to the rear. It rested on short wooden stilts at ground level and was obviously portable if necessary. I assumed a cesspit lay beneath it at first. The smell certainly suggested it. More barrels, badly stained and much the worse for wear, stood close by.

'The house of office,' announced Mr Bambridge.

'The toilet,' I heard. I picked up his words and their simultaneous translation in weird stereophonic unison: perhaps due to my recent transcendent experience, or the bizarre juxtaposition of terminology and meaning.

'You will find two seats of ease within,' he said with a grim smile. 'We piss for the saltpetre-man and the tanner, and shit for the night-man.'

I learnt later that the high water table of the great sandspit beneath Port Royal precluded the existence of cesspits; and urine and faeces were collected in separate leather buckets beneath the crude seating in the makeshift wooden stall. Their contents were stored separately in barrels for collection, together with the products of numerous chamber pots. The urine was used for tanning leather and extracting saltpetre for gunpowder, and the solid waste hauled out of the town by the euphemistically named night-men. The barrels by the well contained drinking water brought in on boats by watermen from the main island of Jamaica, while the well itself drew only brackish water for general use from the sea-saturated sand below.

Opposite the inventive latrine, three rough-hewn doors were set into the rear brick wall of the building. Each door had small window openings over them, but light was restricted by more upmarket floors cantilevered out above them.

'These are the downstairs servants' quarters,' he said, 'they are not what I would wish for you, but all I have spare at present. You may stay here until you can improve your situation.'

He opened one of the doors to reveal a small whitewashed room, illuminated only by the diminutive, ineffective window. Lumpy bedding of stuffed sacking and a blanket lay on the floor. The only other furniture was a small wooden trunk.

'I will have more bedding brought to you,' Mr Bambridge said. 'Have you any belongings you wish to bring here?'

'No, we lost everything we had,' I told him.

'The Lord preserve us,' he said sadly. 'Very well, I will try to obtain serviceable breeches and jackets for you both, and I will advance you money for shirts and stockings.'

'Thank you again sir,' I said, truly grateful for his kindness.

'If you wish to venture into company before sleeping, ask at the kitchen in which bar you may drink, and tonight you may have your choice at my expense.' He eyed us gravely. 'I judge you sincere in accepting employment. I advise you to avoid the rum punch, and to retire in good time to rise for work tomorrow.'

He turned to go but glanced at the holster on Billy's belt, frowning at its unfamiliar appearance. 'If you carry a pistol sir, you will have no need of it while under my protection. It is more likely to bring you trouble than prevent it.'

'We will gladly take your advice,' I said, 'in both the matter of the rum punch and the pistol.'

I sank down thankfully on the bedding as he left, and Billy seated himself on the trunk.

'Well, the smell is not great,' I said with a sigh, 'but at least it is somewhere to stay.'

'It ain't so bad,' said Billy.

The 'house of office' was less than twenty feet away, and the odour was quite noticeable even with the door shut. I supposed he was used to the smell of camp latrines, or perhaps too relived to have secured a bolthole to care.

'I'm getting sleepy after all that food,' I groaned, 'and everything is still hurting thanks to your friend Mr McCreedy.'

'I did not like the man,' said Billy, 'and I did not like what he did. But I guess he had his job to do. You sure seemed mixed up in something mighty strange.'

'It is Jacqueline's stepfather who is mixed up in something strange,' I said. 'He's a time traveller like me, but I'm kind of new at all this stuff. He knows what he's doing, and he's up to no good.'

'He's from someplace else as well?' cried Billy in amazement, 'how many of you fellows are there! Is Miss Johnson one of these time people too?'

'No she isn't,' I said a little sadly, 'Jacqueline didn't really know much about him, and neither do I.'

'I can't get this right in my head,' said Billy perplexedly. 'I thought everything was upside down enough, what with the war and all. You mean there are people popping up from other places all over?'

I laughed, wincing at the ache in my ribs. 'I really don't know Billy,' I said, 'I've only known it can happen for a few weeks myself, and I come from a time when science is very advanced – compared to the eighteen sixties anyway.'

Billy was silent for a moment. 'You really come from the future?'

'Yes.'

'So did we win?'

'Win what? Oh you mean at Gettysburg – or the whole war?'

Billy looked discomforted. 'Well, both I guess.'

'Gettysburg was a kind of a draw, but the North won in the end.'

'The Yankees won? That ain't possible!'

'Well, they had the industrial power, and that was what counted. Armies got better weapons as time went on. Industrialised warfare, that's what they call it. There were terrible wars, world wars. But America became united, and it's the most powerful country in the world in my time.'

Billy looked unconvinced. 'United?' he said disdainfully.

There was a knock on the door as a servant arrived with more of the rough bedding, and a tallow candle in a pewter holder. The clouds had largely cleared, but the sky appeared to be darkening. I asked the time and he replied it was before seven in the evening. I was tired and aching badly, but it was early, and I hoped to learn more about the place – and the year – we had arrived in. I even felt a tingle of anticipation at seeing a bit more of our unlikely new location. It reminded me of how I had felt when Charles had forced me out on that fateful Friday evening. My chaotic adventures were changing me, I supposed, although I did feel more secure with the offer of work and somewhere to stay. Billy needed a little persuasion to venture into the bar though. He was suspicious of doing anything in this strange new world. But he didn't want to be left alone either.

We made our way to the kitchen, where I caught the eye of the girl who had served our food. She led us into an interconnected warren of public rooms, all of them permeated by a haze of tobacco smoke and body odour. Those at the rear appeared the least salubrious, and the girl directed us to a fairly utilitarian bar there, where another young lady beamed upon us and offered us our choice of drink. I glimpsed other, much grander rooms nearer the front of the Inn. Long haired men lurked there, with flamboyant bows and sashes adorning oriental silk costumes. There were ladies too, in elaborate dresses and hairdos, displaying lace and jewellery. Many had thin clay pipes clamped in their mouths, even some of the richly dressed women, and I wondered if it served a secondary function as a form of deodorant.

Our bar was unpretentious, its partition walls scratched and worn and the brick floor strewn with straw, but I was glad to be out of the limelight. We chose tankards of the pungent beer, and took our seats on benches at a battered wooden table. Three men sat opposite us playing dominos, puffing on their pipes and refilling pewter tumblers from bulbous wine bottles. They spoke laconically amongst themselves, and directed only casually curious glances at us.

Billy and I made small talk at first, while we surveyed our surroundings. The men at the other table were dressed little better than we were. Their hair was long and greasy: tied back behind the neck on two of them and falling in untidy curls to the shoulders of the third. They wore knee-breeches and loose, shabby shirts with wide, open collars. Crude darning showed on their clothes, and there were tears in their stockings. Each wore one or more earrings, and their shoes were square toed, buckled, worn and scuffed. The curly haired character had a rather crumpled Tricorn hat embellished with feathers, kept on the bench beside him. A sheathed sword was propped up against it, and at least one of the others had a dagger dangling from his belt.

'Billy,' I said finally, 'Mr Bambridge called this Port Royal, which is a seaport in the West Indies. It's a good few hundred miles from America, and from what I can see, we are more than a hundred years before your time.'

Billy hunched defensively as the alien reality took on a more specific identity.

'Try not to worry about it,' I said, attempting a reassuring grin. 'We got here and we can get away again. Let me tell you what happened to me, and we can take it from there.'

I told him the tale over the next couple of hours, keeping my voice low and constantly back-tracking to provide a great many explanations about life in the twenty first century. As before, I avoided mentioning the Mindworm, and kept quiet about mysterious cosmic events too. Billy had enough to take in without additional reasons to suspect our mutual sanity.

'So you can't just use this Portal thingummy to take us back?' he asked.

'It's not so simple,' I replied. 'I can't make it do what I want. It seems to make up its own mind most of the time, and I don't know where we would end up. I need more time to learn about it.' I paused for a moment. 'There's another thing too. I don't think it was an accident that I ended up at Jacqueline's place, and it may not be an accident that we have come here either. I think we need to stick around for a while.'

Billy looked unhappy. 'These people are strange,' he complained. 'They talk funny, dress funny and smell funny. How are we gonna to fit in?'

'Think of it as an adventure,' I said cheerfully, 'that's what my friend Charles would say. He'll be jealous when he knows we've been here. He would love to see a pirate.'

'A pirate!' exclaimed Billy in alarm.

'Shh,' I hissed, as all three of our neighbours glanced across at us. 'Don't say things like that out loud! I expect they are used to all sorts here, and we'll be fine if we don't draw attention to ourselves. Besides, we've got Mr Bambridge to look after us. Why don't we have another drink?'

Billy sat thoughtfully while I got our tankards refilled.

'Mr Walton...' he began, as I returned.

'Call me Richard, please,' I begged.

'I was thinking. Do you reckon I might see those horseless cars and flying machines and all?'

'That's more like it!' I said with a smile. 'Who knows, maybe you will.'

We finished our drinks – the third since we had sat down – by which time Billy was decidedly more reconciled to his fate. We were a little tipsy as we made our way back to our room. I had no idea when we might be called in the morning, but it was not yet ten o'clock, and I hoped we would have plenty of time to sleep. We borrowed a candle stub from the kitchen to light the way to our door, and collapsed thankfully onto our bedding. Billy was asleep before I was, and I spent my last waking moments worrying about him. I felt responsible, despite the inescapable logic that bringing him here had saved his life.

It seemed a short time before we were roused next day. Daylight revealed Port Royal toilet paper to consist of a thick piece of rope in a bucket of filthy water. I washed my face and hands with the briny water from the well, encouraging Billy to do the same, after which we were presented with a welcome breakfast of bread, cheese and coffee in the same ante room as before. Billy's face lit up as he sipped from his steaming cup.

'Hey, what kind of coffee is this?' he asked in amazement, 'I don't remember when I tasted anything this good.'

'Bless you, that's just what we drink in the kitchen,' smiled one of the serving girls, who seemed to have taken a shine to him. 'If t'is real coffee you want, I might find you some later.'

Mr Bambridge arrived as we were finishing. He promised us working clothes later in the day, and we set out on foot for our first real look around outside. My body was stiff and sore, but our novel surroundings were a welcome distraction. I was surprised at the size of the place. The sandy thoroughfare onto which The Three Crowns faced was Queen Street, one of several parallel routes running lengthways through the town. Port Royal straddled a wide promontory at the end of a long curved sand-spit, which reached out from the Jamaican coastline to enclose a vast sheltered bay.

Some two thousand buildings large and small were crowded upon it: churches, municipal offices, warehouses, banking and merchant houses, markets and a number of forts. But by far the most numerous commercial premises were a riotous array of shops. They overflowed with exotic goods from all over the world. The town also boasted taverns, inns, coffee and eating houses, and brothels of every conceivable variety.

We crossed Queen Street and entered a side road between a fortified goldsmiths shop and one labelled 'pewterer', which displayed a surprisingly exquisite array of decorative plate and vessels behind a leaded glass front window. The side street was narrow and dirty, and some of its houses primitive wooden structures in poor condition. It was still early and there were few people about, but they presented a wide assortment of race and style. Most seemed ordinary folk: men and women carrying baskets of goods, or trudging to a place of work. Some wore coarse canvas garments little better than sackcloth – slaves or transported felons, I guessed with a shock. Several girls and older women covered their heads with embroidered caps, and wore aprons incorporated into their outfits. Many appeared to be tradesmen. Others were sailors with long pigtails down their backs, or soldiers in grubby uniforms.

A few swaggered in bucket-boots, with ribbons and feathers in their hats and swords at their sides. Others were undoubtedly ladies of the night, returning in worn finery from some assignation or another. We passed men and women of African and Asian descent; including two black soldiers that made Billy stare. A couple of guys even looked like American Indians. There were drunks too, lying asleep or dead at the side of the street. We emerged into another broad, gritty thoroughfare running lengthways through the town. It reached even further back along the extensive promontory than Queen Street. This was Thames Street, which ran behind the warehouses and quaysides of the inner, harbour side of the town, between Fort Carlisle and Fort James. Other forts were placed along the Southern side, facing out to sea, while Fort Rupert guarded the land approach across the long sandy peninsular.

A colourful panorama unfolded as we crossed Thames Street. The warm Jamaican sun peeped over the rooftops, and green mountains were piled up behind each other on the distant mainland. The salty tang of the ocean became stronger as we cut through the long row of warehouses facing the harbour. It provided some relief from the less savoury aromas lurking around the town. Beyond them the waterfront stretched away in both directions: a haphazard accumulation of wharfs and jetties. A vivid blue-green sea, and wooden ships festooned with rigging created a startling Technicolor vision of the past. Mangroves encroached intermittently between docking facilities along the shoreline, and a multitude of brightly coloured seabirds, some of them huge, flapped noisily above us uttering mournful screeches. The water was surprisingly deep: some large ships were tied up at the quaysides. Numerous premises were opening for the day. Men prepared ropes, pulleys, slings and nets. They readied davits on board ships, and wooden cranes on the shore.

'These are my storehouses,' said Mr Bambridge proudly, indicating three impressive timber constructions. 'I have cargo due for both landing and loading in the coming days, so you will not be idle.'

We toured the buildings. He identified stacks of merchandise, and introduced some of the men working there. Jonathan was the guy in charge, a short balding man of cheerful bulk and an industrious air. He was briefed on our circumstances and duties, and then our new employer excused himself to attend other matters of business. The day began slowly, with a brief explanation of shipping and warehouse operations from our new overseer. He started us off on some general reorganisation of goods and sweeping up until mid-morning, when some cargo was ready for unloading. Then the heavy work began. We heaved on ropes, pushed barrows, hefted bags on our shoulders, and rolled barrels for hours.

My injuries made the work difficult and painful, and I frequently had to pause to rest. Jonathan was remarkably accommodating about it. I initially presumed this was purely due to Mr Bambridge's patronage, but as the day wore on I learned that the story of the twins rescue from the runaway wagon was known, and well thought of.

'Those two young rascals are always up to mischief,' mused Jonathan, as we sat munching our lunch. We were eating hunks of bread, and biting out of raw onions like apples. 'But we are all fond of them. Thank the good Lord you were able to act as you did. It doesn't bear thinking about, else.'

The young rascals themselves appeared at the warehouse in the afternoon, shrieking and laughing, with their harassed lady guardian beaming tenderly upon them. Nathaniel and Aurelia were their names, and they thanked me dutifully: glancing up with sky-blue eyes from beneath luxuriant eyelashes, and stifling giggles between themselves. Mr Bambridge arrived later still. He informed us that he had found second hand clothing, but it was still being washed, and would be sent to our rooms in the evening. He added that we would also find stockings and shirts waiting for us, which he would deduct from our wages. We worked on, with increasing pauses in my case, until about six. I felt fit to drop when Jonathan called it a day.

I could barely summon the will to walk as we made our way back to the Inn. But Billy was more animated, and stared about himself in wonder. Port Royal became a very different place as evening approached. The streets thronged with flamboyantly dressed individuals, all in a mood of riotous gaiety. There was shouting and laughter, and much flaunting of exotic silks, extraordinary hats, ribbons and jewellery. People were already drunk, and ribald ladies flirted outrageously with unsteady men. The place seemed full of sailors bent on being parted from their money as quickly as possible. Some were festooned with weapons: flintlock pistols and knives stashed in their belts, and swords dangling from extravagant shoulder sashes. They would have looked decidedly menacing had they not been preoccupied with making merry. Bawdy comments were exchanged with ladies leaning from upper story windows, and one intoxicated individual sat on a doorstep with a keg of rum, offering drinks alternatively to passers-by and an enthusiastic parrot.

'I never imagined anything like this Mr Walton,' said Billy in awe. 'These ain't God fearing folk at all.'

'Please call me Richard,' I pleaded for the umpteenth time, 'and you're right. I do seem to remember this place had quite a reputation.'

'Have you figured out what year this is yet?' he asked, a plaintive note creeping into his voice.

'Not exactly, but it is well before the eighteen hundreds. America is still an English colony.'

'This sure is mighty strange Mr – Richard,' said Billy. 'The sooner we get out of here the better.'

'Right now all I want to do is sleep,' I groaned.

I could hardly keep my eyes open to eat a plateful of stew back at the Inn, and shuffled wearily to our room to collapse on my bed. I awoke for a while after dark to find Billy cleaning his revolver by candlelight. We spoke a little, but I soon dozed off again. It seemed hardly a moment before morning arrived. It was a routine that soon became familiar: carrying us back and forth to the dockside.

The work continued unabated: more physical labour than I had ever done in my life. My body's protests gradually faded, and I began to engage more with life around me. I not only outgrew the effects of the battering I had received: my muscles strengthened and hardened with each day that passed. A new vitality infused me, and the sheer novelty of our surroundings buoyed my spirits. There was much to learn, and in my case the physical monotony was sometimes alleviated by time spent on clerical duties with Jonathan. We worked with a port authority tallyman, checking the shipping lists as the cargos were loaded and unloaded. The transfer of goods to and from distant lands was meticulously documented, while the tallyman recorded the harbour dues payable to the Crown.

The year I learned, was sixteen eighty nine. I had never realised what an extraordinary place Port Royal had been. It overflowed with wealth. Goods from all over the world were on display – gold and silverware from Europe, ivory, gemstones, spices and dyes from Africa and India, and beautiful porcelain, jade statues and fine silks and brocades from China and Japan. It was an English Crown Colony fuelled by blatant avarice: a mind-boggling alliance of official due process, galloping commerce and rampant banditry. Pirates both sanctioned and illicit roamed the streets: the crews of privateers endorsed by the Crown to raid French and the Spanish ships, and their more shadowy cousins – officially outlawed but still keeping Port Royal well stocked with goods.

About mid-morning on our fourth day of work a cannon discharged with a dull thud from one of the forts, and a carnival atmosphere broke out all over the town. Jonathan immediately abandoned what he was doing and began to close up the warehouses, and our fellow workers rushed to join what was clearly a customary exercise. In minutes we were being swept along by a jubilant throng of all ages and stations in life: everyone hurrying along the dockside waving and cheering as a sleek ship rounded the end of the headland into the bay. Its decks and rigging were packed with men who waved in their turn, and the ship docked to a roar of approval from a crowd of many hundreds. Uniformed dignitaries arrived puffing for breath and pushed eagerly to the front, escorted by a file of soldiers. I hesitated to ask about obvious truths from those around me, and shrugged at the mild bemusement on Billy's face.

A section of the ships bulwark was swung back and a gangplank heaved over the side, crashing onto the quay to allow costumed officials to tramp formally aboard. They were closely followed by other well-dressed individuals, all equally radiating acumen and greed. A protracted inspection began, involving much avid gesticulation and recording of information. It continued unhurriedly despite the background murmur of the crowd, which grew relentlessly louder in proportion to its size. Cries of 'make way!' preceded the arrival of carts bearing barrels of alcohol: the ubiquitous rum punch, and the focus of the crowd shifted to accommodate high spirits of a different kind. The tempo quickened; impromptu singing and dancing breaking out as horses and carts, escorted by additional soldiers, arrived to force their way through to the ship. Heavy crates, rolls of linen and chests of valuables were manoeuvred down the gangplank and loaded up.

'That's it lads,' bellowed someone from the ship. 'Our good King, the Admiralty and the Governor have got their share, and now so will you!'

An animal roar greeted his words, accompanied by much good-natured toasting and downing of liquor. The official contingent had barely trundled their wares off the wharf when the ship's crew poured from the vessel, carrying goods of every kind. A bewildering array of merchandise appeared: rolls of silk, bags of spices, tobacco, jewellery, exquisite crockery, fine tableware, weapons and numerous other curiosities. The word 'plunder' sprang easily to mind, and it was plunder sanctioned by the Crown. Licensed piracy: looting the merchant ships of England's enemies, and greatly enriching the English establishment and the citizens of Port Royal in the process.

The next few hours were a frenzy of haggling, goods and coin changing hands, drunkenness, arguments, and riotous good humour. The mood was infectious. We had no money and could not participate in the bargain hunting, but Billy availed himself of the rum punch and gazed with amazement upon the scene. I did not feel like drinking. The notion of plunder was not alien to him, but it troubled me. It seemed weird that these were someone else's belongings. Of course its owners might have robbed or cheated in their turn, but there was an ugliness about the revelry which I found distasteful. I thought of the selective blindness in my own time: of westerners frivolously consuming bargains extracted from the captive labour of undeveloped countries. This seemed remarkably similar in some ways. Still, the spectacle was extraordinary, and I enjoyed the break from work.

After three weeks had passed I was feeling fit and healthy, and familiar enough with the rumbustious reality of Port Royal to feel relaxed and at home. I had even stopped noticing the perennial body odour, most of the time at least. Billy and I had taken to negotiating rides with the watermen over to the mainland once a week, to bathe in the river. There was a lot of sickness in Port Royal, and I learned it was common for newcomers from Europe to become ill soon after arrival. No small number died within weeks. But those who survived seemed to take it for granted, as a sort of rite of passage. There were not many old people in evidence. I thought a lot about disease at first: of its transmission to me and Billy from the environment, and vice versa. There was no sign of any problems though. I wondered if the Portal was protecting us somehow, or if passage through mysterious other-worldly dimensions affected these things.

Despite our social acclimatisation, Billy was becoming increasingly restless, and I had begun to try and connect with the Portal again. But I sensed nothing from it. I could only wait and speculate about what might lie in store for us: and happily or unhappily, fate did not keep us waiting much longer. Billy and I divided our free time between exploring our new world, and talking over a drink at the Three Crowns. One evening we encountered a commotion at the entrance, which heralded the arrival of an important guest. Servants struggled with an extravagant array of baggage, and Mr Bambridge himself materialised to greet the august visitor.

To my surprise it was a woman, and one arrayed in the most sumptuous clothing I had ever seen. The midnight blue of her voluminous overskirt was so dark it was almost black. Its fine satin was looped and draped up over a petticoat of exquisitely embroidered floral silk brocade, rich in colour and shuttle-woven in gold and silver thread. The outer gown hung off the shoulder to reveal an equally adorned bodice beneath: confined by an ornate inner panel which hugged the stomach, and flaring to display ruffled lace gathered at her breast. The few wealthy ladies I had seen in such attire lacked her luminous flamboyance, and she had contrived to lower and emphasise her neckline in a manner far more provocative than the more staid arrangements of her peers.

Ruffled lace was also gathered generously at the sleeves on her forearms, and the whole immaculate costume clung sensationally to a figure that was simply stunning. Embroidered silken shoes peeped out below her petticoats, and pearls and gemstones glittered about her person. Her hair was a lustrous platinum blonde and intricately styled, a mass of curls piled high and falling in a gleaming cascade to her shoulders. Flawless teeth flashed behind perfect lips and her eyes sparkled with mischievous delight. She was enough to fascinate any man, but it was not that which transfixed me. It was the unmistakable flood of déjà vu which coursed through my being at the sight of her.

Chapter 9

SHE DID NOT react to me at all. I was standing at the foot of the main staircase and her gaze swept right over me: no doubt on the lookout for persons of suitable status and affluence. Lady Seymour was her title, I learned via backroom gossip. She had come in on a privateer from somewhere in the Americas, and was seeking passage back to England. I nudged Billy, and nodded in the direction of the shabby bar we haunted at the back of the Inn.

'Well Billy, I know something at last,' I said, as we sat down with our tankards. I still felt a little unbalanced by the dazzling vision of feminine charm.

Billy raised his eyebrows inquiringly.

'That lady who has just arrived is mixed up in all this.'

'You know her?' he asked in surprise.

'Not exactly,' I admitted, 'but I had the same feeling when I met Jacqueline, and the girl who started it all.'

'You reckon?' he said. His eyes twinkled in a way I had not seen since we arrived in Port Royal. 'She sure is pretty.'

'It's not like that,' I said, unaccountably irritated. 'I had the same feeling about Jacqueline's stepfather. It's like meeting someone you know from somewhere.'

He shrugged, 'so what are we gonna do then?'

'I'm not sure,' I said, 'keep an eye on her I guess.'

We had upgraded our wardrobe through some judicious haggling with a bunch of privateers, but it was nowhere near the quality required to merit association with the likes of Lady Seymour. Neither did we have the money to keep up with the lavish entertainment that went on around her. She had a suite of private rooms upstairs, and seemed to enjoy the company of a group of admirers in the best public rooms on the ground floor.

Fortunately though – or perhaps unfortunately of course – she seemed disposed to be on good terms with Mr Bambridge, which led to the twins and myself crossing her path. A couple of days after her arrival, Billy and I returned to the Inn to glimpse Nathaniel and Aurelia jumping up and down before Lady Seymour's table in the prestigious front lounge. Their excitement bubbled over as they caught sight of me, and they ran to pull me over towards her.

'This is him, my Lady!' cried Nathaniel, dragging me eagerly towards her table. 'He saved us.'

'No, no,' called Mr Bambridge in the background. 'Do not bother Her Ladyship!'

'Do not fret sir,' laughed Lady Seymour good naturedly. 'Let me see this hero.'

I stumbled awkwardly towards her, with a child tugging on each arm. An unaccustomed waft of expensive perfume and clean skin hit me. She was still smiling as she looked up, her gaze efficiently cataloguing my body and clothing. There was an electric familiarity as our eyes met: an intensity of remembering similar to that I had experienced with Jacqueline. But I was surprised by a shared, almost eerie sense of looking in at the world – a knowing detachment from its everyday concerns. She was not from this time, I felt suddenly. Something else bothered me too. The Mindworm seemed very interested in her: perhaps even involved in the magnetic attraction riding the airwaves between us.

She looked suddenly uncertain, her merriment fading.

'Do I know you sir?' she enquired: a swift evaluation going on behind her eyes.

'No my, err, Lady,' I achieved, trying not to react to various resonations in my being.

She frowned, further discomforted by the hint of irony I failed to keep from my tone. She seemed to consider this briefly, before reverting to outward convention.

'I am impressed by the story the children have told of your bravery. Mr Bambridge is greatly indebted to you'

'I was happy to be of service,' I replied.

She looked at me carefully. 'Have you been in Port Royal long?'

'No, not long my Lady.'

'Where did you ship from?'

'Ah: England my Lady.'

She regarded me curiously for a moment, which Mr Bambridge interpreted as an awkward gap in the conversation.

'I am happy to say, my Lady, that your desire to secure passage back to England has given me an excellent idea. In prevailing upon the good captain to agree to your berth on the Merchant Royal, I came to realise it would be a timely opportunity to send my niece and nephew back home too. Nothing could be safer, with the rest of the fleet and the escorting squadron – and my old friend has found room for them.'

A shadow seemed to pass over her face. 'Is that – wise Mr Bambridge?' she asked haltingly, 'to send them on a long voyage at such a young age, so far from everything they know?'

He seemed surprised at her concern. 'Why I believe it will be for the best your Ladyship,' he said earnestly. 'I have been worried about them here in Port Royal. I don't deny I'll miss them a great deal, but my sister will care well for them in Kent. They will be much better growing up there, safe and sound.'

She appeared to consider the matter a moment longer, before dismissing it with a shrug. Then she smiled once more: 'I am sure you know best sir,' she conceded.

She returned her gaze to me, and I grew alarmed that she was about to ask awkward questions about my background.

'Thank you, my Lady,' I said hastily, executing an impromptu bow and turning to go. She seemed about to speak, but nodded graciously, and I made my exit in relief. Billy and I retreated to our accustomed lair at the back of the Inn, and ordered a beer.

'Well,' he asked intently, 'did you find out anything?'

'Yes, quite a lot really,' I mused. 'I don't think she is from this time for a start.'

'Well dang me, you time people are everywhere!' Billy exclaimed, and I gave a reluctant laugh.

'I'm not sure that's true,' I said, 'but they do seem to be everywhere I go. Like I told you, I don't think it's a coincidence. We seem to be here for a reason. I discovered something else too. Mr Bambridge has got her a passage on a ship bound for England. We had better find out when it's due to leave.'

'Why would she want to get on a ship, if she has got one of these here time thingummies?' he said, puzzled.

'Yes, I'm wondering about that,' I agreed, 'but I'm not sure she has one. I didn't get the same reaction I did with Jacqueline's stepfather. There's something else too: Lady Seymour did not seem happy that Mr Bambridge is sending the twins back to England with her.'

'I guess she don't seem the kind to want kids larking about,' shrugged Billy.

'I think there was more to it than that,' I said. 'Let's see what we can find out about this ship.'

It was not hard to find information, real or imagined, about the Merchant Royal. In fact I was amazed I hadn't heard about it already, because the whole town seemed to be buzzing with it. The Governor was due to retire, and rumoured to be returning to England on the ship with his substantial official share of the bonanza raked in by the industrious privateers. Along with this he was transferring the even more substantial Crown share of the same, in company with various other alleged fortunes, official and unofficial, and a great many more luxury items. Several ships were sailing, and the convoy was due to be escorted by Navy warships. Numerous other wealthy entrepreneurs, including Mr Bambridge, were taking the opportunity to transport some of their accumulated wealth back home at the same time.

I was turning this over in my mind next evening, when Billy begged to see a cock fight in a yard behind a nearby tavern. It was not my idea of fun, but he was still uneasy about going anywhere on his own. Much enthusiasm was being vocalised due to the betting on the fortunes of the unfortunate contestants. I was marvelling somewhat disparagingly at the avid expressions on the faces of the crowd, when I was startled to discover Lady Seymour's features among them. It was not just her presence which surprised me, but the huge delight she seemed to be taking in the murderous contest. She appeared to revel in the excitement, her eyes flashing as she reached into her purse to place money on a bird.

I was equally taken aback by an unexpected pang of desire at the sight of her. I sensed an almost animal magnetism between us which I had never experienced before. I could easily imagine it would mean trouble, but such things have a way of eluding sober scrutiny. Then my attention was caught by something else entirely. Her sleeve caught on some part of her elaborate costume, jerking her hand from the purse, and a shiny object fell to the ground.

She looked aghast. I was already moving towards her, and stooped to retrieve it without thinking. I stared at what I held in my fingers. The device looked simple enough, but it reeked of technology. It was most definitely alien to seventeenth century Port Royal. She stood frozen as I straightened up, and our eyes locked for a moment in a patently candid regard. Then I forced a smile.

'A plain trinket for such a beautiful lady,' I said, and slid my eyes determinedly from hers in a show of artless ignorance. She gazed at me for a moment longer, betraying indecision, before forcing a smile herself.

'Thank you sir,' she said prettily, 'it seems you are forever coming to the rescue.'

'A pleasure my Lady.' I bowed, and retreated. One of the men I had seen her with at the Inn appeared from somewhere behind her. He seemed suspicious, and I moved over to Billy. We watched for a while as blood, feathers and ferocious rivalry were unleashed. It entertained the ring of insatiable spectators, but the mysterious Lady Seymour was more subdued now, and I caught her eye on me several times.

'Well Billy, I think we are going to have to try and get on that ship,' I said later, as we sat in our room.

'I don't know about that,' he said darkly, 'I ain't no sailor. Why don't you just ask her what she's doing? She ain't a killer like Miss Jacqueline's stepfather.'

'I don't know what she is,' I admitted, 'but I don't trust her. And I don't know who else she might be mixed up with either. I can't get anywhere with the Portal at the moment. It just doesn't seem to respond at all. So the only thing I can think of is to try and follow her.'

I decided to approach Mr Bambridge.

'I hesitate to trouble you after all you have done for us sir,' I said awkwardly, 'but there is a great favour I wish to ask of you.'

'Yes, yes,' he beamed, 'there is little enough I have done for you in fact. You have earned your bread fair and square. If it is within my power to be of help, I will do so gladly.'

'Billy and I would very much like to return to England,' I said, 'and I wondered if you might speak up for us to work our passage on the Merchant Royal, or another ship sailing with her.'

He looked surprised, then pensive. My spirits began to sink, but he brightened suddenly and chuckled.

'I was thinking you would stay and help me with my interests here in Port Royal, Master Richard,' he said. 'Jonathan has spoken well of your grasp of business and accounts.' He paused, stroking his chin thoughtfully. 'But upon reflection, I would welcome a report of my affairs at home. I am also having difficulties with Mary. She does not wish to accompany the twins to England and I am worried they will be unhappy with a stranger. They will be reassured if you are aboard, and you may assist in escorting them to Kent.'

I had not expected his rapid acceptance of the idea, and found myself backtracking a little. 'Will they take us aboard the Merchant Royal? We are not experienced seamen.'

'There will be no difficulty,' he answered affably. 'Captain Hammond was telling me yesterday that he had lost more men to sickness than he could replace. I have business with him in the morning, and I will speak to him then.'

'When does the ship sail?' I asked, trying to adjust to the new pace of events.

'It is hoped within the week,' he said. 'I will be sorry to lose you. But the more I consider it, the better the scheme seems to me. I will speak to you of my interests in England: there may be an advantageous position for you there.'

Billy was less enthusiastic about our good fortune, but seemed to be growing in confidence in his role as a time-displaced person.

'Well, I guess when you get that Portal to work, we might as well be on a ship as anywhere,' he said, before pausing thoughtfully. 'Hey, would we come out in the water somewhere else?'

'I have no idea,' I admitted, 'but let's not think about that. The Portal is designed for this stuff and I suppose it knows what it's doing.'

'What do you mean it knows?' asked Billy, entangling me in a convoluted discussion about computers.

Work continued, and so did glimpses of the enigmatic Lady Seymour. She glanced speculatively at me when our paths crossed, but I avoided her eyes and she made no effort to pursue it. We heard numerous stories about her from the servants. Scandalous goings on appeared to attach themselves to her legend at every opportunity. How much truth there was to them I had no idea. But I had little difficulty in believing the most scandalous tale of all. Speaking in hushed tones to all who would listen, one of the upstairs maids assured us that Lady Seymour had a full warm bath prepared in her room every day. Numerous expressions of astonishment greeted this revelation, followed by much conjecture about the diseases she would contract by opening her pores in so reckless a manner.

Mr Bambridge called me to his office in the town, and began to discuss his business operations. It provoked a fair amount of self-recrimination, as I had no expectation of making good his plans. It became apparent that he was sending a substantial store of wealth in coinage and bullion for safe keeping at home, as well as luxury goods for the English market. There would be a lot of work involved in managing the English end of his business interests, and part of me regretted that I would not be able to follow it through. Mr Bambridge had considerable ambitions, and many possibilities presented themselves in a world full of new opportunities. I found a certain amount of fascination creeping in regarding his affairs of business. It surprised me, especially when I knew all of these complicated material matters could vanish in an instant.

Billy grumbled about our prospective maritime adventure, but he seemed to develop a greater interest in the ships we worked around. It reassured me that he was adapting to the extraordinary life we were leading. He also reflected more deeply on his old life when a slave ship docked one morning. Its appearance was announced by a gun much as the privateer's vessel had been, but the town's response was more muted. The vessel was accompanied by a vile stench which our fellow workers recognised from afar, and waves of misery seemed to accompany the odour. We watched as huddled groups of black men and women had buckets of seawater hurled over them on the decks; washing away some of the detritus from the unthinkable conditions below. They stumbled wild eyed and terrified down the gangplank onto the rough flagstones of the docks. Low desolate moans and sobs sounded constantly. Chains clanked and rattled as men and women were herded into separate, barred pens like cattle, brutally threatened and struck with whips and clubs. The stark horror of it sickened me, and the romantic image of Port Royal died in my mind.

Some townsfolk did hurry to see this new batch of merchandise: pushing and grabbing amongst the shattered human cargo in search of bargains. Captives called out piteously to one another, relations perhaps, or life partners. For me the whole desperate scene evoked images of the Jewish Holocaust. I sensed no mysterious depth of consciousness creeping up on me, yet I did feel part of a long, strange human journey through time. I had experienced people inflicting lethal violence on each other, and that was shocking enough. But this casual, callous cruelty against a whole people: negating their humanity and turning them into a mere commodity, seemed inconceivable. Being out of time let me view the present world with fewer filters of habit and prejudice: the unquestioned absurdities and contradictions of accepted behaviour. It was the slavers and their eager customers who were tribal and primitive, and their prey the bewildered victims of ignorant savages.

It all seemed so unnecessary and stupid, as though a group of actors had become possessed by their roles, and begun to murder each other on stage. I wondered what it was all about, this ability to love some and hate others. We were born the same, we laughed the same, we cried the same, yet we learned to look for differences and despise each other. It seemed extraordinary that intelligent beings could be so crass and insensible.

Billy stood awkwardly beside me, and I wondered about the slavery he must have grown up with in the southern American States.

'I know what you're thinking,' he said.

'Do you?' I asked.

'You ain't like most folks Mr – Richard. You worry about other people. Coming back when I got hit was just plumb crazy; and right when we've jumped through heaven and hell, off you go again, running under them horses. Most folks wouldn't put themselves out for other people – even if they could fly.'

'It's not flying, Billy, I just move quicker.'

'Well, it don't matter how fast you move, you can't do nothing for these poor souls.'

'You believe they have souls?' I asked in surprise.

'I don't exactly mean that,' he said, 'leastways, I don't know what I mean.' Then he brightened. 'But I guess they'll become Christians now.'

I laughed bitterly. 'So these Christians are doing them a favour?'

He looked uncomfortable. 'These slavers ain't God-fearing men. I ain't seen nothing like this. We never had slaves, but those I seen seemed happy enough. They were settled, just like other folks.'

'But they are worked like animals, and this is where they come from,' I said grimly, 'God knows what it's like in those holds.'

'It's cruel, right enough,' he admitted, 'but I guess it's the natural way of things. Says so in the Bible, that's what my Pa said.'

'I bet the Bible doesn't say that white men should kidnap black men and get rich by making them work like dogs,' I said impatiently. 'Anyway, the Bible was written a long time ago, by people in primitive societies. We should be better than that. No one even knows who wrote it, or when.'

Billy looked shocked. 'You mean Jesus didn't write the Bible?' he said incredulously.

I laughed sourly. 'No he didn't. The New Testament was put together hundreds of years after his death, and the Old Testament was written before he was born. All religions had their books written by unknown people over hundreds of years, except for Mohammed. But there is some question whether a certain amount of editing went on there as well.'

He stared at me. 'Heathens have Bibles too?'

'Heathens are just what people call other people who don't believe what they do,' I said. 'There are millions of people in the world who think Christians are heathens too. I think the truth is that no one really knows. After all, that place we went through, with all that light and power: that isn't in the Bible either is it? The Bible might talk about the kingdom of heaven, but it doesn't say what it is, or that you can go there when you are alive. It doesn't say you can have different lives in different times and places either.'

'But that's just you time people and your Portal thingamabobs,' he objected. 'It ain't natural.'

'Actually,' I remembered, 'many early Christians believed in reincarnation, which is kind of similar.'

'What's that then?' he asked doubtfully.

'It means your soul lives through many lives; and only reaches God when it has learned all its lessons I guess.'

'You're kidding me!' said Billy, 'how come that's not in the Bible then?'

I chuckled cynically. 'I suppose the people who put themselves in charge of Religion didn't fancy the idea of being reborn poor and unimportant.' I nodded towards the crude cages: 'or as a slave.'

'Seems I got a lot of things to think about,' he muttered.

'Haven't we all,' I sighed. 'Let's get out of here.'

The days before we sailed dwindled, and my sessions with Mr Bambridge intensified. He had arranged our placement with the crew of the Merchant Royal without difficulty. We had been on board to meet the ship's Master, who had cheerfully dismissed our inexperience, and consigned us to haul the ropes and learn as we went on. The twins were delighted that Billy and I would be sailing with them. They bombarded us with gleeful speculation about the adventure ahead every time they saw us. I felt bad about our probable disappearance from their lives, and tried not to think about it. It was surprisingly difficult to detach myself from the concerns of our temporary new world.

Finally we stood on the dockside with our meagre possessions slung over our shoulders in canvas bags. Nathaniel and Aurelia scampered around their unenthusiastic new nanny, and Mr Bambridge wiped a tear from his eye as he wished us a safe voyage. A carriage arrived behind us piled high with baggage, and I was unsurprised to see Lady Seymour emerge languidly from its elegant interior. She stood stock still as she caught sight of our party. Her gaze fixed on me, and she slowly approached us.

'Good day Mr Bambridge,' she called out with a doubtful smile, 'am I to take it that our hero is sailing with us?'

'Why yes, Lady Seymour,' cried Mr Bambridge happily. 'They work their passage back to England, and the twins are very glad of it.'

'I see,' she said, drawing nearer and watching me carefully. 'I am sure we will all be pleased to have such men among our crew.'

I smiled and nodded, but could not resist allowing my gaze to linger for a sceptical second longer than necessary. Her eyes widened, and she gave me a hard, shrewd glance before turning to ascend the gangplank. A train of lackeys followed, struggling with her possessions. Billy and I boarded soon afterwards, waving goodbye to the twins as they were taken to their cabin, and to Mr Bambridge on the dockside.

We descended below decks to stow our bags: into a very different world to that of the paying passengers. Stumbling down steep, rough wooden steps in near darkness, we bent our heads low beneath skull-cracking beams. Our lungs seemed to strive for oxygen in the malodorous fug that lurked everywhere below decks. The sleeping accommodation stretched barely a foot and a half across – space to sling a hammock that required half the crew up and working to grant room to sleep in any comfort. We stored our belongings in a shared, battered sea chest before returning to begin work on deck: shoved into position like dumb puppets, ready to haul ropes and raise sails on command.

Heavy mooring cables were cast off, and the ship began to drift from the dock, a couple of minor sails flapping lazily in the breeze. Crewmen darted about on the rigging with practiced ease. We got the order to heave, and larger sheets of canvas began lurching upwards to catch the wind. The silence in which the vessel gained headway seemed strange at first: the absence of rumbling engines unnatural. Lesser sounds played on the ear instead – rippling water at the bow, the snapping of canvas, and a low hum as ropes took the tension of the sails. A deep groaning of straining wood started up in the bones of the ship.

Seagulls followed for a while, and a few dozen souls continued to wave from the quay as we moved out towards the headland. I glimpsed the stalwart figure of Mr Bambridge and felt a stab of guilt. I hoped everything would work out OK for him, and for the twins. Another five merchant ships set sail with us, shepherded by three naval vessels: two sleek business-like craft, and a larger warship with a triple row of gun-ports either side of its broad, curved hull. The Governor had elected to travel on this ship at the last moment, apparently because it provided a bigger cabin, but a detachment of soldiers was present on the Merchant Royal as additional guardians of his loot.

The slow, plunging roll of the ship became livelier as we moved out into the open sea, and I detected a twinge of discomfort in the pit of my stomach. I glanced at Billy. He looked equally ill-at-ease, and my optimism dropped a notch. I had been pleased we had got onto Lady Seymour's ship, but a bout of seasickness threatened a dose of realism. I began to feel doubtful, out of my depth in more ways than one. Chasing time travellers in the seventeenth century seemed suddenly crazy, and I wondered where it was all going to end. The impossible scale of the quest I had embarked on came sharply into focus, and a trickle of sadness oppressed me as I thought of Alex and Jacqueline. The pursuit of people I hardly knew through inexplicable realities I did not understand seemed reckless and naive.

At that moment I glanced up at the high poop deck at the rear of the ship, which housed the cabins of the officers and the more privileged passengers. It overlooked the quarter deck below, and my location lower still in the waist, at the centre of the ship. Behind the poop deck's ornate wooden rail stood Lady Seymour, looking directly down at me. An almost electric connection seemed to crackle between us. I sensed a lot more substance to her than her carefree persona suggested, and felt an urge to abandon my detective work and ask her for help. Whether it would be wise or not I was unsure. I reasoned that time travellers did not all have to be like Jacqueline's stepfather: that she must understand so many things I did not know. It was hard to recall why I had been so suspicious of her, and when I struggled to remember I felt a familiar stab of resentment at the back of my mind. It was the Mindworm I realised: spinning another of its webs.

'*She is a woman of fire and passion,*' it said quite brazenly in my head, '*not like that strait-laced Jacqueline.*'

An image, not of Jacqueline but of Mellissa, came to mind. I had found nothing mundane about Jacqueline. But Mellissa's brand of routine petulance was cast into the shade by the coquettish mischief sparkling in Lady Seymour's eyes. '*What would it be like to have a woman like that*'? I wondered.

'*Exactly,*' said the Mindworm, with much satisfaction.

I shook myself free in annoyance, and Lady Seymour turned away as if recognising a spell had been broken. I welcomed back the forgotten nausea as a pragmatic reminder of reality. I was committed to this voyage now I told myself, foolhardy or not. I would just take it one day at a time.

Our sea sickness was less intense and prolonged than I feared, and we settled into a hard and demanding routine. It took the skin off our hands and gave me even more aches and pains than our labours in the warehouse. But the age of sail proved to own a spirit of adventure after all. Braving the vast, untamed majesty of the sea in a great sailing ship seemed to awaken something in my soul. I felt a wild, pure joy as the sails ballooned, taut and radiant in the sun. The restless might of the wind lent its blessings, and the boat hummed under its elemental power.

The days passed, the salty tang of the sea blew fresh and clear, and the sunlight twinkled merrily on the wave crests. The flotilla of vessels kept pace like protective siblings, but a shadow seemed to lurk behind our carefree progress. Billy caught one of the crew at our sea chest. The man claimed he had mistaken it for his own, but Billy felt others were unnaturally interested in us too. He stowed his gun and ammunition belt away in a hidey hole he had found.

Nautical mysteries of vocabulary and know-how sorted themselves into approximate meaning, and Billy and I began to venture into the rigging as our experience grew. Our strength and agility flourished, and we laughed at our new, tanned incarnations as we climbed high above the deck in the sun. Billy had been used to a hard life, and took to the new regime effortlessly. I had to struggle more, but my body seemed to fill out daily. I had never felt so fit and healthy, and my physical confidence blossomed. The days passed with only fleeting glimpses of Lady Seymour. But we often spoke with the twins: brought out on deck during our brief moments of leisure by their reticent nanny.

The same good health could not be claimed by many of our shipmates however. A sizeable queue of seamen soon built up outside the surgeon's lair deep inside the ship. Most exhibited the painful symptoms of sexually transmitted diseases, the bounty of riotous self-indulgence in Port Royal. They were ineffectually treated with hideous concoctions of mercury and arsenic, and had the costs deducted from their pay. Such afflictions were deemed just retribution for a sinful departure from the path of righteousness and honest seafaring.

Billy and I had avoided a similar fate, as available short-notice female company had not been conducive to alluring attraction. One look at the condition of Port Royal's wanton women would have driven away even the most red-blooded twenty-first century Romeo. Billy was also surprisingly prudish and shy about these things. I was initially sceptical about such virtue in a hard-fighting, slave-subjugating soldier. But I later came across the account of an incident during the American Civil War which contradicted my assumptions. A group of starving Confederate soldiers had approached a house while foraging in Union territory, and the door was opened by a doubtless frightened, but strikingly beautiful young lady. The soldiers became so smitten and bashful at the sight of her that they left without asking for a bite to eat. I could easily imagine Billy being one of them. How quickly the world seemed to have changed for the worse, despite the advance of scientific enlightenment.

The benign weather faded after a long pleasant interlude, retreating before a distant, murky band on the horizon. A new, fickle mood played in the wind and the waves, and many of us were sent aloft to reduce sail as evening fell. It was a difficult, nerve wracking job in the growing dark. The rigging swung with increasing vigour: the masts' lateral movement violently multiplied by their height above deck.

A heavy blow came from nowhere. It sent me sprawling as I struggled for a footing on a rope slung beneath a wildly plunging spar. I clung dazedly to the beam, my feet treading empty air as I strained to look behind me in bewilderment. I had been struck on the head and shoulder, and could not understand where it had come from. I caught sight of a dark, bulky figure struggling with his own foothold on the rope. I recognised him: a sailor who had also signed on at Port Royal. I thought he might have fallen against me until I glimpsed the shape of a hefty belaying pin in his hand, and any further doubt vanished as he lashed out at me again.

This time his aim was even worse. He struck my arm as the heaving ship flung both of us about. But the pain was numbing, and it loosened my grip. Bright sparks swam before my vision, and I scrabbled to plant my feet on the swaying rope beneath me. Things were not looking good. I felt panic rising, and reached out desperately for the Portal, but nothing happened. My assailant raised his arm for another blow, but a third figure clambered up from below him. He seized the man's ankle, and wrenched one of his feet from its purchase on the rope.

The man twisted, clinging awkwardly to the spar with one arm, and aimed a blow at his new opponent instead. At the same moment my own feet found the foot-rope, and I shuffled sideways hard against him, hugging the spar for all I was worth. I thudded into him, almost losing my footing again: but he lost his, and dropped the weapon. He grasped frantically at the spar but missed his grip, and fell with a wail. With the masts leaning far from the perpendicular, he dropped straight down into the sea a long way below.

'Man overboard!' came a shout from the deck.

'Good riddance,' cried Billy angrily. 'Are you hurt? That was a cruel blow.'

'He missed,' I gasped, feeling my head gingerly. 'Well, mostly he missed. He caught the side of my head and my shoulder. It hurts all right, but I don't think it's bad. It was lucky you came when you did.'

'I saw him climbing over to you, and I reckoned he was up to no good,' Billy growled. 'I seen him watching us the last couple of days.'

'Thank goodness you did Billy. I'd have been dead if you hadn't.'

'Well that makes us even,' he grinned.

A weird perception formed in my head: a complex image of connections and consequences woven through space-time. I glimpsed a subtle latticework of changes and adjustments to the fabric of reality. I had saved Billy's life in eighteen sixty three and now he had saved mine in sixteen eighty nine. Somehow everything seemed related: cause and effect interlinked. I smiled ironically to myself, and winced at the aching numbness from the blows of the belaying pin. Or maybe that wallop had just scrambled my brain. It was hard to make sense of the crazy life I was leading.

'Did anyone else see what happened?' I asked, still rather dizzy and shocked.

'I don't know,' said Billy, 'it's pretty dark, and most of them are back on deck.'

'But why did he do it?' I wondered. 'I suppose it's something to do with the delightful Lady Seymour. She suspects I'm not from this time, but why try to kill me?'

'She's up to something all right,' Billy replied: 'her and a few others by the look of it, and it don't take much to figure out what it is.'

'What do you mean?' I said.

'There's a pile of treasure on this ship,' he answered matter-of-factly.

'But what would time travellers want with treasure?' I asked, perplexed.

'I don't know,' he said, 'but one thing I do know: where you get a whole lot of money, you get a whole lot of trouble.'

I thought about it. I had needed money, but it had been easy to get plenty to live on. I could not imagine why people with such easy access to wealth would need to travel to the seventeenth century and engage in a complicated plot to steal the Governor's bullion.

'Maybe they are trying to stop someone else from stealing it?' I suggested.

Billy looked sceptical. 'Maybe,' he said.

'Well,' I said, abandoning the subject, 'a couple more ties and the work will be done. We'd better just say he fell when we get down.'

The man's demise had been seen, but apparently not the fight that preceded it. No attempt had been made to save him. It would have been impossible to halt the convoy, or to find him in the growing dark. A group of seamen were waiting for us, including the First Mate, as we dropped down onto the deck.

'Who fell?' he demanded gruffly.

'Tom,' I said briefly.

'What happened?'

'I don't know. I heard him call out, and he was gone.'

'What about you?' he asked Billy.

'I didn't see nothing. I guess he slipped,' said Billy with a shrug.

'I would have expected it from one of you two,' the First Mate muttered, 'but that Tom was a right seaman. Learn a lesson from it. Hold on up there.'

We nodded dutifully, and he called out to everyone: 'there's still work to do. Looks like a hard blow we're in for.'

I glanced around at the others. They were dispersing to go about their business, shaking their heads over the unfortunate Tom. All but one, who directed a brief but significant glance back up at the poop deck. I followed his look and there sure enough stood Lady Seymour, an unreadable expression in the shadows of her face.

Chapter 10

THE STORM GREW steadily in intensity throughout the night. The ship rolled in all directions in a progressively alarming manner, with increasingly massive waves braking over the superstructure. All but one tiny sail had been stripped from the masts, and the wind howled through the rigging like some kind of wild, elemental demon. Horizontal sheets of rain lashed viciously across the decks, saturating the air so densely it was difficult to breathe. All who could do so remained below decks, hunched defensively in the gloom, and waiting miserably for the ordeal to pass. Billy said nothing but the looks he gave me spoke volumes. All of his fears had been justified. Sailing was not for him. Or for me, for that matter: I soon decided the joys of skimming the ocean in fine weather could never make up for that nauseous fear and helplessness in the wildly careering darkness.

Slowly the hours passed, the screeching of the wind rising to a shrill banshee shriek. Several men were sick and I was close to it myself. So was Billy, from the rare glimpses I had of him in the dim, swaying light of the storm lantern. The elements roared, the ship cowered before their wrath, and men trembled and prayed. The treacherous Portal might as well not have existed. I could feel no trace of it though I strained to reach it repeatedly. If it had responded, I would have grabbed Billy and gone anywhere, Lady Seymour be damned. The only distraction was relentless spells on the pumps: two-man see-saw affairs, on which shattered men laboured continuously to expel water welling through the tortured seams in the hull.

I lost count of the long bouts of pumping. I was so exhausted I hardly knew what was happening. There was little room to sling the hammocks, and I sat stupidly on the streaming floor, dozing fitfully against the shuddering timber bulkhead. The storm assaulted my mind asleep or awake. I dreamed I was awake and thought reality a dream, an endless, discordant succession of pain and terror. Dawn brought no relief, not even the daylight that usually penetrated in some measure below decks. The nightmare went on and on. One man went mad, bellowing incoherently and drooling at the mouth. He reminded me bizarrely of the two screaming men at the club where I had met Alex. For a moment I wished I could transport them to the ship, and really give them something to scream about.

I fell asleep on the pump and was dragged away, only to be slapped awake what seemed like moments later to take my turn once more. Our endurance dropped drastically, and after only five or ten minutes my muscles refused to function. More and more of us lay in a stupor, no longer caring about the storm or the water creeping into the ship. Eventually I plunged into a sleep so deep that nothing could wake me.

Light was filtering dimly from above when consciousness began to return, and for a few confusing moments I thought I was back in the cellar in Gettysburg. I thought I heard Jacqueline calling me, but it was the keening of the wind, now low and mournful. The ship was still rolling from side to side, but the movement seemed more leisurely. The first mate climbed wearily down the companionway, and I called over to him.

'Is it over?'

'Depends what you call over,' he said grimly. 'There's seven feet of water in the hold, and we have lost most of the masts. We're still making too much water. Seems there's wood rot and shipworm a-plenty, and the hull has taken a pounding. We're trying to haul a sheet under her, so get on deck if you can. How much it will stem the flow I cannot tell.'

I staggered stiffly to my feet, and shook Billy awake. He stared blearily at me, his face haggard and grey.

'We have to get on deck,' I said.

'You mean we're still afloat?' he muttered darkly, 'feels like we sunk a long time back.'

We emerged onto the swaying deck under a cloudy grey sky, the wind now little more than a stiff breeze, and the ship rolling and pitching almost sedately on slow, leaden waves. Half the foremast had gone, along with the yard. The mizzen-mast was mostly missing, and only the lower main-mast remained. All that was left of the rigging was a tangled ruin of tackle and cordage. There was no sign at all of our little squadron. The ocean was empty in every direction. Visibility was still not good, but the storm had raged for thirty six hours, and I imagined we might have been blown vast distances apart.

Thirty men struggled at the bulwarks to pass a sail under the bows. We fought alongside them for an hour to work the heavy canvas back under the hull, with a line of messengers reporting on the leaks from the depths of the ship. Finally the captain was satisfied, but pressed us straight into constructing temporary jury-masts and repairing the rigging. We had sat down to a late, unappetising breakfast of hard tack when I felt a tap on my shoulder, and looked around to see the Captain's steward behind me.

'Begging your pardon,' he said diffidently, 'but Lady Seymour sends word that the children have need of you.'

Her name and the summons flustered me. Conflicting thoughts circled in my head, but I realised guiltily that I had forgotten about the twins. I had been absorbed in the exigencies of the moment, and should have thought to see how they were. I followed the steward into the unfamiliar labyrinth of cabins at the rear of the ship, hurriedly crunching through my remaining breakfast. The facilities were considerably better than ours, but still badly lit, pretty claustrophobic and rather damp. The man led me to the twins' tiny cabin, where to my astonishment Lady Seymour was sitting on Aurelia's cot.

She looked up, her face a curious mixture of exhaustion, mistrust and discomfiture. Her wrinkled skirt and bodice had once been elegant, but were plainer than any I had previously seen. Her hair was swept back untidily, her elaborate blonde curls reduced to a mane of wayward twists and whorls.

'They insisted I call for you,' she said rather self-consciously.

The children sat up immediately, arms outstretched, chorusing 'Uncle Richard' and burst into tears. I clasped them to me awkwardly, with my eyes fixed on Lady Seymour.

'I am not their uncle of course, but they have become attached to me,' I said slowly. 'The storm must have been terrible for them. But how are you here? Where is their maid?'

'With my own,' she said in annoyance, 'both of them more dead than alive, and overflowing with hysterics when they can do anything at all.'

'You have looked after these children yourself?' I asked in surprise.

Embarrassment briefly eclipsed her weariness and caution, and she shrugged. 'It was little enough. I gave them – medicines that I had to calm them, and told them all would be well.'

'And will it?' I asked.

She matched me stare for stare. 'I would like to know who you are Mr Walton.'

'Is that before or after you push me into the sea?'

She flushed. 'I – was glad you did not fall,' she said, her voice a little unsteady. 'It was not my idea. I wish the children were not here either. In fact I wish I had never set foot on this ship at all.'

An electric charge seemed to crackle between us. I sensed an inner connection which undermined our differences. She seemed lost in the moment, her pupils expanding. I continued to comfort the children, but could not tear my gaze away. I felt myself softening towards her, but a hint of the Mindworm's presence sent alarms bells ringing, and I backed off hurriedly.

'So what exactly are you doing here?' I asked, more harshly than I intended.

She looked a little startled, and drew back behind her veil. Lady Seymour pouted back at me once more.

'This game must end soon,' she said, 'but I doubt it will end well.'

She got to her feet, stooping a little in the low cabin, and swept haughtily by me. I sat with the children for several minutes, turning her words over in my mind. She had all but admitted she was a time traveller. It was shocking how hungry I was for that admission – to have someone to share the mystery with. Or, I thought uneasily, perhaps there was more I wanted to share. The magnetic attraction between us was a distraction I could have done without.

We continued to labour with the masts and rigging, carrying a spare topmast up from the hold, and lashing it into position from precarious temporary perches. The pumps were constantly manned, and when the water was down to a few feet we rearranged cargo in the holds to salvage some of the more valuable merchandise from the flood. A ship was spotted in the late evening. We had some sail up, but the vessel was upwind and we were not in a position to manoeuvre towards it. It was tentatively identified as the 'Bonaventure', one of our fellow merchant ships, but it was in a sorry state. All of its masts had gone. It was dead in the water, with a single jury-rigged replacement still incomplete. We watched it drift out of sight in the encroaching gloom, and halted our own work for the night. Exhausted, we retired gratefully for some much needed food and sleep.

Morning dawned, still cloudy and overcast. The sea remained choppy and the wind blew in random, uncertain gusts. No one could agree on the mood of the weather and the damp, dismal realm below decks was filled with gloomy rumour. Still, the pumps had got the water down below three feet in the hold, and some order had been established in the masts and rigging. The ship's routine regained some of its natural rhythm, and the officers could be seen discussing the best course of action. It was approaching mid-morning when a cry from the mast announced a sail on the horizon, and an hour later before cheerful speculation began to turn to dismay.

The ship was lean and fast, and bearing down on us with surprising rapidity. It was smaller than the Merchant Royal but heavily armed: its line of squat, heavy canon far outclassing the handful of twelve pound guns we carried. There was a style and air about it that had been all too familiar at Port Royal. It was no surprise to see its deck bristling with men.

'Well Billy, we seem to have got ourselves some pirates,' I said to him in a low voice. 'You had better get that gun of yours loaded.'

'I'd rather you got that Portal of yours primed and ready,' he said with a grimace. 'I don't fancy our chances with this bunch of fresh fish. They ain't going to put up much of a fight.'

I was extremely apprehensive myself. My previous experience of combat had been brief and unexpected: all over before I had fully grasped what was happening. Waiting for fighting to begin, and on such a scale, was quite terrifying. Apart from checking that the children and the ladies had been sent to a safe refuge below the waterline, I had no idea what to do. So I resorted as usual to striving for a connection with the Portal, and anger soon replaced resignation when it remained mute and inactive.

The soldiers gathered on deck, sixteen of them with an officer, cleaning and checking their muskets. Some experienced seamen were put to last-minute work on the rigging and sails, to try and get us under way. The captain and officers armed themselves with pistols and swords, and the rest of us were issued with an assortment of cutlasses, axes and belaying pins. I eyed the cutlass I was handed in alarm. It was an ugly, brutal looking thing: the wooden handgrip grimy and scored, and the brass hand-guard dull and dented. But its broad blade was heavy and wickedly sharp. I felt a little as I did in dreams, where weapons rarely worked, and wondered if I could really use it to hit someone.

The pirates gained rapidly on us, their ship growing in size with alarming speed. A cannon banged at its prow: a request or a warning, but one our ship's captain ignored. Some of our own guns replied, shrill and ineffectual to my ears, and the approaching ship slewed around to let fly with a booming broadside. Several balls crossed above us without apparent harm: but they screamed through the air with a hideous sound like tearing canvas, which sent a chill right through me. It felt much more personal than Gettysburg. The pirates came on again while our seamen fumbled to reload their guns. This time all our guns fired when the order was given, but with no visible effect on our foes. They were ominously silent. I feared their next broadside would be close and devastating, and so it was.

They were barely a hundred yards off when they swung to bear on us again. Their ship vanished in an ear-splitting firestorm, and a moment later our vessel lurched under a rain of hammer blows. Ruinous crashes sounded below, and clouds of wooden splinters exploded everywhere. There were terrible screams and shouts, and debris fell from the rigging. Men were ripped apart, flung mutilated onto the decks. Others stared in disbelief at great shards of wood protruding from their bodies. All of us staggered in shock: stupefied by the noise and violence and slipping in great splashes of blood and gore.

The pirate ship swung in towards us again. A mass of men crowded its decks, and a host of weapons glinted evilly in the sun. I looked for our company of soldiers. Two or three had been injured by splinters, but the remainder readied their muskets in disciplined calm. But a shocking moment later a swathe of carnage erupted in their ranks: inexplicable, bloody slaughter. I stared in bewilderment, unable to grasp what had happened. Then I glimpsed seamen at a smoking swivel gun up on the quarter deck. They had fired point blank with a lethal charge of grapeshot into the waist of our ship, and were hurriedly reloading. A bloody hand hung limp through the balustrading. There were bodies there: the captain and his officers.

I knew instantly that Lady Seymour and her associates were responsible. I felt a flash of rage and a flood of déjà vu. The scale of the threat and the cold blooded betrayal overwhelmed me. Fear, wrath and hatred took root in my heart. For a moment my perception seemed to fracture: part of me watching in bemused detachment while another self demanded bloody retribution. The weird dichotomy prevailed for a second or two, and then rage took hold. A cold-blooded ferocity filled me. I felt the Mindworm's glee and did not care – I revelled in its might. I had leaped onto the quarter deck before I realised the time dilation effect had triggered, and hacked at the first man without really knowing what I was doing. I chopped viciously into a second man at the mounted swivel gun, and severed the arm of a third as he tried to bring a pistol up towards me.

I was conscious only of deadly, focused fury. Reloading the swivel-gun was simple. The Mindworm knew all about weapons. The barrel had been sponged and the cloth powder charge forced in. I had only to ram down a bag of musket balls and a wad; spike and prime the powder bag through the touchhole, take aim and apply the slow match. I looked down. The pirate's bow nudged at an angle against us, and a flurry of grappling hooks sailed over the bulwarks of our ship's waist below. A hoard of men poured over the rail, and I swung the barrel to fire full into them with shattering effect. I stamped hard on the trembling face of the one-armed man as he scrabbled feebly for his pistol, and leapt down to the lower deck.

The sounds of the fighting had slowed to a sullen background roar. Sluggish animal grunts and languorous screams merged with prolonged sonorous booms and the dull reverberation of metal on metal. But my cutlass seemed to hum with power. Billy straight-armed his revolver and shot down six men one after another. I struck as many before he had finished, and then consciously slowed my movements into a deadly dance, taking my subjective time to slash at men with callous efficiency.

The crew fought with newfound courage as the pirates' charge faltered. They began to retreat, some falling overboard in an attempt to escape the sudden carnage. We hacked at the grappling ropes, and the first mate's men aloft released the mainsail at the same moment. The ship jerked forward in the wind. I cut the final rope, and we pulled abruptly away from the disorganised pirates. They had been hit hard without getting fully alongside, and in moments there was fifty yards of sea between us again.

'Well that gave them something to think about,' said Billy, reloading his revolver.

It was a complicated process involving separate balls, paper cartridges and percussion caps, and I realised as I watched that real time was flowing once more. I looked around. Dazed men stood everywhere in shock. The shattering violence, Billy's repeating gun, and the frenetic destruction I had inflicted were more than their shocked minds could process.

The Mindworm still fuelled my feelings. I was possessed by a manic blood-lust: blazing with implacable hatred. I sensed its satisfaction with my murderous passion, but not with my loyalty to the crew of the Merchant Royal.

'They are slaves of those who control the weak,' it insinuated, *'why protect the ship for their masters? Those you fight are bold and daring, join them and share the gold.'*

'I fight for who I chose!' I snarled back.

I turned to the confounded crew. No one seemed to be in charge. The first mate was still making his way down from the rigging.

'They will be back!' I bellowed, 'get to the guns!'

They stirred into uncertain activity.

'You sure are a devil when your blood's up,' said Billy conversationally. 'I'd have taken a lot more care around you if I'd known. Are you going to fly again when they come back?'

'I don't know,' I said impatiently, 'but I have an idea. Follow me.'

I led him swiftly down into the small forward hold. 'Here,' I said, 'I saw these yesterday.'

One-gallon glass demijohns were stacked in rows, big round green bottles with long narrow necks in wicker jackets, filling a quarter of the storage space.

'What are they?' asked Billy.

'Good quality brandy.'

'We gonna get drunk?' he asked hopefully.

I smiled grimly. 'No.'

A vicious ripple of cannon fire thundered out at point blank range. The sound was muffled slightly in the hold, but the overpressure pounded my eardrums. The ship staggered, its timbers groaning at the catastrophic weight of metal smashing through its side.

'Quick,' I grunted, 'grab as many as you can.'

We stowed our weapons in our belts, clutched two of the bulky bottles in each hand by their crude wicker casings, and rushed back onto the deck. Random, mediocre bangs rang out we raced along the ship: one or two of our canon returning the pirates fire.

'The muskets!' I roared at a group of crouching sailors, 'the soldiers' weapons – pick them up!'

Several moved to obey, but I paid them no more heed and bounded up the steps to the quarterdeck with my load.

'What are we gonna do?' asked Billy, panting slightly as he put his bottles down.

'Knock the neck off one, and pour it over the jackets of the others,' I said fiercely. 'We'll light them, and throw them when the bastards get near enough.'

I reloaded the gun with grapeshot as quickly as I could, ignoring random musket balls whizzing through the air about me. Another broadside smashed into us, killing many in the waist below. I looked up to see the pirates coming in to board again, and glimpsed a dozen muskets aimed at us.

'Down, Billy!' I yelled, and we dropped to the deck as a hail of shots splintered the ornate balustrading and ricocheted off the swivel gun.

'OK,' I shouted, slicing open a powder bag with my cutlass, 'chuck some gunpowder on each bottle too.'

'There you go with that 'oh kay' again,' grumbled Billy, 'silliest word I ever heard.'

There was a heavy thud as the pirate ship struck our hull again. I blew on the slow match, and touched the brandy-soaked gunpowder on the wicker covering of the first demijohn. It ignited with a whoomph and I seized it by the neck, hurling it over the balustrading with all my strength. I heard it strike the pirates' deck: the sharp crack, and cries of consternation.

'Fast as we can!' I bellowed.

Billy held a demijohn by the neck towards me, and I fired it up. He threw three in a row, and then we changed roles, as the flames were scorching. I threw another three, and had to fling the open bottle too when it caught fire. I peered over the rail, blowing on my stinging hands. Pools of ghostly blue flames danced on the pirate deck: a larger conflagration near the mainmast. Piles of rope were burning fiercely and a cache of gunpowder ignited in a sudden flare. I seized the cask of powder bags by the swivel-gun and heaved it over at the burning deck for good measure, then chucked the last demijohn after it.

Chaos reigned among the brutes swarming over the waist bulwarks. Some turned back to fight the fires, and others peered behind them to see what was happening. Desperate fighting had erupted where the first mate had rallied the remnants of the Merchant Royal's crew. I let fly once more into the midst of the boarders with the swivel gun, and leapt down with Billy to join the vicious struggle.

I had no idea if the quick-time effect would trigger again, but it made little difference with the relentless aggression that burned in me. I smashed into the melee with insatiable violence, hacking and killing with a ferocity that some distant self observed in mute astonishment. Billy shot down man after man, and then seized a fallen sabre and wielded it with pugnacious determination. The pirates wavered a second time, shaken by heavy casualties and growing shouts of alarm from their ship. A glance suggested that burning spirit had seeped through gaps in the deck planking, for smoke was billowing up through a hatchway. More of their crew turned to fight the fires and we pressed our advantage, driving the remaining boarders back across the bloody deck. We cut the grappling ropes free again, and the ships drifted apart once more.

I turned to Billy. 'We'd better get some more demijohns.'

He nodded significantly up towards the quarterdeck and I followed his gaze. Lady Seymour stared back at me, her face a mask of horror.

'Get away from there!' I yelled, bounding up the steps towards her.

'What have you done?' she gasped, as I reached her.

'Stopped them for now,' I retorted angrily. 'You had better get back below decks.'

'If that boat sinks, we will all die,' she said bitterly.

I frowned, and started to speak: then felt rather than heard the giant force that seemed to lift the Merchant Royal right out of the water. I flew dreamily across the sky, stunned and stupefied, and plunged deep into salt water. For long, uncomprehending moments I hung there, suspended in cool green nothingness. Then I rose slowly through a curtain of silver bubbles, watching patterns of light playing across the undulating surface above me. I knew I was in the sea, but not how or why. Bursting out into wind and spray brought the first glimmers of understanding. There had been an explosion – a massive one. I gasped in a deep lungful of air and looked about for confirmation. Small pieces of debris were still falling into the water all around me. A great cloud of smoke obscured the sky, and I glimpsed the dark silhouette of a ship

– the Merchant Royal – fifty yards away. All her masts were gone now, and she seemed down at the bow. I could not see the pirate ship. It had been on the far side, but I suspected it no longer existed. The quantity of floating wreckage testified to that. Their powder magazine must have ignited I realised, and then I remembered Lady Seymour.

'We will all die,' she had said, and I wondered how prophetic her words had been. I searched quickly all around me, and spied a bundle of flimsy material ballooning with air some distance away. It had to be her clothes, and I struck out in that direction, my arms weak and clumsy. I found her floating on her back, buoyed up a little by the air in her torn and ragged clothing. Her eyes were closed, and I could not tell if she was breathing.

'Lady Seymour!' I yelled, and heard my voice only faintly. I was almost completely deaf. She did not respond. I tried to keep her face out of the water and towed her awkwardly towards a large section of decking that floated a few yards away. It was some twelve feet by eight, and still affixed to parts of its supporting beams. I heaved the top half of her body up onto the planks, and struggled clumsily after her, feeling dizzy with the effort.

The makeshift raft was far from stable. It dipped low beneath us; with water sloshing right over it, but it was better than nothing. It was some moments before my breathing was steady enough to check her pulse. She was alive, but her heartbeat was rapid and erratic, and her breathing laboured. I thought I could hear bubbling in her windpipe, and struggled to heave her further onto the raft. I turned her over into the recovery position, wondering if I would be able to resuscitate her on the unstable platform if it became necessary. But she vomited seawater without regaining consciousness, and her vital signs settled down. She looked angelic, like a sleeping child. The curls had washed out of her hair, and the long voluminous skirt she had been wearing had vanished. A colourful petticoat and bodice were shredded and torn, with only a silk slip below that intact.

I looked up as soon as I was sure she was OK, and got a shock. The Merchant Royal was a lot more sluggish in the current than we were. It was a hundred yards away, and we were drifting further all the time. I stared in disbelief, trying to think what to do. I knew I could probably recover the strength to swim the distance soon enough, but the unconscious girl was another matter. It crossed my mind to abandon her. She had after all tried to have me killed – or at least not prevented it, and she had been involved in the pirate attack. But I knew immediately I couldn't do it. I also realised I was myself again: or at least, more myself. The Mindworm was no longer orchestrating my actions, although I still felt mired by its nature. But I had no time to consider it further. I had to make a decision.

The only scenario I could envisage was to swim over myself, and try to return in a boat. I attempted to bring her around, shaking her and slapping her face: gently at first, and then more vigorously, but she did not respond. I looked again to gauge the distance to the ship, and realised another problem would be getting up its high sides. I would need help from someone aboard, or a suitable dangling rope. But as I contemplated this, I froze. A triangular fin skimmed the water near the ship. There was a sudden commotion, and the shark's head broke the surface. It shook violently from side to side amidst boiling pink foam. There were bodies and parts of bodies in the sea, and a lot of blood. Another fin appeared and then another. Swimming was definitely cancelled.

I was horrified. I had always had a thing about sharks. I shouted to the ship but still had little hearing, and had no idea if there was any reply. I thought I saw people moving, but could not be sure. I could not imagine a worse position to be in – unless I was actually in the sea of course – and looked about wildly for some miraculous way out of it. It was then I noticed a length of mast floating not far off, still attached to ropes and spars in the water. I felt for my clasp knife, thankfully still in its pouch on my belt, and decided to try and improve the makeshift raft. It felt better to have something practical to do, and I set about catching the trailing rope.

The mast stump was more than sixteen feet long, and eighteen inches in diameter. Our wooden refuge felt a lot more stable when I had lashed it alongside the decking. I utilised some of the rope, weighted with bits of wood, to snag other chunks of flotsam and jetsam and reel them in. I retrieved several broken structural beams, numerous planks and a couple of spars with strips of ripped canvas sail attached. It took me a couple of hours to construct a more satisfactory craft.

When my involuntary companion awoke, the Merchant Royal was still in sight but a long way off, too far to see what was happening on board. Lady Seymour opened her eyes and gazed vacantly at the sky for a moment, before jerking around with a start.

'What –' she began, and stared in shock at the raft and the sea. 'What happened?'

My hearing had returned, more or less, and I smiled bleakly. 'Your friends' ship blew up.'

She eyed me in shocked silence, and I thought inconsequentially that she looked beautiful even with her mouth open. Then her eyes flashed in fury.

'You idiot!' she screamed, 'you ruined everything!'

I felt the Mindworm slide into my consciousness as though enclosing me in a suit of armour. I was entirely unaffected by her tirade, and regarded her impassively.

'By not allowing them to kill us all, you mean?'

'It wasn't supposed to be like that,' she raged, 'and they were all dead anyway!'

'Because they aren't from your time,' I asked, 'is that why you don't care?'

She glared at me, and then put her head in her hands, saying nothing.

'Are you all right?' I enquired coldly.

'My head hurts,' she said shortly, and lapsed into silence.

'I can help with the Portal too,' the Mindworm reminded me.

'No!' I rejected the suggestion without thought, and then wondered why. It occurred to me that the inroads the creature had made during the battle were not absolute. It wanted more, and apparently needed my cooperation to do so. I did not want to think about what had already happened, and had no wish to get further entangled if I could help it.

'No thank you,' I repeated to the voice in my head, *'you have been useful, but some things I would like to do for myself.'*

'As you wish,' it said smugly.

We drifted on, the inert hulk of the Merchant Royal shrinking slowly towards the horizon. The only good thing about our predicament was that the shark fins had disappeared, and thin clouds high in the sky filtered the heat of the noonday sun to a bearable level.

I felt better than I might have expected in the circumstances. I was sustained by the hope that the Portal would work if things became desperate, and by the knowledge that Alex and the Portal's original owner had already experienced my future existence. Even the thought that Alex had known about the Mindworm helped. I fell to wondering if my actions had changed things – if the Mindworm had changed things – or if Alex had changed things for that matter. I remembered what she had said: *'It may just work out in a different way.'* It was confusing to think about, and impossible to make sense of. I hoped I might learn more from my unhelpful companion. I supposed things were hard for her too.

She finally stirred, and looked around as if appraising her surrounding for the first time. 'That's the Merchant Royal out there,' she said dully, 'why are we in the water?'

'We were blown off the quarter deck.'

'Oh yes. My head still hurts and my ears ... how did we end up on this floating rubbish tip?'

I felt rather affronted. 'It was a lot of work to put this raft together, not to mention getting you onto it.'

She looked a little less venomous. 'You pulled me out of the water? I suppose you must have. How long have I been out?'

'An hour or two: it was a hell of a bang.'

'No one helped us? Couldn't they see us?'

'I don't know. They might be injured or unconscious – or dead. I shouted when we were closer, but I couldn't hear anything because of the blast. I thought I saw someone moving on board later but nothing came of it.'

'Couldn't you swim?' she asked with a harder look, 'you could have left me.'

'I thought about it,' I admitted with a wry grin, 'but that was before I saw the sharks.'

She shuddered. 'Sharks? What a nightmare. Have you got a beacon? Is someone coming to get you?'

I felt inclined to be cautious. She obviously knew things I didn't, and I had no wish to demonstrate my ignorance.

'I've got something,' I said, 'how about you?'

She nodded. 'My main App is in the ship. I still have an implant, but it's no use unless they send another boat. Who are you working for – the Keepers?'

'Not exactly,' I said in a neutral voice.

'Well what are you doing here?'

'Nothing to do with you and your pirate friends – our paths crossed by chance.'

She looked unconvinced. 'Don't tell me you're just an observer. You must be on a force team at least. I saw you with that cutlass. You used it like you were born to it – and how did you set fire to their ship?'

'How do you know I did that?' I asked coolly.

'I just do. You were running around like you were Napoleon or something.'

I shrugged. 'Molotov cocktails: lots of really good brandy.'

She sighed. 'All that treasure lost.'

'Never mind the treasure,' I said coldly, 'what about the twins?'

She had the grace to look contrite. 'I'm sorry about them. I wasn't happy that old Bambridge put the children on the ship. But the Merchant Royal sank with all hands: that's just history. These things have happened all down through time. All we were going to do was take the bullion off.'

'And you're quite happy as long nothing happens to you?'

'Well, aren't you?' she asked sulkily.

We sat in silence again for a while, our makeshift raft rocking gently in the swell.

'What happened to my skirt?' she asked finally.

'It must have been blown off,' I said.

A trace of her old saucy self gleamed in her eyes. 'Are you sure?'

'I had a lot of other things to think about,' I said shortly.

She pouted and switched tactics. 'So is someone coming to look for you?'

'Not immediately,' I improvised again.

'What does that mean?' she demanded, suddenly angry. 'We're all in the same game here. If you haven't got back-up we are just as dead as the crew of that ship over there.'

'Our situation is not good,' I admitted, 'but in this game as you call it, you never know what's around the corner.'

I was not going to tell her about the device I carried, not without knowing a lot more about her. Her time incursion had obviously been instigated by a third party; and I felt it would be giving too much away to reveal that I possessed a Portal: especially when I did not know how to use it.

'It has got to be the Keepers,' she said, 'I can't see you as a rogue.'

I was angry. 'I don't like to see people slaughtered just for money.'

'No one was supposed to die,' she retorted, 'well, maybe just a few. They didn't expect the crew to put up much resistance away from the fleet.'

'Didn't expect much resistance?' I said scornfully. 'The captain and the soldiers were murdered before they had a chance to do anything.'

'I don't know what happened…I didn't like the men he sent, but I didn't think…' Her eyes filled with tears, mostly for herself, I guessed. 'But what does it matter now? We are as good as dead too.'

'You must know what kind of people you are dealing with,' I said, unmoved. 'You have only yourself to blame.'

'I have never been involved in anything like this,' she retorted fiercely. 'I actually work for a Keeper, but he's a free-timer. Most Keepers are a boring lot according to him. Is that why you are here? Were we breaking their precious rules?'

'Why do you want the Governor's treasure?' I asked. 'There are much easier ways of acquiring money.'

'Do you always answer a question with a question? – tradable goods for early time periods of course. I know the Keepers wouldn't approve, but there's more to life than glorious posterity.'

'Hmmm,' I said.

'Anyway it's a waste,' she said defiantly. 'Half a million silver Spanish pesos, five hundred bars of gold and silver; rubies, emeralds and pearls, and a lot of jewellery besides – all at the bottom of the sea.'

'Not just the Governor's treasure then,' I said, staggered at the quantity of riches she described.

'No, there was the Crown's share too, and a lot of other people shipping their assets back to England.'

'So you were on the ship so they could trace your beacon?' I guessed.

'Yes, and to make sure the right men got on board, as well as manage any problems.' She laughed sourly. 'I made a good job of that, didn't I?'

'You took a risk with that storm.'

'Not really, the Bonaventure reported sighting the Merchant Royal after the storm.' She scowled. 'But they didn't tell me how bad it would be, even with my shots. And it was all for nothing.'

'There is also the little matter of trying to get rid of me before the storm started,' I said lightly.

She looked uncomfortable. 'That was Tom's idea. I tried to talk him out of it, but he insisted. He didn't want to take any chances with so much at stake.'

'Why pick on me?'

'You were suspicious, you didn't fit in.'

'So why try to talk him out of it?'

She eyed me with some hostility. 'I'm not actually fond of people dying you know, and besides I – liked you.'

I regarded her ironically. I noticed a change since my rampage with the Mindworm. I was no longer afraid of the magnetic attraction that exuded from her. I felt more confident and unfazed by her sexuality. But I seemed to have lost something too. I was unsure exactly what. But it put me in a stronger position where she was concerned, and I figured it an advantage for the present.

'What's your real name?' I asked suddenly.

Her eyes narrowed. 'You ask a lot of questions,' she said, 'I think I should shut up until I know a bit more about you.'

'Fair enough,' I agreed.

'So am I?'

'Are you what?' I asked.

'Going to learn more about you?'

'Not unless I know more about you too.'

Resentment flashed in her eyes, but she smiled coolly and said no more. The silence was broken only by the lapping waves. After a while she began to examine her clothing, and stripped off the ragged remains of her petticoat and bodice, leaving only her slip covering her. The ruffled lace on display at her sleeves and upper chest proved to belong to this garment, but otherwise its fine silk did not do a great job of concealing her body. I was unsure if she was just making herself comfortable or trying to manipulate me, but I looked away anyway.

It seemed absurd for two people on a tiny raft adrift in the ocean to ignore each other, but I shrugged and let my attention drift to the Portal. I was fed up with the endless struggle to access it, and probed idly without really thinking. A single green icon blinked unexpectedly in the air before me, and my mind ramped up immediately. I tried to grasp the connection, and the contact slipped away. But for once I felt reassured rather than frustrated. *'I am operational,'* I felt it was telling me, *'I will act if appropriate.'* It appeared a little too independently minded for my taste, but at least it seemed to be monitoring the situation. *'What about Billy and the twins?'* I appealed intently, *'I need to help them.'* But there was only silence.

Chapter 11

THE CLOUDS BECAME lower and thicker, and the waves more restless again. It was warm though, and our clothes were drying out. It occurred to me that we had nothing to eat or drink, or any shelter from the sun – and almost immediately afterwards that we had no privacy to take care of natural bodily functions either. I checked out the fragments of sail attached to the spars and ropes on our floating woodpile. There were two sizeable pieces of canvas, a roughly oblong section about seven feet by five, and a slightly smaller triangular piece. I thought about it for a while. With a little judicious cobbling together of rope and planks, I decided I could construct a crude awning. It would give shade from the sun, and catch rainwater to drink. It would also be possible to adjust it to form a partition of sorts. Lady Seymour reanimated herself to ask what I was doing, and did not look impressed when I explained.

'How long are we going to be on this thing?' she demanded irritably. 'Do you really not know when you will get help?'

'I'm afraid not,' I said wearily, 'so we might as well make the best of it.'

I managed to get the framework up after an hour or so, and started sewing the two pieces of canvas together. I bored into them with my knife, and pulled unravelled strands of rope through the holes.

'Let me do it,' said Lady Seymour suddenly, after watching me work in silence.

I looked at her in surprise. 'You want to sew?'

She smiled a little wanly. 'I have lived other lives than this one.'

'I suppose you have,' I said evenly, 'but this one seems to suit you well.'

Her eyes flashed, 'why should it not?'

'Actually,' I said more playfully, 'it does suit you well. It's your friends I object to.'

She looked annoyed. 'As I told you, nothing like this has happened before.'

'What normally happens?' I asked caustically, 'you charm men into parting with their gold?'

'Something like that,' she admitted candidly, 'who are you to judge me?'

'I have no particular reason to judge you,' I said. 'I just don't know how far to trust you.'

'Then we understand each other,' she said. 'Now give me the knife – or don't you trust me with that either?'

I smiled involuntarily, and she reciprocated after a fleeting, uncertain pause. Someone quite unexpected seemed to live behind the impish flirtatiousness she normally broadcasted, but which was more real I could not be sure. She sewed the strips of canvas together with surprising deftness, considering the crudity of our tool kit, and helped me fix up the awning. It was completed just in time to catch a little rainwater from a brief downpour in the late afternoon. We were very thirsty by then, and pulled down one side of our canvas sunshade to eagerly drain the welcome liquid into our upturned mouths.

She started to laugh as we drank our fill, and I found myself chuckling too. We didn't speak, but I supposed she found Lady Seymour guzzling rainwater from an old sail in her underwear amusing. The shower washed much of the salt away from our ocean dunking too, which was agreeably refreshing. We sat in silence as the clouds drifted away, and watched the sun begin to set in a glorious crimson sky. There were downsides to our liberation from thirst though. My body's demand for food swiftly replaced that for water, and we were soaking wet once more.

My unpredictable raft-mate's slip took a while to dry again, and remained rather transparent for quite some time. I did not need the Mindworm to kindle an awareness of her physical proximity, but was determined not to show her any weakness. I did not want to give her any advantage in our dealings together. I remained wary, and angry about her part in the murderous pirate attack. The gravity of our predicament actually robbed it of much superficial titillation. I also sensed a deeper connection between us at times, an affinity on more than a sensual level. I mistrusted this as well, wondering if it might be another weapon in her battery of charms. Yet I sometimes felt she was uncertain about it herself.

The incongruity of the situation was laughable. Twenty four hours earlier the idea of being alone with a scantily clad Lady Seymour would have been unimaginable. But for the present I found the reality unexpectedly tranquil. The silence between us had become almost companionable. We sat peacefully together on our unsteady maritime refuge, our clothes drying slowly in the warm evening breeze. Hunger was gnawing at me, and I decided to try and break the deadlock between us: to take my mind off food if nothing else.

'What if I tell you what I can about myself, and you do the same,' I suggested, 'then we can talk about something at least.'

She acquiesced with an almost imperceptible tilt of her head, committing to nothing, but there was a guarded curiosity in her gaze. So I launched into a meandering version of my uneventful tale, deliberately vague about dates and places. But somehow I included details I had not intended: my parents' endless arguments, my father leaving, my mother's illness and death. I apologised for straying into such personal stuff, but she waved it away, seemingly content to listen. I realised I had never articulated these things so openly before, and surprised myself with long forgotten thoughts and feelings. They were the memories of a far more hopeful being that had started out in life long ago.

'So what about love,' she teased lightly, as I talked about university and work; subtly adjusting the details, and my profession from architect to surveyor. 'What of the romance in your life?'

'Not much to speak of,' I admitted. 'My friends told me I took the wrong things too seriously, and the right things not seriously enough, whatever that means.'

'You were afraid, and did not think to put women at their ease,' she said, wrinkling her brow thoughtfully.

'I suppose,' I said. 'One girl told me I worried too much about my mother. I ended up with a partner I did not feel much for at all.'

She laughed bitterly. 'It seems there are some similarities between us,' she said. 'So how did you become involved with a Portal Master?'

I said a little about it, hoping it would encourage her to speak.

'It happened by chance,' I said, 'he materialised in front of me. He was injured, and I helped him. He asked me to do more, that's all.'

She nodded, but seemed absorbed in her own thoughts. For a while I doubted she would say anything at all. But finally she began to speak, haltingly at first. She had been born in Manchester in the early twentieth

century, an only child. Her father had been a failed businessman who
shot himself during the economic depression between the wars. She and
her mother had been taken in by his brother in London, her mother to
become an unpaid drudge and herself the sexual plaything of her uncle.
She spoke in a flat, matter-of-fact voice devoid of feeling, quite unlike
the teasing, sensual tones I was used to. She was partly rescued by a great
aunt who sent her to a boarding school. There she spent four years
under a strict Christian regime, only abused during the holidays, until
she was expelled at sixteen following a liaison with the music teacher.

Her great aunt disowned her, and after a couple of months contriving
to avoid her uncle's attentions, he announced he had found her a
position in service at the house of a business acquaintance. She had been
appalled at the idea of becoming a domestic servant, and mistrustful of
her uncle's friends. Appeals to her mother were useless. Her spirit had
been broken by the ruin and death of her husband. She would not listen
to sexual allegations against her brother in law, and insisted that only his
kindness was keeping them off the streets. The domestic position was
everything she feared and worse. She was expected not only to submit to
the sexual demands of her new employer, but to appear during dinner
parties for the perusal of male guests: and to be delivered discretely to
anonymous addresses for their gratification afterwards.

She had been desperate to escape but had nowhere to go, no money,
connections or experience to make her way in the world. Then one
evening a man appeared at the dinner table who seemed different from
the others, a man who seemed larger than life in every way. She was not
surprised to be delivered to his exclusive Mayfair flat the next evening,
but she was surprised by what happened next. He made no sexual
advances. He talked to her instead, asking her about her life. He already
had a good idea of her circumstances, and coaxed from her hopes, fears
and dreams that she had never told anyone. Then he made her an offer.
He could take her away from her present life, give her everything money
could buy and show her things she had never dreamed of. She could not
refuse of course, but he went further.

'He told me he was no saint,' she said: 'that my looks would be useful
to him. He offered me an important role in his affairs. But he also told
me neither he nor anyone else would touch me without my permission.
That's what really did it for me. I told him that if what he said was true I
would do anything for him, and I have.'

'So he was a – Portal Master?' I asked.

'Yes. I realised later that he played me masterfully. But I have no complaints. He gave me everything he promised and more.'

'So he wanted what – your beauty and your brain?'

She smiled sourly. 'I didn't know I was pretty. I always wanted to look ugly, so my uncle and his friends wouldn't want me. But he showed me that beauty could give me power, and I enjoy having power over men.'

'I can understand that,' I said, 'you have been treated badly by them. But are you happy? You asked me about romance, what about your own life?'

'I don't know about love,' she replied idly, 'men have such stupid weaknesses. Those who say they love me just make fools of themselves.'

'I suppose they love the way you look all right.' I smiled grimly. *But not who you really are,*' I thought.

It was strange. Not long before I would have felt awkward and tongue-tied in her presence. The Mindworm provided a certain confidence, but there was more to it than that. Once I was past the sexual allure, I sensed a rapport that I had not really experienced before. It was instinctual and intuitive: a kind of sharing and understanding of things beyond words. She appeared conscious of it on some level, but uncertain of its nature. It was as if she did not really know herself, and I thought I could perceive the lost child within her. It protected me from her earthy siren's song in some ways. I was not immune to it, but I was aware of the vulnerable girl she had once been.

'I hardly know who I am,' she said self-mockingly, oddly mirroring my thoughts. 'Now I have said more to you than I have said to anyone except Saul – my Portal master.'

'So he values you – uses you to connect with people and influence them?'

'Yes, he values me as long as he gets what he wants. He rewards me well. I have tasted the best things in life, and taken great pleasure in it. I have enjoyed amusement, intrigue and power, and I have seen wonderful things.'

'But there was a price: like the fate of the Merchant Royale?'

Her eyes clouded. 'Yes there was a price, but never one like that. It always felt like a game – like acting in a Holovid or a play. It was about subterfuge, skill and manipulation, not murder. People might die but that was their destiny. We did not cause it, certainly not on such a scale.'

'I could understand if it was to prevent greater disaster, or to create positive change,' I said, 'but what can justify this kind of meddling with people's lives?'

'Now you talk like a Keeper,' she said scornfully, 'who knows what they meddle with? Saul is a free-timer: he has faith in the elasticity of space-time. But he is a Keeper too of sorts, and they are a mysterious lot.'

The sun was disappearing on the horizon. Darkness was gathering over the sea, and stars were appearing between the wisps of cloud overhead.

'I am hungry,' she sighed, 'how long can this nightmare last?'

'I am trying not to think about it,' I said. 'Thank you for talking. You are different to the woman I imagined.'

She laughed softly; a genuine, tinkling mirth. 'And you are different to the man I imagined. I thought you such an innocent, even if a suspicious one. But you can be strong and bold, and yet – kind.'

Oddly, her words reminded me of Jacqueline. She had said something similar: 'kind and strange' and I felt a lump in my throat as I remembered she had laughed about it too. I thought how odd my life had become: here I was, out under the stars with another extraordinary woman, albeit a very different one.

We lay on our backs looking up at the night sky, with the sea lapping all around us.

'Anna,' she said sleepily after a while, 'you can call me Anna.'

'Is that your real name?' I asked.

I thought she wasn't going to answer at first. 'Yes,' she said finally, 'it's short for Annabelle.'

Sometime during the night she moved over and nestled up against me. I felt the Mindworm's suggestion: urging me to take advantage of the physical intimacy. It insisted she would respond favourably, and I thought it was probably right. But I resisted its insidious agenda. I was still unsure about her, and thought it prudent to keep my distance. It was no easy task. I recalled too well the raging intensity the creature had ignited in me on the ship, and tried not to imagine how that might translate into the pleasure of lovemaking. Instead I grinned ironically at the lovely lady's embrace. If the truth be told, despite my suspicions, I had been touched by the story I had heard. I thought of the little girl wanted only for her body, and felt a simple human need for comfort in her touch. Her situation was desperate, and there was nothing else for her to cling to.

Next morning she was more aloof again, as if regretting the confidences of the evening before. The bathroom arrangements did not help: much clumsy rearranging of the awning into a crude privacy screen achieving largely theoretical results. We took turns to face out to sea, and sang loudly with our hands over our ears to counteract embarrassing noises. But it helped to break the ice. After an hour or so she was better company once more. She complained of hunger though, and I was ravenous myself.

'We could try to catch some fish,' I suggested. Our makeshift raft seemed to have attracted a few aquatic hangers-on, which I spotted from time to time.

'We have nothing to fish with,' she said sceptically.

'We'll see,' I said, determinedly positive.

I remembered watching a low-tech survivalist TV show about fishing and felt there was nothing to lose by trying out some of their ideas. I set about fashioning a hook from three splinters of wood, meticulously honing a small and a medium sharp, barbed spike and binding them tightly to a larger shaft with thin strands of rope. The whole thing was about three inches long, and formed roughly the shape of a penknife with two partly opened opposing blades: the larger blade open further than the smaller. It created an upward-angled hook with a smaller, inner spike facing downwards to help prevent a fish pulling itself off. The trick was to chamfer the bottom of the shaft so the main hook could be bound firmly to it at the correct angle. I untangled a slender rope strand five or six feet long, salvaged a brass eyelet from a scrap of sail as a weight, and tied the hook at one end and a wooden grip at the other. The only problem was bait.

'We'll just have to try a bit of cloth,' I said. 'If we can just get one fish, we can cut bits off it to catch more.'

Anna looked distinctly unimpressed.

'I can't believe you will catch anything with that thing,' she said, 'it looks like something out of those survivalist Holovid shows.'

'Well, we won't be any worse off,' I said, trying not to look like an amateur Holovid survivalist. 'At least it will be something to do.'

I sat hopefully for a while, trying to see through the surface glare on the sluggishly heaving sea. I thought I could see one or two shadowy shapes moving near the dim fluttering speck of the cloth bait. It was a couple of feet down, so it was hard to tell. Then, with a sudden thrill, I felt a tug on the line and pulled back firmly.

'I got a bite!' I yelled excitedly, but the line instantly slackened.

'You've caught a fish?' exclaimed Anna incredulously.

'Well, no,' I admitted crossly, 'but something bit on it.'

I pulled the line in. The cloth fragment had disappeared, but the hook seemed intact. I re-baited it and tried again. I waited twenty minutes or so before another determined tug startled me, and I dragged the line backwards. This time there was considerable resistance, and I pulled feverishly against it, cursing when the line went slack once more. I retrieved the hook to find the main barb had come off, and stared at it in annoyance. Eventually I shrugged and started carving another one, this time putting a notch in the chamfered bottom surface and a triangular protrusion on the 'hook' to key it better into place.

Anna sat watching me. 'You don't give up do you?' she asked with a jaded smile.

'No,' I said shortly. 'Why don't you fish this time. I'm going to try and make a spear.'

She grimaced, but cast the line back in when it was ready. I carved a couple of larger wooden spikes about six inches long, following the grain to make the point as sharp as possible, and formed a barb near the end of each one. I intended to bind them like fork tines to the end of a shaft, and began to hack one laboriously from a length of wood.

'Oh I've got one!' squealed Anna, and I saw her line was stretched taut, with a dark, shadowy shape twisting back and forth beneath the water.

'Don't let it get under the raft,' I yelled, 'keep pulling it up!'

'I am pulling it up!' she shouted indignantly, and hauled the fish out of the water with an inelegant flourish. It landed flapping at her feet, some kind of macho Mackerel about two or three pounds in weight, and I stabbed wildly at it with my knife. She giggled and shrieked, seriously rocking our ungainly craft in her efforts to get out of harm's way. Then I had the twitching fish pinned to the raft, and we stared gleefully at each other like two children with an unexpected Christmas present.

'Congratulations,' I said, enjoying her simple delight.

She frowned. 'How do we eat it?'

'Raw I guess,' I said. 'It might be tastier if we baked it in the sun – even better if we could salt it – but it would take too long to evaporate the sea water, and just make us thirstier.'

'Ugh!' she said. 'But I'm hungry enough to eat anything.'

I gutted and filleted the fish, a cherished skill from long gone fishing days. We munched energetically on chunks of raw fish, ravenously hungry and anxious to swallow the unfamiliar flesh as quickly as possible. It felt wonderful to get something into my stomach, despite a lingering, queasy aftertaste. It felt nowhere near enough, but thirst quickly became a greater priority. Soon, when I wasn't fishing or surveying the horizon for ships, I was watching the few wisps of clouds crossing the sky, and praying for them to thicken.

It got worse as the day became hotter, and we abandoned our fishing activities to sit listlessly under the canvas shade. Thirst became increasingly unbearable. My head ached, and my whole body seemed sucked dry of moisture. Time dragged by. We said little. Anna became increasingly irritable, and I snapped back at her when she started blaming me for our predicament all over again. By mid-afternoon my tongue felt thick and dry, and my concentration was faltering. My mind began to wander amidst growing bouts of dizziness. The cloud cover slowly increased, making it at least a little cooler, and I fixated on the sky: willing the drifting banks of moist air to grow fuller and darker.

I had fallen asleep or passed out, I wasn't sure which, when I began dreaming of beautiful, precious moisture. I tried to lick my parched lips, and awoke to find the air rich with the promise of rain. Great, dense clouds were rolling everywhere.

'Anna,' I croaked, reaching over and shaking her. She stirred and looked blankly at me, her eyes full of tortured confusion. Then she gazed rapturously above her. We staggered together, gripping the canopy as the first drops fell, and in moments a vast deluge was beating down on us. She drank first, gulping down streams of water channelled from the canvas, and I quickly followed. Water had never tasted so good, and we laughed hysterically as the life-giving draughts filled our parched bodies. In between drinking our fill we let the water pour over our heads, finally sinking down in sated relief beneath the bounteous downpour.

It rained for an hour, and we smiled happily at each other as the drops gradually ceased. Then my eyes fell to her see-through slip, and I busied myself with preparations for further fishing operations. It was a strange situation: marooned together and racked by hunger and thirst, with suspicion, mistrust, camaraderie and a powerful magnetic attraction waxing and waning between us. She caught my look and conflicting emotions flickered in her eyes.

I sensed it strengthened me not to cross that barrier: that it confused her practiced guile, and touched something more genuine and less assured in her. But it was not easy, and the Mindworm's predilections did not help. The extreme situation helped to concentrate my attention though. In fact much of the time I just thought about food and water. I thought about Billy and the twins a lot too, and tried to glean what information I could of Anna's time travelling mentor, and the life she led under his direction.

We sat and fished, and talked from time to time, each guarded about our current life, but speaking of memories and feelings from earlier days. I caught another fish after dark, using a piece of our earlier catch as bait. I had forgotten about the line in fact, absorbed in conversation, and almost lost hold of it when the fish struck. It was different from the first: flatter and bulkier with silvery scales. I cut it up in the moonlight, and we lay down to sleep with relatively full stomachs. After a while she moved over to me.

'Don't you want me?' she asked; a slight catch in her voice.

'Not unless it means something,' I said, reining in alternative suggestions from the Mindworm.

She was silent for a moment.

'I'm scared,' she said finally.

'Me too, but something can still work out.'

She was suddenly crying uncontrollably, her whole body shuddering against me.

'What's wrong?' I asked, stroking her hair.

'I don't know – everything,' she sobbed.

We slept, closer than we had ever been, yet next morning she was distant again. The day passed slowly. We said little, dozing fitfully under the awning. I got up every hour or so to scan the horizon. Thirst's incremental torture began again, and I brooded glumly on the fact that we had no means of storing water. At one point Anna sat up and started to scream obscenities: cursing me, Saul, the raft, the weather and the slow, hopeless journey across the endless ocean. It ended in tears and I comforted her again, feeling a little guilty that I could draw some reassurance from the presence of the Portal. I caught another fish, and speared one too, dropping tiny pieces of previous catches into the water and lunging down at the blurred shapes which rose to investigate. A couple of light showers finally relieved our thirst, although it was barely enough to satisfy our need. We were trapped in a surreal routine: days and nights rocking on the crude floating platform, the sound of lapping water, the hunger and thirst, the fish, the sun and the rain. That evening she seemed calm again, almost serene, and we lay gazing at the stars in the night sky.

'They're so beautiful;' she said dreamily, 'time makes no difference to them. Wherever you are they are always there.'

'I guess it depends what kind of time you are talking about,' I said, remembering watching the same stars with Jacqueline and the Lieutenant's men. It had been one of the occasions when mysterious depths of consciousness had touched me, and the glittering patterns of light had seemed like the diamond-pure notes of an unimaginable symphony, playing out over an infinity of time.

'Have you been to Atlantis?' she asked in the same absent manner.

I froze inwardly. I had no idea if she was serious, trying to catch me out, or making some kind of a joke.

'No,' I said casually, aiming for neutral ground.

'Neither have I,' she said. 'Saul said he'd take me one day, but I'm not really interested. It sounds so pretentious, all those stuffy Keepers making speeches. I don't like the idea of being on that island either, even if it won't blow up for a thousand years.'

'I suppose I can agree with you there,' I murmured, trying to fit these nuggets of information together in my mind.

'I wish I knew who you are,' she sighed; and after a long pause, 'I wish I had met you a long time ago.'

A surge of conflicting feelings arose in me: tenderness, misgivings, compassion, desire and doubt. Then I saw she had fallen asleep, and smiled at the bitter-sweet emotions she evoked in me. They seemed encapsulated in the child-like peace of her features in the moonlight. She did not seek physical reassurance that night. She slept a couple of feet away, and this time the irony lay in my own trickle of disappointment. But I felt good about it too. She no longer seemed as frightened as she had been. Next morning she was different somehow, more relaxed and reconciled to our lot. She helped steadfastly with the fishing, and was philosophical when we lost both a fish and the hook. We chatted inconsequentially while I made another, and she stabbed determinedly with the spear at the darting shapes rising to nibble at our bait. She even made fun of the monotonous diet of raw fish when we caught one, and was stoic about our ever-present nemesis of thirst.

I was scanning the sky in the afternoon, and so involved in trying to estimate the likelihood of rain that I ignored the dark smudge on the horizon at first. Then I did a double take, and stared at the apparition, desperate to confirm its existence.

'Hey!' I said shakily, 'I think that's an island!'

Anna scrambled to her feet, and we stood bracing each other on our rocking craft. 'Oh yes!' she cried, 'are we moving towards it?'

'We must be,' I said, 'in the general direction at least. I'm going to have a good try at getting there whatever happens.'

I set to work straight away, shaping two planks into paddles, and deciding which parts of our floating home could be cut away to make it more manoeuvrable. A couple of hours later the island had grown considerably. It was bigger than it had first appeared, with a group of hills at its centre, and we were nearer to it than our low vantage point had suggested. Unfortunately it was also moving slowly across our line of sight. The current was carrying us at an angle that might miss it entirely. Finally I could make out foliage on the shore, and decided we were close enough.

'Here we go,' I said, looking earnestly at Anna. 'Are you ready?'

She nodded tersely, gripping her paddle.

I cut away the big length of mast and the smaller section of decking, retaining the main platform and the spars and planking I had lashed around its borders.

'Not too fast,' I said, 'we don't want to get tired too soon.'

We began to paddle towards the tantalising green haven as it rose and fell from view behind the ocean swell. Nothing seemed to happen at first. There was little sense of progress. We must have been paddling for fifteen minutes before I was sure the island was looming closer, and moving less swiftly towards the left of our view.

'I've got to stop; I've got to stop,' gasped Anna, sinking onto to the deck.

'Don't worry,' I panted, 'have a break and start again when you can.'

I clambered from one side of the raft to the other, paddling half a dozen deep, hard strokes at a time. Anna joined in again, and we struggled to drive our ungainly craft forward. The island drew closer. Anna stopped a second time but resumed paddling only minutes later. I kept going somehow, thankful for the weeks of hard labour which had strengthened my body. It went on and on. The island grew larger and larger, filling my vision. I heard water breaking on submerged reefs, and the raft rebounded from something solid with a jolt. We were pushed back and forth, waves pouring over us as we paddled frantically. Then we were aground, wood grating on coral. A wave lifted us, and we were suddenly floating peacefully inside the reef. We were utterly spent and crouched breathlessly, turning slowly to each other with disbelieving grins. We had done it.

We paddled on as our strength returned, heading through brilliant aquamarine water towards a magnificent beach of pristine white sand. A riot of greenery crowded against its borders fifty yards from the shore. I could already glimpse heavily laden coconut palms, and big, melon-like fruit bunched close to the trunk of smaller trees. We pulled the raft a little way out of the water, and my feet dug deep into the hot sand as we ran to investigate the abundance of sweet sustenance.

The melon-like bunches of fruit were low and easy to reach. I pulled one down and attacked it with my knife. It was about the size of a football, with a rubbery, green skin. I split it to reveal an inner core of dark sticky seeds immersed in thick pink flesh. They had a not unpleasant bitter-sweet taste, and seemed like heaven to us. We pulled three of them apart, wolfing down the chunks of fruit greedily. Then, sticky with juice, we ran back down to the sea. We splashed our hands and our faces, and we splashed each other, the water sparkling brilliantly in the evening sunlight. Afterwards we fell laughing together on the sand, drunk with the miracle of our deliverance. But laughter died as I drank in her beauty, illuminated as she was by sheer joy and exuberance. She stared back at me, her eyes still and inviting.

The need of the moment carried all before it. I felt the Mindworm riding the explosion of desire, but its satisfaction was irrelevant. The torrent of passion was mine. We coupled hungrily on the sand, lost in an all-consuming intensity I had never known. Ecstatic sensuality possessed me, and we sought to devour each other in an aching frenzy of need. The release was shattering, and we clung together afterwards, each uncertain where it had taken us. I had crossed the line, had the greatest sex of my life with the enemy, and she seemed equally confounded.

'I have never felt that with anyone,' she gasped, sounding close to tears.

'I somehow doubt that,' I said lightly; trying to distance myself from the event.

'Oh stop it!' she said fiercely. 'You said it should mean something. I know about sex: sex is what I do. I never had – feelings before.'

'Not even for rich important guys?'

She began crying for real then, and I felt a wave of affection for her. Either she was a great actress, or a broken girl reaching out from somewhere dark and lonely. I kissed her, and felt something poignant and tender, but how profound or enduring I wasn't sure. I had never felt such an intense attraction to a stranger before, and I often wondered about it in later days. There was undoubtedly something special about her. It was as if some elemental aspect of my being was mirrored in hers, some essential key to completeness. Yet the reflection was a deceptive one, a tantalising curtain of veils illuminated by an elusive inner core. In some other universe, in some other life, we might have been soul mates. In this one I was naive and confused and she was lost, and a danger to both me and to herself.

Chapter 12

THE NEXT FEW days were like living in paradise. The good fortune of our deliverance, the perfect weather and exotic surroundings all fuelled a reckless abandonment to sexual and emotional need. Anna's body was infinitely desirable, and her emotional high intoxicating. Winning the interest of a beautiful woman was a heady experience, and I revelled under her caresses. But I also felt a surprising self-assurance in handling her, while she clung to me with child-like desperation. The past few weeks had changed me. I felt strong and capable: my body muscled and suntanned, and I seemed to have ripened into a new maturity. The Mindworm was augmenting my ego of course, and whispering to me about subtle techniques of mastery over the opposite sex. But my new confidence felt surprisingly natural: the awakening of a more vital sense of self. Much had closed down in the course of a mundane and dysfunctional life. Now I felt startlingly alive: confident, vigorous, and proficient.

Everything I turned my hand too seemed to work. We drank coconut water and found wild pineapples. I started a fire with a bow-drill, caught crabs to cook, and built a shelter with saplings and palm leaves. My long forgotten interest in survival techniques had a chance to shine, and I derived great satisfaction from putting it into practice.

Anna did not share such enthusiasms, although she was glad enough to reap their benefits. As time went by she started to ask again about my supposed time travelling mentor, and the purpose of my presence in Port Royal. Our love-making lost some of its simple intensity, and she began to become more inventive. She certainly knew a great many things that had never occurred to Mellissa. The Mindworm delighted in the sensual bonanza, but its coarse machinations shone an unforgiving light upon her failings too.

It was a strange business sharing the creature's perceptions. It was no longer running riot with my emotions as it had during the pirate attack, yet it still shared my life in a way it had not before. It seemed entwined with my natural feelings, influencing and colouring my moods, but they remained recognisably my own. Or at least, I thought they did. I sometimes sensed an unsavoury taint to my awareness: as if clean linen had been handled by greasy fingers. I knew the Mindworm was enhancing physical and emotional sensations, but Anna's attraction seemed self-evident and all-consuming, and my satiation natural and instinctive.

For my part I shared some of the Mindworm's cynical understanding of humanity. It detected a subtle sense of power and dominance creeping into Anna's behaviour. I didn't think it was purposeful, at least not in any calculating way. It was rather an unconscious drift back into her habitual inclinations: the practiced courtesan re-emerging from the briefly born-again Annabelle.

She was supremely unaware of the compromises she lived with, even after the bloody debacle on the Merchant Royal. We spoke of it once or twice, and she continued to explain it away as unintended and mismanaged. She regarded herself entitled to a life of pleasure and luxury amid the pain and misfortune of others, and even to capitalise on it at their expense. I could understand it to a degree, given her unhappy background. But I winced inwardly at times to see how unaware she was of her own self-absorption. I couldn't help comparing her to Alex, and even to Jacqueline.

I remembered Alex's fiery sense of mission and destiny: *'there is a lot more at stake here than just you, more than you can imagine,'* she had said, and I shivered involuntarily as her words came back to me. I felt guilty about Billy and the twins too. I had all but forgotten them for the first couple of days on the island, but I became increasingly haunted by images of the ship going down.

There was nothing I could do of course, apart from fruitless appeals to the Portal. But these things helped to prevent me succumbing completely to Anna's spell. Her sexual magnetism was irresistible, and there seemed now no reason to resist her. But deeper ardour faltered under uncaring remarks and casual mercenary ambition, despite her fundamental emotions appearing genuine. She was troubled by our liaison too, because I did not command power or riches, and was at cross purposes with her benefactors. It confused her, but the extreme nature of our encounter on the high seas had impacted at a primal level, and its effects remained profound.

We found a stream close by, and could drink and wash to our hearts content. I had caught a turtle, and we had meat to eat and the shell as a cooking pot. Life seemed idyllic, but we both knew it wouldn't last. The end came suddenly after eight days on the island. We were lazing in the shade one afternoon when Anna suddenly sat up.

'My implant is buzzing,' she cried, 'someone is coming!'

I sat up, struggling to get my thoughts together, 'how long?'

'Soon,' she said, 'they won't have pinged until they're near.' She looked at me curiously, 'don't you track on passive?'

'Sorry,' I said, trying to conceal my ignorance, 'just trying to decide what to do.'

We had talked a little about the future. I had suggested she leave her present employment and find other interests than wealth and mercenary intrigue. It was not something she could easily contemplate. She had grown dependent on her time travelling mentor. He was at the hub of everything she knew. She had a mansion of her own, beautiful possessions, servants, and any lover she desired. She tried to persuade me to share in her life instead. The impasse was insurmountable, and constantly deferred. Now the time was up.

I looked at her intently, 'I'm going to have to disappear.'

She took me into her arms. 'Come with me – I'll explain everything to Saul. We could have such fun together.'

I shook my head.

'Please,' she said, tears glistening in her eyes.

'I don't think you will be able to explain everything,' I said, unable to hide the sadness in my voice.

'Am I going to see you again?' she asked.

'I wouldn't be surprised,' I said with a rueful smile.

We leaned into a farewell kiss more poignant than any we had shared so far.

'What are you going to tell them?' I asked finally.

She smiled and shrugged, tears trickling down her face. 'I'll tell them the truth. I was carried off by Tarzan and he disappeared into his mysterious jungle home.'

I laughed. 'Well if I was Tarzan, you were a great Jane.'

'You saved my life,' she said. 'I never thanked you.'

I grinned. 'Yes you did.' I took her hand to kiss it. 'Goodbye my lady. I'll keep an eye out – make sure you get off all right.'

'What about you?' she asked.

'I expect I'll be gone soon too.'

I scooped up my possessions, and headed up into the trees and higher ground. I turned to give her a final wave. She waved back hesitantly, and I turned back towards the hillside feeling a real pang in my heart. She was not an easy woman to walk away from.

I made my way upwards through the dense vegetation, following a circuitous route through an entanglement of palms, squat green fruit trees, broad leafed bushes and thorny plants. After several hundred yards I had climbed a hundred feet higher, and found a rocky outcrop with a good view of the shore below. I saw the ship immediately, half a mile out to sea. It was one of the smaller and faster vessels the privateers habitually used, curving smoothly in towards the reefs off shore. It dropped anchor and quickly lowered a boat. Half a dozen men navigated a passage through the rocky barrier we had missed on our landfall, and disappeared from sight behind the vegetation lining the beach. Minutes passed, and I began to wonder if I should put a greater distance between us. Then the boat reappeared, carrying a full complement of men as well as Anna. She sat aloofly in the stern, a coat over her light coloured slip. She was looking back at the island, and I could imagine she felt my eyes on her.

It was surreal to watch the wind take the ship's sails, and silently spirit the vessel away. I sat and stared as it faded into nothingness on the horizon, and continued to do so long after it had disappeared. Dusk was approaching, and I was unsure what to do. I was uneasy about snakes, and thought of returning to the beach to sleep. But I feared Anna's accomplices might return to catch me unawares. I wanted to trust her, but there was still much I did not know about her life, and there was the chance her friends might have their own ideas. Time passed, and I didn't move. The stars began to come out and it saddened me to remember how Anna and I had watched the night sky on the raft together. I felt very alone. I vacillated about what to do, and ended up dozing fitfully on the rocks through the night, waking often from disjointed dreams about our time together.

I went back to the beach early next morning, and wandered up and down kicking at the sand dispiritedly. The signs of our occupation had taken on a new poignancy, and fed a dull, aching pain in my heart. I swam in the sea and caught up on some sleep, then sat brooding at the waves with no particular aim in mind. I dozed again in the afternoon, and tried to get some exercise by running along the sand. But my heart wasn't in it, and I ended up walking a long way along the shore and back again. I spent a while trying to connect with the Portal and gave up in disgust. I picked at a melon, but did not feel particularly hungry. I had lost Anna, and I had lost Billy and the twins as well. I had left Jacqueline behind, and I didn't know when I might see Alex or Charles again. Life seemed to have ground to a halt, and I began to feel completely at a loss. I seemed to lack the will or inspiration to do anything.

When the stars came out again I sat and watched them with a heavy heart. I was surprised how much I missed the conflicted Annabelle, and smiled ironically. It had been an unlikely relationship from the start. I had known that. I had thought I had her measure: that the intensity we shared was an end in itself, easily forgiven and forgotten. But I began to realise that she had got to me after all, sunk a bitter-sweet barb which left sadness and regret. Now an emptiness beckoned which seemed to suck the joy from everything.

'*You should have gone with her,*' said the Mindworm.

'*Hmmm,*' I thought noncommittally, wondering if this was the price I was paying for compromising with its agenda. I knew I had empowered the Mindworm by allowing it to empower me. It had fired up my ability to take on the pirates – and to take on Anna in some ways. But there were things I had done during the fighting that I didn't want to think about, and I was beginning to think my liaison with Anna had done me no favours at all. I feared my entanglement with the Mindworm might have repercussions beyond the mere blunting of human decency, but I felt too emotionally wrung out to care. I wanted solace from loneliness and my impossible quest. If one of those demijohns of brandy had been handy, I might easily have drowned my troubles, and awoken to more of the same.

I gazed up at the night sky again, and thought about the way it had looked that night with Jacqueline and the lieutenant's men: how those distant lights had awakened from cold, glittering splendour to pulsate with life and secret purpose. They seemed to soothe me now, and offer a more detached perspective on my troubles. I felt a slow shift of perception, and an anticipatory shiver in my spine. Something was happening. Minute whorls and tingles of excitement began to erupt and dissipate themselves all over my body. A static charge enveloped me. My hair stood on end, and tiny spikes of sensation seemed to be tugged upwards all over my scalp, like iron filings towards a powerful magnet. Part of me wondered if lightning was about to strike. But the sky was clear, and a sudden inertia held me in place.

Energy was vibrating everywhere, and I thought of the Portal. But the force which immobilised me resonated with something deeper, more fundamental. A weird oscillation developed: a bizarre juxtaposition between a single pinpoint of perception and a vast ocean of light. A sense of presence grew: overpoweringly intense. For an inexplicable moment I seemed to look down from that immense, starry splendour into the inner workings of my microscopic existence. Then I was stunned by a dazzling, laser-bright interrogation of multiple aspects of my being. It was over in an instant, but the sheer power of the event left me shattered.

I floated numbly, completely disoriented, before a flood of sickening memories regurgitated themselves with a stark, physical immediacy. The appalling reality of the fight on the ship came back to me: an animal stink of murderous desperation, and the hot, choking stench of blood and entrails. I saw human features obscenely contorted in horror and agony: living bodies hacked brutally apart under my cutlass. I had fought for the lives of my shipmates, but I was appalled at the callous satisfaction I had felt. My actions seemed incredible: savage and bestial, and debasing everything I cared about. I felt violated, and a foul oppression lingered in my being. Even my sense of taste and smell seemed fetid and vile. After long, haunting moments the horror slipped from me, and I was left empty and drained.

But anguish of a different kind surfaced: a suffocating fog of aching desire. Anna's features materialised in my mind's eye, infinitely alluring. But my perception changed and her gaze became blank and sightless; her face transformed into a glittering mask. She became a porcelain doll, with terrible fractures generating tiny fissures throughout her being. I sensed bleak desolation, a terrible loneliness and deep, obsessive insecurity. Hatred and self-disgust, fear and humiliation arose in me. Anna's pain I realised; and a crowd of bizarre sexual images filled my vision. Compassion flooded me at the sad, degrading eulogy to the death of love. I was released from her then, and felt the Mindworm's resentment, but I hardly noticed it. I fell into currents and whirlpools of light which flowed far beyond my comprehension.

Normal consciousness returned only gradually, and left me serene and unconcerned. I had sat on the beach all night, oblivious of time, and bathing in the rich, vibrant moonlight. I felt surprisingly energised, despite not having slept in any way that I recognised. Sunrise was a glorious revelation. It was as if I had never truly seen it before: an immaculate orb bringing light and life to a brand new world. Everything was transformed by its miraculous beauty, and I felt wholly reborn and revitalised. I had been freed from yet another net spun by the Mindworm. How, I had no idea, but I was grateful for it. Yet strangely I took it somehow for granted. I barely questioned my good fortune. Perhaps I had come to expect extraordinary things rather than marvel at them; or was punch-drunk by the mysterious and unexpected. At any event, I continued on my way in blinkered fortitude.

The sea was a vast swathe of blue all the way to the horizon. It was still quite empty of sails, and I finally took stock of my position. I was alone, but no longer lonely: back to my old self again, yet changed. Something was different. A new self-confidence outshone my hopes and fears. I had affection for Anna, and wished her well, but her memory no longer constricted my heart. Tendrils of doubt could brush my mind if I let them: but I could shake them away. I had been thrown into an impossible situation, and had no idea if I could have acted differently. Now I could consider the future, if not with *joie de vivre*, then at least with equanimity.

Sometime I assumed, the Portal would come back to life. Until then I decided to explore the island: perhaps find somewhere better to base myself. I debated whether to follow the shore or climb the hills for an overview. I elected eventually to climb. I would be more vulnerable, and have a more limited field of vision on the beach. The hillside rose to adjoin a higher landmass, perhaps the highest on the island. I estimated it would take until the afternoon to get to the top, but I took frequent breaks, and failed to reach it after climbing all day. The vegetation thinned as I got higher, and I harvested some fruit to take with me. It was cooler higher up too, and I had fewer qualms about snakes. At any event I was too tired to care, and stopped as soon as it became dark. I was lulled to sleep by the heat of the day discharging slowly from a big slab of rock.

I was awake at dawn, and soon began climbing again. The island was bigger than I had thought. The coastline meandered for miles in both directions before it began to curve back out of my line of sight. I reached the summit around mid-morning, and collapsed in some satisfaction. I was finally able to see the whole landmass spread out below me. It was roughly oval, and my route had crossed its narrow axis. I guessed it to be some thirty miles long, and more than fifteen across. There were numerous coves and outcrops on the far coastline, and several separate, smaller islands scattered in the distance in either direction.

Distant movement caught my eye, and I focused on it with a stab of alarm. Smoke curled into the sky from the shoreline far below: an inlet to the right of my viewpoint. Close by, perhaps a few hundred yards out, a dark shape crouched on a reef. It was too far to make out clearly, but it had to be a ship. If so it was aground, and a sudden, unreasonable hope flared in me. Whatever ship it was, some of its occupants were on the shore, and I had to know who they were. I hurried down the far slopes with endless scenarios whirling in my head. I stopped seldom, and ran where I could, making much better time than I had climbing the other side. But the descent still took the rest of the day. It was growing dark before I neared the shore, but I pushed on, unable to rest until I knew the truth.

I stumbled out onto the sand some distance from the fire, and crept softly towards it with my heart in my mouth. I could see only two or three figures around the flames, and feared the worst until I heard the high pitched voice of a child. Moving nearer I could make out two children with an adult, and broke into a run.

'Hey,' I called, 'hey, it's me, Richard!'

All three jumped up, peering out into the darkness. I saw that the man held a pistol, and a moment later I recognised Billy.

'Mister Walton, by Jiminy!' came his amazed tones.

He stared in astonishment, but the twins rushed towards me.

'Uncle Richard! Uncle Richard!' they squeaked in feverish excitement.

I grasped them tightly, an enormous lump in my throat; and they clutched at my clothes as I struggled towards Billy, my hand stretched out towards him.

'I thought I told you to call me Richard,' I said, grinning hugely.

'Is it really you Mr – Richard?' he exclaimed, pumping my hand feverishly. 'You got more lives than a cat!'

'You too,' I grinned, 'I can't believe it!'

'I guess the good Lord is looking after us,' said Billy, grinning himself.

'Where are the rest of the crew?' I asked, looking around.

His face fell some. 'They took to the boats,' he said, 'abandoned ship.'

'Left you – and the twins?' I asked incredulously.

'The twins wouldn't get in the boat,' he said. 'The crew were getting as jumpy as a lot of old hens. These two ran off, and I went after them. By the time we got back they were all away.'

'But why abandon ship?'

'We were taking on a lot of water. The hull started coming apart in the storm, and all them cannon balls didn't help, never mind the explosion.'

'But it didn't sink, obviously.'

'No, the water slowed after a bit. I don't know why. I patched up the leaks best I could o' course, and pumped till I dropped. It never seemed to get much lower or higher, but we stayed afloat: drifted for days. I thought the current would carry us past the island, but it brought us around the back, and here we are.'

'I can't tell you how happy I am,' I said, ruffling the twins' hair, 'I was thinking the worst about you all. This is just great.'

'What about you,' asked Billy, 'was it true you floated off with that Lady Seymour?'

'There's a lot to talk about,' I said, 'but first things first, have you got any food?'

'Sure, plenty from the ship.'

I tucked into ship's fare, the monotonous salt pork and biscuits now a luxury, and swilled it back with fine brandy, and some coconut juice. The twins bombarded me with inconsequential questions, and we all chatted happily until they sank into a contented doze around the fire. Billy and I talked on.

'So you didn't see me drifting away?' I asked. 'I shouted, but the explosion deafened me, and I couldn't hear anything or see anyone.'

'I was out for the count after that ship went up,' said Billy, 'and a lot of other folks were knocked stupid, or worse. I couldn't see much by the time I came to: just bits and pieces floating a long way off, and a lot of them nasty old sharks.'

'Yes, the sharks were why I didn't swim back,' I said. 'We were on some of those bits and pieces. I knocked up a kind of raft, and we were on it for days. We paddled for the island when we saw it. We weren't dragged around the back like you.'

Billy eyed me quizzically. 'You two must have got real well acquainted,' he said drily.

I gave a wry smile, 'You could say that.'

'So where is she?'

'Her friends picked her up.'

He looked alarmed: 'from this island?'

'Yes, but they headed straight on back out to the horizon on the far side. We had no idea you were here.'

'They didn't come after you?'

'They didn't know I was here either. Or she told them I was already gone.'

He raised his eyebrows.

'It's a long story,' I said. 'So how did you get ashore – you've got a boat?'

'Yep, the small dinghy: but I had to fix it up some. I thought the ship would break up when we hit. It came apart a bit more, but settled in the end. I figured to get the twins and whatever else I could ashore as soon as may be.'

'You did well. That was good of you to go back for them when the crew left.'

'Tell the truth, I didn't much fancy getting in them boats neither,' admitted Billy. 'They were so mad on taking the treasure with them. Loaded almost down to the water, they were.'

'Really? So they took it all?'

'Are you kidding?' laughed Billy, 'I've been bringing what's left ashore, but I ain't got half of it yet.'

I stared at him. 'You've been bringing it ashore?'

'Sure have,' Billy shrugged. 'It sure looks pretty too, more money than I ever dreamed of. It don't seem right just leaving it there. That ship will come apart in the next storm. I've been bringing some back along with everything else.' He grinned. 'I figured I could at least die rich.'

'Billy you are a marvel!' I laughed, 'even if we do just die rich.'

'So what do we do now?' he asked, 'is that contraption of yours ever going to work?'

'It did give some signs of life a while back,' I said. 'But we should be alright here while we wait.'

'As long as them pirates don't come looking for the treasure,' said Billy. 'They might get to thinking that if you drifted hereabouts, the ship might have done the same.'

'Anna – Lady Seymour – thought the ship had gone down,' I said. 'That's what this was all about: they knew the history of the Merchant Royal. The ship sank with the treasure, disappeared without trace. They wanted to get the treasure off before that happened.'

'Just what I said!' cried Billy triumphantly. 'They were after the money, same as everyone else.'

'I don't think it's that straightforward,' I said. 'It's not just about getting rich. There's something more going on, but I haven't figured out what it is.'

'She didn't tell you?' he asked.

'No, not much anyway,' I admitted, 'but she let slip a few things.'

I gave Billy a slightly edited version of what had passed between Anna and me in the past week or so; and he regarded me speculatively.

'You sure are full of surprises,' he mused. 'I'd have thought a lady like that would've eaten you alive.'

'She's not really a bad person…' I began, which set him off laughing.

'Well some of her friends sure are,' he said after a moment. 'So let's hope they don't think again about what happened to the ship.'

I was pretty worn out by the journey over the island, and fell asleep soon afterwards. I awoke to a glorious dawn, and the wondrous recollection that Billy and the twins were alive. I sprang up with a light heart and rekindled the fire, discovering that Billy had salvaged some decent coffee and a grinder. There was fresh water too, and I put a pan on to heat. The aroma of fresh coffee awoke Billy, and we were soon enjoying its rich, bitter-sweet flavour. We took scalding sips from silver mugs as we contemplated the new day.

'I got them from the captain's cabin,' said Billy, indicating the mugs.

'You have been busy,' I said, looking around at all the paraphernalia stacked on the sand. 'Where have you put all your new found riches?'

'I'll show you in a minute,' he said.

He took me on a tour of inspection of the camp before breakfast, the treasure being the first port of call. Numerous large gold bars were piled neatly on the ground close to the tree line, and nearby a great heap of cruder silver ingots. Next to them stood several solid wooden chests, each a couple of feet long and about eighteen inches high, with several smaller caskets nearby.

'Them gold bars are heavy,' said Billy, 'around twenty, thirty pounds I reckon. I got nigh on a hundred of them. There's more on the ship, and more silver too, and a fair few of these things . . .' He threw back the lid on one of the chests to reveal it full of silver coins.

'Good grief!' I said, 'what about the small ones?'

'Ah!' he announced proudly, 'I saved the best till last,' and flipped the lid of one of the smaller caskets open. A heap of gemstones sparkled in the sun, some of them spilling out onto the sand. They radiated a strange, hypnotic beauty that was almost frightening. It reminded me of the potency of the lottery ticket: the manifest empowerment of human hopes and dreams.

'Well,' I said a little breathlessly, 'now all we need is somewhere to spend it.'

I had not thought until that moment about what would actually happen if the Portal activated. It occurred to me that I would probably be unable to take more than one person with me, never mind the treasure. It really shook me up. I could hardly bear the thought of abandoning Billy and the twins again.

'You reckon you could get us all through one of these here doorways?' asked Billy, seemingly reading my mind.

I found it hard to meet his eye. 'I don't know Billy,' I said, 'if the worst come to the worst I'll come back.'

'Well I sure hope you learn how to use it sooner rather than later,' he said.

He looked thoughtful for a while. 'What's going to happen to the twins?' he asked, 'once you have figured out how to use that thing I mean.'

'I'm not sure,' I admitted.

'Poor old Bambridge will be grieving,' he said.

'I know,' I said, 'and he probably wouldn't have put them on the ship if it wasn't for me. I feel really bad about it. I don't really know what I'm doing, that's half the problem.'

'Well, it seems you didn't ask to get mixed up in all this either.'

'That's true,' I agreed, after a pause, 'and it makes me feel a bit better I suppose. I guess we can only take things as we find them. In the meantime it might be an idea to build a more permanent camp away from the beach, and get rid of any signs that we've been here – just in case the pirates do come looking.'

'I was thinking the same myself,' said Billy. 'It sure will be good to have another pair of hands to work with.'

We collected some fruit for breakfast, and woke the twins. They seemed to take my miraculous resurrection for granted, and we had a high old time of it, laughing and joking about our life as shipwrecked sailors.

'Can I help build the jungle house?' asked Nathaniel.

'And me!' exclaimed Aurelia.

'Of course you can,' I said, mentally allocating triple the time for the job.

We left them playing on the beach – with strict instructions to stay away from the jungle – while Billy and I set off in the rowing boat. It was strange to clamber on board the ship again. Battle damage and ugly dark bloodstains were apparent everywhere; and the chaotic detritus of abandoned possessions bore witness to the hurried departure of the survivors. I couldn't resist checking out Anna's cabin, and felt a tinge of sadness at the sight of her belongings. Someone, perhaps her maid, had ransacked it. A cupboard and chest of drawers were thrown open, and a couple of dresses, some fancy silk underwear and an empty jewel box lay on the floor. I was interested in clues about her other life, but found nothing. The bullion strong room was even more of a mess. Wooden chests large and small lay about, mostly broken open, with gold bars, silver ingots and the ubiquitous silver coins scattered in many places. Gems twinkled here and there on the floor, while a number of intact heavy chests still lined the walls.

'They took a lot of gold. It's mostly silver that's left – the bars and the coins,' said Billy. 'They took jewellery too, but it was dark in here. They dropped stuff all over and skedaddled.'

'I think it's best to get it all off,' I said, 'we can bury it somewhere. Let's burn the ship when we've taken everything we need. Hopefully it'll leave few signs that anyone has been here, unless they come looking carefully.'

We made many journeys back and forth to the ship over the next couple of days, taking off the treasure, and all the food, drink, weapons, tools and materials we thought necessary. After some debate we fired the Merchant Royal in the afternoon. We hoped the brightest flames would have died down before dark, and the worst of the smoke drifted away by morning. It was strange watching the ship burn: a harsh note of finality to an extraordinary experience, one many of its participants had not survived. We picked a site several hundred yards inland from the beach, and carried all our goods there bit by bit, obliterating all signs of occupation on the shore. A shallow cave, with a flat rocky ledge before it, formed the foundation of our intended home. The site was perfect for our needs, with a stream running nearby, and fruit trees in plenty. We had been working on it for a couple of days when the Portal burst into life.

First it was a couple of glowing icons in the air, then half a dozen more, and a distortion wave was flowing over me before I fully realised what was happening. Everything was vibrating: the finite boundaries of the material world dissolving into an ocean of possibilities. I clung to my present reality in shock. The thought of leaving Billy and the twins behind horrified me, but the sense of falling into timelessness intensified.

I tried to fix the point of departure clearly in my mind as my consciousness merged into the void. Power crackled all around me. I floated in formless realms, still clinging to the image of the island. The patterns of icons were changing, and another impression swam into my vision. A subtle, shimmering membrane appeared: a thin screen of energy. It was the surface of a tangible reality, and I looked into a modern western interior as though from behind a two-way mirror. A deep, crawling sensation passed through my body, and the image opened out into three-dimensional solidity. And into a startlingly familiar form: Charles' astonished features stared back at me.

'Richard!' he gasped, 'what's happening?'

I hardly understood it myself. I was standing within a halo of glittering particles: a circular opening, around which the fabric of reality continually reformed itself in constant molecular fluidity. Behind me our island basked merrily in the sun, and before me stood Charles, as large as life in the lounge of his flat. It was evening. The curtains were drawn, and the TV was on.

'Well...' I began.

'Is that somewhere else?' he exclaimed excitedly, 'can I have a look?'

'Hang on a minute Charles,' I said. The Portal was scanning both him and the building. The bugs had all disappeared apart from one, which blinked dimly and fitfully. A luminous rotating sphere engulfed it, seemed to give it a jolt, and the blinking stopped.

'OK,' I said, 'the bugs are gone.'

'Thank goodness!' said Charles, 'I've been in anti surveillance mode for months. It's been exhausting.'

'Months?' I said, surprised, 'has it been that long?'

'Nearly three anyway, I was really worried. But never mind that – this is wonderful. Can I have a look?'

'Let me check first,' I said, unsure exactly what was going on. I turned and moved carefully back through the opening. The crawling sensation passed through me again, and I stepped into warm sunshine. I felt a burst of joy. Somehow the Portal had made a gateway.

'Billy!' I yelled: only to discover him and the twins crouched nearby like frozen statues. They were staring fixedly at the exotic doorway, which sparkled oddly in the open air.

'Is that one of them doors?' asked Billy dubiously.

Charles pushed past me, quivering with excitement. 'Oh wow!' he said, 'this is just … oh wow!'

'Billy,' I said, giving up any attempt at managing the situation, 'this is Charles.'

Billy brightened at seeing a real live person. 'Well I'll be jiggered!' he said, 'I never thought I would be meeting you Mr – Charles, sir!'

'Uncle Richard, you and that man came through the air!' trilled Aurelia.

'Be he a ghost?' asked Nathaniel in awe.

Charles looked equally taken aback by his audience.

'No he is not a ghost,' I said to the twins. 'This is, err, a special door to another place – instead of going on a ship.'

'Be it a fairie door?' asked Aurelia fearfully.

'No – just an ordinary, special door,' I improvised. 'It goes to a normal place, just quicker. And speaking of 'quick', we had better get a move on. I don't know how long it will stay open.'

The twins' mouths opened in a uniform 'O' as they absorbed this new information.

Billy sidled up to the opening, and peered through it. 'What's that place?' he asked diffidently.

'It's where Charles lives,' I said.

'What in London?' cried Billy in amazement, 'with all them flying machines and all?'

'Who are all these people?' asked Charles in confusion.

'Billy is from the battle of Gettysburg, and the twins are from Pirates of the Caribbean,' I said blithely: 'Billy – why don't you show the twins that you're not afraid to go through the door. It tingles a bit, but it won't hurt you.'

Billy eyed the anomalous opening with misgiving, but squared his shoulders and edged into it. He halted when he felt the unnatural resistance, and then pushed through it. I took hold of the twins' hands, and led them after him. They crept along with their eyes screwed shut, clinging fiercely to me.

'There!' I said, as we stood in twenty-first Century London, 'that was easier than a ship wasn't it?'

Billy and the twins stared wide-eyed about them, their gaze travelling slowly up to the electric light, and over to the TV screen. Charles popped back through the gateway behind me.

'Can I bring that musket?' he asked, his eyes gleaming, 'it looks amazing, and there's a real sword too!'

'I don't think it's worth the risk,' I said.

Billy's attention switched from his novel surroundings. 'What about the treasure?' he said.

Charles' eyes grew large. 'Treasure?' he mouthed.

Between them they persuaded me. But I insisted on being the other side of the gateway. Billy and Charles dragged the chests into the flat on a rope, and I threw the heavy gold and silver bars through to them. Once we started it seemed a good idea to leave no trace of treasure at all. We laboured for what seemed an age, and I smartly followed the last of it into Charles' flat with a sigh of relief.

'Uncle Richard,' sang out Nathaniel, 'it did be a fairie door. There be a magic light, and a magic picture with witches in it.'

I glanced at the TV, and Harry Potter whizzing about on a broomstick.

'They're not magic, just, err, special,' I said. 'There are lots of special things here. You just haven't seen them before.'

'You can say that again,' said Billy. 'I hardly know if I'm awake or dreaming.'

'So you can do time-doors now,' said Charles, 'that's great! Are you going to close it?'

'I don't know how I opened it, never mind close it,' I growled.

A flurry of icons shimmered in my vision: the gateway shrank to a tiny point, and vanished.

'It seems easy enough,' said Charles, as I stared.

'And you've been saying you can't work it all this time,' said Billy.

'The damn thing has got a mind of its own,' I said, embarrassed. 'It only works when it wants to.'

'What about this?' asked Billy, blinking at the ceiling light. 'How does it work? My, it's as bright as day!'

'Electricity,' I said, reaching for the switch, 'watch this.'

I flicked it on and off a couple of times, enjoying Billy and the twins' amazement: then wished I hadn't, because the twins called for me to do it over and over again. It seemed odd they were just as astonished by electric light and the TV as they were by the gateway.

'There's a lot of new stuff to get used to Billy,' I said. 'This is a hundred and fifty years in the future for you, and much more for the twins. We will need to have a good, long talk about everything and decide what to do next. Charles – for a start, now the bugs are gone and we are all rich, I guess you can give up your day job.'

'Just what I was thinking,' beamed Charles. 'We've got even more money coming because I'm selling Aunt Jane's cottage. I've been planning it all in my head – you know, anti surveillance – but now we can get a super house somewhere!'

'Did you give any reason why you were selling?' I asked, 'I mean in case anyone was listening.'

'Of course,' said Charles, affronted that I should doubt his counter surveillance skills. 'I said I didn't like the place anymore, because of your disappearance – not to the buyers of course – to the people at work. And I said I was thinking of moving abroad, you know, for when I give up my job.'

'You had a lot of faith that I was coming back,' I said with a smile.

'Not really,' he said sunnily. 'You might be a bit dull sometimes, but you are usually reliable.'

Billy chuckled. 'Well, if that's the case, you might find he's not as dull as he used to be.'

We got a big order of pizza delivered and had a slap up party, disturbed only by the twins endlessly turning the lights on and off. Thankfully they were distracted by the TV while Billy and I pieced the story of our adventures together for Charles. I felt immeasurably relieved to have arrived back home, even if I had no idea how I had done it. I felt more confident I might learn to navigate the mysterious highways of time, and solve the enigma of Alex's dramatic appearance.

'You have changed a lot,' said Charles, 'you even look different. It's not surprising with everything you've been through. Just imagine! Pirates! It's not fair.'

'I don't remember feeling particularly happy when they were coming at us,' I said, glancing ironically at Billy.

'Me neither,' he agreed. 'It's bad enough having them cannon balls lobbed at you across a big old field, never mind sailing right up to you eyeball to eyeball.'

Charles looked unconvinced. 'Anyway, it seems these 'Keepers' are time travellers from Atlantis,' he said excitedly, 'and some of them are bad guys.'

'The 'Atlantis' thing really threw me,' I admitted, 'but I couldn't make much sense of it from what Anna said. Surely Portal technology must come from the future. There must be easier ways to make money too. All that killing…'

'Maybe they just, you know, like to collect ancient treasure,' suggested Charles, 'like people who steal expensive paintings.'

'Could be,' I mused, 'Anna said they were a strange lot. But she said the treasure was tradable goods for early time periods.'

'Maybe they wanted the treasure because it was lost: because no one would know they had taken it,' said Charles.

'That might make sense,' I agreed, 'but what would they want to trade it for?'

'Most probably something else they don't want anyone to know about,' said Billy. 'Hey! Is that one of them horseless carriages?'

He pointed at a car cruising along the road on TV.

'Sure is,' I grinned, 'you could probably see plenty of them if you just look out the window.'

'Really?' he exclaimed, his face lighting up. He darted over to pull the curtains aside, and stared speechless at the cars speeding through neon-lit streets below.

'Let me see, let me see!' cried the twins, scrambling to join him, and were struck dumb in their turn.

Nathaniel turned to me in awe. 'Uncle Richard,' he said in hushed tones, 'this whole world be special!'

Chapter 13

'WHAT ARE WE going to do about the children?' asked Charles.

'I don't really know,' I admitted. 'I'll have to think about it. I could try and get them back to their uncle, but they are supposed to be dead. I don't know how we could explain that.'

'But how can we look after them?' said Charles. 'What about, you know, school and stuff?'

'I don't think we need to worry about that,' I said, 'not for now at any rate.'

'I don't think it's that easy, looking after kids,' he said.

'Oh how hard can it be?' I said airily.

It was nine o'clock next morning. Charles had phoned in sick to work, and we were discussing the more pressing steps of our largely unformed master plan. Billy and the twins were still finishing breakfast, and playing with Charles' blending machine. Their role for the morning was going to consist mainly of watching TV. Charles was about to nip out with some cash to buy a new laptop for himself, and some clothes for me. I would then concentrate on enlarging our wardrobe and buying supplies, while Charles occupied himself with creating a new internet identity, and in opening a business account with Sophia's certified cheque.

The twins were delighted with the new clothes I brought them, even though my size estimates and fashion sense were rather approximate to say the least. But mostly they were excited about food, and I felt a little guilty about introducing them to items calculated to please rather than to nurture health and sobriety. I took Billy on his first walk out into the twenty-first century the next day, and grinned at the strange, crab-like gait with which he proceeded along the pavement. He flinched at passing cars, and eyed people and shop windows as if they were unnatural and dangerous apparitions. He also stood staring in awe at every plane that appeared overhead, often causing bystanders to search the sky for the source of his astonishment. Strangely it was the huge supermarket nearby that seemed to move him most.

'It just don't seem right,' he said, staring at the vast stacks of food piled high to tempt and titivate.

He was probably thinking of the thousands of starving men he had marched with a hundred and fifty years before, but I felt a similar unease myself. A glimpse of the changes that time could bring made me wonder how long this era of ease and plenty would last.

Charles registered 'Golden Enterprises Ltd' via a registered office service provider with a Post Office Box address; and a company bank account with credit and debit cards without much difficulty, once the certified cheque's bona fides had been established. We bought a car for cash – Charles still being hot on counter surveillance – and drove around searching for a new 'HQ' as he insisted on calling it. The car journeys were events in themselves: a constant chorus of astonished gasps and questions from Billy and the twins at practically everything we saw.

We decided on a house in Essex a little way outside the M25, a sizeable, slightly ramshackle five bedroom detached house, with a secluded garden and a couple of outhouses. It was an early twentieth century mock Tudor affair, with a half-timbered façade, tall chimney stacks of uncertain style, shaded, leaded windows under low eaves, and a blackened, timber-framed porch. The interior was surprisingly airy, and bore only superficial references to its supposed Tudor heritage: a prominent wooden staircase, occasional artificial ceiling beams, a few areas of light wall panelling, and an inglenook fireplace taking up a third of the lounge. It had a badly conceived, but convenient kitchen extension at the rear, and character and space enough to make a pleasant home.

We dropped the asking price by offering to pay outright and forego a building survey, and Billy, me and the twins moved into a short-let property nearby to wait for the sale to go through. Our main preoccupation was to create as small a footprint in the public domain as possible, and we dispensed with rental references by paying three months' rent up front, on top of an extortionate deposit.

Charles' comments regarding the twins proved wearily prophetic. He remained in his flat in London, winding down his 'moving to France' cover story, and sneaking around to visit us via ingenious surveillance-proof routes. But Billy and I found ourselves facing our greatest ordeal yet: hostage to a pair of boundlessly overactive firebrands, full of giggling mischief one moment and fighting like banshees the next. We bribed them with sweets, spoiled them with electronic goods, and failed miserably in the nutritious cooking department by living on takeaways. I was aware of the moral quicksand we were descending into, but had no idea what else to do.

Otherwise I was concerned that the sale might fall through, or that I might be whisked away by the Portal before we could establish ourselves. We arranged a hidey hole where we could leave information about our whereabouts, but I hoped it would not be necessary. The six weeks fast-track sale promised by the estate agents stretched to seven, but was at last agreed, and the owners consented to final completion and vacation of the property two days after that. Charles confirmed the sale of his flat too, and gave away or dumped most of his possessions. Counter surveillance tactics apparently decreed starting again from scratch, and he began covertly ordering all sorts of interesting and extravagant acquisitions from the internet.

The treasure was the principal item for transfer to our new house, and I endured a meticulously planned security operation spread over a couple of days, in which carloads of gold, silver, gems and cash were transported by circuitous routes. We locked the treasure in one room, and arrangements for a more discrete depositary were added to a list of 'items for discussion'. Our most practical problems were some necessary repairs and redecorations; and on the time team exploration front we talked about initiating some historical research into the activities of Jacqueline's stepfather. This was primarily Charles' department, but he was much more interested in building an observatory in the loft, and a lot of time was spent in agreeing a postponement of this cherished dream.

We had barely got settled in when the Portal burst into life. It happened while I was musing over Alex's appearance right back at the beginning of the whole crazy adventure. There was no warning, and there was nothing I could do about it. I was alone, and had no chance to let anyone else know either. I was surfing the kaleidoscopic ocean before I could fully take in what was happening. But in some ways this strange, enigmatic realm appeared less chaotic and disorienting to me. I thought I might be moving into the future, but I had no control over my destination. I was carried relentlessly through labyrinthine tunnels of light, and expelled back into material corporality with startling finality.

This time readjustment into a new temporal environment was more confusing. I staggered blankly in a modern landscape both unfamiliar and odd. Exotic high-rise buildings of novel and streamlined design incorporated decorative archways and reliefs which seemed Asian in style. Yet mirror-glass exteriors were dull and mottled, with absent panels glowering like missing teeth. Elegant facades were discoloured. Shop logos were un-illuminated, and their interiors largely devoid of customers and goods. Great expanses of glazing were cracked and grimy, and broad pavements grubby and strewn with litter.

The people in the street were not numerous. They looked Indian, and were clad in a strange mixture of classic saris and pyjamas and chic tunics. But most were threadbare and stained, and some wore little more than rags. There was little vitality in their features, and this was reflected in the run-down vehicles nearby. The sleek contours of automobiles were dull and battered. Most were stationary, parked at the curb. Many were wrecks, missing wheels or doors, and the few in motion were in little better condition. There was no reverberation of petrol engines. Vehicles ran slowly and silently, making disjointed mechanical creaks and rattles as they weaved around pedestrians straying aimlessly in the road.

The people themselves regarded me with a kind of vacant curiosity, apart from one elderly lady who stared at me in alarm. I assumed she had seen me materialise, and gave her what I hoped was a reassuring grin. She blinked several times, and then turned to hobble rapidly away, giving one last fearful look over her shoulder. I chuckled despite my sudden displacement in space-time. She reminded me of the lady with the dog, back at the beginning of my interesting new existence.

After a few moments I noticed some people were moving more purposefully than others, and all in the same direction. I decided to walk that way too, and after a hundred yards or so I became aware of a ghostly clacking sound that was weirdly familiar. A little further on the noise became more audible and defined: like the tapping of numerous keyboards, and with sudden excitement I recalled a similar effect when Alex had dulled the noise from the club. As I turned into an open square, it seemed to incorporate the clipped off tones of human speech as well.

A large crowd had gathered there, and as I approached its outer fringes the mysterious noise transformed itself into the rich cadence of a male human voice. It was crystal-clear and seemingly right next to my ear. Disconcerted, I stepped backwards. The faint chattering resumed: a tiny fraction of the volume that had resonated a moment before. It was some kind of audio field I realised, broadcasting within a localised area. I moved forward again. The words were meaningless for a brief instant, then the Portal kicked in and understanding blossomed.

'...beyond our irresponsible materialistic childhood into a mature organic society, in harmony with the Living Earth. We must learn from the disasters that have overtaken us – learn to develop an eco-culture in tune with the natural world. These calamities have been created by humanity's ignorance of its true potential. We have lived at a gross level as selfish, egocentric individuals, and have yet to evolve into maturity. We have pursued personal power and narrow materialistic goals, but within this chrysalis of ego exists a potential for far greater things...'

The voice was vital and forceful, and accompanied by a tingling sense of déjà vu. I listened initially because of that significant familiarity, and to gain information about the times and the place. But the speaker's personality began to intrigue me as well.

'...we are like a blind child playing in the dirt,' he continued, *'oblivious of the power and beauty of the cosmos. Our material pursuits are but a temporary diversion in the ancient journey of humanity. We must turn from our hi-tec obsessions to embrace the Living Earth: open ourselves to the rhythms and energies of the planet which created us. Only through harmony with the Living Earth will the seeds of destruction be neutralised, and our true evolutionary potential come to fruition ...'*

The term *Living Earth* cropped up repeatedly, and interested me because of some of my own experiences. But the multitude of woes that appeared to have rained down on humanity was horrifying. I could barely make out the orator in the crowd, but his voice clearly catalogued natural catastrophes, depleted natural resources, collapsed economies, starvation, wars, pollution and drug-immune plagues. Even so, the message was surprisingly up-beat: proclaiming a new era and a new hope for humanity. It did not seem precisely religious or political, although its intensity suggested elements of both. A powerful sense of gravity and presence resonated in the man's words, and he spoke of extraordinary things with a matter-of-fact delivery that carried certainty and conviction.

His vision did not seem so outlandish in light of the fabulous realms I knew existed beyond the fabric of everyday life. I wondered if he might be a time-traveller, and moved forward to get a closer look. The speech ended to enthusiastic applause. People were milling about trying to talk to him, and it was hard to get near. I got close enough to see he was tall, bearded and well built, and that no mirror-like reflection of a Portal emanated from him. But his personality was decidedly larger than life, his vision unconfined by the limitations of the everyday world, and the energy resonating from him triggered a decided response.

I felt a keen excitement and an urge to learn more – followed by a stab of alarm at the effect he seemed to be having on me. I retreated to reassess the situation. The movement caught his eye, and he glanced at me. For a moment a direct connection seemed to pulse between us, and he gave a slight smile. I felt a subtle sense of recognition: as if we both stood outside the human drama, looking in. Then he turned to speak to other people.

It was all quite mystifying. I walked away a little, watching the crowd disperse, and tried to understand what was going on. Finally the man began to move towards the far side of the square with a few remaining hangers-on. I thought about trying to speak to him, but hesitated too long. He conferred briefly with one or two people, and then got into a vehicle and was driven off. I felt I had missed a chance of some kind, and wondered what to do next. But one of the people he had spoken to walked purposefully towards me: a youthful guy in a strikingly elegant outfit of an unusual style. A ripple of déjà vu passed through me, and I was instantly alert.

'Hi', he beamed as he approached, 'do you speak English?'

'Yes,' I admitted, 'I'm from England.'

'Guru-ji asked me to speak to you,' he announced proudly.

The speech, I thought, would have been in a local language I was unlikely to understand. But I wondered if his Guru-ji intended something on a level other than mere translation, and decided to play along.

'Did he say why?' I asked.

'Oh no,' he replied, 'just that I speak to you. It is enough that he suggested it. I am honoured: it is only the third time he has spoken to me.' He looked at me speculatively. 'Do you know about Guru-ji's teachings?'

'A little,' I said cautiously.

'Did you come from Central?' he asked. 'It is unusual to see a foreigner out here.'

'No,' I said, ignorant of my surroundings as usual, 'I am, err, travelling across country.'

His eyes widened. 'Really – a roamer; I have never met one before!' He smiled in delight. 'I have an amazing idea, will you be my guest – come back with me to Central? I must hear about your adventures, and I can talk to you about *Living Earth*.'

I considered his suggestion for a moment. His open smile was infectious.

'Why not?' I said, 'I am Richard.'

'I am Ravi,' he grinned, 'it is very good to meet you.'

'Same here,' I agreed.

'Do you have transport?' he asked.

'No,' I admitted.

'Excellent,' beamed Ravi, 'we can travel together. My car is very close. Are you staying around here? What about your belongings?'

'My rucksack is missing,' I said: a carefully crafted part-truth. I disliked telling lies.

'And still you stopped to hear Guru-ji speak!' said Ravi admiringly. 'Do not worry. There is everything you need at my apartment.'

I couldn't help staring at the suit he wore. It was a comfortable looking tunic with a cell-like structure, something like a seamless skin of ultra-fine translucent scales. But it possessed a subtle luminosity, and its appearance shimmered with incremental transformations of detail, texture and elusive flecks of colour.

He looked down. 'I know,' he said apologetically, 'I should not be wearing a tec-suit: but Guru-ji says I should show that *Living Earth* has hi-tec followers too.'

'I am, err, sure it is the inner person that really matters,' I agreed politely.

'Thank you, I was sure you would understand!' he said happily.

We walked to a battered vehicle parked some way along the street where I had first appeared. It was electric, and the motor made considerably less noise than its other components as it rumbled and squeaked out into the pot-holed road. There were few other moving vehicles. The chief hazards were pedestrians, dogs and the odd cow, most of which seemed less than healthy and largely oblivious of traffic.

The condition of the car mismatched the quality and style of my new acquaintance's clothing, as did the ramshackle house we pulled into a few minutes later. But all was revealed when we drove under a crumbling archway into a small yard at the rear. Here stood a spectacular vehicle, something like a cross between a two-seater sports car and a jet fighter. Much of its roof and upper passenger space was encapsulated in gleaming, curved mirror-glass, and mysteriously, no wheels were visible. Instead, squat matt-black rectangular grills angled outwards and downwards from beneath the front, sides and rear. Above them ran a swathe of low, sleek bodywork gleaming in a psychedelic spectrum of colour. It enclosed the lower third of the vehicle front to back, and curved upwards over the centre in a wide, overhead band.

'My sky car,' said Ravi simply, 'I cannot leave it unattended in this area. This is the house of a *Living Earth* brother.'

'Great,' I said casually, trying not to stare.

A lady appeared from the house and Ravi greeted her, thanking her for the use of the car. He turned to his 'sky car', and a kaleidoscopic flash from his tec-suit replicated itself in perfect sync along the car's lower bodywork. The mirror-glass blister ahead of the overhead structural strip hinged smoothly upwards. Soft, gel-like translucent seating was revealed, and a control panel that seemed made of glass. We climbed in, and a holographic display began to do complex things above the glistening dashboard. The mirror-glass screen came down, sealing us inside with a satisfying clunk. A subtle vibration pulsed through the vehicle. A strange sense of lightness enveloped me, and we lifted smoothly off the ground.

'Very nice,' I achieved, feeling oddly ill at ease. We appeared to be hovering in mid-air without any substantial propulsion or support. There was a low hum, and broad, stubby wings slid from the bodywork on either side. I detected a further sound, and turned to see an elongated tail protruding at the rear.

'Latest dark-tec,' said Ravi, with an incongruous mixture of pride and distain. 'Ultra-lightweight body: graphene composite of course. Highly efficient thrust, it can accelerate fast if we need to.'

'Dark-tec?' I asked.

'Dark technology,' he said. 'You must know of it, even if you don't use it.'

'Not really,' I improvised. 'I mean, I've heard of it of course, but I don't know much about it. I'm not much of a scientist.'

'Multi-dimensional physics stuff,' said Ravi dismissively, 'manipulation of the high energy matrix.'

'Maybe you had better go back a few steps,' I suggested.

'It's so boring,' said Ravi, 'I'd much rather talk about *Living Earth*.'

'I'd like to hear just a bit about it,' I pressed.

'Oh very well,' he said. 'It's relevant to *Living Earth* too, I suppose.' He paused, absently tapping his knee. 'Well, the dimensionality of space-time is restricted, relative to its energy state, right? It has to be, for the lower order energetic processes to function.'

'Back another step?' I asked, 'think of me as a technical dinosaur.'

'How wonderful to live such a simple life,' he sighed. 'So: you understand the transitional cycles of space-time relative to exponential energetic decay? – the step-down processes from the beginning of creation?'

'You mean changes from the high energy state of the big bang to more relative processes in the physical universe?' I enquired hopefully.

'Well yes,' he agreed. 'The time constant is subject to decay-mode variables of course, but basically these are finite processes generating the causative force of time and the evolutionary cycles of matter. At this level the multiple dimensionality of the high energy matrix is folded within the structure of space-time. Surplus to requirements you might say. But this is not actually the case: it is playing an important part in maintaining its stability.'

'Err – the high energy matrix?'

'Ultra-dense energy states that transcend space-time: the existential motherlode which gives birth to the universe in the first place. Space-time is an essentially temporary manifestation, enveloped within the multi-dimensional matrix like a bubble in an ocean. But it remains in a volatile state, and requires a control mechanism to manage runaway energetic processes. The hidden dimensions remain integrally connected to the high energy matrix via micro-wormholes in the quantum foam. They act as a kind of feedback loop: maintaining the additional mass and energy required to stabilise the primary momentum of the universe. We think black holes are doing something similar on a higher order of magnitude.'

I nodded with as little apparent confusion as possible, my mind lagging some way behind.

'Dark energy and dark matter are just old names for the additional force and mass deriving from the high energy matrix. Dark technology taps into it with the Gadhavi field generator: which was invented – he shot me an arch look – by my great uncle.'

'Your great uncle'! I repeated, trying to look suitably impressed.

He nodded sulkily, 'and all his relations are supposed to follow in his footsteps.'

I grinned. 'I'm guessing that doesn't fit too well with *Living Earth.*'

He smiled reluctantly. 'No. That is, according to their understanding it doesn't. They don't believe that creation can be purposeful, despite the algorithms that dark-tec finds in subatomic processes.'

'Algorithms?' I asked.

'Yes. It started with quantum computers. They began registering systematic sequences that no one could account for.'

'So they deciphered them?'

Ravi laughed.

'Only in part: most of them are without intelligible references. They seem to function in various inter-dimensional transition processes. All we know is that it can affect the energy state and behaviour of molecular structure. It's a bit like the early work with DNA, before they discovered it could be reprogrammed. They are just isolating bits which create certain effects, and experimenting with them.'

'With flashy sky cars?'

'Yes,' he shrugged, 'and the sound system we used back in the square. At present dark-tec works best in generating changes in lighter molecules like Oxygen and Nitrogen. It can synchronise them into patterns which reflect sound waves more efficiently, and focus them back into the required audio zone. It also generates lift for this baby by altering molecular resistance around us.'

'It still uses kinetic propulsion though?'

'Yes. The Gadhavi drive envelops the required air volume for the mass and velocity load, and energises the forward and overhead molecular mass to create a low anterior pressure wave. The air mass is conducted back through the propulsion unit, and the energy converted to thrust. The air molecules below and to the rear are condensed at the same time, creating a posterior zone with maximum thrust resistance. It is very efficient.'

'I see,' I lied, but assumed this represented the first forays into the mysterious processes manipulated by the Portal. 'Very impressive, but I wonder how much is known about the high energy matrix itself? I'm guessing what they really want is to become God, and re-create the universe!'

Ravi laughed delightedly. 'Of course,' he said, 'science is always trying to assume command of creation.'

'So you believe in God?' I asked. 'You sound more like an engineer than an evangelist.'

'I believe life is purposeful, and is evolving towards something beyond human existence,' he said. 'That is what *Living Earth* is all about. But I trained as an engineer, and most of my relations are in science and engineering.' He looked rather mournful. 'We are all supposed to be going for a monopoly in dark-tec applications.'

Daylight began to fade as the sky car whispered over vast areas of suburban decay and neglect, and the dark tint of its mirror-glass gradually lightened into crystal-clear transparency. A distant vision of light began to impose itself on the horizon: a fantastic, luminous cityscape of bewildering complexity. Immaculately illuminated buildings of astonishing height and form revealed themselves as 'Central' unfolded before us.

Aircraft of diverse size and shape criss-crossed invisible, orderly lanes at multiple altitudes between the grandiose constructions, glittering like darting schools of fish. Radically sculptured profiles confused the eye: unimaginably complex structures flaunting majestic visions of power and aesthetic precision. Some shimmered with abstract fractal patterns, or displayed a multitude of exquisitely fashioned multifaceted surfaces. Others reflected their surroundings in almost painfully bright perfection. Further creations writhed gracefully in artistically mesmerising configurations: some kind of elaborate articulation utilising discrete levels and segments moving around a central core. A few mimicked unlikely organic creations, or had their outer skin encrusted with eccentric root-like membranes. I tried to appear undaunted as we fell in with other gleaming sky-cars flitting between the towering edifices. I was uneasy too about small drones which randomly flew near and vanished. Finally we closed upon the upper realms of a dream-like spire, its curves and contours falling lazily about it like melted toffee. An opening unfolded smoothly before us, and we slipped silently into an eyrie-like, aerial parking module.

'Home!' cried Ravi jovially, as we walked through into a spacious apartment. I was startled by a reply in sensuous, surround-sound female tones. My surprise, and the initial delay in the Portals translation made me miss the words entirely.

Ravi laughed, 'you must address our visitor in English.'

I looked around; already half suspecting the sound was not human.

'Greetings honoured guest,' came the voice again, now identifiably too perfect in pitch and delivery to be a real person. 'May the *Living Earth* enrich your life!'

'You see,' chuckled Ravi, 'the house-mind is already converted!'

'– and may master Ravi allow you a word in from time to time,' concluded the house dryly, still evidently possessing a mind of its own.

The apartment was an oddball pastiche of contradictions to say the least. The walls and ceilings flowed with luminous curves and designs, their elegant contours enclosing stylish fitments, gadgets and appliances. Yet cheerfully jarring with this was a haphazard display of mysterious rustic objects. Rough-fashioned timber chairs and a table stood about, their grain polished to rich glowing hues. Odd, antique implements were mounted along one wall, and crude fibre matting lay on the floor. One entire face of the living area wall gleamed darkly slick and translucent from floor to ceiling, curving gracefully to include an external arc of the building. Ravi waved a hand: it grew crystal clear, and the view was stunning.

But I was diverted from the stunning panorama by a curious, rippling green hue reflecting from the walls around me; and turned to discover that Ravi's suit had come alive with a rich layer of mildly undulating, brightly glowing leaves.

'Ah!' he said, a little embarrassed, 'I forgot. It is a personal setting: it reflects my mood.'

I waved away this mild eccentricity with a grin, imagining Charles let loose with a chameleon suit of this kind. Ravi arranged his features into a more formal bearing, and his suit assumed its previous enigmatic appearance.

'I am so happy you have come,' he beamed.

'I am happy to be here,' I said, still overwhelmed by the vast technical constructions towering outside his immaculate window on the sky. I nodded towards the infinitely more modest fabrications scattered around the room.

'Presumably the natural look is related to *Living Earth?*'

'Of course,' he said proudly. 'I have been collecting pre-tech antiques for two years, and the furniture and matting I made myself. I have a workshop with many authentic tools and have been practicing cabinet-making and marquetry.'

'But why authentic tools – it is so time consuming,' I said. 'Surely you could produce these things with machines.'

'Of course,' he agreed, 'but the quality of experience would be missing. It is a labour of love to work with my hands: to discover the shapes in the wood, and infuse the essence of my being into my creations.'

I thought privately that the essence of his being could do with a little more tweaking in the expertise department. Yet the simple delight he exuded at his achievements was endearing.

'So *Living Earth* is all about going back to Nature,' I said. 'Isn't that a bit unrealistic: a luxury that your hi-tec culture allows you to indulge in?'

'No, no!' exclaimed Ravi with sudden fervour. 'I will be happy to explain, but first you must have something to eat and drink. What would you like?'

'Well I'd quite like a beer,' I said without thinking.

Ravi looked shocked. 'Alcohol?' he said disapprovingly, 'but it degrades sensitivity: lowers the quality of awareness!'

'Ah, sorry, well anything you like,' I backtracked. 'Perhaps something that, err, improves sensitivity?'

'Yes, yes,' he said happily, 'I have a wonderful infusion for the liver.'

'The liver?' I asked in surprise.

'Yes. Its well-being is essential to the quality of life, just as its name implies. Have you never given thought to the unconscious meaning of words?'

'No, I can't say I have,' I admitted. 'So *Living Earth* is about a better quality of life?'

'You could say that, but a better quality of consciousness would be more correct.' He busied himself with an array of sophisticated culinary appliances. 'It is a matter of developing our inner faculties. After all, tobacco smoking died out when people began to recognise how destructive it was – and alcohol is just the same. Now that we are emerging from the dark age of materialism, we should be enhancing our awareness: not deadening ourselves to life's subtleties with toxic chemicals.'

'I think we needed to deaden ourselves with toxic chemicals to survive the dark age of materialism,' I laughed, thinking of twenty four hour office e-mails, fraught meetings, and endless campaigns to achieve more with less.

'Exactly!' agreed Ravi, undaunted. 'We believe our hi-tec science is the knowledge of a tree that has outgrown its roots. It is failing us without a proper foundation: without a complete understanding of the meaning of existence.'

'So *Living Earth* is a belief system, a religion?' I asked.

'Well, yes and no,' said Ravi, handing me a glass of mysterious liquid. 'We believe religion is an incomplete projection of the true evolutionary potential of humanity – that the life process has yet to reach its goal.'

I thought about this without much enthusiasm. 'So you give up trying to figure out how the universe works, and sit around waiting for it to tell you one day?'

He chuckled good-naturedly. 'Not at all: we still value science, but look where the mismatch between scientific progress and social wisdom has taken us! Everything driven by egocentric desires has collapsed. We believe humanity has become trapped in an obsessive circular diversion: we cannot see beyond the manipulation of matter and self-centred ambition. *Living Earth* sees our destiny as something which will transcend matter entirely. Rather than trying to dominate the material universe, we believe we should work with it to allow its evolutionary potential to come to fruition.'

I took a sip of his 'liver juice'. It was pleasant, but failed to trigger any astonishing new perceptions of reality. 'So it is a matter of faith?' I suggested.

'No,' he insisted. 'It is a matter of maturity, of developing our sensitivity to the true potential of life. We have to grow out of a childish preoccupation with ego-projection and material toys.'

'What kind of sensitivity?' I asked, trying to grasp what he meant. 'Do you mean mystical, or spiritual?'

'We see no difference between scientific enquiry, religious belief and spiritual experience,' he said. 'Each is a different perception of the same reality.'

'Are you talking about different dimensions of existence?' I asked, becoming more interested.

'Higher dimensions of existence, yes,' he said, nodding excitedly: 'the evolutionary potential of the *Living Earth*.'

'What makes you sure that higher dimensions of existence exist?' I probed.

'I feel it within myself when my connection with the *Living Earth* is strong,' he said, his eyes shining, 'especially when I am in Guru-ji's presence. Science is also uncovering the truth, for those with the eyes to see.'

'Do you think your Guru-ji has real knowledge of these higher dimensions of existence?' I asked curiously.

'You have seen him, did you not feel it?'

'I felt something, but it could just be charisma. He has a powerful personality.'

'His words have power, but it is the power to awaken our own potential. That is the truth I feel.'

'Where do you think he gets this knowledge of a higher existence?' I wondered.

He shrugged. 'Some say he is among the first in whom the awakening has begun: others that he is a messenger come to reveal the destiny of the Cosmos.'

'You mean like the founder of another religion?'

'Perhaps, in a way: as I told you, we believe all religions are partial visions of humanity's future. But now we are close to its final manifestation.'

'So what does he say about this knowledge he has?'

'He says we must each discover it within ourselves.'

'Hmm,' I murmured, considering this. 'What about science, did you say it was revealing this truth?'

'Science has shown that sentience exists at every level of life,' he said earnestly. 'It has revealed the cooperation of extremely sophisticated processes in Nature to evolve progressively higher forms of consciousness. We believe the ultimate purpose of creation is to evolve consciousness on a universal scale. Indications of this are observable in scientific data, if we know what to look for.'

'Well,' I said doubtfully, 'it's a nice thought, but I notice you are using the word 'believe' and that is not science.'

Ravi looked slightly affronted. 'The evidence will not exist on any specific, relative level, if we are dealing with a fundamental universal truth. Our science is historically quite limited: extremely compartmentalised. The encoded patterns we recognise in human DNA relate only to individual physical existence. The greater bulk of it is regarded as accumulated junk in a random evolutionary process. But *Living Earth* does not consider life to be random. In our view this DNA is neither surplus nor random, and only appears meaningless because we do not have the capacity to decipher it. We believe it relates to processes beyond our current understanding.'

'What kind of processes?' I asked.

'Those not designed for individual physical sequences, but universal functions at high energy levels. It is programmed for collective interaction – for a shared super-consciousness – and can only be understood as a higher function of humanity as a whole. It is like a language whose elements and syntax has to interlock collectively across the human race to be understood.'

'I see,' I said, still seeing very little. 'So does science recognise such a high level language in DNA structure?'

Ravi looked uncomfortable. 'No, not yet: it is not at that stage.'

'So how do you know about it?'

'Through Guru-ji's knowledge, and the experience he awakens in us of course,' he said brightly. 'All knowledge of higher levels of existence will be experiential in nature, if that is the goal of the evolutionary process. We have only to learn to live in harmony with the planet that gestated us to move towards transcendence.'

'It all sounds rather vague to me,' I admitted. 'Surely you must do something more specific than sitting around waiting for something to happen.'

'Yes, did I not say?' he exclaimed. 'We feel the power of the *Living Earth*. It is an energy which flows through everything that exists: which makes the whole body vibrate. We feel it in Guru-ji's presence. And we feel it in special places on the Planet. You must know of them: in India many are found in natural rock formations, and in your England the ancients marked them out with big stones. We are awakening to these things now on a collective level.'

'You mean stone circles?' I asked, surprised by the sudden switch to something that actually existed.

'Of course: have you not visited them? Did you not feel something?'

I had in fact, on both counts. I had once accompanied an obscure university society outing on a sunrise trip to Stonehenge. It had been a spur of the moment thing. I was at a party and had been invited to join them afterwards. I had experienced something pretty weird when the sun rose: a kind of vision of a chanting man in white robes, his voice resonating with everything around him. But I had indulged in a couple of joints a few hours previously, and assumed it to be some sort of hallucination. I didn't feel like sharing this with Ravi though.

'Err…yes…that is, I did visit Stonehenge.'

'They represent part of a terrestrial energy system, but probably you did not feel it. Our sensitivity is numbed and atrophied. We have to open ourselves to feel the power that created us. We must have a thirst for something deeper.'

'So you have an actual, practical experience?' I asked curiously.

'Actual yes, though subtle of course. It is – what do you call it in English? – a threshold effect. It is like a current that seems to vibrate in everything. I do not feel it all the time, but increasingly often, and more strongly.'

That did get my interest. I had more pressing things to think about just then, but I could see I was going to have to learn more about Ravi and his living religion.

'Food preparation complete,' chimed the house-mind graciously. 'No responsibility taken for ingredients or cooking instructions.'

'Thank you,' cried Ravi happily, incongruously bestowing sentience on an artificially intelligent creation. He dished out a decidedly mushy, but undoubtedly organic-looking meal from sleek designer gadgets onto crudely glazed china plates.

'I am still reorganising towards a more integrated organic lifestyle,' he explained a little self-consciously. 'Soon I hope to move to a more natural habitat.'

Ravi's sunny disposition reminded me of Charles in some ways. I found his company enjoyable and amusing, despite his constant enthusing over the amazing potential of *Living Earth*. He had given me a lot to think about, and we talked on as we ate, and continued far into the night. I learned more about the steady decline of humanity's fortunes; trying not to give away too much of my ignorance of contemporary affairs. It was relatively easy to deflect his supposed interest in my travels among the global detritus of mankind's failed material adventure. A few vague anecdotes, and enquiries about his real interests, sent him off on inexhaustible discourses of his own. The gaps in my knowledge were steadily filled.

'Central' stood in what had once been an exclusive outer suburb of New Delhi in India, and was now a small city in itself, surrounded by the vast decaying hulk of the old sprawling metropolis. The date was twenty sixty seven, and a general economic and social malaise seemed never to have really escaped the financial crisis in the early years of the century. An initial, ragged recovery had degenerated into fitful pockets of growth and decay amid a widespread jumble of corruption and inertia. Pollution, terrorism and social unrest had eaten into the crumbling edifice of industrial nirvana. Natural resources had been depleted, and mutated viruses and drug resistant diseases grown more plentiful. Population had declined, and shifting weather patterns driven many survivors from their traditional lands. A nomadic way of life haunted by starvation had become commonplace.

Only a progressively shrinking elite had maintained their privileged lifestyle, and benefitted from continued advances in science and engineering. But even their superior technology had failed to protect them from being overrun and destroyed in some places by enraged hordes of disenfranchised people. Yet still, declared Ravi in high-pitched incredulity, hi-tec societies continued to insist that technical innovation was the only salvation for humanity.

Living Earth had first emerged some years previously in central India with the appearance of Guru-ji, whose words had steadily gained ground among the disillusioned masses struggling amid the wreckage of the Western dream. Ravi himself had first gone to hear him speak a couple of years earlier in Madras, and had become an instant convert. He had gone on to attend several more public addresses by the Great Man, and got to know a number of his closest followers. He had also worked hard to spread the word among his hi-tec friends and acquaintances in Central, with indifferent success. But he had a number of interested contacts in other hi-tec enclaves around the world.

'Guru-ji has praised me for recognising the excesses of hi-tec ambition,' he said proudly. 'He has told me I have a great responsibility to persuade fellow Central citizens to listen. Tomorrow I am visiting an important family relation in the Senate, who has agreed to talk to me.'

'And the best of luck,' I thought sceptically. The scintillating spectacle of the brilliantly illuminated city provided a surreal backdrop to his words. I couldn't imagine the proprietors of these mega-towers of Babel listening to anything he had to say. The extraordinary scene reminded me of the huge chasm of time and space separating me from people I had left scattered in the past. I thought about Alex, and wondered if she came from this time: if she was even now somewhere close by. I remembered Jacqueline too, left far behind two hundred years in the past. A melancholic loneliness swept through me, and I sensed a stirring of interest from the Mindworm. It occurred to me that Anna might also have seen this time: could also be in this dazzling place. I felt a flicker of desire and determinedly repressed it. There were enough complications in the giant jig-saw puzzle that my life had become.

Chapter 14

AT LEAST, I thought things were complicated enough until next morning, when Ravi burst into my airy guest bedroom to share his latest revelation.

'I woke up and it came straight into my mind!' he exclaimed excitedly. 'I thought, of course! That is why Guru-ji sent me to you!'

His great idea was for me to accompany him to the meeting with his senator relation. I was supposed to give a greater perspective on the plight of people in the countries I had passed through on my travels: the fact that I had made only the vaguest comments about these things seemed to have escaped his notice. But I checked my natural reluctance to agree. I had learned that chance encounters often delivered unexpected connections in this crazy expedition through time. So I smiled and let his enthusiasm carry me along.

We saluted the new day with an excellent cup of tea, and a rather overlong meditation. Ravi sat cross-legged on the floor with his eyes shut: occasionally touching the floor mat in an apparent attempt to absorb its environmental purity. I spent the time taking in the grand vista of the future city, which was bathed in the morning sun. It looked less spectacular in daylight somehow, more contrived and overstated. The elaborate buildings seemed to radiate a kind of arrogance, especially considering the wasteland beyond its borders. Afterwards we had a leisurely breakfast of luscious fruits, and more deliciously fragrant tea.

'I am so happy to have this chance to talk to Senator Gadhavi,' said Ravi, reverently chewing a succulent slice of mango.

'But what are you going to say to him,' I asked, 'surely he is going to be interested only in practical matters?'

'*Living Earth* is perfectly practical,' he said. 'We believe in a self-sufficient local economic model, with small interlinked markets across the country. We advocate a sustainable society with low tech needs; and an inner quality of life rather than outward material acquisition. We can still pursue hi-tec expertise, but not at a frantic pace, and not to accumulate unnecessary and unsustainable material possessions.'

'I expect he will just see that as stagnation,' I said. 'People like to believe they are building a glorious future.'

'But they will be,' insisted Ravi. '*Living Earth* will lead us to a more glorious future than we can imagine.'

'OK, you win,' I laughed. But inwardly I considered his words more seriously. I thought of my own experience of strange, inexplicable dimensions of being, and wondered if they were connected with Ravi's *Living Earth*. But it confused me that he seemed to be talking about something quite different from opening up doors into the past and the future.

'I think you should wear different clothes for the meeting,' he said, 'I have plenty of tec-suits.'

I slipped into one and found it amazingly comfortable. It adjusted itself to my size, and made me feel cool and relaxed.

'It will reflect your mood and interact with others, unless I disable the response reflex,' he said, looking enquiringly at me.

'Yes, please do,' I agreed hastily. I didn't want to turn myself into some kind of kaleidoscopic beacon of alarm and confusion.

He tapped a luminous touch-screen under the skin of his wrist. He had shoes for me too, which were also cool and comfortable. They were made of a lightweight, tactile substance which seemed to both grip and ventilate my feet with equal efficiently.

'I hope you don't expect too much from me,' I said awkwardly, 'I'm not sure I can say anything that will help.'

'Oh don't worry,' he said, 'the more I think about it, the more certain I am that Guru-ji meant you to be there. Would you like another cup of tea before we go?'

'No more tea thank you,' I smiled, 'it was excellent, but I've had quite enough.'

'Best quality Darjeeling, completely organic,' said Ravi absently. 'I will prepare a few things for the meeting, and we will be ready to leave very soon.'

Launching the sky car from a building many hundreds of yards high was rather different from rising from the ground in a sensible manner. The vehicle seemed to dip noticeably as we slid out over the yawning void, and my stomach dropped much further than that. My body literally crawled with horror at the thought of the abyss below, but the craft skimmed nonchalantly off across the dreamlike city.

'How, err, reliable are these sky cars?' I asked, as my faculties began to accept that death was not necessarily imminent.

'You have not spent much time in them?' inquired Ravi cheerfully. 'They are very safe. There is an auxiliary one-time landing boost-jet, three hundred and sixty degree three-step airbags, and even an automatic parachute, but I do not recall anyone in Central ever having to use them.'

We had only been in the air a few minutes when we began to close with a vast, hive-like edifice, a carefully choreographed latticework of cell-like units, all interlinked into a complex mass of unlikely elevations. Ravi flew unerringly down into one of a bewildering array of landing platforms, and we climbed out of the vehicle: he bristling with excitement, and me gaping like a glass-eyed fish out of water. We entered a huge foyer where people loitered, strolled, or scooted about on neat little floating platforms. Nearly everyone wore tec-suits, or tec-dresses, or something in between, and it looked a bit like Christmas in a children's store. Garish, multi-coloured exchanges flashed between people everywhere. Tec-suits projected holographic images and rippled with all kinds of transformations in illumination, style and shape. I began to think I stood out more with my suit remaining neutral.

A guy with a self-important air at an expansive reception station waved in our direction as we entered. Simultaneously, a couple of serious-looking guys started towards us, apparently concentrating on urgent inner information. Their tec-suits glowed a uniform, officious blue.

'Master Gadhavi and companion please report to the reception desk,' announced a pleasant, sense-surround voice; and in the sudden stab of alarm which gripped me I failed to register if it had been in English or translated by the Portal.

'I am here by appointment,' said Ravi peevishly to the man behind the counter. They were speaking in Hindi it seemed, not that it made any difference.

'Of course Master Gadhavi,' said the man smoothly, 'but your companion is not, and he does not appear to have an implant.'

'Oh!' said Ravi, giving me a shocked look. But he made a quick recovery. 'He is from out of Central, but he is my friend. He is here to speak to the Senator regarding the subject of our meeting.'

'One moment,' said the man, an index finger suspended in the air like a baton. He spoke to himself for a few moments, and then beckoned imperiously with the said digit. Ravi appeared to participate in a conversation with the supercilious meeter-and-greeter and an invisible third party for some moments. The discussion was insistent and animated, and when it broke off each looked disapproving for apparently different reasons.

'The Senator says you may accompany me,' announced Ravi stiffly. 'All of this protocol is overcomplicated and unnecessary.'

The upholder of complicated protocols begged to differ, by his expression. But he said nothing, and we made our way over to a bank of elevators. Ravi requested a destination, and we were whisked away in bizarrely alternating horizontal and vertical trajectories. It seemed only moments before we were deposited into a luxuriously furnished waiting area. It contained an elegant secretary, her tec-suit arrayed in elegant saffron petals, who was also talking into the air. She nodded graciously at Ravi and waved us towards a large oval doorway, which obligingly parted itself along its vertical axis and retreated into the wall on either side.

We entered a spacious, elongated office with a fabulous city view many times the area of Ravi's apartment window. The huge transparent screen was tinted a golden brown against the morning sun, and bathed the entire space in a comfortable brass glow. A good looking Asian man: a somewhat more filled out and matured version of Ravi, smiled genially from behind a lavishly contoured desk of seamless transparent material. His tec-suit radiated a business-like dark grey glinting with impeccably illusive flecks of colour. He stood, his gaze flickering uncertainly over me, but waved an expansive arm to include us both in his greeting.

'Ravi my boy, how nice to see you,' he said grandly in English, 'and a very good morning to you sir. Please take a seat.'

'Thank you uncle,' said Ravi, 'this is my friend Richard. I am sorry for the disturbance below, but I did not see any harm in inviting him.'

'No harm, just unexpected,' said the Senator urbanely, 'we have to be a little careful with outsiders these days.'

Ravi bristled. 'Outsiders are just people who are suffering through no fault of their own,' he said.

'Quite so, quite so,' said the Senator smoothly, 'and I have invited you to my private office to discuss your views. The family is becoming concerned that your commendable interest in the welfare of the greater population is interfering with your work. I need hardly tell you and your, ah, friend, that our advances in dark-tec are the key to the problems that we face, and – '

'No, no!' interrupted Ravi. 'You do not understand – they do not understand that...'

A handful of luminous icons floated before me, and I knew something had changed in the room. I was somehow aware that certain electronic systems had been compromised, and as I tried to make sense of this, an Asian man slid into the office through a small internal door. His tec-suit broadcast the same intense blue as the security men in the lobby, and he held different, nasty-looking devices in either hand. We all stared at him in surprise. He stared at me too, apparently startled himself, before whipping the smaller gadget towards Ravi. There was a crackling hum, a glittering flash, and Ravi was flung twitching to the floor.

'No!' cried the Senator. 'Help: security!' He put a hand to his ear with a look of surprise, and turned to reach something on his desk. The intruder hesitated, the second device wavering between the elder man and me for a fraction of a second. Then he jerked it towards the senator. A wicked hiss spat across the room, and Ravi's uncle grunted in shock. Blood misted the air and he collapsed.

For the first time I consciously willed the time dilation effect into being. Everything slowed, and I was out of my seat and running as the man pivoted dreamily back towards me. The weapon swung around with somnolent grace. I knocked it upwards. It flew from his hand, and I punched him hard. The pain as my knuckles connected with his face shocked me back into real time, and I nursed my hand with a curse as he crashed into the corner. He looked stunned for a moment, and then his eyes searched desperately for his hardware. The weapon he had used on the senator had fallen several feet away, and I rushed to scoop it from the floor.

I seized it, and twisted to see the man regaining his feet. I had forgotten the other weapon. He levelled it at me, but it flashed feebly and did nothing. So I brandished my prize at him, wondering if it was as simple to use as it looked. He obviously thought so, because he backed off, glaring at me. He turned and ran for the same door he had emerged from. I hesitated, unwilling to shoot at an unarmed man, and he was gone.

'*Stupid,*' said the Mindworm. But it did not seem to have used the situation to try and gain control.

I kept the weapon trained on the critical door, glancing down to check how it might operate. I reflected for a moment, and then flipped the gun back towards the ceiling behind me and squeezed the trigger. It spat viciously, and a cloud of fragments descended. Now I could say he had fired it as I tackled him. I thought it might make my unlikely intervention more believable. Just as I wondered what to do next, I felt a sudden pulse from the Portal, accompanied by a faint tingling in my body. I shivered: I had felt much the same thing when Jacqueline's stepfather had disappeared from the Major's office in Gettysburg. Someone had just opened a doorway in space-time.

A chime sounded on the desk, and I heard the receptionist's tones. 'Senator, surveillance and communications have malfunctioned. Is everything all right?'

'Help – get help!' I called out. 'Ravi and the Senator have been shot!' A second later an alarm shrieked all around me.

Seconds ticked by, steeped in adrenaline and uncertainty. Both Ravi and the senator seemed semi-conscious, and were making incoherent sounds. I wanted to help them, but dared not leave the door unguarded. Finally I sensed muffled, forceful vibrations outside the big oval doorway. I hastily dropped the weapon, and stood with my hands held high. Even then it seemed touch and go when half a dozen security men burst in. They were bristling with weapons, mostly pointed at me, and seemed unhappy there was no one to shoot.

'What happened here?' one of them barked in English.

'A man came through this door,' I said, indicating it. 'He shot Ravi and the Senator, and left the same way.'

'Whose is this weapon?' he demanded, eyeing the one in the floor.

'His,' I said simply. 'I made him drop it. But he had another one.'

He looked unconvinced, but indicated swiftly to the others, and they took positions around the side door. They burst through it as more security personnel arrived, but it soon became apparent they had found nothing of interest. A medical team rushed in and quickly went to work on the casualties. Ravi seemed to be recovering gradually, and was helped onto a chair, shaking his head groggily. But the Senator was in a more serious condition, and they began concentrating all their attention on him. Ravi was questioned briefly, but could only say 'a man came through that door,' in a bemused voice. The Senator was rushed off on a gleaming medical trolley, and Ravi and I taken separately away. I passed through a blur of unfamiliar environments, accompanied by an efficient but unresponsive escort of three. We flew in a larger craft across the city, and I was deposited alone in a spacious but secure holding cell in an equally spacious and secure building.

Time passed slowly. I wondered how Ravi and the Senator were, and repeatedly played out events in my mind. The weapon used on Ravi seemed only meant to incapacitate. My own presence appeared to have been unanticipated. I wondered if there had been an intention to kidnap the Senator. I supposed he had been trying to call for help when he was shot. But if he was wanted alive, there had been no attempt to stop him with a warning. Then there was the sympathetic tug on the Portal. The man himself had not owned one: there had been no bright, mirrored recognition. Yet I was sure that someone had opened and closed a doorway.

There were too many unknowns to connect, and I soon began to consider how it might affect me instead. I was obviously due for a grilling, and they had some pretty advanced technology. I hoped they would not be able to detect the presence of the Portal. Or, it occurred to me with sudden dread, the Mindworm: they might believe I was some sort of programmed assassin. My ruminations did nothing for my peace of mind, and I tried to put them aside. I could only trust that the Portal would pull me out if things got too dicey. I chuckled bitterly to myself – I had certainly made some unexpected connections. I just hoped that something useful would come out of it all. It seemed a lot of trouble to go through for nothing.

They came for me after three or four hours. I was marched to the inevitable elevator and following that into a gleaming cell, which was encased in mirror-bright reflections from floor to ceiling. It was pretty much a perfect cube, but slight curves on its adjoining structural planes created tiny reflected distortions, and its surfaces were patterned into a jigsaw puzzle of smoothly adjoining sections, both curved and angular. I had no doubt that numerous persons and devices scrutinised everything that took place there. Rectangular sections of the bright, metallic floor rose smoothly upwards as we entered, arranging themselves in a fluid, logical sequence. The contours of a sleek, shiny seat and a desk took form, while opposite them a more sophisticated and technically mysterious seating appliance constructed itself. I had no doubt it was loaded with additional sensors and instruments, and was destined for me. If that wasn't enough, a circular section of the ceiling extended downwards a metre or so, and hovered over the super-chair like an inquisitive hair-drier.

I was placed in the chair. It was equipped with arm rests, no doubt to collect even more forms of data, and disconcertingly, the 'hair-drier' adjusted itself a little closer to the top of my head. The guards departed without speaking, and I was left alone with unpleasant memories of Mister McCreedy for company. I fervently hoped I wasn't about to face something like that again.

But when a man did enter the cube, I was surprised to like him on sight. His tec-suit appeared unresponsive like mine, and he seemed a relaxed, straightforward kind of guy. I tried to discount this initial impression of course, for he was clearly a professional. He took the seat behind the desk with practiced ease. Perhaps in his thirties, of average height and a little overweight, he had an amiable, open face, lined with a certain amount of experience. His expression was mild but his eyes were shrewd, and an unusual depth of perception lurked in their depths. I felt a little more comfortable, but remained uneasy. I could sense buzzing and tingling sensations in various parts of my body, and imagined that any anxiety or subterfuge would be highlighted in gratuitous detail.

A flash of concern about the Mindworm conjured a subtle inner response.

'*This machine will not detect my presence,*' the creature smirked, '*but if you allow me control I can mask any reactions you wish*'.

I ignored it irritably, and waited to see what would happen.

'Good afternoon,' my interrogator said in excellent English. 'My name is Inspector Chaudhri, and I am investigating the attempted murder of Senator Gadhavi this morning.'

I noted the 'attempted murder' with some relief. Aside from my natural wish for his health and welfare, his testimony would be vital in confirming my innocence.

'Is the Senator going to be all right?' I asked.

'He is seriously injured, and under sedation,' replied Inspector Chaudhri evenly. 'However, he did confirm that a fourth person entered his office and shot him.'

'Thank goodness,' I said in relief, 'I was afraid you wouldn't believe me.'

'There are a number of things I find hard to believe,' said the Inspector, 'and one of them is that your own and young Ravi's presence was a coincidence. The interference with the surveillance system and interpersonal communications is another puzzle.'

He gave me a hard look. 'Perhaps you would like to describe your version of events.'

I started to do so, describing my confrontation with the gunman fairly confidently, but gradually finding myself on weaker ground. I put my success in disarming the intruder down to luck, but faltered a little in recounting the lie. He raised a sceptical eyebrow, and asked why I had accompanied Ravi in the first place: who I was; how I knew him, and steadily backtracked into increasingly difficult territory. He regarded me gravely for a full minute after my vague fabrications had wavered into embarrassing silence. Finally he stood up.

'That will be all for now Mister Walton,' he said. 'I will want to speak to you again soon. Perhaps you will have remembered a little more about your past by then.'

I was taken to my cell, where an un-organic but extremely welcome meal was provided. I dozed fitfully on my bunk for several hours, after which I was awoken and returned to the bright interrogation cell. This time the Inspector was accompanied by an additional extruded chair and an apparent subordinate, who said nothing as I was taken once more through my story. They then both began firing questions at me about my personal history, with if anything a more disastrous performance on my part than before. I eventually became annoyed.

'My life has no bearing on this case at all,' I said in exasperation. 'I am just a wanderer. I have little interest in politics, not a lot in Ravi's *Living Earth* campaign, and none at all in assassinating people. Would you be happier if I had not tried to stop the attack?'

The subordinate continued to stare impassively at me, but I was surprised by a glint of humour in Inspector Chaudhri's eyes.

'No Mr Walton,' he said at length, 'we would not be happier. I am confident that you acted to disarm the assailant, although exactly how remains uncertain. A number of other questions also remain unanswered. I am afraid you must continue as our guest for a little longer.'

I was returned to my cell for a second time, where I spent time brooding over my fate as the plaything of a wayward hi-tec dog collar, which took me for walkies through space-time instead of the other way around. I had another meal and slept restlessly through the night. Breakfast consisted of an unidentifiable but palatable cooked vegetable dish, and I braced myself for another round of questions for which I had no answers. It was two or three hours before that time arrived, and I set off resignedly with my escort. This time the Inspector entered the cube at the same time that I did, and only a single chair remained facing my own hi-tec interrogation model. We took our respective seats, and he regarded me with a half-smile before he began to talk.

'Well Mister Walton, your friend Ravi has been very active on your behalf, and you are no doubt aware that his family has a great deal of influence in Central. Senator Gadhavi has also been speaking of you in glowing terms. I am inclined to believe that you played no sinister part in his attempted assassination, but there remain some extremely puzzling aspects to this case. You are clearly holding back a great deal about yourself, and the reason for your presence here in India.'

He paused and eyed me significantly. 'I suspect that you will shortly be released. However, a number of things have happened in this city of late which I am uneasy about, and until I know more I must include your appearance among them. I will be keeping an eye on you of course, but I would like you to review some profiles for me while you are here. I would be grateful if you would identify anyone you recognise. But your reactions will be closely monitored, and it will do no good to withhold information.'

A small square section of celling extended itself downwards between the Inspector and myself; suspended like a gleaming, rectangular stalactite. It emitted an elusive vibration, felt rather than heard, and the startlingly lifelike hologram of a man shimmered into existence in the air in front of me. He looked unpleasant, but was a stranger, and so was the person who followed. I relaxed a little, and watched a succession of men and women replace each other every few seconds. The Inspector watched with an undoubtedly deceptive, lazy eye until the images stopped.

'Good,' he said, 'it clears the air a little that you do not know these people. There are one or two more before we finish. These will be surveillance images rather than profiles.'

A less well-defined series of holo-images appeared, which included extraneous background detail – a man leaning against a wall, two men in a conversation at a table, a woman speaking to someone at a reception desk. I began to relax again and was caught completely off guard. Flags must have gone up from every sensor in the room: for there was Alex in a tec-suit. She was staring straight at me, crouched purposefully on a balcony.

'Well now, how interesting,' murmured the Inspector, 'someone else with no chip, and a habit of being at the right place at the right time.'

'Wh – what do you mean?' I stammered. I felt I had been hit by an express train.

'Why don't you tell me, as you obviously know her,' he suggested.

'I do know her,' I faltered, 'that is, I have met her. But I don't know who she is.'

The inspector raised a sceptical eyebrow. 'Would you care to elaborate?'

I thought furiously. 'I met her for only a few minutes.'

'It must have been a memorable encounter,' he commented drily. 'May I ask where and when this was?'

'In London, err . . . some months ago.'

'I see,' he said, prompting me gently, 'and this was significant because . . .?'

'She warned me that some nasty characters meant me harm.'

'Was she correct?'

'Yes.'

'Did she assist you with this problem?'

'No. Well, maybe she did, someone did.'

'But essentially she disappeared?'

'Yes.'

'Did you discover who these 'nasty characters' were?'

'No.'

'But you were not harmed?'

'No, I escaped them. I have been … wandering ever since.'

He regarded me silently for a while.

'Well,' he said finally, 'you appear to be telling the truth as far as it goes. But there is always so much more you are not saying.'

'I know nothing about her presence here,' I said, and then blurted 'but I would like to know why she was here, what she was doing. Can you tell me anything?'

He smiled a little sadly, as if acknowledging that my desperation was genuine.

'I cannot disclose operational information,' he said, 'but I also know little about her. This surveillance Holo was taken about six months ago.'

He joined his palms as if in prayer, and examined his finger-tips thoughtfully.

'I have reason to be thankful to this young lady myself,' he mused, 'but I don't like mysteries.' His eyes twinkled, 'mysteries I cannot solve, that is. But this is one more piece of the puzzle.'

I smiled reluctantly, 'for me too.'

He regarded me for a moment longer, as if considering whether he should say more. Then he stood up suddenly.

'I thank you for your cooperation Mister Walton, such as it has been. I will say goodbye only for the present, as I have a feeling we will meet again. You will be returned to your cell, but it should not be for long.'

He offered his hand and I shook it. I felt he was a good man. I was banged up again for the rest of the afternoon. Time crawled sluggishly, despite the relief I felt at my impending release. Then Security men arrived: there were a few formalities, and life recommenced. It seemed no time at all before Ravi was bounding up to me with his face alight with pleasure.

'I am so happy you have been released!' he exclaimed, 'it was infamous that you were arrested. But even I was questioned. What a thing to happen! Guru-ji must have foreseen it. It was so important for you to be there: you were the hero of the hour!' His eyes darkened. 'But they are not saying it. There is a security clamp-down. They are saying only that an assassination attempt was prevented, and everyone will think it was thanks to them. It is very unfair.'

'I don't care what they say Ravi,' I said wearily. 'I am just glad to get out of there.'

'Yes but it would be a chance to say that *Living Earth...*' he caught my eye and smiled sheepishly. 'I am sorry Richard. We should go home and rest.'

We made the short journey back in silence. Ravi nobly restrained himself from speaking, and I munched sparingly at an unidentifiable but aesthetically arranged meal he had prepared. I had a long soak in the apartment's enormous circular Jacuzzi, which also enveloped me in a mysterious, electromagnetic buzzing sensation that relaxed me considerably. I begged off talking about the events of the past couple of days until morning. I wanted to wind down after the attack and the ensuing interrogation, and my mind was full of the image of Alex on the balcony. Ravi, briefly nonplussed, hit on the idea of playing me choice selections from his Indian classical music collection, which he assured me would become a mainstay of *Living Earth* culture in the future. This suited me fine, and I allowed the abstract melodies to soothe me while I digested the first real clue in my hunt for Alex. I did not stay up late, and dreamed of Alex all night.

I woke early next morning, and wandered into the living area to find Ravi talking to the house mind in a considered, formal manner.

'Ah Richard!' he cried, 'Are you feeling better? I was just updating my diary: I am keeping a journal of the rise of *Living Earth*. Would you like some tea?'

I couldn't help smiling. We sipped tea, and finally compared notes about the events of the past two days. Ravi knew a great deal more than I did. Much had apparently been wheedled out of various security sources by members of his extended family.

'They used a horrible weapon on my poor uncle,' he said, 'it fires high velocity flechettes. Luckily he was some distance away, and had turned towards the intercom. The damage was mostly in the shoulder area, but it was extensive. How fortunate that he missed you when you tackled him. You were very lucky – and courageous.'

'I guess I didn't have time to think,' I said evasively. 'But how come he didn't use it on you?'

'That is one of the strange things about it all,' said Ravi, 'although naturally I am relieved he didn't.' He shuddered. 'The Rayser was bad enough.'

'It is not lethal?' I asked.

'Not unless you have a serious heart problem. It creates an ionised path for the charge to paralyse you. The pain was terrible, and I lost all control.'

'It didn't work on me,' I said. 'He tried to use it when I picked up the other weapon.'

'It would not have had time to recharge,' said Ravi. 'Thank goodness you were there, that is all I can say.'

'What does security think?'

'They are unsure about me as I am, err, unconventional, and they are especially unsure about you. But everything seems to back up our story, except that they have no surveillance record of the intruder, no DNA or fingerprints except yours on the gun, and no idea how he got in and out of the building.'

'No idea at all?'

'There is only a small bedroom suite and a washroom through that door. There are service ducts above the ceiling, but the access panels were in place. It's a real mystery.'

It was an obvious mystery to me, but I said nothing.

'What do your family think?'

'They think it was a political attack on us all, an attempt to assassinate my uncle and blame it on me,' said Ravi. 'If the assassin had killed my uncle, and left the gun in my hand the circumstantial evidence would have been overwhelming.'

'– And the gunman an apparent figment of your imagination?'

'Yes,' he agreed.

'What about the purpose of your visit to your uncle?'

'What do you mean?' he asked.

'It could have been an attack on *Living Earth*.' I wasn't quite sure where I was going with this, but I felt a sudden tingling in my spine.

Ravi looked unconvinced.

'You think? You mean: to stop me speaking to my Uncle … '

'No, to portray you as a *Living Earth* fanatic who had murdered him.'

His eyes went wide. 'I had not thought of that,' he said, grimacing in bemusement. 'Could people be so wicked? But why would they care? It is a small movement, and few take us seriously.'

'I don't know, it's just a possibility.' I said. But I was thinking that someone from the future might have a reason.

Ravi's face suddenly lit up. 'Guru-ji must have known!' Then he looked unhappy again. 'There are people, even among my own relations, who are delving into bad things. They talk about hi-tec solving the world's problems, but all they want is to preserve their own status and lifestyle. They are playing with their subliminal hypnotics and their Mindworms . . .'

I went cold all over. 'Ravi,' I choked: 'they are working with Mindworms?'

He looked stricken. 'I should not have said! It is secret family stuff – Richard, you will not speak of this?' He paused suddenly and looked strangely at me, his face full of horror. 'Where have you heard about Mindworms?' he asked hoarsely.

I made a decision. 'Ravi,' I said carefully, taking him by the shoulders. 'It is I who has to ask you not to speak to anyone, or at least to be very discreet. I have been infected with a Mindworm, and I am trying to find someone to help me.'

He stared at me in alarm 'You mean they are implementing them? Who did this?' He looked searchingly into my eyes, uncertainty and suspicion clouding his normally sunny countenance. 'How do I know you are telling the truth? This whole thing might be a plan to infiltrate the Mindworm program! My family are always warning me I am too trusting, and I thought...' Tears sprang into his eyes.

'Ravi,' I reminded him gently, 'it was your Guru-ji who asked you to speak to me. I am just a traveller: someone looking for help.'

He thought about it. 'Yes,' he said doubtfully, 'but...you really have a Mindworm? Is it malicious? Does it... control you?'

'No,' I laughed bitterly, 'although it would like to. It keeps trying to influence my feelings and moods. I am told it has been programmed to degrade my personality, make me less effective in everything I do.'

'But what is the purpose of that?' asked Ravi in bewilderment.

'I don't know – maybe an experiment?' I suggested. I didn't want to tell him the whole story. I was getting the weird feeling that something significant was happening: that I was walking through a temporal minefield of cause and effect.

'You say it is programmed to degrade your personality,' said Ravi. 'Who told you that: was it someone in Central?'

'No, in London.'

'Stansted City? But they are supposed to be some way behind our tec level, and they do not have our resources.'

I decided to provide a bit more of the truth. I suspected his family would find out about Alex after my interrogation anyway.

'I didn't say the Mindworm came from there. I was just told about it there.'

'Who told you?'

'A girl I had never seen before.'

'What? She just came up and told you just like that?'

'Yes. She said that I had been infected with a Mindworm, and that people were watching me. She warned me to get away, and she told me to seek help.'

'Is that why you are wandering?'

'Yes.'

'And you have never seen her since?'

'Not until yesterday. I recognised her in a surveillance Holo the security Inspector showed me.'

'Oh my goodness,' breathed Ravi, 'this is unbelievable.'

He sat with his head in his hands for a few moments.

'That is why I was so pleased to discover *Living Earth,*' he said. 'I hate the tec race: all the secrets and hypocrisy and manipulation.' He sighed. 'I am sorry Richard. You are right: Guru-ji had faith in you, and I should not have doubted you. I must trust that the ego phase of evolution will fall away, and our greatness will shine in the future.'

He sat, uncharacteristically solemn for a moment or two more. 'I think I may be able to help you,' he said. 'But they are not going to like it.'

Chapter 15

RAVI LEFT THE apartment almost immediately. 'I am not sure how long I'll be,' he said. 'Just make yourself at home. Leela will help you with anything you need.'

Leela was the house-mind. I asked to view documentaries about recent history, and sat fascinated as a ceiling projector displayed panoramic Holo-images of slow-motion disaster on an epic scale. Two hours went by before sounds of arrival filtered in from the car-port. Two serious looking Asian guys accompanied Ravi, both a little older but with a recognisable family resemblance. There was a marked increase in the almost constant ripples of déjà vu I was feeling when they arrived. He introduced them as distant cousins of some sort, while they stared fixedly at me with an intense, almost proprietary air. We all sat down, and they launched into a barrage of questions without any preliminaries at all. I was unsure exactly what their investigation might reveal, but I tried to refer mainly to direct interactions with the Mindworm, and kept supplementary background detail to a minimum.

The Mindworm itself appeared wrong-footed by the situation. It seemed to have a curious mixture of affinity and reservation towards these men. They were stunned by my descriptions of direct interaction with the creature's mentality, and by its manipulation of my faculties. We had been speaking for only twenty minutes or so when they sat back, seemingly both excited and alarmed by my revelations.

'You were right about this Ravi,' said one. 'It seems our secret project is not so secret after all. If Mr Walton's claims are true, someone is ahead of us in a number of respects. We must take him back to the laboratory.'

My interrogators had arrived in a separate sky car, and Ravi and I followed them on a journey permeated by constant and confusing waves of déjà vu. It was certainly a surreal and fatalistic trip: a pivotal moment playing out against the glittering backdrop of Central, that stunning anachronism of the age of plenty.

'You have certainly stirred things up,' Ravi said. 'They didn't want to believe me. It helped a lot that you intervened in the attack on the Senator, but they were very upset that I had spoken to an outsider about the program. They are singing a different tune now though.'

We landed on the roof of a relatively modest establishment, six stories spread over a couple of thousand square yards or so. But it was isolated by a high surrounding wall, and its security arrangements were impeccable. I was scanned, fingerprinted, DNA sampled and obliged to shower; and my tec-suit exchanged for a simple white tunic and an identity badge before I could enter the main complex. Once beyond these preliminaries, it became apparent that the facility extended many floors below ground. Security guards were assigned to me, and I felt I was entering a secretive world where an unsanctioned exit was off the agenda. I began to seriously wonder if I had done the right thing.

We stepped from an elevator into an immaculate laboratory containing another half a dozen of Ravi's partial clones, including two women with their own imprint of the family features. All wore the ubiquitous white tunics, and shared similar expressions of concern and anticipation. The place also contained a few close relations of Inspector Chaudhri's technically mysterious metallic chairs, and I experienced a certain amount of anxiety at the sight of them. But I derived some satisfaction from the flickers of uncertainly I sensed from the Mindworm. It seemed curiously subdued: not comfortable with the situation at all. I was introduced or re-introduced to Ravi's relations, several of whom I had problems telling apart, and we got down to another question and answer session. Waves of déjà vu resonated within me. This time, however, I had some questions of my own. I felt a surge of anger quite separate from any manipulation by the creature inside me.

'What is the purpose of Mindworm technology?' I demanded bluntly, 'why do you want to control people in this way?'

Shocked looks and denials abounded. Of course this was not intended: it was to aid learning; to supplement memory; to aid language and technical skills; to counter psychotic conditions and addictions; to curb violent tendencies. Like any technology, it could be misused destructively: there was a need to study the potentials in order to develop countermeasures, etcetera – the usual story.

'*Mindworm* is a derogatory term used by one or two cynics among us,' explained one of them. 'We prefer the term 'cybernetic enhancement'.

Essentially it is a quantum computer with self programming and interactive biological capabilities. It is small enough to migrate within the brain and construct links between critical neural pathways, transferring information and stimulating, or curbing particular behaviour patterns.'

'Well the creature migrating about in my brain doesn't seem to be enhancing anything except my testosterone level,' I said grumpily.

They tittered politely, and began to run me through some of the same accounts I had given the original two. They all seemed fascinated by the direct interactions I described with the Mindworm; and extremely curious about the ways it had tried to influence me, and my efforts to resist it. I continued to edit the space-time locations from these confrontations, hoping the unlikely truth would not come out in the course of their investigation. Civil war conflicts and pirates were portrayed as local power squabbles and bandits encountered in my travels. I desperately wanted to get rid of the wretched thing, and was prepared to risk much to achieve it.

Finally they were ready to carry out a preliminary search with complex hardware: ultra-high definition scanning at microscopic levels. I got uneasily into one of the elaborate chairs, and my head was clamped into immobility. A bulbous super-scanner was manoeuvred over me, and the hunt began. It took a while before the Mindworm was cornered. There was a sudden, excited exclamation, much muttered astonishment, and the room seemed to undulate with a powerful pulse of déjà vu.

'*Oops,*' I thought. I had the distinct sense that something significant had happened, and I could only hope it was for the best. But the examination gradually became tedious. I felt the Mindworm react to various attempts to establish connections with it, sometimes with apparent cooperation, and at others with spikes of resentment and defiance. But I was out of the loop, unable to see the visuals from their complex instrumentation. My input consisted mainly of grunts: 'try this' or 'we need another link' from those around me.

'It's armoured!' someone exclaimed at one point, as I felt a particularly aggressive response, but I had little idea what it meant.

Next came a sudden gasp from one of the women. 'I am detecting some kind of exotic dimensional activity associated with the device. What can that mean?' But only puzzled murmurs answered her. For a while I was worried they might be detecting the Portal, but they seemed completely oblivious of its existence.

'Does he understand Hindi?' asked one of them suddenly.

'I do not believe so, perhaps a few words,' Ravi answered.

'Yes, there are neural responses,' observed someone else, 'perhaps the cyberbot is translating.'

'Do you understand what we are saying, Richard?' asked Ravi in English.

There was too much at stake to tell the truth. 'No,' I improvised, 'but I think the Mindworm understands it. I feel a kind of familiarity about the words.'

'It has established pathways everywhere,' commented another, still speaking in Hindi, 'perhaps it is some kind of feedback.'

'I don't understand this,' the first speaker continued in Hindi. 'These are some of our codes, but they have more advanced processes built onto them, and there are some levels I can't access at all.'

'Someone has been stealing our work?' asked another.

'Someone has developed it beyond our present capability, and turned it into a weapon,' replied the first. 'I don't see any benign functions programmed at all.'

'But if it is so powerful, how has he been able to resist it for so long?'

'That's the strange thing: it does not seem configured to take outright control. It may be designed to subvert the personality incrementally.'

'An experiment, perhaps?'

'Possibly, but the cyberbot's purpose may have been compromised when its existence was revealed to the subject – to some extent anyway.'

'But how was it revealed? Why would the subject believe a stranger? It must have sounded a wild tale.'

'I don't know, we will have to interrogate him further. Perhaps the female carried equipment which exposed it somehow.'

'We should be able to interrogate the cyberbot directly.'

'We can't at the moment. It responds to some lower level code, but we are locked out of its higher functions. It is very robustly protected.'

'Err, excuse me guys,' I said, feeling it was time I intervened, 'do you mind telling me what's going on?'

'Please excuse us Mister Walton,' the designated spokesman said smoothly in English. 'We are examining the cybernetic augmentation device. It has some features that are unfamiliar to us, and we are trying to identify them.'

'But can you get it out?' I asked impatiently.

'We are not at that stage yet. But we would very much like to remove it, I assure you.'

'I bet you would,' I thought. I was pretty sure by then that the Mindworm had originated from some future time. Its current existence obviously represented a considerable leap forward in their work. Yet it did not seem to typify a straightforward linear advance of their ambitions. Either they were destined to become rather twisted, or someone in the future had hijacked their aspirations, and developed them for their own use.

'This is serious,' the man said, reverting to Hindi, 'someone has gained access to our work, and is ahead of us in many respects. Not only ahead, but developing a destructive weapon. We must learn everything we can from it.'

'Anil,' said Ravi, also speaking in Hindi. 'All Richard wants is for you to extract this horrible thing. Then you can examine it to your heart's content.'

'We will certainly try,' came the reply, 'but it has incorporated itself deeply into the neural pathways. In the meantime we are pulling all the information from it that we can.'

I did not like the sound of that, and willed them with all my might to find a way of making the wretched creature compliant. They spared no pains in their attempts to do so, and continued for what seemed an age before calling a halt.

'We are all in need of a break Mr Walton,' said Anil finally in English. 'We have learned quite a lot, and we need to run the data through some computer simulations before proceeding further.'

I was only too happy to comply, and got up wearily from my latest torture chair. Ravi and I were escorted to a cafeteria on a higher floor, where I enjoyed my tastiest meal in a while.

'What terrible food this is,' Ravi remarked, 'how I would love some nice fresh vegetables.'

'What do you think is going to happen?' I asked, eating rapidly.

'I don't know,' said Ravi unhappily. 'It is shocking that this Mindworm is so sophisticated. I doubt it was created in Stansted City. Houston Park or Dallas Towers might have the resources. It may even be one of the Siberian or Chinese enclaves. But someone with monstrous intentions seems to have gained access to our program.'

'Well, at least you have discovered what is going on,' I said. 'How long do you think it will be before they can try to remove it?'

'Not for a while,' said Ravi, 'the computer analysis will take some time. It would probably be an idea to get some rest.'

I felt pretty tired, and he organised a small room with a bed and bathroom facilities where I could lie down. He went off to talk to his kin, and I slept deeply for an hour or so, dreaming complicated Mindworm dreams. I awoke to lie staring at the ceiling for a while, wondering what was going to happen next. Ravi looked in a little later, and we returned to the cafeteria for a coffee.

'Any news?' I asked.

'Yes: they are nearly ready for some further investigation, but it is too soon to talk about extracting it,' he said. 'There is some news about the assassination attempt as well. They have discovered false fixings on one of the service duct hatchways next to the Senators office, and found the Rayser dropped some distance inside. There are a number of possible escape routes from there. So at least we know how he got in and out.'

'Hmm,' I grunted. Either that or someone had provided the clues after the fact. I couldn't help remembering Jeremiah heaving the chair through the Major's office window. '*A plausible escape route,*' he had said.

All too soon I was back in the torture chair, and events proceeded much as they had before. There were more muttered suggestions and experimental procedures, exclamations of surprise or dismay, and occasional gasps of excitement. Time dragged on. Any sense I had of the Mindworm drained steadily away, until I was able to detect only the faintest, occasional reactions from it. When they stopped work at last I was surprised to find it was late evening. I felt utterly exhausted, and only too glad of their suggestion that I sleep again while they ran another round of analysis and tests. I forced down some food and crawled into my designated bed with only a desire for oblivion on my mind, and slept right through the night without waking. Ravi stayed in the complex too, and woke me next morning.

'They finished running the programs only a few hours ago,' he said. 'They are getting a little sleep now, but want to be up to run some new checks in about an hour. Come and have some breakfast.'

Much to my disappointment Ravi had procured some fresh fruit for us to eat, and I munched through it with as much enthusiasm as I could muster. Back in the chair I looked upon the shattered features of the lab team with a certain amount of satisfaction. But an eager light burned in their eyes despite their weariness, and they were raring to go. We plunged into another session, had a short break and then went on until lunchtime. I was really beginning to feel I had had enough by then, but Anil smiled encouragingly, blinking away his own exhaustion.

'I think we need to run only one more series of tests to be in a position to start the extraction process,' he said.

That cheered me up a lot, and I set off to the canteen with Ravi in a better frame of mind. I even felt sufficiently up-beat to insist on an unhealthy, appetising meal.

'I should make allowances for the stress you are under,' he said solicitously, after a moment's reflection. 'That is the problem: we eat bad things that taste good to compensate for our poor quality of life.'

The final computer analysis took longer than expected. Some kind of hiccup required more poking about in the chair, and they wanted to go back over some of my experiences with the Mindworm before the tests could be resumed. I spent quite a lot of time drinking tea in the canteen with Ravi, and it was late afternoon before the final session began. This time I took my place in the chair with great anticipation. I could hardly believe I might be getting rid of the Mindworm.

'We have established motor control of the cyberbot, and shut down most of its core functions,' said Anil. 'We are now disconnecting its neural network, and will attempt to manoeuvre it via the auditory nerve into the auditory canal, and out through the ear.'

'Sounds gruesome –' I began. But an instant later I was lost in an explosion of all-consuming agony. I was only dimly aware of my body thrashing in the chair, and barely recognised the distant screaming as my own. Shocked exclamations and urgent activity around me seemed equally disjointed and meaningless, until everything went white and I was gone.

'Richard... Richard!' A voice was calling me, and I stared stupidly into Ravi's anxious face.

'Well, that went well,' I croaked, as memory trickled back.

'Thank goodness,' said Ravi, 'we thought your heart would stop.'

'I thought my head would blow off,' I groaned, 'what happened?'

'You have been unconscious for some time,' said Ravi, 'but your vital signs seem normal now.'

'I am afraid the cyberbot is more resilient than we expected,' said Anil contritely. 'It seems to have auxiliary systems which overrode some of our programming. It re-established enough control of its neural network to overload the pain receptors in your brain.'

'Tricky little blighter,' I quipped, with a light-heartedness I did not feel. I could not bear the thought of being permanently haunted by the creature. 'So what's the prognosis?'

'I'm afraid we cannot remove it at the present time. We need to build models using the data we have accumulated, and carry out a lot of experiments. I really do not know how long it will take.'

'Have you negated its capabilities?' I asked.

'Again, without further study I cannot say. It may even have deliberately destroyed its higher functions. We will need to work with you over an extended period. However, its capabilities have certainly been degraded. It may be able to repair itself, but to what extent it would succeed, and how long that might take remains unknown. I believe its more complex processes will remain inoperative, at least for the time being.'

I digested this slowly. I couldn't hang about as their guinea pig in Central indefinitely. I had to get back to the others, and I had to find Alex. I wondered if they would try to confine me. I would escape sooner or later of course, but doing so unobtrusively might be awkward.

'So am I free to go?' I asked.

There was an awkward silence. 'We do need to work with you,' said Anil slowly. 'We can offer you excellent accommodation here in Central, everything you need.'

'I would certainly be happy to spend time here, and to return from time to time,' I said, 'but I have my own life to lead and my own answers to find. I have friends that depend on me. I need to be free.'

They all looked worried. 'There are still many unknowns regarding the capabilities of the cyberbot,' said Anil, 'we would be very concerned at such technology being at large in the world. There is also your own safety to consider. You may be reacquired by the agents behind this travesty, and they may gain information about our own program from you.'

'This technology is already at large in the world,' broke in Ravi angrily. 'Hasn't Richard got enough problems, without taking away his freedom? He is suffering partly because of things we ourselves have done, and such agents obviously already know of our program. Remember: he came to us, and has provided us with critical information.'

His extended family seemed a little chastened by his outburst.

'Believe me Mister Walton; we have no wish to make things more difficult for you than they already are,' said Anil after a difficult silence. 'Perhaps you would like to rest, or take some refreshments in the restaurant? We will have to discuss this.'

Ravi remained for the conference, and I was escorted by security to enjoy some more illicitly tasty goodies away from his eagle eye. He joined me after thirty minutes or so, just as I finished licking the remaining evidence of some fancy chocolate éclairs from my lips. He looked suspiciously at the crumbs on my plate.

'Well?' I asked, before he could say anything about food.

'Much as you might expect,' he said with a sigh. 'Actually it is not so much them I am worried about as the politicians – when they get involved we will have security all over us. Luckily the lab team are so absorbed with these new revelations that they haven't really talked to anyone else yet.'

'So I am not under arrest?'

'No,' he said, giving me a significant glance and a minute shake of his head. 'They are just going to give you a medical check-up, and then I am taking you home. I said I would bring you back in the morning.'

I sensed something more behind his words, and shrugged casually. 'OK,' I said.

They gave me the physical all clear, and I travelled back with Ravi in his sky car. We sat silently of an unspoken accord. The novelty of the extraordinary city was not what it was: a menacing undercurrent now seemed to lurk behind the glittering façade. Once docked in the carport, Ravi skipped through to the apartment.

'Hi Leela,' he called jauntily, 'may the *Living Earth* enrich your life!'

'Thank you for your kind wishes, Ravi. My current level of enrichment is quite satisfactory,' responded the musical voice of the house-mind.

'Excellent!' said Ravi, turning to me with a smile. 'No one is listening in, or has attempted to tamper with Leela: we can talk.'

'But she said the 'enriching your life' thing when I first came here,' I said.

'She just does that to humour me,' he explained, 'it's only a code when I say it.'

'OK, so what's up?' I asked.

'I don't think we can count on things remaining this casual for long,' he said seriously. 'Luckily the family political department are worrying about their own skins after the assassination attempt. They are not up to speed with the developments in the lab: and those in the lab are too excited and exhausted think of anything else. But once they all get together, I think you are going to become a bird in a gilded cage.'

'So I should leave now?'

'Yes, but it is not as simple as that. There will be security sub-routines monitoring us; it is just not yet a high status alert.'

'Which means what?'

'They will be tracking my chip and my sky car's ID,' he said. 'You don't have a chip – yet. I am thinking of asking a friend in the building if she would give you a lift out of Central. But I am worried about your well-being. You said your belongings were stolen. Have you any means of finance? I cannot use my own credit, it would be traced.'

'Don't worry, I can look after myself,' I said, touched by everything he was trying to do for me. 'Will you get into trouble?'

'I will just claim that you disappeared. Nothing much will happen to me. I may be scolded a little by the family, but that would be nothing unusual. After all, you are not a criminal, and you have been of great service to them. What concerns me more is that I have not spoken sufficiently about *Living Earth*, as Guru-ji asked.'

I grinned. 'You have spoken quite a lot,' I assured him, 'and who knows, maybe all these other things were part of his plan too.'

Ravi looked taken aback, and then beamed delightedly. 'Do you think so?' he exclaimed.

I laughed. 'I have no idea,' I admitted, 'but it has certainly been a pleasure to know you.'

'Also from my side,' he said earnestly. 'I hope we will meet again, and you will come to fully appreciate Guru-ji's vision.'

'Sure,' I smiled, 'and I may well see you again. It is not all over with the Mindworm yet, after all.'

'Where will you go – back the district where I met you?'

'Yes, anywhere around there,' I agreed. It made little difference to me really, either the Portal would activate or it wouldn't. 'How will I get to your friend? Can you contact her without being traced?'

'The house-minds will communicate,' he said, 'they love intrigue, and guard their networks jealously. There will be nothing obvious for security to spot. Leela will guide you through the tower via a discrete ear-piece. It will take only a few minutes of travel.'

I changed back into my original clothes, and we had a farewell cup of his excellent if over-plentiful tea. I shook his hand. 'Thank you for everything,' I said, and he gave me a heartfelt hug.

The minutes of travel seemed to take a while, as I was hurtled in vertical and horizontal directions in several different elevators.

'This will confuse them,' chuckled Leela in my ear, guiding me step by step to another apartment door geographically remote from Ravi's home on the topmost levels. I was expected. The entrance door slid open before I reached it, and a sweet young Asian lady beckoned me inside with a mischievous look.

'Hello, I am Neeta,' she giggled in English. 'You must be Ravi's mysterious friend. Goodness knows what he is up to this time.'

I felt a little uncomfortable, and she gave me a candid glance. 'Don't worry: I am happy to do this for him. He is an excellent person despite his obsession with *Living Earth!* He has been very kind to me.'

'You know where we are going?' I asked.

'Yes of course,' she smiled, 'we will be on our way in a moment.'

Her sky car was not as flashy as Ravi's, but it was nimble and smooth, and we soon joined the fleets of vehicles navigating Central's airways. I kept my head averted when drones flew near, but they seemed unconcerned. We skimmed out of the city at roughly the same time of day as I had entered, when it looked at its most impressive. The last red-gold rays of the sun played upon its dreaming contours, and its extravagant luminescence was just beginning to shimmer in the dusk. But its illusion of permanence and grandeur was rapidly left behind, and we were soon suspended over a sea of decay and disrepair once more. A few lights gleamed fitfully below us as diesel generators laboured into life. Neeta seemed sombre. She glanced down at the grim reality beneath us, and back at me.

'At least Ravi cares about all this,' she said softly.

We touched down on a low hill close to my original point of arrival. There was little visible habitation on its slopes, and it seemed preferable to descending among a bunch of dispossessed people in the dark.

'Are you sure you will be all right?' asked Neeta, peering doubtfully out into the encroaching gloom.

'Yes, I'll be fine,' I said, although my certainty was hardly rock-solid. I jumped out and her craft rose into the air, swiftly disappearing into the growing darkness. I stood alone, feeling exposed and tired. The deepening nightfall seemed oppressive, and the locale alien and intimidating.

'OK,' I said to the Portal, 'I guess it's time for you to do your stuff.' And I was genuinely surprised when it did.

The luminous icons looked extraordinary against the night sky, beautiful and potent. But I sensed something familiar about them too: an intuitive recognition of significance and meaning. They were coordinates, many of them, I realised. I wanted to get back to Billy and Charles: to try and get at least a few more things worked out before being dragged off into the blue again. Some of the icons reminded me of home – at least they seemed to. I felt the reality of space-time dissolving, the energy vibrating through my being. *'I had better be going where I think I am,'* I thought. And I was. I emerged from the inexplicable ocean of power into a bright sky that hurt my eyes, and the garden of our new home beneath my feet. I felt a wave of relief. I had done it. Or at least, I thought in mild annoyance...it had happened.

It was late morning by the angle of the sun. I was close to the back door, and walked towards it wearily, twisting the handle and throwing it open with a sigh.

An Asian girl with pleasant features and an amiable manner looked around from the kitchen sink. She was momentarily disconcerted, but quickly recovered.

'Ah,' she said, 'you must be Richard. They said you might turn up.'

I gaped back at her in shock and surprise. Seeing an Indian girl here in the house seemed surreal after everything I had just been through. For a moment I wondered if I had come back to a different reality.

'Who are you?' I asked stupidly.

'Priya,' she said sunnily. 'I'm the home help.'

'The what?' I was completely confused.

'Well, the home everything,' she said rolling her eyes. 'You should have seen the place when I first started.'

'Richard! Wonderful, you're back!' exclaimed Charles, hurrying into the kitchen, 'I thought I heard your voice.'

'I see we have a home help,' I said pointedly.

'Yes, Yes, Priya has been marvellous,' he said cheerfully, 'I don't know what we would have done without her.'

'I am sure she is excellent,' I said stiffly, 'but shouldn't we have discussed something like this?'

'We had to do something,' retorted Charles, 'it was getting impossible.'

'Couldn't you have waited until I came back?' I demanded.

'We didn't know how long you'd be,' he said indignantly.

'Well how long have I been?' I asked irritably.

There was a muffled explosion of laughter from Priya, swiftly repressed.

'Sorry,' she said.

'I think we should continue this conversation elsewhere,' I said warily. 'I apologise Priya. I shouldn't be talking like this in front of you. I'm sure your services have been greatly appreciated.'

There was a pounding down the stairs, and Billy dashed into the room.

'Mr – Richard, by all that's holy, you're back!' he boomed, grinning from ear to ear.

The twins crashed in after him.

'I told you it be Uncle Richard!' cried Nathaniel.

'Did you come through a magic door?' asked Aurelia breathlessly.

'Now Aurelia,' said Charles sternly, 'what did I say about magic doors?'

'Oh!' said Aurelia, looking stricken. 'You said: don't talk about them in front of Aunty Priya.'

'No!' exclaimed Charles crossly. 'I mean, yes! But that means: don't talk about not talking about them in front of Aunty Priya either!'

'Aunty Priya?' I asked in bewilderment.

'Well I am a kind of honorary Aunty,' explained Priya. 'It's quite normal in my culture, and as my role here is somewhat ambiguous, it seemed the easiest thing.'

'I'm getting a headache,' I complained. 'Charles, come out into the garden and talk to me for a minute.'

I made my way outside, annoyed and confused. 'What on earth have you done Charles?' I demanded. 'You have brought a complete stranger into the house!'

'It's all very well for you to talk,' said Charles, 'you weren't left here with those two child-sized tornadoes, and Billy isn't much better sometimes. I was going out of my mind!'

'Well I didn't plan on going off, it just happened!' I said. 'How long has it been anyway?'

'Nearly two months!' he said hotly. 'I said it would be difficult, but I didn't realise how bad it would be. You have to watch them every moment – and they always want something!'

'OK, OK,' I said, 'maybe it was tough. But what does she know? What have you told her? What on earth does she think about you and Billy and the kids?'

'Well I thought about saying we were a gay couple,' said Charles, 'but when I tried to explain it to Billy he went ballistic.'

I couldn't help laughing. 'Yes I suppose he would,' I said. 'So what did you do, advertise for Mary Poppins?'

'Well sort of,' he said a little sheepishly. 'I advertised for a temporary 'Person Friday' to help out in an unconventional family situation.'

'And what did you say the situation was?' I asked curiously.

'I didn't!' he said triumphantly. 'That was the clever part! I just said we needed someone to come in each day and help to look after the kids, and do a bit of housework. Just until some family problems were, you know, sorted out.'

'What about Billy?' I asked, 'I don't suppose he had ever met an Indian before – I mean an Indian from India.'

'Well he acted a bit funny at first. But I think it was more because she was sort of, you know, modern: knowing lots of stuff and telling him what to do. But he was so thankful that someone was helping with the kids that he didn't mind. He really likes her now.'

'You were lucky you didn't get someone too nosey,' I said. 'People might suspect all kinds of things, what with two men and two young kids.'

'Yes of course. But I was careful,' he said knowingly. 'The others wouldn't have done at all.'

'How many were there?' I asked, fascinated.

'Oh, loads rang up,' he said, 'but she sounded just right.'

'You only interviewed one person!'

'You could see she was up for anything. She's a graduate: Masters actually, can't get a job at the moment. Great sense of humour: she was right up our street, I could just tell.'

'You have got a University graduate poking about everywhere!' I said in dismay. 'What did she graduate in?'

'History,' said Charles.

'What!' I exclaimed, 'and she is hanging out with refugees from the American Civil War and the seventeenth century Caribbean!'

'Oh! I see what you mean,' said Charles, 'but she doesn't know anything. No one takes any notice of what children say anyway, and everything is locked in the treasure room.'

'Hmm,' I said, 'it seems a bit of a mess to me. But I suppose we will just have to live with it for now. I need to get you up to speed about my trip, and we need to try and decide a few things.'

'Sure!' said Charles excitedly. 'Priya is taking the kids to the park soon, we can talk then.'

Priya was tucking in the children's clothing, which had become unaccountably dishevelled as usual, and regarded me curiously as we re-entered the kitchen.

'Sorry about that,' I said, 'it's just that I wasn't expecting you. Charles has been telling me what a help you have been.'

'I'm happy to be here,' she said with a twinkle in her eyes. 'Work is hard to come by at present, and the children are delightful.'

'Aunty Priya,' whispered Aurelia, 'can I go in the treasure room now?'

'Aurelia,' Priya whispered back, 'what did I tell you about that?'

'But I'm whispering,' insisted Aurelia.

'Ha, ha, kids,' chuckled Charles nervously. 'We just call it that because it's full of, err, junk.'

I looked at Priya and encountered a glance awash with pure intelligence.

'Priya,' I said, 'have you been in the treasure room?'

'Yes,' she said.

Chapter 16

'BUT IT'S LOCKED!' gasped Charles, turning pale.

'The twins know where you keep the key,' explained Priya, 'they bring the jewellery out to play with.'

'It's, ah, imitation,' said Charles desperately.

'And did you dust all the imitation gold bars while you were there?' I asked drily.

'I did as a matter of fact,' she said, 'it seemed a shame not to: they are so beautiful.'

Charles made a series of inarticulate noises, and Billy laughed outright.

'Priya,' I asked, 'what do you think is going on in this house?'

It was her turn to laugh uncertainly. 'I really can't make up my mind. I was a little worried at first, but the twins were so obviously happy, and Charles and Billy such an artless pair, that I couldn't believe anything weird was going on. But there were so many mysteries. Great wads of cash stuffed all over the place. Billy confused by the simplest electronic gadget. Children of eight who think electricity is magic, speak archaic English, and are unable to read or write. Then I found Aurelia playing with jewels and golden trinkets, and walked into a room stacked with an absolute fortune in gold and silver bars, not to mention chests full of Pieces of Eight for goodness sake. The only thing I can think of is that you stumbled across a treasure horde, in a sunken wreck or on an island somewhere.'

'Why didn't you say anything?' I asked.

'I didn't know what to do,' she said frankly, 'it blew me away, to be honest. I went around on autopilot for a couple of days. I couldn't believe it was real. I had heard about you of course, Richard, and got the impression that everything revolved around you somehow. So I decided to wait until you returned. I had to find out what was going on. And

258

anyway,' she finished lightly, 'I needed the money. Charles was paying me far too much.'

'If you needed money,' I said carefully, 'you could have just taken some. No one would have noticed.'

She didn't even react to the implied aspersion. 'I don't care about money – apart from what I need to exist, of course. I would work for nothing to be a part of something like this. I have so many questions.'

There was a hint of desperation in her eyes now. It was easy enough to understand. She had stumbled into an improbable world of mystery and treasure, and she wanted in with the whole of her being. I smiled. I felt she was someone rather special: uncorrupted in spirit and pure in her desire for knowledge and adventure. I believed I could trust her, but I hesitated to pull her into the whole cosmic merry-go-round we were stuck with.

'If that's what you want Priya, I would say welcome aboard. But things are not quite what you think. There is a whole lot of other stuff going on here, and some of it is dangerous. There will be no public recognition either: it's not going to make your career or anything like that.'

She looked disconcerted. 'It's not criminal is it? But you don't seem …'

'We are not bad guys,' I said neutrally, 'but there are bad guys involved somewhere down the line. There is much more to it as well. We're talking about something far more extraordinary than lost treasure.'

'Ha, ha,' she laughed nervously, 'I can't imagine anything more extraordinary, except perhaps aliens or time travel.'

No one laughed with her. Even the twins looked on in in silence. She stared around in confusion.

'Oh come on –' she began.

'You still want in?' I asked. 'We can give you money instead – set you up in a little business or something if you want. Once we have got ourselves sorted out, that is.'

'But you can't really mean –' she began again.

'Are we allowed to talk about magic doors now?' asked Nathaniel.

'Nooooo,' breathed Priya: connections sliding together in her brain. 'Everything in that room… the musket and the cutlass …'

'Are real,' I agreed, 'and so are Billy and the twins. Billy is from the Battle of Gettysburg and Nathaniel and Aurelia are from Port Royal, sixteen eighty nine.'

Her eyes were huge. 'But how ... what ...'

'I'll tell you everything,' I suggested, 'and then you can ask questions.'

'Aunty Priya,' Aurelia sang out, 'can we watch TV if we're not going to the park?'

Priya nodded with absent impatience.

'You can watch it in here,' I said to them, spying a new TV screen attached to the kitchen wall. 'We are going into the sitting room.'

We made ourselves comfortable on the plush lounge furniture Charles had ordered in, and I began the tale. Again I didn't mention the Mindworm. I was still reluctant to admit I had been infected by the horrendous thing. I hoped in fact that the technical assault it had endured in India had put it out of commission for good. I could no longer sense its presence at all. Charles and Billy fidgeted somewhat as they knew much of the story already, while Priya's expression vacillated between cautious scepticism and hopeful wonder. They all listened intently as I talked about my most up-to-date adventure – which required some major editing. I continued to keep quiet about intermittent excursions into other, inexplicable realms of experience too. I had no idea what to make of them myself, and there were enough mysteries to go around for the present.

Charles was thrilled by my description of the surveillance Holo-image of Alex.

'That's amazing,' he said, 'so are we going back – I mean forward – to look for her?'

'Pardon me Mr – Richard,' said Billy, 'but I reckon...'

'Billy,' I interrupted, 'calling me Mr Richard is just the same as calling me Mr Walton.'

'Begging your pardon Mr, ah, Richard,' he said, 'but I can't help thinking we ought to be getting ourselves a bit more settled before we go junketing off someplace else.'

'You're right Billy,' I agreed, 'but Priya is supposed to be asking the questions. Let's give her some time to find her feet in all this.'

'Before I buy into this whole thing,' said Priya, 'which I don't say I do a hundred per cent, are you saying this Portal thing doesn't always work? A bit convenient isn't it, an invisible Portal that doesn't work? I mean it's not like a blue box that's bigger on the inside...'

'It seems to have its own agenda...' I began to say: but stopped as glowing icons began to wink merrily on and off all around me.

'Well, OK,' gulped Priya, as a glittering aura of exotic particles encircled an unconventional opening in the centre of the lounge. Sunlight and greenery glinted on the other side.

'Wow, great! Where does it go?' said Charles.

'I don't know,' I said huffily, 'maybe it's a short cut to the park.' I got a little stiffly out of my chair. 'Come along, Priya, it seems the Portal wants you to see this.'

She rose glacially from her seat, her eyes riveted on the twinkling ring of dysfunctional reality.

'I'm coming too,' insisted Charles, 'I've only ever been anywhere once!'

'OK,' I agreed, 'but we'll just have a look. Billy, could you stay here? We need someone with the twins if we can't get back.'

'Be happy to stay,' said Billy, regarding the doorway with misgiving.

'Is it – real through there?' faltered Priya, torn between fascination and alarm.

'Let's see,' I smiled, taking her hand. But it was an effort to walk through. I had had enough of adventures for the time being.

She flinched at the weird crawling sensation of the interdimensional membrane, and we stood among wild grasses on a wooded hillside. But it was the sour reek of polluted wood-smoke that greeted our nostrils rather than fragrant nature. A tragic panorama shimmered distantly below us: a vast, sprawling city of odd crooked little houses, belching dark, broiling clouds of smoke into the sky. The firmament hung heavy with evidence of the conflagration as far as the eye could see. A low, sullen roar rumbled like far-off thunder, and a thin haze of smoke lurked everywhere, right down to the ground at our feet. Miniscule tongues of angry red flames flickered and flared amidst the blackened shells of countless miniature buildings. It was a dreadful, cataclysmic vision. Ragged crowds of refugees were gathered in fields and hedgerows beyond the outskirts. They stood among jumbled barrows and carts of possessions, their tiny figures bowed in shock and despair. We stared dumbly at the appalling scene, the sense of disaster a huge brooding weight that seemed to crush the human spirit. Even Charles was silenced.

'Is that – can that be the great fire of London?' breathed Priya in awe.

'Quite possibly,' I said, 'are you satisfied? Because I don't want to be stuck here, and there is nothing we can do.'

'I don't know if I can believe my own eyes,' she said dazedly.

'No problem,' said Charles, jerking into action. He dug out his phone and snapped away at the scene.

Priya remained reluctant to move, standing spellbound a long moment more before I shepherded her back through the doorway. She turned for a final glance before stepping back into surreal normality. Then she stood in the lounge, transfixed by the shimmering aberration in space-time, until it obligingly vanished. I indicated her seat, and she sank dumbly back into it. We all sat in silence for a while.

'I suppose there aren't really any words for this kind of thing,' I said finally.

'No, there aren't,' agreed Priya in a subdued voice, but a new light was dawning in her eyes. 'I see what you mean: it's totally amazing but its – frightening too.'

'So do you want out?' I asked.

The light in her eyes cranked up to full beam. 'No, I absolutely want in,' she said, grinning crazily.

'OK' I said, surprisingly cheered by this unexpected addition to our little band. 'So now we have to decide where we go from here. Firstly, what do we do about the twins? I have been wondering if we should try to return them to their uncle in Port Royal. But what about the problems it might create?'

'What do you mean?' asked Billy.

'Well, it's a pretty ignorant and superstitious society for a start,' I mused. 'Their unexplained reappearance from a missing ship might set off some kind of witch-hunt. It might also cause some sort of disturbance to space-time. I mean, I don't know how this stuff works, but my feeling is we shouldn't create obvious historical changes if we can help it.'

'Can we change history?' asked Billy in astonishment.

I laughed sardonically. 'That's a good question, and probably one to debate when we have more time on our hands. But apart from anything else I think we should avoid attracting attention to ourselves. There seem to be a lot of people up to all sorts of dubious stuff out there.'

'The kids have adjusted to life here amazingly quickly,' said Charles, 'they might not be able to cope with going back.'

'Can I say something?' asked Priya.

'Absolutely,' I grinned, 'you're a fully paid up member as of now. Salary somewhere between zero and anything you want.'

She flashed an appreciative smile. 'Thanks, well, I agree with you all, but there's something else: you said they came from sixteen eighty nine? Port Royal was destroyed by an earthquake around that time. You could be sending them back to their deaths.'

There was a short silence.

'Poor old Mr Bambridge,' I said.

'That's hard,' said Billy.

'So you doubly saved them,' said Charles brightly, 'first from the earthquake, and then from the pirates. It must have been meant to happen.'

'What does that actually mean Charles?' I inquired a little impatiently.

'I have no idea,' he beamed, 'but it's good isn't it?'

I smiled reluctantly. 'Yes I guess it is.'

'So the twins don't go back,' said Priya. 'That could lead to some complications with modern bureaucracy.'

'Modern bureaucracy doesn't matter to time travellers,' said Charles imperiously. 'We can live anywhere we want. Well, I mean we can eventually – once the Portal works alright.'

'Maybe: but I think they should start learning to read and write,' said Priya.

'Billy, what about you?' I asked suddenly. 'Do you want to go back – to your time I mean?'

He looked startled. 'I don't rightly know,' he said, 'do you think you could get me back?'

'I don't know that either,' I admitted, 'but if I could, would you want to go?'

He scratched his head, with a kind of bemused wonder in his eyes. 'You know what?' he said, 'I quite like it here. I mean it's strange and all, but there's plenty of grub and no one taking pot shots at me. That old television sure is something, and then there is all that gold! It's like a dream come true.' He shrugged. 'Course, I'd like a good gallop on a horse once in a while, and to see some real countryside. But if I can still go back sometime if I want, I reckon I'm happy to stay for a while and help you out some.'

'All those famous battles you could be in,' said Charles wistfully. 'The American Civil War must really have been something to see.'

'Well I don't mind watching it on this here TV,' said Billy deprecatingly. 'But it's kinda different when there's dust itching all over, and bullets parting your hair. Anyhow, it ain't the same when you know what happens.'

'Fair enough,' I smiled. 'I'm glad to have you with us. So that settles things for now.'

'What about the historical research into Jacqueline's stepfather?' said Charles.

'Well, what about it?' I asked.

'I haven't done much,' he said. 'But I thought I should mention it, because it was on the agenda.'

'Saying you haven't done much isn't much of a report,' I said a little irritably: 'why haven't you done much?'

'Counter surveillance of course!' said Charles. 'I had to find internet cafés with avoidable cameras, to hide my tracks. Then I decided I needed some hacking training as well. It's a work in progress.'

'OK,' I sighed. 'There is something else, too, before I forget. I'm fed up with arriving everywhere without a bean in my pocket. I was thinking of sewing some gold and jewellery into my clothes. What do you think?'

Billy came up with the idea of opening up a fairly broad leather belt and concealing hammered strips of gold about half an inch wide inside, and Priya sewed a dozen precious stones into the leg bottoms of a couple of pairs of trousers. I also bought a small canvas rucksack in which I kept a change of clothes, a sheath knife, a few toiletries and some biscuits and water. I tried to keep it with me. I wasn't sure I would be able to grab it in time if I unexpectedly took off, but at least I felt a little more prepared.

We discussed what would happen next and I had to admit that I just didn't know. I explained that I was beginning to feel more familiar with the Portal in some ways. I tried to describe the intuitive, almost subliminal sense of function and meaning I was starting to sense in the holographic icons it projected. But I was a long way from understanding how to control it.

'It made a doorway back to my flat from that island,' objected Charles, 'it must have been because you wanted it to happen.'

'I suppose so,' I agreed, 'but there doesn't seem to be any real pattern to it. Sometimes I try my hardest, and nothing happens at all. But at other times it does what I want almost before I think of it. The worst is when it just takes me off somewhere at random.'

'It doesn't sound random,' said Priya thoughtfully, 'you seem to end up in times and places where other time travellers are operating. It's almost as if something is guiding you there.'

I felt a tingling in my spine, and shivered at the unexpected touch of a profound depth of consciousness. 'Could be,' I wondered aloud, 'but that doesn't tell us much at the moment.'

'It may be something to do with the dying time traveller who started it all off,' continued Priya. 'You said he recognised you from the future. He could have known all sorts of things about you, and what was going to happen to you. Maybe it is programmed into the Portal.'

'What difference does it make if it's going to happen anyway?' asked Charles. 'Or maybe those men outside the cottage wanted to change something.'

An eerie image of the Mindworm came unbidden to mind. I tried to sense its presence, but felt only a cold emptiness.

'I think there's some truth in what you're saying,' I said, guiltily aware of how much I was hiding. 'But we don't really know enough to make sense of it. I guess we'll just have to keep going, and hope for the best.'

'What about the Portal making doors instead of you just disappearing?' said Charles, 'that's new isn't it. Did you do anything different when you came back to my flat?'

I thought about it. 'I didn't know where I was going, and I didn't want to leave Billy and the twins behind. I tried to hang on to the island, and when your flat popped up the two were joined together somehow. It was a bit like they were on different ends of the same bit of rope.'

'Aha!' said Charles.

'What do you mean 'aha'?' I demanded.

'I don't know,' he said cheerfully, 'it was just, you know, something.'

I rolled my eyes.

'Well, what about the fire of London then?' he asked, undaunted.

'I don't have a clue,' I shrugged. 'It may have been at the back of my mind that some action from the Portal would prove it was real -- and don't say 'aha' again.'

He caught himself just in time. 'But it must be connected: sort of something to do with your unconscious mind.'

'I have another question,' said Priya. 'You said the portal can translate languages telepathically. So why can't it do the same with itself, so you understand how it works?'

'I have no idea,' I shrugged again, 'maybe it's just more complicated, and takes time. The little man from the future said I would find a way.'

'It's not just a language I suppose,' said Charles. 'I mean, the Portal operates in other dimensions. It must be a sort of multi-dimensional language which opens pathways to space-time coordinates. Our minds may not be able to grasp those concepts at all. It would be a bit like a cave man trying to fly a jet plane.'

'Wow, Charles,' I said. 'How can you go from 'aha' to something like that? You really surprise me sometimes.'

'I've been reading up about all this kind of stuff,' said Charles, visibly swelling with pride. 'Something else I've been wondering is where it gets its power from. It must use a massive amount: from what Ravi was telling you in India, they must tap into this 'high energy matrix' itself as a power source. I wonder how far these Portals come from the future?'

'Hopefully we'll find out before too long,' I said. 'Meanwhile I guess we carry on as we are. I'll try to learn more about the Portal, but I have a feeling it's something I have to kind of grow into. Speaking of learning things: Priya, do you think you could help to teach the twins to read and write?'

I noticed Billy looked a bit uncomfortable. 'What about you Billy?' I added, 'did you ever learn to read and write? I suppose there wasn't much need for it when you were growing up.'

'Sure wasn't,' he said reticently. 'I was helping out on the farm or out kicking up with the boys. I guess I could learn my letters – give it a go anyway.'

'I'd be glad to help the twins, and you too Billy,' smiled Priya, 'But I'm not sure how good a teacher I'll make.'

Charles had been busy buying a lot of fancy electronic gear, and was constructing an elaborate infra-red alarm and surveillance system around the house and garden. This was all about making Time Travel HQ secure against unspecified future threats, and the Priya debacle had suggested additional security measures too. He began planning a network of hidden dumps in the surrounding countryside to conceal the bulk of the treasure. He started hiding smaller amounts in the house and garden too, and I helped out with some practical suggestions and investigative work.

I became even more involved in building alterations as the days went by. We decided that Priya should have a room to stay overnight, at least some of the time, and Priya herself felt that the twins should have separate rooms, which was something they had never experienced. With the treasure room gradually being liberated, we had five rooms to play with, two of them quite large. So I sat down to plan various changes that would give us six bedrooms, with a couple of extra bathrooms too, as we had only one upstairs, and a small shower room and toilet on the ground floor. It took a while, as I had a number of assistant designers with conflicting agendas, but we eventually arrived at a workable scheme.

It seemed unwise to get outside builders involved, and I was confident I could complete the work myself. In fact I looked forward to getting my hands dirty, after years of working on computers and drawing boards. I enjoyed buying the materials and tools, and was soon emulating Charles in obtaining unnecessary shiny new gadgets. But when I actually started the work I found it a little overwhelming.

Fortunately, Billy had just finished sitting through an extremely long documentary series about the American Civil War for the second time, and was keen to have something to do. He proved surprisingly – or perhaps not so surprisingly – good at picking up practical skills, and was a tireless worker. Even Charles became interested. He took great delight in acquiring basic building skills, including plumbing, and soon picked up a working knowledge of domestic electrical wiring. He wisely pointed out that he and Billy should be in a position to complete the work, as I might disappear at any moment. Eventually I pretty much ended up in my architect's role after all, producing reams of suggestions, diagrams and instructions.

It was just as well. One afternoon five or six weeks after my return I felt suddenly energised and alert, and luminous icons began to glow around me. I realised what was happening, and after a momentary panic remembered the haversack, and grabbed it. Across the room, Billy looked up from his work under a bath. We locked eyes through a flutter of holographic images, and the Portal began to open other realities. '*I really need to find Alex,*' I thought, as the familiar disorientation washed me away.

Again I fell through an ocean of power, hurled relentlessly through magnificent landscapes of strange swirling energies. It was weird to feel suspended from time and to know it flowed with lightning speed beyond these tunnels of light. I felt a little more at home now in the nameless void. I seemed to recognise some of the patterns, and sense how my will might impose order and direction. Yet some other force seemed to direct my passage. Then I glimpsed patterns of icons which seemed familiar: felt myself entering a locale that I recognised. Finally I even knew ... exactly where I was.

But not when. Clear, bright countryside: earthy aromas, sky, trees and grass. I stood once more in the fields behind Jacqueline's farm. It shocked me at first, and I felt a flare of anxiety. I feared something had gone wrong, that I was back where I started, doomed to travel in some endless loop of time. Then I realised the season was different. It was colder, and the crops had been harvested. I had no clue exactly how much time had passed – or even if I was preceding my previous visit. I wondered what complications that might create if so.

Once again there was only one course of action: to walk down to the farm. I felt suddenly more upbeat. I found myself looking forward to seeing Jacqueline again. The thought that her stepfather might also be there was more sobering, but somehow not as alarming as it might once have been. It was early in the day, and there was no dusk to conceal my approach. I briefly debated waiting until nightfall, but decided to fling caution to the winds. So I hung my haversack on my shoulder, and made my way down for the second time over the gently sloping fields.

Everything seemed very quiet. It was strange to be there in daylight hours, and I began to feel no one was home. I was on edge as I crept through the outbuildings. Glancing into the stables, I saw a couple of horses in their boxes, but still had the feeling the place was deserted. I made my way quietly around to the front. There were no horses tied to the hitching posts by the front door. I listened, but could hear nothing in the house. Finally I knocked, but the silence continued. Then, as I raised my hand to knock again, I heard the faint thud of footfall on the staircase inside. My heart began beating surprisingly fast, but it was Mary's round form that opened the door.

She stared first with incomprehension, and then confused recognition, followed by an odd, sullen indifference.

'Hello, ah, Mary – if I remember correctly. I visited once before.'

She blinked. 'The Englishman,' she said flatly.

I felt relieved: at least I seemed to be following some sort of normal timeline.

'Is Miss Jacqueline at home?'

Her eyes hardened. 'No, nor is she likely to be.' A tear trickled down her cheek despite her stern glare. 'No thanks to the likes of you coming and going. This used to be a respectable farm.'

I felt a stab of alarm. 'Has something happened to Jacqueline?' I asked anxiously.

She narrowed her eyes, regarding me disdainfully for long seconds. Then her features softened into doubt and puzzlement. 'You don't know?'

'Don't know what?' I insisted urgently.

'They are going to hang her, poor dear, for murder,' she said fiercely, and then burst into tears.

Cold fingers of horror crept inside me. 'What!' I gasped incredulously. 'How can that be possible?'

'You ask that Jeremiah,' she said angrily. 'Nothing good has happened in this house since he turned up.'

'Did he have something to do with it?' I demanded, suddenly furious myself.

'It was his man, that no-good Jack Sweeney,' she muttered, crossing herself. 'If the mistress shot him he surely deserved it, black hearted fellow that he was.'

'Where is Jacqueline?' I asked hoarsely.

'In the town jail,' sobbed Mary, tears tracking down her face. 'They are going to hang her on Saturday.'

'No they are not!' I snapped, 'nobody is going to hang her!'

My outburst brought her out of her grief. She looked at me fearfully.

'Don't worry Mary,' I said vehemently. 'I mean it. I will not let her hang. How far is it to town?'

'Ten miles,' she said uncertainly.

'Can I borrow a horse?' I asked.

'You still ain't got a horse?' she asked in bemusement.

'No,' I admitted with a fleeting smile. 'But do you want me to help Miss Jacqueline or not?'

'You really think you can?' she asked doubtfully. 'You can have a horse all right. Why should I care? That Jeremiah's taken himself off: says he's ashamed to see his stepdaughter hang.' She spat violently out of the door. 'He's the one who ought to hang if you ask me.'

Mary was beyond wondering about my ignorance of the neighbourhood in general and horses in particular. She helped me saddle up, and carefully repeated the directions into town. Before leaving I extracted a strip of gold from my belt, and hammered it into a little nugget. I wanted to see Jacqueline, and I expected to have to persuade someone to let that happen. I found the town easily enough, but riding was just as painful as I remembered. I felt ridiculous too. My equestrian accomplishments were as woeful as ever, by the looks I was getting.

It also seemed absurd that I intended to bust someone out of jail. Echoes of the theme music to 'The Good, the Bad and the Ugly' repeated mockingly in my mind, and I almost missed the presence of the Mindworm. I could easily imagine what it would have to say about it. But I burned with a cold resolve. Somehow I was going to do it: the thought of Jacqueline hanging was inconceivable.

I directed a veritable laser-beam of determination at the Portal.

'Don't you dare let me down,' I commanded it, *'when the time comes you had better do your stuff.'* I was too fired up to countenance failure.

It was a small town, pretty much the classic long main street, with saloons, boarding houses and stores. The buildings were constructed mostly in wood, but there were a few brick buildings in evidence too. A network of embryonic side streets were coming into being here and there: a settlement girding its loins for the explosion of the twentieth century. The jailhouse was at the far end of town, a single storied building with a crude, hand-painted sign bearing the legend 'Sheriff's Office'. It was built with the usual raised boardwalk; a necessary refuge from an abundance of horse manure and muddy weather. I slid awkwardly off the horse, tied it to the ubiquitous hitching rail, and clumped up the steps to the entrance. A thin, sneaky-looking guy of around thirty lounged disinterestedly behind a desk in the front office.

'Howdy.' He greeted me laconically, working at his mouth with a toothpick, and left any further conversation to me.

'Good day sir,' I said formally, 'I have called to have a few words with Miss Jacqueline Johnson.'

His expression soured. 'Miss Johnson ain't supposed to have no visitors,' he intoned stonily. 'Where're you from anyway?'

I hammed up my Englishness. 'I am a distant English relation, and I have come a long way to speak to her.'

'Sorry, no can do,' he said in a bored monotone. 'You gotta go through the Sheriff.'

I leaned forward in a confidential manner. 'There is no need to bother the Sheriff. I need only see her for a very short time. I would be most grateful to get this over with, and be on my way.'

I slipped the gold nugget from my pocket, and displayed it between finger and thumb. It was about the size of a large grape. But it possessed a gravity all of its own, and a hypnotic lustre that fascinated the eye. It certainly fascinated the shifty-faced officer of the law.

'That real?' he asked with unconvincing nonchalance.

'Sure is.' I tossed it to him.

He caught it deftly, tested its weight, and bit on it with one of the few teeth he had left. His features froze into an inscrutable mask of inner calculation.

'Just a short time you say?'

'Yes, I'll be in and out before you know it.'

He paused: a final show of reluctance, and then jerked a thumb at the back of the office. 'Through that door,' he said.

'I am greatly obliged to you sir,' I said graciously.

'Make it quick,' he smirked, 'you're lucky I got a kind heart.'

I pulled back the door with a thumping heart. I wasn't sure what would happen next. I wanted to speak to Jacqueline, I knew that much. I also wanted to see exactly where she was. I wasn't sure what I was going to do, but it seemed likely that the Portal would be involved, and I wanted a clear image of her location in my mind. My last thought before facing her seemed oddly irrelevant. I hoped she would be pleased to see me.

Chapter 17

THERE WERE TWO barred cells, one containing a crudely constructed timber cubical in a corner, presumably a hastily constructed privy. Jacqueline sat on a low fixed wooden bed, gazing dully at the floor. She looked subdued and withdrawn, and glanced up disinterestedly as I walked in. A whole gamut of emotions flashed across her face: surprise, pleasure, confusion, sadness and despair. I was surprised myself when my heart gave an unexpected lurch at the sight of her.

'Richard!' she gasped, 'I thought you were dead. I can't believe you are here… why are you here?'

'I wanted to see if you were all right,' I said a little lamely.

'That's kind of you,' she said, getting to her feet. Her eyes were suddenly glittering with tears. 'But I'm not all right, as you can see.' She moved to grip the bars of her cell, her fingers absurdly sensual and delicate against the ugly ironwork. Everything about the setting seemed completely wrong.

'Mary told me what happened,' I said after an awkward pause. 'I suppose your stepfather is involved.'

'Yes of course,' she said wretchedly. 'You were right about him. He tried to force me to marry one of his men, and sent him to … compromise me when I refused.'

'He tried to rape you?'

She coloured, and nodded briefly.

'But you had your little gun?'

'I didn't mean to kill him. He tried to take it from me, and it went off.'

'You seem upset he is dead.'

'I feel bad about it. I am a murderess, I suppose.'

'Well, I don't feel bad he is dead at all. What is bad is that the law has condemned you for it. Didn't you explain what happened?'

'I tried of course,' she said. 'But Jeremiah had men to say that I planned it. He has a story that I became strange after my mother died, with witnesses to uphold it. He even had a man swear that I threatened to kill Jack if he would not marry me.'

'What about the things we talked of at Gettysburg,' I asked grimly, 'did you see a lawyer?'

'I did, but he turned that against me too. He had a doctor testify I was imagining things.' She gave a sad little grimace. 'I was starting to wonder if I was really deranged after all – but now I have seen you I feel myself again. I thank you for coming, even if it is too late.'

'It is not too late,' I said fiercely, 'I am not going to let you die here.'

She smiled wanly, 'there is nothing you can do.'

'I can get you out,' I said.

'Don't be foolish Richard,' she said quietly.

'I mean it,' I insisted. 'Would you come away with me to a different life?'

She gazed blankly at me for a moment. There was a subtle shift from puzzlement to misgiving. Something like the old Jacqueline surfaced: a glint of steel in her eyes.

'And what might I have to do in such a different life?'

'Nothing,' I said hurriedly, 'that is, whatever you want. This is me remember, the man without experience in paying compliments to ladies.'

She stared a moment longer before the martial light faded, and then smiled sadly. 'You have changed,' she said. 'You are not the same man you were. You are harder, more reckless perhaps.'

'A lot has happened since I last saw you,' I admitted. 'I cannot promise you safety or comfort, but it would be life – and I can show you things you have never dreamed of.'

She gazed at me intently. 'You really mean it. Please don't do anything rash Richard.'

'But if I can do it,' I insisted, 'would you come with me to another life?'

She laughed bitterly, 'you are still as crazy as ever.'

'But would you come?' I was surprised at how important it was to me.

'How can I answer a question like that?' she asked helplessly.

'Yes or no,' I said with an anxious smile. 'But I warn you, I am going to try and save you no matter what you say.'

She eyed me candidly for a few seconds before returning my smile. Her lip trembled. 'Yes I would go with you Richard, but I doubt I will ever see you again.'

'It may be – something unusual. If something strange happens, don't be frightened, and don't hesitate. Do you understand?'

'Yes – no! Richard, you are not going to do anything stupid?'

'I am not going to abandon you.'

Large, slow tears welled in her eyes. 'Whatever happens, I thank you for that.'

She stood clutching the crude metal bars in a heart-breaking vision of loveliness. Her long dark hair fell densely about her shoulders like a curtain of night. An astonishing depth of beauty smouldered in her eyes: her lips somehow a perfect alchemy of purity and passion. The intensity of the moment caught me by surprise, and I forced such inappropriate imaginings aside. I tried to remember only my anger at the thought of someone wanting to destroy her.

'It is the least you deserve,' I said awkwardly. 'I am leaving now but I will be back, I promise.'

She nodded, plainly struggling between hope and disbelief.

'What is the security like here?' I asked. 'Is there usually only one guy in the office?'

'There are three,' she said disparagingly. 'One deputy like a rat and the other is a stupid lump of a man. The Sheriff is like a fat pig. One of the deputies is always here, often the Sheriff too.'

I chuckled. 'Now you have to run away with a madman. Let's hope the rat and the pig don't follow, or we will look like a circus.'

'How can you joke at a time like this?' she said furiously. 'Richard, can you really take me away from here? I am going to die in two days.'

'You are not going to die,' I said firmly. 'Be prepared to live.'

I turned to go just as rat-face peered nervously through the door to the cell block.

'Just leaving,' I said, raising my hands in the air.

I got back on my horse with as much dignity as I could muster. I was already near the outskirts, and continued on out of town in the opposite direction I had entered. I made less of a spectacle of myself that way, and there was higher ground over there. I thought it might help me to look down on the jailhouse. I reached the crest of a long rolling slope about a mile beyond the outermost buildings, and turned the horse loose. I was a hundred metres or so above the trail which led from town, and I could see exactly where the Sheriff's office stood.

'OK,' I said grimly to myself and to the Portal. 'This is it.'

I put both arms through the haversack straps, and hoisted it onto my back. I had turned over a number of scenarios in my mind. It was around midday, and I intended to try and materialise in the jailhouse a few hours forward in time, in the evening. I had considered attempting to overpower the guard in 'speed mode,' and unlock the cell door, before fleeing to another time and place. It would leave a 'plausible escape route', but there were a lot of unknowns. I could not be certain I would be able to activate the time dilation effect when I needed to, or 'fire up' the Portal at the right time. It seemed too complicated.

I decided the 'plausible escape route' was not that important. I didn't intend coming back. I would risk everything on one continuous sequence of action: to materialise in the prison cell, grab Jacqueline and take off immediately. I visualised myself swooping down into the cell, and taking flight again in one, smooth movement, like a bird. I fixed the image of the cell intensely in my mind. I didn't bother addressing the Portal. It knew what I wanted. Not what I wanted – what I demanded. I insisted on it with every ounce of my will.

I was haunted for an instant by the shadows of past failures with the Portal, but I refused to entertain them. This felt different. I was not blundering about in the unknown, or running from problems. I was embracing life: committing to an action of meaning and purpose which resonated in every cell of my being. The icons glowed even in the sunlight. Some part of me recognised some of their meaning, and felt I was intuitively applying their functions to the brief space-time jump into the jail. It was simple. But even as material reality began to lose its solidity, I glimpsed more complex calculations whirring in the background – coordinates unfolding on a greater scale, as if of their own volition. They were beyond both my comprehension and my interest. I cared for only one thing – to reach Jacqueline, and take her away from that ugly, squat building in nineteenth century America.

I did not even lose sight of the everyday world. I perceived its existence like a thin film of gauze as I glided down towards that fateful building through accelerating time and diminishing daylight. I passed through its diaphanous roof, dissolving the veil of timber and pitch to reveal the stark reality of Jacqueline's cell. She was sitting on the bunk staring vacantly into space, an opened book on her lap. I alighted in front of her, and the cell solidified around me. She focused on me with a start, and I remembered how the little man from the future had materialised outside Charles' cottage: the wave of disorientation, the energy vibrating everywhere, the subtle patterns of colour and the sparkling golden dust. And most astonishing of all, a person, appearing out of thin air.

'Jacqueline!' I hissed, 'it's me. Come here, quickly.' Energy crackled all around me. I hovered on the cusp of alternative realities, not wanting to move in case I lost the connection.

She sat frozen, staring in utter incomprehension.

'Jacqueline!' I hissed again. 'It's me, Richard. You must come with me, now.'

She was very pale. 'R – Richard?' she faltered.

'Yes,' I whispered urgently. 'Don't think. Trust me. Come here, quickly.'

I held out my hands. She stood up as if in a dream. I motioned frantically at her. She glanced hesitantly around at the dark, dingy cell, and then stepped forward with sudden determination. She looked terrified, but I pulled her towards me.

'Don't be frightened,' I urged, 'it will be all right. Just hold on.'

I hugged her tight. She tensed and then yielded. I felt a surge of joy, and icons flickered all around me, too fast and intricate to grasp. I had no thought of where we were going, but something drove us into the maelstrom. We plunged on and on, miraculously preserved from the ocean of power swirling around us. I felt Jacqueline's terror. She clung tightly to me, and I hugged her in return, trying to reassure her in the only way I could. Then we fell into burning sunlight, and hot, scorching sand.

We were still locked tightly together. I half expected her to push me away as she had after the gunfight in her house, but she didn't move. I carefully released my grip, and lifted her arms from around me.

'I am sorry about that,' I said gently, 'but I had to get you away from there.'

'I don't understand,' she whispered. Her whole body began to tremble.

'Of course not, how could you?' I smiled.

'I thought I was dead,' she said, staring confusedly around at her surroundings. 'What is this, where are we?'

'I don't really know,' I admitted. 'But where ever it is, it's very hot, and I think we should get into the shade over there.'

A huge rock stood a few yards away, its shade a welcome haven in the burning sunlight. She allowed me to help her to her feet, and continued to stare around herself in bewilderment as we stumbled towards it.

'What do you mean you don't know? Have I been unconscious? Are we in the desert?'

'There is no easy way to explain,' I said. 'The most important thing is you are not in jail, and you are not going to die.'

She paused, wide eyed. 'Oh! Am I really free? I did not think…but is that fat Sheriff not chasing us?'

'No one is chasing us,' I grinned, 'we are far away.'

'But where…' she faltered, 'I – I saw something very strange. I saw you in my cell, and there was light and…' her pupils dilated wide, 'there was a terrible, unimaginable place.'

'Yes I know,' I said. 'Do you remember when I couldn't explain how I arrived at your farm?'

She nodded haltingly, sweeping her hair absently behind one ear.

'That was because I got there just like this: through a strange place that – at first – seemed terrible and inconceivable. I arrived in a field behind your farm just as we did here, with no idea where I was.'

She frowned in slow confusion. 'That doesn't make sense. Am I dreaming?'

I tried to smile reassuringly. 'I know it is difficult for you. But I couldn't leave you there. I couldn't bear to think of –'

I stopped talking as I realised her gaze was fixed mistily on me, as open and trusting as a child.

'I am thankful to escape that awful cell, if only for a while,' she sighed. 'If this is a dream it is a nice dream, and I am glad you are in it.' She smiled absently. 'You were the one person who was nice to me in all that nightmare, except Mary of course. I was so sad when you did not come back at Gettysburg – all of that terrible shooting.'

'I'm sorry,' I said. 'I didn't mean to go, but it was the only way I could get out alive.'

'Richard you are full of riddles,' she murmured, closing her eyes. 'But I feel safe with you. It's so hot. I think I must sleep a little.'

She nestled comfortably against me, resting her head on my shoulder. I held her gently, feeling wryly privileged. I supposed she was in shock. It was hardly surprising after such an overwhelming experience, especially with everything else she had been through. I wondered how long it had been since Gettysburg, and felt a fierce anger at Jeremiah Serrano. She slept for forty minutes or so, and woke with a start, just as I was considering a surreptitious attempt to reach the water bottle in my haversack. She froze for a moment, her head still on my shoulder as she tried to orientate herself.

'Richard?' she asked hesitantly.

'Yes,' I said, 'are you feeling better?'

She sat up in alarm, edging away in embarrassment. 'Oh!' she said, 'it wasn't a dream.'

Then she looked around in astonishment. 'Richard where is this place?'

'I don't really know,' I admitted. 'We have travelled in time and space: I don't think we are in America anymore – or in the nineteenth century.'

She stared at me incredulously. 'What on Earth do you mean?'

'I tried to tell you before,' I said, 'but you were rather shaken up.'

She blushed. 'Richard, I am not sure what has happened, but I do not think I was quite myself. I may have been – over familiar with you.'

I attempted to laugh it off. 'Don't worry; you were a perfect lady as always.' The words came out awkwardly, and it was my turn to flush. 'It is, err, extremely disorientating I know. You were bound to be shocked.'

She frowned in concentration. 'There was that terrible place …'

'The same thing happened to me,' I said. 'I arrived at your farm just like we have arrived here. It was the only way I could get you out of jail, and away from the trouble you were in.'

'Can this really be true?' she asked dazedly, 'am I really free of that hateful place?'

'Yes, we are far away, in another time and place. You remember that you agreed to come with me to another life?'

'Of course,' she said a little caustically. 'But I did not expect you to whisk me off in a hurricane.' She scooped some sand from the ground, and allowed it to trickle through her fingers. Her voice dropped to a whisper. 'I hardly dare believe this is real … am I truly going to live?'

'Yes,' I said, my voice a little uneven.

Tears welled in her eyes and I felt a prickling in my own.

'I don't understand it at all,' she said.

'I don't understand it either,' I admitted. 'But I can tell you what happened. I acquired a device that opens a kind of doorway between different locations in space and time, with that 'terrible place' in between. I don't really know how to control it. It took me to your farm in nineteenth century America. Now it has taken us here, and I have no idea where we are, or if this is the past or the future. It is all rather relative I suppose, depending where you start from...' I trailed off rather incoherently.

'You are telling me the truth?' she asked doubtfully.

'Yes, absolutely.'

She regarded me curiously for a moment, wiping away her tears with her fingers, and then, strange girl that she was, she started to laugh.

'Oh Richard, I thought you odd before, and now I find you more so than ever! Only you could tell me you are travelling between different worlds, with no idea where you are going or how you are doing it!'

She struggled helplessly with her mirth, gained some control, glanced at me and went off into another peel of hysterics. I felt rather hurt, and tried to quell her hilarity with a stern time-travelling look. Eventually she took pity on me.

'I am sorry Richard,' she said unsteadily, 'I fear I am still not quite myself – not really myself at all. Please give me a moment.'

'There is a lot to get used to,' I agreed, partly mollified. 'It's best to just take it a bit at a time. I can guarantee you are safe from the fat sheriff, but not what is going to happen next.'

'Where is this device you say opens these doorways?' she asked, practical once again.

'I am wearing it but you cannot see it. Once engaged, it seems to maintain itself in a dimension outside of material reality. I am aware of it, and can communicate with it sometimes, but that is all.'

'Well then,' she said, considering this, 'how did you acquire it?'

'It's a long story,' I said, 'but I am not sure this is the time to tell it. It is very hot here, and I have only a little water in my bag.'

'Yes I am already thirsty,' she agreed. 'But what can we do? To go out in the sun would be worse.'

'Maybe I could have a look around,' I said. 'There seems to be a trail passing by here. I could follow it a little way in each direction.'

We were sitting on one side of a wide, shallow sandy depression in the land, with no sign of higher terrain on the horizon. The large rock we rested beneath seemed akin to a low rocky outcrop thrusting up from the sandy ground behind us. Before us a trail of sorts ran across our field of view, trod hard by hoofed animals over a long period of time, I guessed. I tried to gauge the time of day by the sun, and thought it approaching midday.

'Perhaps I'll wait a while,' I said.

'Can you hear something?' asked Jacqueline suddenly.

'No,' I said, listening, 'what do you hear?'

'It sounds like bells,' she said.

I listened again, and a faint tinkling sound came to my ears. 'It could be,' I agreed.

'And animals,' she said.

I began to make out a slight, irregular reverberation which grew progressively more distinct, until a lone horseman appeared from behind a rocky outcrop further down the trail. He looked Arabic or Egyptian, dark skinned and clad in light, flowing robes enlivened with splashes of colour. A close-fitting leather helmet, reinforced with metal studs, extended down over the back of his neck. Metal also glinted on buckles and his belt, and on a small round shield slung on one elbow. A spear rested casually on his shoulder, the point gleaming dully in the sun. But both hands held the reins, and he scanned the way ahead with vigilance. He was far enough off to miss us at first in the shadow of the rock, and advanced ahead of a ragged caravan of camels and mules. More outriders were strung out around them. Most of the animals carried substantial loads. Bulging sacks, or great wicker baskets were slung astride them, and a mournful tinkling of bells announced their progress.

'Oh my,' gasped Jacqueline. 'You are right, this cannot be America.'

The foremost rider saw us and halted suddenly. He turned, signalling the caravan to stop, and motioned to a couple of his fellow horsemen. All three cantered towards us, one of them with an arrow nocked to his bow. I stood up, wondering out of habit if I might need the Portal, but forcing myself to relax. I hoped events were unfolding as they should, and tried to keep faith with the mysterious destiny that dogged my footsteps. The first rider called out to us.

'Greetings strangers, fare thee well?' translated the Portal after a fractional lag, and then I got into the swing of it.

'Greetings,' I replied robustly, concocting a hastily spun tale in the same style of address. 'Ill fortune has been ours: our camel master and guide have left us. We have lost our possessions and are abandoned here.'

The two bowmen rode suspiciously around the rock, and scanned the rocky outcrop behind it.

'Why are you are abandoned?' probed the horseman doubtfully. 'From where do you hail? You speak Greek well enough, but strangely. Your attire is foreign, and your hair oddly shaven. I have not seen your like before.'

'I know not the reason,' I improvised. 'I had few possessions to steal. I was born far away, in the, err, North.'

All the while I was aware of Jacqueline's hand clutching at my arm, and her astonishment at my apparently one-sided conversation with the unintelligible desert warrior.

'What is your profession?' he queried.

'I am a scribe and a scholar,' I said, unable to think of anything else.

He raised his brows. 'Indeed,' he said inscrutably.

'I judge them to be alone,' announced one of the other men.

'Wait here,' said the first, 'I will return.'

He spurred his horse, and cantered back towards the halted caravan.

'Richard,' said Jacqueline anxiously, 'who are these men? How do you understand each other?'

'I will explain later,' I said, 'don't worry.'

I was unsure if the Portal would translate automatically to those around me if I spoke to her. I suspected not, but didn't want to take the chance. Instead I tried to make sense of the time and place we were in, searching my mind for a connection between spoken Greek, camels, spears and bows and arrows. I knew the Greeks had been active in the Middle East in ancient times. Looking at my surroundings, I guessed this could be Egypt, or a neighbouring country. I thought the time might be any point prior to the expansion of the Roman Empire throughout the Mediterranean.

I saw the horseman returning to us with another individual on a camel, and felt uneasy. I wondered if they meant to take us as slaves. I saw the second man was older and stouter than the first as they drew nearer. He did not look menacing: in fact he appeared fairly affable, though shrewd.

'Greetings Oh learned one,' he hailed me. 'Athan tells me you have met with misadventure.'

'That is true,' I agreed.

He regarded me with keen interest, and I wondered why. 'Do you journey towards the pearl of all cities, or away?' He asked.

'I have not yet reached there,' I prevaricated, rather fed up with having no idea what I was talking about.

'You are a master of letters? You have knowledge of languages, the arts and the sciences?' he asked.

'I have knowledge of languages, and some of the arts and sciences,' I agreed cautiously.

'I carry scrolls among my goods that I would have you examine, if you are willing,' he said. 'For my venture too has suffered unexpected misfortune, and it may be that we can help one another.'

'I will look at your scrolls if you wish,' I said warily. 'But I do not know if I can help you.'

I was not particularly confident. I had no idea if the Portal would translate written language, but having declared my profession, I felt it would invite suspicion to decline. He turned to raise a hand, and a youth led a heavily laden mule towards us from the group of standing animals. On closer inspection the load was not as great as it first appeared, for the wicker baskets held only capped leather cylinders. The man inspected several of these containers and selected one. He carefully removed a substantial roll of papyrus, and handed it to me.

'Can you tell me the subject and author of this work?' he asked, and I thought I sensed some anxiety on his part too.

I carefully unrolled part of the scroll. The letters, even their shapes, were initially meaningless, but I felt a kind of familiarity about them. I remembered the unexpected historical reconstructions that had formed in my mind's eye during my initial interrogation at Gettysburg, and other glimpses of the past. I tried to reach for the experience again, and felt something stir on a deep and nameless level: somewhere beyond the telepathic empathy of spoken words and a shared understanding of everyday needs and wants.

A great pool of consciousness opened up to me: multi-layered and multifaceted. The letters acquired meaning, but I saw far beyond their syntax. It was like entering a timeless, collective home of humanity, a storehouse of brilliance and revelation: sublime moments in the arts and sciences which seemed to resonate with the essential beauty of life itself. I knew everything about the document I held in my hand: who had written it, where and when, who had influenced, inspired and frustrated him; what he had wanted to achieve, how he had built his ideas; his joys, fears, strengths and weaknesses. I even knew the constituents of the inks he had used, where the papyrus was made and the type of reed stylus he preferred.

It was astonishing. I supposed it to be some function of Portal technology, and was awed by its comprehensive, even omniscient nature. It seemed to contain an imprint of everything that had ever occurred in the history of the planet. My mind boggled at the complexities of acquiring, storing and displaying that kind of data, even over a vast time period, and with unlimited technological resources. I could not imagine the processes involved, but they certainly came in useful at that moment. I made a show of examining the long papyrus scroll, rolling it carefully back and forth to consult various columns of text, although I knew everything there was to know in an instant.

'This is a play of Euripides,' I said at length, *'Orestes,* one of his later works. It is an original scroll, written by Euripides' own hand.'

'All praise to the Gods!' the man cried out joyfully, 'Henuka did not play me false, and a true scholar has crossed my path!' He reverently replaced the scroll into its leather carrying cylinder, radiating immense satisfaction.

'Know that you are not alone in your adversity,' he continued, 'and our misadventures may act now for the benefit of both. For I journeyed far to purchase this store of scrolls, and the man of knowledge who accompanied us took sick and died. Henuka of Thebes owned these works and sang their praises, but I could not be certain of their merit. He drove a hard bargain and I feared to lose them, but I likewise feared them to be of little worth.'

He paused and smiled upon Jacqueline and myself. 'The custodians at the Great Library may also play upon my ignorance, and cheat me of their true value. I would pay you well, and extend my hospitality and protection to you and your woman, if you take service with me.'

I felt a prickle of excitement. There was one Great Library in particular it would be absolutely incredible to see, but I tried to rein in my hopes.

'This is my wife,' I informed him, deciding it was the safest option. 'We would be happy to join you until your business is completed.'

'Excellent, excellent,' he said, 'I am Servertis, merchant of Tyr, and here is my hand.'

'My name is Waltonis,' I improvised, gripping his hand, 'of, ah, Europa.'

'Well met, good Waltonis,' he said. 'The sun is approaching its zenith. We were soon to stop and wait out the heat of the day. Therefore we will halt now, and make good the loads to accommodate your wife and yourself. We hope to reach fair Alexandria before full sun tomorrow.'

I felt a rush of excitement: hardly daring to believe he spoke of the fabled Alexandria of Hellenistic times.

'Who rules in Alexandria?' I asked with feigned indifference.

Servertis laughed, 'the squabbles of the Ptolemies follow one another like night and day, if that is your meaning. But honest merchants and scholars may ply their trades in peace.'

He turned his camel back towards the caravan, waving his hand, and the whole cavalcade began to dismount and unpack.

I turned to Jacqueline. 'Everything is fine,' I said with a triumphant grin. 'I have got a job!'

She looked blankly at me. 'Richard what are you talking about? Who are these people?'

'I am a scholar, special adviser to the merchant Servertis of Tyre,' I chuckled. 'But wait until you hear where we are going.'

'Don't tease me,' she pleaded. 'I already feel I am about to lose my mind.'

'Sorry,' I apologised with a grin. 'It seems we have gone back two thousand years into the past. We are a day's journey away from ancient Alexandria, in Egypt.'

'The city of Alexander?' breathed Jacqueline incredulously: 'the home of the lighthouse of Pharos and the Great Library?'

'Yes,' I said, 'I can hardly believe it myself.'

Her face was a delightful mixture of wonder and disbelief. 'I am so surrounded by marvels I hardly know what is real,' she whispered. 'But if this is a dream I don't want it to end.'

Chapter 18

THE CARAVAN RAPIDLY transformed itself into a small temporary village. The camels, mules and horses sank down, or stood grumbling beneath dirty awnings strung outside a jumble of much repaired but surprisingly spacious round tents. There was little for the animals to eat and drink from transported stores, and their masters also made do with simple fare. People appeared to want to do little except doze indolently in their stuffy shelters from the boiling sun.

I had a few minutes to give Jacqueline a rather garbled explanation of how the Portal translated speech, and how I had tapped into the extraordinary databank of art and culture. I also had to admit that I had passed us off as husband and wife, which she did not take kindly to at all.

'How dare you Richard,' she said in sudden fury. 'I trusted you to behave with propriety! My gratitude towards you does not give you any rights over me, or entitle you to take advantage of my situation.'

'I am only trying to help you!' I protested. 'This is not nineteenth century America. I daren't let you out of my sight: you don't understand the language, and it is others who may try to take advantage of you. Besides,' I grumbled, 'where I come from, the boundaries of 'propriety' as you call it are very different. There is much more personal freedom between the sexes. After everything that has happened between us, you should know you can trust me.'

She remained cross for a while, but gave ground grudgingly in the face of the practical realities we faced. There was little time to spare for such considerations in fact. We were invited into my new employer's tent for refreshments. Fortunately he was too pleased by the stroke of luck represented by our appearance to enquire much into our personal histories. I told him we hailed from a remote region in the mysterious wilderness of Europa, and that I had learned Greek from a travelling scholar. I credited this worthy figment of my imagination with the awakening of my interest in intellectual enquiry, and with assuming the position of my mentor for some years during further studies in Greece.

It soon became evident that the Portal did not translate to others when I spoke to Jacqueline, and I attributed the language we shared to our origins in barbarous foreign lands. Even our clothes did not seem to arouse much curiosity, apart from Servertis commenting on the fine quality of the stitching. Jacqueline's dress was plain enough, and I wore a simple t-shirt and trousers. He merely said we could replenish our wardrobe when we reached the city.

We shared a light meal of figs, tough gritty bread and water, and soon everyone lay down or sat dozing in the baking heat. Even the occasional breeze stirring through the tent was hot, but Jacqueline and I were running on too much adrenaline to sleep.

'Richard I still can't believe this,' she whispered, stifling a giggle at the chorus of snoring all around us. We lay facing each other on one side of Servertis' tent, still trying to adjust to our novel surroundings.

'I know how strange it is to be with people from another time and place,' I whispered back, 'I felt just like this when we left your farm with the Lieutenants men.'

She regarded me with a mixture of awe and curiosity. 'Where are you really from?' she whispered.

'I do come from London, but from the future,' I said quietly.

Her eyes widened. 'Really?' she mouthed, 'how far in the future?'

'About a hundred and fifty years ahead of your time,' I said, 'from the year two thousand and seventeen.'

She stared. 'Is it – different then?'

'Very. Science has advanced a lot.'

'In what way? Tell me what is different.'

I grinned ruefully. 'Well, as you may guess from my performance on a horse, people don't use them much. We drive in very fast horseless carriages called 'cars'. We travel by air in flying machines, and we talk to each other from anywhere in the world just as you and I are talking now.'

She smiled doubtfully, 'oh, that cannot be true!'

'I can assure you it is,' I chuckled.

She looked suddenly annoyed. 'So you lied to me about your telescope! There must be great telescopes that show the stars and all their secrets!'

'Shh!' I hissed, 'not so loud! Would you have believed me if I told the truth? Yes, we have great telescopes: we even have telescopes out in space which transmit pictures for us to look at on the ground.'

Wonder battled scepticism in her eyes. 'Oh, you are lying again!'

'No I'm not,' I chuckled quietly. 'They show us wonderful things, but not all the secrets of the universe. More is discovered all the time. You can definitely see those pictures if we get back there – and there is someone you might like to meet.'

'Who?' She asked uncertainly.

'Billy is there with my friends.'

'Billy!' She exclaimed in surprise, forgetting herself again, and hurriedly lowered her voice. 'I thought him dead or wounded at Gettysburg.'

'We were about to be shot when the Portal took us away, just as it did you and I from the jail. Poor Billy had a dreadful shock.'

'So you saved him as well?' She smiled. 'It seems I misjudged you. I thought you needed saving, with your odd, unworldly ways.' She laughed softly, 'and now Billy has seen horseless carriages and flying machines? What must he have thought?'

'He stands gaping in the road, watching aeroplanes fly over. Everyone stares to see what amazes him so much.'

She chuckled, 'how extraordinary life has suddenly become. I would truly not be surprised to awake and find it all a dream.'

'No, it's quite real,' I said, and then frowned a little. 'As far as anything is real that is.'

'So you have discovered how to travel in time as well? It is astonishing!'

'Not us, this technology comes from my future.'

'Then how did you obtain it?'

'As I told you, it is a long story. We can perhaps talk about it tonight.'

We lay quietly, eventually dozing a little, until the camp began to stir in the late afternoon. Servertis parcelled out various goods amongst the animals until he had two camels uncluttered: enough for Jacqueline and me to ride on. We mounted with some difficulty – considerably more on my part than Jacqueline's – and the caravan lurched collectively off into the still, sultry afternoon. The shadows began to lengthen as the waning sun dropped lazily towards the horizon, bathing the plodding cavalcade in a surreal orange glow.

I smiled a little hesitantly at Jacqueline as we undulated unevenly along at the mercy of the camels rolling gait, and she smiled broadly in return, apparently fully enjoying the adventure. The bells on the animals tinkled dolefully in the twilight, and we pushed steadily on as the bejewelled night sky slowly ignited above us. A three-quarter moon lit our way, and an unaccustomed joy began to grow in me. I felt deeply happy that Jacqueline was safe, and a keen excitement at the thought of the legendary city we were approaching. For the first time in my excursions out of time I felt fully alive to the miraculous nature of it all: enchanted by the magical reality of each improbable moment. But I had a sneaking suspicion that part of the magic was sharing it with Jacqueline.

We continued for several hours into the night, until the moon began to sink behind some distant hills. Then we halted to make camp again. This time fires were lit, and appetising aromas were soon wafting around the tents. We ate with our hands, taking salted meat fried with lentils and olives from communal dishes onto simple metal plates. It was supplemented with more of the tough, gritty bread: doubtless laced with powdered stone from the grinding process. I welcomed the beer we were given to wash it down with, although Jacqueline choked over it a little. Afterwards we retired to a smaller tent shared by two other couples, with crude dividing curtains granting some privacy.

'It's only one night,' I said to her as we crawled into our makeshift boudoir. 'Maybe we can arrange something more suitable when we get to Alexandria.'

'It's all right Richard,' she said softly. 'I realise I was being unreasonable. In fact I have been more than unreasonable. I never thanked you for trying to protect me in that awful gunfight in my house, and now you have plucked me out of that terrible jail. You must think me ungrateful. I am not. I have experienced many difficult and unpleasant things these past few months, and I find it hard to know who to trust. But I do want to trust you. I did not mean to laugh at you either. I am fully sensible of everything you have done for me.'

'Harrumph,' I murmured, clearing my throat awkwardly, 'I guess we have both experienced difficult things lately. I don't mind you laughing at me. It's true that I don't know what I'm doing half the time.'

'But you have the courage to do what you think is right,' she said with a smile in her voice.

'Do I?' I wondered in surprise. It seemed more to me that some things I just could not bear to walk away from.

'Yes,' she said, 'some might say foolishly so.'

I somehow failed to brush her words away with a jokey response. 'Well, I certainly struggle with things I don't understand,' I achieved after a moment's silence, 'especially since the Portal appeared in my life.'

'I am waiting for you tell me how it happened,' she reminded me.

So I began the story, speaking in hushed tones. Once again I left out the Mindworm. I was particularly reluctant to speak of it to a woman like her, who seemed far above such loathsome things. I also mentioned little about Anna, somewhat to my surprise, but sensed Jacqueline's smile when I spoke of the twins.

'You have adopted two children?' she whispered in amusement, 'whatever next?'

I saved the most dramatic news for last.

'My stepfather a time traveller!' she hissed in fierce astonishment. 'It seems absurd. Yet somehow I do not find it difficult to believe. It would explain many things about him. But why should he involve himself with my family?'

'My friends back in London are searching historical records for something that might explain it,' I said quietly. 'But so far everything about him seems a mystery: especially his unscrupulous and destructive behaviour. There are other time travellers involved in the attack on the Merchant Royal and the Senator in India too. I can't understand how people with such advanced technology can act so maliciously.'

'Yet from what you say, the young lady who first brought you warning, and the poor man who bequeathed you the Portal, were of a very different mettle,' she said.

'Yes,' I agreed, yawning, 'which is heartening, but yet another puzzle. I would love to have some answers for a change.'

We drifted off to sleep, and I dreamed that Jacqueline and Anna were each calling me from different directions, while Jacqueline's stepfather laughed in the background. It was still pitch black when people began to move around, and Jacqueline called my name in a low, panic-stricken voice.

'I'm here,' I said, and she sighed thankfully.

'I thought I was still in the jail,' she said. 'I don't know which seems a more impossible dream: being here or back in that hateful cell.'

The dying embers of the fires were rekindled to brew a strong, pungent tea flavoured with mint. We dipped a couple of handfuls of the rough bread into it, chewing, sipping and struggling to wakefulness as the camp was packed up. We were on our way well before the sun began to lighten the horizon, and had covered a good distance before the heat of the day really began to build.

There was a hypnotic monotony to the camels lurching stride, and I periodically emerged from trance-like daydreams to see that Jacqueline appeared in much the same condition. Finally, in the late morning, I noticed small groups of palm trees and scrubby bushes appearing along the trail, and soon afterwards we crested a low rise to gain our first glimpse of the fabled Alexandria.

It was a sight I would never forget. The distant masses of cream-coloured stone shimmered like a mirage in the sun. The outer defensive wall was a couple of miles away, and ran right across our line of sight for an astonishing distance. Regularly spaced, square guard towers marched along its length, and it adjusted itself to minor changes in direction with impressive precision. We were approaching from the west, with the sea to our left and the great inland lake that connected to the Nile some distance away on our right. The city walls turned away from us at these natural boarders to its domain, and disappeared off to enfold the distant haze of buildings they defended.

'The Pearl of the Mediterranean!' exclaimed Servertis, waving his arm expansively as he brought his camel alongside mine. 'May our visit be a prosperous one.'

I smiled at him, and at Jacqueline, whose face was alight with wonder. The lighthouse of Pharos was unmistakeable. The offshore island on which it stood curved around beyond the great mass of the city to our left, but the hexagonal and rounded forms of its upper two tiers were easily recognisable: soaring high above every other building in the fabulous metropolis. There were great wooden galleys in the western harbour, nearest us, and several manoeuvring out to sea. Their size astounded me, their very existence unbelievable. The bold, bright motifs on their sails, the legendary curves of sterns and prows and their precisely arrayed banks of oars looked unreal, almost hallucinogenic against the sparkling blue of the sun-kissed Mediterranean.

The great city really did seem like a waking dream as it opened out to us. Its western gate was towards the seaward side of the line of fortification we faced: a huge opening fifteen feet high and twenty across. It stood in a mighty wall of limestone blocks double that height, and its guard towers were higher still. Two lesser gateways stood on either side. Soldiers strolling along its ramparts looked impassively down upon us as we approached, the blazing sun glinting occasionally on their weapons and armour. The ponderous central gates hung open. They were massive: their dense, heavy timbers clad in silvery cupronickel plating, and studded with solid bronze bolts. A huge, metallic disk of a brighter, silver hue was fixed above them, engraved with the phases of the moon. Soldiers and officials milled about in the grand entranceway, and our caravan mixed with a stream of travellers converging on it from several directions.

'It is clad in pure silver,' said Servertis, catching my glance at the great metal disc gleaming above our heads, 'this is the Gate of the Moon. The disc over the gate of the sun is clad in gold.'

He had papers to show the official who approached him. 'I am licensed by the master of the Great Library himself,' he announced, 'I deal directly with the Mouseion.'

'The dogs would take all if I had not this licence,' he muttered as we moved on, indicating the scrolls stacked high on the animals behind us, 'and I would receive only bad copies for my trouble.'

We rode into a truly breath-taking sight. A monumental royal highway stretched before us, running unbroken through the city into the far distance. Easily ninety feet wide, it was paved in massive slabs of white granite, and lined by stunning colonnades of round, red granite pillars, each several times the height of a man. Through the colonnades we glimpsed parks, pavilions and cloistered walkways: elegant visions of brightly painted architecture, stone reliefs and statues both Greek and Egyptian. These varied from the stately and dignified to the grotesque and bizarre: images of grandeur, beauty, grace, pathos and demonic glee. Streets of more modest proportions intersected the great royal thoroughfare to transverse orderly city blocks.

It was meticulous urban planning on a staggering scale, and everywhere thronged an extraordinary variety of people, more colourful than the extras of a Hollywood movie. It was unsurprising that Servertis had not commented much on our clothing. Everything imaginable seemed to be on display. The inhabitants of Alexandria appeared to come from every nation on earth: Indians, Chinese and Africans, and Middle Eastern and Europeans of every variety; many apparently retaining at least some elements of their national costume.

Martial horsemen trotted casually on gorgeous mounts, their weapons and accoutrements jingling ominously. Prosperous merchants in sumptuous costumes, studious men in elegant robes, men and women rich and poor wandered everywhere, or conversed earnestly between themselves. We passed a hugely extravagant compound: a great stadium laid out beyond the colonnades on our left. Its extensive grounds and outbuildings were alive with athletes, exercising, wrestling and practicing with weapons. Extensive running tracks extended all around its boundaries, its closest border paralleling the great highway itself, and perspiring men pounded determinedly in and out of view behind the line of pillars.

'Oh my goodness!' exclaimed Jacqueline, averting her eyes, for the athletes were naked.

'Ah yes,' I said, somewhat embarrassed myself. 'This is the ancient Greek world after all. If it's any consolation, I think they ran naked to demonstrate how pure they were – something like that anyway.'

'Yes of course,' she said, her colour heightened. 'I was just unprepared. It is very different from reading about it in books!'

Young and not so young ladies, as well as men, also seemed to be admiring the purity of the athletes. The women reclined like birds of paradise on hand-carried palanquins, and seemed to revel in frivolous fun and enjoyment. More simply-dressed souls hurried on errands: servants or slaves; and goods flowed constantly into the city. Some like us led goods-laden animals, while horse-drawn carts of various capacities hauled everything from fruit and vegetables and sacks of grain to part-completed statues. Jacqueline urged her camel closer to mine, looking totally elated.

'Oh Richard,' she exclaimed, 'I truly feel I am living in a dream! I think my heart is going to burst with happiness!'

I grinned broadly. 'So you are glad you came?'

She laughed gaily. 'It is magnificent beyond anything I could have imagined! It is almost more than I can bear. No matter what happens I will always remember this moment.'

I absolutely shared her joy: Alexandria really was a dream come true – the dream of one of the most extraordinary human beings who ever lived. Half-remembered tales of Alexander and the history of this wondrous city rose to mind. I felt impatient to explore and experience all that I could.

But niggling fears remained: the mysteries of the Time Portal and the dark happenings that surrounded its existence. I knew I would have to stay alert to the unknown and unexpected. I sighed inwardly. It had been a while since I had felt free to simply enjoy myself. But thinking back, I hadn't done a whole lot of enjoying when I'd had the chance. Now I was experiencing incredible things, but at the cost of new dangers and responsibilities. For a moment I wondered if it was worth the price. Then I looked at Jacqueline's radiant features, and knew I wouldn't change it for anything.

We turned right, down one of the side roads, itself thirty feet wide, and made our way into the south-eastern part of the city. Here shops and houses lined the street fronts; substantial lots of fifty feet apiece, constructed in stone blocks, and mostly two stories high. The shops overflowed with everything imaginable. Pungent wafts of incense and perfumes excited our senses. We saw food, wine, spices, weapons, ornaments, jewellery, sandals and fabrics for sale within the space of a few minutes, and business was brisk. It seemed to be a time of plenty. We negotiated smaller backstreets into a district of warehouses, boarding houses and stables; and finally halted to unload our goods and arrange quarters for the animals and ourselves.

'Now we will rest,' said Servertis, thankful to have reached the journey's end. 'There will be food and drink, such as it is in this place, but later you might like to view some of the wonders of the city. Have you any coin? I can advance a small amount for such things as you may like to enjoy. In the morning we will start work on the scrolls, and perhaps two days afterwards we will begin our business at the library.'

I thanked him for his kindness, and accepted the few coins he offered me. I did not want anyone to know about the gold and jewels I carried. We ate with the others and were allotted our accommodation. Jacqueline and I were to share a small first floor room at the rear of our lodgings. It was more intimate that the tent had been, and I sensed her discomfort as we entered.

'Don't worry, there are two beds,' I said lightly: although the simple wooden pallets with their thin straw-stuffed padding and flimsy patched blankets looked barely worthy of the title.

'That's all right Richard,' she said awkwardly, 'actually I am more concerned about bathing and getting some new clothes.'

'I'm not sure about contemporary sanitation facilities,' I said. 'Alexandria was pretty much built from scratch on the most enlightened principles of the time. I think water cisterns and drainage went in right at the beginning, and there should be communal latrines emptying into sewers locally, if not from the buildings themselves. I don't think there will be any domestic bathing facilities though. There should be communal baths, maybe even with hot water. Separately for men and women I mean. We will have to investigate. I seem to remember that people rubbed oil and sand on themselves and scraped it off to get clean.'

'Ugh!' said Jacqueline, and then sharply: 'Richard! You are not getting undressed?'

'Calm down!' I said, 'I'm just taking my belt off.'

I explained about my hidden financial reserves while I extracted a strip of gold. 'I used some of this to get in to see you in the jail,' I said, 'I have some jewels as well. I will try and get some more local currency with them.'

Jacqueline looked impressed, 'not the lost boy any longer I see.'

I grinned. 'Not quite as much as I used to be, at least.'

We each lay down on our rugged little beds, gazing at the ceiling.

'Will we really go out to see Alexandria this evening?' she said wonderingly, 'I can hardly believe it.'

'I am really looking forward to it,' I said, 'and you deserve a treat after everything you have been through.'

She was silent for a while. 'So you have been living this strange existence for some time,' she said eventually. 'I suppose you have become used to it.'

'Not really,' I admitted. 'I still find jumping into to new situations a bit of a nightmare. True, it can be surprisingly easy to get involved in the everyday life around you. But there is also the uncertainty of other time travellers. You never know what might be going on behind the scenes.'

'What of the girl who started all this. Do you think you will find her?'

'Yes. She told me I would see her again.'

'What do you – hope from her?'

'Hope? I don't know – to get some more answers, I suppose.'

'You don't have – an affection for her?'

'No … yes … I don't know: she said she was not the girl for me, whatever that means. She is a mystery in every way. It drives me crazy sometimes.'

'Do I really look like her?'

'Very much so,' I admitted ruefully. 'She could be one of your descendants, or an ancestor perhaps.'

'But you think she is from the future?'

'Yes I do. She knew a lot about me, personal things. And I know she was in India about fifty years after my time.'

'She knew personal things about you?'

'Yes. She even knew about my girlfriend, and that she was having a fling.'

'Girlfriend?' said Jacqueline, 'what a strange expression. You – live together as man and wife?'

'Well yes – that is, we were at the time – except that we still had separate homes.'

'And by a fling I presume you mean that she had an affair?'

'Yes, she was involved with another man.'

'It all sounds rather sordid,' she sniffed, looking around our little room with considerable misgiving. She was more hesitant when she spoke again. 'You said there was more personal freedom between men and women in your time. What did you mean exactly?'

'Well, relations between the sexes are generally more relaxed, and people live together before marriage – or without marriage at all if they wish. It is common for people to have several partners during their life.'

She looked dismayed, 'but what of the sanctity of marriage?'

'That idea doesn't really exist anymore. Some people still like to get married in church, but many are not religious at all. I suppose science is the new religion in my time.'

She looked bewildered. 'How can science be a religion?'

'Well it's not, but it has discovered many wonderful things: created amazing technologies, and greatly improved our health and comfort.'

'So you live wonderful lives which have no purpose?' she said tartly.

'Well, I wouldn't quite put it like that,' I replied defensively.

She was silent for a while.

'I don't think I would like the future,' she said finally.

We slept for couple of hours, and awoke a little apprehensive but excited at the prospect of exploring the city. I located some fairly basic, but efficiently designed latrines at the rear of the boarding house, but there were no separate arrangements for ladies. They were not in a good condition at all, but Jacqueline was unfazed. She vowed to make them 'decent' when she got hold of some work clothes.

We soon set out on our evening of adventure, but our priorities were to find somewhere to wash, sell some gold and buy some clothes. I was particularly keen regarding the clothes, as I imagined we would be easily identified by any time traveller who might be in the city. Enquiries about washing revealed there were public baths for both men and women. The best were at the great gymnasium, but there were similar facilities at numerous lesser establishments. We made our way to the nearest, and found a pleasant building boasting a few decorative columns and reliefs, with the 'gymnasium' consisting largely of massage parlours and groups of chatting acquaintances. The bath houses were attached at the rear, with the women's facilities smaller than the men's.

Jacqueline was a little daunted by the processes which might be involved, for I warned her she was unlikely to experience the privacy she was used to. But she was determined to bathe. I paid the wizened creature guarding the ladies' entrance with some of Servertis' money. I skipped the costly additional option of perfumed oil, but added a coin for looking after my non Greek-speaking wife, explaining that she was ignorant of city life. The woman accepted this with a gummy smile, and professed herself happy to acquaint Jacqueline with their modern amenities. I waited outside as she entered. I had no idea how safe my valuables might be in the place, and preferred to transfer them to Jacqueline when she had finished. She emerged after little more than thirty minutes looking very happy if rather wet, with her hair fixed in some sort of twist at the back of her head.

'I can't tell you how good that was Richard,' she beamed, 'so simple and yet so effective. The good lady was very kind. They first poured water onto heated stones and the steam opened the pores of the skin, then I passed through to a place where I could douse myself in cold water. There was no soap of course. There was another lady scraping a hideous mess over herself, but I felt no inclination to try it. I felt quite sufficiently cleansed. The way it is planned is quite sensible and pleasant.'

'Great,' I said, transferring my small change and belt to her as unobtrusively as possible. 'Keep this safe and wait near the women's entrance. Call on the old lady for assistance if anyone troubles you. I'll be as fast as I can.'

I repeated her experience, although the 'steam room' was rather crowded with laconically conversing men. I risked the jewels in my trouser seams, and somewhat to my surprise, my clothes remained where I had left them. I re-joined Jacqueline in less than twenty minutes.

'We must get ourselves some towels for the future,' I said, 'but it's quite warm, so I guess we will soon dry.'

'It is so good to be clean,' she replied, 'damp clothes are no hardship.'

'Now for the money,' I smiled, and asked a passer-by where I might find a gold merchant. The directions took us back onto the broad royal thoroughfare and further into the city, where an equally epic highway crossed it at right angles. This marked the centre of the teeming metropolis: with this new, great artery leading down towards the harbour in one direction, and back towards the inland lake in the other. We crossed over into the south western quarter of the city, and soon found more goldsmiths than I could ever have imagined existed. A whole district seemed crammed with stalls and workshops specialising in gold, all huddled together, I supposed, for security. Guards similar to those accompanying Servertis stood idly about, but few of the venues seemed to be merchandising jewellery, or buying and selling gold. Most appeared to be roughly constructed workshops, with clients bringing in gold to be fashioned into ornaments of their own, or of others design.

I spied one reasonably upmarket establishment, and wandered in to find an interested proprietor rubbing his hands in greeting. No doubt we looked suitable birds for plucking, and the good – if unusual – quality of our clothing seemed to excite him. Sure enough he looked very pleased with himself when we left. I had exchanged about a third of my gold and a couple of emeralds for a small number of gold and silver coins. But they were sufficient for our immediate needs in my estimation. The coins were struck to a surprisingly high standard, and Jacqueline examined them in great fascination.

Next we looked for somewhere to buy clothes, and again found many similar establishments situated in close proximity to each other, not far away. Trades of a feather, I learned, stuck together. In fact these places sold mostly cloth rather than clothing, as lengths of material seemed to be mostly what ancient Greeks wore. The fabrics were far from mundane though. There were diverse qualities of cotton, wool and silk: in rich colours and patterns as well as cream and plain white, and many had elaborate borders.

We made a fairly conservative choice of garments, our options simplified by much that was unisex in form and function. A kind of undergarment consisted of a wide, rectangular tube of light cotton, fixed over the shoulders and upper arms by broach pins. These hung down to the ground and were secured around the waist by a belt – or in Jacqueline's case, a platted leather girdle. They were pulled up through this restriction to achieve the required length around the ankles, and the superfluous material left hanging loosely from the waist.

Over this hung a rectangular length of cloth of better quality, front and back, through which the head passed. This was white with simple borders in our case, and was folded and pinned at the shoulder with one side left open. A heavier, more voluminous version could be secured around the body like a cloak, but we had no need of it. Loin cloths and breast bandages were also optional extras, which we did agree to, amidst a certain amount of embarrassment on Jacqueline's part. We changed separately into our new outfits in a storage space packed with wooden crates, amusing the proprietor with our coyness, and in no time at all we were admiring each other's new costumes.

Jacqueline seemed born for the part. The clothing added a new grace and dignity to her, and I couldn't help noticing that her garments were more diaphanous and figure-friendly than the stiffer material of her nineteenth century dress. Her sexuality had always been refined and understated, and unexpected, fluttery tendrils of desire unsettled me at the sight of her. She seemed self-conscious about it herself, and I tried to ease her discomfort.

'You look wonderful as an ancient Alexandrian,' I said encouragingly, 'I would like to buy you some nicer stuff, but we are not supposed to be rich.'

She smiled a little uncomfortably. 'That's quite all right Richard. There is no reason for you to spend money on me. We don't need much at the moment, the climate seems perfectly warm. But I will need another, um, dress – and a pair of sandals if that's all right. These shoes won't do at all.'

'Of course,' I said, 'we'll find the sandals in a minute.'

We left our old and additional new clothes in the shop for a few hours, where the smiling owner assured us they would be safe. He obligingly agreed to keep our shoes too when we brought sandals nearby. But just to be sure, I informed him that we would return to purchase more of his wares when I was paid for unspecified trading transactions. In no time at all it seemed, we were wandering the streets as bone fide Alexandrians. I felt much more relaxed knowing we now blended in with the environment; free to immerse myself in the extraordinary sights and sounds all around us, and Jacqueline obviously felt so too.

'Here I am, living and breathing, and yet I cannot believe this is real,' she sighed.

I smiled at her simple wonder. I felt a constant bubble of joy that she was alive, well and happy.

'It certainly feels surreal,' I agreed, my eyes devouring fresh marvels everywhere I looked. The distant image of the legendary Pharos caught my attention.

'I would love to try and get a closer look at the lighthouse,' I said.

'Oh yes please, Richard,' she said excitedly.

We strolled together towards the sea, asking directions a couple of times. The route to this iconic landmark of the ancient world took us back a little way around the harbour. Here began the great mole, the famous Heptastadion which had been built a mile out to the island. It was a wide, robust construction; boasting even a water aqueduct, with bridges spanning strategically crafted gaps that allowed ships to pass between the two harbours it created. Scores, probably hundreds of ships crowded the great sheltered bays on either side of this extraordinary promenade. Some were massive warships, with several banks of oar ports and wicked-looking rams jutting from their elaborate prows. They did not look primitive at all. The timeless spirit of human ingenuity had worked its magic on the limitations of wooden architecture, and they projected royal power and prestige with brutal elegance. The sheer scale of artistry and industry which they represented was awe inspiring.

Dozens of smaller ships were moored on either side of the Heptastadion as we walked its length. Most bobbed quietly with the gentle harbour swell, the day's bustling activity almost over. But here and there men still laboured on various tasks, or called out to each other in casual good humour from ship to ship. We were not the only sightseers wandering to and from the celebrated lighthouse, and no one took the slightest notice of us. Pharos proved a long, unevenly shaped island with the towering, iconic construction standing at its north-eastern tip, where it marked the entrance to the north eastern harbour. A temple stood where the vast mole reached the rocky island, and from here a good level road ran towards the astonishing edifice at its far end. We walked towards the great lighthouse in reverent silence. It grew steadily in height and substance as we approached; its reality confounding centuries of fable and folk-law. It was mind-blowing – the height of a forty story building with an internal staircase and elevator, built two thousand years before Manhattan took to the skies.

Of course, the elevator was basically an internal shaft through which fuel was winched for its nightly beacon, but the building was still a technical masterpiece. We came to a halt a hundred yards or so from the wide rectangular walls enclosing the vast courtyard at the base of the tower. Four identical bronze statues faced outwards on raised platforms at each of its four corners: a man with the upper body of a human and the tail of a fish, holding a trident, and raising a conch shell to his lips. *Triton son of Poseidon and Amphitrite, herald for his father* – the mysterious depository of knowledge welled up from within me uninvited.

A broad ramp climbed from where we stood, cresting the high enclosing walls of the courtyard and making an entrance eighty feet up the first massive leg of the tower. A team of horses laboured up its slope hauling a waggon laden with wood, men following its progress with big wooden wedges, ready to check any back-sliding. Built in huge limestone blocks, the massive inward-inclining square base section formed half the height of the great monument. The width of the octagonal central section was two thirds that of the base, and the final round tower half of that. The building's pale façade was rich with sculptured reliefs, and topped by a sturdy, open columned turret with a dome-shaped roof sheathed in copper. From its apex a tall bronze stature of Poseidon himself stared out to sea, presumably granting safe passage to the seafarers of fair Alexandria.

'Oh my, to think I should be seeing this,' breathed Jacqueline in awe, 'why it must be taller than the State Capitol building we are constructing in Washington!'

'Yes, I believe it is,' I laughed: intoxicated by the impossible reality of that great wonder of the ancient world looming over us. The final rays of the setting sun gleamed poignantly on the god-protector of Pharos, and simultaneously the huge brazier in the turret below flared into fiery life. The moment seemed perfect, and something magical ignited in my own heart. I turned instinctively to Jacqueline, and it was like looking into a mirror. I wanted to say something, but the words did not come. I held her gaze for slightly too long: something or everything hovered between us, and then we both smiled self-consciously and looked away.

'Let's go back to the city,' I said.

We were silent for a while as we walked back to the Heptastadion, but the novelty of our exotic surroundings soon returned our mood to one of carefree contentment. It was dark by the time we wandered back to the great crossroads in the centre of the city. Huge oil lamps had been lit to mark important buildings and monuments, and the moon bathed the city in an exhilarating, luminous glow. More of the lounging females on their palanquins were in evidence, some of them truly spectacular. They were adorned with delicate silks and glittering ornaments, their faces aglow with alluring face-paints and their hair piled high in elaborate ringlets above their heads. Most seemed dressed for revelry, and eagerly making their way to festive destinations.

We found an eating house and feasted on fish, lentils, olives and figs, and I splashed out on some slightly tart but not unreasonable wine. I grinned suddenly, remembering Ravi's disapproval of alcohol. It was weird to think of him far up along the timeline in his dreamlike, shining metropolis.

'What is funny?' asked Jacqueline, and I told her.

'How strange it is,' she said. 'It seems that time is like a huge building with innumerable separate floors, with many different people existing in many times and places. I hardly dare think what it means. It has overturned my life utterly. Somehow it must all make sense, but I cannot imagine how.'

'Well, let's just enjoy the present,' I said, 'and let the mysteries sort themselves out in their own time.'

She sighed. 'I have always longed for knowledge and adventure. Yet I did not consider that my heart would be in my mouth at every turn. I can hardly digest the wonders I have seen for the alarming nature of it all!'

'You do an excellent job of digesting the wonders you have seen,' I laughed, 'and you seem knowledgeable about a great many things. What education did you have?'

'I did not have a formal education as such,' she said, 'very little anyway. My interests come mostly from my father. Both my father and uncle were clever; but my uncle was more the engineer and my father the philosopher. My father used to read books of all kinds to me, and when he – died – I took to reading them myself. They reminded me of him.' She paused, her eyes suddenly sad. 'Richard, we have travelled into the past. Could I...'

'... go back to see your Father?' I finished for her. 'I don't know. I have no idea what the consequences of something like that might be. It's certainly not an option at the moment. I don't have that kind of control.'

She remained pensive. 'But what is it all about, our lives? – People living and dying in different times and places. I took comfort from thinking my father was in heaven: but what is heaven? If I went back and saw him would he really be alive? Am I am really alive now? It is all so confusing.'

'You can't really think about it, that's for sure,' I said. 'I suppose Ravi would say that the consciousness of each human being is just one small spark of a greater potential within us all. He doesn't know about time travel. But if he did, I'm sure he would say we are all equally alive; and each lifetime is part of a progression towards a glorious future in which the essential nature of the whole human race, past and present, will participate.'

'What a wonderful thing to say Richard,' she said, her eyes shining. 'How profound you can be sometimes. I would never have guessed it when I first met you.'

'Actually,' I confessed, as a slow rush of energy crept through my body, 'I am not quite sure where that came from.'

Chapter 19

WE COLLECTED OUR clothing from the shop, and strolled back to the boarding house in a companionable silence. But the growing empathy between us became a little constrained as we entered our room. I knew Jacqueline felt uncomfortable about our enforced intimacy, and the situation was highlighted by our period costumes. She was clearly conscious that her clothing was less formal and more revealing than she was used to.

I tried to lighten the moment. 'I hope I don't snore.'

'I am sure I am too tired to notice,' she said politely. 'I wish you goodnight,' and she lay down to turn away from me. I did the same, but I remained very aware of her presence just a few feet away. The silence in the room was charged with imaginings, and I sensed she was as much a part of it as I was.

Servertis banged on our door at an early hour next morning, requesting that I start work with him on the scrolls as soon as possible. I left Jacqueline sleeping, and grabbed something to eat downstairs before making my way to his room. It was much larger than ours, and crammed with scrolls, which he had sorted out according to category and contents. It occurred to me that I might not be able to access the mysterious data source at will, and I felt a certain amount of trepidation as I sat down with him.

But I needn't have worried. Everything slid into action without any problem at all. I tapped into the astonishing storehouse of knowledge with little effort or sense of disorientation. In fact I could not comprehend the mechanics of the process at all. I remained comfortably anchored in the dependable reality of space-time, and simply scanned each document without thinking at all. I felt only a cool lucidity and a subtle sense of depth and expansion in my awareness. A handful of icons glowed occasionally in my peripheral vision, but there was no obvious translation or interpretation required. The facts crystallised faster than I could say them.

Even when Servertis queried my pronouncements, or quoted alternative sources, a host of supporting details and explanatory circumstances surfaced in my mind's eye. In most cases I was able to lay his fears to rest, but he had bought a few turkeys as well. Mostly he already suspected these items though, and was well ahead in his investments overall. It was extraordinary to find myself commanding such abilities. I had always thought of myself as someone of no particular vision or creative excellence, and it was exhilarating to tap effortlessly into such an inexhaustible mine of knowledge and expertise. We worked for three or four hours, with Servertis laboriously recording my comments, until finally he called a break.

'We have made excellent progress,' he beamed. 'We can continue our work this afternoon, and I will visit the library tomorrow to make arrangements for an audience. I thank you greatly for your assistance.'

I went in search of Jacqueline, and found her helping a slightly bemused servant girl to prepare food in the kitchen. 'They have so many herbs and spices here Richard,' she said happily. 'Could you ask Phaedra if I may accompany her to the market, and learn more about the produce of this city?'

'Of course,' I said, pleased that she had found something which interested her. 'I have more work with Servertis this afternoon, but perhaps we can go out again this evening too.'

She gave me an unaffected smile which lit her up like a cathedral, and I felt an answering pang that was beginning to worry me. I had never been in love, even wondered at times if it was something made up in the movies. But I strongly suspected I was beginning to fall for her now. It worried and confused me. I could not assume she would reciprocate my feelings of course, but it raised all kinds of questions beyond that. I was trying to find Alex and pit myself – laughingly – against an unseen army of time travellers with a mystifying and deadly agenda. Jacqueline was an old fashioned kind of girl. She would want stability, respectability, a family – not to mention safety. Just when I could not imagine my life becoming more complicated, it seemed I had found a way to achieve it big-time.

My afternoon session with Servertis was intense and lasted a long time. It was approaching sunset when Jacqueline and I wandered out once more to soak up the sights and sounds of Alexandria. Ironically, or perhaps not so ironically, she was talking about marriage.

'It sounds so awful Richard, this future you describe. Can everyone really live without marriage?'

'Not everyone, only about half the population in my time, in England.'

'But what is to keep them together?'

'Err, well, they often don't stay together.'

'So why don't they get married?'

'Around forty percent of marriages don't last either.'

'What is the matter with you all?' she cried, aghast, 'what becomes of the children?'

'I don't know; they stay with one parent or the other, or sort of alternate between the two.'

'But you said people might have several of these 'relationships'. What happens to the children then?'

'They all sort of all alternate between each other I suppose. It gets a bit complicated.'

'I can't understand why people would behave like that,' she said. 'My father believed that citizens would grow more enlightened and closer to God as science progressed.'

'Hmm – well you have two problems there. Firstly, science has more or less cancelled God, because it says life is a random and meaningless process. And I'm not quite sure about the 'enlightened' part either.'

'What do you mean?' she asked.

'People are not called 'citizens' any more for a start, they are called 'consumers'.'

'Whatever do you mean Richard,' she asked, 'what is a consumer?'

'People who buy stuff all the time, you know, consume things.'

'Oh, you are teasing me,' she said sceptically. 'I have never heard anything so stupid.'

I got rather bogged down in a long, convoluted description of twenty-first century market economics, necessarily touching on many of the problems faced by the 'outsiders' of Ravi's time.

'But does no one have a personal sense of honour?' Jacqueline demanded finally.

'Of course they do,' I said indignantly, 'it's just a bit – blurry I suppose. People get swept along by events.'

'But are events not swept along by great people?' she asked: 'by leaders in society, politicians, writers, philosophers?'

'Not really, no,' I admitted, 'we are swept along by bankers and businessmen: it is actors and musicians whom everyone admires.' I paused thoughtfully. 'Actually, for some reason politicians are still subject to moral judgement. But no one takes them seriously where anything else is concerned.'

'It sounds like a madhouse,' she said in exasperation.

'Well from our perspective, the morality of your time was hypocritical,' I said. 'People preached noble ideals, but acted differently in private. Now we are more open and honest about our behaviour.'

'As your woman friend was to you in London,' she said bitingly. 'Why could people not become genuinely virtuous, rather than abandoned? It seems to me that your moral deprivation has become as gigantic as your shamelessness. Not only do you occupy your days in becoming mindless consumers, but you destroy the world to do so.'

I laughed awkwardly. 'You look magnificent when you are angry,' I ventured to say, in an attempt to escape the argument.

'Stop trying to change the subject,' she retorted, but I glimpsed a flash of embarrassment. 'Besides,' she continued, 'I thought you did not know how to pay compliments to ladies.'

'It's difficult not to pay compliments to you,' I said cheekily, and to my surprise she blushed outright. We had another moment where we could not quite meet each other's eyes, and I sought for a distraction.

'I was reminded today of something we must see in Alexandria,' I said.

'And what might that be?' she asked lightly.

'It's a surprise,' I announced. 'I have the directions.'

I led the way to the crossroads of the two great city highways, and over into the north western part of the city. This was the royal quarter, home to the palaces, centres of arts and learning, temple complexes and extensive gardens of Alexandria's royal rulers. We passed into a park enclosed by a high wall, which sheltered numerous imposing mausoleums. At its centre stood a magnificent structure that made my heart thump in my chest. It was about the size of a medium parish church, an elaborate, rectangular edifice of classic Greek design, enclosed with marble columns and standing on a huge, stepped marble platform. Soldiers in glittering armour and gorgeous royal trappings stood on the steps. People were gathered in and around it an atmosphere of reverence, and something was taking place within the screen of pillars.

'What is this place?' asked Jacqueline quietly.

'The tomb of Alexander,' I said.

She sucked in her breath in a small 'oh' of wonder. We edged nearer, and I could make out dignitaries and priests busy with rituals within the mausoleum. Oil lamps were lit and prayers were chanted. Finally these luminaries filed away, and the crowd moved forward to file one by one up the steps under the uncompromising eye of the honour guard. It seemed that we were permitted to pay respects to the city's legendary founder, and I pushed forward myself, pulling Jacqueline by the hand. I could hardly believe our luck.

We ascended the stepped plinth in stately procession, my anticipation swelling into a heady exhilaration. The interior of the mausoleum overflowed with extravagance. Marble deities, greater-than-life size, stood in each corner in attitudes of blessing and respect. The sarcophagus was solid, worked gold and ivory, and everywhere elaborate decorative adornments glittered and shone. Gold, silver, pearls and precious stones gleamed in the soft light of the oil lamps. The lavish sarcophagus was open, and upon it lay Alexander, his hands clasped in dignified repose on his stomach.

The body was encased entirely in sheets of dense, gleaming gold, skilfully moulded to follow the contours of the form below. A palpable aura of greatness pervaded the place, and it gripped the imagination. His life had been an explosion of visionary genius. He had driven armies far from their native lands, toppled empires, and brought many new things into the world, including this fabulous city where his body lay. I wondered where such power had come from: how one man could have shone so brightly, and transformed the lives of so many. I felt a kind of sadness too, that such gifts had been squandered on war and conquest. It seemed tragic that he had died before perhaps achieving greater things for himself and his empire. I considered what might have constituted a more fitting legacy of human excellence, and then laughed inwardly. I was beginning to remind myself of Jacqueline.

Impatient nudges from behind made me conscious that we were blocking the way, and we made our way back down the broad steps, lightheaded with awe and disbelief.

'That was incredible Richard,' she said, as we walked away. 'To think that I have seen the lost tomb of Alexander: whatever next!'

I couldn't help smiling at her delight. I told myself that I should just enjoy her natural enthusiasm for all things exotic, magical and mysterious, and stop reading personal significance into it all. But her excitement was enchanting, and her joy intoxicating.

'Yes, that really was something,' I agreed. 'But I think it will do for our quota of astonishing ancient artefacts for today. Let's go and find somewhere to eat.'

'I am sure you are right Richard,' she smiled, 'I am so much up in the air that I hardly know what is up or down any longer.'

We found a nice eating place with outdoor tables, and a garden roofed over by vines intertwined with light trelliswork. It granted shade during the day and filtered moonlight by night, supplemented by clay oil lamps which threw a cosy pool of light onto each table. The lamps were a slightly grander version of the domestic design I saw everywhere in the city: a shallow rounded body tapering to a spout for the wick, with a central opening for oil and abstract decorations etched into their earthen body. The glowing contours and shadowy voids cast by the flames conjured a timeless beauty, and it struck me that no additional device from my twenty-first century world could have rendered the scene more perfect.

Or perhaps it was sharing it with Jacqueline that made it so. The intensity of feeling reminded me of a vivid interlude in my late childhood, when a family with a young daughter had moved in next door to me. We had spent an enchanted summer swapping dreams and stories at the bottom of her garden. Then she was plucked away by a family crisis, and I returned to the numbing antagonism between my parents. I had not thought of her for years. But now I recognised that same, simple hearted openness and magical joy: of hardly knowing where one personality ended and the other began.

I felt an irresistible pull which frightened me. I thought of the violence which my haphazard adventure had already led to: the carnage which could erupt from nowhere at any moment. This was no walk in the park, and I shuddered to think of the risks it might pose to her.

She felt it. 'What's wrong?' she asked.

'Oh, nothing really,' I shrugged. 'Just wondering what it might be like to have an ordinary life, without fear and danger.'

'I doubt that such wonder and adventure comes without a price,' she said, uncharacteristically sombre. 'But there is little I would not trade this moment.'

Her words could have meant many things, but they made my heart swell with love for her. I was shocked by the intensity of feeling which blossomed: an overwhelming desire for oneness and completion. Every molecule in my being seemed to ache with a desire for fusion and procreation, and suddenly there was nothing I wanted more than to make a home with her: for her to bear our children. It was as alarming as it was wonderful, and a part of me wanted to run a mile.

So I had fallen in love I thought. And perhaps because it felt such a perilous thing, I tried to rationalise its grip. The Greeks had many words for love I remembered, each with a different meaning. I tried to recall them, and the ancient concepts welled dutifully from the mysterious depths within me. *Eros:* sexual passion, with its loss of control, and *Ludus:* the casual affection of children, friends and acquaintances. There was *Pragma:* the deep understanding between long-married couples; and *Philia,* the deep comradely friendship between brothers in arms. There was the love between brother and sister, between parents and their children. Most mysterious was *Philautia:* self-love, narcissistic and destructive, or positive and outgoing; and finally *Agape:* the selfless love of all people.

The fine shades of perspective and meaning crowded in on me, and I wondered how they had been reduced to the guilt-ridden Eros of my own time. Now all of them seemed to shine like multiple facets of a single, many-splendored jewel blazing in Jacqueline's soul. A deep and poignant ache grew in my heart. It was like glimpsing an Aladdin's cave of treasures I could not believe might be mine.

So I tried to ignore the elephant in the room, and spoke inconsequentially about the wonders of Alexandria. She drank little wine and I abstained too, afraid that I might say something I would regret. Even so there were moments where it seemed something was going to happen. An irresistible force seemed to be pushing us together. I longed to reach out to her, but did not have the nerve to do so.

Jacqueline had a way of blasting me out of the water in a blaze of altruistic indignation, but the following day it was her convictions that were on the firing line. We were visiting the Serapeum, the temple of Serapis, which was the patron god of Alexandria. Servertis was off at the great library, arranging an appointment to view the scrolls. He and I had completed our preparatory work, and Jacqueline and I were free to roam the city. The Serapeum was the most important temple in Alexandria, built on a low hill in the south west of the city. I remembered being fascinated by the place while studying the history of Architecture, for it was a temple to an invented God, deliberately created for the brand new city of Alexandria by its founding Ptolemaic Dynasty. The idea that an entire city population would happily take to worshiping a manufactured deity had always seemed extraordinary to me, and I was curious to see it.

Even the outer precincts of this august establishment were immensely extravagant: a huge rectangular, colonnaded court of grey granite, not unlike the outer courtyard of the great lighthouse, with extensive annexes constructed behind the enclosing pillars. The main temple stood in majestic isolation in the centre of this great compound, with its own massive columns contrasting strikingly in red granite. The inner sanctum was guarded by vast, lavishly embossed bronze doors worked with gold, and they swung ponderously open by invisible means at our approach. It was a fashionable form of technical wizardry, engineered by pulleys and weights, and intended to increase the sense of mystery and the size of the temple donation.

Within the lavishly decorated inner vault towered a statue of the god Serapis, a huge bearded man three times life-size, seated on a fabulously ornate throne with a bizarre, three-headed dog by his side. The statue was constructed in wood, and finished with superbly worked metal and precious stones. Its body was dark blue, and its clothes and sandals decorated with gleaming gold and silver. I felt a flicker of recognition in the baffling store of knowledge within me. The name Serapis was an amalgamation of Osiris and Apis, aspects of the Egyptian god of the Dead. He had been given the form of Zeus, the most powerful of the Greek gods, and was accompanied by Cerberus, the three-headed dog which guarded the entrance to the Underworld. So – a made-to-measure compromise unifying the beliefs of the Greeks and Egyptians in Alexandria: a political divinity. An image expressed in a staggering exhibition of wealth, which created a reality all of its own. I shrugged. I supposed it was not the first or the last of its kind.

Jacqueline found it quite disturbing though, and we had a long, rather surreal argument about Religion on the elegant marble seating in the wide courtyard outside, surrounded by glittering, statues embellished with a fortune in jewels, silver and gold. I pointed out a few home truths regarding the history of Christianity, including the cruel death of the accomplished lady philosopher and scientist Hypatia at the hands of a Christian mob in the streets of Alexandrea, and the butchering of every man, woman and child in Jerusalem when the Crusaders captured that city. While my new library of inner knowledge was overflowing with facts about the historical, political and intellectual development of religious ideas, I was surprised to find little information about their original exponents. There seemed a strange, confusing resistance to learning anything about their personalities and intentions regarding the movements created in their name. Our conversation wandered over the similarities and contradictions among religious ideas around the world, and the differences between belief and understanding.

'I find this all horribly confusing,' Jacqueline said at last. 'I was brought up to believe that Christianity is the only true religion. I can't accept that it is wrong or false, or just like any other religion.'

I couldn't help laughing. 'Really Jacqueline, just think how bigoted you sound! Everyone believes their own religion is the right one – or maybe it's just a coincidence that Hindu's are all born in India or whatever!'

'My mind is in a complete whirl,' she complained. 'If I hadn't experienced so many strange things myself everything you are saying would sound mad to me. Surely you do not mean that God and heaven do not exist?'

I smiled. 'No, not necessarily. I am just saying that maybe they are something different to what we imagine.'

'Harrumph!' she sniffed disapprovingly. 'I was quite happy with Reverend Hamilton and his Sunday sermons before all of this strange travelling in time began.'

I felt an absurd pang of disappointment. 'Were you really?' I asked.

She looked at me for a long moment: her pupil's fathomless whirlpools, as dark as night.

'No,' she said.

Next morning I set out for the Great Library with Servertis, accompanied by a couple of guards and a donkey laden with the most valuable of his precious scrolls. It was situated in the royal quarter of the city, down towards the harbour, and less than a mile beyond Alexander's tomb. There was actually another, smaller library annex at the Serapeum, attached to the temple which Jacqueline and I had visited the day before. We had toyed with the idea of looking around it, but in the end we had sauntered lazily about the streets, talking of nothing in particular and soaking up the intoxicating ambience that seemed to linger in the most inconsequential parts of that fabulous city.

Now I felt a growing buzz of excitement as we approached the Great Library itself. It had fired my imagination in my student days, as it had so many others over the centuries. Envisioned at the founding of the city by Alexander's general Ptolemy when he claimed Egypt for his own, this legendary institution had grown to become a haven for all of the fledgling arts and sciences of the ancient western world. Little had been known of its physical construction and appearance, but tales abounded of its philosophers, poets, astronomers and mathematicians, and its innovative students of practical and intellectual knowledge of all kinds. The place was maintained by the royal treasury, and enjoyed a funding regime like none other in history, something very apparent as we arrived within its precincts.

The extravagant profusion of gardens, waterways and pavilions was mind-boggling. Carefully tended trees and a rich profusion of exotic foliage leant cooling shade and fragrant colour to elegant marble walkways, watched over by statues grave and heroic, and refreshed by sparkling pools of lotus flowers. We passed terraced plots of saplings and sprouting plants of all kinds, each identified by carefully labelled sticks, and diligently examined by serious young men. Nearby a grey-haired dignitary strode about a secluded, paved enclosure, mouthing a poem or a speech to himself.

Large numbers of people, mostly men, converged from every direction: a shared air of profound and eager enquiry written over their features. I flashed back to the London morning rush hour – the blank faced automatons speed-walking out of the tube station to work – and the contrast was dismal. It was an illusion of course: these seekers of truth thronging the graceful avenues of the Royal Gardens could only be a privileged elite, but the euphoric air of renaissance and discovery was exhilarating.

We turned into a broad, leafy avenue to pass a long single-story construction more than two hundred feet in length. Its walls were featureless apart from intermittently carved animal and botanical reliefs, and it had a shallow-pitched terracotta tiled roof with a beautifully engraved frieze, picked out in blue and maroon. The end of this structure butted at ninety degrees against the front corner of a large building of two lofty stories, which stretched back some distance to the rear. Its frontage was perhaps a hundred and twenty feet across, and presented an elegant and elaborate vision to passers-by.

A rich gallery of Ionic marble columns; each bearing engraved pediments and entablatures, decorated its rich façade. Paired columns stood one before the other, supporting alternating segmental entablatures brought forward on the first story. Broken pediments were similarly constructed on the second; the columns standing four-square beneath them to frame graceful statues within. Nine sublime female forms, each equipped with devices musical and creative, gazed out demurely at us. I recognised a Lyre, a tragic mask, a writing tablet and a globe and compass. The encyclopaedic memory stirred within me: *The nine Muses*, I knew, *the nine daughters of Zeus, each the personification of separate disciplines in science and the arts.* I began to see their origins: how they had been added to the Greek Pantheon as creative mythology developed -- but withdrew from the unfathomable storehouse of knowledge to escape the mass of information.

Generous door and window openings filled the flanking wall spaces, with three great entranceways standing adjacent to one other at the centre, served by a single set of broad marble steps traversing the front of the building.

'The Great Library,' said Servertis with a smile, waving effusively at the imposing building, 'the Mouseion adjoins at the far end.'

The Mousion – the place of the Muses supplied the enigmatic depths within me: the forerunner to the Museums of my time. The low single-story construction continued on from the main library building, running another two hundred feet along the avenue to stand against the front corner of an even larger building that had already grabbed my attention, and which confounded my knowledge of Greek architecture.

It looked older than the library, and boasted a classically imposing front elevation: a great row of Doric columns capped by a vast, sculpture-rich pediment. They encased an inset gable wall, with substantial entranceways and first floor window openings sheltered within. Marble steps ran between each thick, fluted pillar, accessing an inner entrance platform that spanned the width of the structure. It was easily a hundred and fifty feet across, but what really stunned me was the great dome above the building.

It was set towards the front of the building's long axis, which stretched back two hundred and fifty feet or so. The huge vault (for the time) was about seventy feet in diameter and thirty five high, clad in an exquisite mosaic of carefully cut light-coloured marble, so perfectly fitted to its rounded contours that the grouting barely showed. The marble was a beautiful pinky-white, with smoky red-brown rectangular key patterns running horizontally about its curves at intermittent levels. At its crown sat a round, golden cupola with an open parapet granting spectacular views of the city.

The dome rested upon a larger rectangular third floor structure behind the huge front pediment. It was a bit like a penthouse addition, with window openings and entranceways accessing a wide surrounding balcony and a narrow curved stairway up to the cupola. It contained the dining hall, I learned later; its weight and that of the dome carried down through the building via massive columns and supporting walls. The rear area of the Mousion extended in two parallel separate blocks to let light into the studios: two-storied constructions with conventionally tiled roofs.

'The place of heavenly observations,' said Servertis, catching my gaze. 'There they pass every night, charting the movements of the stars and the planets.'

I later discovered that the dome had been constructed using sturdy terracotta tubes, each slightly cone-shaped and about five feet in length. They were inserted into each other, and curved into diminishing parallel arches before being encased in mortar. A second, lighter layer of arched clay tubing had been added crossways over the first, and similarly covered. It was a daring expansion on a simple vaulting technique previously used on a much smaller scale, and typical of the unbridled spirit of innovation which thrived in the city.

The Library and Mousion formed part of a massive complex which incorporated a whole series of lesser structures that faced each other across the broad royal avenue. Further elaborate edifices, walkways and gardens stretched far to the rear on either side. A faint, sour animal tang and indistinct barks and grunts drifted on the breeze from the sea. This vast academy of learning boasted a menagerie, I remembered from my student days, and even an outdoor amphitheatre.

The long, single-story constructions extended around behind the main library building and the Mousion to form a huge inner courtyard, divided by a central section which cut across to a rear library entrance. Sheltered inner colonnaded walkways opened onto the compound, their inside walls stacked with bibliothekai: shelves holding many of the thousands of papyrus scrolls that made up the library. The more valued scrolls were stored in a similar fashion in the main building.

'The acquisition halls are further along, nearer the docks,' said Servertis, 'many additions to the library come by sea, and by royal decree, all ships that dock here are searched for scrolls so that copies may be taken of items of interest.'

'Do the owners get the original back or the copy?' I asked.

'It depends on its importance, and how many coins change hands,' he said with a sly smile. 'Fortunately I have a royal licence. I need no copies, and the coins will flow in my direction.'

We continued down towards the harbour, past a series of rectangular, single story buildings which Servertis identified as lecture halls. The walls featured generous, cooling openings to the outside air, and I glimpsed eager young men taking their places on tiered stone seating surrounding raised central platforms, on which speakers were preparing to teach. Our donkeys were a little jumpy at the indistinct sounds and odours of the unseen menagerie, and we worked our way awkwardly through the throng of budding academicians. Thousands of people were milling about on the Mousion campus. It was another twenty minutes before we progressed beyond the oncoming tide and reached the two substantial buildings that processed the steady influx of literature into the library.

I was to become quite familiar with these acquisition halls in the days that followed. Each was a little over half the size of the main library building, and their organisation and industry was typically impressive. They were both two-storied but more functional, with fewer ostentatious external embellishments and the upper floors less formal mezzanine-like levels. The structure closest to the harbour had an almost warehouse air to it: a spacious public receiving bay within its front screen of plain granite columns equipped with a broad marble countertop and overseen by sober-faced clerks. They discussed or argued matters with visitors or officials tasked with searching incoming vessels: examining and recording scrolls and stacking them in temporary racks behind them.

Beyond this first line of engagement lurked an extensive array of tables and benches populated by a contingent of Alexandria's celebrated 'Grammarians' - philologists and textual scholars. They further examined and catalogued the influx of scrolls, and lodged them in more respectable and exact storage facilities lining the walls. Wooden steps led up to the second level, where dozens of scribes laboured to create copies of books seized from incoming travellers.

There were hundreds of thousands of scrolls stored in the various departments of the Mousion campus, each many yards long when fully unrolled. The magnitude of the operation was extraordinary. It seemed glorious and unreal – a surprising co-existence of altruism and hubris: a determined labour of love on an industrial scale.

Servertis led the way into the second building, further back from the waterfront, and acquired the assistance of a couple of porters to carry his leather cylinders of scrolls from the donkey panniers into a private receiving room at the rear. Here he introduced me to Hephaestos, a jovial, middle aged individual with a carefully crafted beard who engaged us in polite conversation until a couple of his associates joined us.

We then entered into much the same process I had been through with Servertis: unrolling scrolls on a large marble table top and standing about arguing the case for each one. Once again my mysterious new ability to trawl collective data from deep time manifested on cue, and the esteem of my new acquaintances grew grudgingly but perceptibly. The discussions became heated at times, mostly where Servertis and money were concerned, but my role was advisory, and I happily left the bargaining to him. Some of our wares were put aside for further deliberation by others, but by the end of the morning prices had been agreed for most of the scrolls we had brought with us, and Servertis seemed well satisfied.

He smiled when Hephaestos called a halt for the day, and announced that we would visit the Mousion to eat. I could hardly wait. I felt electrified by the kind of quivering anticipation I had previously attributed solely to the likes of Charles. The unique communion of philosophic souls and eclectic treasures which its reputation suggested literally intoxicated me with excitement. The guard was sent home with the donkeys, and Servertis and I set off for our lunch; he gleefully counting money in his head, and me hardly able to believe I was not dreaming.

The Mousion easily surpassed my hopes. I arrived dumbstruck at the grand entrance hall of a glorious temple of high culture. The marble floor was laid out in a sumptuously rich mosaic of intricate rectangular patterns and mythical imagery, its images conjuring magic and mystery. Lavish fresco designs and even more magnificent mosaics adorned the walls and ceilings. Ahead of us stretched an immense, regal staircase, separating left and right to rise to the floor above. There was little natural light in many parts of the Mousion, and ingeniously fashioned, highly polished silver mirrors amplified the light from immense oil lamps. Elegant statues of bronze and brilliantly painted marble gazed beatifically upon the abundance of art and beauty, and reflected splendour gleamed from decorative surfaces on every side.

Three fabulous wall mosaics caught my eye: their workmanship immaculate, the tesserae enriched with squares of ivory, gold and silver and semi-precious stones. One, to the left of the entrance hall, celebrated Alexander's victory over the Persian king Darius at Issus. Another on the right portrayed the founder of the Ptolemaic Kingdom in Alexandria in all the royal splendour of an Egyptian Pharaoh. The largest mosaic loomed high above the division of the staircase: three mysterious female figures which seemed to glow with an uncanny sense of presence and power. Above them in bold letters was the legend *'The place of the cure of the soul'.*

The three Muses – the information welled up unbidden within me – *the powers of the Great Mother of prehistory: Mnēmē the Goddesses of memory, Aoidē the Goddess of song, Meletē, the Goddess of contemplation...* I retreated sharply from the vast pool of intelligence. Not to avoid information overload this time, but to escape an abrupt pull into alarming new depths of being. Mere information seemed to realise a critical density, and ignite into raw energy. I had almost lost myself in some indescribable depth of existence. *'What was that?'* my mind yelped, and I shivered unaccountably. I didn't want to know.

I tried to force my attention back to more mundane wonders as Servertis indicated the spacious ground floor studios, which opened out beyond massive doorways leading from the majestic entranceway. But his rambling description of the Mousion and its annexes; its rigorous debates on all things mathematical, medical, astronomical, literary and musical now largely passed me by. I had been reminded again of realities and forces beyond my comprehension, and realised how distracted I had become from my quest. Jacqueline's company and the marvels of the extraordinary ancient city had captivated me, and I had forgotten my purpose.

I followed Servertis up the magnificent staircase with a sizeable part of me tempted by the idea of taking life at face value. A second, less spectacular stairway led up to the great dining hall at the top of the building, where a central circle of columns supporting the great dome above divided its customers. The food served here was gratis to all visitors at the Mousion, and I again wondered at the egalitarian spirit that permeated the establishment. Later of course, I learnt that a closer eye than I realised was being kept on the social credentials of those entering the library complex. It was the residence as well as the workplace of many of its occupants. Accommodation arrangements existed throughout the Mousion-Library complex. There were royal pensioners among the learned and accomplished in Alexandria's great palace of the arts: jobs for life underwritten by the Ptolemy dynasty, in a pursuit of excellence unmatched anywhere in the known world.

And it was here, while eating a simple meal of fish, bread and dates with Servertis, that the next piece of the puzzle dropped unexpectedly into place. I recognised the subtle reflection of the portal first, coming from someone at a table some distance away. It took slightly longer to recognise the unfortunate little man who would die in my arms in the far distant future.

Chapter 20

I FROZE, CONFLICTING thoughts racing around in my head. I was alarmed: wondering if he wore the same Portal I did – if such a thing was possible – and if some kind of violent reaction might take place if we got close to each other. Then it occurred to me that the portal reflection must be visible to him too, and I shrank involuntarily in my seat, eliciting a curious glance from Servertis. Ironically the movement seemed to draw the man's attention, and he glanced over in my direction. His gaze lingered for a moment, but he turned away without interest and I relaxed, though still disconcerted.

'Is something wrong?' asked Servertis.

'No,' I said, attempting to feign a casual air, 'but I have remembered a – err – private errand I would like to attend to.'

He regarded me shrewdly. 'As you wish, Waltonis,' he said, 'I had thought to show you the library after our meal, but it can wait until tomorrow if you prefer.'

'Thank you,' I said, appreciating his discretion as much his easy-going nature. 'It has been a lifetime's wish to see the treasures of Alexandria, and I look forward to visiting the library.'

He seemed content with this, and left with a smile a short time later. I remained uncomfortably in my seat, unsure what I was going to do, but determined not to let the man out of my sight. My quarry was deep in conversation with a striking young man who appeared passionately absorbed in the subject at hand. His hair was a tousled cluster of bright blonde curls, and his tunic frayed and marked with stains. They talked for some time before quitting their table, and I followed discretely as they sauntered down to the ground floor.

They parted in the grand entrance hall: the dishevelled young man disappearing into one of the ground floor studios, and my time traveller leaving through the main exit. I continued to follow him, staying fifty yards or so away, and trying to keep as many people between us as possible. I was barely aware of the Portal reflection at that distance, but I didn't want to take any chances. He strolled casually along, apparently enjoying the sights and sounds around him. I couldn't help a wry smile as I recognised something of the holidaymaker abroad in his manner. But the darker connotations of my connection with him nagged at me, and I remained nervous of a confrontation.

The next development really threw me. As my quarry ambled past the grand library entrance he was hailed by a man and a woman descending the steps towards him. To my astonishment, the tell-tale glimmer of a portal reflected from each of them too. I was still trying to process this when another man exited the library emanating a similar aura, and passed the three of them without so much as a nod of recognition. I stood and stared. Suddenly there were time travellers everywhere. It was a few seconds before I realised how exposed I was, and I moved further away, my mind racing as I surveyed the trio from the corner of my eye. I supposed I could understand why time travellers might be attracted to ancient Alexandria, but discovering four of them in close proximity like this was overwhelming. I had no idea what to do, and when the trio began to walk away together, it simplified matters merely to follow them, taking care to remain at a safe distance.

It was easier to track three people together, and I dropped back further still, keeping them in sight for ten minutes or so, until they entered a property on the outer fringes of the royal quarter. I lingered for a while on the chance that someone would reappear. But after some minutes I thought I detected a faint reaction from the Portal. It could have been a response to a door opening in space-time, and I realised they could now be somewhere else entirely and abandoned my pursuit. But it was a striking development, albeit an inconclusive one, and I hurried back to Jacqueline big with news.

I was surprised to find her rather muted when I spilled the story out to her. She seemed to regard it as more of a threat than a breakthrough. When I thought about it, I supposed her impression of other time travellers had been shaped by her stepfather, and I could understand that she had no great desire to probe into their affairs. She was still high on her deliverance from a hideous fate. My news served to remind her of her narrow escape, and she was reluctant to put her head into the noose once more.

'Do we have to pursue these people Richard?' she asked. 'Now that we know they are here, should we not try to escape to some other place?'

'I agree we should be careful,' I conceded, 'but I don't think it an accident we are here and have discovered them like this: especially the man who gave me – or will give me – the Portal. There is much more to this than our own concerns. The fate of other people and events in the future may depend on what we do. After all, had I not acquired the Portal, you may not have escaped your stepfather's intrigues. There is also the girl who warned me about the bad guys. She said a lot more was at stake than my own fate – more than I could imagine.'

'Harrumph!' she said huffily, 'yet you know little about her either.'

But she no longer spoke of fleeing the mysterious time travellers in the city. We went out for a meal in the evening, and she agreed to accompany me the next day to carry out a little detective work at the Mousion and the Library. I reasoned that we could split up if necessary to follow people, and she could get close to time travellers without being recognised as one of their own. But I could see it was weighing on her mind. She was quieter than usual and drank more wine than she normally did. I realised how frightening this all must be for her, and tried to reassure her.

'I'm sorry for dragging you into all this Jacqueline,' I said, 'but in a way you were already involved.'

'I know Richard. I have no reason to complain. It's just very unsettling to live like this, to be in a strange place...' she flashed a quick smile, 'however fascinating... with all of these peculiar people and their fantastical machines popping up everywhere.'

We talked for an hour, knocking back a lot more wine as I tried to get her to relax and feel less insecure. I succeeded, but realised too late that I was exchanging one problem for another. She became increasingly confiding, and the Aladdin's cave of impassioned nirvana that I was trying not to think about grew increasingly palpable. The joys and dangers of Alexandria blurred into a happy backdrop, and the emotionally charged field between us expanded and intensified. I tried to will myself to break the spell, to get us up and out somewhere distracting, but my best intentions seemed rooted in an agreeable inertia.

'Perhaps I will adjust to all this in time,' she was saying, 'so many of the things I believed in my life have been turned on their head.'

'I forget I have had more time to get used to it,' I admitted. 'I remember how strange everything was when we were riding with the Lieutenants men – and at Gettysburg.'

'How awful I was to you,' she said ruefully, 'yet you still tried to help me: when you were lost and alone with no idea what was happening to you.'

I coloured slightly. 'I just blundered from one situation into another really.'

She smiled wistfully, her pupils dark with emotion.

'You did much more than that. You tried to do what you thought was right even when it put you in danger. You went back for Billy who was your enemy...' she paused ...'and you came back for me'.

A profound silence fell. I felt I should point out that I hadn't precisely come back for her, but I couldn't make a sound. The space between us pulsated with expectancy and my heart began to tremble.

'Jacqueline...,' I began: my voice was uneven, and some invisible force seemed to propel me towards her.

'Here I go again,' I quipped to myself, *'doing what I think is right despite the danger.'*

Everything seemed to slow down, and for a moment I thought I had triggered the time dilation effect. I kissed her, braced for rejection, and felt a flash of joy as she acquiesced after only the smallest hesitation. It was everything I could have imagined. She clung to me and the depth of feeling was overwhelming; the softness of her lips, the fragrance of her being utterly intoxicating. It was infinitely more intense than anything I had felt before: almost ridiculously so – as if we were physically dissolving into each other's beings. Then she broke away, and we stared at each other in shock, each breathing unsteadily.

'Richard...' she faltered: an echo of my own affirmation of a moment before. 'I – I should not have done that, I think. I fear I have drunk too much wine. I hope you don't expect...'

'...that I can have a casual relationship with you? Not in a million years.'

'I mean it. I hardly know what I am feeling. So many extraordinary things have happened... but I have come to care for you so much.'

'Me too,' I said, my heart singing.

'You have been a gentleman and I honour you for it. I can easily imagine how it must be to cast all caution aside. But you must know that I cannot – I will not...'

I smiled at her. 'Jacqueline, I would never ask for more than you are willing to give. Forgive me, I could not help myself. I know this is not the time or the place.'

'This time and place have been wonderful. I will always treasure them. Of course you are right, everything is so uncertain. Perhaps if we find somewhere safe, where things are more normal...' She blushed, leaving the sentence unfinished.

'I will come knocking on your door carrying flowers, and do everything that is right and proper,' I laughed, giddy with feeling.

She turned a multi-megawatt smile on me, which pushed *finding somewhere safe and normal* several notches up the agenda. The evening continued in a happy dream, our words charged with a new depth of tenderness and meaning. It wove an enchantment into the night, and the magical setting of Alexandria sealed the moment with a timeless poignancy.

We walked back to our lodgings in a comfortable silence. Yet things felt different as we entered our room. I wanted to respect her principles, but was unsure how it would work in reality, given our enforced intimacy. I was pretty sure she was a virgin, and that it would be immensely important to her. The last thing I wanted was for her to feel pressure, or to become more insecure and confused in our present predicament. But even so there was a decided emptiness in turning away from her to sleep. I lay for long minutes trying not to think about it, until she finally spoke.

'Richard?' she whispered. She didn't ask if I was awake.

'Yes?' I said a little breathlessly.

'If you were to – hold me, would that be acceptable? I mean would you...'

'Yes,' I said, preparing to summon up considerable reserves of idealistic resolve, 'I would like that.'

I moved my crude bedding over to hers. I hugged her and we lay on our sides facing each other, with our hands lightly intertwined. She gave a little sigh.

'Thank you Richard,' she said, and I felt a gentle contentment. No resolve required.

Morning was a little trickier. I awoke to find her snuggled into my shoulder, and my body seemed to have awakened to the situation somewhat before I had. I carefully extracted myself from her embrace, and called upon the unused resolve from the night before. She began to wake as I moved, and by the time she raised herself on one elbow, peace reigned on the carnal front.

'Oh Richard, I slept so well,' she said cheerfully. 'I feel much happier about looking for your time travellers today.'

I smiled, 'that's the spirit. Wait outside the Mousion about an hour after noon, and I'll come as soon as I've finished with Servertis.'

My day at the acquisition hall proceeded much as before, except that I glimpsed yet another time traveller in one of the other parts of the building. They seemed to be gathered around the Library complex like bees around a honeypot. It didn't seem to be mere sightseeing.

Servertis turned to me and smiled when our business was concluded for the day. 'It is best I accompany you to the Mousion again and to the Library if you wish to see them with your wife,' he said, 'the stewards know me, and will not question your right to be there.'

Jacqueline was waiting for us opposite the Mousion, looking remarkably relaxed on one of the elegant red granite benches that lined the royal boulevard. My heart surged with joy at the sight of her, and I felt equal to anything the day might bring. We entered the Mousion, and I watched her stare solemnly at the great mosaic of the three Muses. I turned to Servertis before she could ask me anything about it.

'May we visit some of the studios before we go upstairs to eat?' I asked. I was hoping we might come across the young companion of my time traveller there.

'Certainly,' he beamed, and we followed him through one of the high doorways that lined the great entrance hall. The studios were airy and elegant, but functional in character. Some were larger than others, even occupying two or more connected rooms, and we had to pass through several to reach the furthermost studios at the rear of the building. Each area was dedicated to different branches of study. Students and their mentors gathered about worktables strewn with models and scrolls of astronomical configurations or anatomical forms, while musicians, playwrights and poets loudly practiced or debated their disciplines. It was hard to credit the living reality of it all as the stuff of legends passed before our eyes. I watched Jacqueline light up in wonder, gazing about in enthralled absorption.

Deep within the maze of studios we came upon a large workshop teeming with people tinkering about with an array of mysterious devices. I knew that a whole range of air, water, steam, mechanical and even magnetically operated appliances were being constructed by the enquiring minds of Alexandrian scholars. Evidence of their inventiveness and industry was apparent everywhere. But what really leapt to my attention were the familiar features of the passionate young man I was looking for. He was frowning now with concentration, and filing methodically at something on the work bench before him.

I nudged Jacqueline, and tried to draw her attention to him as discreetly as possible. She seemed to understand: I had described him to her in some detail the night before. I toyed with the idea of going over to see what he was doing, but decided it would be better not to draw attention to ourselves for now. Instead I thanked Servertis for showing us around, and indicated that we were ready to eat. We had an enjoyable meal, with Jacqueline asking numerous questions about everything we had seen while I interpreted Servertis' responses to her. He was a little surprised and patronising about her interest, but answered readily enough. There was no sign of my unfortunate friend, or of any other time travellers in the Mousion, but we passed a guy with a Portal walking towards us as we set off to the Library. It was a man I had not seen before, and he glanced at me as we passed, but showed little more than mild curiosity as he did so.

We ascended the entrance steps of the great library into a hall even larger than that of the Mousion. There was another grand staircase, and another interior abounding with glorious mosaics and paintings and statues of hybrid Ptolemaic Hellenistic-Egyptian splendour. As in the Mousion, opulence and beauty presided everywhere, but many of the subjects were more academic in nature: images taken from the natural world, or celebrated famous landmarks, authors and artistes. It reflected perhaps the more pragmatic ethos of recording reality, rather than its inventive interpretation.

The library was divided into business-like departments according to subject and contained many thousands of scrolls. It even featured a directory section, listing the collection alphabetically by author and genre. The works were stored in rows of bibliothekai stacked around the walls to the rear of busy library staff, who stood upon raised platforms behind wide marble front shelves. Each scroll was equipped with a small dangling tag containing information on the author, title, and subject. Men, and fewer women, numbered among both staff and clientele, and literary works were delivered to the front shelves to be unrolled and studied, or taken to be perused on luxurious couches or laid out on sumptuous tables.

The main library rooms on both floors contained the more valuable scrolls. Countless others were stored in the dense rows of bibliothekai lining the inside walls of the long colonnaded walkways enclosing the gardens at the rear. There were numerous lesser rooms too, fulfilling other functions in the relentless expansion and maintenance of the great library: translations into standardised Greek, repairs to damaged acquisitions, and the careful copying of stored manuscripts nearing the end of their shelf-life.

It was through an open doorway into one of these workrooms that I glimpsed a female with the tell-tale reflection of a Portal shining from her. She was seated at a table with her back to me, but I thought I recognised her from the day before. Jacqueline caught my expression as I glanced into the room, and her happiness seemed to dim a little. But she continued to gaze about herself in fascination as we continued our tour, and we covered the main building areas without discovering any more time-travelling brethren. Even wandering about the gardens at the rear produced no further results, so we thanked and parted from Servertis, and Jacqueline and I took up positions on an outside bench some distance from the main library entrance.

'There was one of them in a back room,' I confirmed, 'I think it was the woman I saw yesterday.'

'Is this the way life always is?' Jacqueline asked obliquely, 'alarming or tedious duties dragging at one's heels when the most wonderful things are happening?'

I chuckled. 'It does seem that we can't have one without the other sometimes. Maybe that's what life is all about. It is full of beautiful things, but if we abandon our obligations and grab for them, we might lose...' I thought about it, uncertain how to complete the train of thought.

'...everything,' completed Jacqueline absently, and then shivered. 'I hope it will not be so.'

'Well,' I said after a pause, 'listen to us, grumbling about the adventure of a thousand lifetimes!'

I turned and smiled at her, reaching for her hand. She closed her fingers over mine, colouring a little as she returned my grip. Then we settled back resolutely to see what the future would bring. A steady stream of people passed by, with no presence of a portal in evidence. An hour passed, and the sun began to hang lower in the sky. Evening approached, and I was beginning to wonder if we should give up for the day, when the elusive light of twin portals shimmered from two figures at the top of the library steps. I identified the woman from the day before as they descended; and then, with a curious mixture of alarm and excitement, the second figure as my ill-fated mentor. We had somehow missed him in the building. The woman lifted her hand in farewell and parted from the little man, who somewhat to my surprise adopted a position on a bench on the opposite side of the boulevard to us. He was not close, but I knew he would notice the tell-tale signs of my Portal sooner or later. So, much to Jacqueline's amusement, I slunk carefully from my seat and hid behind a couple of palm trees nearby.

'Stop giggling,' I hissed.

'I'm sorry Richard,' she whispered back, concealing her mouth behind her hand. 'It's because I'm nervous. But you do look so ridiculous, sneaking about like that.'

Our quarry remained seated for ten minutes or so, until the wild-haired youth approached from the direction of the Mousion. They greeted one another warmly and moved off together, heading back the way the three time travellers had gone the day before.

'You follow them, but not too close,' I said to Jacqueline, 'I'll be further back. I don't want him to see my Portal.'

We all trailed along, moving with a fair number of people heading in more or less the same direction. I could not see our quarry, but kept Jacqueline in sight about fifty yards ahead of me. The course she took led past the house which the three time travellers had entered the previous day, and we soon left the Royal Quarter to cross the vast, colonnaded Canopic Way. We passed between the prestigious buildings lining this great East-West civic artery, and began to enter the less impressive streets beyond. I could see that Jacqueline was hanging back. I presumed she was feeling more conspicuous in the less crowded streets, but when I caught up with her she was peering around a corner into a narrow street beyond.

'I saw which house they entered,' she said, 'it is the ninth or tenth on the left, the one with the blue coloured door.'

'Should we have a closer look?' I asked.

'I'm not sure,' she said. 'Someone else is already doing that. We were not the only ones following them.'

I felt a stab of unease, and peered around the corner myself. I could not see much, just a handful of passers-by glancing incuriously at a man with his back to us, who lurked some way along the street.

'We had better move,' I said after a moment, 'he might notice us if he comes back this way.'

We retraced our steps into the larger thoroughfares behind the Canopic way before we stopped to talk.

'I only noticed him when the crowd thinned a little, as we left the royal quarter,' said Jacqueline. 'It suddenly struck me that he appeared just as intent on them as I was. I wasn't certain, but I distanced myself just in case, and sure enough he stuck to them like glue.'

'So, things are becoming more complicated,' I mused. Little did I realise how much more complicated they were about to get.

It was early evening by now, and men of business and learning were starting to be replaced by more ostentatious individuals in the streets, clearly bent on recreation and entertainment. One of the extraordinarily flamboyant Alexandrian ladies was borne regally towards us, lounging indolently on a palanquin conveyed by four impassive footmen. Her conveyance was impressively designed and adorned, and she glittered with even more extravagant accessories herself. Her gown was of dazzling white silk, heavily embroidered with gold thread and festooned with bejewelled golden trinkets. Her brilliant blond hair was piled high in fashionable ringlets, her face fluorescent with cosmetics, and she looked so startlingly beautiful that for a moment I simply stared in fascination.

I clocked a glowering look from Jacqueline in the corner of my eye, and quickly withdrew my glaze, but my attention had not passed unnoticed on the palanquin. Its occupant fixed me with a penetrating glance and stiffened.

'Richard!' she said.

My heart seemed to seize, and I felt like a proverbial rabbit in the headlights.

'Anna?' I croaked.

'Down!' she snapped in Greek, and the footmen lowered the conveyance to thigh level after a startled look. She hopped off with practiced ease, trapping me in a nightmare scenario between herself and Jacqueline. They eyed one another ferociously, and I had the alarming impression I had become the prey of two feral beings.

'H–Hello Anna,' I achieved, 'you are, err, looking well.'

She seemed to drip vitriol for a moment, but mastered herself, and was suddenly overflowing with sweetness and light.

'Richard dear,' she drawled, 'how nice to see you. Are you going to introduce me to your friend?'

I glanced at my frozen-faced 'friend' in embarrassment. 'Yes, um this is Jacqueline. Jacqueline this is Anna.'

'Not a local then?' asked Anna, inclining her head in exaggerated politeness, 'or have you taught her English?'

'I speak English perfectly well thank you,' said Jacqueline icily.

'What brings you to ancient Alexandria Anna?' I asked, struggling to recover my presence of mind.

'You mean business or pleasure?' she enquired acidly.

'I suppose,' I said neutrally. 'Look Anna, it's nice to see you, um, doing well. But I hope this doesn't mean there is something nasty waiting around the corner.'

She looked at me inscrutably for a moment. 'It depends what you are poking your nose into,' she said tersely, but I glimpsed a film of emotion in her eyes. 'Richard,' she began again, a catch in her voice, 'how long has it been for you?'

I shrugged, a little more nonchalantly than I felt, 'a month or two.'

A tear glistened on her cheek. 'It's been less than two weeks for me.'

I couldn't help feeling something. 'I'm sorry,' I said.

She glanced at Jacqueline, and then back at me. 'Can you meet me tomorrow? Say at Alexander's tomb, a little before evening oblations? I'll tell you what I can.'

'OK,' I agreed, a little uncomfortably.

She nodded, more in control of herself again. 'I'll see you tomorrow then,' she said, laying herself back onto her palanquin with a coquettish smile. 'Bye.'

Jacqueline turned stiffly towards me as the exotic procession resumed its course. I swallowed. I knew I was in trouble, if not exactly sure how much.

'Perhaps you forgot to mention this lady when you related your adventures?' she enunciated frostily.

'No, I mean not really…' I hedged, 'I told you about her, we were shipwrecked, she was working for a time traveller…'

'You hardly mentioned her!' she exclaimed angrily, 'I had no reason to suspect…' She stopped and glared at me, hands on hips. 'Just how long were you alone with that creature?'

'Well,' I said reluctantly, 'only a week or so, less than two anyway…'

'And no doubt you had one of your relationships?'

I found myself unable to say anything, and her face crumpled in pain and fury.

'I didn't know you then,' I protested. 'Well, that is I did but not very well. I had no idea if I would ever see you again, and you had not…we had not…'

'Am I just another relationship?' she demanded furiously. 'To think that I wanted to…I thought that…I should have known better!'

'Jacqueline,' I pleaded, 'the circumstances were extreme – and I did not love her.'

It came out all wrong, and did me no favours at all.

'Oh this is all so sordid,' she stormed, 'I must have been mad to think you honourable!'

'Please Jacqueline,' I begged, 'please listen to me. I have never felt anything like I feel for you. I have not tried to … seduce you or anything have I?'

She glared at me, boiling with distain. 'How would I know? I am inexperienced in such matters. No doubt you have any number of strategies.'

'I don't have any strategies,' I said dolefully. 'I just love you.'

She hesitated, and stared at me flatly, her breathing still unsteady. But something more like her usual self seemed to surface.

'I love you Jacqueline,' I repeated. 'I have never said that to anyone.'

She registered the words, but pain and suspicion lurked in her eyes.

'But you are still going to meet her tomorrow?'

I hesitated. 'I should, yes. She may be able to help us.'

'I would not trust her with anything,' she growled, 'least of all you.'

Chapter 21

WE WALKED HOME in silence. I made a couple of attempts to speak to her but she rebuffed me impatiently, and I began to get angry myself. The darkness was complete by the time we entered our bedroom, and the oil lamp cast a dismal light. My anger had degenerated into lingering misery, and I watched her turn away from me with a heavy heart. The room was deathly quiet; the only sounds those of distant revelry. I blew out the light and lay for a while waiting for the sound of her regular breathing. I was finally beginning to drift into bleak, fragmented dreams when she spoke.

'Richard,' she said, 'did you mean it when you said you loved me?'

My throat choked with emotion and I could hardly speak, yet I almost laughed at the erratic trajectory of her logic.

'Yes,' I croaked.

'And you do not love that woman?'

'No.'

'And yet you have had a – a relationship with her – recently.'

'Yes,' I admitted cautiously.

'How could you do that if you did not love her? For all her brazenness she has feelings for you.'

'I don't feel good about it,' I said, cursing the complications the Mindworm had brought into my life. 'We thought we were going to die. She told me how terrible her life had been. I felt sorry for her. And when we reached the island we were so happy...'

'I suppose the fact that she is beautiful had nothing to do with it?'

'Of course it did. She wanted comfort and it was difficult to, err, resist.'

'No doubt I am easier to resist.'

I was surprised at the jealousy in her voice, and laughed bitterly. 'Jacqueline, you could not be more wrong. I desire you very much, but that is the least of it. What I feel for you is something very different. It makes me wish I had never been with anyone before. With you it would be something so special: sacred even. I feel that in every cell of my being. Anna is no threat to you.'

'Oh, she is certainly a threat to me,' said Jacqueline, and I heard the rustle of her garments as she turned to face me. 'But I am pleased that something is sacred to you. I may be inexperienced, but I am not ignorant, nor am I stupid. But thank you for what you have said Richard – I am sorry for my behaviour. I don't know what came over me.'

I sighed with relief. 'Jacqueline, I thought I'd lost you.'

I could sense her smile in the darkness. 'And I thought I'd lost you: that you were not the man I thought you were, and this Anna had a claim on you. I have never felt so unhappy.'

I felt my heart was about to burst, and I reached out to her in the darkness, finding her clutching fingers doing the same. We hugged and kissed with a desperate urgency, clinging to each other in breathless need. I struggled to contain myself as the kisses became deeper and more demanding.

'Jacqueline,' I groaned, 'we need to stop. We agreed –'

'I know what we agreed Richard,' she whispered urgently, 'but everything is upside down in my life. Everything except you: I don't want to lose you. If you truly love me, I will consummate our union.'

'No!' I heard my voice say, 'not like this.'

My need for her was something more profound. The meeting with Anna had reminded me forcibly of that. Jacqueline was uprooted from the life she knew, adrift and vulnerable. I didn't want her to regret her actions, or feel she had to secure my loyalty. Even so, I surprised myself.

'You don't want me?' she asked in surprise.

'You know I do,' I sighed. Given our close proximity she could hardly be unaware of it. 'But I want it to be perfect, especially for you. I want it to be what you always wished for.'

'How can that be?' she replied edgily, 'we don't know what is going to happen from one day to the next.'

'I don't know,' I said, 'but I'm going to do everything I can to try and make it happen.'

'Are you sure you are – happy with me? Happy to wait I mean?'

'Jacqueline,' I said carefully, 'you are like a miracle to me. Just to be with you is more than enough for now.'

We kissed again, more gently this time and it was heartbreakingly beautiful. So beautiful that cold fingers of fear crept into me at the thought of losing her.

I awoke first next morning, and watched the morning light gradually illuminate her features, the soft sound of her breathing barely audible. I felt a kind of awe at the beauty and mystery of her, and wondered about the magical alchemy of love. Science reduced it to a commonplace urge to reproduce, and I suppose I had always looked at women as somewhat exotic (if occasionally baffling) playmates with interesting bodies. Now I seemed to touch something deeper, something more primal. I remembered reading that in European prehistory woman were regarded as powerful and magical beings associated with the Moon and mythologies of the Goddess, the Earth Mother. Some sources even claimed the term 'honeymoon' originated from frightened men quaffing mead to face the mystical terrors of their wedding night.

Gazing at Jacqueline's features now, I did feel that some ancient mystery slept within her: something awesome which hovered just on the cusp of recognition. I shivered slightly, reminded unaccountably of the three muses in the Mousion. It was as if she triggered something primeval in me too: that our existence represented more than just our personal fears and desires. I was suddenly glad that we had not plunged into a tempestuous affair: that there was something more profound between us. I felt I was getting to know a trusted friend and partner as well as a lover, with a strange enchantment binding us that resonated with the elusive sense of destiny winding through my life.

She awoke slowly, stirring languidly in my arms, until her eyes suddenly shot open. 'Oh!' she gasped, staring wide eyed at me for a moment. She looked more than a little mortified. 'Oh – we did not.'

'No,' I smiled.

She looked shyly at me. 'Thank you for not taking advantage of my – mood,' she said hesitantly. 'I was so jealous of that woman.'

'Well I had hoped it was the attraction of my manly physique,' I said, only half joking.

She smiled herself. 'Don't worry Richard. You are not alone in having physical desires. It's just that my principles are very important to me.' She looked a little disconcerted. 'At least they usually are.'

I grinned. 'That's good to know – I think. But if the situation was reversed, with you and another man, I would find it difficult too. Let me tell you Anna's story. Perhaps then you'll know there is little to be jealous about.'

'Harrumph,' she said. But she listened.

I had one more session to attend at the acquisition halls with Servertis, and arranged to meet Jacqueline outside the Mousion afterwards for lunch. The day passed uneventfully, apart from sighting yet another time-traveller near the library. This one favoured me with the usual mildly curious glance, and an infinitesimal nod as he passed. The Great Library seemed to be time-travel central station: or at least visited often enough by temporal tourists to make such encounters unremarkable.

I sat outside the Mousion with Servertis for a quarter of an hour or so after our business concluded, until an acquaintance of his walked by, and they went in to eat together. Jacqueline arrived ten minutes later and we did likewise, after which Servertis left on other business, and Jacqueline and I visited the menagerie across the way. I was expecting low levels of animal welfare, and was surprised by the lavish quarters constructed for them. But the measure of comfort was manifestly more human than natural. The animals were decked out in rich, gem-studded leather harnesses, and the enclosures over-embellished with royal portraits and insignia. It was meant to reflect their royal patronage more than anything else, but the spaces were large and clean, and we lingered there pleasantly enough until it was time to visit Alexander's tomb.

Jacqueline agreed to maintain some distance as a lookout during the rendezvous: something she patently had mixed feelings about. I stood at the back of the crowd, fidgeting a little as I waited for Anna to appear. I was unsure of her loyalties, and what form any possible betrayal might take. For the first time in many days I searched tentatively for the Portal, but felt nothing. I could only remain alert and hope the damned thing would work if it needed to.

The evening rituals at the mausoleum had only just begun when Anna arrived. I failed to recognise her at first. She wore a plain, unadorned robe; her hair was pinned up simply behind her head, and she looked uncharacteristically pensive.

'Is our English friend not with us today?' she asked silkily, glancing around her.

'She has something else to do at the moment,' I said.

'I could see it was personal,' she went on with a brittle smile, 'but another do-gooder like you. Was she the reason you wouldn't come with me? I had the impression she was not entirely informed about our little dalliance.'

'No she wasn't the reason,' I said, 'you chose not to come with me too, remember.'

She regarded me candidly, her eyes glinting with emotion once more. 'Yes I remember. That beach is all I see when I close my eyes.' She sighed bitterly. 'I made the only decision I could, and I have suffered for it – in more ways than one. They weren't very happy with me. I must be crazy to be here now.'

'What did you tell them about me?' I asked.

'As little as possible: what did I know anyway?'

'And does your presence here mean there any more nasty surprises around the corner?'

'If I did know anything, why should I tell you? Are you going to claim it's just another coincidence you have turned up again?'

'As far as I know it is.'

'Doesn't your Portal Master tell you anything?'

I laughed cynically and evaded the question, 'does yours?'

She grimaced. 'Not everything; no.'

'Well then, I guess we're in the same boat.'

'Again?'

We shared a poignant moment. I tried to dismiss it with an uneasy smile, and returned determinedly to business. 'So is there anything I should know?'

She hesitated for a moment. 'Stay off the streets for the next few days. There may be some crowd trouble. A lot of crowd trouble: political stuff.'

'Because…?'

'I don't know, and I wouldn't dare to tell you if I did. There something behind it obviously. I'm out of here tonight.'

'So you have done your job.'

She flushed. 'Yes.'

'Anna,' I said impulsively, grasping her shoulder as she turned to go. She stared back defiantly.

'If you are ever in trouble, I will be glad to help if I can.'

A small smile flickered briefly and she was gone.

I looked around, uncertain if her associates might be present, with or without her knowledge. All seemed to be clear though, which could not be said for Jacqueline's expression, which was apparent from a considerable distance. But she had her feelings under control, and merely grimaced as I approached her.

'OK, that's over,' I said.

'Did you get what you wanted?' she asked, unable to keep the derision from her voice.

'Jacqueline that is beneath you,' I grinned. 'What I want is you.'

Her reserve thawed slightly, and she smiled reluctantly.

'Does everyone say this 'Oh Kay' in the future? How odd people are.'

'Well it started in America I think. Anyway, don't change the subject. I spoke to Anna and she warned me there may be civil unrest coming.'

'Civil unrest: do you mean rioting? '

'I don't really know what it means,' I said, 'but I wouldn't be surprised. She said to keep off the streets.'

'So we won't be able to follow your time traveller anymore?'

'Let's see. I think we should risk watching for him again tomorrow. If we see him we'll follow him, and if we don't learn any more I'll risk talking to him.'

We stopped to drink a little wine. Jacqueline returned to her abstemious ways, and we simply enjoyed each other's company – at least where veiled references to Anna were absent from the conversation. Then we returned to our lodgings to speak to Servertis about winding up our business arrangement. He asked me about my plans, and whether he might be able to use my services again. I told him I had no plans as such, but promised to check at the acquisition hall for news of his whereabouts in the future. I enquired about his own plans as well, and mentioned casually that I had heard a rumour of possible trouble in the streets.

He looked at me curiously. 'You are an interesting man, Waltonis. I too have heard such things today, but from a highly placed source. Not someone I would expect you to have knowledge of – or access to.'

I tried to shrug it off. 'It may be just a coincidence; or perhaps some street rumours have good sources too.'

'Perhaps so,' he said mildly, 'although my men have not heard of it. For my part I will leave the city in the morning. It has been a pleasure to know you Waltonis. May the Gods watch over you, and may your life be blessed with good fortune.'

Jacqueline and I slept early: back in chaste, would-be lover's mode. Surprisingly I found I quite enjoyed it. I treasured the gradual progression of tenderness and trust. It seemed sweeten the miracle of her entry into my life, and I wanted to savour every nuance.

We waved goodbye to Servertis and his entourage, and explored more of the city during the morning. After that we returned to the Mousion complex to have something to eat, and to look around for our various persons of interest. A quick scout inside the studios revealed the earnest young man at his work, and in the Library we spotted the original owner of my Portal in conversation with the same lady time-traveller. So we settled down outside on the main boulevard with a good view of the library entrance. We chattered happily and inconsequentially for an hour or two – apart from a slightly tricky diversion into the finer points of twenty-first century morality and persons on desert islands – until I spotted the young man approaching from the Mousion. He sat down almost opposite us for a while, and jumped up at the sight of my original Portal master descending the Library steps. They headed off in the same direction as before, and we followed in much the same manner, although I stayed closer to Jacqueline this time.

We traced the same path to the same house, but without any sign of extraneous company. Jacqueline and I watched the premises for a few minutes from a safe distance, but no one else arrived other than a young woman whose appearance suggested she might be a servant. She disappeared inside, and I made the decision to attempt direct contact.

'I'm going to try and talk to the time traveller,' I said to Jacqueline, 'perhaps you should wait here.'

'I most certainly will not,' she replied sharply, 'what happens if he takes you off somewhere?'

'I don't think –' I began, before registering the look in her eye. 'Err, OK, fine: why not?'

I banged on the stout wooden door. Nothing happened for thirty seconds or so, when it was cautiously opened by a stranger. He was shorter than I was but stocky, his face roughly shaven and full of suspicion. I was little confused, but felt it too late to back out.

'I am looking for a…friend, a small man with a short beard. I believe he may be here.'

Alarm flickered briefly in his eyes, swiftly replaced by a studied, blank expression. He glanced at Jacqueline, and then leaned forward to look up and down the street.

'He is in the back,' he said finally.

The window shutters were closed, and I felt a stirring of unease as he led us through the darkened front room towards a curtained entranceway into the rear. I stepped through into a space barely any brighter. An oil lamp burned on a table and a little light fell onto the floor from partly open rear shutters. Much of the room remained dim, and it took a moment to comprehend the scene in the murk. The little time traveller lay motionless on the floor, and the young man groaned semiconscious beside him, bound hand and foot. The lady we had seen enter the house sat trembling on a stool, and a second grim-faced guy stood pointing a Rayser straight at me.

The time dilation effect kicked in, and he seemed to stand frozen as I began to streak towards him. But he had fired instantly. The bright flash of the Rayser blossomed slowly, but not slowly enough. It hit me with agonizing precision, and I felt every jolt as the charge burned its leisurely way around my body. My muscles locked in agony, and nothing worked any more. Everything went yellow and then white, and the floor came up and hit me hard.

'Richard! Richard, are you all right?' Jacqueline's voice gradually penetrated a chaos of pain, confusion and dysfunctional reflexes.

'Oww,' I groaned blankly. My limbs trembled: there was no strength in them, and little darting sparks obscured my vision. The world began to make sense slowly. The solid ground appeared docile and inert again, which seemed a good sign.

'Oh thank goodness,' she said shakily, 'I thought you were dying.'

I began to feel a little more myself, and managed to sit up with her assistance. Both of the nasty rough men lay crumpled on the floor, one twitching and moaning and the other still and silent apart from his ragged breathing. The young man lay still bound, but alert. He and the ashen faced girl were staring at us open mouthed.

'What happened?' I gasped.

'These foolish men did not expect trouble from me I suppose,' said Jacqueline with considerable satisfaction. 'One went out to the street at the front, and I hit the other on the head when he bent over you. I believe he intended to tie you up. I took his energy gun, and shot the first man as he returned.' She brandished the Rayser triumphantly.

'Jacqueline, you are a marvel,' I said in amazement. 'What on earth did you hit the guy with?'

'This thing,' she said, picking up a complicated bronze assemblage from a table. I heaved myself up, and took it from her.

'Quite heavy,' I said, hefting it in my hand. It was around twelve inches long, six inches high and getting on for three wide; with numerous interconnected bronze cogwheels, levers, spindles and dials mounted between associated plates and framework. Parts of it were a bit bent and smeared with blood and strands of hair.

'What have you done to my astronomical calculator?' the bound young man cried, suddenly coming out of his stupor.

I looked over at him. 'Was this yours? I must ask your forgiveness. I think you will agree the need was rather desperate. Can you tell me what was going on here when my, ah, wife and I arrived?'

He stared at me for a moment, 'will you remove my bonds?'

I smiled apologetically. 'Of course, I am sorry. I have barely regained the use of my fingers as yet.'

He looked at the Rayser in Jacqueline's hand with a curious mixture of fear and reverence. 'It is a weapon of the Gods: it flung a sacred fire, and I was felled as if by the hand of a giant.'

I grinned ruefully, moving over to tug at the ropes that bound him. 'I would say more by the kick of a mule myself.'

He sat up stiffly when I eventually released him. 'I am Kosmas, apprentice engineer of the Mousion. This is my uncles home, and I live here as caretaker while he is abroad. I have just returned from the Mousion with my friend Aton, who lies here. Will he live? I do not know what these dogs did to him.'

I leaned cautiously over the comatose time traveller: more than a little concerned about the Portal we shared. I feared some cataclysmic reaction might occur if I touched him. He bore no signs of violence, and was breathing slowly and steadily.

'They must have used something more than the, ah, special weapon: drugs perhaps.' I said, 'What exactly did they want I wonder?'

'I can only suppose they wish to steal my astronomical calculator,' said Kosmas. He turned to the still shaken girl. 'Chrysanthe, please forgive me. This was to have been the happiest of days, and now all is overturned. I may not be able to secure your freedom after all.'

The girl cast a look of soulful despair at him. She seemed a sweet person, and they made an attractive pair.

'You are a slave?' I asked her.

She stared fearfully at me without saying a word. 'Yes,' Kosmas answered forlornly for her, 'Aton promised to pay me enough to buy her freedom if I made him a copy. We wish to marry.'

I addressed her again, 'what did these men do to Aton?'

She spoke this time, but so timidly I could barely catch her words. 'Both Kosmas and Aton they struck with the lightening. But with Aton I believe they – they also pressed an evil potion into his veins.'

'Hmm,' I mused, 'I wonder why. It seems unlikely this was just about the theft of Kosmas' device, however beautiful.'

I looked at it more closely. It was amazingly complex: I could see dozens of gears within it. 'Will you be able to repair it?' I asked the despairing suitor.

'I can repair the mechanism,' Kosmas replied gloomily, 'but it will take time, and I do not know if Aton will recover. Also when this attack is reported my master will learn I have made a copy. He will claim ownership and I will lose my position.'

'Do not give up your dreams yet,' I said. 'I do not think they meant to harm Aton seriously, and he is unlikely to report this attack.'

'You really believe so?' he asked hopefully, 'but what of these thieves lying here? We cannot just release them.'

'Don't worry, we will find a way to sort it out,' I said reassuringly, although I wasn't at all sure how.

I felt a tug on my Portal at that moment, and had a bad feeling about it. An alarmingly familiar sense of disorientation swept over me, and the air in a corner of the room began to distort into the diaphanous patterns of an energy field.

'Stop them Jacqueline!' I yelled instinctively, scrabbling for the second Rayser lying on the floor. She didn't hesitate, bringing up her own weapon, and both of us blasted the emerging rift in space-time. There was a violent purple flash and a dramatic disturbance in the energy patterns. Then everything became still; with only some remarkably beautiful light-trails fading from existence.

'By Serapis the Magnificent...' gasped Kosmas, as the exotic fireworks display vanished. 'These are truly the weapons of the Gods!'

'What was it Richard?' asked Jacqueline nervously.

'A Portal opening from somewhere,' I said shortly, 'couldn't take any chances.'

I wasn't sure if we had done something terrible to an ally or prevented another assault of some kind, but I dismissed the thought with a shrug. I didn't want to take any chances, especially where Jacqueline was concerned.

'It was surely an evil spirit from Hades,' exclaimed Kosmas in awe. 'To think that I have seen such marvels: what manner of people are you that wield the thunderbolt of Zeus himself?'

'Perhaps I can explain later,' I replied, 'we must decide what to do about Aton and these men.'

'I think we should tie up these Yahoos first,' said Jacqueline angrily, lapsing into good old nineteenth century slang. 'One of them seems to be recovering, and the other might be playing possum.'

I nodded. 'Help me tie these two men up, Kosmas,' I said to him. 'Jacqueline, you had better keep your – err, energy gun ready, just in case.'

Kosmas and I went to work with the ropes, and we had only just finished when Jacqueline alerted me to the noise outside. I listened and detected a distant clamour, but could put no meaning or direction to it, so I hurried through to the front door. The confused reverberation was still unclear but my brain began to recognise separate sounds. People shouting, distant screams and the clash of metal: conflict in the city, and not far away either. I ran back to the others.

'There is rioting or fighting out there,' I said. 'Can we barricade the front door?'

'There is a bar for the door,' said Kosmas quickly, 'I will put it in place, and secure the shutters.' He rushed to do so while I checked on the unconscious time traveller. He still seemed to be breathing regularly, but I could get no reaction from him at all. The noise outside was getting nearer and I eyed Jacqueline uneasily. The perils we were facing seemed to be piling up. I thought about activating my own portal, and reached within myself. To my surprise there was a tenuous connection, but it threw me into a new dilemma. I was unsure if I should try to save the other time traveller too, and felt concerned about Kosmas and his beloved as well. The only way to get us all out of there would have been to create a fixed doorway, and I had no idea if I could make that happen or not.

The roar of violence outside grew louder. I felt increasingly conflicted, lacking the focused clarity I had experienced when I rescued Jacqueline from the jail. I had no doubt I would choose her above anyone else, and yet the little time traveller represented my past and my future: was perhaps the key to everything. The uncertainty and culpability was unbearable. I reached again for the Portal. Something was happening with it, but I felt no control. The sounds in the street rose to a crescendo, and a brutal impact made the front door shudder.

'Can we get out of the back?' I asked Kosmas urgently.

'There is no escape that way, the courtyards are enclosed,' he cried, his eyes wide with horror. 'But the fighting may pass us by.'

He had barely uttered those words when there was another crash against the front door. The shutters began to rattle violently too, and I peered into the front room to see sword blades being forced through and worked deliberately to break them up. Fighting was taking place all along the street now, and it seemed particularly ominous that people were taking the trouble to break into our refuge. We were approaching a crisis point, and I could still not see a clear course of action.

I glanced at Jacqueline. She looked pale but smiled resolutely, and my heart was seized with fear and love for her. Then, abruptly, I was humming with energy from head to toe and a weird sensation began to emanate from the Portal. I sensed a powerful force permeating the room and everything began to slow down, much as it did in the time dilation state. But the process continued: time wound down slower and slower while the energy level soared exponentially. Sound regressed into a low background rumble, and there was a strange weightlessness. Everything in the room seemed to hang on an endless moment, and abruptly all was still. Reality was suspended in silence, as though frozen in a sea of glass.

It was profoundly odd. I was without thought, without movement: my body fused somehow within the molecular structure of everything around me. I was one with even the still, thickened air I no longer breathed. A beautiful, soft lightening emerged from my Portal, tracing a leisurely pathway through the frozen tableaux towards the static form of the time traveller. Some distant part of me waited for a deadly reaction as the two Portals were united. Instead, a luminous band of energy formed between them and began to writhe slowly and purposefully, the entire dazzling trail pulsating in unison. A timeless interval passed, and the extraordinary display began to fade. Time lurched back into motion, and there was a furious exchange of icons between the two Portals, almost too rapid to see.

My Portal began purr like a gold-standard limousine, and I sensed a reciprocal vibration from the time traveller. There was an unusually smooth alteration to the quality of space-time, and the subtle rainbow patterns of an energy field melded instantly into a perfect circle. A hole opened in reality, and the warm sunshine of another time and place flooded the darkened room. The noise of the furious assault on the front of the house returned in full flood, and deliverance shone bright before us. I galvanised myself into action.

'Kosmas,' I yelled over the din. 'You can escape through this doorway, you and your woman, if you choose.'

'What is this wonder?' he cried, torn between terror and astonishment. 'Have the Gods come down to walk among us?' Chrysanthe cowered terrified beside him.

'It is a door to another place,' I bellowed. 'What more do you need to know? I am going, and taking your friend Aton. Come with us if you wish to live. There is little time.'

I cast any fears about the twin Portals aside. I heaved the inert time traveller over my shoulder, grabbed the Rayser and looked around for Jacqueline.

She called to Kosmas herself. 'Come quickly, you must take your lady away from here!' Her words were unintelligible to him, but her meaning was clear.

He looked wildly about him as sounds of destruction echoed violently inside the house. I knew they would be upon us any minute, and stumbled through the hole in space-time with Aton. Jacqueline was close behind. The sun was dazzling, and I look little heed of my surroundings. I laid down Aton's limp form and whirled around to level the Rayser at whoever might follow us. An anxious second passed, and then another. Finally Kosmas appeared, blinking in the light and grasping Chrysanthe by the hand. I noticed with a flash of amusement that his other hand grasped his machine. There was a subtle adjustment by the Portal, and the doorway blinked shut.

'It is Mount Olympus itself,' breathed Kormas in awe, 'I am truly walking with the Gods.'

Jacqueline and I gazed about in little less surprise. I paused only to move Aton into the recovery position before turning to take in the vista that surrounded us. The sun shone down fiercely. We stood upon a circular expanse of immaculately fitted, polished black Gabbro: a dark, granite-like stone streaked with lighter crystals of iridescent greys and blue-greens. About a hundred feet in diameter, the circle was bordered by oddly gleaming red-tinted bronze pillars; each about a foot wide and nine high, and spaced six feet or so apart. Beyond the pillars lay a great expanse of equally pristine shining green marble, also of a darkish hue, and exquisitely laced with lighter tones of green and grey, even white crystalline patterning. Several strange vehicles, their design both elegant and bizarre, were stationed just outside the circle of pillars. Each was about the size of a large van and had bulbous, insect-like front modules, flanked by twin bulging side carapaces which curved around to the rear. There were no visible wheels, and every surface reflected the fiery sunlight in an impenetrable red-gold sheen.

The surrounding landscape was beautiful but strange. The polished green marble area surrounding the pillars was vast, and hinted at greater aesthetic delights: my eyes traced the graceful patterns of embedded mosaics on a scale too large to decipher, their king-sized tesserae glowing in vividly luminous colours. Low, jagged hills ringed the horizon. They rose behind oddly familiar structures of colourful design that bordered the huge square enclosing us. The buildings looked Minoan I realised, yet seemed more uniformly put together, and the odd red-gold metal glinted in many places. But by far the most astonishing sight were three great pyramids that towered into the sky beyond the square, the same red-bronze gleam blazing from every facet in the hot sunshine. Out in the square itself a group of men regarded us inscrutably. They wore immaculately white flowing robes, bordered with brilliant patterns that I had seen once before. I did not need the bright reflection of their portals or the waves of déjà vu to know who they were.

'Not Olympus,' I said, 'but little less unlikely. I believe we have arrived in Atlantis.'

Chapter 22

ANOTHER OF THE strange vehicles sped silently towards us across the square.

'A horseless chariot!' gasped Kormas. 'We will be struck down for trespassing in this place.'

'I do not think so,' I said, more lightly than I felt. 'I believe I may have a right to be here.'

'I trust you are correct Richard,' said Jacqueline, but her eyes shone as she gazed about herself. 'Will these wonders never cease?'

The horseless chariot halted just beyond the pillars: its sides flipping out and upwards like outstretched wings. A double row of outward-facing seated men leapt from the vehicle on either side, all gripping lethal-looking hi-tec weapons in their hands. None reflected the bright presence of portals. Each was dressed in richly hued red tunics, some of them overlaid by stylized red-gold armour evocative of Grecian mythology. They were tall and bare headed, and several had ornate swords sheathed at their sides. It all looked rather theatrical, and there was an air of hurried disorganisation about them, as if they were actors caught unprepared between changing scenes. But there was nothing disorganised about the way they held their weapons, and I suddenly realised we were still holding Raysers.

'Drop the gun,' I said urgently to Jacqueline, quickly letting go of mine, and both clattered to the ground.

'Identify yourselves,' barked one of the soldiers. I thought he spoke in English, but was unsure at first if the Portal was translating or not.

'We are fleeing from danger, and accompany your citizen Aton, who has been injured,' I called back. 'He needs medical attention.'

A second vehicle zoomed across the enormous courtyard to disgorge more soldiers in various states of unpreparedness, also clutching hi-tec weapons. Some wore magnificent Grecian helmets on their heads. The man who had shouted looked abruptly over to the group of time travellers, and I sensed they were communicating. His lips moved and he held up a hand, visibly relaxing his companions. One of the time travellers: an older man of perhaps sixty, walked towards us. He had a full head of grey hair and an autocratic air, and looked down his long nose at us in a rather superior manner. But his features were not severe, and his eyes were alight with interest.

'Greetings,' he said, 'I am Lysias. What injuries does Aton have?'

'I think stunned with a Rayser, and possibly drugged,' I replied.

He raised his eyebrows, but let it pass. 'You have brought outsiders with you, and your Portal is unrecognised,' he stated.

I noticed he used the same term as Ravi's uncle had for the disenfranchised masses outside the hi-tec enclaves.

'Our lives were at risk,' I said, 'one of my companions is my wife, and the other two are friends of Aton. I acquired my Portal only recently.'

He glanced at the unconscious time traveller, and looked us over carefully. 'Friends of Aton you say? And your wife?'

A third vehicle shot into view from a new direction.

'Medics,' he announced, 'they will assist Aton'. He turned to me. 'You carry many temporal echoes. We will have to debrief you in depth.'

The third vehicle looked much like the others, but two narrow front sections sprang outwards to allow a man and a woman to jump from it. The rear also flipped open, and they hurried around to extract equipment before running over to Aton's supine form. The female asked me what had happened and I gave her what information I could, while the man unrolled a segmented red-bronze cylindrical bundle next to the patient. It stiffened into a long rectangular platform with angular modules at either end: a stretcher I guessed; and they began to go through a rapid physical assessment of his condition with a number of instruments.

'Did you understand what they said?' I asked Jacqueline.

'Enough to know that you introduced me as your wife,' she said, looking slightly pink. 'It seems a form of English, but there are unfamiliar words and pronunciations.'

'It is hard for me to tell I suppose, when it is close to my own language,' I said, 'the Portal translates so seamlessly.'

I turned to Kormas, who stood nervously clutching his would-be bride.

'Aton is a citizen of this place,' I said, 'I have told them you are his friend.'

'I hope they will not blame us for his fate,' he muttered anxiously.

But Lysias's interest had been diverted. His gaze alighted on the astronomical calculator in Kormas's hand, and he darted forward with a delighted cry.

'What can this be?' he asked excitedly, reaching out to Kormas' shrinking form. 'Do not be alarmed. I wish to see the instrument.'

Kormas looked astonished that Lysias appeared to speak his own language, and offered up his pride and joy hesitantly.

'Oh!' sighed Lysias, taking the device carefully into his hands, 'An Antikythera mechanism! It is perfect – no, alas it is damaged, how tragic.'

'It was used as a weapon to strike down the man who attacked Aton,' said Kormas, unable to keep a certain amount of indignation from his voice. 'He was to pay me for making it.'

'You made it?' cried Lysias joyfully. 'You can make an authentic repair?'

'Of course,' said Kormas, perking up. 'I am apprentice engineer at the Mousion.'

Lysias's companions came forward eagerly to examine Kormas's handiwork, and he glowed in surprise and delight at their muttered sounds of appreciation.

Meanwhile the medical duo completed their examination. They extended the telescopic legs of a slender tripod which positioned some sort of projectional device over Aton. It emitted a subtle hum and his loose garments floated a few inches into the air a second or so before his body did the same. They slid the rigid platform under him and it rose smoothly upwards to hover waist-high off the ground. One of them guided the floating stretcher effortlessly out of the circle of metallic pillars while the other collected their instruments. They slipped Aton into the rear of their vehicle and the female hopped in with him. Her companion jumped in front and they shot off.

'Excellent,' said Lysias, rubbing his hands. I was unsure if he was referring to Aton's delivery into care, or the imminent restoration of Kormas's creation. 'Now we will take you somewhere more comfortable, where we can discuss your situation.'

The side panels flipped up on two of the unused vehicles as he spoke, and Lysias ushered us all towards it. Jacqueline approached it with little less awe than Kormas and Chrysanthe.

'Are these like the horseless carriages of your time?' she asked, 'how do they move without wheels – and with no driver?'

'We still use wheels,' I said. 'We do have vehicles that can travel without drivers, and even without wheels, but they are not in common use.'

Something else not in common use was an integral seat relocation system. The central line of back-to-back seating efficiently rearranged itself into three forward facing rows before we could board. Each row utilised four seats apiece, and Lysias indicated we should occupy the central section, while a couple of soldiers entered the back and he moved into the front. Another innovation was a mild force field which maintained the environment inside the vehicle while the side panels were open. There was tingling resistance as I passed through it, and I found myself in a delightfully cool refuge from the baking heat outside.

Even so my impression of Atlantis was underwhelming to say the least. Apart from Portal technology their science seemed little different to that of Ravi's Central, and considerably more contrived. The others flinched at the unexpected force field, but soon smiled at the novel coolness as the vehicle set off across the square. Jacqueline seemed reassured about the benevolence of our hosts, and looked a little like a child entering Disneyland. But Kormas and Chrysanthe were still pensive and overawed.

'What is to become of us?' she whispered to him, 'are these Gods?'

'Not Gods,' I interjected, 'just clever people with great knowledge. I do not believe they will harm us.'

'You mean they are philosophers?' asked Kormas. 'They pursue the arts and sciences as we do in the Mousion?'

'Yes,' I said. 'Imagine what you might discover if you pursued knowledge for a thousand years.'

Kormas stared wide eyed at his surroundings. 'Oh,' he breathed, 'that is indeed wonderful.' He thought for a moment, 'yet they value my calculator, which must seem primitive to them.'

'Yes,' I agreed, impressed at his astuteness. 'They seem to revere the history of their art.'

I tried to decipher the vast mosaic design in the outer green marble expanse without success as we sped over it. Several other time travellers had entered a second car, and both vehicles drove to one side of the great courtyard, some hundred and fifty yards from the central circle of pillars.

The huge square was surrounded on all sides by the Minoan-like terraced constructions, with central gaps fifty yards wide accessing it north, south, east and west. The buildings themselves were two and three storied angular constructions, with flat roofs and long, rectangular parapets. Asymmetrical round columns: wider at the top than the base, were clad in the red-tinted bronze and much in evidence in various sizes along cloisters and balconies. Vibrant designs decorated parapets and massive, angular structural pillars, and window openings were large and square, with a pristine clarity reminiscent of the immaculate glazing of Ravi's tower block in Central. More force-fields preserved the inside air temperature, as similarly glazed doors with ornate red-bronze frames slid back on the ground floor.

The section we entered was a lounge area writ large: luxury on an extravagant scale, and supplemented by a well-stocked cafe with serving staff. Sweeping walls and soaring ceilings were alive with vivid murals. Even the heavy ceiling beams that criss-crossed rows of massive, asymmetrical red-bronze columns glowed with colourful patterns and designs. It was a stunning tour de force, yet the only 'customers' I could see in the vast open area were three time-travellers sipping beverages and watching a large projected hologram together.

A bank of elevators waited to take non-existent hordes to the higher floors. Lysias and the two soldiers ushered us into one of them, and four other time travellers followed. It accommodated us all easily, and Jacqueline, Kormas and Chrysanthe took in yet another technical novelty. We stepped out into the even more surreal setting of an ultra-modern office and control room. Sophisticated information terminals projected virtual data displays into the air in multiple locations: some scrolling streams of information, and others displaying high definition images of the circle of pillars in the square in a variety of electromagnetic wavelengths. The centre of the room was dominated by a giant 360 degree holo-image of the pillars, which hovered above head height and featured rapidly changing data-symbols of all kinds. Half a dozen men and women were at work there, two of them owning Portals.

'Well Mercedeh,' said Lysias, to a lady time-traveller seated at an impressive instrument array, 'we have an interesting situation here.'

'Yes,' she agreed rather stiffly, 'an injured First Citizen, two outsiders and an unregistered Portal Master and his wife: quite an enigma. It will have to go before the council, but we will make an initial assessment now.'

'What will this initial assessment involve?' I asked her warily. 'The two, err, outsiders have never been displaced in time before, or encountered hi-tec culture. They are confused and frightened.'

'We are quite used to that,' she smiled – rather condescendingly I thought. 'We will merely log an account of your arrival here and the events that preceded it. These two – she indicated Kormas and Chrysanthe – will be interrogated separately to yourself and your partner of course, but we will not be harsh. We will know if their story is genuine.'

I turned to them with what I hoped was a reassuring smile. Both stood with their mouths open and their eyes filled with fear and wonder.

'Don't worry,' I said quietly, 'you have nothing to fear. They will talk to you separately from us: just tell them the truth.'

I felt less relaxed about my own position. I had no idea if I should speak about Aton's future fate, and the fact that I now wore his Portal – I could hardly get my head around that anyway. Or where these people stood regarding the direct or indirect activities of other time travellers I had encountered. Their reference to my Portal being 'unregistered' was puzzling, as their technology was obviously quite advanced, and presumably capable of probing us in all sorts of ways. The lady time traveller, Mercedeh, had suggested as much regarding their interrogation of Kormas and Chrysanthe. I felt a stab of alarm as the memory of the Mindworm surfaced. I feared they might detect its presence, or traces of its previous existence. It could raise a whole lot of complications, not least with Jacqueline. Finally I decided, as usual, to say as little as possible and hope for the best – a situation I was increasingly fed up with being stuck with.

Lysias and Mercedeh indicated that Jacqueline and I should accompany them into a separate office, while a couple of other time travellers ushered Kormas and Chrysanthe into another. I half expected to be strapped into some sort of interrogation chair as I had in India, but they merely seated themselves on low, puffy armchairs set around a beautifully etched transparent coffee table, and invited us to do the same. The chair seemed to mould itself to my body: the seat even rose in height to accommodate the length of my legs. I sank into a delightfully tactile material, but felt anything but comfortable. I glanced at Jacqueline and she gave me a trusting, upbeat smile, but it only made me more anxious. I wondered what I had got her into now, and found it difficult to return her optimism.

'Would you like something to eat and drink?' inquired Mercedeh, by way of an introduction, but I shook my head. I just wanted to get it over with. I looked enquiringly at Jacqueline, and she gave a quick shake of her head as well, so I knew they were communicating with both of us.

'Very well,' Mercedeh said, 'we will begin. Your rights as a portal master will of course be respected, as will those of your wife. You are not obliged to answer our questions, but if you wish assistance from us, and indeed if you wish to claim citizenship of Atlantis, it will be in your interest to be open and informative with us in all respects.'

'Fair enough,' I said as evenly as possible, my mind trying to predict where the conversation was going.

'Firstly, why is your Portal unregistered?'

'I can't answer that,' I said, 'I don't really understand the question. I haven't had it for long.'

Neither Mercedeh nor Lysias responded openly to this, but I thought I recognised a flicker of unease in their eyes. Mercedeh continued quite calmly however.

'How long has it been in subjective time since you acquired your Portal?'

I thought about it. 'I can't say exactly, a little over three months I suppose.'

'Can you tell me about the circumstances in which you received the Portal?'

This was a real problem, full of unknowns. I decided to risk a reasonably truthful version, with a few alterations and omissions.

'A woman, a stranger, came up to me one day and warned me that I was about to inherit an artefact of great value and that others would try to stop me acquiring it. The next day a badly injured man materialised in front of me. He called me by name although I had never seen him before. I saw men running towards us and warned him. He took me away to another place and time, a relatively short distance. He was very weak. I asked him to explain what was happening and he said he couldn't tell me. He was only concerned about giving me the Portal, and he used the last of his strength to do so. Then he died.'

This time Mercedeh and Lysias exchanged grim glances. I wasn't sure if it was my story that troubled them, or other things they were reading from me.

'How did you learn to use the Portal?' she asked.

'He said I would find a way,' I said.

'And have you?'

'Not really. It sometimes does what I want, but it mostly works randomly – or doesn't work at all. I don't usually know where I'm going to end up either.'

They both looked aghast: staring at me as if I was some kind of hybrid laboratory specimen.

'Can you describe the Portal Master?' asked Mercedeh finally.

It was another dilemma: the biggest of all. I wondered what my rights as a Portal master actually were. She had said it would be in my interest to be open and informative, and I wondered if that implied I could choose not to be. I shrugged inwardly. They might know I was lying, but I decided not to tell them about Aton – at least not until I had learnt more about him, and what the consequences might be. I gave only a vague description, and was glad I had done so, for a moment later, Lysias said something which startled me.

'It is a serious business. With your Portal unregistered we cannot track the timelines. If the same Portal was to appear in the same time and place from different points of origin it would cause serious disruption to space-time, and here in Atlantis its effect on reality could be chaotic.'

That really shook me. Not only was the same Portal twinned in Atlantis without obvious repercussions, but they were not even aware of it. I was astonished. I could not comprehend how they could be so wrong about their own technology.

'What does registering a portal involve?' I asked uncertainly.

'All Portals have a unique holo-signature,' he said. 'The technology built into the travel-port interacts with them to maintain sequential continuity. That is what we monitor in this control station. It not only maintains the integrity of space-time, but keeps order in our affairs. If we randomly entered and returned from multiple space-time locations the timelines would become hopelessly compromised. We could return before we set off, or months after we are expected. Our lives and our work would be impossible – and that is the least of it. If we disrupt each other's time lines the changes will multiply and create unpredictable repercussions for all of us.'

'So why does my Portal not have this holo-signature?' I asked, puzzled. 'Is it not incorporated during manufacture?'

'Yes they were all made with unique signatures,' Lysias affirmed. 'But there is a facility to delete this along with their time jump history in certain circumstances – if there is a danger of the information falling into the wrong hands for instance. It was thought a hypothetical possibility, but in the event a handful have chosen to utilise it, free-timers or rogues – or even perhaps in a few cases for the purpose intended. Some Portal Masters have just disappeared, and their fate may never be known.'

'Does that mean I will never know the history of my Portal, or why it was given to me?'

'You may discover some of it when you encounter those in your subjective future,' said Mercedeh. 'Otherwise that information is likely gone forever.'

'The Portal's previous owner may have cached some data,' said Lysias thoughtfully. 'His statement that 'you would find a way' could be significant. Each Portal has significant interactive protocols and capabilities, and it's possible he wanted to retain specific causal links and patterns in the timeline.'

'A number of things are possible,' said Mercedeh, 'especially given the extraordinary circumstances in which you encountered him. You have many temporal echoes, and he would have been aware of that: you were known to him from his own past, and there might be other complications. He must have had good reason to take the action he did.'

'What are these temporal echoes that you talk about?' I asked.

'I think you must know them, even if you do not recognise the term,' she said. 'It is the disruption and rewriting of timelines: the perception of repeated futures and altered standpoints in consciousness. It is what takes place when the progression of space-time is disturbed, and the fate of its passengers readjusted.'

'Déjà vu,' I interposed.

'Yes – and an experienced Portal Master can detect its presence on the timeline of those affected.'

'I can see I have a lot to learn,' I said, 'that is if you are willing to teach me.'

'Portal Master Rights are inviolable,' said Lysias. 'We are bound to uphold them. We will teach you what we can. Indeed, we would not risk you tumbling at random through space-time. But citizenship of Atlantis would require certain agreements and responsibilities.'

I began to wonder about the inviolable rights of Portal Masters. It occurred to me that there was something anonymous and impenetrable about the mirrored reflection radiating from each of them. It might actually be the Portal that was inviolable I realised: rendering its user immune from penetration by technological snooping. A doubt arose in my mind as I thought back to my interrogation by Central security, and the investigations by Ravi's phalanx of scientific relations. But I supposed that even then the Portal might have manipulated the situation in my best interests. After all, had I confounded their technology it would have sent even more alarm bells ringing. At any event, I became more relaxed about representing myself as I chose.

'About Atlantis,' I said, 'what exactly is this place, where and when? What is it all about really? I mean – ancient Greek guards in Hollywood outfits with ray guns – or something.'

Lysias gave a coy smile. 'You might say it is a little indulgence of ours. We are on the island of Thera in the Mediterranean, in the early third millennium BCE. We wanted a base to carry out our operations free from disturbance. The guards are partly for appearances sake, to deter the locals. But they also have superior skills and weaponry, and more specialised duties.'

'And the volcano blows in a thousand years or so, should you leave any traces behind,' I said, remembering Anna's words.

'Exactly,' said Lysias with a self-satisfied air.

'So you come from the future,' I said.

'Yes,' said Mercedeh crisply. 'But your education can wait. I want to hear of your actions following the acquisition of your Portal, and especially the events immediately preceding your appearance here.'

I launched into a relatively brief history of my adventures, saying nothing about Charles, Billy, Priya or the twins, other than as incidental characters in the tale. I did not mention recovering the treasure from the Merchant Royal either. I could not omit Jacqueline's stepfather of course, as I feared word of our dealings might get back to Atlantis by other means. Mercedeh stopped me when I described our meeting and asked about his appearance. I could not really be vague about him, and the two time travellers shared a dour look as I described him.

'It sounds rather like Apollonius,' said Mercedeh, and turned to Jacqueline, 'so this man is your stepfather. How long ago in subjective time did he come into your life?'

'If you mean the normal time of the everyday world, about eighteen months,' she said.

'And you had no reason to suspect him before Richard appeared?'

'No. I did not like him or his associates, that was all.'

Lysias and Mercedeh looked pensive. 'If it is Apollonius he is a free-timer. We do not have much contact with him.'

There was something that was bugging me. 'If you come from the future, why do you all have odd ancient-sounding names?' I asked.

I caught a flash of the strange, haughty disposition that seemed to lurk among the citizens of Atlantis. 'We have adopted formal names when referring to ourselves here,' said Mercedeh, 'it is useful when we operate under so many aliases in diverse times and places.'

'And what exactly is a free-timer?'

'They believe that alterations to space-time will spontaneously readjust themselves,' said Lysias, 'and up to a point we would agree. However, we consider it wise to avoid such things, and take active steps to guard against significant alterations to the temporal flow. You might describe them as somewhat self-centred and hedonistic individuals, whereas we feel a responsibility for the collective destiny of humanity.'

'Why don't you stop them if you believe their behaviour is unwise?' I asked.

Lysias and Mercedeh looked scandalised. 'A Portal Master's rights are inviolable,' they practically chanted in unison.

'We would know if substantial changes to the collective time line were taking place,' said Mercedeh more reasonably, 'and they are aware of this, as well as the fact that we would intervene if necessary. However there is a third category: rogues, who are totally irresponsible, even maliciously destructive. We are not sure if any still remain, but we would certainly hunt them down if we learned of their existence.'

'What would happen if you caught one?' I asked cheekily, 'would their rights would not be inviolable?'

They squirmed uncomfortably. 'The last known rogue was killed while resisting attempts to capture him. It would have been a matter for the council, but he would probably have been confined behind a temporal barrier here in Atlantis for an indefinite period.'

'You would not remove the portal?' I asked in surprise.

'It would be very difficult, if not impossible, and it would probably be damaged,' replied Mercedeh. 'The Portal must be freely given. That is why we respect your status.'

When I recounted my time in Alexandria, I described Aton as just another time-traveller I had followed in an attempt to gain more information about them. I made no mention of the strange luminescent connection which had formed outside time between our portals either, reserving this for future consideration. When they asked how I had opened the doorway to Atlantis, I just shrugged and said it had happened in the same random way as everything else. I asked them in fact if they knew how I had been making these apparently arbitrary time jumps, but they would only say it would be looked into during my Portal 'training'. Neither did I say anything about my clandestine meeting with Anna at Alexander's tomb, in case it got her into trouble somehow.

'I think we have all the information we need for now,' concluded Mercedeh after an hour or so. 'There are some very disturbing aspects to your story, and we will have to examine them more closely. But for now I think we can all relax a little. Information from the other two corroborates your version of events: at least as far as their part is concerned. We will also have to speak to Aton of course. I am informed he is responding well to treatment, so we will be able to do that before long. In the meantime I thank you for your cooperation. Lysias will look after you, or delegate others to do so. The guards must still accompany you I'm afraid. We have to follow protocol until the Council rules on your case. In the meantime I am sure you will find much to interest you here in Atlantis.'

She had obviously received information from elsewhere by invisible means. I did not doubt they had all kinds of advanced technology at their disposal, and found their willingness to confer privileged 'portal master' status on me rather startling, even a little creepy. I felt I had been accepted into an elite priesthood, which viewed itself as beyond human accountability. But it was certainly useful in avoiding unwelcome interrogations and intrusive hi-tec scrutiny. I was pleased that my status seemed to protect Jacqueline too. We filed out of the office to discover a still overawed Kormas and Chrysanthe waiting for us in the main control room. They looked hugely relieved to see us, and we all took the elevator back down to the ground floor with Lysias.

'Some refreshments I think, before we do anything else,' he said jovially, and ushered us over to the large, staffed snack bar, where he encouraged us all to try various interesting looking delicacies and beverages.

'My goodness, what luxury,' exclaimed Jacqueline, 'do we not have to pay for this?'

'There are no payments required in Atlantis,' chuckled Lysias, 'all of our needs are freely met.'

'What about those who are not portal masters?' I asked, 'the soldiers, those in the control centre, and this young lady attending to us. Are they paid for their services? Where do they come from?'

'They come from many places: many times and places that is,' he said. 'Suitable people are offered positions when necessary, and are amply rewarded. Indeed, for many just to be here is reward enough. The facilities here are without comparison.'

Kormas and Chrysanthe sat nibbling at their food in bemusement. I could hardly blame them. Even without the hi-tec trimmings, the space we occupied was palatial.

'What will happen to these two?' I asked Lysias, indicating the couple with a slight nod.

'It will have to be decided officially,' he said mildly, 'but I imagine they will be offered a place here if they wish it.'

I smiled warmly, feeling an unaccountable burden slip from my shoulders. 'That would be very kind,' I said, but a question occurred to me. 'I don't imagine they would refuse,' I went on, 'but should they do so, would you return them to their previous existence, with the knowledge of all that they have seen here?'

The smile he returned was somewhat thinner than mine. 'Each case would be judged on its merits. If necessary that knowledge would be removed. However, as the myth of Atlantis already exists in the established time-flow, there is little to fear in any time period. Wild tales would merely be regarded as a sign of madness.'

'I see,' I said, glimpsing a less than altruistic edge to this carefully crafted utopia.

'How long has your Atlantis existed – in subjective time I mean?'

'More than sixteen years,' he said, 'children have been born here and many will inherit the role of their parents, both Portal Masters and Second Citizens. Others are also qualifying themselves for new responsibilities.'

'I assume Second Citizens are the hired staff,' I said, 'how many people live here?'

'About two hundred Portal masters, many with families,' he replied, 'and there are about six hundred Second Citizen families or individuals, including a hundred and fifty guards.'

'But surely the population will overflow before long,' I said, trying to do the maths in my head, 'how much living space do you have here?'

'We are on a central island surrounded by a lagoon, which is the centre of the volcano's caldera, with the rim forming an outer ringing island,' said Lysias. 'The central island is over five kilometres long and more than three wide. We have sufficient space for our needs.'

'Then you must have reproductive restrictions in place,' I pointed out.

'We have a number of measures in place,' he agreed, 'no couple may have more than two children, and there are incentives to have less, or none. All who come here understand that our work is the highest priority. There has been a gradual increase of population, but we are still well within our capacity to sustain it.'

'So what is your work?' I asked, 'is there any purpose to Atlantis other than a comfortable base to travel to and from?'

Lysias laughed. 'Of course; since space-time technology was discovered we have established three main duties as Portal masters: to maintain the natural time-flow, to preserve the legacy of humanity, and to study the Barrier.'

'What is the legacy of humanity?' asked Jacqueline with interest.

'Why, the irreplaceable creations of human genius,' exclaimed Lysias in surprise, 'the priceless artefacts of the great human journey! We preserve the works of brilliant minds and magnificent talent which would otherwise be lost to posterity.'

'And the Barrier?' I queried, although I already suspected the answer.

'The Barrier is a mystery. It is an anomaly in the future time-flow, where space-time breaks down into exotic particles which we have been unable to quantify. We cannot penetrate it with Portal technology. In fact it is difficult to approach within a few years of its inception, and well before that navigation becomes erratic and unpredictable.'

'How far in the future does this happen?' I asked, a mixture of fascination and foreboding stirring within me.

'Space-time begins to distort about the year two thousand, two hundred CE,' he said. 'We are unsure if it signifies a cataclysmic disaster, a temporal barrier imposed from beyond, or if space-time itself has no reality beyond that unfolding within the universal temporal flow.'

I tried to get my head around it. 'You mean the future might not exist yet beyond a certain point? Who gets to say what the universal temporal-flow is anyway? Is there a cosmic clock somewhere that says when now is?'

Lysias laughed again. 'Welcome to the reality of the Portal Master. It is a highly complex subject, and we are looking at all possibilities. Unfortunately we are not yet certain if the anomaly remains static or is moving ahead of the time-flow. At a certain point the laws of physics start to break down, and we get contradictory readings. Relocating our resources to Atlantis has given us time to study the Barrier, and our knowledge is still in its infancy.'

We had finished our snack by this time, and Lysias invited us all to visit the 'Great Museum'. An empty transport vehicle was waiting outside as we left the building, and we took our seats with our two security minders.

Kormas leaned anxiously towards me. 'Are we to go before the King?' he whispered.

'They have no King,' I answered easily. 'A council will rule on whether we may stay here. For now we are guests, and Lysias is taking us to see their great Museum.'

'Like our Mousion in Alexandria?' he asked eagerly, his expression altering in a flash to one of breathless excitement.

'I am not exactly sure. I think it will be a place where artistic works and inventions are displayed rather than created,' I said. 'These people travel to many places in time, and believe it important to preserve works of humanity which would otherwise be lost. I suppose that Aton wished to display your astronomical calculator there.'

'My Astrolabe?' he gasped, scarcely able to believe his ears. Then consternation struck him, 'but it was created by my mentor, who built upon the previous work of his own master. I cannot claim it as my own.'

'No intact machine exits in future history,' I explained. 'More than two thousand years after your time, the only known example was found badly corroded in a shipwreck on the sea bed. There was not enough left even to be certain how it worked, or what was missing.'

I left him pondering this information and glanced at the others. Jacqueline gazed about her with a beatific smile, but Chrysanthe still looked nervous and confused. I spoke reassuringly to her, trying to convince her that no harm would come to us. Our transport sped through the large opening in the square leading towards the three great pyramids. As we drew nearer I saw that two were smaller, perhaps two thirds of the towering three hundred feet of the first, and set back from it on either side. The sun's reflection blazed in a molten orb of red-gold bronze from their immense angular planes.

I turned to Lysias, 'this weird bronze colour...' I began.

He smiled smugly. 'Another indulgence of ours: the mythical *orichalcum*, of Plato's description of Atlantis.'

'You seem to have indulged yourselves a lot,' I observed.

'And so might you have, on discovering that reality was about to end, and with significant resources at your disposal,' he responded casually.

'It looks like the metal cladding on the buildings around the square,' I said, 'but it must be a different material.'

'Yes,' he agreed, 'the pyramids are clad in smart-glass, which polarises to the desired tint in sunlight and generates all the solar energy we require.'

'Solar energy?' I asked, puzzled, 'if Portal technology can tap into huge amounts of power to open wormholes, don't you have – I don't know – dark energy generators or something?'

'Yes, that would be nice,' he chuckled, 'but the step-down interface resists massive power transfers into space-time. Dark tec can invoke the power spike that opens the way into exotic dimensions which interact more directly with the high energy matrix. But we can't download high power-loads for unlimited lengths of time. We do have generators that can maintain a trickle-down process. But they are prohibitively expensive to manufacture, and can run a few dwellings at the most; nothing like the power consumption we require here.'

We slid to a halt before the elaborate A-framed entranceway to the foremost and largest pyramid. The huge, surreal image looming over us was spectacularly impressive, and I could only imagine how it must seem to the others. We passed through the entrance in a subdued silence, brushing through the subtle force-field into pleasing coolness, and a wonderland of miracles.

Chapter 23

THE OUTER WALLS were translucent behind their bronzed veil: exterior sunlight diffused into an elusive red-gold tint and an otherworldly air. Vast expanses of immaculately clear material glistened everywhere, forming many levels and partitions, to create the illusion of an enormous open space interlinked by glass and light. Two cylindrical elevator-shafts rose through the transparent floors on our left and right, their framework crafted in an elegant latticework of red-gold *'orichalcum'*, while numerous load-bearing columns repeated the design in miniature between every level.

Yet these exquisite works paled before the stunning vision directly before us. At first I thought it a pillar of flame. It rose majestically from an immense holo-projector at the base of the great pyramid, suspended up through its exact centre in a slowly writhing column of light. Perhaps twenty feet wide and more than two hundred high, incandescent rainbows of colour played throughout its length: bright mercurial hues like those of heated copper flowing and intermingling in dream-like slow motion. Its radiant image drifted constantly upwards, but a dazzling enigma crowned its ascent. A brilliantly luminescent cloud of particles consumed its progress: an invincible stasis which absorbed its tides like a sentinel galaxy at its head.

The great, undulating mirage left me speechless – more than speechless, stunned: hypnotised by its ethereal beauty. I knew immediately what I was looking at. Those diaphanous, psychedelic currents represented tunnels of light flowing between past and future. And at its peak lurked the invincible wall of power I had glimpsed in my bed-sit long months, or lifetimes ago.

The entire projection was encased within a crystal-clear conduit some thirty feet in diameter, which ran seamlessly up through six of the seven pristine floors of the great pyramid. The topmost level rose to its peak, spanning the space above the slowly swirling mass of light at the head of that great column of unearthly fire. Its floor passed some twenty feet above the topmost strata of the astounding display, and the *orichalcum* elevator shafts reached the sixth floor on either side. Spiral stairways of a similar latticework design ascending to the topmost level. Encircling the central viewing cylinder on each of the six lower floors were circular work-stations festooned with technology. The ceiling heights were on the same grand scale: thirty feet or more, and dwarfed the tiny figures working there.

I finally tore myself free from the mesmerising sight. 'Wow!' I said to Lysias.

He acknowledged my praise with a satisfied smile.

Jacqueline remained awe-struck, open mouthed and enthralled, while Kormas and Chrysanthe stood like statues, hardly appearing to breathe. My professional interest, architectural and temporal, began to kick in.

'How are the glass floors constructed?' I asked, 'I am wondering about their structural integrity.'

Lysias looked gracious. 'It is clear-glass, a type of transparent graphene: extremely light, stable and strong. The outer smart-glass envelope is basically the same – it just contains some additional engineering. It is not very apparent, but there is more clear-glass partitioning between each level than you might think, which provides additional structural support. The *orichalcum* columns are stronger than they look as well.'

'It is certainly amazing,' I conceded, 'and the holo-projection especially so. I recognise the time-stream and the barrier on an intuitive level, but not the detail or specific processes it depicts. What is its purpose exactly?'

'It represents a huge amount of quantum computing power, integrated with temporal sensor links installed from fifty thousand BCE to the barrier distortion zone,' he said. 'It is an out-of-time projection of the space-time flow, which facilitates both our policing of temporal disturbances and our study of the barrier.'

'You mean you can detect disturbances in the time flow throughout this period?'

'Of course; and with a certain degree of precision regarding both time and place. The spectrum streaming tells us quite a lot. If anything starts to look ugly, we send in teams to investigate and diffuse the situation.'

'Why just the last fifty thousand years?' I asked, 'is there a limit to how far Portal technology can reach in time?'

He gave a superior smile. 'There are limits, but not fifty thousand years. It is more like ten times that amount. We could expand the scale of time-stream analysis, but detail would be harder to perceive. Most of what is important to us is contained within this time period, and that also applies to those who may wish to meddle with the time-flow. The infrastructure for the kind of excitement they like to indulge in does not really exist before that time. But more fundamentally, the elasticity of the time-flow diminishes as one travels back in time. The further back one goes, the more set in stone it becomes, as it were. Much beyond fifty thousand years it becomes impossible to change things. At least: one can make local changes, but causal effects are not transmitted and amplified by the time flow. There is tremendous resistance to the alteration of key events, and also an established redundancy which renders such things superfluous. The roots of the tree have made multiple links and grown beyond them, one might say.'

'Oh! What are all of these statues and exhibits?' exclaimed Jacqueline, starting to come out of her trance as I digested Lysias's words.

I looked about me. I had taken in little other than the pyramid's construction and the vast holo-projection. Now I zeroed in on the multitude of items on display all over the palatial structure, some of them not far from us.

'May we have a look?' I asked

'Of course,' said Lysias.

We moved towards an extraordinary life-size assemblage of bronze figures, a charioteer complete with chariot, attendants and horses. One of which I suddenly realised, was familiar to me.

'I have a feeling I've seen this guy before,' I said, pointing to a willow-thin, mildly obtuse-looking young man in a Greek outfit, who stood holding the reins.

'Heniokhos, the Charioteer of Delphi,' agreed Lysias.

'I remember the brown eyes,' I said, 'but not the copper lips and eyelashes and the silver headband, not to mention the entire assembly of chariot, grooms and horses. Last time I saw him he was very publicly all on his own in the Delphi museum.'

'He was acquired during the European riots of twenty thirty two,' he said, 'we saved the rest from the fifth century BCE earthquake.'

'Do you really go to that much trouble?' I asked, 'I mean, it's an amazing piece of work, but surely you have so many greater possibilities in life with the technology that you have.'

An ecstatic gleam: almost a messianic fervour shone in Lysias's eyes. 'Nothing is more important save the mystery of the barrier!' he exclaimed. 'The works of human genius are bright jewels in the darkness of time, unique milestones in the ascent of humanity. They must be preserved for...'

'...posterity?' I finished for him, unable to keep a hint of irony from my tone.

'It is no abstract posterity,' he said, 'you will learn, if you are fortunate, that these unique works occupy great importance in the minds of the great and the wise of the future. We are keeping these things in trust for them.'

'Keepers,' I said, remembering my conversations with Anna. 'Is that why so many time travellers were present in Alexandria – I mean, the great library was lost, wasn't it?'

'You have heard the term Keepers before I see,' he smiled. 'Yes, we are substituting the original documents for excellent copies. But there is more to authentic historical knowledge than mere physical artefacts; they are only material confirmation of a great human legacy.'

I supposed he was talking about the extraordinary reservoir of knowledge I had tapped into. 'Will that kind of knowledge form part of my Portal training?' I asked.

I saw a flicker of surprise, 'You know of the archive?'

'I have had a little experience of it,' I admitted.

'That is remarkable,' he said, 'few high citizens have the skill.'

'I hope I can learn more,' I smiled, unaccountably pleased at the revised estimations going on behind his eyes.

We wandered among the objects on display like kids in fairyland, and I resolved to bring Priya there one day if I possibly could. Weapons, clothing, jewellery and armour were particularly fascinating in their mint condition. There were thousands of carefully preserved artefacts: the ground floor alone was ninety thousand square feet, and the overall storage capacity was staggering. We had barely scratched the surface of the surreal museum when Lysias called a halt. He announced that we could return when we wished, but there was something particular he wanted us to see.

He led the way to the nearest spectacular elevator shaft with our guards in tow. Its *orichalcum* framework glowed a rich, red gold, its fractal design confounding the mind with exquisite detail as we approached. The elevator itself was clear-glass, and cast the illusion that we rose on enchanted air. Jacqueline, Kormas and Chrysanthe looked horrified as we sailed smoothly up past floor after towering floor through the gleaming latticework cylinder. I felt a little weird myself. We seemed to hang suspended high in the air within a vast crystal cathedral, with little that was solid in any direction above or below us.

The floor area shrank with each level we ascended, reducing to about eight thousand square feet where the elevator shaft ended on the sixth floor. We emerged somewhat shell-shocked, to follow Lysias up the nearest *orichalcum* spiral staircase to the seventh level under the apex of the pyramid. Even here the floor area was comfortably spacious for a small party like ours, and there was plenty of headroom with the narrow pinnacle forty feet above our heads.

A range of comfortable seating had been configured to facilitate the view in every direction, and was supplemented by a few exotic plants and a couple of swivel-mounted telescopes. The floor here was actually opaque, although its crystalline structure blended in well with the overall transparent theme. It screened the barrier's blazing fire some twenty feet below, and afforded a better view of the stars at night. The telescopes themselves – a suitably impressive land-view model and a larger star-gazer – were also brand new antiques. Jacqueline smiled at me as she spotted them. I knew we would return sometime when the stars were out, and I added Charles to my list of would-be visitors.

'From here you have a good view of Atlantis,' announced Lysias. 'Visibility is not ideal with the smart-glass polarised at present, but it is sufficient to familiarise yourselves with the island.'

And there it was stretched out before us: laid out a little too neatly for my taste, but an impressive and idyllic oasis of hi-tec order and exclusivity. From here the vast mosaic design in the great square was instantly recognisable, and it surprised me. A gigantic depiction of the signs of the Zodiac encircled the ring of *orichalcum* pillars in the centre of the square.

'Astrology?' I asked in surprise, 'is that another of your ironic statements?'

'Yes and no,' he chuckled, 'it looks beautiful, don't you think?'

'Yes,' I agreed, 'quite magical even, but somewhat unscientific.'

'Science at certain levels is quite magical,' he smiled. 'I suppose it was a quixotic impulse. But it does represent an archaic view of the cosmos, and there are still future wonders to be discovered.' He grinned artfully: 'we have found some interesting correlations between genetic traits and celestial configurations at critical periods of gestation.'

It was my turn to smile. 'Fair enough,' I said.

The pyramids stood on the north side of the great square, and further north, behind us, were hundreds of acres of beautifully landscaped countryside, complete with lakes and wooded areas. The island itself was roughly potato-shaped, about a third longer than it was wide, and we were situated perhaps two thirds along its length, with the built up areas on the greater part of the island lying south of us.

'It is mainly for pleasure and relaxation,' said Lysias, as I took in the carefully sculptured wilderness to the north, but we also keep livestock and grow vegetables. Some citizens enjoy working with nature, and it supplements our food supply. There are even First Citizens who have built themselves dwellings there, in preference to the main living quarters.'

'How do you get the rest of your supplies?' I enquired, 'and what about water?'

'We have a separate goods Portal, with storage and distribution facilities,' he replied, indicating the area to the west of the great square, over to our right. 'There is also a desalination plant, waste recycling facility, power management centre and extensive repair, restoration and storage units for historical artefacts. The large buildings you see closer to the main square are public facilities: the council chambers, leisure complex, library, food halls and holovid complex, etc. The main living quarters lie to the south.'

'And what about the other two pyramids?' I asked, indicating the two smaller versions of the king size edition we occupied.

'They also generate power and contain more of our treasures,' he said.

An obvious feature from that height was the high white wall running all around the island perimeter. It had a broad walkway along its crest, protected by battlements and broken by watchtowers in numerous places. Several hundred yards of bright blue water surrounded the coastline, enveloped in its turn by an outer ringing island of low irregular hills.

None were more than three hundred feet high, and there was a wide opening out to sea to the south west. The main living quarters Lysias had indicated lay opposite us, beyond the south side of the square. It looked much like a large housing estate, except that the properties looked substantial and aesthetically pleasing, and the gardens extensive. I could even glimpse swimming pools dotted about here and there.

Large numbers of smaller buildings on either side of the main estate were in closer proximity and more regimented order: the homes of Second Citizens I presumed. The quasi-Minoan style seemed applied to many constructions, including the larger public structures to the west of the square. Other sizeable creations stood south east of us, one of them I later learned, the rather grand guards' headquarters. Behind these buildings four large towers rose in close proximity to the sea, obviously part of the outer perimeter wall.

'The towers protect the main gates,' said Lysias, following my gaze, 'and they open to the harbour. We purchase some commodities from the locals, significant artefacts, fish, even Syrian olives – and a surprising amount of copper, once they discovered we had a need for it. We required a lot of it for the manufacture of *orichalcum*, and we liked the idea of using authentically mined ore from this era.'

'How big is the harbour?' I asked, 'do you have any ships of your own?'

'The harbour is not large,' he replied, 'the longest quay is a hundred metres. We have a couple of small boats and a larger vessel for the open sea, which is about sixty metres in length. It's bigger than anything the locals have and made to look very warlike. Along with the guards in their splendid equipment, it serves to keep visitors suitably awed – and cooperative.'

'So out of all of this will grow the legend of Atlantis,' I said dryly.

'Yes, a delightful paradox, is it not?' he chuckled, 'but we have more important matters to concern ourselves with here: the legacy of humanity and the future of reality itself.'

'So I am beginning to see. Everything about this place is certainly extraordinary.'

Lysias looked pleased, 'you may return here and inspect the storage Arks whenever you wish. However, I believe I should take you to your temporary living quarters now.'

Jacqueline, Chrysanthe and especially Kormas had been examining the view in detail through the telescope, while I discussed it in general with Lysias. We separated Kormas from this new plaything with some difficulty, and were soon being transported by the invisible elevator once more. Outside we clambered back into our transportation with Lysias and the guards, and were whisked across the square to the main residential district on the far side. The vehicle left the green, polished marble of the plaza to enter a broad southbound roadway paved with flat round crystalline stones, perfectly fitted together. They were a glowing, rich pinky-cream, with sunlight glinting from sparkling quartz flaws. Lush, neatly cut green grass embankments set them off beautifully, but the aesthetic style looked a little contrived. Tall, boxy, latticework *orichalcum* sculptures spaced on either of the road would later reveal themselves to be street lamps.

I found myself humming random refrains from the song *follow the yellow brick road* for no particular reason, and we proceeded between smaller, more densely packed homes to our left and far more luxurious and comfortable establishments laid out on our right.

'These are Second Citizens' homes,' announced Lysias, indicating the less ambitious houses. 'There are about two hundred and fifty units here, and a similar number on the far side of the complex. There are also more units in other parts of the island'

The 'units' actually looked rather pleasant, each a couple of stories high with the flat roof, simple chunky design and painted plaster finish I associated with many houses on the Greek islands of my own time. They were not small either, each home possessing a ground floor area of around eighteen hundred square feet, and standing in garden plots three or four times that size. The style was repeated in subtly different configurations and pastel colours throughout the estate. There were balconies, garden seating shaded by vine-laden trelliswork, lush green lawns and colourful shrubs in the shade of pine and olive trees, and graceful palms.

'We have gardeners who attend the gardens of First and Second Citizens alike,' said Lysias. 'Most Portal Masters are concerned with far more important things, and Second Citizens sometimes neglect them. It is better for morale that they are well maintained.'

The 'Second Citizens' homes were comfortable, but those of the 'First Citizens' were extravagantly large and luxurious. There were more than two hundred of them: also two storied, but easily encompassing seven thousand square feet of ground floor area, and set in grounds five or six times as large. The houses were more individualistic, similar to the Minoan style I had seen around the public square, but with wider variations in layout and decoration. There were eccentricities too: statues and pavilions of early civilisations – presumably copies – sprinkled with other mysterious artefacts and whimsical landscape designs. Unusual trees and colourful foliage clustered around unlikely ground formations, with artistic ponds, fountains and even streams complete with quaint bridges in attendance. Many had the swimming pools I had seen from the top of the pyramid, and reminded me of Hollywood homes I had seen on the internet. We turned unexpectedly into the drive of one of these spectacular establishments, and before we knew it, were being welcomed by a middle aged couple at the main entrance.

'This is Galen and Myia, who will help to look after you during your stay here,' said Lysias.

'This is our temporary accommodation?' I asked Lysias in surprise.

'Yes,' he smiled loftily, 'we retain guest houses for those of a certain rank. You are entitled to it as a Portal Master of course – and your wife naturally. Aton's dependants may also stay here for now. Should you be granted citizenship, you would be entitled to a property such as this on a permanent basis.'

Jacqueline raised her eyebrows at that, her eyes laughing at the extravagant change of fortune in our surreal scramble through time. One of the things I loved about her was her cheerful scepticism of wealth and comfort; but even she gave a squeal of delight when she saw the grand en-suite bathroom attached to our huge master bedroom. The bedrooms were all upstairs, and Kormas and Chrysanthe had been allotted individual bedrooms close by: a little less splendid than ours, but regally luxurious by their standards. They were also discretely situated next door to each other.

'These people have wealth and generosity beyond compare,' said Kormas in awe. 'To make us welcome in such a manner is beyond all understanding.'

'It is because Aton and I both have the rank of Portal Master here,' I said, 'which means we have command of the doorways into other times and places. If you are granted residence your accommodation would be less grand – like those painted houses we passed on our way here.'

He looked stunned. 'Granted residence – in this place?'

'I believe it is possible,' I said, 'of course you would have to work – perhaps in the Museum.'

'But...but,' he stammered, 'how is such a thing possible? – And what of Chrysanthe, I could not let her return to her wretched life. I promised I would free her.'

'If you are accepted here then she will be too,' I smiled, 'and if not I will help you both find somewhere safe to live, or at the very least make sure you can buy her freedom.'

He and Chrysanthe clutched each other with tears of hope and astonishment shining in their eyes, and I wondered how many more refugees in time I would find myself feeling responsible for. I thought of all that had happened since I had met Alex, and remembered my initial despair at the impossibility of the quest I faced. I smiled at my naivety in pursuing a mystery on such a scale. I could not have been more ignorant or ill-prepared. Now I had survived a whole series of unlikely adventures. I had discovered the inconceivable Atlantis, and I was about to learn the secrets of the Portal. I glanced at Jacqueline and felt a rush of joy. I had already achieved more than I could have imagined, and admitted something to myself that I had really known from the first. From the moment I had first awakened to the extraordinary mysteries beyond the illusory veil of the everyday world, there had been no turning back.

Lysias informed us that new clothing would arrive shortly, and that a meal was being prepared which would be ready when we had bathed and changed. I went with Kormas to instruct him in the mechanics of his state-of-the-art Atlantean bathroom, and had to experiment a little to work it out myself.

'Are you happy with separate bedrooms?' I asked him. 'I suppose they are uncertain about the status of your relationship with Chrysanthe, and have chosen adjoining rooms in case you wish to be together.'

'Of course we will sleep separately,' he said, looking rather affronted. 'We wish to observe all of the proprieties until we are free to marry. I would not honour her with anything less.'

'Yes, naturally,' I agreed hurriedly, wondering if it was possible for a slave to observe all of the proprietaries in ancient Alexandria. Perhaps it had been. She certainly looked innocent enough. I also wondered what kind of marriage rituals might be available in Atlantis, but left that for another day. I went in search of Jacqueline, and discovered her bouncing up and down on the huge double bed in our magnificent bedroom.

'Oh! Richard,' she exclaimed, blushing a deep red. 'This bed has – ah – the most remarkably soft mattress!'

'I expect it does,' I grinned, enjoying a moment of moral superiority. 'Do you want me to sleep on the floor?'

She was silent for a moment, looking adorably embarrassed.

'Do you know Richard, I am quite shocked at myself. I seem to have grown used to…sleeping with you…' she coloured again, 'that is, in the way that we have been. It would be strange to sleep apart and yet…'

'Let's see how it goes,' I said, determinedly ignoring the preferable scenarios advocated by my more red-blooded self. 'I will sleep on the floor if necessary. You are safer if we are thought to be married – the inviolate rights of the Portal Masters and all that – and I still have a lot to learn about this place. I don't want to leave you alone any more than I have to. It all seems very nice here, but we know there are time-travellers up to no good in other times and places.'

She smiled awkwardly, 'that is very sweet of you Richard. I am sure it will be fine on the bed.'

'You might be interested to know that we are not the only chaste pair here,' I informed her. 'Kormas and Chrysanthe are sleeping in separate rooms until their relationship is formalised too.'

'Really?' said Jacqueline. 'Ah, I feel better then. It is not just Christians who believe in these things.'

'Apparently not,' I said ruefully, 'maybe we can have a double wedding.'

She looked doubtful. 'But there is no Christian church here.'

I burst out laughing. Despite our wide ranging discussions about the relative merits of various religions, she habitually returned to her childhood convictions.

'No doubt Kormas and Chrysanthe will think the same about the rituals they are used to,' I said.

She looked rather annoyed. 'A Christian service is different from a pagan ritual.'

'Why?' I asked.

'Christianity came after paganism, it is more enlightened,' she said primly.

'Well, Christianity could hardly have come before,' I pointed out, 'because it invented pagans. Before that they were just ordinary people.'

'Don't be silly Richard,' she said crossly.

'I'm not being silly,' I objected, dipping briefly into the baffling depths of knowledge within me.

'Words like 'pagan' in the Bible were only approximate translations from other languages,' I said, 'and the meanings themselves changed over time. The word 'pagan' originated from Roman army slang for something like 'country bumpkin.'

'Oh you are just using your horrid Portal to find out things,' she retorted, 'and it's just telling you about words, not what it's really about.'

I didn't really want to argue, yet heard myself pushing it further: 'OK, if you say Christianity is more enlightened, what about Islam, which came after Christianity? By your logic it should be more enlightened still.'

'I know nothing of Muhammadans –' she began impatiently, and then paused, considering. 'Richard, I wonder if it might be blasphemous to see what your Portal says about Jesus...'

'I'm sure it's not blasphemous to try and find the truth,' I said, 'but I have tried before, and it doesn't seem to work with people like him.' I reached inside myself and attempted to put my attention on that iconic figure of Western spiritual tradition. To my surprise, I seemed to penetrate deeper this time. An odd image appeared: a bright, stylised outline of a human being, which put me in mind of Leonardo da Vinci's Vitruvian Man.

'There is nothing there, just a kind of archetype...' I began, before realising the image had begun to pulsate with a strange sense of depth and intensity. For a moment I hovered on the edge of something beyond my understanding. The memory of a similar pull into the unknown before the Three Muses in Alexandria came back to me: a sense that I was swimming beyond the shallows into open ocean –

A vast tree blossomed in eternity: a timeless song of immaculate beauty and power which intoxicated me with wonder. I glimpsed fabulous realms where glorious high-dimensional beings functioned with the power of will. I saw impossible things: dazzling, amorphous forms of blinding splendour; pristine intelligence and ecstatic bliss; pre-nascent creation and mystic fire. This was the true Atlantis if anything was. My whole being sang with the certainty of it. And there was more...much, much more...

'Richard! – Richard! Are you all right?'

I shook myself free with a huge effort, only gradually becoming fully aware of Jacqueline's urgent tones.

'Richard!' she exclaimed again, 'what happened? You looked as if you were not there at all: completely still and empty – it frightened me.'

I smiled uncertainly, still dazed and vacant. The impact of the vision dwindled slowly, slipping away like a half-remembered dream. 'I'm not sure what happened,' I admitted in confusion, 'there didn't seem to be any information, but there was something strange …'

'How can that be?' she asked, puzzled, 'so much is known about Christ and his life. He was a public figure, there must be information.'

'I don't understand what it was: something not human.'

'What do you mean?' she asked.

'It wasn't just an absence of information: there was something else – a different state of being.'

'But we went through that different state of being when you took me to Alexandria,' she said and shivered, 'it was horrible.'

'Well, that state is strange,' I said. 'But this was beautiful – more than beautiful, absolutely wonderful.'

'Do mean Divine?' she asked, suddenly eager.

'Who knows?' I shrugged, more light-heartedly than I felt. 'It was certainly mind blowing.'

'Oh you are teasing me again,' she said crossly, 'what does 'mind blowing' mean. Is that another of your made-up words?'

'I didn't make it up,' I said, 'it means something so amazing that you can't think about it, and it was certainly true in this case.'

'Well perhaps it was heaven then,' she said, 'did it look… holy?'

'I don't know,' I laughed, starting to feel more myself again. 'But it sure seemed a long way beyond human ego problems.'

She considered this, her features vacillating between excitement and confusion.

'What about trying someone else?' she said finally, 'Abraham or Moses – or even Muhammad.'

'I don't know…' I began dubiously, but my attention wandered back over these ancient personalities of its own volition. Curiosity overruled caution, and one of them slipped into focus. The mysterious depths stirred once more, and there it was: the same enigmatic icon. This time

I felt the hair rise on my body and a creeping excitement all the way up my spine. I pulled back quickly.

'It's the same,' I said in surprise.

'What is?' asked Jacqueline.

'One of the other people you mentioned,' I replied, 'it's the same icon with no information, and the same strange feeling.'

'Which one?' she asked.

I laughed, 'does it matter?'

'Yes of course, they were from different religions.'

'No they weren't, at least, they all have common roots in Judaism.'

'Surely not Muhammadans?'

'Muslims, they call themselves in my time. Yes, they all trace their history back to Abraham.'

'How strange that they are all different then,' she said. 'I can see that I must learn more about these things. I suppose I must seem quite ignorant to you.'

I shrugged. 'Not really, perhaps I know a little more history than you, but I have never actually thought much about religion.'

'So who was it then?' she persisted.

'I don't think it matters,' I replied. 'I get the feeling it would be the same for all of them.'

A chime downstairs announced the arrival of our clothes, and Jacqueline abandoned her mystical quest to disappear eagerly into the bathroom with her new outfit. She remained there for a very long time, and apologised profusely when she finally emerged, but looked absolutely radiant. She had indulged in the plethora of hairdressing accessories, and her dark, gleaming locks flowed like black satin once more, alive with rainbow sparks of reflected light. She reminded me of Alex again at that moment, but I was fully engaged in the present, overwhelmed by Jacqueline's fragrance and beauty.

I had given up waiting and gone in search of another bathroom, taking a fraction of the time that she had to get clean and changed. But I was delighted to see her able to pamper herself after all of the shocks and hardships she had endured. We had been supplied with high quality garments, not unlike the richly embroidered robes worn by wealthy Alexandrians, but considerably better equipped with hidden fastenings: not to mention snuggly fitting underwear. Wonderfully comfortable soft sandals completed our wardrobes, and she moved with a natural dignity that made me feel a little like my old gauche, unworthy self again. Intermittent flashes of gold and gems on delicate clasps and brooches perfectly complemented the magical enchantment of her smile. I could not have been more awestruck if she had been royalty.

We walked downstairs, despite discovering an elevator, just to enjoy the sensation of being able to move in cleanliness, comfort and style. There we found Kormas and Chrysanthe, totally stunned by their own new garments. They were less luxurious and ornate than ours, but Kormas gazed upon his lady in the utmost satisfaction.

'We are truly blessed by the Gods, whatever you might say,' he exclaimed in wonder. 'I fear this is a dream from which I may awaken at any moment.'

'Not before you have eaten I hope,' I smiled.

Galen emerged from the extensive realms of the kitchen department. 'The meal is simple as we had little warning,' he said, 'would you like to eat out on the patio or in the dining suite?'

I looked out to see that it was growing dark. 'It might be nice outside,' I thought aloud, 'is there lighting there?'

'Naturally,' he answered, and a fairy grotto of subtle colour lit up the space beyond the expansive clear-glass patio doors. They slid apart to reveal comfortably elegant tables and chairs, all glowing transparently with a soft inner radiance. Carefully conceptualised shrubberies grew in a raised-bedded landscape of natural stone, all illuminated by a display of concealed lighting. It seemed a little over the top to me, but my three companions rushed forward with cries of delight.

'It seems we are eating outside,' I said lightly.

I offered to help Galen and Myia bring the food out but they wouldn't hear of it. I also asked if our two somewhat taciturn guards would like to join us, and was informed with a look of discomfort that they would eat in the kitchen. So I wandered outside with the others, and took my seat to be waited upon as a rather self-conscious Portal Master. Dish after dish arrived in rapid succession: numerous artistically arrayed meat and vegetable preparations accompanied by a raft of condiments.

Galen asked us what we would like to drink, and surprised me with the assumption that I would not be drinking alcohol. 'We keep a supply of alcohol of course for the companions and guests of Portal Masters,' he announced urbanely, 'perhaps they might enjoy a nice wine. For you there is a choice of fruit juices and flavoured carbonated extracts, or water, carbonated or still.'

The others didn't understand him, and I glossed over it, asking for fruit juices for everyone. I wondered if it was some health thing akin to Ravi's liver juice. I guessed that Portal Technology had evolved from the hi-tec enclaves of his time, and wondered with a smile if this was some legacy of his fervent enthusiasm for *Living Earth*. I thought about trying to access the 'archive' to see if I could find out what had happened to him, and then wondered if it worked for events in my subjective future: or if my location in space and time made any difference to the information I could access. It was complicated to think about, and I decided in the event that I preferred not to know his fate.

Instead I wondered about the extraordinary vision I had had up in the bedroom. In fact, it had been far more overwhelming and immersive than any mere vision. It seemed extraordinary that I could have experienced something so astounding, and yet understood so little about it. I sighed. More mysteries, just when I thought I was finding some answers. But I smiled at the unlikely scene we made: four refugees in time eating together on a luxurious garden patio in Atlantis. Far out in the night the three great pyramids were alive with light. The smart-glass had reverted to perfect transparency in the darkness, and they completed the surreal backdrop to the improvised celebration of our deliverance. But the light in the principal edifice was different. The rainbow hues of the immense holo-projection bathed its interior in an eerie luminescence, and its haunting presence seemed to warn of fates from which even Atlantis was no sanctuary.

Chapter 24

THE RESONANT BONHOMIE of a surround-sound voice woke me next morning.

'Portal Master, the High Council requests your presence in the council chamber in two hours.'

Jacqueline and I stirred. We had spent a blessed hour lying in each other's arms and talking before falling asleep. The sense of peace and order in Atlantis was as welcome as its comfort and conveniences, and I dared to imagine how it might be to love her in the blissful mundanity of ordinary life. Yet I did not feel I could relax completely, nor forget it was the extraordinary nature of the quest I had been thrown into which had brought us together. So far it seemed I could not have one without the other. Another tricky part of our relationship had encountered a close call towards the end of our conversation, which I blamed on the seductive nature of the overly comfortable king-sized bed. I had resolved to invent an eccentric preference for sleeping on a more Spartan model on the floor.

Lysias arrived an hour later, in what I had come to think of as a 'buzz wagon' on account of the rather insect-like appearance of the Atlantean people carriers. It was only while watching it arrive that my conscious mind finally made the connection, and I remembered the strange armoured men who had run at us across the field outside Charles' cottage. I couldn't believe I hadn't seen it before. There was a definite similarity in style, and it made me more cautious than ever.

We had finished a relatively perfunctory breakfast and I was ready to go. Lysias looked cheerful enough, and I waved goodbye to Jacqueline feeling reasonably confident that all would be well. The council chamber was much as I expected: grand, cavernous and largely empty. Five austere countenances examined the officially recorded findings and recommendations. They duly proposed and agreed that I be offered instruction and advice in the mastery of the Portal, and commended my timely services to a valued First Citizen. An investigation was initiated into the circumstances of the assault upon Aton; Kormas and Chrysanthe were offered sanctuary and employment in Atlantis, and our military escort was dismissed. The way ahead seemed clearer and more straightforward.

'Aton would like to see you all,' said Lysias, as he and I strolled down the imposing marble steps outside the council chamber. 'I have sent for your wife and friends, and they should arrive shortly.'

Sure enough, they turned up in a buzz wagon a couple of minutes later, and I informed Kormas and Chrysanthe of their good fortune as we were whisked off together to the hospital. Their faces reminded me of Kaltrina and Sophia, when they realised the lottery win was for real.

Aton sat propped up in bed in a comfortable private suite. He looked a little pale but his eyes were bright with interest. I had grown used to the background energy in Atlantis. A ubiquitous hum reverberated faintly but permanently all around me. But it grew suddenly in intensity as I approached him, and I felt something more than mere déjà vu: a dizzyingly intense and confused remembering, much like I had experienced with Alex. Aton tensed, and his genial expression acquired a wary edge.

'The temporal echoes are very powerful,' he said. 'I am experiencing sequential dissonance. We must be careful how we interact my friend. Perhaps the investigation will throw some light on the situation, but in the meantime we should have as little contact as possible. I thank you for the assistance you have rendered me and young Kormas here, but it seems the dialogue I had been looking forward to will have to wait, or proceed by other means.'

'I feel it too,' I said, 'and I have felt it before from someone else with a Portal, just before I acquired my own. I am happy I was able to be of service, but I have many questions.'

Aton's eyebrows elevated themselves significantly, and the caution in his expression grew sharper.

Lysias cleared his throat. 'Temporal dissonance in advance of technical inception is of even more concern. It seems that temporal displacements of a serious nature are involved. Many of your questions will be answered during your debriefing and Portal instruction, and other investigations will be made. It is best you do not discuss this with Aton, as the time-looping seems to affect both of you intensely.'

The urge was strong to say something to Aton about our fateful future meeting. But just coming out with it seemed impossible. I felt such a conversation should be confidential, at least. Besides, there were too many things I didn't understand – including apparent contradictions in the Portal Masters' knowledge of their own technology. My principal loyalty was to Jacqueline and Alex, and to Charles, Billy, Priya and the twins. My priority was to learn all I could about the Portal before deciding anything at all.

Kormas remained for a few minutes of conversation with Aton, while Lysias spoke to Jacqueline and me out in the corridor.

'Your Portal training will begin tomorrow morning,' he said to me. 'I will look after Kormas and his lady from this point on. You two may spend the rest of the day as you wish.'

We wandered out into the sunshine hand in hand, and began somewhat inevitably to make our way towards the three red-gold pyramids that dominated the surreal refuge in time.

'Richard how long do you think this Portal training of yours will last?' Jacqueline asked.

I laughed, 'funny, I was just thinking the same thing.'

'I was thinking about our marriage,' she said coyly.

'Me too,' I smiled.

'Do you feel I am wrong to think of propriety when we are living such an odd existence?'

'I am more concerned about dragging you into this odd existence in the first place,' I admitted.

'It seems that fate has connected our lives Richard, and for my part our time together has already exceeded anything I could have hoped or prayed for – or even imagined.' She waved her free hand at the gleaming pyramids. 'Just look at this sight! Here I walk in Atlantis, with a good and kind man I have come to love with all my heart.'

My own heart swelled with joy, but a niggling doubt quibbled. 'I'm not that good ...' I began, but she silenced me with a kiss.

We spent a leisurely day wandering through the waking dream of artefacts in the pyramids, talking about everything and anything, and eating and watching holo-vids in the extravagant lounge facilities around the main square. Historical documentaries fascinated her, and when we looked through lists of old movies she picked 'Gone with the wind' and sat through it completely entranced. I teased her afterwards: reminding her how she had scoffed at the idea of people watching soap operas about themselves. When it began to grow dark we took the elevator to the sixth floor of the main pyramid and climbed up to the final level, where the gleaming telescopes stood pointing at the night sky.

'I remembered our discussion about telescopes at that horrible house of Mr McCreedy's when I saw this,' I said, pulling her close.

'Yes,' she murmured, and then added provocatively, 'when you lied to me.'

'What would you have thought if I told you I was from the future?' I smiled, 'you already thought me mad.'

'I suppose I thought you a little – unusual,' she admitted reflectively, 'but I liked you very much. You were the first real gentleman I ever met: kind I mean, and thoughtful.'

'How strange that time with you seems now,' I said. 'It terrifies me that I might never have seen you again. And when I found you in that jail cell, I thought my heart would break.'

'And mine felt such hope and despair I cannot find words for it. I think I loved you from that moment, though I did not know it.'

We were no experts with the big telescope, and spent much of our time looking at the moon.

'You know we can watch holo-vids of the stars and the planets,' I said. 'You can see a thousand times more than with this thing.'

'I dare say Richard,' she said. 'But this is very special, just you and me and the telescope under the night sky. I can hardly believe it is real, and yet I feel so wonderfully alive: I have never imagined such contentment – or happiness.'

The stars seemed to shine down in benediction over us as we walked hand in hand back to our guesthouse. I had never felt such happiness either. There was certainly something sacred and profound in our goodnight kiss that night, and I felt no need to take to the mattress on the floor to preserve my good intentions.

Next morning I was off for Portal training quite early, feeling a little like a student again. I reported to Mercedeh in the travel port control office as requested, and she introduced me to another female Portal master, a somewhat severe, athletic looking woman of around forty. I was beginning to notice that most of these 'high citizens' of Atlantis seemed to be middle aged or older.

'This is Intakaes, who will be responsible for your training,' said Mercedeh with a bland smile.

I received an even less generous acknowledgement from my instructor, who barely nodded. Her eyes were a steely green, her lips determined, her jaw firm, and she wore her greying hair in a short, elfin style. My enthusiasm dropped a notch.

'Pleased to meet you,' I said, putting out my hand.

She raised her eyebrows slightly, but otherwise ignored the gesture.

'We will begin with a background de-briefing,' she said shortly, 'and then move on to discuss your own experience in concurrence with some preliminary training.'

'Sure,' I agreed, 'where is it going to happen?'

'Follow me,' she said.

A couple of minutes later I was in one of the other offices, watching a holo-vid of a thin, gangly man about thirty with weird, intense eyes and unkempt spiky hair.

'Portal technology was the creation of Valentin Dementyev, a secretive and obsessive genius who was born in the Siberian enclave in twenty one hundred and three,' Intakaes was saying. 'He developed the basic concept in his twenties, before defecting to Houston Towers in pursuit of the technological and material resources he required to perfect his work. Some bad blood was created over it, but he succeeded in creating a working model about eight years later. The fundamental tenets of time travel were established, and the technical flaws ironed out over the next ten years. Some fifty Portals were made and of course the barrier was discovered. Then problems began to emerge. There was conflict and disagreement about the barrier and the preservation of the time flow. Some Portal Masters went rogue and others elected to become free-timers. Chaotic timelines created some serious space-time anomalies. A majority, including Valentin, elected to enforce order, and the decision was made to establish Atlantis.'

She looked at me expectantly, 'do you have any questions?'

'Yes,' I said, 'lots, but I can't put half of them into words yet. What about Valentin whatshisname, the Portal inventor, is he here in Atlantis?'

Her face fell slightly. 'He disappeared. We don't know what happened to him. He vanished from his laboratory one night. It was not unusual, he was in the habit of going on impulsive time-jumps and remaining absent for unpredictable periods. But he never returned. He was not the only one: a number of other Portal Masters have disappeared too. Space-time is a dangerous place, especially in primitive time periods, and there are risks of a different kind in the vicinity of the barrier. Of course things have been much better since Atlantis was built. We maintain sequential continuity, and monitor time-jumps meticulously. Even so several Portal masters have gone missing. We investigate of course, but there are limits to what we can do.'

'How long has Atlantis been here, in subjective time I mean?' I asked.

'Sixteen years,' she said, 'plus the two years it took to build the main infrastructure.'

'And your numbers have expanded to two hundred Portal Masters since then?'

'No, that was done at the inception of Atlantis. We manufactured all the Portal technology we could, including what we required to construct the travel port and the time-flow complex in the great pyramid. It largely exhausted our supply of ultra-rare materials, as well as the hi-tec production equipment we needed. It was a desperate venture, and a lot was sacrificed to make the project a success. Houston Towers couldn't have done it on its own. We entered into agreements with several other enclaves, and all of us depleted our ability to keep the outsiders at bay in the process. Each enclave wanted some of their own people instated as Portal Masters of course, as well as placing physicists, technicians and other representatives in Atlantis. It was part of the contract we made. But we all understood that our own collective future was at stake.'

'How were the Portals initially assigned?' I asked curiously.

She smiled: a not altogether pleasant expression. 'Competition,' she said, and I thought I detected a rather self-satisfied smirk.

'OK, I think I've got the political background,' I said. 'What about how the Portal actually works?'

She laughed, 'I can't really answer that one. As I said, Valentin was a genius. It's high-end dark-tec of course. It draws energy from the high energy matrix, and utilises it to expand and access wormholes. All you need to know is how to control it, and that is part of Valentin's genius. Some intuitive functions of human consciousness are far more proficient at navigating multi-dimensional topographies than any quantum computer.'

'OK, I don't think I got much of that at all,' I said. 'How many multi-dimensions are there, and how can we 'intuitively' know how to navigate them?'

'To be honest, we're not entirely sure,' said Intakaes, 'At least seven dimensions appear to be engaged, possibly more. Plus time of course, which alters its relationship to space according to localized energetic loading. The capacity for multi-dimensional navigation appears to be related to the unconscious mind, which by definition we cannot consciously direct and control. As I said, it is intuitive: almost an art form you might say. We have to learn to accept unconscious input while steering the process with our attention. It's a bit like any skill: you have to develop an ability to act with single minded focus and intent.'

'You say that time alters its relationship to space if the energy level increases?'

'Yes, time is the first dimension to manifest changes as the wormhole begins to open. It expands into the past and the future, and the brain can somehow recognise this and quantify it intuitively.'

'How does time expand?' I asked, 'I don't even know what that means.'

'Don't you?' she enquired archly. 'Not even in life-threatening situations?'

'Oh,' I said, 'you mean when everything speeds up.'

'Everything doesn't speed up,' she said: 'you do, and it is a limited and temporary effect that can be triggered by the Portal. When the wormhole begins to expand space-time reverts to a fluid energy field, and you become aware of every part of it. In a way you exist in every part of it. Your consciousness resonates within this field, and you can reach through it to touch any point in space and time. Your point of arrival is merely exchanged for your point of departure – or coupled together if you establish a doorway.'

'OK,' I complained. 'I think that's about as much explanation as I am up to for now. I mean, I don't actually understand how any of the electrical gadgets at home work, but I can use them. How do I actually use the Portal?'

'To master the Portal you must focus and apply conscious attention, while trusting your intuition,' said Intakaes. 'You will have to separate your mind from habitual emotional and physiological reactions, and take control of your cognitive processes.'

She waved a hand and a holo-projection appeared: a human brain and spinal cord linked with a Portal. It depicted illuminated pathways linking various functions of the cerebral cortex and the central nervous system.

'Portal interaction penetrates the spine to commandeer sensory and motor neuron pathways in the peripheral nervous system,' she said briskly. 'It interrelates with the cerebral hemispheres via the thalamus...' Her voice droned on, and I found myself entering the unconscious mind in quite the wrong sort of way. It reminded me of struggling to stay awake during lectures at school and university. I managed to zero back in as she started to talk more about techniques.

'...the sympathetic system impacts the focus of our conscious attention, and is largely out of control in the primitive human condition. It is involved in storing information and planning future actions in the right and left hemispheres of the brain respectively, and our minds are chaotically distracted by dissatisfaction with past events and anxieties about the future.'

She looked encouraging: 'to take control we must pay conscious attention to these processes in a particular way. We must learn to be continuously present with immediate experience, and able to consciously direct our awareness.'

'Will I need drugs or some kind of implant to do that?' I asked.

'No,' she said disapprovingly, 'you need practice. And you need precise and clear attention and control. The quality of your consciousness is very important. No caffeine, nicotine, alcohol or any other toxins.'

'Seriously?' I groaned.

'Yes,' she said firmly.

'Hmm,' I mused. 'This wouldn't have anything to do with *Living Earth*, would it?'

Intakaes grunted contemptuously. 'I was briefed on your adventures in India. A healthy diet is the only sensible thing about those people.'

'What happened to them? Did *Living Earth* catch on?' I asked, remembering Ravi's zealous optimism with a half-smile.

'They continue to gather converts right up into the final years – into to the barrier distortion field itself, if that's what you mean,' she said dismissively. 'Their madness seems to suit all that chaos.'

'Are things very bad there – or then?'

'Portals get difficult to navigate some years before the barrier is fully manifested: closer, and space-time starts to deform. The physical characteristics of material structures begin to alter; eventually distorting significantly. Objects can blink in and out of existence. Time warps too. A moment can last hours or hours pass in a moment. Human faculties become unreliable. Hallucinations are common. It is a nightmare.'

I was shocked. 'So it's not just a barrier to time travel. It's the end of everything!'

'It could be,' she said flatly.

'And *Living Earth* still keeps the faith?'

'They embrace it. They sit on the ground and claim that the Earth reassures them.' She snorted derisively: 'idiots.'

'So what do I have to do apart from eating and drinking uninteresting things?'

'You have to work hard,' she said stiffly. 'We have programmes and techniques which will help, but the more we practice becoming actively attentive, the more associated neuro-pathways will develop in the brain. It's like building up mental muscle.'

'What about the icons the Portal projects?' I asked, 'is that a computer language I have to learn?'

'You need to understand and use them, yes,' she said. 'We have subliminal applications which will speed up your ability to do that. But the icons are more than just a language. They are an interactive medium with a semi parapsychological affinity with the brain. They can identify locations in the time flow, monitor the portal's actions and control its functions. You must learn to manipulate them with a focused mind, in multiple dimensions. It is an intuitive skill which is difficult to teach.'

'Oh good,' I said drily, 'any idea how long it is going to take?'

'It depends on your aptitude,' she said, 'it should take only weeks to grasp the basics, but it will be months to develop real finesse.'

'Well I had better get started then,' I sighed.

Jacqueline gave a sigh of her own when I delivered the news to her some hours later.

'At least we will have some stability in our lives for a while,' she said at length, 'and there is so much to see in these Ark's of theirs. It is absolutely fascinating: such a privilege. There are many interesting things to learn.'

'It's not a lack of interesting things to learn that is the problem,' I grumbled.

'I know Richard,' she smiled. 'Let us see how your training progresses. Much has changed in my mind since I met you, and I may feel differently as time goes on. I have come to see that it is the respect and commitment to a 'relationship' – she laughed as she said the word – which matters, not the outward form of a ceremony. And there is no self-righteous congregation to disapprove. I have come to know and trust you more each day, and that is what is most important to me.'

For the first time in a long while I thought of the Mindworm. As far as I could tell it was no longer functional, but I wondered if it was right to get so involved with Jacqueline when any doubt existed. I went through a complicated loop in my head, where I traced the origin of the wretched thing from the future back into the past of a life which I had presumably already lived – at least up to the point where I became some kind of threat to the perpetrators. It seemed to me that if I existed now in fear of the theoretical harm the creature might cause, I might change significant things in my time-line just as much as if it was controlling me. I supposed this might aid my mysterious enemies as well, and could have all sorts of unpredictable consequences. It gave me a headache, and I pushed the whole tangled mess out of my mind. Such ponderings mostly just ended up with hoping for the best, which amounted to my basic compass in life anyway.

So the days passed with Intakaes taking me step by step through my previous experiences with the Portal: explaining what had been going on technically, if not how I had actually triggered these amateur forays through space-time. I struggled with attention-focusing exercises, familiarised myself with the Portals luminous projected vocabulary, and learned how to nudge some of its simpler functions into action with my mind. I could only practice low-energy procedures in Atlantis: Portals were not allowed to be fully activated outside the orichalcum pillars of the travel port. On the couple of occasions I did accidentally trigger space-time distortions, alarms went off and Intakaes had to contact the control centre to restore the peace.

There were plenty of opportunities to talk about the vagaries of temporal technology, and I found such interludes just as vital as everything else. They also made welcome breaks from the tedium of developing a muscular brain.

'…if you start to think about the thought, or get annoyed with yourself for not being able to retain focus,' Intakaes' voice was saying, 'it stops you paying attention, and takes you away from the present moment. '

'Err, could I ask you something?'

'What is it now?'

'This whole déjà vu business – disrupting time-lines and all that: what is it about actually?'

'It can mean a number of things,' she said. 'Basically, if anything changes in the time-flow, you unconsciously remember both realities. You recognise on some level that you are repeating experience in a different way. Even small changes can trigger the effect. The changes themselves have repercussions along the timelines, and alter reality as the scenario plays out. Normally space-time adjusts itself to absorb these changes, and maintains the integrity of the time-flow within certain parameters. It is a kind of damper effect which prevents the anomaly escalating exponentially. Everything connects back together – more or less. That's what the free-timers rely on.'

'Lysias said that if we disrupt each other's time lines the changes would multiply, not be smoothed out,' I objected.

'He was talking about interactions between Portal Masters' timelines,' she replied. 'The repercussions are still ultimately smoothed out, in the sense that the ripple effect is eventually contained. But they are initially magnified, and can create dramatically unpredictable changes in our lives, and in the lives of those around us. The greater the number of Portal Masters involved, the greater the disorder can become. But there is also more resistance to it happening in the first place.'

I wanted to know why these effects were magnified, and what resisted the changes. It was complicated as usual, and the answer appeared to be that essentially no one really knew. Spontaneous events just seemed to conspire to prevent such disruptions taking place, but if this buffer was forced beyond a certain point the backlash could be intense.

'We think the effects are amplified by interactions between Portals in higher dimensions,' she said. 'Even two separate Portals operating in the same time and place have some effect on each other. Altering each other's timelines seems to generate violent repercussions.' She paused and sighed. 'This is where we have really missed Valentin's genius. Portal Technology was still relatively new when he disappeared. There was so much more to learn.'

'When did he disappear?'

'While Atlantis was being constructed,' she said sadly. 'He never saw his master project completed.'

I asked her about Lysias's assertion that there would be serious disruption to space-time if the same Portal was to appear in the same time and place.

Intakaes grimaced. 'Yes, there was a terrible incident in which a Portal Master simultaneously materialised in the same time and place from two separate space-time locations. He – or they – vanished, never to be seen again, and reality was horribly distorted among those nearby. Portals were damaged and people lost months or even years out of their lives: vital records and priceless artefacts disappeared, and work and study programmes were hopelessly disorganised. Some lost knowledge and skills, relationships ceased to exist, and others developed bizarre personality changes. It was a mess. There have been near misses too, with less chaotic but nevertheless regrettable consequences.'

'Was that here in Atlantis?'

'Of course not, it was one of the reasons Atlantis was built: the sequential continuity of the travel-port guards against such a thing. If something like that happened here with so many portal masters present, the repercussions would be unthinkable.'

'Are you sure it was the portals that caused the damage?' I asked cautiously. 'Maybe it was the same person in the same place rather than the portals?'

'We have experimented with that,' she said. 'A Second Citizen was transferred to increasingly synchronised space-time coordinates without any drastic repercussions at all. The doppelgängers were simply unable to approach beyond a certain distance from each other, and began to lose consciousness when the limit was reached. We found it impossible to move them into physical proximity even while unconscious. The inertia field was approaching an infinite value.'

'Was this courageous voyager a volunteer?' I wondered.

'Of course,' she said smugly, 'he was happy to take the risk for an extravagant remuneration. He did very well out of it.'

'What about two different people using the same portal?' I asked, adopting my best theoretical poker face.

She laughed. 'Unlikely. We have not had the opportunity to experiment of course. No one has passed on a portal to another in our present subjective history, and they are too valuable – not to mention irreplaceable – to risk damaging. But logic dictates that it is the Portal which interacts with higher dimensional realities. We merely navigate.'

'Does timeline disruption occur only if we interact directly with our other selves?' I asked. 'What about acting indirectly: through other people I mean – arranging for particular information to get to our past self, or making changes to circumstances we know will affect our future?'

'Whose future?' asked Intakaes slyly, 'it is actually our own past. How will such actions affect our present self? Will they alter or negate our current timeline and its associated events? It's complicated, and exotic feed-back can complicate it still further. In answer to your question, even indirect action can initiate bleed-back, but the closer we get to actual intersection, the worse things become. There can be noticeable effects where our doppelgänger closes to within a couple of days and a few miles of itself. The subduction zone really starts to intensify a couple of hours and a few hundred metres out...'

'Subduction zone?' I enquired.

'The bleed-back threshold.' She delivered a flinty smile. 'It's a term we borrowed from geological tectonic mechanics. We found the reference to such fundamental forces rather appropriate: particularly their disastrous potential to shake the foundations of our lives. The repercussions become increasingly violent and unpredictable the closer we approach the nexus point.'

'Something strange did happen once when I returned to the place I had been,' I said, realising I had forgotten to tell her. 'I felt weird and kept getting flashbacks from what I had done before, and at one point I was thrown several days and a few miles away.'

'You were very lucky,' she said, 'as you seem to have been in so many ways. Perhaps you got away with it because you were not fully integrated with your Portal. It could have been much worse. Returning to intersect your temporal pathway at any point can trigger a kind of inter-dimensional short-circuit which releases high-energy bleed-back up and down the timeline. We can follow a winding pathway between the past and the future, but the proportionally changing variable of our progression must remain linear. The effects of transecting our time-line can vary to an unpredictable degree, and it can further complicate the changes that knowledge of past and future events can create. We avoid such encounters as a matter of course. But the repercussions are worse where the Portal of one or both incarnations are engaged with high-dimensional realities when the encounters take place – particularly so in the case of the latter.'

I often tried to get my head around the nature of existence itself in my conversations with her. 'But what is reality actually?' I asked. 'How are we able to change things – to set the lives of so many people on different courses without them being aware of it? It's mind boggling!'

'It's certainly difficult to think about,' she agreed. 'It's related to the ability of the unconscious mind to navigate high dimensional domains. Once you enter the quantum level, reality becomes a sea of abstract harmonic frequencies: time and space cease to have meaning. Yet consciousness remains: we retain the ability to resonate with these exotic dimensions. We're still not sure why – consciousness itself is still something of a mystery.'

'Yes, if we enter a wormhole, we are beyond space-time, I get that,' I said. 'But how can we affect material processes – cause billions of tiny interactions between people and objects to unknowingly re-arrange themselves into different sequences of events?'

'We don't,' she said smugly. 'We merely temporarily transcend their limitations. Space-time follows the laws of cause and effect. You could say life is a complex illusion we are immersed in. Raising our energy level into higher dimensional frequencies frees us from its subjective constraints, and experiencing space-time from a transcendent perspective enables us to act with greater knowledge and understanding. The natural laws simply absorb and flow around any changes we make, and continue in their course accordingly.'

She thought for a moment. 'It is a bit like this: imagine you are standing on a beach watching the sea, with the sunlight glittering on the waves as they come rolling in. There are millions of variables creating that scene, multiple laws of physics interacting in limitless combinations. They are all perfectly synchronised, working together effortlessly and spontaneously. Picture that as everyday reality. Then you walk into the water. Around you, the scene changes a little. You obstruct part of a wave; divert a little wind, block a bit of sunlight. Some patterns in the light, sea and air around you are altered, but the changes are cancelled out a small distance away, and re-absorbed by the prevailing environment.'

I thought about it. 'Yes, but I don't understand why those around us don't experience these changes as anomalies of some kind.'

'We experience them as temporal echoes, as you know. But ordinary people do not, because their stream of consciousness is anchored in the collective time flow. Life is not what it seems. All levels of reality are interconnected and interdependent. When exotic dimensions were first projected mathematically, we used to imagine them as curled up within space-time like some sort of rather useless, invisible appendages. Now we see space-time as curved around them, like the outer skin of an onion, and within these inner dimensions, the past, present and future all meet in the same place. If we intervene on relative levels of reality via exotic realms, everything readjusts simultaneously. As soon as you act, it has already happened.'

'And no one notices anything?'

'Some notice little things: subtle inconsistencies and contradictions, if their unconscious mind is more attuned to it. But such glimpses are dismissed as fanciful or mistaken if they do not conform to the shared consciousness stream. The mentally disturbed can sometimes be aware of profound happenings in the collective psyche too. But they do not understand them, and their perceptions are ignored in much the same way.'

'What about activating the Portal soon after materialising somewhere – to move on to another space-time location,' I asked, 'does that create this bleed back effect?'

'There can be some high-dimensional interaction,' she said, 'but as long as the time-line remains progressive such problems do not occur.'

At one point, she herself brought up the 'sequential dissonance' I had experienced with Aton.

'I spoke to him about it,' she said, 'it is worrying.'

'What does it mean?' I asked.

'Trouble,' she said: 'sequential looping. What you experienced is a kind of feedback loop in which two time-lines bleed back into each other. One or both of you either have or will enter each other's timelines in a significant, contradictory trajectory – out of subjective time sequence.'

'You mean it's a kind of paradox?'

'It is more the risk of a paradox; which for a Portal Master could mean time-line disruption raised to a significant power.'

'I would have thought it a constant danger, what with so many Portal Masters travelling about everywhere.'

'The risks are very low,' she said stiffly, 'we keep careful track of our time-lines, and practice sequential discipline at both our destinations and travel port departures.'

'It all sounds rather stifling,' I grinned. 'I suppose I can understand why the free-timers want to do their own thing.'

'Any hi-tec function will have fixed performance parameters,' she sniffed, 'even the aircraft of your time could only maintain stable flight within critical configurations. Portal technology is no different. Free-timers are extremely irresponsible, but fortunately the risks are low for them too. There are few of them, they are aware of the dangers, and they know we are watching the time flow for significant incidents. Of course Portals have been improved too, after some of the early mishaps. They monitor the time jumps and intervene if necessary.'

I learnt a lot of things from such off-hand conversations. The fact that the Portal could adjust itself to avoid people and objects when it materialised was one. It could even push them aside in emergencies. Another was atmospheric pressure differentials where doorways opened between different space-time locations. I wanted to know if air would rush through the opening if there was a big enough contrast in the respective pressure zones. 'No,' was the answer: any more than it did when travelling through the time flow. The exotic transition membrane of a doorway continued to embody the high dimensional topography between the two locations, and acted as a barrier to such latent forces. Only living beings and kinetically charged matter could penetrate the doorways.

Absorbing the Portal's icon vocabulary was relatively easy with the technology available. I spent several hours each day working with a device that interacted directly with the brain in a similar way to the Portal. It imparted visual mental impressions of icon images and their functions, and allowed me to practice manipulating them without activating the Portal itself. On a secondary level it monitored my chattering mind and discordant biofeedback readings; knitting them into a unified, harmonious background tone when I tuned my wayward faculties into the required configuration. It was a bit like learning to play a musical instrument: orchestrating desired responses in specific combinations with focused recognition and intent. I still had to absorb and ingrain the information in the old fashioned way, repeatedly running the process through my consciousness. But each repetition established it more deeply, and with increasing competence and speed.

I asked how the Portal translated speech and Intakaes described a sophisticated capability monitoring neural oscillations associated with verbal communication in the brain of a Portal Master and encountered individuals. There was a missing link in the theory it seemed, and in their comprehension of this aspect of Valentin's multi-dimensional technology. Exactly how this electrical activity in the brain was decrypted into mutual meaning and intent was not understood, and never precisely explained by its creator in satisfactory scientific terms. In his usual oddball fashion he described a mysterious dimensional coefficient resonating with the nervous system on an interactive universal constant: a shared consciousness he related to the psyche's ability to navigate the abstract realms beyond space-time.

The Portal Masters didn't like this idea, believing it semi-mystical or religious in nature: an occasional eccentricity which they tolerated in their erratic genius. Instead they had concocted a convoluted counter-theory involving the Archive, which had been unknown at the inception of Portal technology. My own experience at Port Royal involving a self-aware universal sentience linking all forms of consciousness favoured Valentin. But I kept quiet and filed it away in the unsolved conundrum department for future consideration.

Intakaes' training program was quite intense, and I was pretty tired in the evenings. Jacqueline kept herself entertained during the day, visiting the pyramids and watching holo-vids, but the novelty of these pastimes began to wane after a while, and she started looking for other things to do. I had taken her to the extensive gym facilities and swimming pool in the leisure complex, the first of which she found 'unladylike' and the second utterly scandalous.

'They might as well be naked,' she hissed, averting her gaze from the minimally decent figures cavorting around in the pool. The sauna, beauty parlour and various exotic therapy treatments did not appeal either, and she took to going for walks in the parkland areas and getting to know the second citizens working in the farm at the other end of the island.

'I can hardly believe it Richard,' she said one evening, 'but I am beginning to tire of Atlantis.'

'I can believe it,' I said moodily, having had a particularly gruelling day.

'Oh, I'm sorry,' she chuckled ruefully. 'I do not mean to belittle your trials with the tyrannical Intakaes.'

She leaned towards me in a conciliatory manner as she spoke, resting her hand lightly on my thigh in the most delightful way, before whipping it away again with a mortified expression.

'Don't worry,' I grinned, 'I am much too worn out to be seduced.'

'Richard!' she exclaimed, blushing hotly, 'I was not...I forgot, that is, I did not mean...'

'I'm only teasing, Jacqueline,' I laughed. 'You look so sweet when you blush like that. Intimate gestures are quite normal when you live together, you know. It is just that we are living together in a rather unusual way.'

'Well I find it extremely confusing,' she said crossly. 'However, to return to my original remark, I find that I cannot like this place somehow, despite its wonders. There is something dull and confining about it. Even these extraordinary treasures from history are starting to seem artificial and out of place. I miss the bustle and exchange of ordinary life, and the satisfaction of work and achievement. There is no natural rhythm of life here. Anything I want is there for the asking. There is nothing worthwhile to do. These Portal Masters look down their nose at me, and from what I have seen their husbands or wives – or these 'partners' of theirs – are even worse. My only friend is Chrysanthe, and if I visit I can only talk to her through her house-mind. And that is another thing: I know your Portal can turn them off, but I feel these house-minds are constantly snooping on everything we do.'

'The house-minds are programmed to be discrete and loyal to their guests,' I reminded her. 'My Portal would only inform me if one did not disconnect when I asked it to.'

'Harrumph,' she grumbled, 'I still don't like it. But I digress once more. Chrysanthe could not be happier. It is her greatest dream to have her own house, and Kormas has the most wonderful career he could imagine. Now I find I am happiest at the farm with the animals and the crops, and I long for your return in the evenings. I hope you will not think me ungrateful. I am fully sensible of –'

I stopped her there. 'Yes, I agree.'

She looked at me searchingly. 'You do not think to accept their offer of citizenship? I can see it would be a great honour and we would want for nothing... '

'I have no wish to stay,' I said. 'I have Charles and the others to think of, and I want you to be happy. There are also things going on here that give me cause for concern. Besides,' I grinned, 'you are right. It is boring.'

Chapter 25

WITHIN A COUPLE of weeks Intakaes pronounced herself pleased with my progress, and began taking me out of Atlantis to practice for real. She opened a door in the circle of *orichalcum* pillars, and we stepped out onto a rolling grassy plain with nothing to see other than a few low hills in the distance. The weather was cool and breezy, and according to the Icons we were in part of what would one day become Ukraine on the Russian Steppes. The era predated Atlantis by a thousand years.

'We are not likely to be bothered by anyone here,' she said, 'I want you to open a door to a point fifty kilometres west of here and ten years into the future.'

We had discussed the differences between travelling within the energy field as opposed to opening a static door between two space-time locations. Establishing a doorway was technically more difficult, and Portal Masters preferred to travel within the energy field. It was more discrete, and greatly reduced the risk of unwanted people or objects passing through a doorway. But she didn't want me getting lost in the time-flow, which would be at the very least a nuisance, and quite possibly far worse. I had used the opportunity to ask how it was possible to take someone without a portal through the time-flow, and it seemed to be yet another thing that no one really understood.

'We think it is something to do with the way the Portal is focused through the human psyche,' she said. 'The Portal Master's transcendent experience appears to interact sympathetically with the electrical field of an adjacent nervous system, and both are enveloped by the wormhole. But they have to be in close bodily contact. If you are just close to someone, or touching them, they will be ejected from the energy field.'

I took my time and fixed my attention in the way she had taught me. Just being around Portal Masters for a while seemed to have made a difference: that constant awareness of a background vibrational hum everywhere around me. It was strange, as if some elusive part of me had to engage on the very cusp of consciousness to initiate the process. It reminded me of trying to conjure a 3D image while staring at an auto stereogram. I began to enter a zone where I could perceive in a certain way: become aware of the Portal, and project my attention to direct its functions. It still felt forced, and I had to be careful not to get distracted, or start second-guessing myself. If I did, I lost the connection. But I had learned to cling onto the link. I felt a brush of contact with the Portal, seized on it a little too forcibly, and then relaxed enough to hold on to it. I almost lost it again as I tried to recognise and manipulate the icons that started to appear. My control felt shaky, and my confidence wavered. But I overcame the uncertainties with a surge of determination, and a veil parted in reality.

Solid structure began to dissolve and power vibrated all around me. But I remained anchored in the present, and tried to reach out into the boundless realm which opened before me. The chaotic flow of possibilities now seemed more imbued with meaning and structure. Time acquired perceptible depth and perspective. A seemingly infinite series of images stretched into the past and the future, like reflections between parallel mirrors. Manifold earths hovered on the edge of existence: multiple times and places shimmering in sequences of chronological progression. The luminous icons imposed a sense of order and control, and helped to steady my rather indistinct stab at Intakaes' coordinates through the amorphous layers of reality. Two separate space-time locations synchronised and locked together, and I was suddenly standing in a perfectly normal world with a perfectly abnormal hole in space-time shimmering before me.

'Congratulations,' said Intakaes. 'Your coordinates are about ten percent out, but not bad for a first attempt. Now as we discussed, you have the option of instructing the doorway to collapse after a set time, or holding it open while we pass through.'

'Which is best?' I asked.

'I would suggest holding it open until we know what is on the other side,' she said drily.

So I simply desired that the door remained open, and we walked through. Unsurprisingly, the landscape was identical, and equally empty.

My next attempt failed completely, and the one after that was more inaccurate than the first. But I gradually made progress: engaging with the Portal more often than not. My practice runs continued over the next few weeks. Intakaes began to allow me to make jumps directly through the energy flow; showing me luminous coordinates projected from her Portal and following me to the destination. On a number of occasions she took me into the great pyramid to explain and relate my experiences to different aspects of the vast holo-projected time-flow. My confidence grew steadily, and my knowledge and skills became gradually more refined under her exacting tutelage. There were many more discussions between times.

'What about disease?' I wanted to know, as it was something that concerned me about Jacqueline. 'So far I have been OK, but presumably we are vulnerable to bacteria and viruses in different times and places?'

'Not really,' she said. 'There is a sanitising effect which takes place when passing through interdimensional rifts: both through static doorways and when passing through the time-flow. There seem to be changes in the molecular structure of the body when it is exposed to high energy realities. You might say it is broken down and reassembled in a more optimum condition. Pathogens are scrubbed from the system and the immune system energised. Not only within your own system – but in those who travel with you. It is related to the sympathetic effect which allows them to enter the wormhole with you in the first place The Portal has a secondary feature too. It samples local pathogens as you enter a new space-time location, and stimulates antibodies to protect you.'

Something else we talked of extensively was the Archive.

'It is the most extraordinary engineering feat,' she said. 'We do not really know how it is achieved: the technology is beyond our own capabilities. It gives us hope for the future in fact, because it suggests that the human race will survive and develop such heights.'

'So you think the technology comes from beyond the barrier?'

'That is one theory.'

'What about say – I don't know – alien intervention?'

She laughed depreciatingly. 'We abandoned twentieth century extra-terrestrial mythology some time ago: at least as far as physical space travel is concerned. For one thing, the material resources of old-style industrial nations no longer exist, and secondly the discovery of high dimensional realities rendered the whole idea obsolete. If we travel to other star systems it will be via wormholes.'

'Have you tried?' I asked, fascinated.

'It's complicated,' said Intakaes a trifle condescendingly. 'We have had to alter our whole approach. Rather than project our ambitions outwards towards the stars, we have had to project inwards into new dimensions of existence.'

'What does 'inwards' mean exactly,' I asked, 'surely higher dimensions are...higher?'

'As I said, it's complicated,' she replied, 'multi-dimensional realities certainly exist in a higher energy state. But from our point of view, they are folded within three dimensional physical structure: four dimensions to be more precise, including time. And as we are creatures of space-time, they are folded within us too.'

'OK, that sounds complicated,' I agreed.

She sniffed impatiently. 'As we have discussed, the Portal draws power from the high energy matrix and raises the local energetic state sufficiently to break down space-time parameters. The exotic dimensions then become accessible: and our inner faculties an instrument capable of navigating these alternative states of existence.' She examined me for a moment to see if I was taking it in. 'For all of its vastness, this physical universe is only a superficial aspect of reality. We live within a finite atomic structure, with apparently limitless potentials existing beyond its boundaries. That is the basic principle of dark tec. The Portal enables us to transcend material corporeality and the key to the whole thing is our own consciousness. The frontiers of knowledge lie within us.'

'So can we travel to places other than this Earth?' I asked.

She grimaced. 'We are still in the infancy of inter-dimensional exploration. We suspect that we are making relatively limited use of its possibilities.'

'Are you talking about other planets or star systems, or some sort of higher existence?' I asked, thinking of the extraordinary visions I had experienced.

'Again, there is no simple answer,' she said. 'The Earth's physical characteristics seem to exert subtle effects in exotic realms too. It is as difficult to break out of the planet's space-time location with the Portal as it is for a rocket to escape its gravity well. There is likely more to it than this of course, and our high-dimensional physicists are struggling to understand this as well as the barrier. But at present all trajectories seem bound to the planet. But there are other avenues of exploration apart from the physical exploitation of space-time.'

'You mean within the Archive itself?' I asked, feeling a stirring of excitement.

'Yes,' she said. 'I had not wanted to raise the subject until your Portal training was fairly advanced. But you have proved surprisingly adept, and developed your skills quickly. I understand from Lysias that you already have some experience with the Archive.'

'Yes, some,' I said, 'it came in handy when I was working with the scrolls in Alexandria.'

'Ah, Alexandria,' she sighed wistfully, 'how I love that city. But I believe you found it possible to access the data without training?'

'Yes, once I started, it did not seem difficult at all.'

'Remarkable,' she said. 'Have you attempted to access it since you began your training?'

'No,' I answered, 'why?'

'I'm curious. Can you try and access it now?'

'OK,' I shrugged, and picked a famous historical figure.

Nothing happened. I concentrated harder. A slight flicker of contact swirled into life, a half-memory of hazy facts and images which quickly faded.

'That's odd,' I said, 'it doesn't seem to work now: not much anyway.'

'Interesting,' Intakaes mused. 'It seems to tally with what we know, and some of the theory.'

'What theory?' I asked, rather annoyed that my Archive trick seemed to have deserted me.

'The Archive was discovered accidentally in the early stages of Portal technology. Few Portal Masters have managed to access it, and even then, generally in a rather intermittent and random manner. A number have dedicated themselves to developing the skill, and a handful have partially succeeded. They theorise that our current Portal technology somehow interferes with the ability to access the Archive, and two or three First Citizens have actually abandoned Portal travel altogether in an attempt to re-train their abilities.'

'So you think I can't tap into the Archive now because I'm learning to use the Portal?'

'We will see. But the indications appear to point in that direction.'

'You might have told me that before we started,' I said tersely.

Intakaes gave a superior smile. 'Portal training is more important, both for your safety and ours. Of course, once you know how to use the

Portal safely, you can choose to stay in Atlantis and study the Archive as much as you like. You don't have to use the Portal to travel if you don't want too.'

'Harrumph,' I grunted, 'I suppose you're right.'

'We are still trying to identify the medium in which the Archive is stored, and the processes involved,' she continued.

'You don't know?'

'At first we thought it was written into the DNA of the human race,' she mused.

'How could that possible?' I asked in astonishment. 'The amount of data is unimaginable – and how could something like that be implemented?'

'It could be implemented, and there is plenty of space for the data. The human genome is several dozen gigabytes in size, and is stored inside a nucleus just a few micrometres across. Storing information on DNA is relatively simple, we can do that by programming the A and C base pairs as a binary '0', and the T and G as a '1'. The Archive is far more efficient though: it seems to use some kind of multi-dimensional holographic key which can be processed directly by the human brain.'

'That is inconceivable,' I said, my head reeling. 'You are talking about technology beyond humanity's wildest dreams.'

'Not our wildest dreams,' purred Intakaes complacently, 'but certainly beyond our present capabilities. And there is more. According to our Archive specialists, there are integrated links to high-dimensional meta-data hubs in place of historical records of key religious figures. We are not sure what to make of that. They have to proceed with extreme care. These hubs may be the key to transcending local space-time constraints, and I am told it is like venturing into an ocean of exotic possibilities. We have already lost our best researcher. He attempted to enter a meta-data hub and lost his mind. He has remained in an unresponsive state for three years.'

I shivered, remembering my own experience. I wondered if I might not have returned either, if Jacqueline hadn't reacted to my absent presence.

'What about travelling to see what these religious figures were really like?' I asked. 'Maybe these high-dimensional hubs are there for a reason.'

'We have tried of course,' she said, 'but their lives are surrounded by multiple paradox anomalies. It is hard to get anywhere near them, and risky to try. There are powerful temporal forces at work around them which repulse any interference with the time-flow – most likely because they generate such exponential collective effects down through the ages.'

I thought about it. 'Are these higher dimensions actually higher levels of existence? I mean: is there an expanded state of being – of intelligence or understanding?'

Intakaes regarded me speculatively. 'Have you experienced something like that?'

'Something like that, yes,' I admitted. 'As if I was witnessing human development from a different perspective: a kind of slow evolutionary progression through time.'

'Interesting,' she said. 'Nekonekh spoke of something similar before he attempted to access the Hub. Such dimensions of existence would appear rather hazardous to explore. I would not pursue such things, certainly not until we learn more about them. There is still a vast amount of uncharted territory in multi-dimensional science.'

'So there seem to be mysteries everywhere we look,' I said. 'You would think that advances in science would make life simpler and clearer, not more complicated and inexplicable.'

Intakaes laughed politely. 'We have to go where the science takes us. Hi-tec advances have brought us many benefits, and pushed forward the frontiers of knowledge immeasurably in a very short time.'

'But what about the rest of the human race?' I asked a little mulishly. 'Most people seemed to be in a pretty bad situation in twenty sixty-seven.'

She regarded me disapprovingly. 'I will not hide the fact that you seem an odd individual for a Portal Master to choose as his successor. True, from your account he was fatally injured and had little time. But he might have been able to reach Atlantis and surrender his Portal before he died.'

'I suppose he had his reasons,' I said with an uneasy smile. 'He already knew me for a start.'

'There has been some debate about asking you to review the database in an attempt to identify your benefactor,' she said. 'It risks crossing time lines, but there are a sufficient number of oddities in your story to worry the Council. Of course it is probable that he exists in our subjective future, and is unknown to us. In any event, it was decided that the time-flow must be allowed to take its course. But if you do recognise the Portal Master concerned, I would request that you inform the Council in confidence.'

I had firmly decided to keep my cards close to my chest by this time. The more I learned, the more complicated the strange mishmash of knowledge and ignorance in Atlantis seemed to become. I was not going to share any information about Aton until I had a better picture of what was going on.

'Sure,' I agreed carefully, wondering if there was a roundabout way to learn more about the strange interaction between our Portals in Alexandria. 'But what if I, err, cross timelines with him sometime? This Portal's jump records no longer exist, so it can't warn me. Will we both blow up or something if we meet, or might something else happen?'

She pursed her lips: a rather un-high citizen-like expression, I thought.

'I cannot imagine how any interaction could take place without great risk. You must remain vigilant. He could have come from anywhere, the past or the future. As I have told you, some Portal Masters have just disappeared. We can only assume that he knew what he was doing. I would make a habit of screening your destination before re-entering space-time. A thin screen of hyper-reality can be maintained for a brief period before you materialise, so you can see what is waiting for you. I believe you have already had some experience of this, from your accounts. Your intuitive skills are quite surprising.'

My training continued and my competence continued to increase, until I found some aspects of time jumping becoming almost second nature.

'Impressive,' she said one day. 'You have become surprisingly proficient in a relatively short period. Just a few more weeks and I think your training will be over.'

I smiled to myself. She didn't know that I had an ulterior motive for getting my wings – and away from Atlantis with Jacqueline – as soon as possible. But I still had a lot to learn. Not long afterwards I had one of my most traumatic jumps ever. Intakaes flashed me a flurry of icons, and I took off almost without conscious thought. I suppose I was over-confident, just wanting to get it all over with, and completely forgot her suggestion that I screen my destination. I shot out of the energy flow to be instantly paralysed by an overwhelming event which I thought would kill me.

I couldn't see. I couldn't breathe. I couldn't even think. A great wall of pain numbed and blinded me: a shrieking, hurricane-force wind, dense with ice-hard snow. All of the heat in my body seemed to vanish in an instant. I shivered uncontrollably, struggling vainly to understand what was happening. Intakaes had directed me somewhere near the North Pole. I knew I had to get out of there, but my mind was as paralysed as my body. I couldn't concentrate. Nothing seemed to work. Only a supreme final effort enabled me to jump again, and I tumbled through the energy flow in shock, with no sense of where I was going. I landed back on the Russian Steppes, still shaking with cold, only to find Intakaes waiting there laughing. My return trip had been programmed all along. I had been too preoccupied with dreams of wedded bliss to notice.

'I did warn you,' Intakaes said. 'It was an important experience. You need to know how to function in an emergency.'

I was still annoyed about it when we arrived back at the travel port, and turned grumpily to commandeer a vehicle home. I initially ignored Intakaes when she beckoned to me, but she repeated the gesture urgently, obviously focusing on an inner dialogue. The Portal Masters communicated via micro-implants, an upgrade I had already decided I would do without.

'One moment Richard,' she said as I halted reluctantly. 'It seems we have a visitor who will be of interest to you.'

I had a bad feeling before I had fully processed this information, and my intuition was correct.

'Apollonius is in the control room,' she said. 'It seems he is indeed the Portal Master whom you encountered. And he is here regarding your wife.'

My misgivings erupted into an explosion of unwelcome sensations. Even the 'temporal echoes' felt threatening.

'Would you like to speak to him now, or in a more formal setting with appointed mediators?' she asked.

'No I will see him straight away,' I said grimly. 'I don't want him frightening Jacqueline.'

'Apollonius has already asked to see her,' Intakaes announced, 'and she has been informed of his arrival.'

'Damn him!' I growled, 'why couldn't they have waited?'

'A Portal Master's right…' she began.

'All right, all right,' I cut her short, 'let's get over there.'

We hopped into a buzz wagon, and zoomed over to the control block in seconds. I was angry, but beneath it there was a flutter of anxiety. This kind of brazen confrontation seemed to be his favoured modus operandi, and I wondered what mischief he was up to now.

I was braced for trouble as the elevator doors slid back, but shock still blindsided me. Jacqueline's stepfather stood there as big and forceful as ever. But beside him was Anna: her face a pale mask, and her eyes glittering with fury. Her presence and rage completely threw me. For a moment I was just confused. Then the implications began to register, and I realised he was involved in far more than Jacqueline's misfortunes. He glanced at Anna, a hint of enquiry on his face, and she nodded heatedly. My pirate-busting identity was confirmed, and alarm tingled through me. It seemed to have the opposite effect on him though. He seemed satisfied, and a mask of affability slid over his features.

'Ah, the mysterious Portal Master himself!' he boomed jovially. 'It seems I must thank you for rescuing my stepdaughter. I was most anxious about her.'

I was flummoxed for a moment. The sheer effrontery of the guy was staggering. Then I felt a surge of anger, and struggled to rein it in. I sensed he wanted to goad me, and forced myself to stay cool.

'I didn't see any sign of you at the jailhouse,' I said carefully.

'Naturally,' he said: his face a mask of artless probity. 'I was planning to free her in a less conspicuous fashion. Inexplicable disappearances from locked cells tend to attract attention.'

'You put her there in the first place,' I said through gritted teeth, 'and you deliberately blackened her name.'

'Not at all my friend,' he replied: now all righteous concern. 'After all, she did kill the man. I had to think of his family's good name it is true – explain the situation in his favour. But Jacqueline would have been hanged in any event, and I intended to remove her from the situation.'

'Well now,' said Intakaes, 'it seems just a simple a misunderstanding. Apollonius may be a free-timer, but he understands his responsibilities as a Portal Master.'

My jaw dropped. 'What about the Civil War spying, and all the people he killed?' I said fiercely. 'What about the attack on the Merchant Royal?

What do they have to do with his responsibilities as a Portal Master?' It had not taken long for me to come close to losing it.

Intakaes looked politely confused, and turned enquiringly to the unabashed Apollonius.

He laughed heartily. 'I am afraid you blundered into situations of which you had little knowledge. You had no understanding of the complexities involved. I was merely investigating the espionage in my stepdaughters time, and I asked my, ah, companion to sail on the Merchant Royal because I feared a temporal rogue was up to no good. I have no need of wealth or political conspiracies. But even as a free-timer, I feel some responsibility for the integrity of the time flow.'

'Exactly how were you upholding the integrity of the time-flow?' I demanded.

'As I said, it was complicated,' he said patronisingly. 'I gather you have little experience as a Portal Master.'

'True,' I said bitterly, thinking of the lieutenant. 'But I have experience as a human being.'

'Ha ha, of course you do,' chuckled Apollonius. 'Incidental loss of life is always regrettable of course, but we Portal Masters have greater concerns.' He turned with a flourish to an unfamiliar First Citizen seated at the control consul. 'How do you like them? They were not easy to unearth.'

'It is a magnificent achievement,' agreed the Portal Master happily, stroking something small and round, and glittering extravagantly with gold and gems. 'Two of the missing Fabergé Eggs are a most welcome addition to the Ark.'

The elevator doors slid open, and Jacqueline strode angrily through them, accompanied by a rather harassed looking Lysias.

'Jeremiah or Apollonius, or whatever you call yourself!' she said wrathfully, 'I want a word with you!'

'Ah, Jacqueline my dear,' he drawled, 'how lovely to see you.'

'Well it is not lovely to see you,' she said furiously, 'you destroyed my life.'

'Come my dear, let us discuss this,' he said soothingly. 'These matters are more complex than you imagine.'

'You lying scum!' I shouted, finally losing control, 'you tried to kill her!'

'Perhaps these matters should be resolved in a more private discussion,' said Lysias hurriedly. 'Or we could arrange a formal mediation.'

'I have a few things to say to my stepfather,' said Jacqueline forcefully, 'and I would be as happy to say them in private as in public.'

'Very well,' said Lysias, indicating the door to one of the offices. 'Speak separately with Apollonius, and if you cannot resolve your differences we will arrange a formal mediation.'

'Hey!' I protested, 'not without me.'

'It may be more conducive to a productive ...' began Lysias.

'It's all right Richard,' interrupted Jacqueline. 'I am not afraid of him.'

'Well you should be,' I muttered through clenched teeth.

Jacqueline stalked into the office behind Lysias and Apollonius, and I became suddenly aware that I had been left with Anna.

'Nice of you to notice me,' she said sullenly.

'I'm sorry Anna,' I said distractedly, 'that guy has caused so many...' I paused. 'If he is your Portal Master, he has been lying to you.'

'Maybe he has,' she snapped, 'but what about you? You had a Portal and you never told me. All that time on the raft, all the Tarzan stuff, and you pretended you were just as stuck as I was. And you had a wife, and never told me that either.'

'Anna,' I spluttered, 'I had only just got the Portal. I didn't know how to use it. If I did I would have got us out of there.'

'Why should I believe you?' she stormed bitterly. 'Saul says it is impossible. Your wife didn't figure much in our conversation either. What was I, just an amusing diversion? I was terrified on that raft; and on the beach I – I thought that you cared.'

Intakaes and the other Portal Master were clearly embarrassed, and strolled off to gain some distance from the raw emotion swirling in the room.

'Anna... it's not what you think...,' the words stuck in my throat. 'I can't explain everything now, but when we were together it was – real.'

She stared flatly at me. 'So do I still mean anything to you?'

I felt a treacherous pang of emotion. 'I care about you, yes,' I admitted. It was the truth, though horribly overloaded with complications.

Her vulnerability surfaced for a moment, and I saw something simple and genuine in her: someone she perhaps could have been. 'If things were different –,' I began.

'Oh please,' she said impatiently. 'I am not interested in excuses. I'm a big girl. I can look after myself.'

I smiled sadly. At that moment she looked almost like a child.

The muted voices inside the office had been growing steadily in volume and outrage, and Jacqueline burst out through the door in the midst of a final tirade: '...don't care about your stupid time flow; you behaved like a pig.'

She stopped dead and glared at me and Anna. Admittedly we appeared embroiled in an emotional turmoil of our own, but I was still shocked when her anger continued in full flood. 'And you are as thick as thieves with this woman, Richard, who seems to be mixed up in everything. You Portal Masters are all as bad as each other.'

Anna laughed, but there was nothing mirthful in her tone. 'You are welcome to him.' she said bitterly. 'Just don't believe anything he says.'

Jacqueline gave me a look which frightened me. 'I am going home,' she seethed, striding towards the elevator, 'or perhaps just to the place where I live.'

'Wait,' I said anxiously, 'I'm coming too.'

I didn't dare look at Anna as the doors slid across her fuming image. I couldn't believe it: suddenly I was surrounded by women who hated me. In five minutes the wretched Apollonius had created mayhem.

'She thought I was already married when I, ah, knew her,' I said anxiously as we descended, 'and that I only pretended to be marooned when I had a Portal. It was difficult – I didn't want to say that we're not married yet, and she doesn't believe me about the Portal.'

'I'm not surprised,' Jacqueline retorted ferociously. 'I'm not sure that I do either.'

'Oh, come on,' I said incredulously. 'You know the truth.'

She glared at me as the doors opened onto the foyer, and I was still pleading with her when they closed again. They opened and closed several times before she began to relent.

'Well, I suppose you are right,' she said grudgingly, as we finally made it out of the elevator. 'But I cannot stand that woman. I cannot stand that man. And I cannot stand the way they keep intruding into our life.'

We stepped into a buzz wagon and asked to go home.

'Now they know where we are Richard,' she said, gripping my arm. 'I don't want to stay here any longer. I want to leave as soon as possible.'

I smiled tentatively, relieved to see something like her usual self resurfacing.

'OK,' I said, 'I guess I am pretty much done with the Portal training. I'll talk to Lysias tomorrow.'

Lysias wasn't happy. He questioned me intently about my reasons, and continually restated and elaborated on the advantages of remaining in Atlantis. Eventually my patience began to wear thin, and he gave ground reluctantly. He suggested that I would probably change my mind, and reiterated that I should return if so. Finally he told me I would be required to announce my decision to the council, and undertake to respect my responsibilities as a Portal Master.

Intakaes looked disapproving but admitted, also reluctantly, that I was becoming reasonably proficient with the Portal. 'You still need more practice,' she warned, 'but at least I have taught you the basics.'

My second formal meeting with the council was as brief and perfunctory as the first, although now charged with disapproval. We said our goodbyes to our various acquaintances. Only Kormas and Chrysanthe were sad to see us go, but they were still ecstatic about their new life, and we promised we would see them again. We visited Aton too; long since recovered from his ordeal in Alexandria. I spoke only briefly to him. I felt even more cautious after everything I had learned and experienced in Atlantis. It still seemed prudent to say nothing to him about the future; but returning his cheerful smile wasn't easy. I also attempted to speak to Lysias and Intakaes about Apollonius's artful performance. But they merely dismissed my fears, referring with various degrees of tact to my inexperience in such matters.

It was a different matter with Leonidas, the head of the guards. I had endured a number of interviews with him regarding both the attack on Aton in Alexandria, and my other confusing entanglements with Portal Masters prior to reaching Atlantis. His sceptical nature and careful attention to detail had irked me. But now I was glad of it, for it was evident that he applied these qualities without prejudice or agenda. He had spoken to Jacqueline in some depth, and was plainly unconvinced by her stepfather's airy assurances. Leonidas was a big, powerful man with rugged features. He had careful, watchful eyes, and was far more pragmatic and approachable than any of his High Citizen masters.

'I will consider these matters,' he said. 'I am less complacent about these free-timers than our First Citizens. They believe everyone as high-minded as themselves. They think a rogue is at work, but I fear there may be more going on behind the scenes.'

I looked at him. There was something other than Aton's identity I had failed to mention in my initial interview at Atlantis. At first I had just wanted to keep the story simple. Then, as is the way with avoiding the truth, I became trapped in the lie. I had also become less trustful of Portal Masters as time went on. Now I wondered whether to confide in Leonidas, and a certain depth of integrity in his eyes convinced me.

'There is something I did not mention about my original meeting with the injured Portal Master,' I said carefully.

His expression did not change, but his gaze became more intent.

'And you did not mention this because..?'

'I don't know really. It didn't seem important at first: there were so many extraordinary things going on. I was overwhelmed at arriving unexpectedly at Atlantis, and was trying to keep things simple.'

He studied me for a few moments, and then nodded. 'Go on.'

'The people who rushed at us in the field when the Portal Master appeared were moving in accelerated time. They must have had Portals; or similar technology. Are your guards able to do that?'

'No, only Portal Masters have this capability. But are you certain? You did not imagine it in the shock of the moment?'

I shook my head. 'I did not imagine it. They had a strange kind of armour on, and several were killed.'

'Armour... killed?' he said doubtfully, 'I cannot imagine Portal Masters risking themselves in this way – or soldiers in armour and moving in augmented time being easily killed.'

'Well, they were all firing these laser beam things. But someone was shooting at them with something bigger, and at a rapid rate: a bit like a machine gun.'

'A pulse gun?' he said incredulously. 'Who was using that?'

'I don't know,' I shrugged.

Leonidas closed his eyes, clasped his hands to his head, and sighed heavily.

'I think you had better describe it all from start to finish – in as much detail as you can remember.'

He was silent for some time after I finished. 'We have these weapons – or something like them. But we have never had to deploy a pulse gun. Apart from anything else they are heavy: not easy to carry around. We have armour of a sort too. But an augmented time capability functioning in ordinary foot soldiers is unknown to us.'

He stood up. 'Come with me.'

I followed him to an elevator, which took us down into a basement level in the Guards headquarters. Here we passed a weapon testing facility and a firing range before arriving at a large armoury. The row of full body armour mounted along one wall sent a creeping chill through me. They were not identical to those worn by the men who had charged Aton and me outside Charles' cottage, but the similarity was obvious. Leonidas indicated the armoured suits and looked back at me with a raised eyebrow.

The colour was one difference. The suits before me had a curious translucent *orichalcum* sheen which defeated the eye's ability to focus somehow: while those on that far-off field had shone like marauding beetles: an elusive blue-black with a faint multi-coloured sheen. Both styles incorporated many-faceted angular segments, moulded to the body's articulations like an old fashioned suit of armour. These were designed to deflect energy beams I presumed; but the Atlantean edition looked a little blockier than the original mystery version. The segmented, exoskeletal contours had contributed to the insectile impression. So had the high neck-shields; together with the disjointed array of instrument pods and antennae encrusting the shoulder-plates and the flat planes of the visor-screened helmets.

'It has given me a lot to think about,' said Leonidas, after I had described the variations to him.

'Will you...talk to the Portal Masters about it?' I asked. 'Will they be angry I didn't tell them?'

He smiled grimly. 'Half of them won't believe you, and the others will lecture you on disrupting time lines. Presumably these people come from our subjective future, perhaps even from Atlantis itself: but it is hard to imagine the circumstances in which that might happen. Such a dramatic intervention itself is unprecedented. It would all seem to suggest something greater than I can conceive of at present, but I will keep my suspicions to myself. There are one or two first citizens – and some of my guards – to whom I can speak more candidly. But these investigations will remain officially conventional and routine for the present.'

He stood up and held out his hand. 'I am sure we will meet again,' he said. 'Be careful; and try to get word to me if you discover anything of any significance.'

I said farewell in the hope that I had found someone in Atlantis I could trust – to some extent at least. We were informed that our new wardrobe was ours to take if we chose. It seemed a shame to leave our immaculate collection of nice flowy robes, but we decided to take only those we were wearing. I intended to travel to the house back – or rather forward – in England, so our appearance would not be an issue. But I did not do so directly, in case the Travel Port tracked my destination. I went first to my anonymous training grounds in eastern Europe before trying to zero in on our refuge outside London. I opened doorways, as Jacqueline still feared the power and magnitude of the time-flow. Also, now that I had some control, I aimed for three weeks after my departure. I felt it would be weird to return too soon after I had left when so much had happened. And I hoped it might be long enough for them to have finished the bathrooms.

Chapter 26

WE STEPPED THROUGH the circular opening into loud birdsong and refreshingly random English greenery. It was a fine spring day. The grass had grown a little longer, and more construction debris was piled outside the kitchen door.

'That is certainly a more civilised way to travel,' said Jacqueline, looking around appreciatively. 'How nice it is to see some untidiness.'

'Yes, all that perfection did get on my nerves,' I agreed, closing the doorway. 'Now you can come and meet the family.'

Instead, the family came to meet us. We heard the distant thunder of multiple footfalls on the stairs, and the back door burst open to disgorge Charles and Billy in quick succession.

'I told you it was him!' exclaimed Charles exuberantly. 'Wow, look – ancient Greece!'

He paused, further comment failing him as the impact of Jacqueline's appearance struck home. She looked stunning in her regal Atlantean robes: radiant with happiness, her magnificent raven-black locks shining, and gleaming gold and jewellery winking splendidly about her person.

Billy squinted in bemusement as recognition gradually dawned. 'Why it's Miss Johnson!' he pronounced in amazement.

'Hello Billy,' she smiled, 'how lovely to see you. But please call me Jacqueline.' She turned to Billy's star-struck companion. 'You must be Charles,' she said, 'I am very pleased to meet you too.'

The back door was thrown open again, and Priya ushered out an excited Nathaniel and Aurelia. 'Uncle Richard! Uncle Richard!' they cried in unison; before adopting the same awestruck gaze as Charles as they took in Jacqueline's appearance.

'This is, err, Auntie Jacqueline,' I improvised.

'Is Auntie Jacqueline a queen?' asked Aurelia breathlessly.

Jacqueline laughed. 'I am not a Queen young lady, but I do feel a little like one at the moment. You must be Aurelia, and this must be your brother Nathaniel.'

They nodded warily, open mouthed at this royal knowledge of their identities.

'What about me,' I asked them, 'do I look like a King?'

'No,' they giggled, 'you are Uncle Richard.'

'Hmm,' I said. 'Well, your majesty, I would like to present you to Priya.' Priya gave a slightly self-conscious wave. Even she seemed a little in awe of Jacqueline. Or perhaps it was the live appearance of yet another historical person.

'Your alarm system seemed to work well,' I said to Charles, 'or did you just happen to look out of the window?'

'Of course it worked!' he said, springing indignantly back into life. 'The cameras are activated by movement – infrared at night – and they set off a silent alarm. We just switch it off if any of us are outside.'

'It sure is a nice surprise to see you again Miss, ah, Jacqueline,' said Billy. 'How about you two come back inside, and tell us what you bin up to?'

Jacqueline and I glanced at each other and flushed slightly, and Billy's eyes opened a little wider as we all turned towards the house.

'You haven't been gone for long this time,' said Charles, as we all settled down in the sitting room.

'It's been quite a while for us,' I admitted. 'You are not going to believe where we've been.'

It took a while to get through it all too. Charles and Priya could hardly contain themselves during our descriptions of ancient Alexandria. Billy was less impressed, and directed some pretty shrewd looks at Jacqueline and me as the story unfolded. Priya seemed to be reading more into my account than I was saying as well. But when I got to Atlantis and my Portal training, both she and Charles became extremely excited.

'Does this mean you can take us somewhere now?' exclaimed Charles. 'That's great! Where shall we go?'

'Alexandria,' breathed Priya, 'could I really go there? –What about the Indus Valley civilisation? My God, to think that I might see them...'

'The short answer is yes, anything is possible,' I smiled. 'But we need to think about the more serious side to all this. The Portal Masters in Atlantis seem unconcerned that some time-travellers are up to no good. At least, they downplay it. I'm not sure if they are naive or hiding something.'

'I tell you what,' said Priya, 'the children are starving. I'll go and make lunch and you can fill in the details later. Come on children, you want to help me don't you?'

Nathaniel and Aurelia had been writhing in increasing dissatisfaction during our conversation, and leapt up to follow her.

I glanced at Jacqueline before continuing. 'There's more. Jacqueline's stepfather turned up in Atlantis. He put on this big innocent act: claimed I am inexperienced and misunderstood what was going on. But get this. It turns out he was the Portal Master involved with Anna and the attack on the Merchant Royal too.'

Billy whistled. 'He's a regular Sam Hill that's for sure.' He took in Charles' enquiring look: 'fella with the horns and the tail,' he explained.

'Ah, yes of course,' said Charles, storing away another choice item of Billy's Civil War slang. 'He was probably mixed up with the stuff in Alexandria as well. He seems to be really bad news.'

'He is a pig and a liar,' interjected Jacqueline vehemently.

I chuckled sourly. 'All he had to do was wave a couple of Fabergé Eggs about, and the precious Portal Masters lost interest in everything else. It was pathetic.'

'Incidentally,' said Charles, 'if you remember, we decided to check out Jacqueline's family history, and I have discovered a bit more.' He turned to Jacqueline. 'Your uncle's name was Jonas Johnson, and your Mothers first name Emeline?'

'Yes,' she agreed in surprise. She had become accustomed to the idea of sophisticated database systems in Atlantis, not to mention the mysterious 'Archive'; but it still seemed strange to her that strangers so removed in space and time could know personal details about her life.

'What else did you discover?' she asked.

'I found a record of you and your mother becoming majority stockholders in Jonas' company – 'Johnson Armaments' – in eighteen sixty. I also found a record of your mother's death in eighteen sixty two. You do not appear in any records at all after that, and Jeremiah Serrano appears as majority stockholder in eighteen sixty four.'

Jacqueline made a very unladylike noise, apparently unable to find the words to express her feelings.

'Never mind,' I quipped, 'at least you escaped the bad Karma.'

'What is Karma?' asked Jacqueline, diverted.

'He who lives by the sword dies by the sword I guess,' I said, 'but the concept is much more developed in …'

'Excuse me,' interrupted Charles, 'I spent a lot of time researching this.'

'Sorry,' I said meekly, 'carry on.'

'Actually, I haven't found out much more yet,' he admitted, 'but I suspect that Jeremiah went on to become more involved in the American arms industry. The company seems to have become amalgamated into a larger one along with a couple of other small arms manufacturers a few years later. I'm still looking.'

'Kinda worrying,' said Billy, 'that man and a gun factory will mean nothing but trouble.'

'Yes,' I agreed, 'but it's hard to figure out why he went to all this trouble. There are so many ways he could get weapons if he wanted to.'

'I'll keep investigating,' said Charles.

'OK, now there is something else I want to mention. I am very happy to say that Jacqueline and I have decided to get married.'

Billy grinned broadly, apparently unsurprised. Charles was less prepared, but lost no time in casting a spanner into the works.

'What about documents?' he asked. 'I suppose you could go off somewhere in the past to do it, but we should probably have ID for now anyway – Billy and the twins as well.'

'Ah!' I said, 'I hadn't actually thought about that.'

'What documents?' asked Jacqueline.

'You will need passports or birth certificates or something,' said Charles.

'Why?' she said in bewilderment. 'Can't we just go to a church?'

'No, now that I come to think of it,' I admitted. 'There are legal requirements. Don't worry; we'll get round it somehow.'

Jacqueline smiled briefly, but remained uneasy. 'Must we really have these documents?' she said doubtfully.

'Yes, if you want a wedding in a church with a minister or a priest,' I said. 'We can get married without a church or a priest, but again, not without documents.'

'But how can we get these things?' she asked.

Charles had been surfing his mobile. 'Well,' he said, 'we could try hacking the General Register Office but that doesn't seem very likely...'

He paused, considering the matter. 'Maybe you could get in there at night with the Portal and... no, still too difficult getting into the system...I know! Of course! That's why he's doing it!'

'What are you talking about Charles?' I demanded impatiently.

'We need documents from the past. Build ourselves into the system. That's what Jeremiah must be doing: positioning himself for the future.'

'OK – I guess,' I said, 'but what about our marriage?'

'You go back twenty-something years, before computing was really big, and register Jacqueline's birth. A marriage certificate will do for identification. I can create something that will look authentic enough.'

'But the birth certificate won't cross reference,' I objected, 'there won't be a corresponding marriage, or parents.'

'Oh don't worry about that,' said Charles blithely. 'Databases weren't very developed then, and they're unlikely to check now. If they do they'll just assume it's a glitch. They are too busy trying to play catch-up with historical records to worry about things like that.'

'So I register Jacqueline as my daughter?' I said. 'It seems a bit weird.'

'It's just a formality,' said Charles tetchily. 'Then all we have to do is make the birth certificate look old, or request a certified copy using the GRO Index reference number. Better do the same for yourself too.'

'Me?' I said without thinking, 'but I've already got one. I mean I can get a copy'

'Counter surveillance?' inquired Charles archly. 'The bad guys may still be looking for you. You need to get one in another name.'

'I don't think that is so likely now,' I said slowly. 'They may have just been trying to stop me getting the Portal in the first place. According to the people in Atlantis, time travellers have to be careful about interfering with the timelines of other Portal Masters. Especially those they have interacted with. Jeremiah or Apollonius or whatever his name is, seems to be the villain in all this, and now he has interacted with me in various ways – and with lots of other Portal Masters too.'

'Never mind all that, Richard!' exclaimed Jacqueline angrily. 'I don't care about these silly Portal Masters. If we have to go through this charade you are at least going to have your real name. I want a proper marriage certificate from a minister.'

I looked fondly at her. She looked almost like a little girl as she said the words. But it put me in mind of Anna, and I shook the thought away.

'OK then,' agreed Charles reluctantly, 'at least get one done with a different place and date of birth. A few years earlier perhaps – and we could do the same for Jacqueline. You can always look a bit young for your age.'

I sighed. 'I suppose so.'

'Oh, whoops!' said Charles, still searching away on his phone.

'Now what?' I asked warily.

'Getting married in a church is not so easy,' he said. 'You need to prove more than six months residence in the parish, or that your parents were married in the church...all kinds of stuff like that. Even then they want you to spend time at church services, and take part in local Christian activities. They recommend giving several months' notice before you want to marry.'

'Oh whoops indeed,' I groaned, glancing at Jacqueline, who looked shell-shocked. 'I guess we'll have to have a think about it.'

'Not a problem,' said Priya brightly, popping back just in time to catch the end of Charles' doom-laden narrative. She also seemed unsurprised at the topic of conversation. 'You can have a church ceremony if you marry in a registry office first. It's just like a real wedding: the only difference is you sign a commemorative certificate instead of the marriage register.'

Priya possessed a surprising amount of random information. This particular nugget turned out to have been mined during a university research project, and was worth a considerable weight in gold. Jacqueline blossomed into smiles, and I happily reciprocated, a flood of relief coursing through me.

'It doesn't make sense,' objected Charles. 'Or does it? I'll never understand religion. It's great anyway!'

'Thank you Priya,' I said reverently, 'you have absolutely saved the day. Now we can get on with the rest of our lives.'

The first thing was to get Jacqueline some clothes, and Priya proved herself indispensable once again. She was a little too petite to lend Jacqueline her own stuff, but went through an online shopping catalogue with her to select some basic stuff for next day delivery.

'Once you have got this we can go out on a real shopping trip,' she enthused: 'nothing like being able to try things on and see what you look like.'

It sounded rather tedious to me, but I looked forward to introducing Jacqueline to the twenty first century. We showed her around the house and garden, and all sat down to have lunch together at the somewhat neglected grand walnut dining table and matching furniture Charles had procured for the dining room. Most of our meals were usually scoffed around the utilitarian kitchen table, or on our laps in the lounge. But somehow Jacqueline's arrival seemed to require something more formal.

'How pleasant this is,' she remarked, 'everything is so much more homely than Atlantis.'

This led to more detail being extracted by Charles and Priya about the minutiae of Atlantean life in general, and the contents of the pyramids in particular. Priya was fascinated by the exhibits I described, and I promised to take her there one day if I could.

'Will you really be allowed to bring guests there?' she asked eagerly.

'Yes, I'm sure I can, within reason,' I said. 'But I'm not sure it is a good idea to reveal your existence, or anyone else's, just yet. We need a better idea of what is going on behind the scenes with all this clandestine stuff.'

A protracted discussion about the whole unsavoury puzzle stretched the meal out considerably. Priya stuck the twins in front of a Blu-ray in the lounge in contravention of her own rules in order to continue the debate. She had taken their education very much to heart, and limiting their intake of child-orientated trivia was a fairly central tenet of her routine. We talked for much of the afternoon, after which Billy and Charles went to finish off some odds and ends on the renovation work. Priya dragged the twins off for some belated lessons, and I introduced Jacqueline to the wonders of myriad-channel TV.

Documentaries about the natural world captivated her most, while news channels fascinated and horrified her in equal measure. Images of vast city skylines, traffic jams and airports stunned her, and she was appalled by the casual coverage of wars, refugees and terrorist atrocities. I didn't dare let her watch late night programs.

'What a terrifying place the world has become Richard,' she said. 'There are so many people. It is like an agitated ant hill: everyone seems to be rushing here and there without any real direction.'

'I suppose it does look a bit like that,' I said, 'especially when we know the future: and yet people have never been better informed. It's quite ironic really.'

'They certainly cannot be informed about anything meaningful,' she said caustically. 'It doesn't seem that human nature has improved at all. If anything it appears to have become worse. It is just as I said to you: all of these marvels of science have created a world that is empty of substance.'

'I wouldn't say that,' I objected, 'you have only had a glimpse of modern society so far. It is incredibly complex and full of contradictions it's true, but there is much human ingenuity and creative genius at work too. Wait until you have had more experience of it.'

'I will do Richard,' she agreed. 'It is just the first impression I suppose. But I do feel it profoundly. These news people relating all these events – they seem clever and witty, but not entirely real somehow. It is as if they are playing a game which they do not particularly care about. There is an absence of sincerity and real vitality which robs it of meaning. It reminds me of Atlantis.'

I laughed a little sourly. 'I suppose we are a little wrapped up in looking cool and playing with our gadgets.'

'I am not complaining Richard,' she smiled. 'I am very thankful to be here with you. I just find this future state of the world rather strange and overwhelming.'

'You will get used to it,' I said easily. 'It can be pretty crazy out there if you are struggling to earn a living, but we don't have to worry about that.'

That evening we had a companionable meal together. It was accompanied by candles and subdued lighting to make Jacqueline feel at home, and classical music which delighted her. She found recorded music far more novel and satisfying than TV in fact. She felt that music created an atmosphere of intimacy and communion, while TV intruded and distracted. I was just happy we were all together at last, and perfectly content to push the unresolved mysteries in our lives to the back of my mind.

Next morning Jacqueline's clothes arrived: a long dress and various other bits and pieces which she disliked intensely; and we set off in the car with Priya to go shopping. Priya drove, and Jacqueline clung to me white-faced in the back seat as we raced inches away from oncoming traffic. She shrieked when we joined a dual carriageway, and gave a huge sigh of relief as we pulled into the nearby town of Brentwood, finally parking by a couple of boutiques near the centre.

'That was nothing like the sensible carriages in Atlantis, Richard!' she gasped. 'I cannot believe I have just travelled at eighty miles an hour.'

'Well don't tell anyone,' I replied with a grin, 'it is against the law. There's a seventy mile an hour limit.'

'Oh!' she said indignantly; 'as if we weren't going fast enough already. And some people were travelling at even greater speeds! What is the need to rush everywhere so fast?'

'I don't really know,' I said flippantly, 'maybe we're just in a hurry to get home and watch the telly.'

'You people are crazy,' she retorted, 'it all seems unnecessary and dangerous to me.'

Her words stilled my ready laughter. Alex had said the same in the alleyway outside the dancehall. *'You people are crazy'* – and it took me right back to her spectacular appearance at the beginning of the whole outlandish adventure. I was supposed to be on some kind of crazy mission, and I asked myself again if it was right to involve Jacqueline in my life. I wondered if it was fair, with so many unknowns hanging over my head. I even wondered if it was a diversion from the path I was supposed to be taking.

'What is the matter?' Jacqueline asked, quickly sensing my concern.

I looked at her and my heart melted.

'Nothing,' I said.

To be with her felt absolutely right: I could not imagine a future without her, and I surrendered to fate with an uncertain smile. Jacqueline spent a couple of hours in the shop with Priya. I was soon thrown out for asking unhelpful questions and trying to hurry the process along. So I went for a stroll before sitting in the car for a while listening to the radio. I thought about trying a little hop forward in time, but the idea seemed rather frivolous, not to mention risky. I was still not totally confident of my skills with the Portal.

Fears about the future trickled back into my mind on the journey home, and again during the evening, until I asked her outright that night as we prepared to sleep.

'Are you sure you want to marry me?'

She stopped brushing her hair and sat absolutely still on the bed.

'Why on earth would you ask that, Richard?'

'I was thinking again about this life we are leading...'

'Is that what was bothering you today?' she asked.

'Yes,' I admitted.

She regarded me levelly. 'I have known that my destiny was entwined with yours from the moment we watched the lighthouse catch fire in Alexandria. I already suspected in fact, but from that moment I accepted and hoped for it. Now, I know we agreed we would not risk kissing at night time until we are married, but I find this to be an important exception...'

A couple of weeks passed in serene suspension from mystery and fear – not to mention freedom from random abduction to far flung places by a wayward Portal. For days we did little but relax and talk about everything imaginable. We began to plan and research for the somewhat unusual official requirements of our wedding, and all went sightseeing together in a couple of choice contemporary and historical settings.

These locations were chosen as much for safety as for novelty and spectacle, and limited by the availability of period costume for hire. But – apart from Disneyland – the twins irritatingly preferred the blue-ray version of reality back at home to the real thing, and Charles' initial appreciation of historical pageantry was soon overtaken by a thirst for more adventurous destinations. Billy remained largely unimpressed by such excursions too. The novelties of twenty-first century life had not worn off for him. The only thing of any importance I did was take him and some digging tools back to where I had left poor Aton's body. It was a day or two after I had left him and he still lay as I remembered, although animals and insects had begun to assault his mortal remains. We buried him deep and concealed it as best we could, and I returned with one less burden on my mind.

Jacqueline was more interested in making preparations for our marriage than anything else. I took her on a rather tedious tour of local religious establishments over a number of days, looking for a place of worship she considered worthy. We eventually discovered a pleasantly traditional edifice of the 'Church of England' which fitted the bill. This was the easy part. Introducing ourselves to the vicar and making arrangements for the 'commemorative ceremony' was a little less straightforward. References to our past whereabouts, occupations and religious track-record were necessarily vague: not mandatory of course, but it made for awkward conversation. We were expected to attend Sunday services from then onwards, which was a little daunting, but I actually kind of enjoyed turning up at the church when it started to happen. I suppose I enjoyed doing most things with Jacqueline, and she was especially happy on these occasions.

Perhaps the mundane ordinariness of it all seemed reassuring in the face of the darker uncertainties that hung over our lives. It also gave me an occasion to contemplate some of the more mysterious experiences in my recent past. The first sermon I heard reminded me of Ravi funnily enough, and I found myself listening for clues about the ultimate nature of reality tucked away among the homely parables and platitudes.

The earliest available date for our church ceremony was six weeks away, and Charles and I started to take action regarding the bureaucratic side of the marriage. We had to record proof of residence and birth certificates at the local registry office twenty eight days before the legal marriage could take place, and a few days after my first sermon I travelled to two different cities in England in nineteen eighty six and nineteen eighty eight. I was armed with local information and fake marriage certificates, and on both occasions the registrar appeared to have no suspicions at all. They registered places and dates of birth for Jacqueline and me in a perfectly routine manner.

Billy and the twins also required identity documents of course, but we had decided to organise that at a later date. The twins' registration in particular would be much more recent, and would require more elaborate arrangements.

We researched and rehearsed everything Jacqueline and I would have to do at the registry office. It was not without its difficulties, as Jacqueline regarded all the rules and regulations as irrelevant, but she was reasonably confident when the registrar walked us through the questions and filled in the forms. Her unusual accent we put down to her French mother and time spent in America, which was, after all, true, and it did not seem to arouse any curiosity. The biggest problem was her clothes. Priya had done her best to find her a wardrobe she could live with, but Jacqueline did not like modern fashion at all. She would not wear short skirts, disliked jeans and trousers, and found everything too gaudy and flimsy. She shifted self-consciously all the time, to the point where I feared it might look suspicious. So I teased her about a fictitious rash and reminded her to make a doctor's appointment, earning myself an indignant glare.

But she found a beautiful wedding dress which pleased her. I even managed to see a picture of it despite her attempts to prevent it. It was a simple ivory corded lace gown, with a low (for her) neckline and a high waist. Its fitted bodice ended just below the bust, and the subtle sheen of its long, loosely fitting gathered skirt skimmed the body in understated elegance. She arranged to have her hair done at the fanciest place we could find, and we splashed out some relatively serious money on a fabulous necklace and earrings. The reception was booked at an extremely up-market restaurant, and the honeymoon arranged at a tastefully converted Regency Manor House Hotel set in exquisite grounds. Everything seemed perfect when the dream ended.

Chapter 27

I WAS CONTEMPLATING opening doorways from one weekend to the next for us all, to shorten the wait until the wedding, when it happened. Charles and I were in the lounge, watching a documentary about changes in global electromagnetic resonances. A couple of Icons suddenly appeared. Something had changed in the house, but I wasn't sure what it was.

'That's funny,' Charles said suddenly, 'I think the surveillance system just stopped working.'

A swirl of déjà vu rocked me at the same moment, and I felt a stab of alarm.

'What do you mean?' I asked quickly.

'I don't know.' He sounded confused. 'I rigged an LED to help me remember to switch it on, and I just noticed it go dead.'

Ripples of déjà vu continued, and I felt a deep uneasiness. I moved towards the windows, and glimpsed a blurred shadow moving outside through a gap in the curtains. I didn't see much, but it was enough: a man with a weapon, moving with stealth and purpose.

'Upstairs, quick!' I said urgently: 'is everyone else up there?'

'I – I think so,' Charles stammered, looking wildly about.

We ran into the hall. I quickly checked the kitchen and dining room, and we raced up the stairs.

'Priya,' I called, 'have you got the twins?'

She appeared with Nathaniel and Aurelia in tow. 'What's up?' she asked anxiously, picking up on my alarm.

'Grab your coats, we've got trouble,' I snapped.

Billy strode out of his room, his face hard and alert.

'Armed men,' I said briefly, and he ducked back inside.

'What do we do?' asked Charles shakily.

'I'll open a door,' I said, 'where's Jacqueline?'

They all shrugged, and I darted into our bedroom. It was empty. I rushed back. Charles had a hold-all, and Billy his pistol.

'Where the hell is Jacqueline?' I hissed.

'Get them out of here,' said Billy curtly, inclining his head towards Priya and the kids. He sighted his revolver down the stairs.

I felt rising panic at Jacqueline's absence, and forced myself to concentrate. Stepping back into the nearest bedroom, I materialised a doorway to the first place I could think of: some rough parkland across the road from a large hospital in East London. I glanced through the opening. Sparse bushes and trees surrounded a small lake, and there was no one around.

'Quick: Charles, Priya, through here,' I urged. They nodded, each clutching a twin in one hand and a bag in the other. They looked pale. The whole thing seemed surreal. The sense of menace was overpowering.

'Go to ground,' I urged, agonising over Jacqueline, 'we'll make contact at the Hastingwood hide.'

They stepped though and I snapped the opening shut, and then flinched as Billy's gun boomed deafeningly on the landing. A flurry of sharper reports rang out, and Billy's gun roared again. I leapt out of the bedroom as he sank to the floor: bright red blood blooming through the back of his shirt.

'Varmint got me,' he muttered, as I stared in shock. I chanced a quick glance over the banisters. The air was full of smoke and a crumpled form in black lay at the bottom of the stairs. But I stayed an instant too long. Just as I registered more figures peering around the corner below there was a flash and a crack, and a numbing impact high on my left arm,

'That's not the shooter,' someone barked. 'No hard ammo. We want him alive.'

'Mister Walton!' called a second voice more smoothly. 'Have you lost someone? There's a young lady here you might not want to leave behind.'

The numbness was spreading in my arm and shoulder, but the rest of me went ice cold.

'Let me see her,' I croaked. My mouth was suddenly dry, and I could hardly get the words out.

Jacqueline was wrenched into view, struggling with two men. One of them had a bloody nose.

'Don't listen to them Richard!' she shouted, 'just go!'

'Come down Mister Walton,' said the smooth guy, stepping forward. 'Nothing will happen to either of you. We mean you no harm.'

I could see four men now, all holding weapons. A couple held Raysers, one an automatic pistol and the other something like the flechette gun used on the Senator in Central. There was no Portal reflection, but I sensed the disquieting presence of one somewhere in the background. I thought of trying to rush them in speed mode, but I didn't like the odds, especially when they held Jacqueline. I glanced around at Billy. He was sitting slumped against a wall, clutching his chest with both hands. Blood ran through his fingers and pooled on the floor beneath him.

'Reckon I'm done for,' he muttered weakly, 'you get Miss Jacqueline.'

I was frantic with frustration and indecision. I was bleeding too, and feeling lightheaded with shock. I knew I had to do something quickly. The bizarre vision I had experienced with Alex returned: my life seen from two separate perspectives. Everything seemed to hang in the balance over a terrifying chasm of uncertainty. I couldn't leave Jacqueline, I knew suddenly. Everything hinged around her, and I might never find her again.

'Sorry Billy,' I gasped in real anguish.

My mind made up, I felt energised, and ignored the sense of chaos swirling all around me. I discounted trying to materialise beside her and jump back out of time. I knew they would detect the energy field forming before I could act. I thought of looping back to the past: for us all to escape before the attack happened. But I also remembered Intakaes' warnings about re-crossing timelines. There was another Portal Master involved here too. There were too many unknowns, and my adversary would be far more experienced than I was. He or she might be expecting me to try something, and counter it in a way I wouldn't expect. All of these things flashed through my mind in an instant. Then an idea crystallised.

'OK, I'm coming,' I called.

I made my way unsteadily down the stairs, grimly focused on my plan. One arm I held high, the other as high as I could. The men moved a little further apart. The man with the pistol continued to cover the landing above me, while the two with Raysers gripped Jacqueline's wrists with one hand, and covered me with the other. The fourth man with the other weapon trained it steadily on me.

The ground floor hall was spacious: high and wide. I was not completely confident of what I wanted to do, but grimly determined. I reached into the time-flow and opened a door matching the full width of the hallway – straight into the heart of the raging ice storm Intakaes had dumped me in during my training. It was a couple of hours and some distance from my first visit, but it made no difference to the violence of the storm. If anything it was stronger. A howling wall of ice-hard snow blasted through the passageway, and I began to blur down the staircase an instant later.

They were well trained. Even in that extreme moment they struggled to respond. Their faces grimaced grotesquely, eyes screwed almost shut as they attempted to see what was happening. I had both initiative and speed, and more room to manoeuvre than when I last faced a Rayser. I leapt the bannister and was racing towards them, my back to the storm, in fractions of a second.

I glimpsed the beginning of the flash as the first Rayser fired: anticipated its trajectory and swerved from the stream of charged particles before it came anywhere near me. The discharge from the second was closer. I felt it brush my hip: a fiery wave of pins and needles which further destabilised muscles and coordination down my left side. It caught me as I weaved to avoid a spreading cloud of flechettes from the other weapon. But my attention was fixed on Jacqueline. Nothing was going to stop me.

I registered only a few stinging impacts from the tiny missiles before I was among the befuddled men milling sluggishly around her. I ripped the automatic pistol from its stupefied owner with my good hand, and smashed it left and right at their blind, contorted faces. Then, in one tenacious final effort, I grabbed Jacqueline and jumped into the time-stream.

It was a slick, fluid operation which would have made Intakaes proud. But there my perfect performance faltered. The explosion of energy and my physical injuries were draining me fast. My focus wavered. Worse, I had forgotten to lock in a destination. The portal destabilised and Jacqueline and I tumbled from the ocean of power almost as soon as we entered it, crashing onto a roadway in a tangle of limbs.

'Oww!' I gasped.

Jacqueline rubbed her knees where the tarmac had torn her dress, looking swiftly around.

'Richard – where are we?' she asked breathlessly. Then she stared at the left side of my shirt which clung wetly to me. 'Oh no,' she gasped, 'you are injured!'

'Shot…shoulder,' I muttered, trying to get my bearings.

'Let me look at it,' she insisted urgently, 'we must find a doctor.'

'Don't think it's bad…not hospital: might look for us there.'

I lurched to my feet and tried to figure out what to do. We were in a built up area – not far from the time and place we had left, I suspected. I realised I was still holding the pistol and dumped it in a garden hedge. I was dizzy, and much of the left side of my body felt weak from the glancing Rayser hit and the shoulder wound. But something else was wrong. My thinking was becoming stupid, I felt clumsy and uncoordinated, and dark blotches swam in front of my eyes. I remembered the sharp impacts of the flechettes, and wondered if they had injected me with something. I started to sway on my feet.

'I really think…' began Jacqueline.

I knew I would soon be unable to function at all, but I fought the creeping oblivion. I couldn't leave Jacqueline with an unconscious and wounded man in a world she didn't understand. An idea swirled dreamily from somewhere, and executing it took a supreme effort of will. I would never have succeeded if it hadn't been a small jump in space-time, and to somewhere I had been before.

'Hold me,' I gasped, clutching drunkenly at Jacqueline, and jumped through the weird yellow haze that was consuming my world. We sprawled together on an extremely plush carpet, right in front of its startled owner.

Or more correctly, its half-owner: 'R – Richard!' she gasped.

'Kaltrina,' I slurred. 'Sorry: nowhere else to go,' and everything faded peacefully away.

The return to consciousness was long and laborious. I constantly rediscovered a sluggish drive to awaken, only to be sucked back into a bottomless pool of forgetfulness. I only gradually became aware of the dull fire in my shoulder. I wondered why it was there, and slowly a little of what had happened came back to me.

'Richard, you are awake,' said Jacqueline.

I felt relief at the sound of her voice, but lacked the energy to pursue it further.

'Richard, speak to me!' she insisted. 'I think your shoulder is all right, but you have been sleeping for twelve hours. I am worried about those little darts. Could they have been poisoned?'

'Muummph,' I moaned, 'sleep'.

'Richard, please!' she insisted. 'I don't know what to do.'

'Think... drugged,' I muttered, my eyes too heavy to open. 'Just... sleep.'

I did that for a few more hours, and felt a little more alert when I resurfaced. Jacqueline was still with me, dozing in a chair.

I heaved myself up, groaning at the jagged bolt of lightning in my shoulder. My head ached too, and my body felt weak and rubbery.

'Ah, you are awake again,' she said hopefully. 'Are you feeling better?'

'I don't know about better,' I grumbled, 'but I think I can stay awake this time.'

'Thank goodness,' she said, 'I have been so worried about you.'

'What about my arm?' I asked, 'it hurts like hell.'

'The bullet went through the muscle. We cleaned and bandaged it. Apparently it may need something called antibiotics, but so far it seems to be healing well.'

'Oh!' I grunted, as memory returned. 'I had forgotten about Sophia and Kaltrina. It must have been a big shock for them.'

'They behaved impeccably, given the circumstances,' said Jacqueline a little stiffly. 'I cannot praise them too highly. Neither can I help wondering how many more young ladies you have tucked away from your past.'

I chuckled weakly. 'They are not 'tucked away'. We just helped each other once. You're not suspicious of them too?'

'Of course not!' she retorted, with a martial glint in her eye.

Then everything came back to me. 'My God...Billy!' I gasped.

'What?' she urged anxiously. 'What happened to everyone?'

'I got the others away, thanks to him. He was shooting at the bad guys. He kept them downstairs. But he was seriously wounded, and I had to leave him to get to you.'

'Oh no,' she whispered. 'Do you think those men will have treated his wounds?'

'I don't know. I hope so, but it's not good either way. Even if they save his life, they may treat him badly – try to get information from him.'

'Poor Billy,' she said, 'is there nothing we can do?'

'Not at present,' I said grimly. 'I can't even think about it at the moment.'

'Where did the others go?' she asked.

'They are all together somewhere in East London,' I said. 'Charles had his emergency bag with him, so they have plenty of cash. They should be OK until we can meet up with them. We arranged where to leave a message.'

'What about you?' she asked, 'is the drug from those horrid darts wearing off?'

'Yes, it seems to be. It was probably something like the stuff they injected Aton with: to make it impossible to use the Portal perhaps. I was only hit by a few of them. But I was hit by a Rayser too – partially, and I was in shock from the bullet wound. It's a miracle we got here.'

'Thank goodness you managed,' sighed Jacqueline. 'I don't know what I would have done otherwise.'

'We materialised in front of Kaltrina didn't we?' I recalled ruefully. 'What on earth did she say?'

'Well, she actually didn't say anything for some time,' said Jacqueline. 'She just went rather pale. I don't think she thought we were real. I had to strike up a conversation with her.'

'I would love to have seen that!' I grinned.

She smiled back. 'Yes, it was somewhat bizarre.'

'How did you explain it all to them? Sophia is here as well I take it?'

'They are both out at the moment,' she said. 'I am uncertain how successful I was in communicating our situation, and Sophia did not witness our, err, appearance. Fortunately you will be able to supplement my no doubt perplexing introduction.'

'I'll try,' I agreed, cautiously manoeuvring myself off the bed. 'But first things first: where's the bathroom?'

Sophia and Kaltrina returned an hour later. They both appeared nervous and eyed me warily.

'I am happy to see you of course, Richard,' said Sophia in her usual blunt way. 'But I am finding it hard to understand what Kaltrina and your...ah...wife have been telling me.'

'I'm not surprised,' I smiled wanly.

'Kaltrina says you appeared out of thin air,' she said, her gaze alive with baffled scepticism. 'She says you have special powers.'

'It's advanced technology,' I said.

'Technology?' she frowned. 'Kaltrina says you are a magician. You have also produced a wife from somewhere, who says you have an invisible necklace. I don't know what to think.'

'Well,' I said resignedly, 'I'm not really well enough to give you a demonstration at the moment. I can try to explain in the meantime, but are you sure you want to know? It involves more bad guys, and you have had enough of that already. We just need somewhere to stay for a couple of days, and we can disappear again.'

Sophia regarded me curiously. 'There was something strange about you before, and now there is something stranger still. But I think you are a good person. I would like to know more, and Kaltrina has her own interest in these powers of yours.'

I glanced at Kaltrina, and noticed a keen, if edgy excitement about her.

'You do?' I asked her.

'There is problem at home,' she said. 'Maybe you can help.'

I shrugged, forgetting my wound, and gasped with pain. 'Ouch! Well, if I can, I will.'

I attempted an abbreviated version of the tale, short on detail and content. Their eyes particularly lit up when I mentioned treasure in the Caribbean: they had no trouble believing I could make large amounts of money appear. The conversation extended itself through the preparation and consumption of a meal, and included catching up on Sophia & Kaltrina's own activities since we had last met. They had started a business buying and selling designer clothes on eBay: using drop-ship companies and buying up complete lines to take control of products.

'It is going well,' said Sophia happily. 'We are expanding.'

I was feeling pretty tired again by the time we had finished talking, and went back to sleep; not waking until early the following morning. I really did feel better by then, and left Jacqueline sleeping to make myself a coffee in the kitchen. I sipped it slowly as I tried to think logically about everything that had happened. My deep unhappiness about Billy lay heavily on me, and I ran through various scenarios as I tried to figure out if I could do anything about it. I felt a better connection with the Portal, and my head was much clearer. But I was still a little weak, and my arm was stiff and painful. I did not feel in a position to attempt anything immediately.

Jacqueline appeared before long, and Sophia & Kaltrina soon afterwards.

'I think I can use the Portal OK again now,' I said. 'I'm not up to any gymnastics, but I can probably go and check on Charles and the others.'

I concentrated for a moment. The hard edges of reality blurred, and I reached through golden tides and flickering icons to a thicket of trees some twenty miles away. We had hidden some of the treasure there, and I held a thin screen in place for a moment to check for unwelcome surprises. Finally a glittering circle opened out into bright countryside, and Sophia & Kaltrina stood like statues, their pupils huge despite the sunlight streaming into their kitchen.

'You may pass though. It is quite real,' I said.

They peered at the apparition cautiously. 'You first,' whispered Sophia in awe.

I did so, and reached my hand back to her. She took it, trembling a little, and flinched at the sudden tingling of the wormhole membrane. Then she sprang through, and began dancing in delight.

'It is true, Kaltrina!' she cried excitedly, holding out her own hand in turn.

Kaltrina closed her eyes, tensing her body as she allowed herself to be drawn through the doorway. She reminded me of the twins, and stared about herself like a child, as if expecting the mirage to disappear.

'There you are, an experience is worth a thousand words,' I grinned.

They didn't answer; creeping about to touch the trees in wonder, while Jacqueline sipped her drink with airy nonchalance on the other side of the doorway.

'I cannot believe it!' exclaimed Kaltrina, enthralled. 'It is a miracle!'

I laughed, and pointed at my injured shoulder. 'But not a fairy tale: there are risks.'

Sophia laughed too. 'Such wonders are worth a few risks.'

'Don't say I didn't warn you,' I smiled. 'Now I need to find our friends.'

The two girls returned reluctantly into their kitchen, and I closed the exotic fissure in space-time. Charles' note was wrapped in plastic: rolled up and secured with an elastic band around the back of a small tree trunk. I jumped to a location near the address he gave me, and made my way cautiously to the building. It was a small hotel only a few miles from Sophia & Kaltrina's place. I asked at reception for the name

Charles had given me, and heard the twin's voices before I knocked on the door.

'Uncle Richard!' they shrieked, sending jolts of agony through my arm as they jumped at me in glee.

Charles and Priya laughed in relief, and the twins eventually quietened enough for me to explain what had happened. The news about Billy dismayed them, and Charles instantly proposed some of the time-bending rescue scenarios that had been running through my own mind.

'I'm thinking about it,' I admitted. 'But I'm not sure what may be possible – or even if it's a good idea. It might just make things worse.'

We talked about the raid: who the perpetrators might have been, what they wanted, and what we should do now they had found us.

'We were lucky to get away,' I said, 'but they must have found out all kinds of things about us at the house.'

'Not really,' said Charles. 'They got a couple of phones, but they were pay-as-you-go and I change them quite regularly. I got rid of the one I had. They can't track where we've been much. I was doing any sensitive research at random internet cafés, and only worked on stuff at home on jump-drives I kept in the panic bag. I keep all the documents, bills, credit cards and stuff there too, and payments went through the offshore company address. There won't be much for them to find.'

'You really are a marvel,' I said in frank admiration. 'Your surveillance system even worked when it was turned off! Thank goodness you took this counter-surveillance business so seriously.'

Charles looked offended. 'You mean you haven't?'

'Not as seriously as you,' I admitted.

'But who are they, and what do they want?' frowned Priya. 'If there are Portal Masters involved, what about all this crossing timeline business? Aren't they taking a bit of a chance?'

'Yes – maybe – I don't know,' I said wearily. 'The point is: what to do now. We need to make new plans. Find somewhere else to live.'

'Such a shame,' sighed Charles, 'just when we'd got our HQ sorted out.'

'I'll talk to Jacqueline,' I said. 'Whatever we do, it had better be quick.'

'Absolutely,' he agreed, 'especially as I am stuck with the twins as usual.'

'Don't worry,' I said, 'if Sophia & Kaltrina agree, you can come to their house. I can open a door here, maybe tomorrow. So be prepared.'

I got the hotel to order a cab for the return trip to Sophia & Kaltrina's house, as I did not want to risk opening a wormhole too close to my recent departure point there. All three girls were still engaged in animated conversation about my magical powers when I arrived, and Jacqueline turned to me immediately.

'Kaltrina expects you to exorcise a ghost for her Richard. I have been trying to explain that you are not a magician or a priest.'

'I certainly am not,' I agreed. 'But I don't know exactly what she means by a ghost either. I can listen to what she has to say. We owe her that much at least.'

Kaltrina was not in any doubt what a ghost was. 'Has haunted house long time,' she said. 'No one can stay there.'

Kaltrina was far less fluent in English than Sophia. The Portal could translate her meaning fairly seamlessly, but much of the time I tended to hear her words verbatim for some reason.

'Why are you frightened of a ghost?' I asked. 'Can't a priest, err, make it go away?'

'Priest scared,' she said. 'Ghost make him go away.'

'Hmm,' I temporised. 'What's the story? Whose house is it? Why does it have a ghost?'

'House of aunt,' she said. 'Aunt's brother die, but he not ghost. Aunt's mother not liking his marriage – trying to poison wife, but mistake – and he die. Mother becoming crazy: thinking son gone away, always waiting, waiting, for him come back. Then died, and still she is waiting.'

'Really?' I said, 'your aunt's mother is the ghost? That doesn't sound very frightening.'

Kaltrina shivered. 'No one can stay in house: she not like if you not son.'

I forgot not to shrug again. 'Ouch! Well, I don't know what I can do, but I tell you what: Charles, Priya and the twins are rather cramped in their hotel rooms – we can make a deal. If you will put us all up here for a few days, I will come and look at this ghost.'

'Of course they can come,' said Sophia, 'and it would mean a lot to Kaltrina if you can help her with her family problem.'

'OK, that's agreed,' I smiled. 'Where is the ghost – Albania?'

'Yes, yes!' said Kaltrina eagerly, 'we go by magic door?'

'Yes, we can go,' I said wryly, 'but it is not magic.'

'Thank you, thank you,' she cried happily.

'Don't thank me yet,' I warned, 'and give me another day or two to recover before we try anything. I will leave it a couple of days before I bring the others over too. Are you sure it will not inconvenience you to have us all here?'

'No problem,' smiled Sophia. 'I can move in with Kaltrina, which will give us two more spare rooms. It will be fun.'

A couple of days later I opened a door back to the hotel – back to the morning after I had left Charles and the others there. I was still recuperating and needed the rest, but I also wanted to maintain reasonable gaps in space-time between wormhole locations. Charles had paid up to date, and they vanished silently from the hotel, trailing through the exotic opening into the house with almost routine equanimity. They received a warm welcome, and we all got down to arranging replacement clothing via the internet, exchanging Sophia & Kaltrina's credit facilities for cash from Charles' emergency bag.

A couple more days went by, and my arm seemed to be healing quickly: presumably the positive effects of high-dimensional travel. In any event, I felt well enough to go and see Kaltrina's haunted house. I had asked Sophia for her view of it all, and she was quite convinced it was for real. She hadn't been to the house herself, but knew of others who had. 'Everyone feels bad there,' she said. 'Some just feel uneasy, and others sick and afraid. No one can sleep there, they have terrible dreams.'

Only Charles and Kaltrina accompanied me. Jacqueline and Sophia had no wish to meet a ghost, and Priya felt she should stay with the twins. Kaltrina wasn't keen either. But she was fired up with the idea of breaking the family curse, and had great faith in my magical powers. Nothing, of course, would have kept Charles away. I managed to open a doorway more or less where I intended, and we walked into a local town to catch a bus to her aunt's village. She lived there with an elder relation, and much astonishment, scepticism and alarm was expressed at our surprise visit. But Kaltrina's insistence gradually gained ground, and the tones of her aunt's protests softened into reluctant agreement.

The house stood alone some distance outside the village, and I felt odd as soon as I saw it. Not in a particularly alarming way. I just sensed a strange resonance: a kind of discordant echo vibrating within me which I could not identify.

It was a good solid building of a traditional style, constructed in rough, well laid local stone. The upper storey was corbelled significantly outwards on all sides to create greater space within, and shaded by the long, overhanging eaves of a pitched, tiled roof. The upper walls were plastered and fitted with large wooden casement windows. Smaller inset windows and a side door lined the ground floor, and a high central archway sheltered a substantial external stairway leading up into the first floor. But the structure reeked of neglect. Traces of mould and decay were beginning to bloom over the woodwork, paint was peeling, and the roof tiles were moss-bound and slipping in places. The windows were dirty and dark.

Charles looked a little daunted, but not sufficiently to dampen his thirst for adventure. Kaltrina's aunt, who had driven us there, became pale and agitated before we got anywhere near it. Her breathing was increasingly panicky.

'Don't worry,' I said to her, 'you don't have to go in.'

The woman laughed harshly, 'nothing would make me go into that house.'

'What about you?' I asked Kaltrina.

'I come in,' she said shakily, 'I have asked you. But tell me if dangerous, and we go quick.'

I took the heavy key ring from the quaking aunt, and the three of us marched towards the house. It reminded me of my amateur ride to the town jail to rescue Jacqueline. It would have been comically surreal if it wasn't for the weird sense of wrongness emanating from the building. Kaltrina seemed aware of the strangeness, and began to move as if her legs were turning to lead. But Charles appeared relatively unaffected. In a rare instance of confidence where females were concerned, he took her hand and smiled reassuringly at her.

I put the first key Kaltrina's aunt had indicated into the lock of the ground floor entrance door. It turned reluctantly. The door screeched as I pushed it open, and simultaneously something awakened to the intrusion. I felt an unusual buzzing in my head, but accompanied by a manic restlessness rather than malevolence. I flicked on the torch I carried, and ran its bright beam over the desolate interior. Dust swirled lazily in the still, pervasive quiet. The rooms were basic and utilitarian, with ancient barrels, old wicker baskets, large empty wine vessels and agricultural tools stacked haphazardly about. The others had torches too, and Kaltrina's beam was trembling; sending my shadow flitting grotesquely about the neglected interior. But the shrill sense of frenetic anxiety seemed muted somehow. I sensed its real intensity was centred somewhere above me.

'We should go upstairs I think,' I said.

'Y–yes,' Kaltrina said, her voice shaky. 'They say she wait there. Still we will face her?'

'Of course!' said Charles determinedly, though his zeal had dimmed a little.

'Sure,' I agreed. It was probably foolish, but I was feeling more curious than alarmed.

We retraced our steps, and trod resolutely up the outside stone stairway. The upstairs entrance door was heavier than the one below, and I heaved it back with a grunt to reveal an expansive but gloomy living area. It had once been nicely decorated. But now prettily carved woodwork and patterned wall-hangings were thick with spider webs and ancient dust, and the heavy silence stripped away the magic of the past.

I sensed the manifestation of some sort of exotic reality. It felt otherworldly but strange: a kind of schizophrenic juxtaposition between the everyday corporeal world and the transcendent dimensions I was familiar with. I tried to grasp its nature, feeling blindly towards a nebulous, almost eerie sense of presence. The habitual focus and intent which drove the Portal formed in my mind. But perception of the phenomenon receded as concentrated effort took hold. I pulled back and attempted to let go of my training. I tried to recall the more passive, nonspecific awareness with which I had summoned the archive in the past. It was easier with a target right in front of me. I felt myself opening to a wider spectrum of experience, and tried to release mental control still further. It felt odd to be exposed to the unknown, but the lurking sense of wrongness became gradually more apparent.

I hit the zone of disquiet and flinched reflexively away. My instinct was to disengage completely, but I forced myself to regain the connection. A bizarre sensation swirled through me: a perpetual stasis looping endlessly back on itself, with no established polarity of flow. I confronted a rambling sentience, despairing, rootless and remote – an interminable, interrupted cycle of completion. Vital existence had faded into a half-life of unrequited need – a chaotic, partial reflection of self which peered into space-time like an exile from the feast.

'Is it you? Have you returned?' Unspoken words emanated from the non-being. The contact shocked me. Not just because of the ghostly setting: for moment I thought it was the Mindworm. It was almost a relief to feel the strange entity lingering there.

'What are you?' I asked, suddenly emboldened.

'Don't go. Please forgive me. Please stay.'

'What are you?' I asked again, *'What do you want?'*

'Is it you? Have you come back to me?'

I sensed a tentative probing, a frictionless interface much like my own. A wave of confusion passed through me, and my world turned inside out. There was a flash of light, and the sudden, intense image of a woman wringing her hands in anguish. Then, just as suddenly, I separated from my everyday sense of self and was looking down into a hologram of my life, much as I had at Port Royal. But something new was going on. A feeble tendril of consciousness reached through the subtle energy field connecting me with my earthbound persona. I felt a tortured struggle for deliverance: a broken link seeking to reconnect, with a whole raft of data stored within it. A superficial glitch resisted, a stuttering, obsessive short-circuit which locked the entity in on itself.

'No... not you... but what...not me...not you...not me...'

The blind germ of consciousness reached through me, and beyond.

'Not alive...not dead...I am...not this...not this...not this ...'

There was a sudden, profound remembering: a thankful foothold on the bedrock of certainty. The accumulated data uploaded itself into a mother-lode of knowledge – a life-time of experience gone in an instant. Joy and sadness washed through me as it departed in a single, convulsive pulse. There was an abrupt expansion of vision. I glimpsed a relentless pattern of births and deaths: each reawakening a joyous new beginning; each final moment a grateful surrender and release. Not just an individual journey, but a collective progression. Myriad interlinked cells growing and evolving in space-time like delicate limbs – a slow, ancient sentience walking itself across countless aeons of time.

The confused, tormented entity had found its way home. It had been a living creature like myself I realised: some essential part of its being misidentified somehow with the material illusion when its physical body died. I had inadvertently released it from self-inflicted exile, and I felt a powerful tug to follow.

It was easy to drift into that blissful peace: into freedom from earthly care. Déjà vu was no longer a mysterious suggestion of another life, but a living reality. I was at home in this limitless honeycomb of succour and light. I had known it over long ages and touched it in my dreams; and other somnolent beings dreamed around me. Impressions peeped from each bright, inner essence: telepathic exchanges sharing ancient memories of primeval seas, swamps teeming with life, baking savannahs and the unhurried advance and retreat of massive sheets of ice. Half-remembered human lives too spoke of struggle and greed, love and sorrow, and the deep longing for knowledge and wonder.

Most of these timeless siblings were engrossed in the outer shell of material existence. Others were withdrawn, rejuvenating after weary or traumatic experience. Some part of me knew what was supposed to happen here: I should slip into a suspended, dreamlike passivity and await my next incarnation on this ancient cosmic journey. But now I perceived this long metamorphosis from a new perspective. I was awakening, becoming aware of the transition of consciousness through abundant life cycles into this immeasurable, enduring realm. Profound inner depths were unfolding: greater dimensions of beauty and splendour that had slumbered through countless ages.

Somehow the microscopic self-awareness of my insignificant human psyche translated into something vast and fathomless beyond the dimensional divide: a single cell coalescing into the higher cognisance of an unimaginable macrocosmic totality. Or perhaps on such inconceivable levels of existence such differences had no meaning, and each nexus of consciousness shared in the experience and understanding of the whole.

I saw everything in a flash of revelation: how my experience with the Portal had been restricted and incomplete. I had not 'used my mind' to steer across Intakaes' fluid energetic field to travel in space-time – at least not in the way I had thought. Rather I had opened a higher dimensional reality in which the abstract energy field was a deeper aspect of my own nature. Somehow the Portal connected with this exotic potential in an artificial and limited way: an intervention which retained my subjective human viewpoint in some ways, and diverted my interaction into the past or the future. We were immortal, high-dimensional beings it seemed – seeded in space-time and dreaming our way into existence on a level of reality beyond humanity's wildest imaginings. The gateway to truth lay not in the past or the future but in penetrating the eternal mystery of the present.

But my exalted state was temporary. I was not yet done with my bemused caterpillar self. I gazed back into the unforgiving reality of space-time. It was a nebulous, dreamlike field of pre-existence, lapping at the shores of eternity. The ocean of stars looked like a vast, ethereal hologram of scintillating neurons, interlinked by diaphanous filaments of light: a universal scaffolding of structured sentience and purpose.

My vision readjusted in dimensional scale as I followed the rainbow tendrils of energy that bound me to the outer, illusory shell of existence. Charles and Kaltrina's dreamlike forms came into focus; shimmering and insubstantial in the unreal matrix below me. They were sitting on their haunches, spellbound, as if in prayer. Exotic energies danced within and without them, weaving them into the tapestry of illusion. They looked exquisitely beautiful; like glowing figures in an artistic masterpiece. I recognised subtle flashes of their human personalities, but these were superficial reflections of something deeper and more glorious. Their bodies were transparent, illuminated from within, and something bright and undying pulsed steadily in the core of their beings, processing experience and understanding.

My own insubstantial body sat cross legged in front of them. Its inner core seemed largely absent: rather it illuminated the surrounding environment. I felt a flicker of concern as I realised how far I had drifted, and turned reluctantly against the tide. I fought the lure of sweet comfort and dissolution. A long time seemed to pass before I came back to myself again, and a subtle song of loss and regret still called as material structure solidified around me.

I felt the weight of the world on my shoulders, and knew I was back. I looked around at the simple mundanities of the traditional dwelling. It looked old and unloved, but no longer strange. The atmosphere was clear, even peaceful. I felt the house needed only a brisk clean and a cosy fire to become homely again.

'You are – OK?' asked Kaltrina breathlessly.

I pulled myself from deep stillness. 'I am now.'

'So many strange things…' she faltered, 'I am very afraid… and you not moving for so long. But now everything changed. I think it is gone.'

'It was certainly strange,' I said slowly. 'I don't know exactly what happened. But you are right, it has gone.'

'What was that?' gasped Charles, jerking belatedly back into life. 'That was...I don't know what it was. My whole life was like a dream: and everything seemed connected somehow. Was the weird woman the ghost? I thought I was dying again, but this time it was amazing!'

'Yes she was ghost,' said Kaltrina, her face ashen. She looked at her watch. 'Such long time: but I am not feeling time – sometimes I think not at all.'

'How long has it been?' I asked, suddenly all too aware of my cramped and aching body.

Charles whistled, looking at his own watch. 'Hours!' he said. 'Were we somewhere else? It was like a sea of light! I could have stayed there for ever!'

'What you do?' asked Kaltrina.

'I'm not sure,' I admitted wearily,

'It can come back?' she asked apprehensively.

'No,' I said adamantly.

'It was spirit?' she asked again.

'Something like that,' I agreed.

'I must tell aunt,' she said, suddenly animated.

'Is she still outside?' I asked in surprise.

'Of course,' she laughed unsteadily, 'but maybe she thinking us dead!'

Kaltrina's soaring mood seemed to complete the transformation in the house. We made our way stiffly out into late afternoon sunshine, stumbling down the rough-hewn steps. Each of us was smiling at a transformation none of us really understood. My memory of the dream-like transcendent realm was already fading; my grasp of its reality dispersing into wisp-like, fragmented images.

We had arrived around lunch time, and evening was approaching. Kaltrina's aunt was comically crouched down in her car; her head peering over the dashboard like an anxious coconut. She viewed us with doubtful suspicion: no doubt as the walking dead. But her niece's blinding smile and ecstatic hand waving eventually enticed her into the open. Persuading her to enter the house was a little more complicated, yet we eventually supported her trembling steps up to the first floor. She explored the interior inch by doubting inch, and only gradually relaxed into disbelieving astonishment.

'Why it feels so different!' she admitted cautiously.

'Yes, yes!' cried Kaltrina excitably. She began to rip grimy curtains aside, and to wrench open windows. One window fell straight out of the house, but neither Kaltrina nor her aunt seemed to mind.

'It is true!' cried her aunt, finally convinced, 'It is all changed!'

The golden rays of the waning sun cast a healing glow as the two women cavorted about the neglected interior. I went out to collect the fallen window, and wedged it temporarily back into place. Soon a rescue party – more relations worried by our long absence – approached cautiously in a battered old pick-up truck. They too received the news of the miraculous exorcism: but were insufficiently convinced to put it to the test with evening coming on. After much excitable discussion it was agreed that a sizeable deputation would visit the property in the morning: an official pronouncement would be made regarding its haunted status, and a thorough repair and redecoration program initiated if all was well.

We returned to her aunt's home in the village. Word spread quickly, and visitors arrived at regular intervals. We were the heroes of the hour, and Charles' and Kaltrina's beams of delight were inversely proportional to my desire to maintain a low profile. I was unprepared for the degree of local community spirit, and post-exorcism de-briefing apparently required a large number of powerfully alcoholic toasts.

Events escalated rapidly into a riotous party. The priest even turned up, and expressed much joy that his official exorcism may have finally borne fruit. I was content to credit anyone with the happy development, and bowed out of the limelight as much as possible. Kaltrina, Charles and the priest gradually assumed centre stage. Charles definitely had more than his customary meagre drink, and he and Kaltrina appeared to be becoming decidedly friendly. I struggled to refuse drinks for what seemed a long time. I wanted to retain the focus and control I needed for the Portal. But I also wanted to try and get my head around exactly what had happened back in the house.

I had got used to the idea that there were altered dimensions of reality, but they had always seemed less real to me than the everyday world. Now I had to get used to the idea that it was the other way around. What I had thought of as myself was some kind of elusive projection; space-time was a vast holographic illusion; and buried deep in the heart of my being was an undying creature from some unimaginable higher reality.

A mind-boggling thing to contemplate, back in the everyday world: though little less likely than time-travel itself. There had certainly been no doubts in my fast-receding memories of that higher existence. It explained other things too, or at least, seemed to – the strange visions; the sense of an extraordinary, timeless being watching through my eyes. And there were other, more powerful experiences that I still had no explanation for at all. It was difficult to think about, and not particularly useful to do so. The horizons of my life seemed to move faster and further away every time I came anywhere close to reaching them.

Chapter 28

CHARLES AND KALTRINA both had headaches in the morning, and gave each other uncertain looks from time to time. They were buoyed up by the continuing excitement though, and we eventually got away after lunch the following day.

'Well?' enquired Jacqueline curiously, as we sauntered in from the designated 'travel port' end of the lounge.

'Ghost gone!' announced Kaltrina triumphantly, 'magic very good.'

Jacqueline looked blankly at me, and I shrugged helplessly.

'Where does science end and magic begin?' I grinned. 'I guess we've got some more answers and some more questions.'

We had a protracted discussion about our Albanian adventure, somewhat handicapped by my inability to put much of it into words. Charles and Kaltrina were just as bad, and had experienced little more than a vision of the elderly ghost and a weird sense of transcendence. Jacqueline was thrilled to hear we had souls that did not die; but less keen on the idea of having to wait to get to heaven.

'After all, many people believe in reincarnation,' I pointed out, 'even the early Christians. I don't need the Archive to know that.'

'Oh they didn't,' she said disbelievingly, 'whatever will you say next!'

'Why is it so hard to believe?' I asked. 'What makes more sense: that we have been evolving towards a higher life form for millions of years, or that that the local vicar is taking us to heaven by reading out sermons on Sundays?'

Jacqueline and I argued about it on and off for a couple of days, but we had more immediate things to worry about: the relocation of what Charles still insisted on calling our HQ. I participated only half-heartedly, because my mind kept returning to the thought of Billy bleeding to death at the old place. The more my wound healed, the more I wondered if I could do something about it. I knew from everything Intakaes had said to me that any attempt to change things would be risky: and from the lofty viewpoint of a Portal Master, unwise. But the way I had been forced to leave Billy there bothered me deeply, and I couldn't get it out of my head.

I mulled over it from every angle I could think of. And the more I did, the more I knew I was going to try and do something to save him. In the end I just decided to go for it: to attempt an intervention just after the point where I had jumped away with Jacqueline. I rationalised that I would not be compromising my own timeline, merely effecting minor changes to associated interactions after I had left the scene. I managed to justify it to myself, in a hypothetical, convoluted sort of way, but I knew it was risky and something I really knew little about. Intakaes 'subduction zone' was a big unknown. I had no idea just how chaotic things might become that near to my earlier self; never mind what the proximity of three different wormholes might do. In the end I guess I just couldn't help myself.

I vacillated about confiding in Jacqueline while I made plans. I did a bit of field work: locating a hospital in France where casualties would be taken during a big terrorist attack a couple of years in the future; and familiarising myself with its layout. I intended to grab Billy and take him there, trusting he would be treated in the confusion, and could be extricated afterwards. If his wounds were not fatal, of course: I refused to think about that. I just had to try.

In the end I told Jacqueline at the last minute. She was scared. She understood something of its foolhardiness. But she demonstrated a steely resolve and a faith in me that constantly took me by surprise.

'If you believe it is possible Richard, then I think you should try,' she said. 'I feel awful about Billy too. But promise me you will come back, with or without him.'

I jumped to a vantage point on a big water tower a couple of miles away from our old headquarters. It overlooked our distant house, and I intended to 'fly' down into it just as I had when I rescued Jacqueline from the jail. I had got the time we were attacked approximately right, and planned to fine-tune the short skim through space-time to the precise time and location I wanted.

My heart rate was up, but I felt calm and resolute as I stood poised for the attempt, and concentrated on the challenge before me. I launched at the right moment, and began to glide down through the same sort of transparent landscape as before. But the flight was not smooth. A strange, shuddering inertia unsettled me: a bit like turbulence in a plane. My focus and control seemed less certain, and it felt more like swimming underwater than skimming through the air. Random energy surges buffeted and swirled around me, and my destination grew increasingly hazy. A paralysing sense of doom seemed to resist my will, but I forced myself on.

Despite everything the distorted image of the building grew nearer. Its structure was murkily transparent, and I could see into the stairs and landing. Time slowed and the moments expanded. I dimly made out the last clouds of ice and snow settling dreamily on the floor. The doorway into the ice storm had closed. My previous self had jumped with Jacqueline, and Billy's indistinct form leaned limply against the landing wall, struggling to raise his heavy revolver.

But the wormhole location still glowed brightly in that lucent, quasi-manifested state. Even the doorway I had opened for Charles, Priya and the twins remained visible, fading only slowly. There seemed a reciprocal attraction between the rifts in space-time: a powerful force reaching out from each of them towards me. I sensed a fourth high-energy source too: the mirror-like emanation of a Portal Master somewhere outside the house. Rainbow bands of writhing energy swirled between all four points. They locked together, and power began to flow in some kind of fantastic feedback loop. I knew I should pull away, and I sensed the other Portal Master struggling to escape, but Billy was so near. I fought stubbornly to reach him, forcing my way through a raging energy storm. He saw me and stared in dream-like confusion. I almost touched him.

The energy flow became brighter: accelerating into a screaming kaleidoscope of light. I knew suddenly that I had gone beyond a point of no return. My consciousness was dissolving into chaos. The light became blinding, and I could no longer see. I was falling, falling: twisting and turning like a leaf in a gale. There seemed no end to it, until with startling suddenness, I awoke.

'Awake at last, sleepy head?' asked Jacqueline cheerfully.

I stared at her. Something was wrong. The whole room was buzzing with déjà vu.

'Are you all right Richard?' she said, puzzled at my stricken expression.

I looked around. Everything looked normal: just wrong.

Her tone changed. 'You are not trying to avoid church are you? I am sure you will enjoy it when you get there.'

'Are we going to church today?' I asked stupidly.

'Oh Richard, you are trying to get out of it!' she said crossly. 'We agreed. You know I won't make you go after we are married.'

'No – no, that's fine,' I said slowly.

I got out of bed and drifted to the bathroom. My best clothes were laid out ready for me, and I showered and dressed in the same, absent manner. I kept searching within myself for the answer: feeling there was something I should know – or something I had forgotten. It was like trying to wake up from a dream.

'Richard!' said Jacqueline sharply, as I wandered off to get some breakfast.

I looked at her. 'What?'

'Your hair,' she said impatiently. 'I don't know what's wrong with you today.'

I looked in the mirror. Sure enough, a dark-haired Boris Johnson stared back at me.

'Sorry,' I said. *'Yes,'* I wondered, *'what is wrong with me?'*

Billy was slurping coffee in the kitchen with a beatific smile on his face. I stopped dead as soon as I saw him.

'What's up?' he grinned, 'you look like you seen a ghost!'

I stared for long seconds. 'Something's wrong,' I blurted stupidly.

His eyes narrowed, and he looked swiftly about. 'What's happening?' he asked in a different tone.

I shrugged uncomfortably. 'I don't know. I just feel there's something weird going on. I don't feel right somehow.'

Billy relaxed a little, and eyed me carefully. 'Well, maybe that's not surprising; what with you going through these here doorways all the time. Maybe you should rest up a little.'

I felt a little calmer. 'Maybe you're right. Strange things do happen sometimes. Perhaps it'll settle down.'

Jacqueline came bustling through, and we had a light breakfast together. The first shock had worn off a bit, and I began to feel a little better. I wondered if Billy was right – especially as he did not know just how strange some of my experiences had been. I even half-remembered strange states of being which seemed quite unfamiliar to me. I hoped I was not being affected by the Portal. I couldn't remember Intakaes having any such concerns, and I would soon have to make a couple more trips into the past to get fake birth certificates. I thought about it as

I munched my toast. She had spoken of bizarre consequences arising from crossed timelines, and from delving too deep into the Archives. That seemed more likely, although hardly reassuring. I tried to keep my misgivings to myself. I thought I was feeling less disorientated, and started to feel more confident that I would be able to cope with whatever was going on. I told myself it could just be some form of temporal disturbance I had not experienced yet. Time, I thought, would tell.

I had anticipated that these Sunday services would be an irksome duty, but the idea of something as mundane as going to church now seemed rather soothing. Jacqueline was happy about it of course, which made me feel good as well. I tried to forget the dark uncertainties hanging over our lives as the vicar rambled through his well-practised routine. It did relax me. I was even amused when his sermon reminded me of Ravi, and found myself listening for clues about the ultimate nature of reality among the homely parables. But the ubiquitous déjà vu seemed to grow stronger, and I tried to think of nothing instead.

Charles and Priya were waiting for me with Billy when we got back from church. 'I hear something strange is happening,' Charles said.

'Well, yes,' I admitted evasively.

Jacqueline looked at me anxiously. 'I thought you were still behaving oddly Richard. What is wrong?'

'I don't know,' I said irritably. 'I feel a bit less confused, but there is still this sense of déjà vu. I feel this all a dream I cannot wake up from.'

'According to your teacher in Atlantis, it means that reality has been changed in some way,' said Priya thoughtfully.

'Yes I know,' I agreed. 'But I have experienced it plenty of times, and it was never like this: never this disorientating and intense – except perhaps in Central, with Ravi, for a while I suppose.'

'There you are then,' said Billy. 'It will wear off again, if it did before.'

'Yes but this is different,' I insisted. 'When I first woke up I felt shocked, as if something bad had happened. In Central it felt that reality was changing. This morning it was more like something was fundamentally wrong: as if something was missing.'

We continued to discuss it for a while, achieving nothing. The conversation went around in circles. Every so often the others would ask how I was feeling, and I found myself manufacturing an increasingly upbeat prognosis just to reassure them. The weird sense of wrongness persisted, and I tried to ignore it. Eventually I found some relief in a few glasses of wine, something I rarely indulged in anymore. The sense of strangeness receded with the alcohol, and I slept.

My dreams were vivid and chaotic, but I couldn't remember anything about them, and next morning things were less disturbing. The oddness was still there but seemed less intense, and at times I forgot about it altogether. Charles and I got on with research and planning for the birth certificate trips, but we agreed to delay their execution on account of my strange state of being.

'I am going to put it all in my book,' announced Charles.

'What book?' I asked distractedly.

'Oh, didn't I tell you?' said Charles sunnily, 'I am going to write a book about all this: not yet, in case it gives anything away. I'm just making notes – in code of course.'

'But if people read it in the future it will give everything away,' I pointed out. 'Isn't that counter-counter-surveillance, seeing as we are up against time travellers?'

'Oh no!' groaned Charles, his dreams of greatness dashed once more. 'I was going to join writing classes and everything.'

The days passed, and Jacqueline busied herself with preparations for the wedding, such as they were. The sense of strangeness continued to recede: the constant déjà vu reducing to a background buzz I scarcely noticed. But an underlying uneasiness haunted me as the confusion faded. Reality felt more stable, but I worried I was losing something in the process. My dreams grew increasingly tumultuous: their impact more intense, but their meaning infuriatingly absent. And so it continued, until the dam burst.

The dream was as chaotic as ever, but in the midst of it I stumbled into an oasis of peace. A golden sun shone down on me, calming and reassuring. Its glow spoke of a different realm, and its presence promised release.

I was puzzled. *'Release from what?'* I asked.

'From illusion,' no one in particular replied, and I began to remember.

I found myself hovering in the air above Charles and Kaltrina. They were looking up at me: and writhing in the air between us was a bizarre, wizened woman.

'Help me!' cried the woman.

'How can I help you?' I wondered in confusion.

'You know how!' she cackled, and vanished in a flash of light.

The dream was so powerful that it woke me. Its impact was immense, and I sat up in confusion, trying to make sense of it. But there was no sense to be made: only disappointment as the sense of revelation dwindled away.

Jacqueline stirred. 'What's wrong?' she asked.

'Just a dream,' I said.

But it was unexpectedly back on the agenda in the morning. Jacqueline and I were having breakfast when she asked me about the dream. I was half way though describing it when Charles looked up abruptly from scrutinising the small print on a cereal packet.

'What did you say?' he demanded excitedly, and I obligingly started again.

'I had the same dream!' he exclaimed incredulously, as I finished. 'Except that me and the girl were looking up at you, and the funny old woman was in the air between us.'

'What did the girl look like?' I asked, a tingling excitement creeping into my spine.

His description was pretty hopeless, but good enough.

'It's her: Kaltrina,' I exclaimed, 'Sophia's friend.'

Charles, Jacqueline and I stared at each other, and tingling excitement threatened to become a flood.

'It does seem extraordinary,' said Jacqueline, homing in on the one incongruent psychic item which seemed to jar her most. 'So this is another girl you have tucked away from your past.'

'I told you about her,' I said indignantly. 'She was one of the girls I split the lottery money with. That's not important. But for me and Charles to have the same dream is a different matter.'

'Yes I am sure it is,' sniffed Jacqueline, 'although it might have been nice if I was in it too. But I don't see how it can help us.'

'I do!' said Charles eagerly: 'we can go and see if she had the same dream too.'

'I don't think that's very likely,' I said doubtfully. 'I don't really know her very well. She's going to think it a bit weird if I turn up and ask her if she's had a dream about me.'

Billy and Priya and the twins joined us, and the conversation wound back and forth between us all, until Aurelia managed to bring matters to a head by announcing that she believed in dreams.

'Why is that dear?' asked Jacqueline sweetly.

'Because of the nice bad lady,' said Aurelia brightly. 'I was scared on the ship, but I remembered my dream that the nice bad lady would look after me and she did.'

She had dreamed that Anna would help her in a storm on the Merchant Royal before it actually happened, and it had helped her feel that everything would be all right when the events began to unfold. The ensuing explanation-come-argument got me into trouble with Jacqueline all over again. But it introduced the idea that dreams might convey valid information regarding other times and places. Priya mentioned that she had dreamt of events before they had happened once or twice, and Charles claimed that he had too – or at least that he thought he had.

Eventually it was agreed that I would visit Sophia & Kaltrina that afternoon, along with Charles and Jacqueline. The later I suspected, was some form of chaperone. I felt a strange dichotomy of expectation as we approached their house in the eastern outskirts of London. Superficially I anticipated a somewhat awkward and embarrassing encounter, while deeper down a more instinctive self was impatient to get there.

Kaltrina opened the door, which seemed portentous. She also appeared startled to see me, with some unstated emotion lingering behind her automatic welcome. But when she saw Charles she gave an involuntary squeak, which he reciprocated at an only marginally lower pitch. It cut right through the social niceties. I barely had time to introduce Jacqueline before she was ushering us in, radiating suppressed excitement.

'Sophia! Sophia! Look who has come!' she called back into the house.

Sophia appeared, and smiled a greeting. She reacted more to Jacqueline than to Charles, and seemed a little puzzled by Kaltrina's urgent attempts to whisper in her ear. Charles meanwhile appeared to be having some sort of face spasm. I eventually divined that his exaggerated nods and winks were directed at Kaltrina, and made a minor intuitive leap.

'Err... Kaltrina, did you by any chance have an interesting dream last night?'

'Ha!' said Kaltrina, turning to Sophia; her right index finger raised high, 'you see!'

Sophia looked startled.

'Not Richard only!' Kaltrina exclaimed out loud, pointing at Charles, 'this one also!'

'Yes!' exploded Charles. 'She was in the dream too!'

The tell-tale stirrings in my spine began again.

'This does seem strange,' said Sophia slowly. 'Is this something to do with your, ah, gift for seeing the future Richard?'

'Well,' I said awkwardly, 'that is what I am trying to find out. It is rather a long story, and I'm not sure you really want to know everything. I just want to share some details about the dream if that's OK: to help us solve a bit of a puzzle.'

'Yes, yes!' cried Kaltrina excitedly, 'old woman and light in sky!'

Just then her phone rang, and she glanced at it impatiently.

'Must speak: one minute,' she said hurriedly, and rushed out.

Sophia began to explain that Kaltrina had already been excited about her dream before our unexpected arrival. 'I did not understand why,' she said, 'but she becomes excitable about many things.'

Kaltrina tore back into the room, chattering into the phone at a million miles an hour. 'Aunt also having dream – not so much – but ghost gone!'

We all stared at her in confusion. 'Err…ghost gone?' I ventured uncertainly.

'Yes. All OK: woman in house gone!' She announced triumphantly.

That did it: the dam crumbled. A powerful force moved through my body, sending tiny whorls of exhilaration racing all over me. The air seemed thick with vibrations, and material structure looked suddenly transparent and unreal. For a moment I thought the Portal was activating. Then I was looking down into the material illusion once more from that blissful, transcendent realm. I understood everything instantly: I saw the two conflicting timelines as uncertain, faltering doppelgängers – irreconcilable, discordant parallel images. Both reflections began to flow and bleed together, and the incongruities resolved themselves in a sudden, convulsive conclusion.

'I remember everything!'

I wasn't sure if I spoke the words. Everything looked much as it had in Albania: exotic energies weaving our physical forms into a subtle tapestry of illusion, while something bright and undying shone in the core of our beings. But now delicate golden ripples emanated between us. There was a shared expansion of being, and an understanding of things I could not put into words. Finally the extraordinary state of being ebbed away, leaving us staring open-mouthed at each other.

'Wow!' gasped Charles elatedly, 'what was that? It was like getting to the next level on a computer game! I think I had your déjà vu Richard! I had my dream again while I was awake. I remember being with you and Kaltrina and that weird woman floating in the air...'

'I saw something so beautiful,' whispered Jacqueline. 'I didn't feel frightened. My life was passing in front of me...so many memories...I felt like a little girl again.'

'Something extraordinary,' muttered Sophia, shaken out of her habitual calm. 'To exist beyond yourself...I never imagined...'

'Magic!' exclaimed Kaltrina, her eyes blazing with triumph. 'We are having dream: so much light coming, and ghost gone!'

'Err...something like that,' I agreed, little less bewildered than the rest of them. The regained memories were a shock. 'How can it still happen? It was on another timeline.'

'What do you mean, Richard – what happened?' asked Jacqueline.

'There was another timeline,' I said shakily. 'Me, Charles and Kaltrina went to Kaltrina's aunt's house in Albania. We went to look for the ghost of a crazy woman. Something similar to what we just experienced happened – a lot of light and energy - and the ghost disappeared.'

'What! I went to Albania looking for a ghost?' exclaimed Charles. He looked puzzled. 'I thought it was a dream?'

'It got erased,' I said wonderingly. 'We were on the run and we were hiding here with Sophia and Kaltrina...but somehow the episode with the ghost still happened, and it bled over into this timeline.'

'What!' yelped a chorus of confused people.

'Let's all calm down,' I suggested. 'I haven't got it straight in my own head yet, and Sophia and Kaltrina know nothing about it at all. We'll have to go through it one step at a time.' I turned to Kaltrina. 'What exactly did your aunt say?'

'Aunt having dream...ghost gone,' she said. 'She going to house with some people: and true! Everything changed!'

I had to decide how much to tell them. When I thought about it, Sophia and Kaltrina had become involved in both timelines at around this point, so I went ahead cautiously.

'I can try to explain, but are you sure you want to know? It involves risks and uncertainties that you might not want, and I don't understand it all myself.'

'Yes, yes, explain,' insisted Kaltrina eagerly.

But Sophia considered me more carefully. 'There were strange things about you before,' she said, 'and now we find stranger things still. But you helped us, and I trust you are a good person. I have already experienced something fantastic, and I would like to know more.'

'OK,' I said, manifesting a doorway into countryside near the Hastingwood hide. 'Well, first of all: I can travel in time – and space.'

Sophia & Kaltrina stood like statues before the glittering circle, just as they had on the last occasion, and we went through the whole scenario again in much the same way. I went first, gave Sophia my hand, and Kaltrina followed. The two of them crept about in astonishment: more sober than last time perhaps, because of the mind-blowing experience they had already encountered.

Jacqueline and Charles looked on in airy nonchalance as they returned.

'Such magic: so wonderful!' said Kaltrina in awe.

I laughed. 'Don't forget the risks.'

Sophia laughed too, just as she had last time. 'Such wonders are worth a few risks.'

The strange feeling of wrongness had disappeared. But now I was simultaneously remembering both realities, and I seemed to hear her words in stereo. 'Don't say I didn't warn you,' I said to complete the sequence. 'Now I need to tell you the short version of a long story.'

There were horrified gasps from Charles and Jacqueline when I got to the part where the house was attacked.

'Oh Richard!' she exclaimed, 'why did you not tell us immediately? Will we be attacked again?'

'No – well, it hasn't happened in this timeline has it?' I pointed out. 'Something changed things, something I did I think.'

'I not understand,' said Kaltrina.

We got into a complicated discussion about timelines; which Sophia and Kaltrina found even more confusing than Charles and Jacqueline.

'It is without doubt a big difficulty for me,' Sophia chuckled uncertainly. 'I think it is too much for my poor brain, all at once.'

Kaltrina was more interested in hearing amazing tales than understanding them.

She just wanted to know more. But Jacqueline was less enthralled.

'The more this goes on, the more nonsensical it seems to become,' she grumbled. 'I don't understand how this so-called exorcism took place when you weren't there – and I would have thought we had enough problems without going ghost hunting in the first place.'

'I'm not sure I would use the term exorcism,' I replied a little crisply. 'I wouldn't call it a ghost exactly either: more a sort of misidentified aspect of a higher kind of consciousness.'

'Well, whatever it was, it was good,' said Charles cheerfully. 'I suppose this exorcism thing still existed when the timeline changed, because it happened outside of space-time. Somehow our unconscious mind remembered it, and we all dreamt about it. After all, if it wasn't for the dream, we might never have found out about the other timeline.'

'Yes, something like that Charles,' I agreed, as yet another round of tingling stirred in mysterious parts of my being. 'I do kind of remember a place where dreams and memories from space-time seem to mix together. But it's hard to get your head around this stuff. I have altered timelines myself, and I remembered both realities – or I experienced déjà vu and knew that reality had changed in some way. But this was different. It was as if reality had been ripped out of existence somehow.'

'Never mind about that,' said Jacqueline impatiently. 'Who attacked us? What happened?'

'Ah yes,' I said, strangely reluctant to talk about it. 'Well, um, there were about half a dozen or so of them, including a Portal Master somewhere behind the scenes. Actually Billy and I were shot...'

'What!' shrieked Jacqueline, 'why did you not tell me immediately?'

'I am trying to get used to the idea myself,' I admitted, 'and some of the details are still coming back to me. I was hit in the arm, but Billy was much more seriously hurt. I got Charles, Priya and the twins away through a doorway while Billy held them off, and then I got away with you. Billy was left behind. You and I came here. I was hit by a bullet and some darts – and a stun gun. It was the only place I could get to. When I got a bit better I tried to go back and save Billy, and I guess this crossing timelines thing happened big-time. The next thing I knew I was back in the house and everything was weird.'

Everyone absorbed this in silence.

Jacqueline spoke first. 'We must get back to the others, quickly.'

'But it didn't happen,' Charles protested. 'We are all OK.'

'I don't care,' she said agitatedly, 'if it can happen once it can happen again. We must all get away from that house.'

'It's true,' I said slowly. 'We don't know who these people were or how they found us. Something changed things. It might have been the false birth certificates that put them onto us: I haven't gone back to change them yet in this timeline. Or someone – maybe even a group of people and Portal Masters – may have lost time and knowledge like we did in the high-energy chaos when I tried to save Billy. We don't know exactly what happened. It may just take longer for them to find us, so it would make sense to disappear.'

We promised to contact Sophia & Kaltrina soon, and drove back to the house; where Billy and Priya had news of their own.

'Two men called,' said Priya. 'They seemed to know something unusual is going on here, and they are coming back to see you.'

'What did you tell them?' I asked tersely.

'Nothing much,' she replied coolly. 'I didn't get a bad feeling from them, but I was careful. They got the idea I wasn't the one they needed to talk to though, and I admitted that you wouldn't be out for long.'

'OK,' I decided, 'everyone pack: we're leaving. Not everything – just basic clothing, money, and important documentation. Anything that ID's us. Charles, can you deal with the computing stuff?'

'Already in hand,' he said. 'I use external hard drives, and keep all the cards and correspondence together. Cash too.'

'Oh yes, of course you do,' I said.

'Are you sure this isn't an overreaction?' asked Priya in surprise.

'There's a lot more to tell you,' I said briefly, 'but later.'

We had barely started packing when the doorbell rang. Billy appeared with his revolver, and the sight brought a lump to my throat. I signed him to wait, and peered through a window overlooking the front door. One of the visitors moved back to look up at the first floor, and I breathed a sigh of relief. It was Leonidas, his Atlantean guard's uniform incongruously replaced with casual contemporary wear.

'It's OK, I know them,' I called out to the others. 'But everyone stay out of sight.'

I ran lightly down the stairs and opened the door.

'Richard,' said Leonidas with his serious smile, 'we thought it was you.' His gaze was candid and amicable, but his underlying demeanour grim.

I recognised the second man vaguely too, although the shining signature of his Portal identified his status clearly enough.

'This is High Citizen Farbod,' Leonidas announced. 'He is leading an investigation into a time-flow anomaly.'

'And you thought I would be involved?' I asked, a little abruptly.

Farbod nodded politely. 'The anomaly coordinates brought us to this approximate space-time location, where we knew you originated. It was an obvious possibility.'

He seemed reasonably straightforward and unassuming for a Portal Master, and my antagonism softened a little. I asked them in. 'Any other citizens you may have concealed out there are welcome too,' I added dryly.

Farbod smiled slightly. 'Their duties keep them outside at present. We must be prepared for any eventuality.'

'So you expect trouble?' I asked, leading them into the lounge.

'It is always possible in these situations,' admitted Leonidas.

I offered them refreshments, but they wanted to get down to business.

'The anomaly is centred around here, in the recent past.' Farbod said. 'Yet you appear largely unaffected, apart from the temporal echoes. What can you tell us about it?'

I had been trying to decide exactly that, and tried to steer a middle pathway as usual.

'We were attacked by a group of people, who included a Portal Master,' I said. 'I tried a number of things to save myself and my friends, including doubling back from the near future, and it set off some kind of reaction. A lot of strange things happened, and the people who attacked us vanished. That's all.'

Both men looked intently at me.

'A Portal Master?' said Farbod, 'did you recognise who it was?'

I shook my head.

'What of the others?' asked Leonidas. 'Had you seen them before?'

'No,' I said. 'Why – do you know who they are?'

They were silent for a moment, before Farbod spoke.

'There have been…repercussions associated with this anomaly among certain High Citizens,' he admitted, 'disrupted time-lines among several, and complete reality loss in one case.'

'What does that mean exactly?' I asked.

'He has lost weeks out of his life,' Farbod said, 'and the time-flow is disordered in some of his associates.'

'How do you know they were associated with the anomaly here?' I probed.

'There are…indications,' Farbod said evasively, 'and the activities of some of these Citizens were already being monitored.'

'High Citizen Farbod has been involved in several of my investigations,' explained Leonidas, 'including those relating to your own adventures in Central and Alexandria.'

Farbod removed a small spherical device from an inside pocket, and cupped it in his upturned hand. It glowed briefly, and a holographic image hovered in the air, centred approximately on my eye line.

'Do you recognise this man?' he asked.

I didn't, but I took a moment to familiarise myself with his features. I shook my head and a new image appeared; followed by several others. One or two looked vaguely familiar from my time in Atlantis, but no one I had spent any time with.

'Are they all Portal Masters?' I asked him.

'Some,' he said, 'others are second citizens, or work with them as outside agents.'

'What about those who have lost memories?' I asked, 'will they recover them?'

'Almost certainly not,' he said. 'Of course such incidents are always unpredictable, and there may be others mixed up in this business. But I imagine their activities have been thrown into some confusion.' He paused, scrutinising me curiously. 'I am surprised that you appear relatively unaffected. Are you certain there were no repercussions? No changes to your perception of reality?'

'Well,' I said, deliberately vague, 'I felt quite confused and shaken up, and it took a while before I was back to normal, but I feel fine.' I certainly wasn't going to get into a conversation about ghosts with him.

'There is a lot of disruption surrounding the event,' agreed Farbod, 'but it would not appear to have been as destructive as it could have been.

You in particular seem to have stabilised very quickly, with a remarkably intact timeline.'

I shrugged. 'Just lucky I guess.'

He regarded me carefully for a time. 'You have certainly been lucky,' he agreed, 'but I would suggest you do not take it for granted.'

'From now on I'm not taking anything for granted,' I said ruefully. 'Do you know how they found me?'

'Any number of ways,' replied Leonidas: 'tracking financial data, archived documentation, infiltrating surveillance systems, face-recognition software, that kind of thing. What we don't know is why they were after you. On the first occasion the Senator appeared to be the target, and on the second it seemed to be Aton. But this time only you and your friends were present. Did your assailants give you any indication what their motive was?'

I shook my head. 'I don't have a clue what they wanted.'

'You have a number of companions in the house,' remarked Farbod. 'They are vulnerable, and a liability. So I am prepared to make you an offer. We will extend our hospitality to all of them, if you will reconsider our invitation to join us in Atlantis.'

Chapter 29

I WAS SURPRISED. It was tempting after our recent narrow escape, but the idea felt stifling, and not necessarily as safe as it seemed. I intended putting it to the others of course, their lives were on the line too. But I doubted that Jacqueline would have changed her views.

'Thank you,' I said. 'It is good of you to offer us sanctuary. But I will have to think about it, and talk to the others.'

'Very well, but please do consider it carefully,' said Farbod, getting to his feet. 'I think that concludes our enquiries for now. Thank you for your cooperation.'

'Be careful,' said Leonidas, bestowing a significant look as they left through the front door.

Jacqueline led the charge down the stairs. 'Who was it?' she asked.

'Leonidas and a High Citizen,' I said. 'They picked up on the fireworks here when the timelines changed.'

'Then why did I have to hide?' she demanded indignantly. 'They know me.'

'Sorry,' I said. 'It seemed the simplest thing to say. As it was they met Priya, and I didn't know who else might come down. I didn't want them to identify any more of us than necessary. They have already detected that there are quite a few people here.'

'Probably some kind of microwave thingy,' said Charles knowledgeably. 'What did they say anyway?'

'I created some kind of anomaly in the time-flow when I went back for Billy, and it registered on their equipment,' I said.

'What do you mean, went back for me?' asked a puzzled Billy

'Ah!' I said awkwardly. 'There's so much going on that we haven't had time to tell you. We found out what was wrong – me feeling weird, and all those funny dreams: we got attacked here. There was a gunfight and everyone got away except you. You were badly wounded. I tried to go back and pull you out of there, and set off a kind of high-dimensional back-lash. We effectively got thrown back in time, with no memory of what happened. It's a bit complicated.'

'Well I'll be...,' cried Billy in bewilderment. 'This here time business knocks a man's horse-sense into a cocked hat, and that's a fact! One minute I'm looking down a gun barrel, and in two shakes I'm off in Jamaica – and now I'm shot, and I'm right as rain!'

'No you ain't – I mean you aren't – shot,' I said. 'But the best part is: the bad guys were affected too. They are confused, and may have lost the memory of what happened. They may not have our location any more. It gives us a bit more time to make plans; and no one is going to try anything with an Atlantean enforcement team around either.'

'I'm sorry you were injured and left behind Billy,' said Jacqueline, 'even if Richard managed to change things. He was shot too. It seems to have been an awful situation.'

'He's bin un-shot too?' marvelled Billy.

'I didn't manage to change things,' I pointed out. 'I took a crazy risk, and we were lucky. Billy was the hero: he held them off on the stairs while I got Charles and the others away.'

Billy scratched his head, looking embarrassed. 'I don't rightly know what happened,' he said in confusion. 'I guess we just thank the Lord we're all in one piece, and take it from here.'

'Yes, what are we going to do now?' asked Priya.

'We've got to move,' said Charles. 'What a shame: just when we'd got our HQ set up. I wonder how they found us?'

'Are we going to play Peekaboo again?' asked Aurelia.

'No we aren't,' said Priya, smiling at the twins. 'Come with me and we'll put a movie on.' She turned to us as the twins rushed ahead, her face abruptly sombre. 'We have got to find somewhere safer for the kids,' she said bleakly.

'We wouldn't be difficult to find, according to Leonidas,' I sighed: 'by hacking into surveillance systems with face-recognition software for instance. Charles was right about that. I thought it far-fetched, but apparently it's not. They might have images of me and you Charles, if it's the same people who were outside your cottage back at the beginning – of Jacqueline too, perhaps, from Atlantis. I mean, these latest creeps didn't have laser guns or weird armour, but they could be connected.'

'They could be out of time sequence,' considered Charles. 'Just because things happen in the past or the future in our timeline doesn't mean they happen that way from a world viewpoint.'

'True – I think,' I laughed reluctantly, 'hard to get your head around. Or they could have just found us on the internet, maybe through the marriage registration. We changed the dates and places of our birth certificates, but I suppose using the same names was a bit obvious. We were careless – took too much for granted.'

'I suppose we didn't know for sure that anyone was after us,' said Charles. 'After we found out about Atlantis, I thought they might sort it all out.'

'They are trying to police the situation,' I agreed, 'but they don't really seem to have any idea what is going on either. Some of the people affected by the 'anomaly' were actually in Atlantis, which means they were involved, or had connections to those who attacked us. Incidentally, we have all been invited to live there if we choose.'

There was a sudden silence, and we all exchanged glances. I could see suspicion in Billy, excitement in Charles, and mutiny in Jacqueline.

'It's fascinating to begin with Charles, and quite luxurious,' I said, 'but in the end it's a rather unnatural and limiting place, with lots of rules and regulations.'

'We would still have horrid modern machines spying on everything we do,' said Jacqueline angrily. 'Can't we live in a simpler time?'

I thought about it. I supposed that having a safe haven tucked away in an earlier time period might be a good idea. It would mean living without modern conveniences, although I assumed we would be able to keep some technology out of sight. But I could see it might be a price worth paying. Charles seemed torn.

'I'll have to ask Priya too,' I said, and got up to get her.

She was quiet for a while. 'I would love to see the place of course,' she said finally. 'But that's not the same as living there, and obviously some of the Portal Masters are up to no good.'

'I want to be free to look for the girl who started all this, and find out what she knows,' I said, 'and I like the idea of basing ourselves somewhere in the past. We could establish smaller places in more complicated times if we need them, and keep them separate from our home base.' I smiled at Charles. 'Just think what fun you'll have dreaming up counter-surveillance procedures.' He perked up a bit. 'And we can still visit Atlantis at some point.'

The conversation rambled on a while longer, but its outcome was not really in doubt. The subject moved on to the requirements of our proposed refuge: somewhere far away from Jeremiah Serrano, not too primitive, and not too developed. Where we could speak the language, and most easily make use of our unorthodox fortune. Eventually we agreed to look for somewhere with a bit of privacy in the English countryside, around the year eighteen hundred.

'Excellent,' exclaimed Jacqueline, her face glowing, 'we could have some land – maybe a small farm!'

I smiled at her. 'Yes, perhaps we could.'

We did not have to look far to find the earthy scent of the farmyard in the eighteenth century. The all-pervading smell of horses in London surprised me. There were other odours too, fetid and bound up with the reek of countless chimneys, yet for me the ubiquitous equine stench seemed at odds with the industrious sense of metropolis. I had returned to Sophia and Kaltrina's house to negotiate a temporary stay with them while we relocated into the past. I offered to compensate them handsomely, but their hospitality had been open and unaffected. The bonds formed in our first encounter, and the magical happenings of the second had brought us all very close. The bags stuffed with cash, great chunks of gold and silver, and handfuls of jewels were merely the icing on the cake.

We had travelled via doorways from house to house, diverting only through empty countryside as a precaution against unknown time-jump tracking technology. Some sort of working arrangement had been organised – part of their dining room had been allocated for jumping and returning, and we had begun a systematic infiltration into the past. Our first trips had been little more than reconnoitres, starting a number of years before our chosen 'insertion date' of seventeen ninety. We had hired costumes, familiarised ourselves with the streets and the population, and acquired more authentic clothing. We bought a house in Compton Street near Soho Square, and used it as a base and entry point into the timeline. It had a useful back yard, into which we could back the carriages we used to transport the treasure from various hideouts.

Next we set about establishing a financial presence, choosing several London bankers we wanted to work with after some careful research.

There were hundreds of private bankers in London, mostly partnerships of two or more businessmen with deep pockets and good connections. We had approached several: concocting carefully ambiguous backgrounds in the murky backwaters of the Americas. They welcomed our ambitions to utilise their services in winding down unspecific, lucrative past enterprises. Our plans to invest in a respectable future as traders and investors in the heart of the burgeoning British Empire cheered them even more: especially when we had a plentiful supply of silver, a useful currency of trade for exotic goods in Asia and China.

A certain amount of our gold bullion was put to work too, but we decided to keep a substantial amount in reserve: intending to store it safely when we eventually settled down. We hung on to a lot of the jewels as well. The chests of pieces of eight were both more valuable and easily disposable than I had imagined. The coin was still acceptable as foreign exchange. Our investments in various joint-stock company shipping ventures were richly rewarding, thanks to maintaining a judicious eye on the historical fortunes of such affairs. Over a few time-hopping years we were amassing rather more riches than I felt comfortable with. I did not intend to let it go too far, as I had no wish to acquire a public reputation. My avoidance of the slave trade had already branded me a little eccentric in the eyes of some of my business associates. But we did well enough: exporting woollen textiles and iron goods, and importing more exciting wares, such as tea, spices, silks, printed cottons and porcelain.

We did not spend a lot of subjective time there to begin with. Jacqueline came to see some of the sights, but after the initial novelty was almost as disillusioned by eighteenth century London as by its twenty-first century incarnation. I guess she was not a city girl at heart. I promised to take her to some choice locations in Europe later, where there was less industry and more culture. But Charles and Priya loved the place. Charles in particular began to acquire a rather extravagant wardrobe, along with a number of choice colloquial expressions. He was even adopted by a couple of unlikely friends, who effortlessly sized him up as a rich new greenhorn-about-town. In no time at all he ran up some eye-watering gambling debts, and announced ambitions to procure a Phaeton and a 'bang-up' pair of horses to get about with. This extravagant item was a tall, spidery two-person carriage with giant yellow wheels; powered by two exquisitely powerful steeds which looked as dangerous as they were expensive.

'They are not named *Phaeton* without reason, Charles,' said Jacqueline crossly, as we sat in Sophia & Kaltrina's kitchen. 'Phaeton was the son of Helios, and he nearly set the earth on fire while attempting to drive the chariot of the sun.'

I tried a less learned approach. 'No,' I said.

'But dash it all, Richard,' he pleaded, 'everyone drives things around there. This would just be a bit…err, quicker. You know: if I see a bad guy, I can get away… or maybe catch him!'

'We're supposed to be working under cover, not driving great bright yellow things all over the place,' I said in exasperation, 'especially expensive ones that are as big a risk to you as to everyone else. These nitwit friends of yours are doing you no good at all.'

'I'm blending in!' protested Charles hotly.

'We're not staying in London,' I said in a more conciliatory tone. 'We can learn to ride horses and drive carriages when we find somewhere to live in the country.'

Charles looked rather deflated. He glanced self-consciously around and leaned towards Jacqueline and me. 'The thing is,' he hissed, 'there's another reason why I'm learning to be fashionable.'

'I see,' I said a touch acerbically, 'and this has to be whispered about because…?'

'Shhh!' he hissed again, with greater emphasis and even less volume. 'The thing is, I was thinking of asking Kaltrina out – you know, on a date. I can't do it here in case of surveillance cameras – so I thought I should do it there – in the eighteenth century. So I wanted to be able to, you know, do stuff.'

'It's nice that you wish to entertain her in style,' said Jacqueline diplomatically, 'but I'm sure ordinary eighteenth century life will be interesting enough for her as it is. I think that she likes you and will be happy to spend time in your company.'

'Really?' said Charles, forgetting to be quiet.

'Yes,' said Jacqueline. 'She finds it very significant that you appeared in her dream, and is unaccountably impressed with your credentials as original companion and agent of the master magician amongst us. Besides,' she smiled, 'I think she suits you very well.'

'Really?' said Charles again.

'Actually,' I said, 'you two were getting on very well on the other timeline. You were the life and soul of the party in Albania, toasting each other and everyone else with great abandon.'

'I was? We were?' gulped Charles, eyes wide.

'I tell you what,' said Jacqueline, 'perhaps the four of us could go out for the evening. I can find something for her to wear.'

Charles plucked up his courage and Kaltrina accepted, aided by a certain amount of micro-management in the ladies department. We decided on a visit to the opera at the original King's Theatre in the Haymarket, just before it burnt down. All went well there. It was a spectacular setting; the performance was skilful and passionate, and much additional entertainment was provided by the audience. Their clothing spanned the entire spectrum of the magnificent to the bizarre, and their behaviour was outrageous. Jacqueline was amused, horrified, and lost in admiration in equal measure, and Charles and Kaltrina exchanged happy and appreciative glances.

But unlike me, Charles loved playing the role of a man of means in Georgian England. I always felt a clumsy imposter, happy if I could get by without razing suspicion. And unfortunately, when we visited a tavern of quality afterwards, he could not resist showing off the worldly knowledge he had gained from his dubious London acquaintances.

He sampled an endless variety of dishes and alcoholic beverages, and sneezed violently and often over a great deal of inexpertly extracted snuff from a rather posh snuffbox. His conversation grew increasingly loud and jocular, and started to range beyond the fulsome praise he bestowed on every dish, drink and inhalation. To my horror, he even began to confide to one of his neighbours that there was more to this world than met the eye. Finally a badly misjudged administration of snuff and a spectacular nasal explosion deposited the entire contents of his snuffbox over everyone within six feet, including the bemused Kaltrina. Jacqueline and I had to practically frogmarch him out to a Hackney Cab.

I did not hide my anger next morning.

'No more showing off, Charles!' I scowled, as his woe-begotten features peered over his bedclothes in painful confusion.

'I'm sorry,' he moaned. 'I forgot that alcohol is, you know, alcoholic.'

'That is not an excuse, Charles,' I said severely. 'It doesn't even make sense.'

'Jasper and Rollo knocked back any number of glasses without getting squiffy,' he said indignantly, 'I didn't realise…'

'Well you had better realise,' I said crossly. 'You were about to enlighten everyone about time travel, and what poor Kaltrina made of it all I hate to imagine.'

Charles looked even paler, if that was possible, and sank back beneath his covers with a groan. 'I won't do it again,' he announced contritely after a while. 'Dashed good thing you were there to stop me!'

'I couldn't stop you,' I pointed out. 'I don't know what I would have done if your atomic sneeze hadn't ended your grand performance.'

'I've gone right off snuff,' he announced after a thoughtful moment.

Kaltrina did not seem totally put off by Charles behaviour, but I got the impression she was a little confused about certain aspects of his personality. I had a conversation with Sophia about it, and she counselled patience.

'Kaltrina is a good girl,' she said. 'I explained that he was nervous, and not used to alcohol. If he behaves like a sensible man, after some time I think he can ask her again.'

After about three weeks of subjective time, we were ready for the next stage of our plan. Billy, Charles and I swayed, jolted and rattled along in the battered Hackney carriage we had hired for the principal work of the day. We were transporting several small crates of silver ingots to the offices of *Messrs Attwood, Spooner and Coales,* at fifty-six Lombard Street in central London. Billy was perched up front outside, managing a disgruntled brace of horses, while Charles and I lurked in the shaded interior with the treasure. We peered out over the shabby half-doors as the grimy streets passed by. The faded crests on the door panels reflected the vehicle's respectable private past. Now it eked out its final days as a cab for hire: rented on this occasion with a hefty deposit minus its cabby, for it was privacy rather than economy that served our purpose.

Billy, Charles and I were on the final 'treasure run' to one of our bankers. All three of us were armed: local flintlock hand guns for show, and Colt Semi-Automatic pistols in case we got into serious trouble. I had gone for a simple and reliable weapon whose misappropriation would create little stir; and overflowing American armouries in world war two Britain had fitted the bill perfectly. They were standard officers' issue: only .32 calibre, easily concealed, and with a smooth design that helped prevent it snagging on clothing. The recoil was relatively mild too, which was useful if the ladies needed to use them. They looked almost effeminate compared to Billy's canon, and he regarded them with some distain. But he kept one on his person at all times. Charles and I were only supposed to carry ours on specific missions at that point, a restriction maintained mostly for his sake. We were all a little nervous about him being around guns, and I thought he'd be less put out if both he and I were officially unarmed. Priya was not keen on guns, and also did without. But Jacqueline wanted one, and kept it hidden in a reticule she bought in eighteenth century London.

Now Charles quivered with excitement at the thought of the veritable arsenal under his coat. He glanced sternly about in search of highwaymen, ancient or modern, and kept surreptitiously checking that his weapons were still there. Fifty six Lombard Street displayed a plaque on the wall with the names *Attwood, Spooner and Coales*. But an outdated sign hung out over the entrance which bore the legend *The Black Spread Eagle,* and a dark, indistinct representation of the creature glowered in its centre. Many London premises, for some reason, continued to be known under their original identity, irrespective of new trades, tenants or owners.

Esdaile Mathias Attwood was one of the few working men I came across in this era who still wore a wig, and a powdered one at that. He was beyond middle age, and I assumed it was because his own hair had departed, as there were few other pretensions about his dress and manner. I quite liked him in fact, and found his shrewd common sense reassuring. He obviously had someone looking out for our arrival because he appeared almost as soon as we did, and had a couple of his own men watching the street in addition to the clerks who unloaded our silver.

'Thankee Mr Watson,' Esdaile said, as I sat down in his office with him once the ingots had been weighed, 'another three hundredweight of silver – and the quality no doubt as fine as before.'

Billy and Charles sat out in the Hackney carriage, filling the role of ordinary henchmen. Charles and I took it in turns to play the front man with our various men of business, and under various names. I had tried to persuade Billy to do so too, but he still lacked the confidence.

'Your funds stand in excess of thirty thousand pounds,' continued Mr Attwood with great satisfaction, 'and another shipment is due next month, the Lord be willing.'

'I must thank you for your diligence and advice in my affairs,' I said. 'This silver bullion concludes my dealings in the Americas, and I am very content with my present financial position and your good offices here in the capital. However, I now wish to diversify some of my business interests, and move some of the principal funds.'

Unease clouded his features. 'May I enquire as to the nature of the proposed investments sir, and the likely capital required?' he asked, trying to mask his concern.

'I am not yet certain,' I replied vaguely. 'I am interested in some of the new inventions in the wool trade, and I have a fancy to invest in a hotel. I also deserve a holiday, and I wish to consider such opportunities at my leisure.'

'May I not be of service in these matters?' he inquired anxiously.

I smiled at him in a way that did not invite further discussion. 'I am a great believer in not keeping my eggs in one basket Mr Attwood,' I said. 'However, I fully intend to leave at least one third of the principal with you, and I am happy to authorise you to invest up to fifty percent of that principal at your discretion in my absence. You may contact me through my house in Compton Street of course, but I may be away for long periods.'

Swift calculations went on behind his eyes, until he finally smiled in resignation.

'Very well, good sir,' he said, with a determined return to affability.

'I will require a bill of exchange, most likely more than one,' I warned.

'A promissory note, of course,' he agreed. 'Just name the place sir, and I am sure I have a suitable colleague who will be able to accommodate you.'

'Up north will suit me very well,' I said, 'perhaps York or Leeds – perhaps even Liverpool.'

'Why bless you, I can manage any or all of them,' he said more happily. 'Would it be credit to your good self, or in coin to the bearer?'

'Now you mention it, all three would do fine,' I said cheerfully. 'Ten thousand in credit in my name to your colleague in Liverpool, and two bills to the bearer for five thousand each in York and Leeds.'

His eyebrows lifted slightly, but he nodded. 'Very well, I will have the documents drawn up by tomorrow.'

I would have preferred to have the whole lot available in anonymous cash, but didn't want to appear any more suspicious or unorthodox than necessary. We were enacting the same scenario with other bankers in the city, using fictitious names and aiming to diffuse our wealth through a network of bankers and trading enterprises around the country. We didn't want to chance anyone becoming interested in the origins of our bullion and tracking us down. We continued to shift money from account to account, changing from credit to cash and fictitious identity to fictitious identity, until we arrived at three main accounts in Northern towns, belonging to Billy, Charles and I, under the names of Messrs Robert Lee, Charles Prince and Herbert Wells respectively. Opening separate accounts for the ladies was too complicated, both socially and legally, and Jacqueline would soon become Mrs Wells in any case.

All of these things were engineered at a frenzied pace from Sophia & Kaltrina's house. They were happy to help of course, and happy to take custody of bags full of banknotes, which we withdrew (with excessive counter surveillance precautions) from our modern-day bank accounts. But the house was crowded, and the constant planning of strategies, the opening and closing of space-time doors, and the changing in and out of period costumes and various disguises – not to mention the twins whining discontent – was both intense and chaotic.

Jacqueline and I barely had time to think of our marriage. It was only after these three hectic weeks, as our relocation plans began to come towards fruition, that we started to talk of it again.

'We can look for somewhere to live now,' I said to her one evening, 'and it will be much simpler to arrange a marriage in the eighteenth century.'

She smiled a little sadly. 'I suppose I must accept a wedding under an assumed name, or some wretched person will find us from the future. I know it is foolish, but somehow it does not seem the same.'

'Don't give up yet,' I said, 'I have some ideas. We may be able to find a way to be married under our own names without it going into historical records.'

I had been researching the matter, and there were all sorts of irregularities that went on with English marriages in the eighteenth century.

'I've been thinking,' said Priya, who had been listening, 'if we really want privacy, it would be better to look for a bigger place with some private grounds: a small manor house or something. The more land you owned, the more control you had over what went on around you. And you could be as eccentric as you liked.'

'Can we not just buy a farm?' asked Jacqueline.

'Not easily,' mused Priya. 'Everything was pretty much owned by the aristocracy and the landed gentry in the eighteenth century. The aristocracy still owns a lot of land even now. Some landowners farmed land on their estates, some land was kept for pleasure – riding and hunting, and a lot was divided into small farms and rented out to tenant farmers.'

'I think it quite disgraceful,' exclaimed Jacqueline, 'it is legalised banditry: the country stolen from the people at the point of a sword!'

'Well, America was stolen from the Indians at the point of a gun,' I said mildly, 'and now a different kind of Aristocracy is stealing America from itself at the point of a cheque book.'

'What about us?' she sniffed. 'We have stolen all that money from the ship.'

'Not really,' I countered, 'we saved it from being lost – or from pirates stealing it.'

'Guys,' said Priya diplomatically, 'we are trying to make some plans here.'

'I am not any sort of guy,' said Jacqueline starchily.

'Very well,' I said. 'Temporarily disregarding the rights and wrongs of treasure hunting, land ownership and gender neutral nouns – how do we actually go about finding somewhere to live?'

'The times are changing in our target era,' said Priya encouragingly. 'Businessmen are starting to make a lot of money, and some of the landed gentry are beginning to fall into debt. A few of them are selling off parcels of land. It's not completely straightforward. Most estates were entailed, and the landlord only a tenant for life, strictly speaking. I think they had to petition Parliament to release the land for sale. But it was not uncommon. All we need is a few acres with a house on it, perhaps one we can build onto. We will not be the only successful businessmen looking for something like that.'

I smiled at Jacqueline. 'There you are then! No problem.'

Charles made elaborate plans for 'operation discrete enquiry.' It was going to be carried out without computer searches of the past, and we set out to look for properties for sale the hard way. We started searching for locations off the main travel routes, around a hundred miles or so from London; beginning around Leicester, and moving up north-west towards the Peak District. It was little different to our banking operation. We went in pairs, swapping between Billy, Charles and myself, checking out local newspapers and making tentative enquiries at lawyers and banking establishments. But little came of it over a number of visits. I was beginning to feel like a permanent performer in a variety show, crammed up backstage with costumes, directions and too many people; when Charles came to the rescue by breaking one of his own rules about interacting with locals.

I had opened a door to pick him and Billy up outside Derby. They had been dropped on the opposite side of town that morning. Charles had been full of plans to hire a gig and practice driving it – with Billy's tutelage – to check out the small town of Ashbourne as well, some thirteen miles distant. My first inkling that something was wrong was a low moaning noise. I felt a jolt of alarm, but it seemed a little high-pitched to be Charles or Billy. Then I heard Billy's tones, soft and reassuring, and stepped through to see what was going on. It was growing dark, and I could not see much at first. Two figures were crouched on the ground, and I had a strong suspicion one of them wasn't Charles.

'Richard,' came Billy's voice, 'we got ourselves a bit of a problem here.'

My heart faltered a little. 'Who is that?' I asked. 'Where's Charles?'

The moaning figure gave a sudden start: 'mercy, t'is a spirit,' it gasped, unmistakably feminine.

'T'is no spirit,' said Billy calmly. 'Don't fret ma'am. He is a friend.'

'What is that ghostly light?' she cried in a trembling voice.

The light from Sophia & Kaltrina's sitting room silhouetted me in a subdued yellow-pink glow. I could easily imagine how eerie it would look in the growing dusk. 'You have nothing to fear,' I said. 'What has happened? Where is Charles?'

'He is returning the gig,' said Billy, 'should be back anytime now. We came across this here young lady on the road to Ashbourne. Her leg has taken a nasty old knock. We took her to a sawbones in the town but –'

'No,' moaned the girl in panic, 'he'll take me leg off!'

'Sorry ma'am, I wasn't thinking.' Billy said contritely. 'We took her to a Physician, and he didn't think her, ah, prospects were too good. Charles says we gotta get her some proper treatment.'

The girl began to groan again, her voice breaking in a way that told me she was near the end of her strength, physical and mental.

'OK,' I decided, 'we'll do that, and try and sort things out afterwards.'

'Hi there!' floated Charles' voice from some way down the rut-strewn track. 'Sorry Richard, I couldn't leave her like that.'

'Now then ma'am,' said Billy firmly, 'I'm gonna lift you up and carry you though this here doorway. It will feel mighty strange, but it won't hurt you. Don't you worry now: we'll get your leg fixed up all right.'

She whimpered, probably too far gone to care; and then uttered a sudden gasp as they crossed the dimensional membrane. Charles arrived, scooped up something from the gloom, and followed me through after her.

We emerged into a typical scenario: Jacqueline and Sophia chatting casually on the sofa, and Priya trying to intervene in a squabble between the twins over the TV. They all stopped and stared at Billy, and at the girl in his arms. It was really my first sight of her too. Her dress was bulky, though ragged and extremely scruffy, and her chestnut hair pulled back in an untidy bun. She had a pleasant, homely face but it was hot and feverish, and her eyes were wild and uncomprehending. She gaped at the ceiling light's rosy glow in plain bewilderment, and her eyes darted around the room seeking constancy and meaning. Then she gave a little cry as her gaze fixed on Jacqueline.

'I knew you was a fairie!' she whispered, and fainted dead away.

Chapter 30

THERE WAS SILENCE for a moment, and then everyone began talking at once.

'Who is she?' asked Jacqueline in astonishment.

'Someone from the eighteenth century,' I said.

'Her name is Henrietta,' said Charles. 'This is her bag.' He put down a pitifully small, battered suitcase.

'She's hurt,' said Billy, carefully lowering her to the floor, and pushing a cushion beneath her head. He lifted the hem of her dress a little to reveal a hideous crater on one side of her leg, not far above the ankle. Easily five inches across, it enclosed rugged pits oozing with puss, and was encircled by an angry wash of dark red, swollen skin.

Everyone sucked in a horrified breath.

'Oh my,' said Jacqueline.

'The sawbones said she'd have the leg off,' explained Billy.

'We'll have to get her to a hospital,' said Priya.

'And someone will have to go with her,' I said with a heavy sigh. 'It's not what we want at the moment.'

'I can go,' suggested Sofia. 'I can pretend to speak little English. Give little information.'

'It's what the girl might say that we need to worry about most,' I said uneasily. 'She already seems out of her mind. They could lock her up.'

'Well, you can just rescue her then,' said Charles, 'you know, zoom in and out once she's treated.'

'We're not supposed to be attracting attention to ourselves.' I reminded him.

'Let's take her into the bedroom,' said Jacqueline briskly, 'we need to get her into some different clothes.'

Billy and I carried her, and she was just beginning to come around as we laid her onto the bed. I heard her confused alarm, and soothing words from Sophia and Jacqueline as we closed the door.

'How will we get her to the hospital?' asked Priya.

I laughed bitterly. 'I don't know. A car will frighten her just as much as a doorway.'

'Perhaps a car will show her that this word is solid and real,' she said. 'She probably thinks she is in some kind of dream-world at the moment.'

'She would not necessarily be wrong,' I chuckled sourly, 'I don't know how real this world is either.'

'Maybe,' said Priya, crisply, 'but we must proceed within its illusory parameters. I suggest we drive the girl some distance, and then call a taxi. That way no one can trace us back here from the hospital should anything happen. And if our nasty friends happen to be using face recognition software, there is no reason to suppose that they know Sophia. There will be nothing for the hospital surveillance system to flag up.'

'I hope she will be all right,' said Charles. 'The poor thing is in terrible pain. She was just sitting beside the road, miles from anywhere.'

'Where was she going?' I asked.

'Dismissed from her place of work by her account,' said Billy: 'walked more than twenty miles on that leg.'

The sound of voices came from the bedroom across the hall. The door opened, and Jacqueline reappeared.

'Is everything all right?' I asked.

'Yes, we have put her in into some new clothes, and she seems a little calmer.'

I saw she was frowning. 'So why don't you look happy?'

'Richard, you remember that odd thing she said to me?' she asked.

I thought back: 'something about a fairy?'

She nodded. 'She thought I was someone else – someone who looked like me.'

A creeping sensation worked its way up through my body, creating little whorls of sensation all the way into my scalp.

'You mean...'

'Yes,' she said, 'it sounds like the same girl again. Dressed like a man apparently: wearing trousers.'

'Really!' I said eagerly, 'what did she...'

'I don't think we can question her now,' she interjected quickly. 'She needs medical treatment as soon as possible. But at least we know that she is not completely out of her mind.'

'Wow!' said Charles. 'So it must have been meant to happen – I mean, we did the right thing bringing her back.'

'It certainly seems so,' I agreed, 'but we must get her fixed up first.'

Billy and I carried her back into the lounge. Her appearance was transformed by a long colourful modern skirt and a light, loose jumper, but she still stared tremulously about at her novel surroundings.

'I told you these people would help,' Billy said to her earnestly. 'Same thing happened to me. They plucked me out of a nasty old war, and I've bin right as rain ever since!'

'You never got back home?' she quavered. 'We are in this fairie place forever?'

'Why bless you, this ain't no fairie place,' he chuckled. 'T'is the same old world in the future, is all.'

'T'is so a fairie place,' declared Aurelia.

'But there ain't no fairies,' explained Nathaniel, pointing to the TV: 'only fairie pictures.'

The girl looked terrified.

'No this jolly well is not a fairie place,' said Charles crossly, 'and of course you can go back home. I tell you what, as soon as your leg is better, I'll give you your back pay to go home with as well.'

He rummaged about in his pocket, and produced a handful of golden guineas. Her eyes bulged: her psychological outlook magically transformed.

'Truly sir?' she gasped.

'Yes truly,' said Charles. 'Just go along with Mistress Sophia to the hospital and let the doctors fix your keg up. Then I will give you five guineas.'

'Oh thank you sir, thank you,' she said breathlessly, her bright, feverish eyes now searching eagerly for someone to get her on her way.

'You go with them, I'm still in my costume,' said Charles, 'I'll call the cab on the pay-as-you-go. Where do you want to get picked up?'

Sophia told him, and Billy lifted the girl. I followed the three of them to the front door, which opened at that moment, and Kaltrina walked in.

'Just a time traveller passing through,' I announced to her elevated eyebrows, and we made our way out to Sophia's car.

We pulled the front seat well back, and sat our patient carefully into it with her leg stretched out before her. Twenty-first century streets left her speechless.

'Well, here we are,' said Billy cheerfully, 'just the good old world in the future. Lots of fantastical machines, but people ain't changed much: leastways, they have, but...'

'Billy,' I said carefully, 'the poor girl is hurt and she has much bigger changes to get used to than you did. What did I say to you when we landed in Port Royal?'

He thought for a bit. 'Just take it one thing at a time.'

'That's right,' I agreed, and gave our terrified temporal visitor a reassuring squeeze on the shoulder. 'Just take it one thing at a time Henrietta. I know this is all strange to you, but you will get used to it. Just think about getting your leg better.'

'Yes sir,' she said distractedly, writhing in discomfort.

'Now, I'm sorry to trouble you, but there is one thing I must ask you before you go.' I was determined to get at least some information from her before we parted company: 'the lady with the trousers, who looked like, err Mistress Jacqueline – where did you see her?'

She looked confused, and closed her eyes. 'Oh, me head hurts so... and me leg is burning.'

I felt bad pushing her, but I was desperate to know. I repeated the question. She stared uncomprehendingly at me, and I thought she was going to pass out.

'The fairie?' she muttered finally, 'why at Abbeydale Hall,' and her eyes rolled up into her head again.

We only waited a couple of minutes for the minicab at the rendezvous. Billy and I carried a faintly groaning Henrietta over, and placed her in the front seat, and Sophia got into the back.

'This girl has an injured leg,' I told the driver. 'Here's an extra fifty quid if you will help her into a wheelchair at the hospital. The young lady in the back will look after her from there.'

I looked in at Sophia. 'Thank you so much,' I said. 'Please let us know how things are going.'

'Yes of course,' she smiled, 'don't worry.' And they were off into the night.

'Sure seems a long time since we turned up in Port Royal,' mused Billy, as I drove Sophia's car back to the house.

'Yes,' I grunted absently. 'Do you know where this Abbeydale Hall is?'

'Is where she worked,' he said, 'somewhere out beyond Ashbourne I believe. Imagine walking all day on that leg of hers. I sure hope they can fix it. She'd likely have lost it in my day.'

'How was she injured, do you know?' I asked.

'Kicked by a cow, by all accounts,' he said.

'And what was all that about back pay?'

'She weren't paid for a year, and then dismissed,' he said gloomily, 'that was another reason we felt sorry for her.'

'I want to see this Abbeydale Hall,' I said. 'We can start looking straight away.'

'Best wait 'til the girl's back,' suggested Billy, 'get the whole story from her. We won't know what we're walking into otherwise.'

'I'll talk to the others,' I said reluctantly.

I was outvoted, and sat about impatiently waiting to hear from Sophia, while Charles, Billy and Jacqueline discussed the situation with Kaltrina.

Sophia rang after several hours. 'All is going well,' she said. 'I have given them her correct name, but a false address where some people I know used to live. I have informed them that she is rather simple minded, and told her not to say anything except yes or no. They are very busy, so hopefully no one will investigate further.'

'How is she?' I asked.

'Astonished by everything, as you might imagine,' Sophia laughed. 'They have x-rayed the leg, and the bone is not physically damaged. They've given her some morphine and broad-spectrum antibiotics. There are some kinds of bacterial tests going on too, and they are going to keep her in for tonight at least. I have showed her how to use the bathroom, which amazed her greatly. She is quite high and happy at the moment, and seems to like all the fuss being made over her. She's getting sleepy now. I'll come home as soon as she is settled in.'

Jacqueline was brooding as we went to sleep that night.

'Why does this girl keep sneaking about on the borders of our lives?' she asked. 'Surely she can make herself known to us, if her intentions are good?'

I had wondered if she was disturbed by Alex's reported appearance.

'She is hardly sneaking around our lives,' I objected. 'This is only the second sighting we know about, and neither occasion seems directly connected with us. The reason she has not contacted us is most likely to do with our timelines.'

'Harrumph,' she grumbled. 'I hope she is not someone waiting to have a relationship with you in the future.'

I sighed. 'Now you are being ridiculous.'

She pouted. 'Maybe I am. I want to get married.'

'Me too,' I grinned. 'It's first on the list when we move to the eighteenth century.'

Sophia went back to the hospital early next morning. 'Everything is fine,' she reported back. 'She is still on morphine, and sleeping or staring at the TV.'

Kaltrina went to keep her company and they spent much of the day with her. 'She just stares at the screen with her mouth open,' chuckled Sophia when they got back. 'Apart from that it looks as if her leg is starting to improve already.'

The day after that the doctor pronounced himself surprised and delighted at Henrietta's progress. I supposed her infection had no defence against modern antibiotics, and passing through the wormhole had probably played a part too. They released her the following morning, and she was walking almost normally when Sophia brought her home.

She had changed more than just physically. She was less timid and confused, and seemed genuinely pleased to see us.

'I cannot thank you enough sir,' she said to me shyly. 'I have seen such wonders, and I can hardly believe how they have healed my leg.'

'I am very happy to see you so much better,' I smiled, 'and Charles has your five guineas.'

Disconcertingly, she burst into tears. It transpired, between sobs, that she was overwhelmed at the change in her fortunes. Her life had been a hard one, and she could hardly believe that so many miraculous things were happening to her. Slowly, with much encouragement, halts and diversions, we coaxed her story from her. Her mother, a brother and her sister had died of a fever when she was ten, after which her father had taken to drinking, and she acquired an unsympathetic stepmother. At thirteen she had been put into service at the local manor house as a live-in scullery maid, and considered herself fortunate to have worked her way up to kitchen maid by the age of eighteen.

At that point the owner of the establishment, Lord Wroxton, had died; and the title was inherited by his eldest son. The house and the estate had been neglected for a long time, but under the new lord of the manor things took a turn for the worse. Lord Wroxton was a rich man but not a wise one. He owned several estates, of which this he considered least important, being the furthest from London. He paid infrequent visits, using it as little more than a hunting lodge and a discrete venue for riotous parties for his friends. He drank, gambled and partied to excess, and cared nothing about the management of his land.

A few years down the line, and his debts had multiplied while his income dwindled. The staff at the house were first halved and then reduced further. Even the land agent was dismissed, and a local lawyer appointed to take over his duties, such as they were. Finally only three servants and a gardener remained. Henrietta was assigned general housemaid duties, under the cook maid and an aged butler. Another year passed in which they had received few funds to run the house and no wages, and his Lordship did not visit at all. Finally the lawyer had appeared to inform them that the house and estate were to be sold. He dismissed them all with a vague promise of payment after the sale.

'I couldn't stay there any more,' she was explaining, 'me leg was bad and the others were leaving, so I...'

'Good grief, the property is on the market!' I gasped. 'Why didn't you tell us Charles?'

Charles looked startled. 'I didn't know!' he exclaimed.

I stared intently at Henrietta. 'Never mind: what happened when you saw the lady – the one that looked like Miss Jacqueline?'

She had been unsettled by my outburst, and it was a few moments before she could continue. 'She – I – I came out the back; and she was standing there, just looking at the house. All dressed in black she was, with trousers like a man, and high boots.'

'Did she say anything?' I asked eagerly.

'Yes sir,' said Henrietta. 'She seemed surprised when I came out the door. Oh, Hetty,' she says, 'are they here already?'

'Hetty?'

'It's what I'm known as,' she said timidly. 'It was ever so strange. She seemed to know me, and I had never seen her before. That's why I thought she was a fairie, what with her strange clothes and all.'

'Yes, it is very strange,' I agreed, trying to contain the excitement this tiny bit of news sent buzzing through me. 'How did she look? Did she say anything else?'

'She looked sad, sir,' she said. 'I was scared. I didn't rightly know if she was human. I just begged her pardon and said I didn't know. She said she was sorry, and not to worry.'

'What...' I was surprised at the emotion which choked me, and caught a suspicious glance from Jacqueline. 'What did she do then?'

'Why, she just walked away. I hurried back indoors, and when I could bring myself to look out again she was nowhere to be seen. I wondered if it happened at all.'

'Thank you,' I said, acting casual. 'Well, that is certainly a bundle of news. We must act on it straight away. Now, where exactly is Abbeydale Hall – and what is the name and address of this Lawyer?'

The house was huge: the front elevation approaching a hundred and eighty feet across. I was uncertain which took my breath away more: its stately dimensions, or its understated elegance and beauty. It was a seventeenth-century Jacobean mansion: its rich, three storied façade awash with large, mullioned windows, protruding bays, tall, ornate chimneys, and multiple prominent dormers and gables. It glowed in dream-like serenity in the morning sun; built in ochre Horton stone – a blue-grey limestone impregnated with iron ore, which gave it a soft orange-brown hue.

Jacqueline, Priya, Charles and Billy had accompanied me through a doorway to have a look at Henrietta's Abbeydale Hall, and we all stood and stared at the vision before us.

A dark, brown-grey slate lined its rooftops. Its two great front bays aligned with an ornate, central porch, and rose through all three stories: each topped with gabled attic windows, and constructed across a serried array of lesser bays and dormer attic glazing. A grand entrance-arch enclosed substantial double doors, framed by four pilasters and an elaborate entablature. It was approached by two flights of stone steps, shallow and wide, and bordered by stone balustrading. Above the steps, the porch rose to match its mullioned windows with the multitude on every floor, its brick-facing embellished with heraldic stone reliefs and additional adornments. A tiny spire rose from the front ridgelines of the abundant rooftops, an almost ethereal touch which bestowed the entire edifice with an insubstantial air, verging on an apparition conjured from a dream. It was love at first sight.

But like love, it was also a kind of madness, and I was quite aware of it. All sorts of reasons why it would be crazy to buy the place whirled in my head.

'Oh Richard...' was all that Jacqueline said, but it spoke volumes. She was crazy too.

'Oh dear, it's gigantic,' gasped Priya.

'Wow! Fantastic!' breathed Charles.

'Dang me, a fella would get lost in that place,' said Billy in awe.

And Alex's ghostly presence asked if we were there already.

We discussed it back at Sophia & Kaltrina's house. The idea that we might purchase Abbeydale Hall propelled Henrietta into new heights of awe and astonishment. She gazed back and forth between us all as if we were gods debating the fate of the world from Mount Olympus.

'But even if we could afford to buy such a place, how could we run it?' wondered Jacqueline. 'I can barely imagine how much work it would be.'

'I have no idea what it would cost,' I admitted slowly, 'but we could probably raise the money.' I turned to Henrietta. 'How many servants were there when you began work at the house?'

'Ever so many sir,' she said. 'There was the butler, the housekeeper, the footmen, the valets, the head cook, the under cook ...'

'Oh, we wouldn't need all that!' interrupted Jacqueline. 'But we would need some help, and it would need to be discreet.' She paused: 'would you like to work in the house again, Henrietta? You could perhaps become the housekeeper, and supervise a cook and one or two maids.'

Henrietta went white. 'M – me!' she gasped, 'housekeeper?'

'I know you are young,' said Jacqueline, 'but you know how everything works in the house. You would be invaluable to us – and you can keep an eye on everyone in the house who does not know we come from another time. You could help to ensure they do not discover anything they should not.'

'Oh...' said Henrietta wonderingly. 'Would you – have such magical machines about the house?'

'No,' I cut in, 'at least, some perhaps: but they could be kept out of sight.' I warmed to the idea. 'Yes, it might work very well. Would you like to be housekeeper Henrietta?'

'Oh sir!' she cried. 'Oh yes I would!'

'What about the grounds,' asked Billy? 'Those old lawns sure were overgrown, and the house needs some fixing up I bet. I saw some window glass missing. We would need some help there too.'

'No problem,' I said, 'I'm sure we could have a few workmen around the place.'

'There must be stables as well,' said Priya, raising her eyebrows enquiringly at Henrietta, who nodded. 'I have always wanted to learn to ride.'

Priya, Billy and Jacqueline all perked up at that.

'And a vegetable garden I imagine,' Jacqueline added happily.

'I'm sure I can build my observatory on the top floor somewhere,' said Charles, 'and all of the other things will be fun too!'

'All right, so it seems to be decided,' I smiled, 'we will go and find this lawyer.'

The Lawyer turned out to be a *'Solicitor and Conveyancer'*, one *Bartholomew Prowting Evans,* with an office in Leek, a small market town some eight or nine miles from Abbeydale Hall. He was a stout, rather shifty looking character, with greasy clothes, a bulbous nose, and a lot of facial hair. I visited with Charles, and his initial, barely concealed disinterest vanished in an instant when he realised our purpose. Golden commission digits danced visibly in his mind's eye, and he bowed and scraped with much enthusiasm.

'You will be happy to know that the petition is passed by Parliament gentlemen,' he wheezed affably, 'and the conditions of the estate act are reasonable. Lord Wroxton is required to fund the construction of a new town hall here in Leek from his side, while the purchaser is to maintain the Hall in a habitable condition, undertake improvements to tenanted properties, and repair particular stretches of fencing and one damaged bridge on the Estate.'

He beamed contentedly at us. 'No doubt you would like to peruse the details?'

A large and ancient map made an appearance, and I tried to make sense of it in the light of hurried briefings from Priya. A sense of alarm began to grow as I attempted to decipher the spidery letters and lines on the faded document.

'May I enquire as to the total acreage of the land?' I asked, with an attempt at nonchalance.

'Of course sir!' exclaimed our new best friend and advisor. 'I grant the estate was never large, and sadly reduced by a sale of land under the previous Lord Wroxton. Yet still it exceeds fifteen hundred acres, which you will allow is at least respectable.'

I rigorously schooled my most deadpan expression. I had not imagined a quarter of that size. Charles' eyes too, I noticed, had adopted a fixed, glazed stare. Mr Evans seemed to take our silence as a desire for further information.

'Ah!' he said, 'you will be wanting the figures? – the annuities?'

'Oh! Err – yes,' I agreed vaguely.

He heaved in a substantial breath. 'Very well, the largest tenanted farm is three hundred acres. There is one of two hundred acres, and two more of some one hundred each. A further three hundred acres are divided into…' His voice droned on, while thoughts like *can we really do this?* and *this is insane*, circled around in my head. Events seemed to proceed of their own volition, and before I knew it we were arranging to visit Abbeydale Hall after a meal. More information bombarded us during this lavish banquet, which would have put me to sleep for the rest of the afternoon if I hadn't been so hyped up over the leap of folly we were contemplating.

A long list of apparent drawbacks to this desirable acquisition; such as deteriorated fencing, depreciated tenant housing, the crumbling bridge, land draining requirements and innumerable repairs to Abbeydale Hall itself, were explained away as trifling matters. Its highly acclaimed positive attributes, via much sleight of hand, appeared to consist mainly of the great advantages such trifling improvements would bring.

But there were prospects which did seem to offer advantage to the investment. The current annual income from the rented agricultural land alone stood at nearly a thousand pounds, which from the sound of things could be very much improved with a degree of investment and better management. There were cottages on the estate, and more respectable houses in the nearby village, which could be rented out with a little (or perhaps more than a little) refurbishment. There was even a promising mine which had been started, although discontinued for lack of capital. And there were several hundred acres of natural woodland; to ride or hunt in, or harvest for timber.

For all of Mister Evan's exhortations, the dereliction of duty by a succession of landlords was clear from the moment we arrived. We had been driven out in a hired shabby-gentile carriage, and the once-impressive stonework at the main entrance to the estate reflected our ride's poor condition. Its stonework was mossy and crumbling, and the driveway potholed and invaded by scattered weeds. Once-elegant trees and shrubbery were steadily returning to the wild, sections of fencing had fallen or were crudely patched, and the lawns had obviously been trimmed seldom and roughly, even in view of the main house.

The house looked a little shabbier too, closer up. But my heart thudded rapidly as we trod the grand entrance steps. Our guide unlocked the imposing double doors with an equally distinguished ancient key; and he heaved mightily against one great, unwieldy leaf, which yielded with a protesting creak.

It was breath-taking. We entered a wide passageway, nine or ten feet high, and festooned with beautifully patterned woodwork. To our left, half-a-dozen widely-spaced, round oak pillars, intricately carved, opened out into a great hall: perhaps twenty feet high, sixty feet long and thirty wide. Flagstones lined the floor in simple geometrical shapes, and half way along its length the left side opened out further into one of the lesser outside bays, lit by an enormous mullioned window emblazoned with heraldry in stained glass. A second window, merely large, and similarly glazed, illuminated the nearer half of the hall.

The pervading musk of wood reminded me of the living vitality of Jacqueline's farmhouse in America: but this was a different odour and carried a more ancient and elaborate potency. The oak was dense, though dusty and dry, and in need of wax and tender loving care. Yet it was extravagantly worked into a unique and exquisite beauty. Decorative wainscoting seven feet high entirely surrounded the walls of both hall and passageway, and a massive carved oak fireplace dominated the right hand side of the great hall. Three wide, heavy timber double doors hung below arched wooden lintels, and bore intricately carved reliefs. They opened out from the passageway ahead of us; from the far side of the hall, and into other rooms on our right. The upper walls and ceilings were plastered – the ceiling decoratively panelled in the great hall itself – and as we wondered into its spacious interior I looked back to see an elevated balcony above the pillared entrance passageway.

'The minstrels' gallery,' announced Mr Evans flamboyantly. 'This is the great hall where the Lord of the Manor received his tenants and guests.'

We continued to wander about the house in a bit of a dream. Spaces not immediately lighted by windows were rather dim, and I constantly wanted to turn on the lights. I had to restrain myself from reaching for switches. But it added to the venerable atmosphere. Vast hallways and wide, stately staircases meandered throughout the building, and huge rooms with lofty ceilings opened out one after another. There was a library, and even a chapel: more lavishly decorated with exquisitely worked panelling, and with more stained glass than even the great hall. Everywhere beautifully worked wainscoting lined the walls, massive, elaborately carved fireplaces flourished, and great oaken doors hung heavy with imaginative designs.

On the first floor ornamental plasterwork was more in evidence, both on the walls and ceiling: much of it painted, and some even gold leafed. Several of the fireplaces were carved granite or marble, and the decor looked less ancient. But everywhere we saw faded elegance and neglect. Three or four of the best bedrooms had been kept in a functional condition, with furnishings including grand four poster beds and serviceable curtains. But many of the rooms were half empty, with broken furniture piled in corners and cobwebs a common sight.

Leaks had come though ceilings from above, and mysterious stains were visible on walls. Window glass was cracked or missing, doors were off their hinges, and in some places floorboards were lying in heaps, in the midst of abandoned repairs. The top floor was effectively the servants' quarters, and in the worst condition of all. There was water damage in many places. Wooden tubs and leather buckets lay about to catch dripping rainwater, plaster was falling away in several rooms, and there were numerous rotten floorboards. Clearly more than a few roof tiles were broken or missing, and some of the lead linings were failing in the valley gutters between the maze of interconnecting rooftops. The place had obviously not been decorated for fifty years.

'Harrumph,' grunted our host, keen to spend as little time up there as possible. 'We must visit the basement I suppose, and the stables and the dairy. Then we must be on our way, or night will set in before we make our return.'

The rest of our inspection was soon over. Most of the basement seemed in quite a reasonable state, although it was hard to tell by candlelight. I guessed it had been used more than anywhere else of late, as the kitchen, the servants' dining room and the storerooms there had been in constant use. The out-building complex containing the stables and the dairy was in good condition too, being a more recent construction. There were coach houses, saddlery stores and servant accommodation apart from the horse boxes and hay lofts. The dairy in the rear section held milking stalls, cheese and butter-making rooms, and numerous utility areas.

The whole thing was so extensive we could probably all have lived there quite comfortably ourselves. It also boasted an adjoining paddock inhabited by a solitary, ill at ease cow: presumably Henrietta's assailant. I enquired if anyone was looking after the creature, and had to be content with a convoluted answer involving one of the tenant farmers. Beyond these buildings was getting on for an acre of snuggly walled but neglected vegetable garden, and in all of these places I could imagine Jacqueline happily employed. It was as if she had got on the right side of a benevolent Genie who had granted her every wish.

We discussed the asking price on the journey back to Leek. I got the distinct impression Lord Wroxton needed money urgently, and we politely haggled back and forth throughout the journey. The material degeneration of Abbeydale Hall looked worse than it actually was, but I made as much of it as I could. But Mr Evan stoutly upheld his brief, and only really began to give ground when I expressed a wish to inspect the tenanted properties on the estate. He was obviously not keen for me to see them, which was a little unsettling. But by now I felt the decision was made, and I made use of his unease to lower the cost of our irrational flight of fancy. In the end we reduced the price of one hundred and fifty thousand pounds by ten thousand. It still meant dipping into our treasure reserves, in addition to the capital we had invested and accumulated, but I was more than happy with the deal. Our new life had begun.

Chapter 31

ONCE OUR REFUGE was secured, the next most urgent item on the agenda was the marriage. It seemed to have been following Jacqueline and me about like some sort of persistent maiden aunt for what felt like a very long time. I was anxious to get the pesky knot tied, and lining this up with the move into our splendid new home seemed ideal.

I had spent a bit of time talking it over with Priya, and she had a number of ideas. We felt safe enough investigating historical Parish records: looking for situations which might be amenable to a degree of tweaking where the rules were concerned, or where record keeping had failed for one reason or another. And we discovered the perfect solution. A church in the town of Worcester in seventeen seventy eight had lost its year's ecclesiastical records to a fire.

'Here's another bonus,' said Priya cheerfully, looking up from her laptop. 'In the surviving records after the fire, the second bondsmen are mostly John Does and Richard Roes.'

I raised my eyebrows enquiringly.

'Blatantly fictitious names,' she explained. 'John Doe seems to have been with us for quite a long time. I don't know what happened to Richard Roe. The second bondsman was the required 'second sufficient witness' who undertook to forfeit a bond – in addition to the groom – if the couple proved legally disqualified to marry.'

'Ah,' I said vaguely.

'Anyway,' she continued briskly, 'it means the priest was not concerned or conscientious about such things. Even if he is a replacement following the fire, it suggests that the prevailing regime is lax. It is unlikely he will want to establish your residence in the parish with any certainty.'

I found rooms for hire in Friar Street, a lovely cobbled thoroughfare near Worcester Cathedral. It was a picturesque place, crowded with thatched, timber wattle-and-daub Tudor houses. The ever-present reek of sewage in the gutters was less prevalent than in London, and its inhabitants seemed more relaxed and cheerful.

The dreamlike imagery of the past fascinated me. It threw me into an oddly compelling reverie, even more so now I knew it was some kind of extraordinary illusion. There was a sense of immersion in a living artistic masterwork: a kind of magical work-in-progress finding its way towards an unknowable future transcendence. Yet I knew what the future would bring: a concrete, steel and plastic wilderness, reaping the whirlwind of its excesses.

I thought suddenly of Ravi: of how he would love the raw, organic simplicity of these humble dwellings, and the rustic folk in the street. I wondered about the whole mysterious business of being alive: of how unlikely it seemed, and how little I ever really engaged with it. Then I shivered, remembering the enigmatic barrier that mocked the grand march of mankind at the end of time. It had shone like a mirror reflecting blinding sunlight: invincible, impenetrable and signifying the futility of all ambition. Or, I wondered, was Ravi right: was it a barrier only to our own self-image, demarcating some new threshold of existence beyond the chrysalis of ego? For a moment I felt the stirrings of the timeless inner being watching my life, but it faded almost as soon as I became conscious of it. Apart from my bizarre adventures with the ghost, I had noticed a gradual disassociation from such unfathomable happenings as my control and precision with the Portal grew. I shrugged. I had more need of the Portal than of abstract perceptions of reality, however profound. There might be time for such contemplation later I reasoned, if I reasoned at all. Right then, I needed to get married.

My goal was a small church, St Swithun's, some streets away from the Cathedral. It was a lovely little place, recently rebuilt in a classicising Georgian style with some Gothic revival elements. The original Tudor tower still stood, re-faced in oolitic limestone to match the new build; and the substantial round-headed windows were spaced in a delightful simplicity of style all around the church exterior.

The Reverend A.G. Matthews was neither unconcerned nor lax. He was of slight build with a thin, sensitive face and lively, intelligent eyes. He smiled benevolently, but looked penetratingly into my own eyes before agreeing to take all the particulars for the banns to be read. His evaluation of my eligibility appeared to be of a subtle nature, and once satisfied he showed little interest in the bureaucratic process. He shook his head with a smile when I asked him if he needed a second bondsman. I liked him and felt bad, wondering if he would fall victim to the fire due to take place in less than two months. But he eased my mind by mentioning that his post was temporary. The resident vicar had died, and he was there for only a few weeks while a permanent replacement was found. He did say that he would like to meet Jacqueline before the marriage service though, and I was happy to arrange it. I felt a little sheepish giving him a false London address for her, but my local address was technically valid, and I sensed these were not his priorities.

Jacqueline loved the old town, although still offended by the primitive eighteenth century English sanitary arrangements. We attended the Sunday morning service two weeks later, with an awe-struck Henrietta posing as a personal maid and chaperone. I saw Jacqueline admiring the church, and I had to admit that its elegance and simplicity seemed the perfect setting for our marriage.

The interior was one single cell, open, light and airy, with no real division between the nave and the chancel other than side screens, supported by four Doric columns. It was lined with box pews, and all the windows contain leaded lights. A canted gallery supported by fluted wooden pillars housed the organ at the rear, and an attractive rib vaulted ceiling soared overhead, decorated with roundels, Gothic motifs and cherubic heads. Jacqueline turned to me as the marriage banns were proclaimed, and the smile she gave me as our names were read out took me right back to Alexandria. We waited outside afterwards, when our amiable vicar came over to speak to us.

'Good day Miss Johnson,' he said, bowing gravely and politely, while his twinkling eyes undertook the same assessment of her character that they had of mine.

'Good day Reverend,' replied Jacqueline, smiling frankly at him. I could see that she liked him, and he gave a little nod of approval.

'It is always a pleasure to see two good people joined in matrimony,' he said softly.

He spoke mildly but I was impressed. He seemed to glow with a simple faith in humanity.

'How happy I am that this man is to marry us Richard,' said Jacqueline afterwards. 'It is as if God has brought him here at just the right time. And it is such a lovely church. My faith in religion is quite restored.'

I smiled at her, wondering if it was a Hindu, Muslim or Christian God who had arranged a nice priest for us. But it did seem an agreeable omen, and I felt good about it myself.

'I have to admit, he seems a pretty special guy,' I said, 'and I like the church too. But there is something even better you must see while we are here.'

We finished our trip with a visit to Worcester Cathedral. Situated on a bank overlooking the River Severn, it was one of the most beautiful religious buildings in England. It represented every style of English architecture from Norman to Perpendicular Gothic, and contained a remarkable array of English medieval features in between. Its elevations were of particularly fine proportions and many of its interiors absolutely breath-taking.

Henrietta approached the sacred edifice as though it was the star-ship Enterprise. She habitually regarded only bona fide eighteenth century manifestations as authentic. Their twenty-first century counterparts she treated as temporary hallucinations: to be tolerated, marvelled at, but ultimately dismissed as insubstantial and unreal. I had to admit that the cathedral's splendour was greatly accentuated in its Georgian setting. There was nothing remotely like it in the city, and the contrast would have been even greater in earlier times.

Jacqueline was mesmerised. 'It is absolutely wonderful,' she breathed, her eyes alive with wonder and drinking in every detail.

'The only flaw,' I thought to myself, *'is that the earliest parts of this cathedral were begun about the same time as the crusades.'* I didn't say anything, because I didn't want to spoil her happy anticipation of the wedding. But I resolved to show her some pictures of the larger mosques sometime. They were just as beautiful, if not more so. We had built magnificent places of worship, and then marched off to kill other people who did the same.

Everyone except Henrietta visited Worcester for the marriage. She was going to preside over her new kingdom at Abbeydale and make sure we all got off and returned from the festivities without the staff noticing. We planned the lead up to it like a military operation. First Billy and Charles purchased a decent second-hand coach and four horses from Nottingham. It was a smart but common model, a 'U' shaped central compartment suspended from the main frame on springs, with large rear and small front wheels. Absurdly it put me in mind of Walt Disney's animated 'Robin Hood', and conjured visions of Prince John and Sir Hiss plotting dastardly deeds within it.

It seated four plus the driver, and Billy drove it from Nottingham – apart from 'giving Charles a go' – to pick up Jacqueline, Henrietta and me from a doorway just beyond Derby. We continued conspicuously on through Ashbourne, passing through the turn pikes, and pausing in Leek to collect the keys from Mr Evans, and order provisions for delivery to Abbeydale Hall. Henrietta also let it be known that there would be openings for staff, even if not on a traditional scale.

We drove up to the hall in silence, each contemplating the enormity of this next unlikely step in our lives. I felt a kind of giddy madness which made me want to shout out loud. I had no idea if we were doing the right thing, but this crazy leap into the unknown seemed entirely in the spirit of the unlikely journey through time which had usurped our lives.

We heaved the front door open, and wandered uncertainly around the cavernous interior. Only Charles and I had been inside before, other than Henrietta of course, and Jacqueline and Billy were lost for words. Room after ornate room opened out before us: a moving feast of extravagant, faded grandeur.

'Are we really gonna live here?' asked Billy finally. 'It's gonna take a week just to see it all.'

'It is perfectly ridiculous Richard,' said Jacqueline, 'and absolutely wonderful.'

'We're going to need a lot of candles,' said Charles.

'Begging your pardon sir,' said Henrietta, 'but we only have candles in the chapel. Everywhere else we use oil lamps. We will need more, but there are some that still work. All we need is wicks and oil.'

'How often was the chapel used?' I asked curiously.

'Oh, never sir,' she admitted. 'But it had to be kept ready in case visitors came to admire it.'

'Well, I would love to admire it,' said Jacqueline. 'Can you show me?'

We spent the rest of the day deciding which rooms we intended to occupy initially, and checking out the kitchen. Jacqueline took one look at the mattresses and insisted we carry them out of the house to burn. Henrietta knew of an upholsterer in Derby, and we scheduled a visit to order more at the top of our to-do list. Jacqueline was dubious about the bed linen too, although Henrietta was adamant they had been washed.

'Washed with what?' asked Jacqueline, sniffing at a sheet suspiciously.

'Well soaked in Lye, in the bucking-tub ma'am,' said Henrietta earnestly. 'I did it myself, me and Jane, the cook's maid.'

'Ugh!' grunted Jacqueline. 'We will order new bed linen at the same time– and the best quality soap.'

'Lye?' I raised my eyebrows enquiringly.

'Ashes and urine, and goodness knows what else besides,' she said.

From then on we kept a couple of people at the house at all times, in case of visitors. We took it in turns to go back through a doorway to Sophia & Kaltrina's place, for creature comforts, and miscellaneous items we discovered a need for, taking care to remove out-of-time objects after use. A sense of normality grew as the days passed. Stores of provisions grew. Mattresses and new bedding arrived. The horses were accommodated in the stables instead of let loose with the cow in the paddock. Priya and the twins were picked up and given a public airing on their journey through Ashbourne and Leek to the Hall too.

We accumulated a scattering of staff. The cook's maid, Jane, reappeared. She had heard that new owners were in residence; and was approved by Henrietta. Astonished by the unconventional ways of the new merchant class, Jane found herself promoted to cook, with her wage increased threefold, up to little below that of her unaccountably well-established friend. We acquired a house maid and a gardener too. The maid helped with general cleaning duties in the house, and Jacqueline set the gardener to work scything the overgrown lawns. A stable man came next, who looked after the horses and doubled as a coachman sometimes. He helped out as a general handyman on occasion as well.

All of these arrangements were in place as the wedding loomed. Sophia & Kaltrina were coming too, and we organised suitable garments for everyone through a relatively anonymous dressmaker near our London house in eighteen century Compton Street. It was twenty years into the future from our designated wedding day, but we explained the less than fashionable styles we wanted as a gesture to eccentrically old fashioned parents. We all entered my hired rooms in Worcester through a doorway, and a trio of hired carriages conveyed us to the church in style: our outfits preserved from the perils of the street. I had become so involved in orchestrating everything that it was not until we actually arrived at the Church door that the impact really hit me: that I fully realised the moment had arrived.

Matrimonial white was not yet a thing, and Jacqueline had chosen an ivory silk hooped dress and an elaborate petticoat. The front-parted, vertical edges of the dress and the hem of the exposed petticoat were adorned with a broad, embroidered pink and gold band, embellished with ribbon and a stencilled fringe. The sleeves ended at the forearms in generously gathered ruffled lace, the neckline was square cut, and her shoulders and bosom decorated with fine lace gauze and ruffled lace trims. Hair was increasingly worn au naturel at this time, but we both wore wigs as it was a formal occasion. Her outfit was completed by high heeled silk brocade shoes and a magnificent, carefully pinned wide hat. She looked amazing.

I felt myself a far less exotic creature, dressed in a long cutaway tailored coat over a waist-length satin waistcoat and dark breeches. I wore an uncomfortable cotton stock around my neck, and my silk stockings stood in rather plain, flat, buckled shoes. But my shirt and sleeves were enriched with fine lace ruffles, and my waistcoat with gold trim.

Charles was a little morose because his much-loved, highly extravagant cravats would not be in fashion for another ten years, and he had to tone down his waistcoat too. He had contented himself with an ostentatious gold watch, chain and seal, and enormous (fake) bejewelled shoe buckles. Priya, Sophia & Kaltrina were hugely enjoying their long fancy dresses, but the twins found their formal clothes irksome after becoming used to casual future wear. Billy's emulation of an English gentleman was in a class of its own. He looked quite ludicrous in a wig; a condition greatly amplified by his entirely self-conscious expression, while his rigid body-language put me in mind of an unenthusiastic robot attempting to imitate a human being.

The simple wedding ceremony seemed just as surreal to me as other, more outlandish adventures in space-time. Partly it was awed disbelief at my formal acceptance by the luminous woman at my side, but it was also the incongruous vision of our small, improbable band and the unlikely optimism in our hearts. Our hopeful quest seemed laughably naïve, and our future impossible to imagine. Yet it did feel auspicious to mark the occasion, and it was nice to share it with our friends in so memorable a fashion.

I thought back to the aimless manner in which I had fallen into sharing life with Mellissa. There had been nothing to seal our alliance: no real recognition of trust and commitment. It had been more of a casual convenience, a sensual diversion without purpose or direction in a rather mundane and meaningless world. Now I felt something very different flowing between Jacqueline and myself. Our marriage represented a vital sense of purpose and destiny, and I could not imagine treading the road ahead without her.

I had offered Jacqueline a honeymoon in pretty much anyplace she chose. But she was adamant that she wanted to start her new life at home.

'I have had enough of adventures for now,' she said, 'Abbeydale Hall is exciting enough for me: there are a thousand things I can see and do there if I wish.' Then she smiled in a way that triggered a sudden fluttering in my heart. 'Besides, I thought a successful honeymoon did not depend on the scenery.'

The idea of dispensing with the usual couple of weeks away somewhere special seemed a little weird, but I had been content to go along with it. We decided to splash out after the ceremony though. We booked a private room at the Talbot Inn in Worcester, a popular hotel and dining institution on the edge of the Cathedral Plaza, close to our hired accommodation in Friar Street. It was a brick and timber structure with sash windows: apparently adapted from three individual houses, and looked better inside than out. The ceilings were loaded with wooden beams, and three separate eating and drinking parlours took up much of the ground floor. A seemingly endless array of serving staff delivered an astonishing banquet of food and drink. The idea of healthy, disciplined consumption was safely off in the future, and I had instructed them to spare no expense.

We ate and drank solidly for two hours without making much of a dent in the feast. Everyone was in high good humour. The twins sampled everything in reach, including illicit sips of alcohol when Priya and Jacqueline weren't looking. Jacqueline seemed high and slightly flushed. She was drinking more than her usual modest portion, and bestowed emboldened tipsy smiles and occasional uncertain, glances on me. She was a little nervous about what was due to happen after the partying was over I guessed.

I had not wanted to compromise my control over the Portal with alcohol when we were displaced in time like this. I had expected to feel I was missing out a bit as the designated driver, but I felt quite untroubled by not drinking and driving at our cosy wedding reception. I was enjoying a deep sense of satisfaction at establishing our marriage at last, and in acquiring a beautiful new home for us all. An inner contentment and serenity crept over me, and the image of happy, laughing faces began to take on a timeless, storybook quality.

Then I saw other people at other times, in other parts of the Inn, and dramas large and small. I knew their names, their hopes and fears. One particular event shone brightly, and I signalled a waiter.

'Did King Charles stay in this inn during the Battle of Worcester?' I asked absently.

'Why yes sir, so we are told,' he answered.

'So, I can access the archive again,' I thought, watching the building's original construction take place with detached interest. But just as I was getting used to the idea, the past receded, and my perception edged towards the future. Repairs and changes materialised in the building as it made its way into the modern world. Yet as cars began to appear I lost traction with this too, and my visions of past and future events retreated into more peripheral aspects of my awareness. I settled into a timeless, perfect perception of the present moment, effortlessly sustained by a mysterious fountainhead of startling potency. There was a subtle quality of vision, a sort of lucidity or transparency about everything, and a fine, solar wind seemed to flow through the room, as though a door was open to eternity.

Once again space-time looked like a dreamlike fairly-tale; but now it seemed self-aware: permeated by an underlying foundation of more essential consciousness. Everyday life took on the appearance of a subtle veil masking a more fundamental ocean of existence. I felt the awakening quicken deep within myself. A vast hybrid being was emerging – seeing without eyes, feeling without form: a cosmic pupa part-emerged from a chrysalis of matter into a realm of light and power. Power flowed without thought or conscious intent, illuminating inner depths of astonishing archetypical beauty and royal pharaonic splendour.

I drank in the energy in the room. Our little band looked like a happy gathering of cosmic caterpillars: humanoid carapaces spilling glimpses of luminescent beauty through the whimsical caricatures of our human personalities. Jacqueline, Sophia, Kaltrina and Charles picked up on it first, presumably because they had shared a similar experience with me not long before.

'Magic!' cried Kaltrina suddenly, looking about in excitement.

'Some kind of high-energy event is taking place,' I agreed, as everyone started to peer curiously around themselves. The hair all over my body stood on end, and I felt amazing. 'But I don't think there's anything to worry about.'

Any resistance to the phenomenon washed away in an instant. It was like the sun coming out: one big personality filled the room and ignited a sense of egolessness in each of us. Self-consciousness was impossible, and a fantastically otherworldly scene proceeded: each personality part of something greater, and sparkling with new depth and magnificence. The twins spoke with stately wisdom. Charles was relaxed and dignified. Kaltrina grinned with supreme contentment. Sophia and Priya stared in open wonder, and Billy gazed about himself like a child at a fairground. Everyone seemed full of light, and brightest of all to my eyes was Jacqueline. She looked incandescently beautiful, and a gentle, radiant energy flowed between her heart and mine.

'I love you,' I said, unable to keep the wonder from my voice.

'I certainly hope so,' she laughed, and her image glowed brighter still.

I laughed with her. I was euphoric. Everyone smiled at each other. It was fantastic, and we existed in a state of profound contentment. I felt infinitely more myself, confident and complete, and a vast, burgeoning potential sought to blossom. But my human shell constrained me: unready to unhook itself from a thousand thorns and affections. I remained tied to the material world and lacked the power to break free, but was ecstatic at even this small glimpse of transcendence. Our collective nirvana continued, taken for granted until the moment came to open a doorway back to Sophia & Kaltrina's place from my hired rooms. We were all laughing and joking: inter-dimensional partygoers on a larger than life excursion through time. Then I reached for the Portal and it was not there. I froze, and tried again. I was suddenly disorientated; my elevated state destabilising into a confused scrabbling for my hi-tec nemesis.

'Is something wrong?' asked Jacqueline.

'Err, no, I don't think so,' I said. 'Give me a minute.'

The others quietened and began to look uncertain, and our collective high diminished.

I struggled to remember the application and concentration of focus I needed. Dimly I sensed the device. It seemed tiny, complicated, constricting: like trying to clamber back into an old skin I had shed. I grasped it, and felt myself adjusting to its constraints like a pilot strapping into a fighter-jet. There was relief as the doorway flared into existence – but an answering shadow of loss and regret. I had no choice, of course. The Portal seemed incompatible with the extraordinary state we had been enjoying, but our immediate needs were clear. We needed it, and other mysterious states of being had to be relegated to the mountain of mystery we faced, for future contemplation.

We dropped Sophia & Kaltrina off, stayed for a while, and then I opened doorways via a diversionary route back to an empty, locked room on the first floor at Abbeydale. It was only a few hours after we had departed, and Henrietta had been warned to keep everyone else downstairs. We were able to sort ourselves out without difficulty: change into more casual clothes, and make our way down to the library. It was our current leisure room, and Charles and Billy seemed inclined to continue the celebration.

It was evening and the light was beginning to go. I didn't think Jacqueline wanted to continue partying, and I couldn't see her rushing into the bedroom and tearing her clothes off either. So I suggested we went outside for a walk. The sky was beautiful, a great wash of colour. Vast swathes of deep mauve-blues marched above us. It was illuminated in the west in bright orange-reds and gleaming golds by the setting sun, and darkened to a profound blue-black in the east, where a rising moon and a smattering of stars glowed like quicksilver.

The rich fragrance of the countryside seemed potent with presence, and I looked curiously about me. Myriad shining specks were dancing everywhere: a shimmering tapestry of tiny cells. I could not make them out precisely, and the more I stared the harder they became to identify. Yet if I relaxed my gaze a subtle platinum haze swarmed and multiplied. They reminded me of pixels on a TV screen: a projection of energy weaving the image of reality. Everything was vibrating. I could feel it deep in my being: not a superficial image, but the surface of an infinite ocean of possibilities.

'What is the matter Richard?' asked Jacqueline. She always knew when something was bothering me.

'Nothing,' I said absently, 'just trying to figure something out.'

She just kept walking and waiting in silence.

Something remained open or awakened in me, I realised. I had not lost my altered state, at least, not completely. It was intriguing rather than surprising: confirmation of something I already knew. This world was an illusion. It was a spontaneous perception, independent of the Portal, which seemed to inhibit such natural manifestations. I wondered if I should resume my Portal training: try to regain Intakaes' muscular brain. I decided not – at least, not yet. We were not going anywhere anytime soon, and I could worry about the Portal later. For now I was comfortable with this new, enriched perception of reality. I turned to the radiant woman at my side and tried to explain it all as best I could.

'Our life has always seemed like a dream to me,' she said, 'ever since you spirited me away from that jail. I do not find it unlikely that more astounding things await us.' She paused thoughtfully. 'I am very happy that we are married at last, and I liked the priest and the church very much. But what I felt was sacred came from inside me – like the light you describe flowing between us.'

'It felt like that to me too,' I said, 'or at least: beautiful and magical. OK, kind of sacred too. Do you worry about your religion? I mean, do you feel you have lost something or gained something?'

She laughed, squeezing my hand. 'Both I suppose. I no longer have the same certainty about truth. I see now that believing something does not make it real. But I feel a new sense of wonder at what it means to be alive in this world. Everything feels miraculous; as if I am just waking up and seeing it all with new eyes.'

'Me too,' I smiled, 'and at the moment there is nothing more new or magical than being here with you.'

She returned my smile, her eyes shining, and I welled up in tears of joy. The moment seemed perfect, and we stood together watching the last remnants of sunlight glow softly on Abbeydale and its quiet parklands.

'I think it's time,' I said softly.

It was wonderful. The episode at the Inn returned, if not in full flood, then in a perfectly acceptable resurgence, with its own blend of narcotic, aphrodisiac and jet fuel. Any fear of embarrassment or clumsiness was dissolved by the intoxication that consumed us. I tried to be gentle, but Jacqueline told me later that she felt little pain. The extraordinary high we were experiencing relaxed her completely.

Sex had always been something of a sensual jamboree for me: an intense consummation of desire, but a physical extravaganza none the less. Now our embraces became a whole new melding of heart and soul. Barriers real and imagined slipped away as our kisses deepened. There were no games, just a supreme tenderness and a slow, blissful dissolution of self. I felt myself immersed in a formless ocean of being: a vast, timeless womb of creation and dissolution. Our bodies moved and communed as one in a timeless cycle of life and renewal. New states of being were no longer surprising to me, but it seemed strange and wonderful that such egolessness could lead to such intensity of being, or that such intensity of being could exist in such boundlessness. This was no frantic build-up to cataclysmic delight: rather a fabulous anthem of life and love that carried all before it.

'Oh Richard!' she gasped, as we lay together in stunned satiation, 'I had never imagined anything like that.'

I laughed a little wildly. 'It was a first for me too. I have never known anything like that either.'

'Have you not?' she asked wonderingly.

'Well, I don't know exactly how it was for you,' I said, 'but it was totally mind-blowing!'

'Oh you and your modern expressions,' she sighed dreamily. 'I did feel part of something greater than myself. I felt as though the whole Earth was alive and giving us its blessing somehow. It was beautiful.'

'Yes,' I smiled, still drunk with the wonder of her. I remembered the primal mystery she had evoked in Alexandria, and its echo in the compelling depths of the three muses in the Mousion. Her simplicity and innocence was the core about which this new depth of experience had flared. But it had awakened some deeper truth. I sensed the primal force that drove spring's first bloom: the primordial hymn which turned the seasons, and endured the long childhood of humanity. Today it smiled kindly upon us, and bent low the fruits of love. But on some fundamental level its nature rang like steel, and I pushed away the sense that this Goddess of life and nurture might demand much from her children in the name of Destiny.

Chapter 32

THUS BEGAN AN interlude so beguiling that I often forgot completely about the future and the past. The mysterious high that had launched our marriage continued to enhance our days like a balm of magical contentment. I checked that I could connect with the Portal every so often, and it remained difficult, but not impossible. I noticed a gradual return of precision and control as time passed by, and that it seemed inversely proportional to a measured dwindling of the profound state of satisfaction I enjoyed.

The changes in the quality of living experience were subtle rather than overwhelming. Everything was the same, yet more immediate: vivid and enriching. It reminded me of pleasant moments from my childhood. Colours were brighter, fragrance more intense, and the simplest things hugely enjoyable. Nature seemed miraculous: the air an elixir of life, water magically pure, flames enchantingly beautiful. I could almost feel the earth bursting with life and potency beneath my feet.

I sensed it was a temporary idyll, and that storms lay ahead. But I was happy to allow time to run its course. I was not inclined to make much use of the Portal in any case. I remembered the lingering traces of the wormholes I had seen when trying to rescue Billy. I was unsure if such repeated activation in a single space-time location might have an accumulative effect that the Keepers, or less desirable persons, would be able to track. I hoped to find out, but for now I was content to put such matters on hold.

One day I asked Henrietta to show me where she had seen Alex at the back of the house. The main building ran back some ninety yards; the flank elevations aligned and flush, with bay and dormer windows looking out on either side. But separate additions extended back to various distances in a more haphazard arrangement than at the front. The ground was higher to the rear of the house; and a sunken courtyard with herb beds rationalised the various gabled ends into a proportional enclosure, with a shallow stairway leading up through a stone balustrade garden wall to the lawns beyond.

'She was here, sir,' Henrietta said, standing at the edge of the lawn, near the top of the stone steps.

'Thank you,' I said softly; and she scuttled back into the house, no doubt anxious to avoid any lurking fairie enchantment.

I stood there and looked back at the house, brooding on the scene. I felt the nearest I had been to Alex since that first traumatic meeting so long ago. She had been close to where I was standing only a few short weeks before. It was tempting to jump back the brief distance in time, but Intakaes' warnings about crossed timelines seemed much more real to me now. I also knew that Alex could have been here in a moment if she wanted to. I still felt compelled to try to sense her presence though, and to wonder why she had come.

It was then that I felt it: some kind of anomaly close by. At first I thought I was imagining it. I moved surreptitiously about, feeling a little self-conscious as I had no idea what I was actually doing. After a minute or so I stood over one particular spot, confident that the strangeness emanated from immediately below me. The perception was difficult to identify: a sense of wrongness, and of a great yawning void in space and time. Feeling both a little excited and a little foolish, I knelt down and probed around in the earth at my feet.

A small area of soil was disturbed and the grass came apart, and a couple of inches down I felt something solid. It extended downwards, and I used a sturdy twig to loosen it. I grew increasingly curious as the excavation deepened, and dug more vigorously. Finally I could move the thing, and it came out with a heave. I held a great, curved tooth: more than three inches wide and almost twelve inches long. It was a ferocious thing, with a thick, robust cross section, a hard point and wicked serrations lining its edges.

But most astonishing was the raw vitality it radiated. Rich, fresh enamel gleamed through the mud along its sharper eight or nine inches. The base was duller cementum: root material, with soft tissue still attached. What I held was impossible. The living tooth of some kind of Tyrannosaurus: a creature supposedly far beyond the reach of any portal.

A sense of deep time engulfed me: of being adrift far from any familiar shore. The Earth vanished and I looked out upon the infinite heavens; a drifting nebula of breath-taking beauty before me. Millions of years passed in moments. Dark energy worked its magic: nudging subtle fluctuations in density within the cloud of interstellar gas and dust into runaway gravitational collapse. Its infinitesimal net rotation increased along the vector sum of its angular momentum, and gravitational efficiency spun the rotating nebula into a thin disc. A concentrated central mass formed, its gravitational potential converted into kinetic energy, and collisions between particles generated heat.

Hottest near the centre, the mass reached a critical point. Hydrostatic equilibrium suspended gravitational collapse, and a star was born. A thin protoplanetary disk – a fraction of the mass of the solar nebula – remained in orbit, sustained by its own rotation. The temperature dropped as the disk radiated away internal heat, and the heaviest molecules began to condensate into tiny droplets. The heavier compounds of aluminium, titanium, iron and nickel formed nearer the sun, the silicates further out, and further still hydrogen-rich molecules condensed into lighter ices: water ice, frozen methane, and frozen ammonia.

The condensates collected into the seeds of planet formation, planetesimals into protoplanets, whose short-lived elements accumulated heat from radioactive decay, melting materials into differentiation by density. I watched, mesmerised, as the abundant ices formed the larger gaseous, low-density outer planets, and the heavier elements denser, smaller worlds in the warmer inner solar system. The growing planets began to absorb or eject the remaining planetesimals, and light-pressure and solar wind from the newly burning Sun began to sweep the nebula clean of dust.

The process continued to refine itself: remaining condensates bombarding the settling planets and complementing the Earths volatile outgassing with huge quantities of impact degassing to build the Earth's oceans and atmosphere. The laws of cause and effect worked like clockwork, but I perceived subtler processes at work too: invisible energies honing the process behind the scenes. Everything was being spun into specific coefficients: resonating with harmonic tones in a universal accord. I could feel the primordial song resounding within the magnificent planets and their majestic Sun: archetypal processes engineered within precise parameters in manifold dimensions.

The Solar system was a nursery, I realised in awe. A precision instrument manufactured by a technology impossible to think about

– perhaps the precursor of the universe itself. The Earth seemed to glow like a self-illumined pearl. A maternal prescience pulsed in its deepest core: a living vision of virgin fertility. Life and nurture were no accident. Humanity's ancient reverence for its earthly home was rooted in something far more profound than mere seasonal fertility.

Terraforming the planet got underway: plants and land creatures building the atmosphere and vast bio-deposits over millions of years. My spectacular overview had been homing steadily in towards this mother earth, and I gazed spellbound as dinosaurs patiently trod the eons.

But a stark aberration jarred my wonder. An outlandish construction loomed in the primeval landscape: a great encampment glowering malevolently amid the casual anarchy of the Cretaceous landscape. At first, impossibly, it put me in mind of a Roman military fortification. Broad, robust walls bordered by a wide trench and some kind of perimeter fence. But as the vision drew nearer, I realised it had some odd features. I had the scale wrong for a start. The walls were thirty feet high and fifteen thick, and the construction two or three miles long and almost as wide. I couldn't make out how it was structured. It looked a bit like roughcast concrete. But the perimeter fence beyond the trench was heavy-duty metal, and it looked like it might be electrified.

It certainly looked dinosaur-proof, which seemed logical, despite its actual existence making no sense at all. The interior of the great compound contained many different buildings, with people and vehicles in evidence. Finally I zeroed in on something that changed everything. Tiny forms were carrying out manoeuvres in an open area – forms wearing dark insect-like armour that I had seen once before, racing across the field outside Charles' aunt's house.

The image faded slowly from view, leaving me kneeling in disbelief; still holding the huge, incredible tooth in my hands. For long moments I couldn't think at all, and when I did it didn't help much. Obviously Alex had hidden the tooth, and it was a message to me. The experience it had triggered was inexplicable. But what I was supposed to do about it all I could not imagine. Witnessing the stunning construction of the solar system hit me harder than other high-dimensional experience somehow: perhaps because it seemed more real to my human ego. I wasn't sure I was ready to face the implications of the gigantic jigsaw that was coming together.

What I hoped for was a nice quiet life in the country with Jacqueline, and an eventual catch-up with Alex when the time was right. Now, as I slowly recovered from the stunning vision, I wanted to push the big picture aside and follow that course. We had plenty to keep us occupied. Every day seemed to bring new situations to resolve. We got a couple more cows and a dairy maid named Phoebe, who helped out in the house when she wasn't milking or making cheese. Jacqueline often worked in the vegetable garden when she wasn't busy with Henrietta. Billy, Charles and I started looking at the repairs needed to put the house in order, although Charles naturally regarded this as inseparable from the construction of his observatory, and was most interested in the attics.

We also began learning to ride, those of us who lacked the skill. I had no wish for another painful and embarrassing exhibition in some distant era, and we figured this could apply to any of us. We also practiced driving the coach and the gig, and started to make use of these various conveyances to visit the tenanted properties on the estate. It was fun to get to know the colourful characters on the farms and smallholdings. We visited the cottages in the local village as well, which had been separated from the estate by previous land sales. They all had one thing in common – those that were still occupied – long, involved complaints about neglect and broken promises; and we began to compile an inventory of required repairs and renovation works which would require years to complete.

Back at the Hall, things were proceeding well. The twins soon settled down to the slow pace of life in the eighteenth century. They had been fretful and petulant after we moved; pining for the gadgets they had become used to. But they became happily absorbed in self-invented occupations soon enough, which often involved little more than some sticks and string and a few stones. They had also been learning to ride. Jacqueline bought a couple of ponies for them, and they often accompanied her with Priya on exploratory rides around the estate. We also acquired some chickens, and before long, a couple of young Great Danes, or Great Danish Dogs as they were known locally, to keep the foxes away.

There were also long, early nights with Jacqueline in our extravagantly carved four poster bed. Autumn was coming on, and some of the nights were chilly. We had a spectacular fireplace in our room; and the tranquil play of its flickering light over the richly decorated interior transformed our boudoir into a fairy grotto of enchantment and delight.

The remarkable depth and intensity of our initial physical encounters levelled out into more human dimensions, but they remained magical and deeply fulfilling. A deep current of love flowed between us, and new subjects of conversation arose with our new physical intimacy. We spoke lazily together about all manner of things, and her innocence constantly surprised me.

'No wonder people have all these relationships, Richard,' she murmured one night, 'this is very agreeable.'

'I don't think people would be having so many relationships if they were experiencing something this agreeable,' I said.

Is it not always the same?' she asked in surprise.

'No, I admitted, 'quality and quantity can be very different things.'

'What do you mean exactly?' she asked wonderingly.

'Well, I could put it down to my great prowess as a lover,' I grinned. 'But I'm sure being in love has a lot to do with it. Lots of people have casual affairs that don't really involve feelings, and some are unable to have normal sex at all.'

'Oh, you are teasing me again, Richard,' she said with a frown, 'what does that mean?'

'I don't feel particularly inclined to go into details right now,' I confessed. 'But many people cannot react sexually to even superficial encounters, and have to enact bizarre and humiliating practices in order to become, err, aroused.'

She stared round-eyed at me. 'You mean they are mentally deranged?'

I laughed. 'No, at least, they are not regarded as such. They can appear perfectly normal. They just do it is secret.'

'But they cannot be entirely well. How can they be happy?' she asked.

'That is not something society concerns itself about too much,' I said. 'Mostly it is how rich and successful one appears that matters. I suppose the real satisfaction we seek is the kind of intensity we are feeling now, and shallow, self-indulgent behaviour the way many people compensate themselves for its absence.'

'No wonder God wants us to lead moral lives,' she said disapprovingly.

'I suppose the idea behind religion is to maintain a better quality of consciousness,' I agreed reflectively. 'But I don't think it's an end in itself: more the foundation for achieving a higher level of existence.'

I also discovered that Henrietta was getting Jane and Elsie the house maid up at five every morning to start work.

'It's what we're used to sir,' she said earnestly.

'What on earth do you do at that time?' I asked in disbelief.

'Well sir, we start with the tea leaves, and then there's always plenty to clean and polish before its time to get the breakfast.'

'Tea leaves? What tea leaves?' I said in bewilderment.

'Why, we spread them on the carpets to pick up the dust,' she said cheerfully.

'We do?' I enquired blankly.

'Damp of course,' she explained, 'and then we sweep them up again.'

'Harrumph,' I grunted. 'Well, we don't have that much carpet, and what we do have needs replacing. I think a couple of times a week will do. And there is no need to get up at five o'clock: seven will be fine.'

'Oh sir, that is much too late!' she gasped, 'we will never get anything done!'

We haggled back and forth, and eventually arrived at a compromise: they would rise at six, unless there was something particular to do, like the washing. (We were sending bulky objects out to a washer woman – whom Jacqueline insisted on supplying with glycerine soap obtained from fifty miles away – but we washed a fair amount of items ourselves each week.)

Jacqueline fell pregnant very quickly, which shocked me for some reason, even though it was an obvious development. Actual reality was very different from its theoretical cousin, and I felt quite unprepared for it. And that was without really considering the perils we faced: the as yet little understood responsibilities we bore, and the unknown foes who wished us ill. But I could not complain about our present situation. I flashed back to my monotonous life before Alex had appeared, and smiled at my ruminations.

We spent a lot of time discussing the mysteries surrounding out lives though, and Priya was particularly interested in the idea of higher dimensions of consciousness. She made me relate everything that had ever happened to me, and wrote copious notes and theories about it all. Occasional visits (by circuitous routes) to the modern world involved the acquisition of heavy tomes about psychology, religion and spirituality for her; and I actually learnt a lot in the course of the discussions we shared. We spoke about Ravi and his *Living Earth* too, and I agreed that we should visit him in the future.

The year wore on, with life at the Hall settling down into a comfortable routine. I quickly became dissatisfied with the plumbing though, and set about designing a new system at idle moments. It seemed extraordinary that such a grand house relied on the daily emptying of chamber pots; while a bath involved so much heating, carrying and emptying of hot water by the servants that we hardly dared ask for one. Jacqueline refused to let anyone empty her chamber pot until she was too indisposed to do so, and applied moral pressure on the rest of us to do the same, with varied results.

Little of any excitement took place, apart from an attempt by a highwayman to hold up Billy and Charles on a coach trip to Derby. The perpetrator fled amidst a flurry of bullets, one of which narrowly missed Charles' foot when his gun went off as he tried to get it out of his pocket.

'I was more scared of him than the varmint holding us up!' Billy chuckled afterwards.

But we decided to get shoulder holsters made up, so we could hide our weapons and still have easy access to them. It occurred to me that we would benefit from professional training in firearms and tactics in such situations. But that was just something else on the 'to do' list. We reviewed the various dramas we had been through and discussed possible future plans, but basically we were just settling into a new way of life. Billy and Charles travelled to London sometimes by way of a change, but the rest of us were happy enough to get used to life in the Hall as the months went by.

Billy enjoyed riding, fishing and hunting when he wasn't working; and work consisted mainly of he and I and a small team of builders engaged in various repair and rebuilding projects. Charles joined in these pursuits sometimes, but he spent a lot of time designing his observatory and reading up about astronomy. He had attended a couple of lectures at the local amateur astronomers' society (which was more than a day's ride away) and had become acutely aware of all sorts of deficiencies in his knowledge of the mechanical skills of the trade.

'I don't understand it Charles,' I said to him one day. 'What is the point when you know all the answers to the things they are trying to find out?'

'I don't understand it either,' he said brightly. 'I just always wanted to do it as far back as I can remember. It's not finding new things for me, but finding out how they did it, and seeing all those beautiful brass telescopes. Actually, what I really dream of is sitting in my observatory and listening to the rain on the glass dome at night, and seeing the moon – you know – behind racing dark clouds.'

'But you won't be able to do any astronomy if it's cloudy!' I said, mystified.

'I know,' he admitted, 'but it's just a picture I've always had in my head. I just want to sort of feel it. But I really want to understand it all too, so I can talk to people.'

The only regular outing was our trip to the village church on Sunday mornings. Even Jacqueline agreed it was mainly to satisfy the locals' idea of what was right and proper. But I enjoyed the homely routine, and quite admired the parson's attempts to extract high-minded homilies from obscure references in the bible.

My nerves became increasingly fraught as the end of Jacqueline's pregnancy approached. Priya and I had read everything we could about the delivery, and we had decided to try and go it alone. Jacqueline was confident she would be able to manage, and I didn't fancy getting local doctors or midwives involved. Too many ignorant practices were still fashionable. Besides, if we hit any major problems I intended to whisk us all to a twenty-first century hospital, and I didn't want any locals seeing that.

There was a false alarm a week before the delivery was due, and we all went into panic mode for a couple of hours. But Jacqueline's pains died down, and we reset ourselves to impatient pre-panic mode once more. It all still seemed unreal, but now the unimaginable actuality loomed over us like an oncoming express train. Then at last it was happening: a whirlwind of anxiety, excitement, pain and expectation. Jacqueline had a no-nonsense, down to earth attitude about it all, and the pain and exhaustion rarely overcame her fortitude. I felt humbled and overwhelmed: awed by the primal struggle of the woman I loved.

Hours passed somehow. Labour had begun in early evening and was still going strong ten hours later. I kept checking nervously for my connection to the Portal: making sure we would be able to get to a hospital if necessary. Then at last the head was crowning. Jacqueline gave an enormous, animal-like grunt, and it was all over. I stared at slick, bloodied perfection: a tiny human being which had appeared as miraculously as if materialised by a Portal. I felt shattered, the powerful swirl of déjà vu almost incidental.

'It's a girl,' cried Priya, swiftly enfolding the child in swathes of linen. The new arrival loudly proclaimed her displeasure at this new environment, and Jacqueline struggled up with a sob to see her. I pushed some pillows behind her, and she took our daughter in her arms, her eyes filled with tears of joy. I struggled to take in the enormity of the event; the room literally swimming with energy from Jacqueline's high.

'Shouldn't we cut the cord?' I asked tentatively.

'Not yet, it's supposed to be better to wait a while,' said Priya. 'Wait until the placenta is delivered. It should be soon.'

'Is everything OK?' I asked, 'not bleeding too much?'

'I don't think she's torn,' stated Priya; 'looks OK to me.'

'I feel fine,' said Jacqueline serenely.

'What about a name,' Priya asked, 'have you decided on one?'

We had talked about it, but had not made any decisions.

'I have a name,' said Jacqueline. 'It came to me today. I would like to remember the place where we fell in love, so I wish to call her Alexandra.'

A surge of emotion rushed through me, and the background eddy of déjà vu lurched into a torrent. I leant forwards, and my daughter gazed gravely back at me.

'Hello Alex,' I whispered, the tears pouring down my face.

The flood of emotion erupted into an explosion of joy. It lit up my being with a radiant intensity that banished every shadow from my life. All but one: a minute, shrinking speck which could not hide in that transcendent fire. The Mindworm crept there like a skulking, reanimated Golem exposed to the light.

*****

'You are what?' roared Apollonius. 'Well get rid of it!'

Anna raised her head defiantly. 'I am pregnant and I am keeping it,' she said.

'How could you be so stupid?' he growled.

'I was careless about my shots,' she admitted. 'With everything at Port Royal and afterwards, it went right out of my head.'

Apollonius paused. 'The shipwreck,' he said. A cold gleam shone briefly in his eyes. 'It's Richard Walton's child, isn't it?'

She stared levelly at him. 'And what if it is? You said I could have anything I want, and I want a child.'

He traded her look for look, giving nothing away now. 'All right,' he said finally. 'But I want you back in shape fast when it's over.'

She nodded. 'Don't worry; I will still be of use to you.'

He smiled lazily. 'Yes, I am sure you will.'

###

Author Note

WELL, OF COURSE I hope you have enjoyed reading the book as much as I enjoyed writing it. Not that I haven't had a challenging time trying to connect all the strands of the tale, and preparing the way for future developments! I have always loved the idea of time travel. When I first saw the original (1960) movie 'The Time Machine' aged ten, it took me a whole week to realise it wasn't real! So I basically set out to write a book I would like to have read myself when I was younger, with some hard-won experiences of a subtle nature thrown into the mix. I can't say I planned it all out in meticulous detail. In some ways the book seemed to create itself – in fact some things I found myself writing about mystified me, and only seemed to fit themselves into the plot as the book progressed. Also I guess I am attempting something unusual in trying to cross the bridge between sci-fi and spirituality (my other great interest in life) which I hope is not too confusing for the reader. I would be interested in your views, and grateful if you could leave a short review at your favourite retailer. You can also connect with myself and other readers directly at www.facebook.com/timequestchronicles.

Acknowledgements

MANY THANKS, AS always, to my wife Grazyna. I am also very grateful for all the feedback and advice from Finbar, Dawn, Sarah, Nigel, Tania, Daniel, Rachel, Ros, Pete, Shirley, Gena, Ghoshal and Marilyn.

Lightning Source UK Ltd.
Milton Keynes UK
UKOW04f0747090118
315789UK00002B/152/P

9 781999 840617